D1194620

DISCARD

Rickety Stitch

— AND THE GELATINOUS GOO —

THE BATTLE OF THE BARDS

Also by Ben Costa and James Parks

Rickety Stitch and the Gelatinous Goo: The Road to Epoli

Rickety Stitch and the Gelatinous Goo: The Middle-Route Run

Rickety Stitch

AND THE GELATINOUS GOO

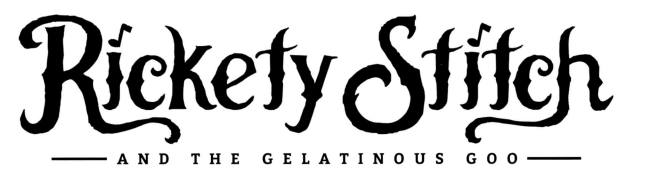

THE BATTLE OF THE BARDS

Created and Written by
BEN COSTA & JAMES PARKS

Illustrated by
BEN COSTA

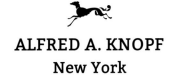

ALFRED A. KNOPF
New York

THIS IS A BORZOI BOOK PUBLISHED BY ALFRED A. KNOPF

This is a work of fiction. Names, characters, places, and incidents either are the product of the authors' imagination or are used fictitiously. Any resemblance to actual persons, living or dead, events, or locales is entirely coincidental.

Text, jacket art, and interior illustrations copyright © 2021 by Ben Costa and James Parks

All rights reserved. Published in the United States by Alfred A. Knopf, an imprint of Random House Children's Books, a division of Penguin Random House LLC, New York.

Knopf, Borzoi Books, and the colophon are registered trademarks of Penguin Random House LLC.

RH Graphic with the book design is a trademark of Penguin Random House LLC.

Visit us on the Web! GetUnderlined.com

Educators and librarians, for a variety of teaching tools, visit us at RHTeachersLibrarians.com

Library of Congress Cataloging-in-Publication Data is available upon request.
ISBN 978-0-399-55619-7 (trade) — ISBN 978-0-399-55620-3 (trade pbk.) —
ISBN 978-0-399-55621-0 (ebook)
The illustrations were created digitally.

MANUFACTURED IN CHINA
April 2021
10 9 8 7 6 5 4 3 2 1

First Edition

Chapter 1
Welcome to Harp's Edge

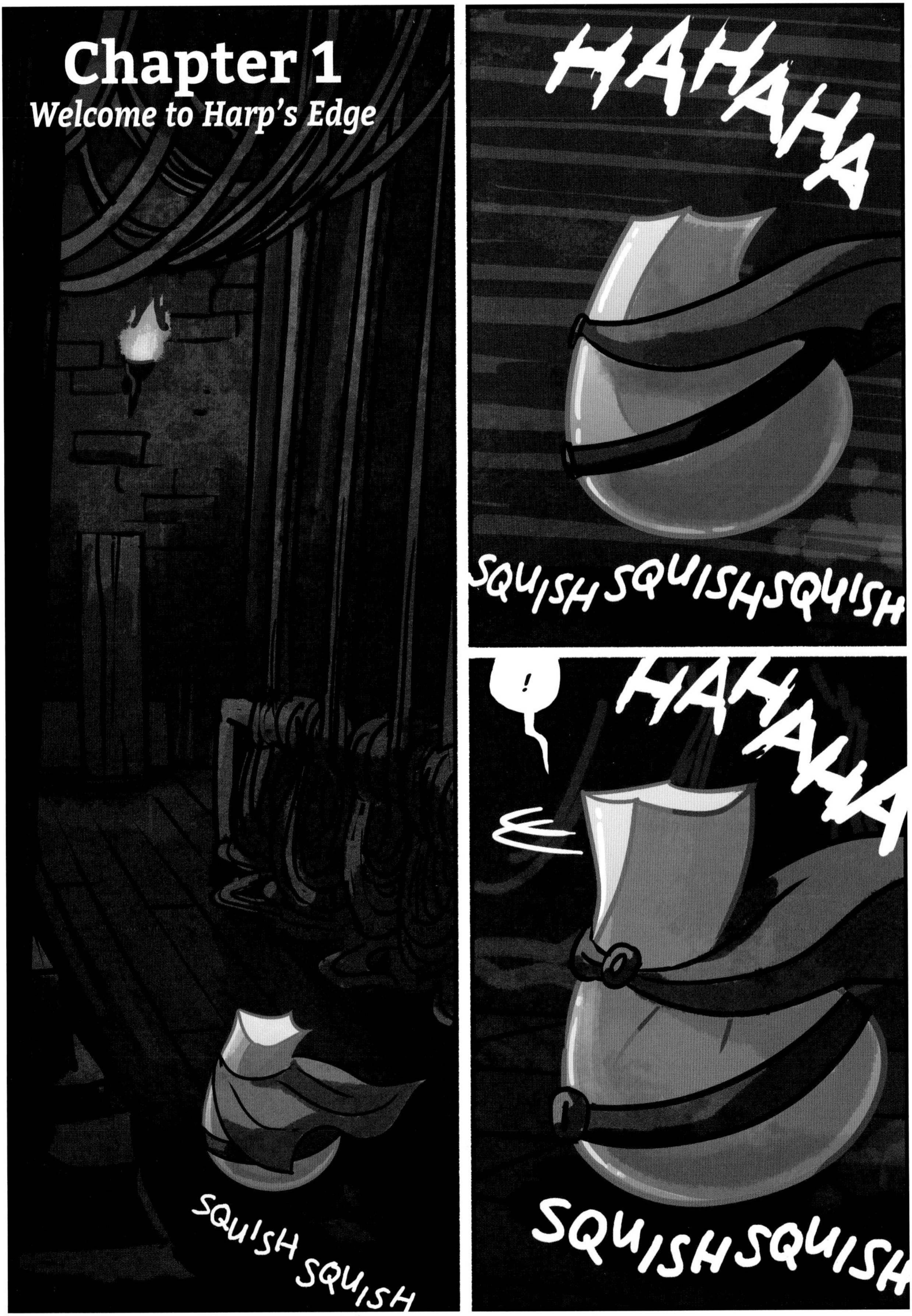
SQUISH SQUISH
HAHAHA
SQUISH SQUISH SQUISH
!
HAHAHA
SQUISH SQUISH

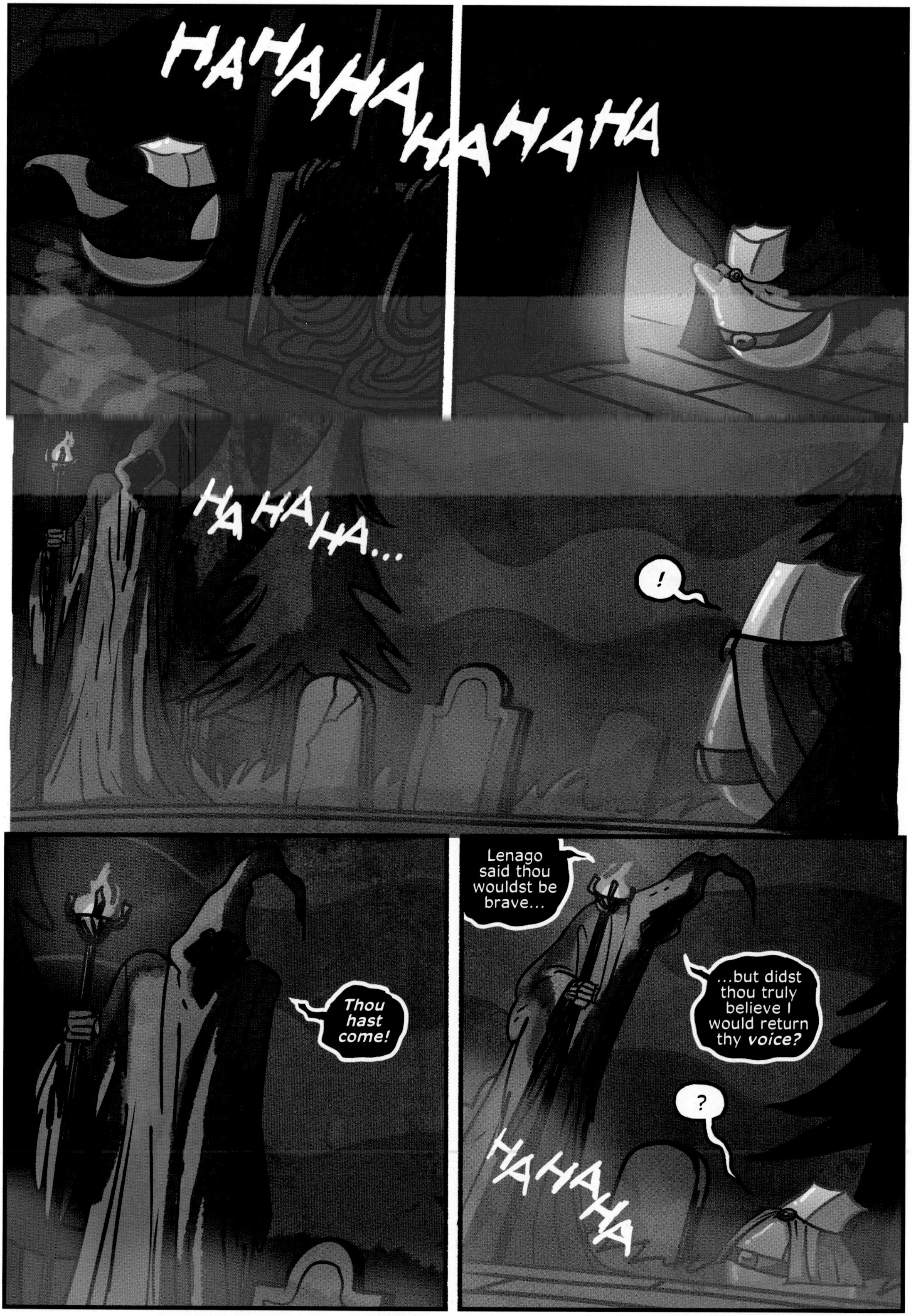

HAHAHAHAHAHAHA
HAHAHA...
!
Thou hast come!
Lenago said thou wouldst be brave...
...but didst thou truly believe I would return thy *voice?*
?
HAHAHAHA

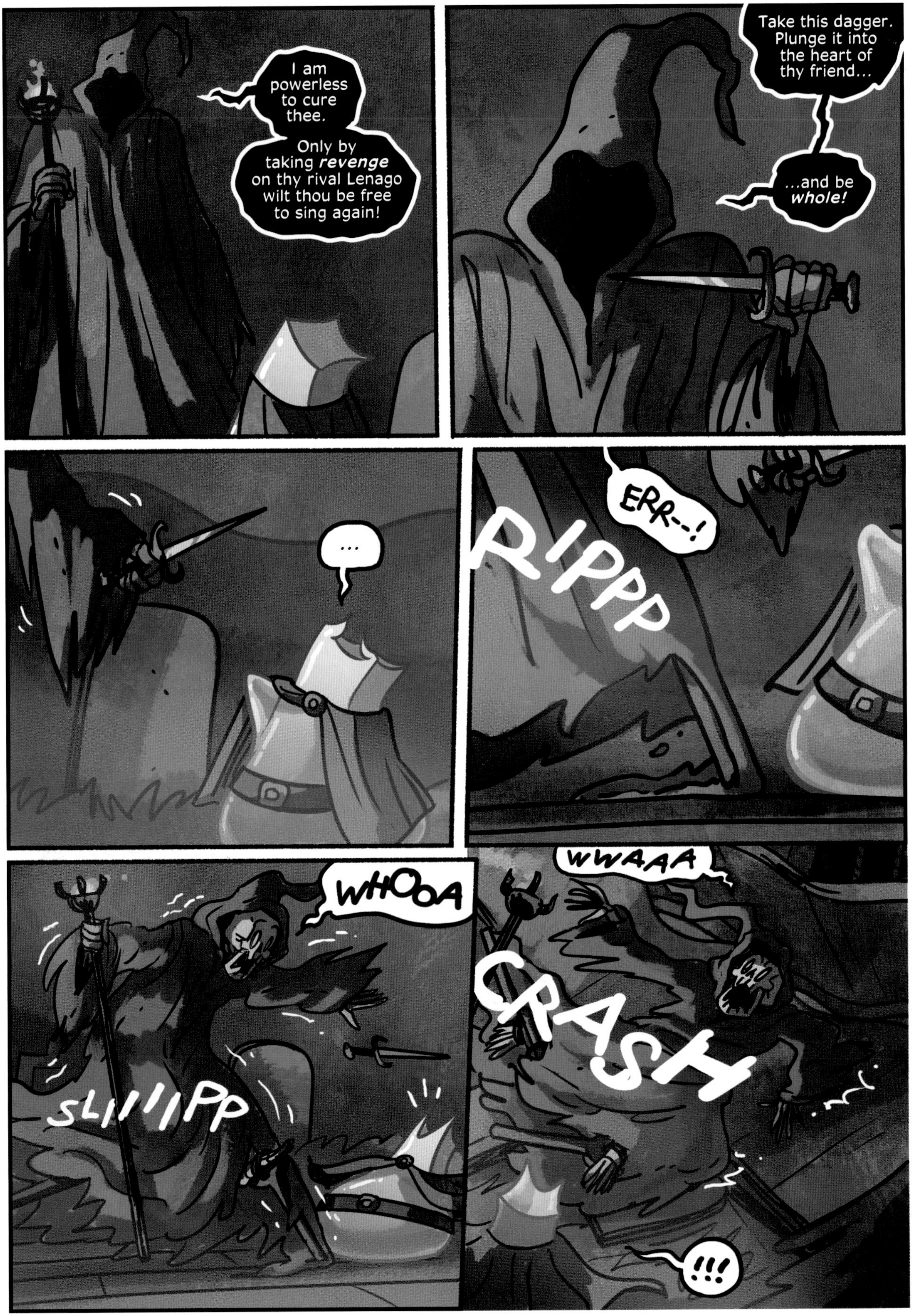
I am powerless to cure thee.
Only by taking *revenge* on thy rival Lenago wilt thou be free to sing again!
Take this dagger. Plunge it into the heart of thy friend...
...and be *whole!*
...
ERR--!
RIPPP
WHOOA
SLIIIIPP
WWAAA
CRASH
!!!

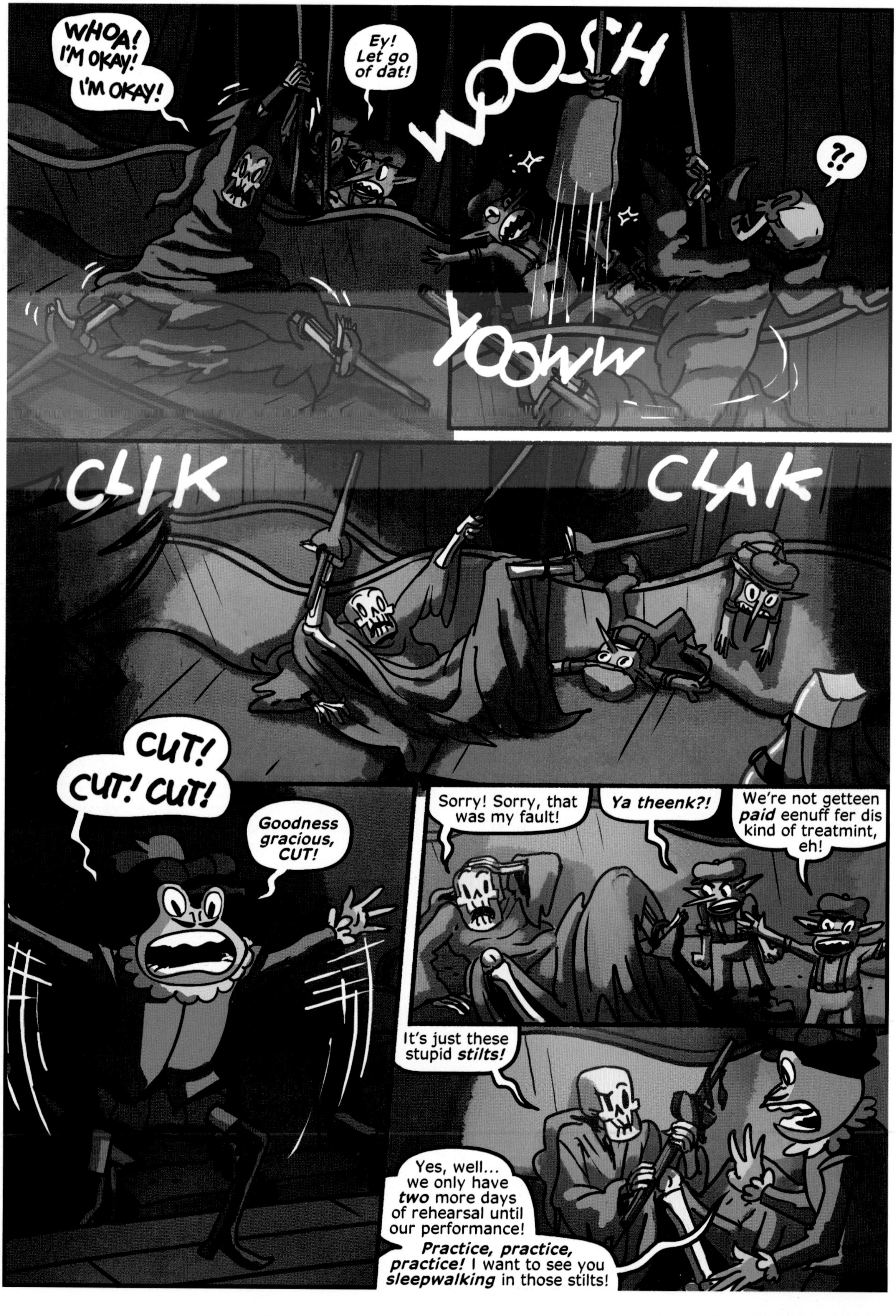
WHOA! I'M OKAY! I'M OKAY!
Ey! Let go of dat!
WOOSH
?!
YOOWW
CLIK
CLAK
CUT! CUT! CUT!
Goodness gracious, CUT!
Sorry! Sorry, that was my fault!
Ya theenk?!
We're not getteen paid eenuff fer dis kind of treatmint, eh!
It's just these stupid stilts!
Yes, well... we only have two more days of rehearsal until our performance!
Practice, practice, practice! I want to see you sleepwalking in those stilts!

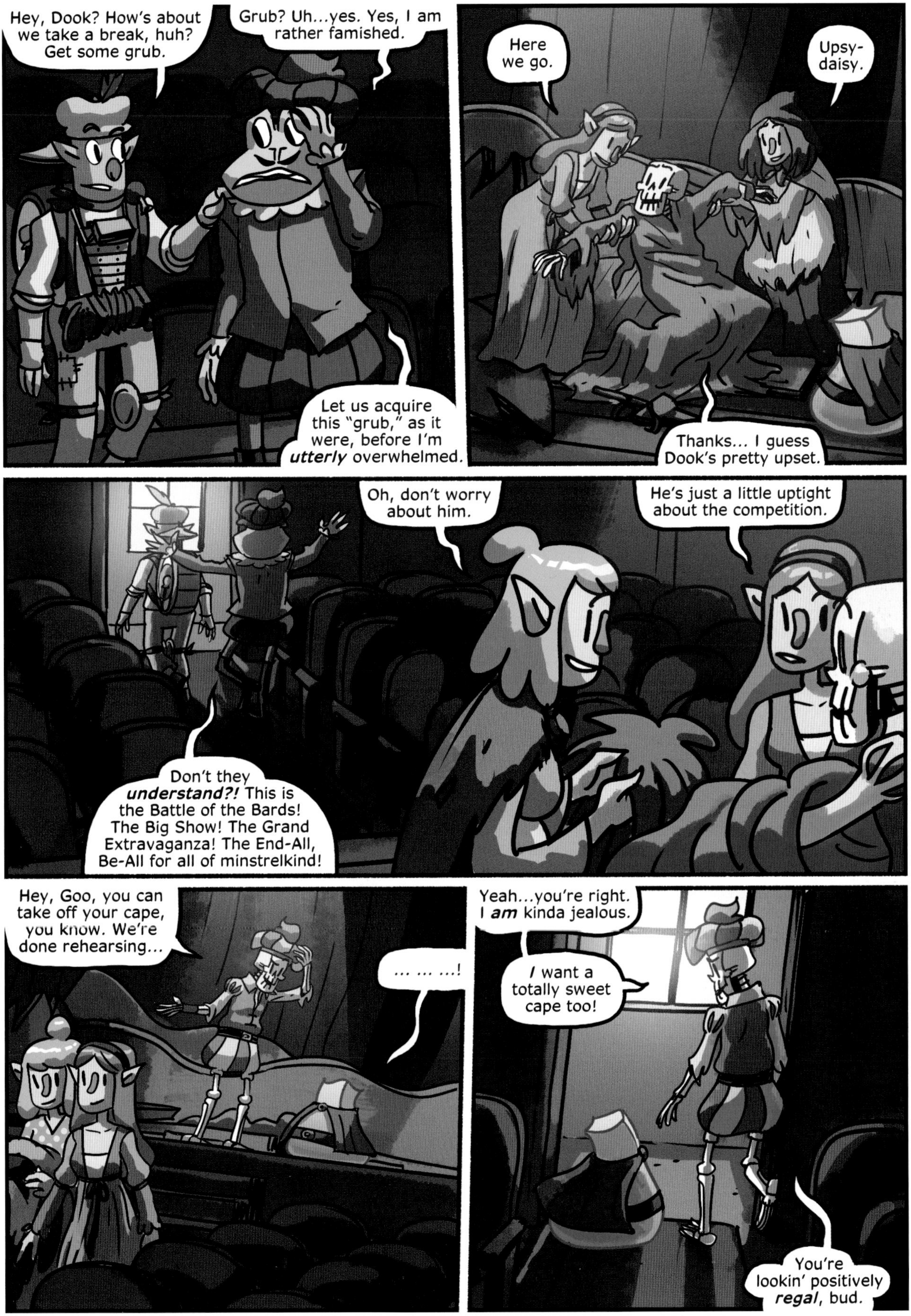
Hey, Dook? How's about we take a break, huh? Get some grub.
Grub? Uh...yes. Yes, I am rather famished.
Let us acquire this "grub," as it were, before I'm *utterly* overwhelmed.
Here we go.
Upsy-daisy.
Thanks... I guess Dook's pretty upset.
Oh, don't worry about him.
He's just a little uptight about the competition.
Don't they *understand?!* This is the Battle of the Bards! The Big Show! The Grand Extravaganza! The End-All, Be-All for all of minstrelkind!
Hey, Goo, you can take off your cape, you know. We're done rehearsing...
... ...!
Yeah...you're right. I *am* kinda jealous.
I want a totally sweet cape too!
You're lookin' positively *regal*, bud.

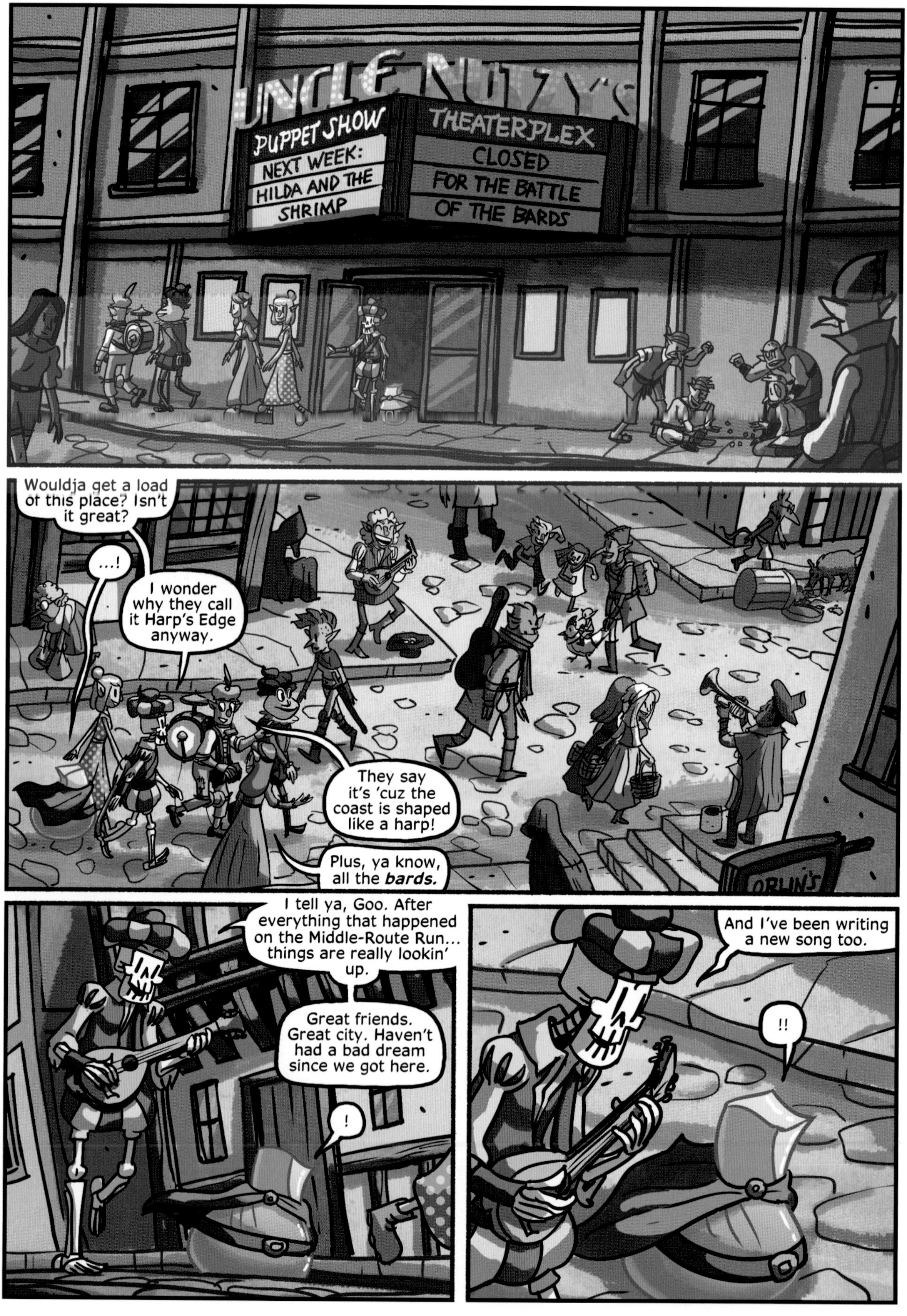
UNCLE NUTZY'S
PUPPET SHOW
NEXT WEEK:
HILDA AND THE SHRIMP
THEATERPLEX
CLOSED
FOR THE BATTLE
OF THE BARDS
Wouldja get a load of this place? Isn't it great?
...!
I wonder why they call it Harp's Edge anyway.
They say it's 'cuz the coast is shaped like a harp!
Plus, ya know, all the ***bards.***
ORLIN'S
I tell ya, Goo. After everything that happened on the Middle-Route Run... things are really lookin' up.
Great friends. Great city. Haven't had a bad dream since we got here.
!
And I've been writing a new song too.
!!

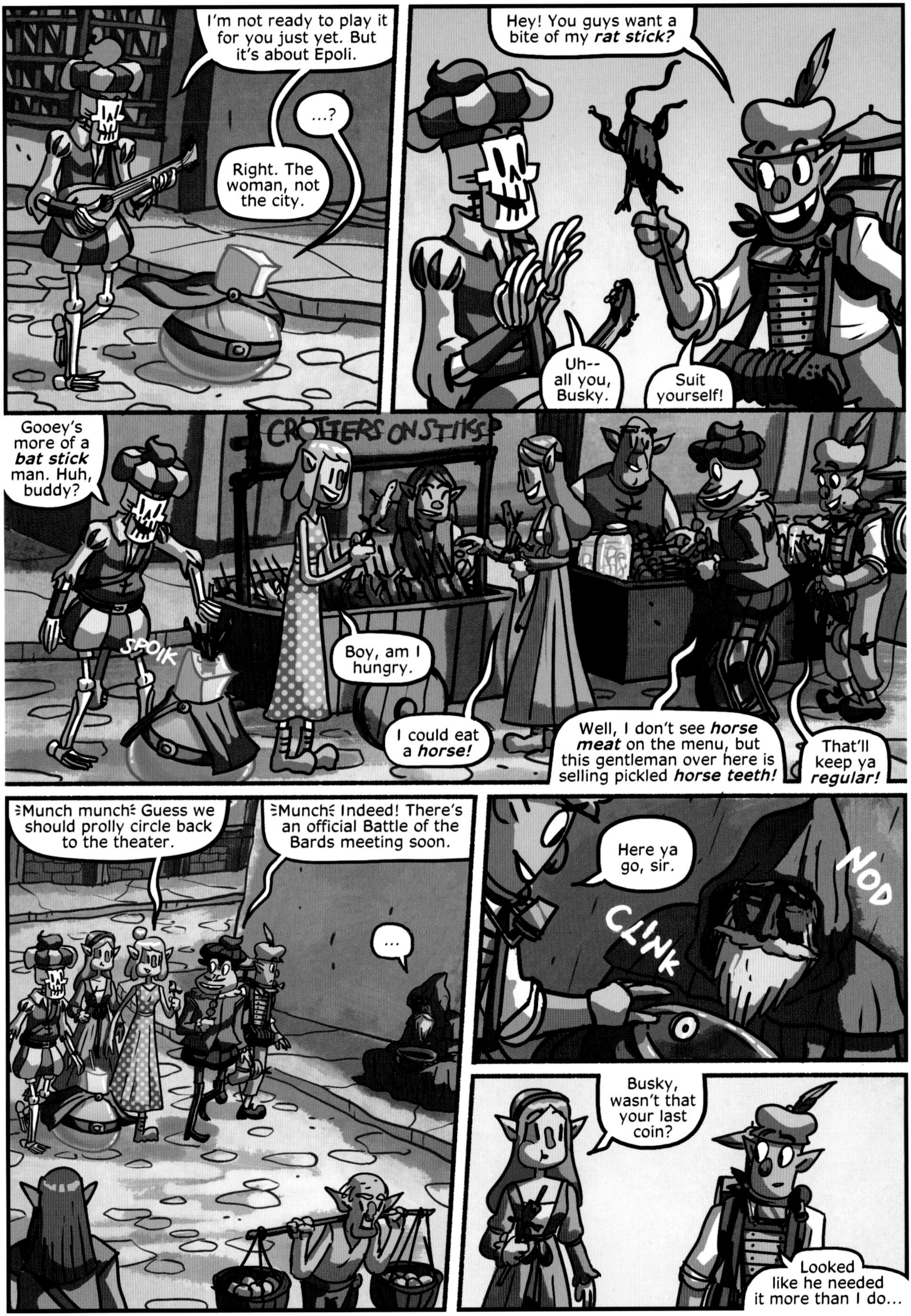

I'm not ready to play it for you just yet. But it's about Epoli.
...?
Right. The woman, not the city.
Hey! You guys want a bite of my *rat stick?*
Uh-- all you, Busky.
Suit yourself!
CRITTERS ON STIKS
Gooey's more of a *bat stick* man. Huh, buddy?
SPOIK
Boy, am I hungry.
I could eat a *horse!*
Well, I don't see *horse meat* on the menu, but this gentleman over here is selling pickled *horse teeth!*
That'll keep ya *regular!*
Munch munch Guess we should prolly circle back to the theater.
Munch Indeed! There's an official Battle of the Bards meeting soon.
...
Here ya go, sir.
NOD
CLINK
Busky, wasn't that your last coin?
Looked like he needed it more than I do...

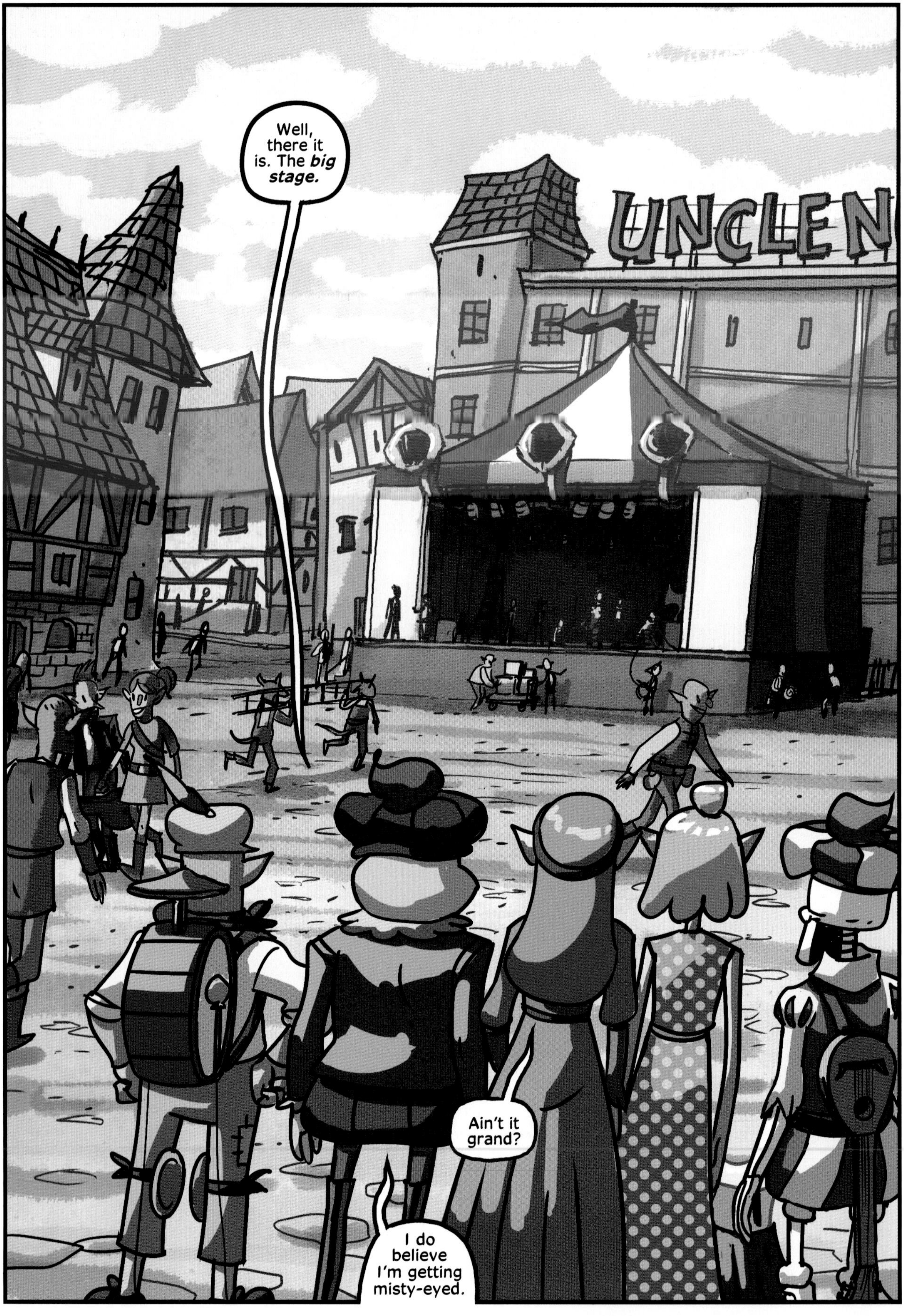
Well, there it is. The *big stage.*
UNCLEN
Ain't it grand?
I do believe I'm getting misty-eyed.

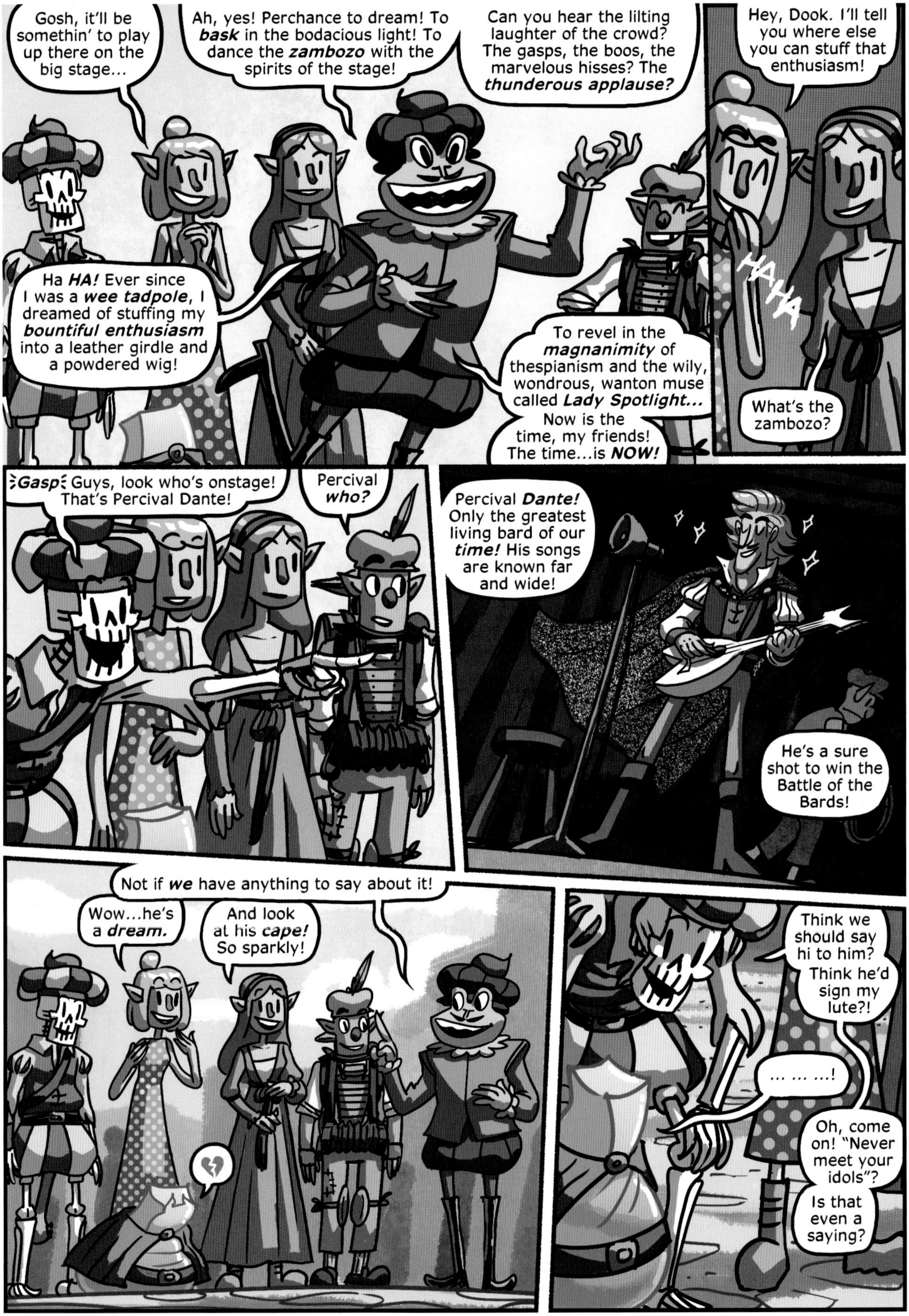

Gosh, it'll be somethin' to play up there on the big stage...
Ah, yes! Perchance to dream! To *bask* in the bodacious light! To dance the *zambozo* with the spirits of the stage!
Can you hear the lilting laughter of the crowd? The gasps, the boos, the marvelous hisses? The *thunderous applause?*
Ha *HA!* Ever since I was a *wee tadpole*, I dreamed of stuffing my *bountiful enthusiasm* into a leather girdle and a powdered wig!
To revel in the *magnanimity* of thespianism and the wily, wondrous, wanton muse called *Lady Spotlight...*
Now is the time, my friends! The time...is *NOW!*
Hey, Dook. I'll tell you where else you can stuff that enthusiasm!
HAHA
What's the zambozo?
Gasp Guys, look who's onstage! That's Percival Dante!
Percival *who?*
Percival *Dante!* Only the greatest living bard of our *time!* His songs are known far and wide!
He's a sure shot to win the Battle of the Bards!
Not if *we* have anything to say about it!
Wow...he's a *dream.*
And look at his *cape!* So sparkly!
Think we should say hi to him?
Think he'd sign my lute?!
... ...!
Oh, come on! "Never meet your idols"?
Is that even a saying?

Chapter 2
A Meeting of Minstrels

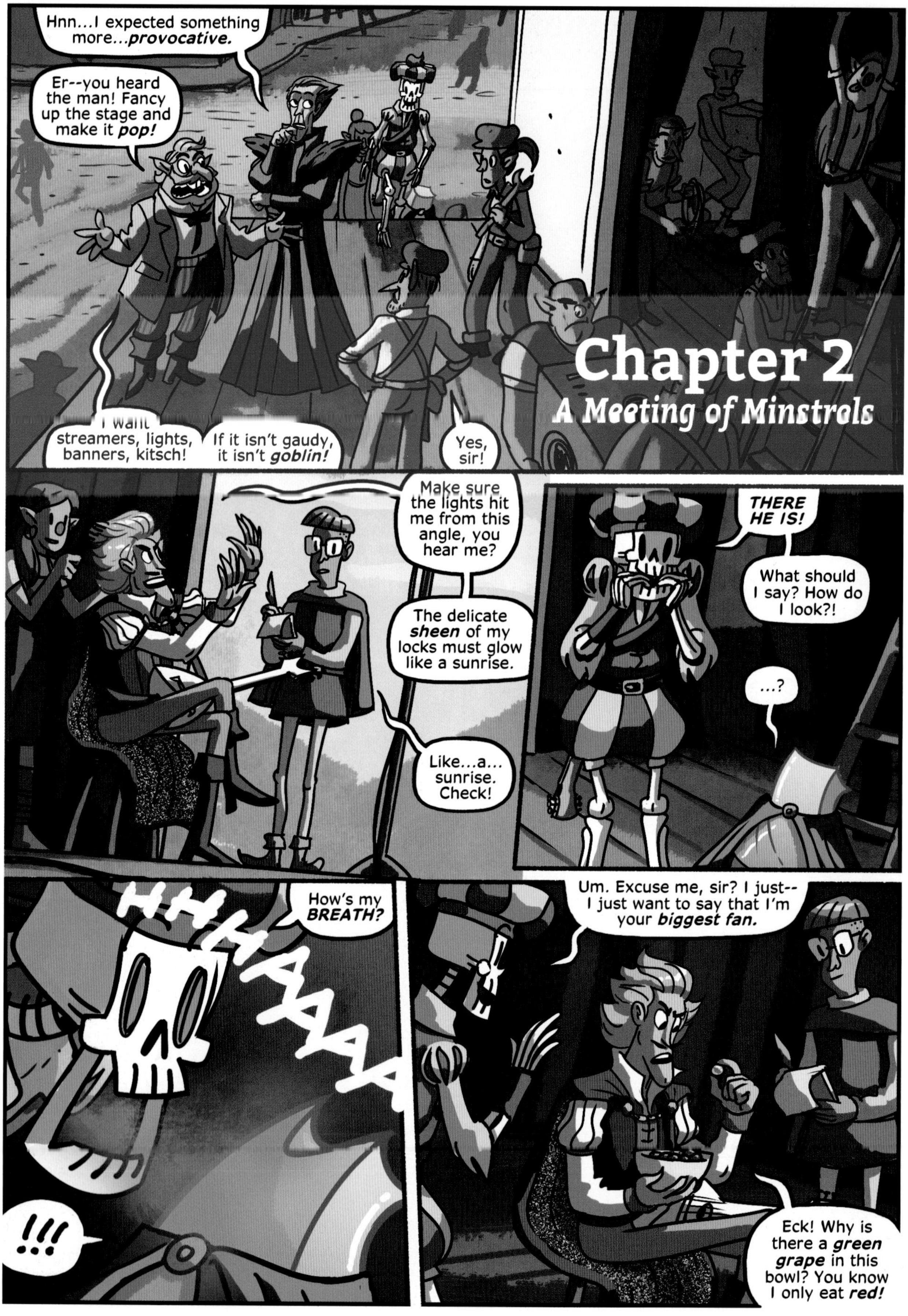

Hnn...I expected something more...*provocative.*
Er--you heard the man! Fancy up the stage and make it *pop!*
I want streamers, lights, banners, kitsch!
If it isn't gaudy, it isn't *goblin!*
Yes, sir!
Make sure the lights hit me from this angle, you hear me?
The delicate *sheen* of my locks must glow like a sunrise.
Like...a... sunrise. Check!
THERE HE IS!
What should I say? How do I look?!
...?
How's my *BREATH?*
HHHAAAAA
!!!
Um. Excuse me, sir? I just-- I just want to say that I'm your *biggest fan.*
Eck! Why is there a *green grape* in this bowl? You know I only eat *red!*

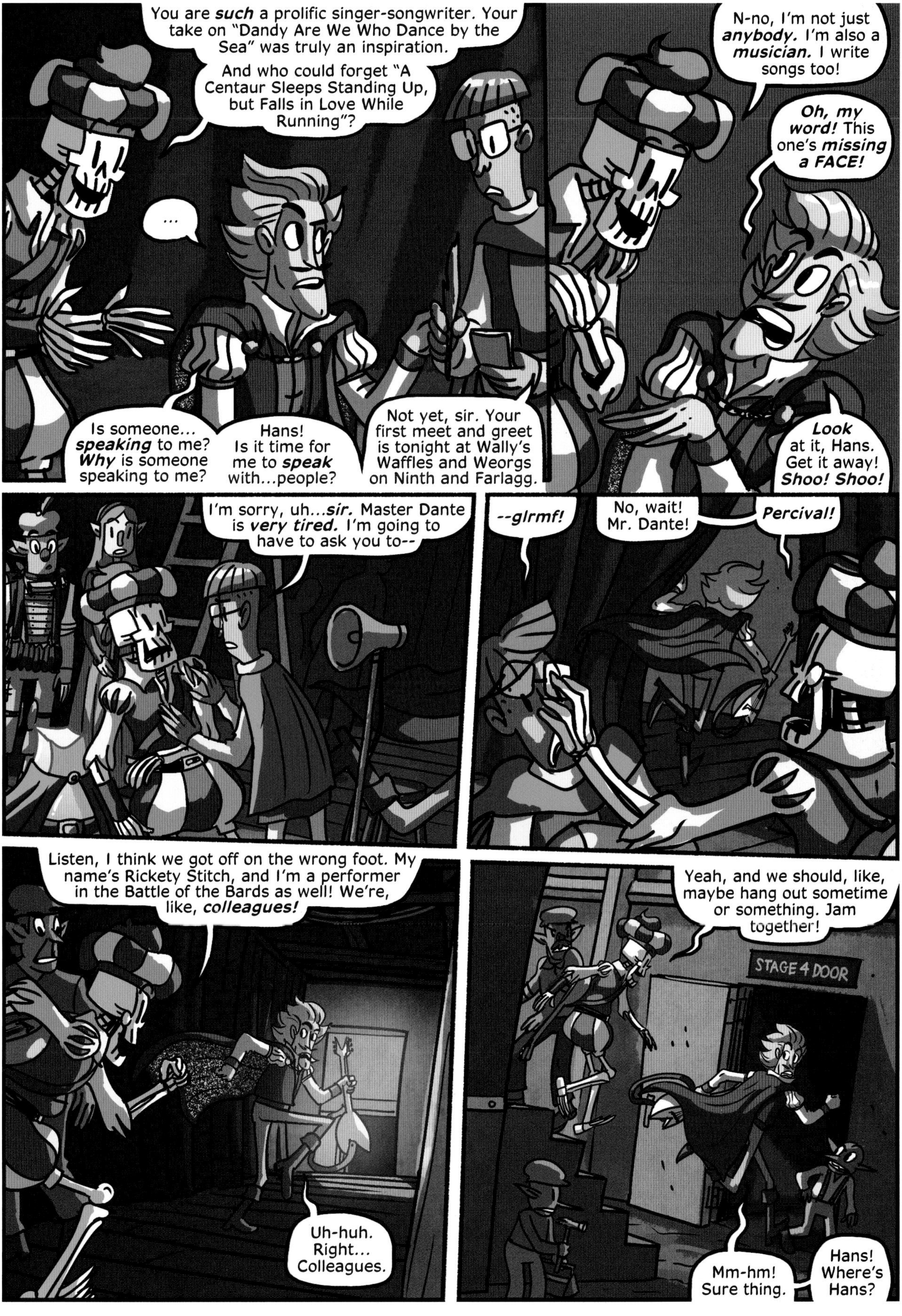
You are *such* a prolific singer-songwriter. Your take on "Dandy Are We Who Dance by the Sea" was truly an inspiration.
And who could forget "A Centaur Sleeps Standing Up, but Falls in Love While Running"?
...
Is someone... *speaking* to me? *Why* is someone speaking to me?
Hans! Is it time for me to *speak* with...people?
Not yet, sir. Your first meet and greet is tonight at Wally's Waffles and Weorgs on Ninth and Farlagg.
N-no, I'm not just *anybody.* I'm also a *musician.* I write songs too!
Oh, my word! This one's *missing a FACE!*
Look at it, Hans. Get it away! *Shoo! Shoo!*
I'm sorry, uh...*sir.* Master Dante is *very tired.* I'm going to have to ask you to--
--glrmf!
No, wait! Mr. Dante!
Percival!
Listen, I think we got off on the wrong foot. My name's Rickety Stitch, and I'm a performer in the Battle of the Bards as well! We're, like, *colleagues!*
Uh-huh. Right... Colleagues.
Yeah, and we should, like, maybe hang out sometime or something. Jam together!
STAGE 4 DOOR
Mm-hm! Sure thing.
Hans! Where's Hans?

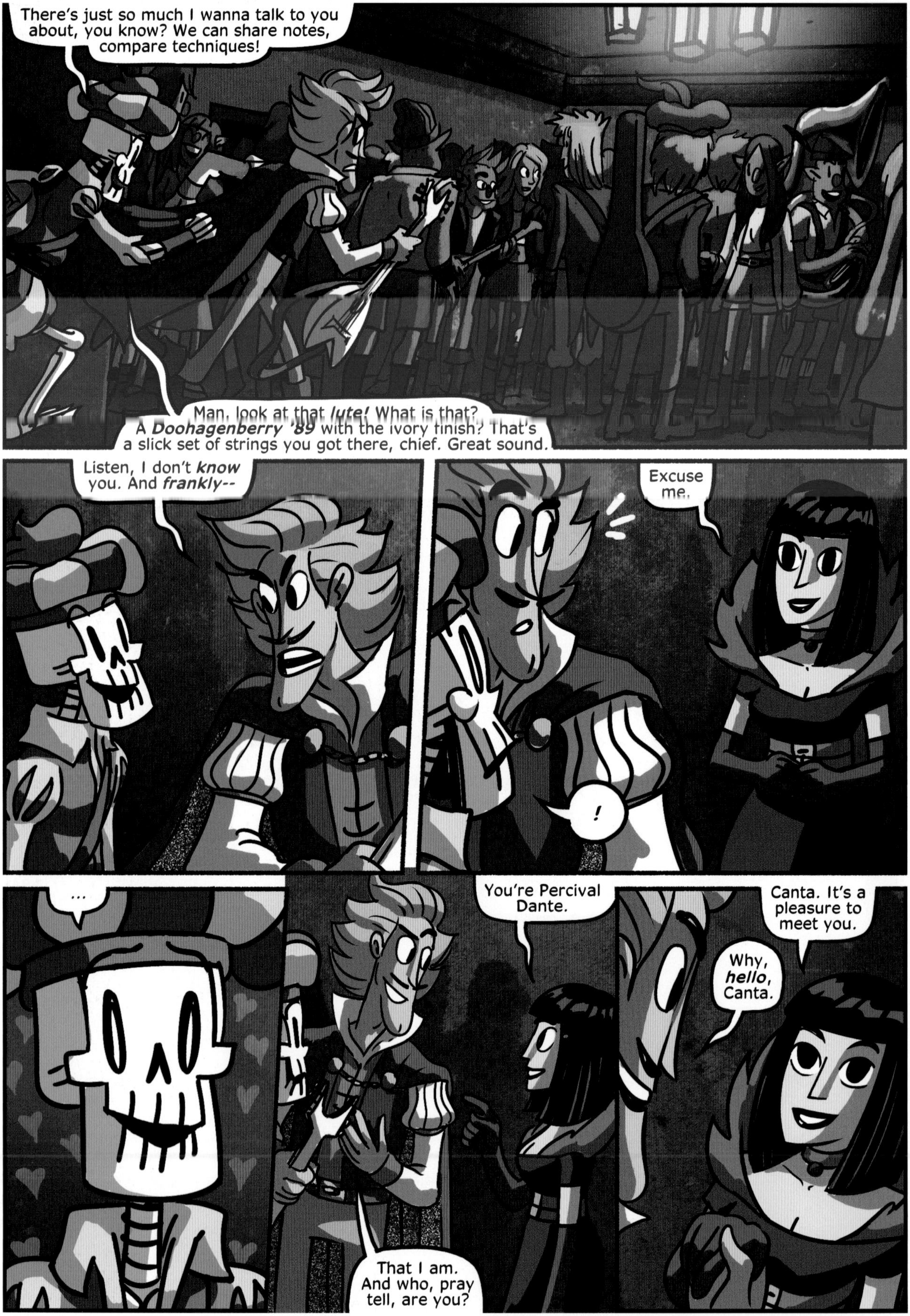

There's just so much I wanna talk to you about, you know? We can share notes, compare techniques!
Man, look at that *lute!* What is that? A ***Doohagenberry '89*** with the ivory finish? That's a slick set of strings you got there, chief. Great sound.
Listen, I don't ***know*** you. And ***frankly--***
Excuse me.
!
...
You're Percival Dante.
That I am. And who, pray tell, are you?
Canta. It's a pleasure to meet you.
Why, ***hello***, Canta.

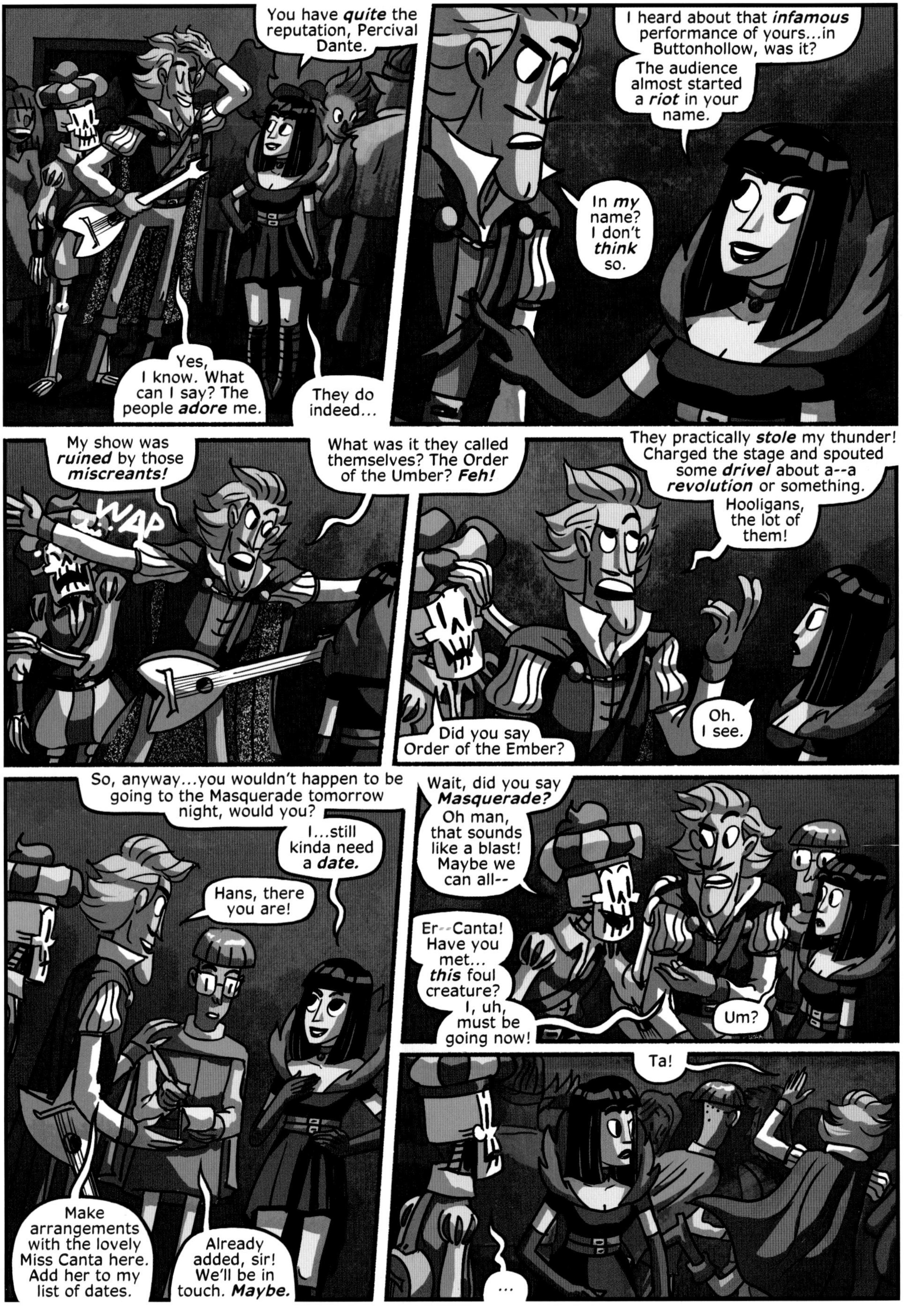
You have *quite* the reputation, Percival Dante.
Yes, I know. What can I say? The people *adore* me.
They do indeed...
I heard about that *infamous* performance of yours...in Buttonhollow, was it?
The audience almost started a *riot* in your name.
In *my* name? I don't *think* so.
My show was *ruined* by those *miscreants!*
WAP
What was it they called themselves? The Order of the Umber? *Feh!*
They practically *stole* my thunder! Charged the stage and spouted some *drivel* about a--a *revolution* or something.
Hooligans, the lot of them!
Did you say Order of the Ember?
Oh. I see.
So, anyway...you wouldn't happen to be going to the Masquerade tomorrow night, would you?
I...still kinda need a *date.*
Hans, there you are!
Make arrangements with the lovely Miss Canta here. Add her to my list of dates.
Already added, sir! We'll be in touch. *Maybe.*
Wait, did you say *Masquerade?*
Oh man, that sounds like a blast! Maybe we can all--
Er--Canta! Have you met... *this* foul creature?
I, uh, must be going now!
Um?
Ta!
...

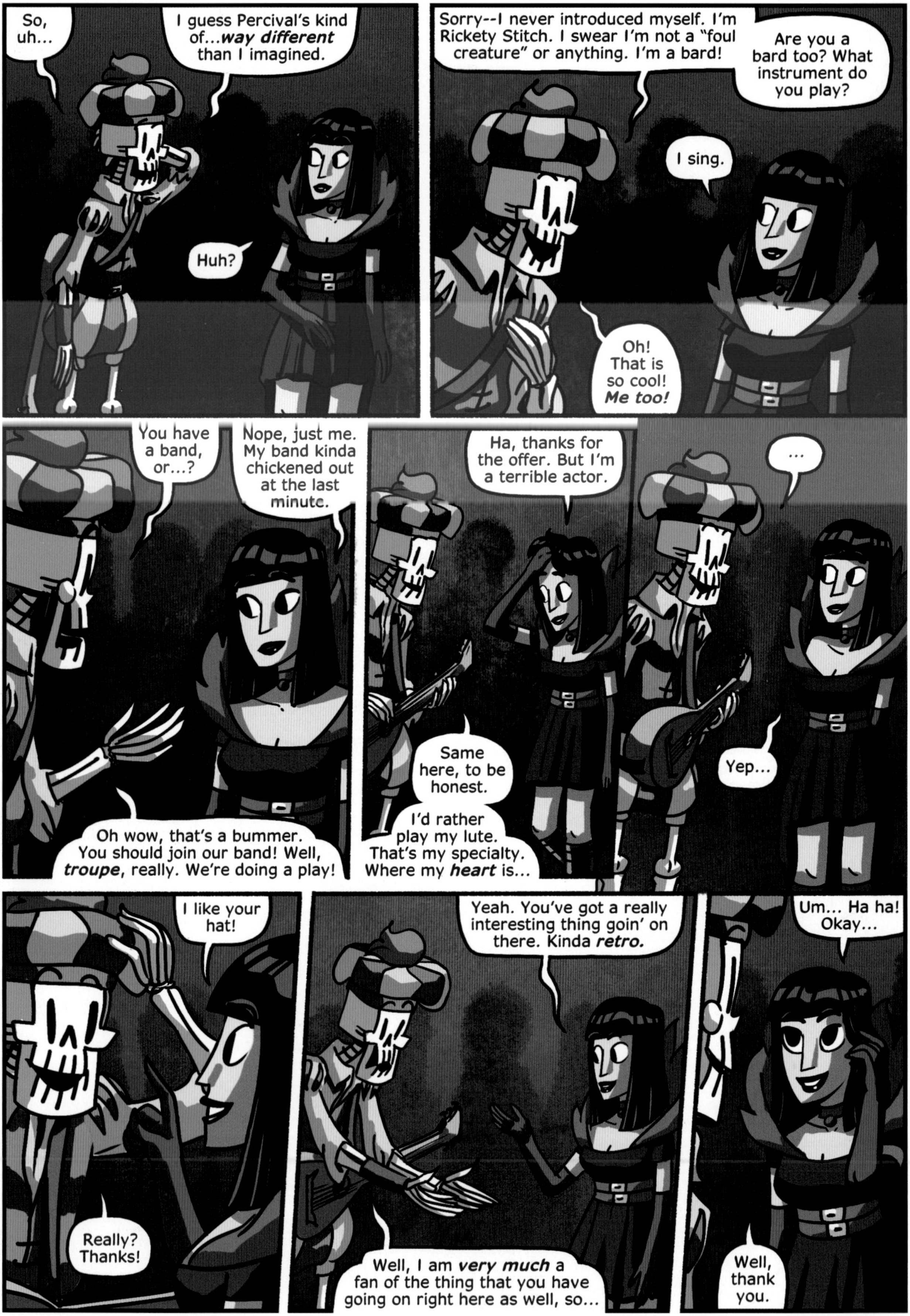
So, uh...
I guess Percival's kind of...*way different* than I imagined.
Huh?
Sorry--I never introduced myself. I'm Rickety Stitch. I swear I'm not a "foul creature" or anything. I'm a bard!
Are you a bard too? What instrument do you play?
I sing.
Oh! That is so cool! *Me too!*
You have a band, or...?
Nope, just me. My band kinda chickened out at the last minute.
Oh wow, that's a bummer. You should join our band! Well, *troupe*, really. We're doing a play!
Ha, thanks for the offer. But I'm a terrible actor.
Same here, to be honest.
I'd rather play my lute. That's my specialty. Where my *heart* is...
...
Yep...
I like your hat!
Really? Thanks!
Yeah. You've got a really interesting thing goin' on there. Kinda *retro.*
Well, I am *very much* a fan of the thing that you have going on right here as well, so...
Um... Ha ha! Okay...
Well, thank you.

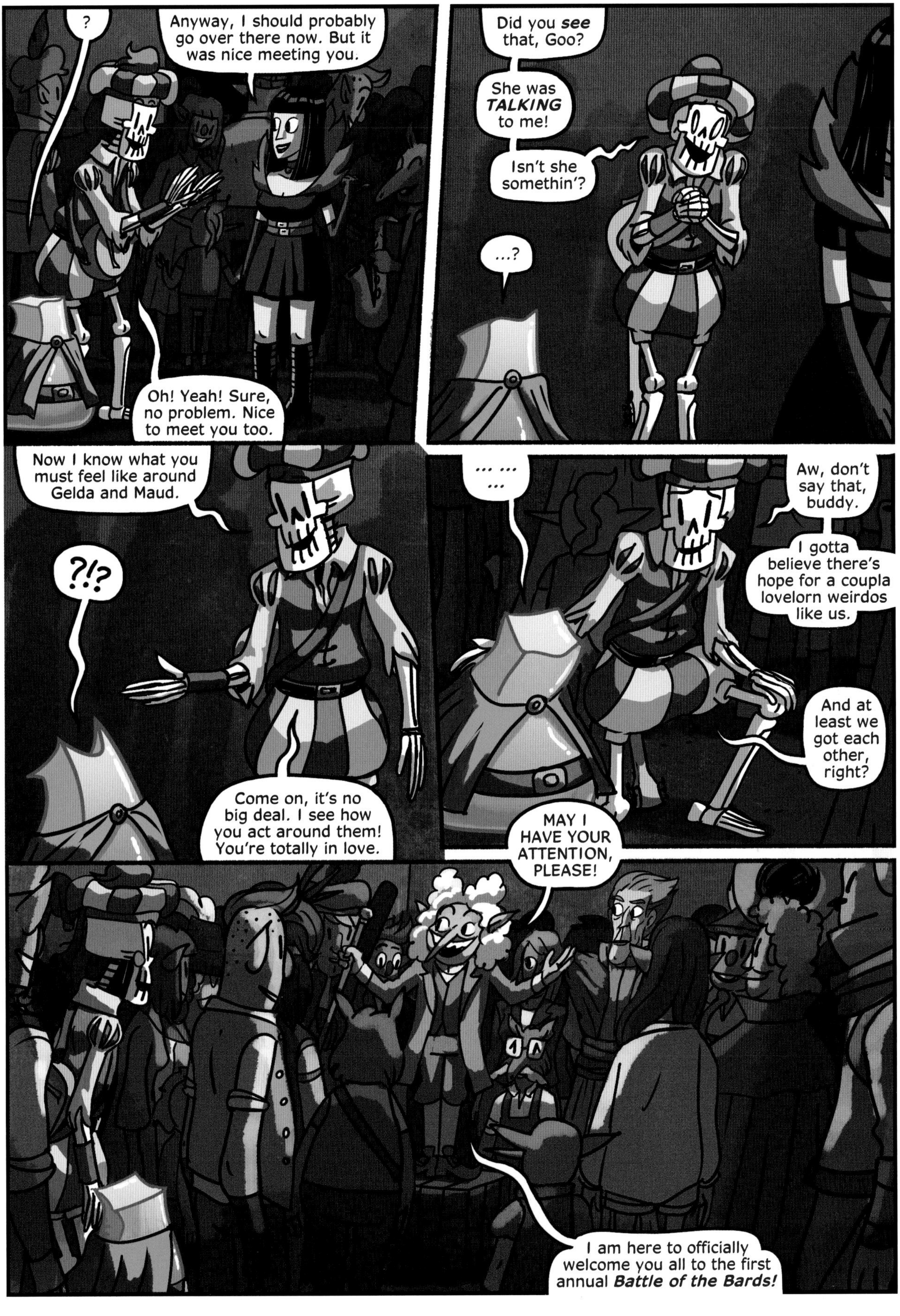
?
Anyway, I should probably go over there now. But it was nice meeting you.
Oh! Yeah! Sure, no problem. Nice to meet you too.
Did you ***see*** that, Goo?
She was ***TALKING*** to me!
Isn't she somethin'?
...?
Now I know what you must feel like around Gelda and Maud.
?!?
Come on, it's no big deal. I see how you act around them! You're totally in love.
... ...
Aw, don't say that, buddy.
I gotta believe there's hope for a coupla lovelorn weirdos like us.
And at least we got each other, right?
MAY I HAVE YOUR ATTENTION, PLEASE!
I am here to officially welcome you all to the first annual ***Battle of the Bards!***

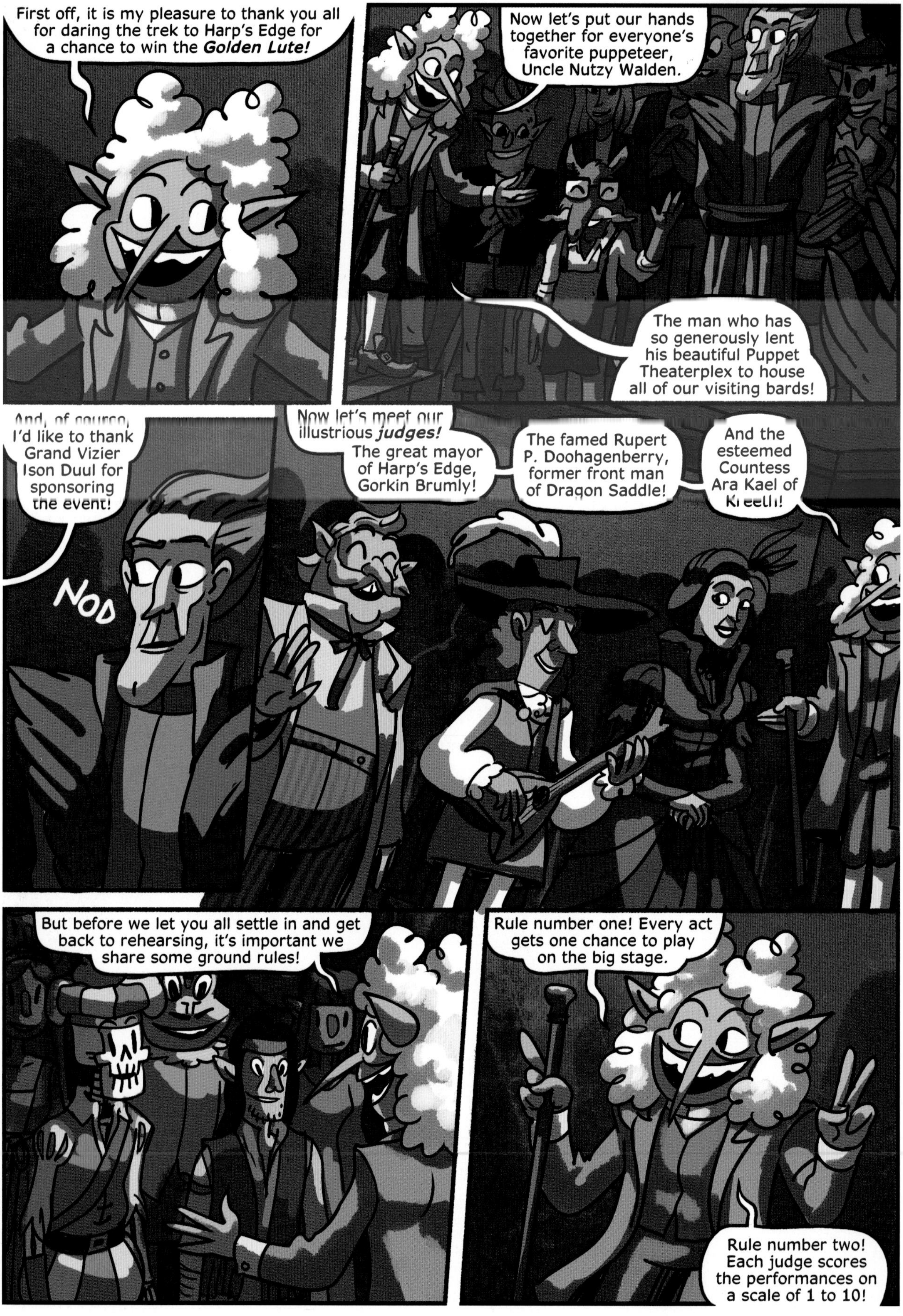
First off, it is my pleasure to thank you all for daring the trek to Harp's Edge for a chance to win the ***Golden Lute!***
Now let's put our hands together for everyone's favorite puppeteer, Uncle Nutzy Walden.
The man who has so generously lent his beautiful Puppet Theaterplex to house all of our visiting bards!
And, of course, I'd like to thank Grand Vizier Ison Duul for sponsoring the event!
NOD
Now let's meet our illustrious ***judges!***
The great mayor of Harp's Edge, Gorkin Brumly!
The famed Rupert P. Doohagenberry, former front man of Dragon Saddle!
And the esteemed Countess Ara Kael of Kreeth!
But before we let you all settle in and get back to rehearsing, it's important we share some ground rules!
Rule number one! Every act gets one chance to play on the big stage.
Rule number two! Each judge scores the performances on a scale of 1 to 10!

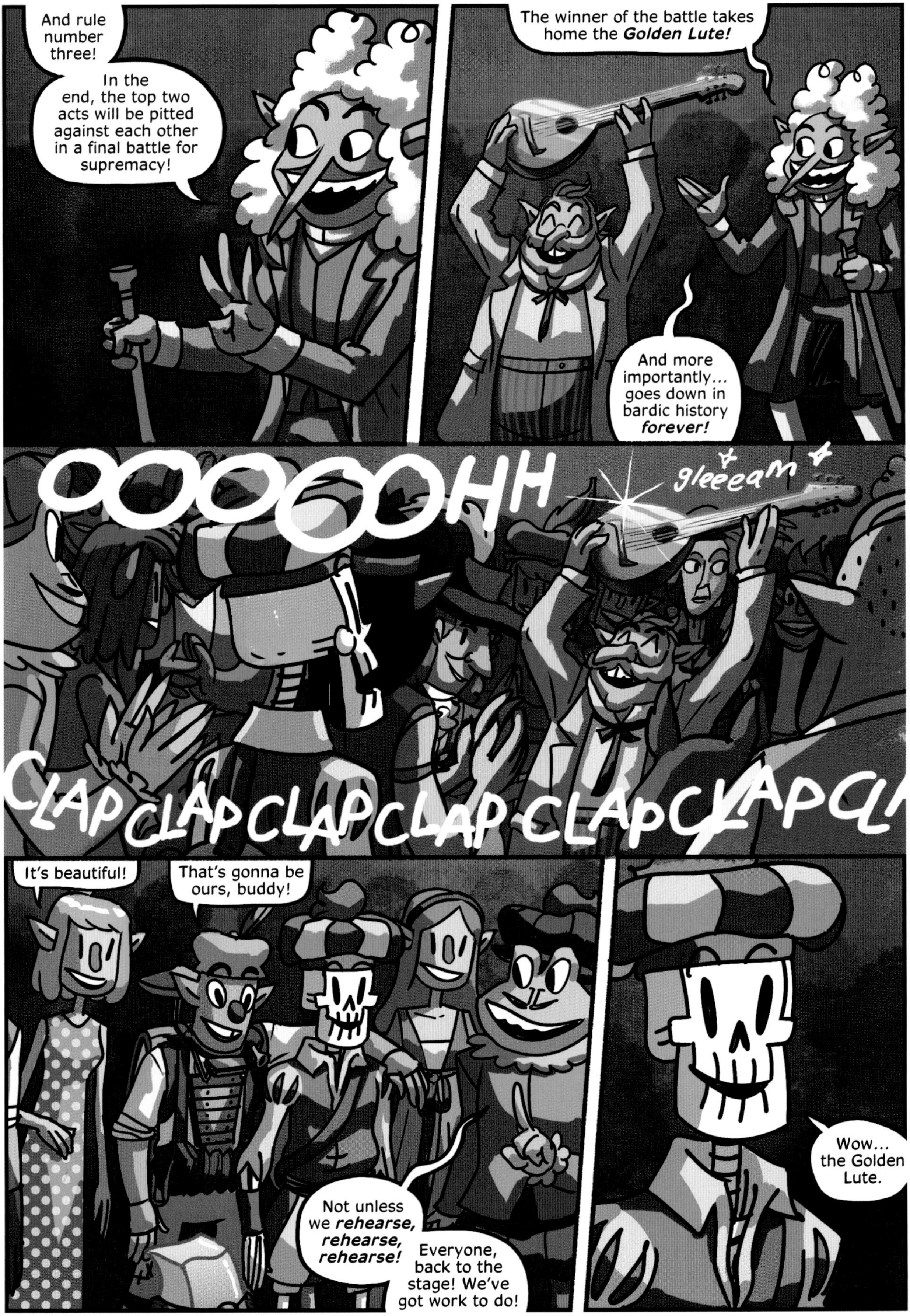
And rule number three!
In the end, the top two acts will be pitted against each other in a final battle for supremacy!
The winner of the battle takes home the ***Golden Lute!***
And more importantly... goes down in bardic history ***forever!***
OOOOOOHH
gleeeam
CLAP CLAP CLAP CLAP CLAP CLAP CL
It's beautiful!
That's gonna be ours, buddy!
Not unless we ***rehearse, rehearse, rehearse!***
Everyone, back to the stage! We've got work to do!
Wow... the Golden Lute.

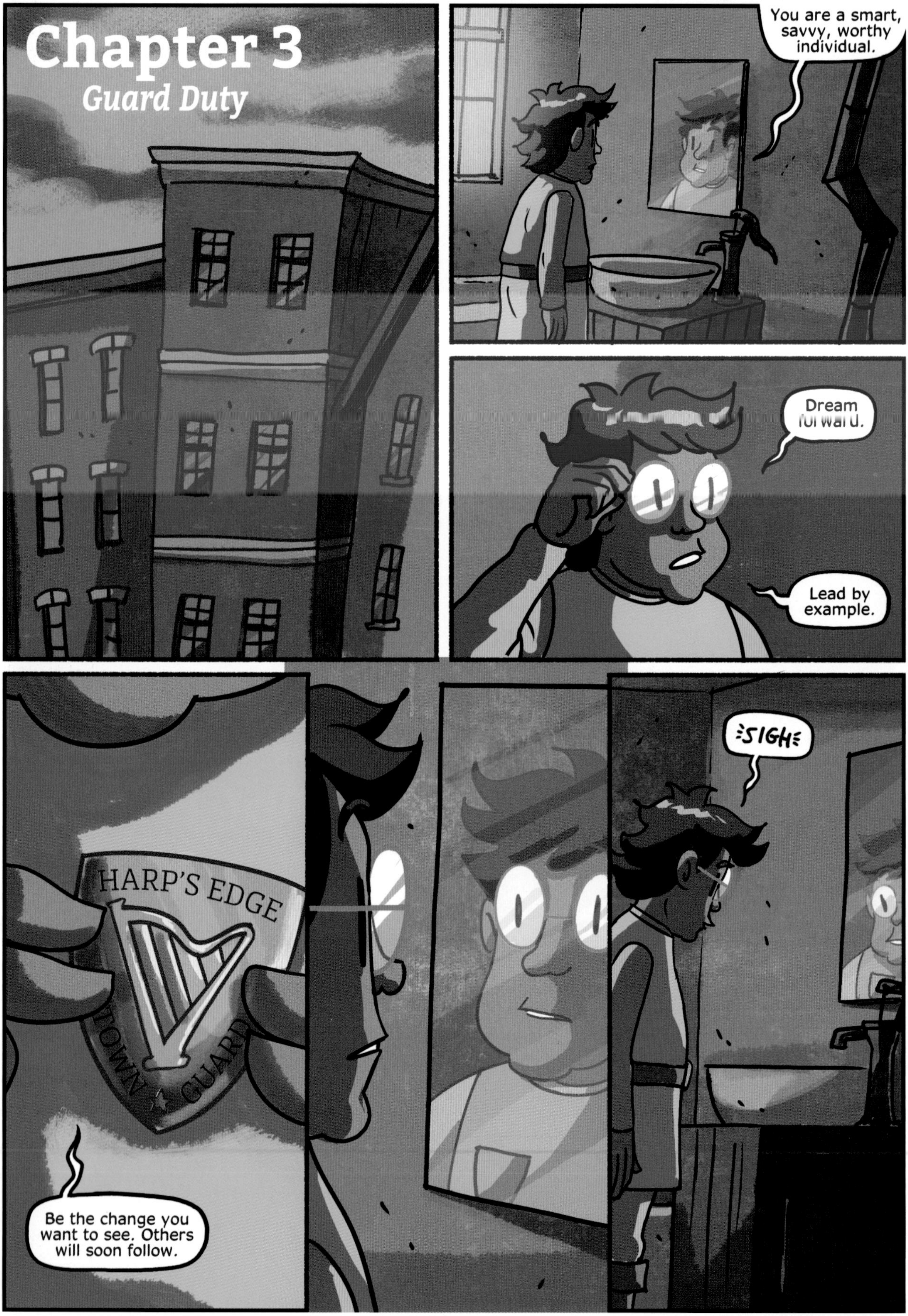
Chapter 3
Guard Duty
You are a smart, savvy, worthy individual.
Dream forward.
Lead by example.
HARP'S EDGE
TOWN GUARD
Be the change you want to see. Others will soon follow.
SIGH

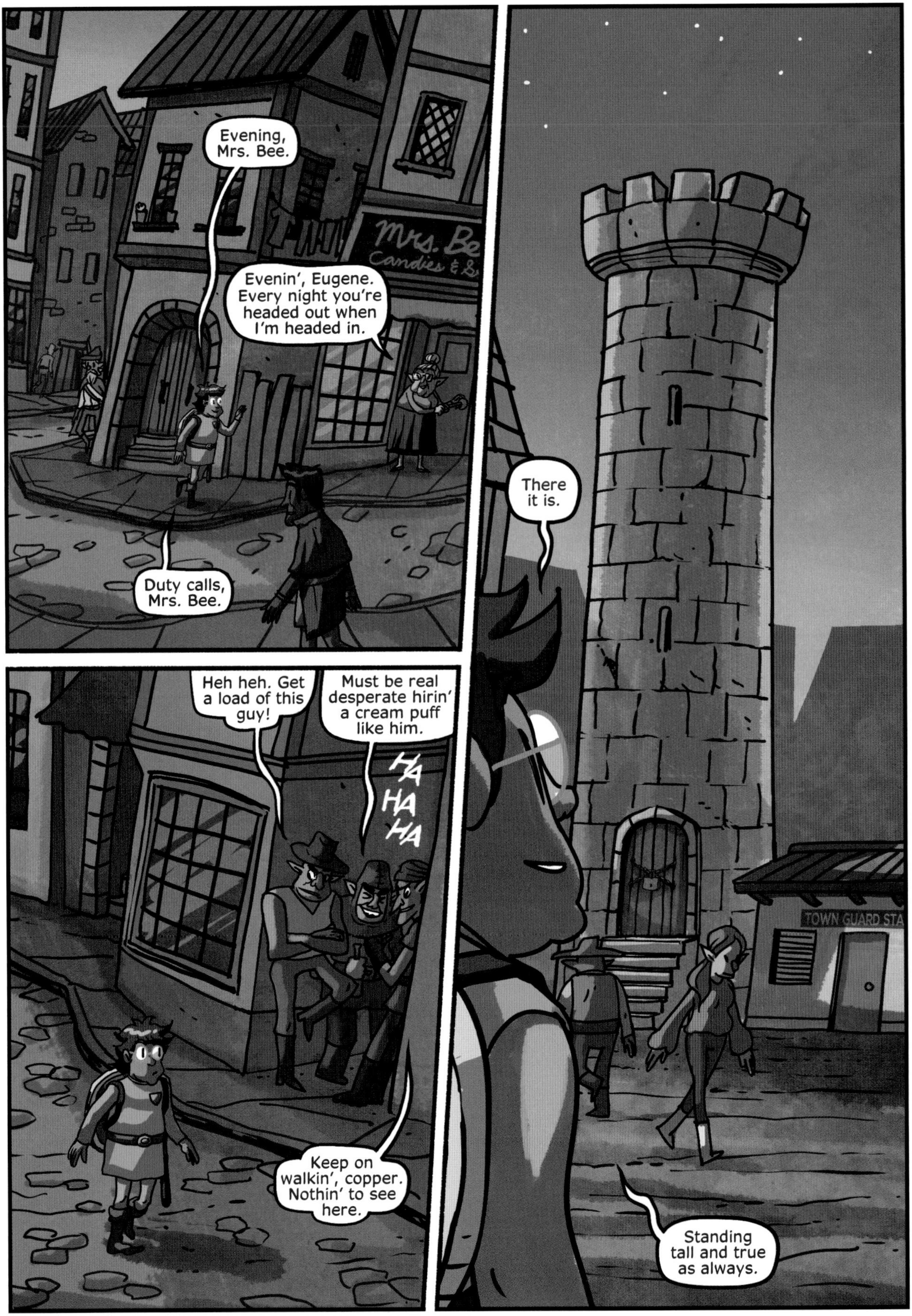
Evening, Mrs. Bee.
Evenin', Eugene. Every night you're headed out when I'm headed in.
Duty calls, Mrs. Bee.
Heh heh. Get a load of this guy!
Must be real desperate hirin' a cream puff like him.
HA HA HA
Keep on walkin', copper. Nothin' to see here.
There it is.
Standing tall and true as always.

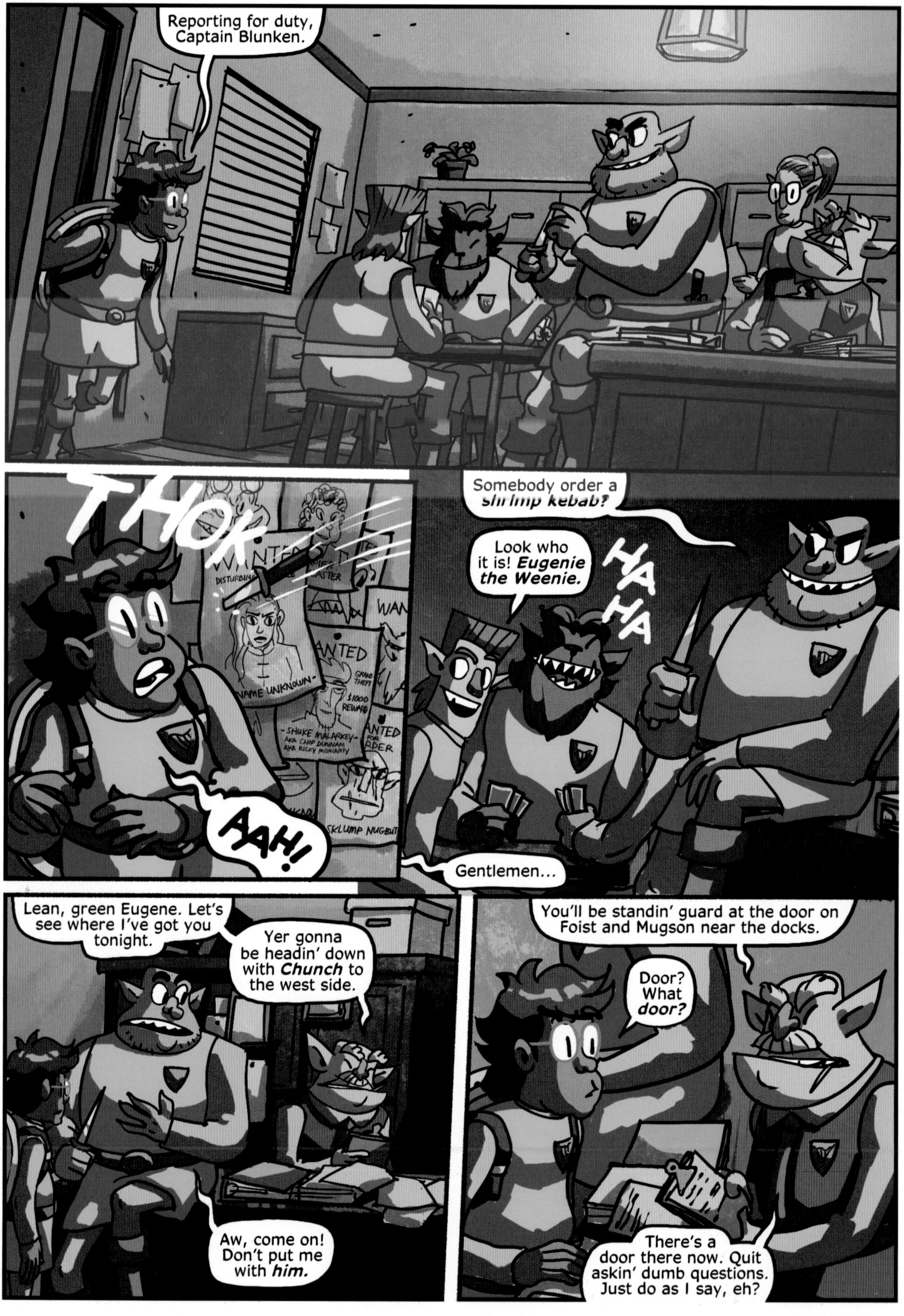

Reporting for duty, Captain Blunken.
THOK
AAH!
WANTED
DISTURBING
NAME UNKNOWN
WANTED
GRAND THEFT
$1000 REWARD
SHUKE MALARKEY
AKA CHIP DUNHAM
AKA RICKY MORIARTY
WANTED FOR MURDER
SKLUMP NUGBUT
Somebody order a *shrimp kebab?*
Look who it is! ***Eugenie the Weenie.***
HA HA HA
Gentlemen...
Lean, green Eugene. Let's see where I've got you tonight.
Yer gonna be headin' down with ***Chunch*** to the west side.
Aw, come on! Don't put me with ***him.***
You'll be standin' guard at the door on Foist and Mugson near the docks.
Door? What ***door?***
There's a door there now. Quit askin' dumb questions. Just do as I say, eh?

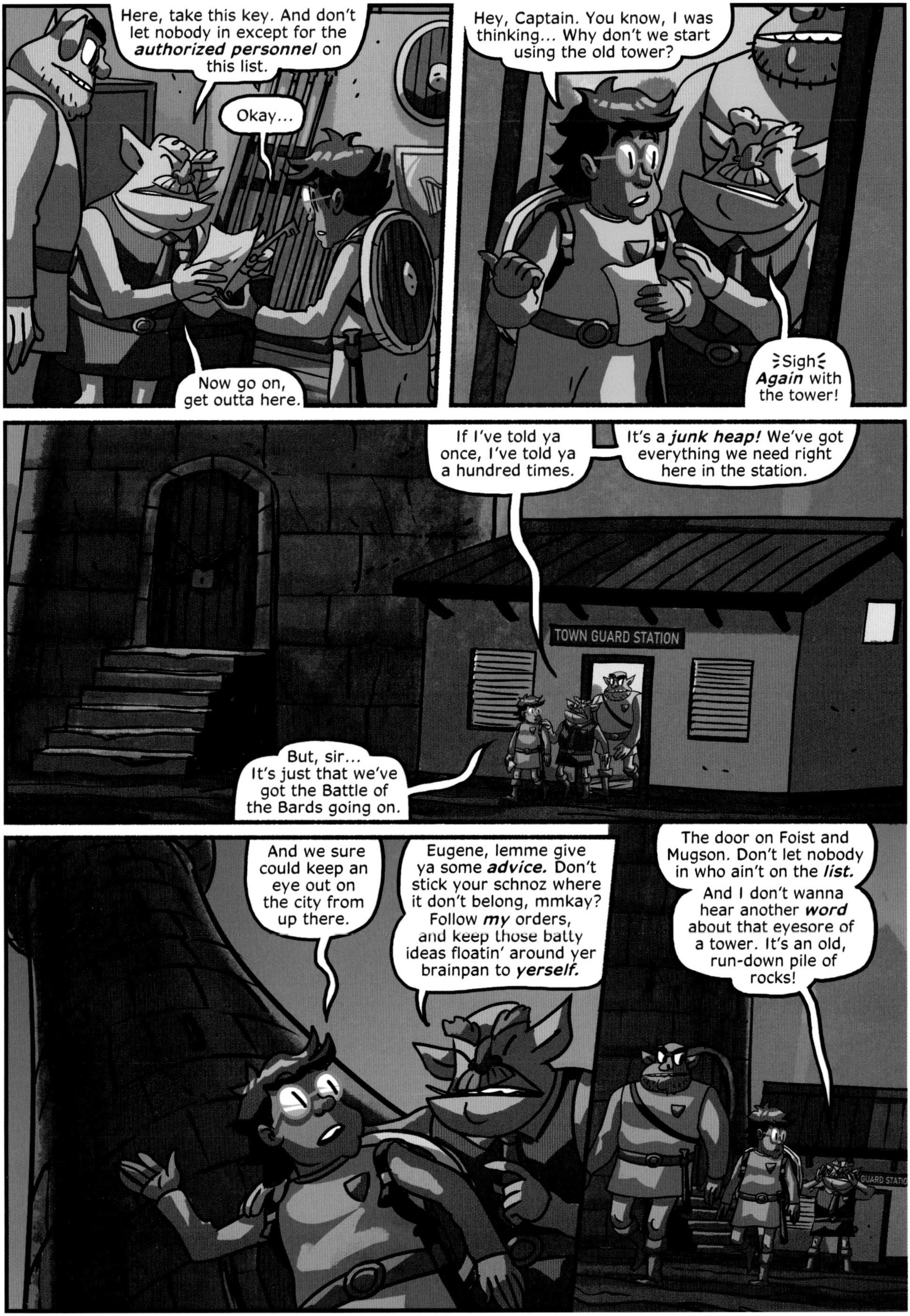

Here, take this key. And don't let nobody in except for the *authorized personnel* on this list.
Okay...
Now go on, get outta here.
Hey, Captain. You know, I was thinking... Why don't we start using the old tower?
Sigh
Again with the tower!
If I've told ya once, I've told ya a hundred times.
It's a *junk heap!* We've got everything we need right here in the station.
TOWN GUARD STATION
But, sir... It's just that we've got the Battle of the Bards going on.
And we sure could keep an eye out on the city from up there.
Eugene, lemme give ya some *advice.* Don't stick your schnoz where it don't belong, mmkay? Follow *my* orders, and keep those batty ideas floatin' around yer brainpan to *yerself.*
The door on Foist and Mugson. Don't let nobody in who ain't on the *list.*
And I don't wanna hear another *word* about that eyesore of a tower. It's an old, run-down pile of rocks!
GUARD STATIO

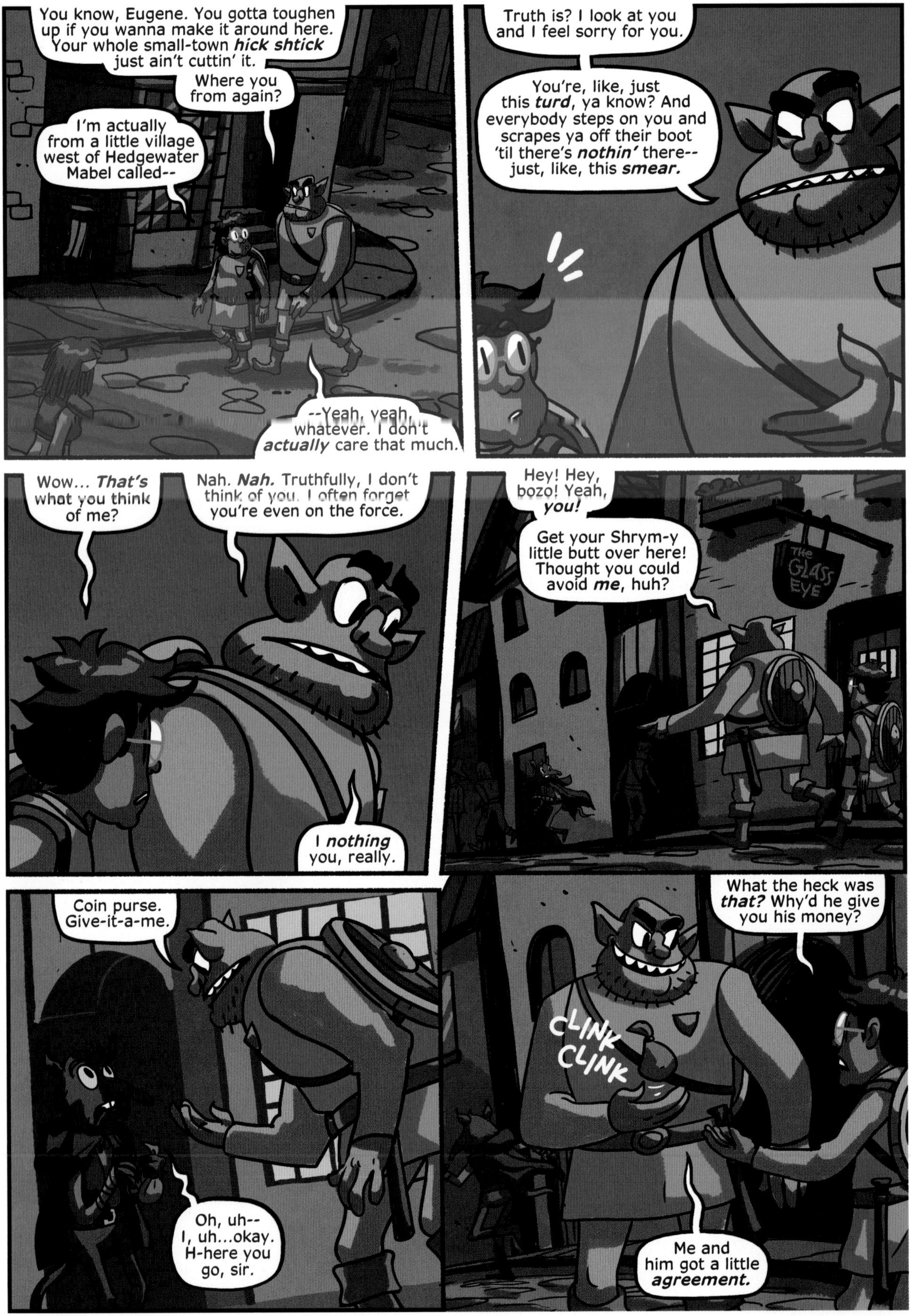
You know, Eugene. You gotta toughen up if you wanna make it around here. Your whole small-town *hick shtick* just ain't cuttin' it.
Where you from again?
I'm actually from a little village west of Hedgewater Mabel called--
--Yeah, yeah, whatever. I don't *actually* care that much.
Truth is? I look at you and I feel sorry for you.
You're, like, just this *turd*, ya know? And everybody steps on you and scrapes ya off their boot 'til there's *nothin'* there--just, like, this *smear.*
Wow... *That's* what you think of me?
Nah. *Nah.* Truthfully, I don't think of you. I often forget you're even on the force.
I *nothing* you, really.
Hey! Hey, bozo! Yeah, *you!*
Get your Shrym-y little butt over here! Thought you could avoid *me*, huh?
THE GLASS EYE
Coin purse. Give-it-a-me.
Oh, uh--I, uh...okay. H-here you go, sir.
What the heck was *that?* Why'd he give you his money?
CLINK CLINK
Me and him got a little *agreement.*

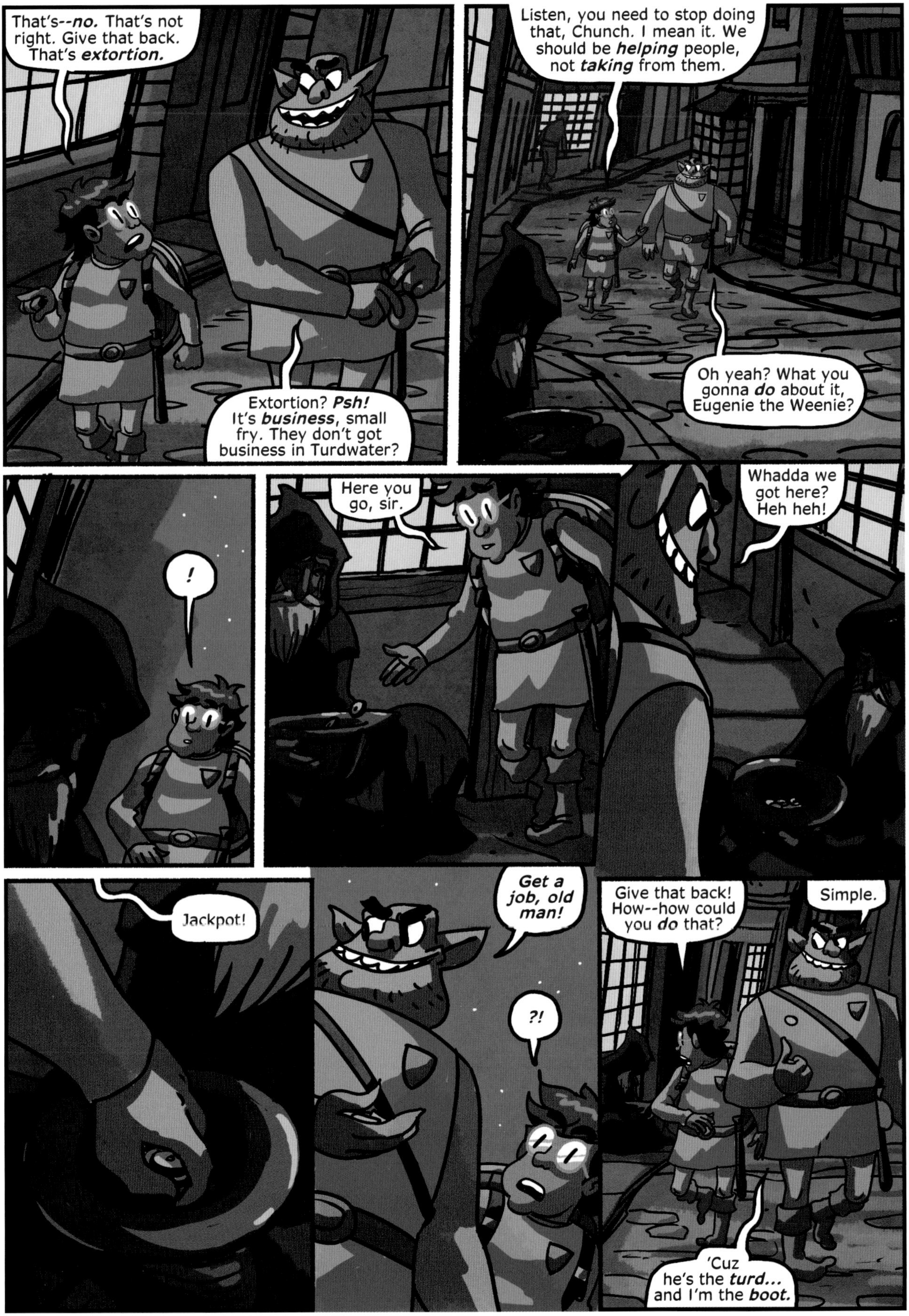

That's--*no.* That's not right. Give that back. That's *extortion.*
Extortion? *Psh!* It's *business*, small fry. They don't got business in Turdwater?
Listen, you need to stop doing that, Chunch. I mean it. We should be *helping* people, not *taking* from them.
Oh yeah? What you gonna *do* about it, Eugenie the Weenie?
!
Here you go, sir.
Whadda we got here? Heh heh!
Jackpot!
Get a job, old man!
?!
Give that back! How--how could you *do* that?
Simple.
'Cuz he's the *turd...* and I'm the *boot.*

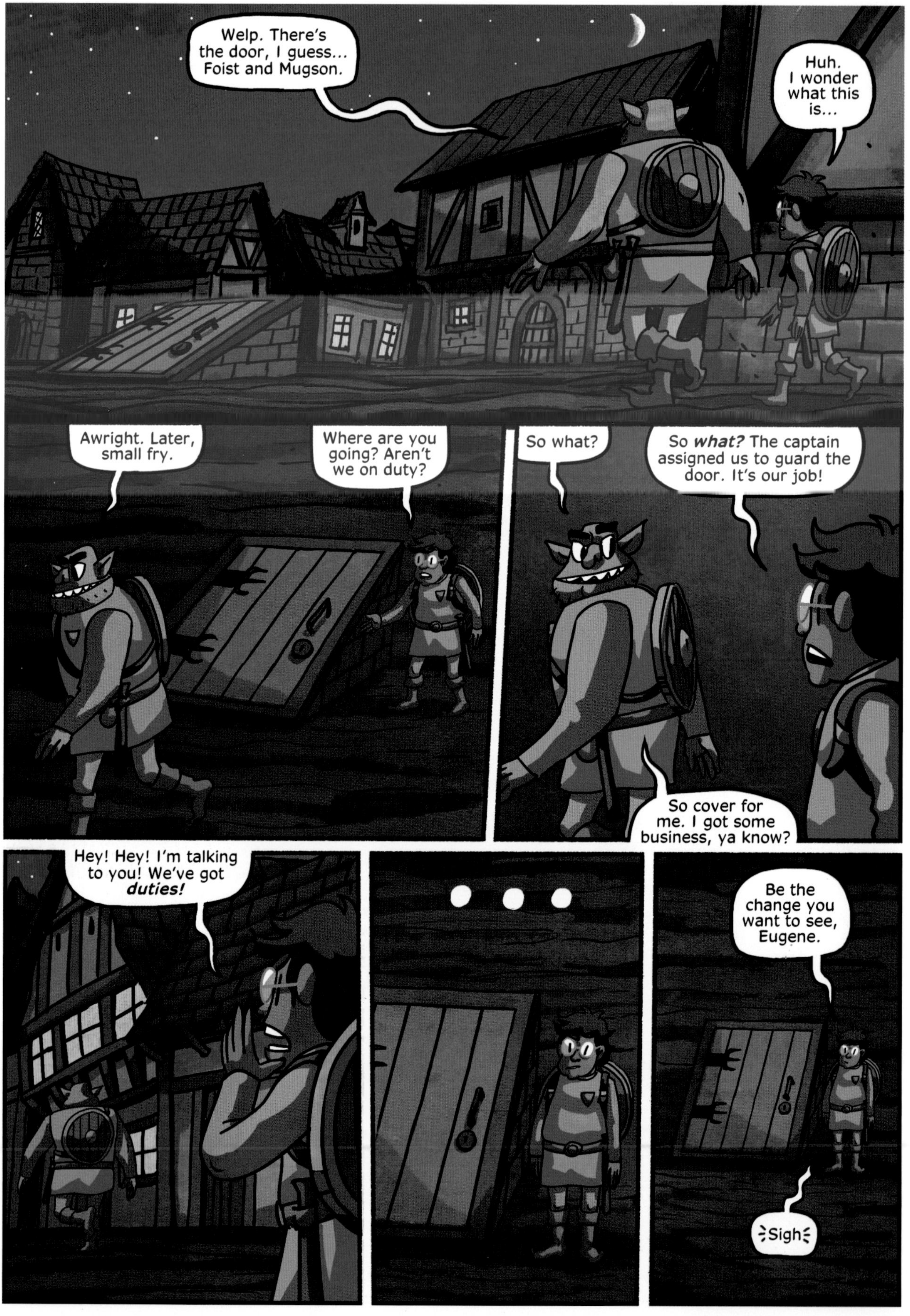
Welp. There's the door, I guess... Foist and Mugson.
Huh. I wonder what this is...
Awright. Later, small fry.
Where are you going? Aren't we on duty?
So what?
So *what?* The captain assigned us to guard the door. It's our job!
So cover for me. I got some business, ya know?
Hey! Hey! I'm talking to you! We've got *duties!*
• • •
Be the change you want to see, Eugene.
Sigh

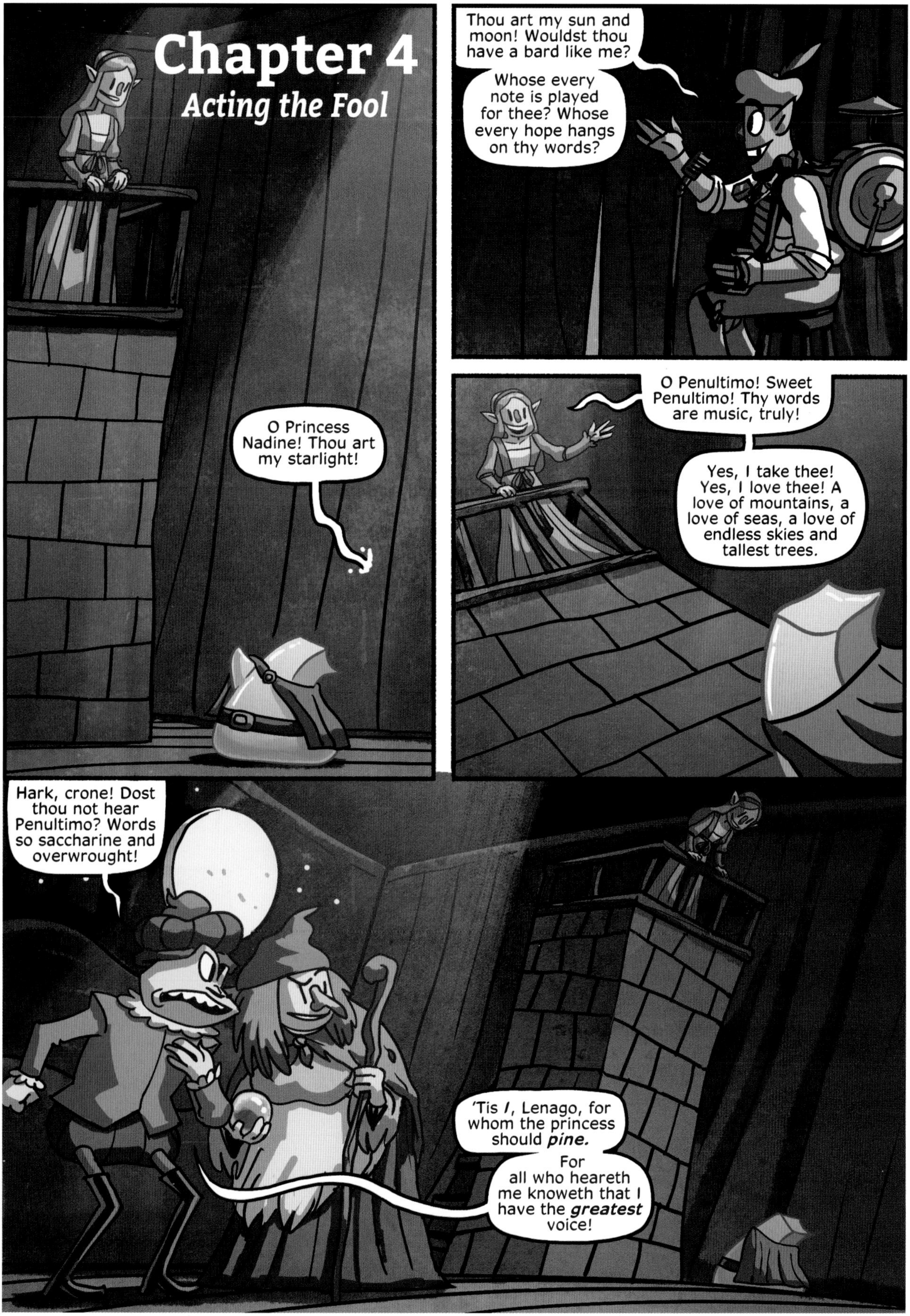

Chapter 4
Acting the Fool
Thou art my sun and moon! Wouldst thou have a bard like me?
Whose every note is played for thee? Whose every hope hangs on thy words?
O Princess Nadine! Thou art my starlight!
O Penultimo! Sweet Penultimo! Thy words are music, truly!
Yes, I take thee! Yes, I love thee! A love of mountains, a love of seas, a love of endless skies and tallest trees.
Hark, crone! Dost thou not hear Penultimo? Words so saccharine and overwrought!
'Tis *I*, Lenago, for whom the princess should *pine.*
For all who heareth me knoweth that I have the ***greatest*** voice!

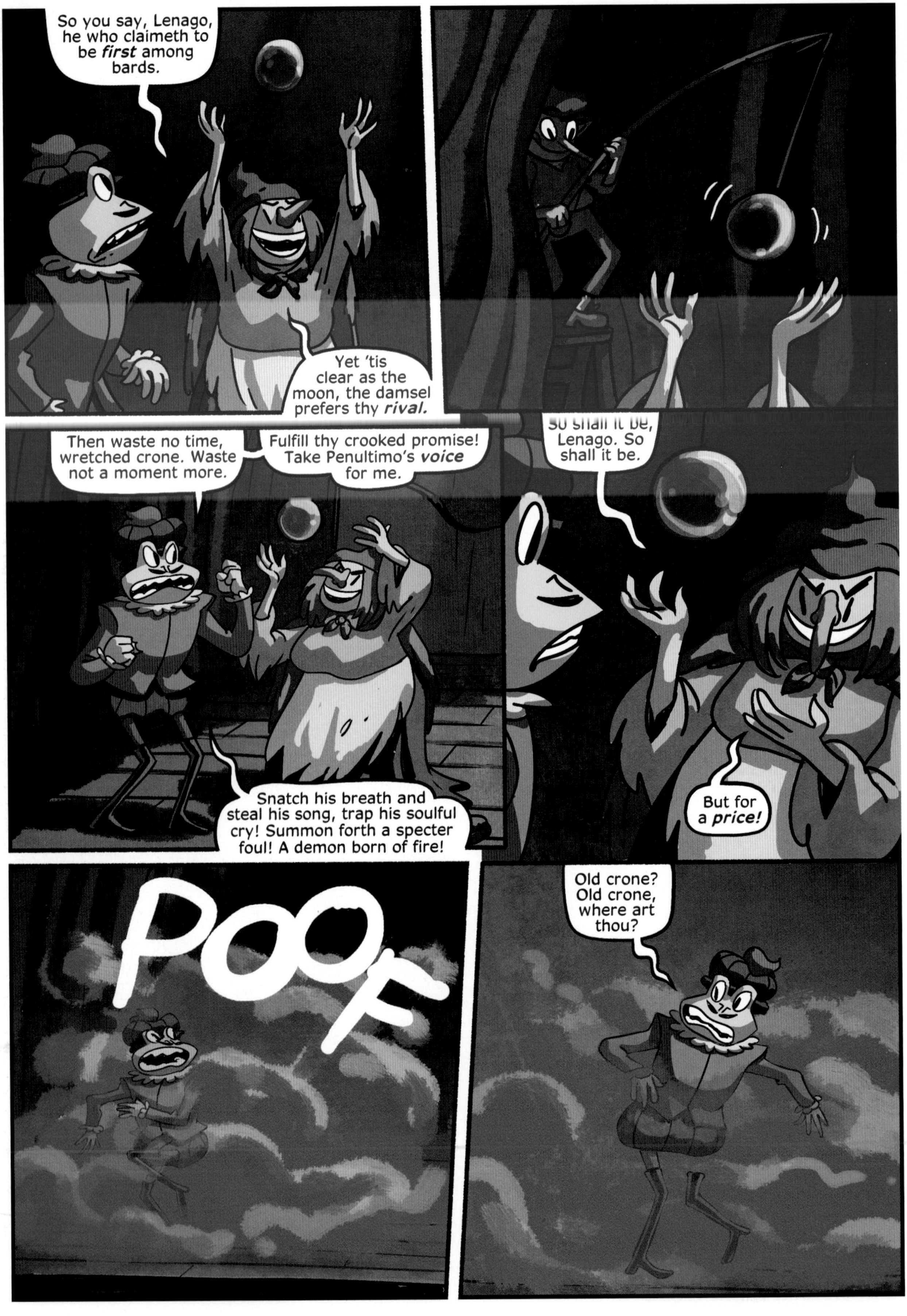
So you say, Lenago, he who claimeth to be *first* among bards.
Yet 'tis clear as the moon, the damsel prefers thy *rival.*
Then waste no time, wretched crone. Waste not a moment more.
Fulfill thy crooked promise! Take Penultimo's *voice* for me.
Snatch his breath and steal his song, trap his soulful cry! Summon forth a specter foul! A demon born of fire!
So shall it be, Lenago. So shall it be.
But for a *price!*
POOF
Old crone? Old crone, where art thou?

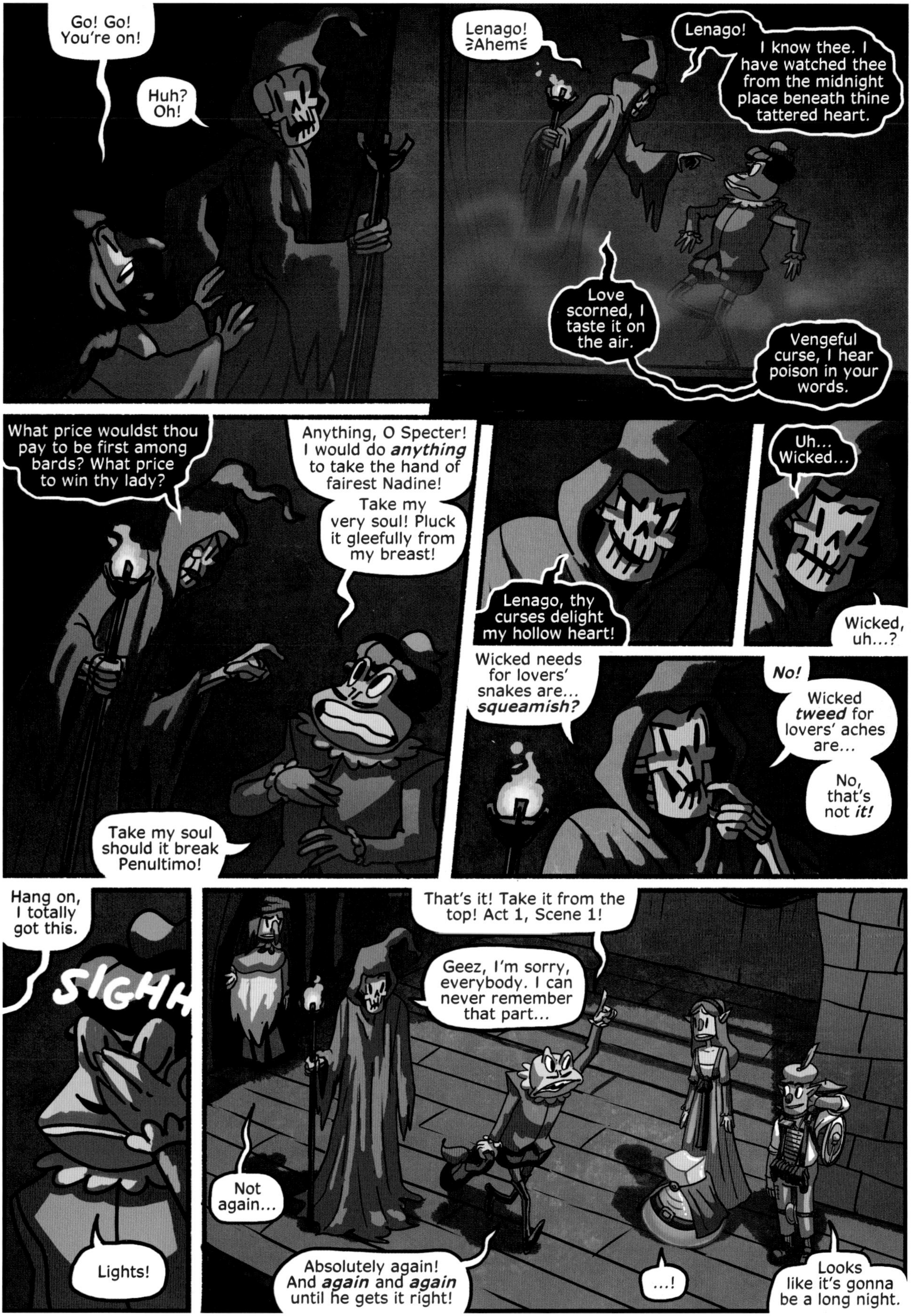

Go! Go! You're on!
Huh? Oh!
Lenago! Ahem
Lenago! I know thee. I have watched thee from the midnight place beneath thine tattered heart.
Love scorned, I taste it on the air.
Vengeful curse, I hear poison in your words.
What price wouldst thou pay to be first among bards? What price to win thy lady?
Anything, O Specter! I would do *anything* to take the hand of fairest Nadine!
Take my very soul! Pluck it gleefully from my breast!
Take my soul should it break Penultimo!
Lenago, thy curses delight my hollow heart!
Uh... Wicked...
Wicked, uh...?
Wicked needs for lovers' snakes are... ***squeamish?***
No!
Wicked ***tweed*** for lovers' aches are...
No, that's not ***it!***
Hang on, I totally got this.
SIGHH
Lights!
That's it! Take it from the top! Act 1, Scene 1!
Geez, I'm sorry, everybody. I can never remember that part...
Not again...
Absolutely again! And ***again*** and ***again*** until he gets it right!
...!
Looks like it's gonna be a long night.

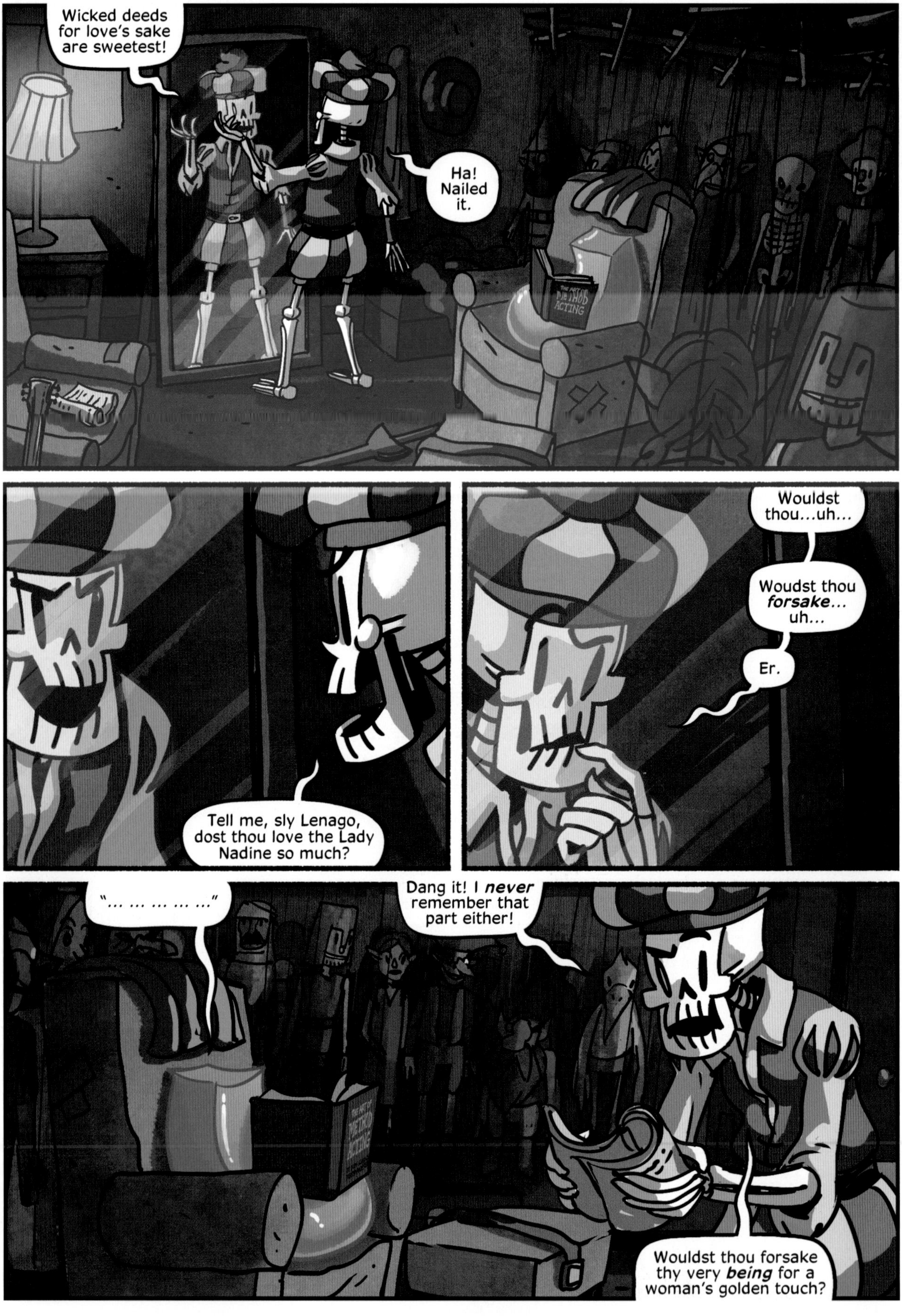

Wicked deeds for love's sake are sweetest!
Ha! Nailed it.
THE ART OF METHOD ACTING
Tell me, sly Lenago, dost thou love the Lady Nadine so much?
Wouldst thou...uh...
Woudst thou *forsake*... uh...
Er.
"... ... ..."
Dang it! I ***never*** remember that part either!
Wouldst thou forsake thy very ***being*** for a woman's golden touch?

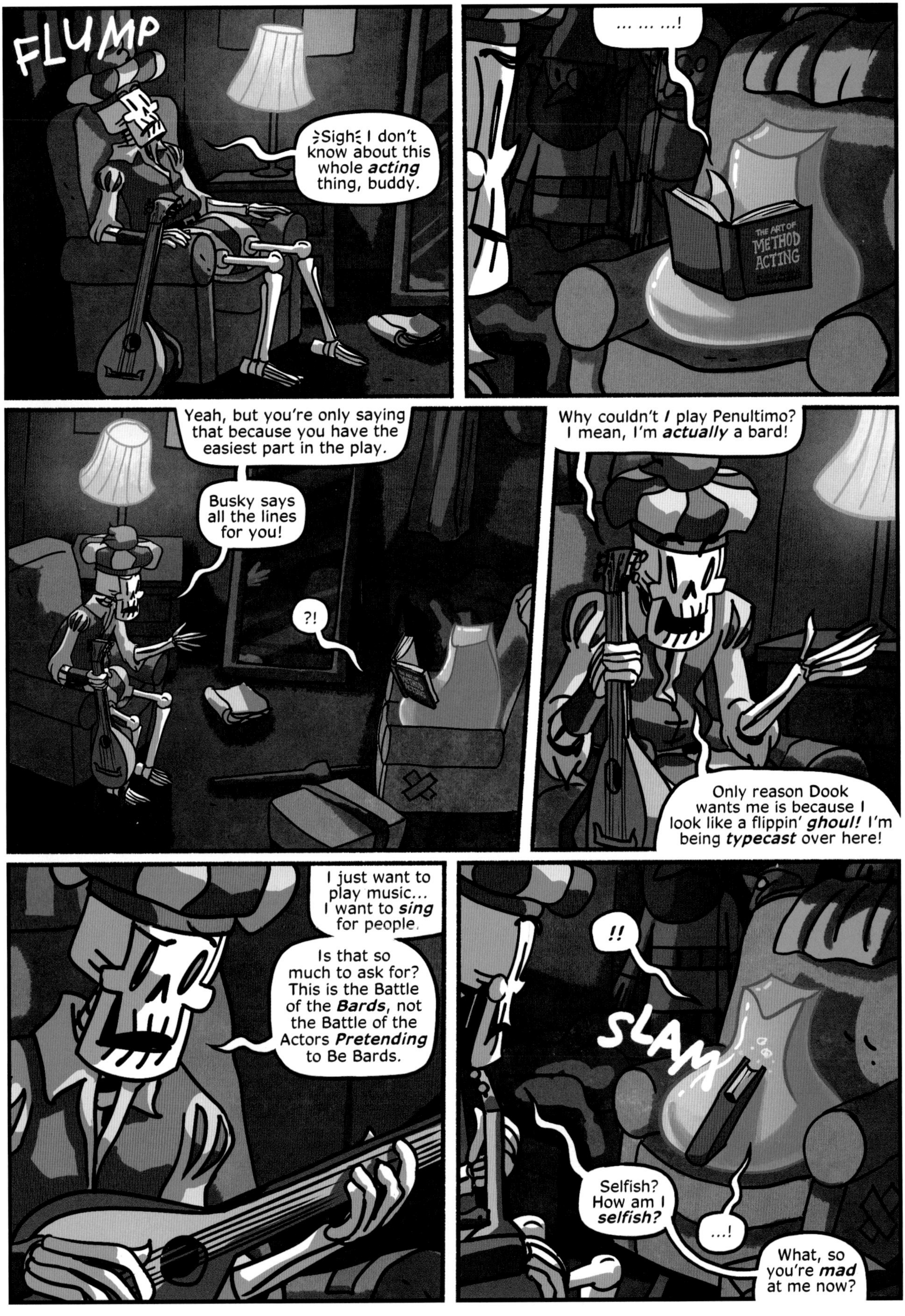
FLUMP
≷Sigh≶ I don't know about this whole *acting* thing, buddy.
... ...!
THE ART OF METHOD ACTING
Yeah, but you're only saying that because you have the easiest part in the play.
Busky says all the lines for you!
?!
Why couldn't *I* play Penultimo? I mean, I'm *actually* a bard!
Only reason Dook wants me is because I look like a flippin' *ghoul!* I'm being *typecast* over here!
I just want to play music... I want to *sing* for people.
Is that so much to ask for? This is the Battle of the *Bards*, not the Battle of the Actors *Pretending* to Be Bards.
!!
SLAM
Selfish? How am I *selfish?*
...!
What, so you're *mad* at me now?

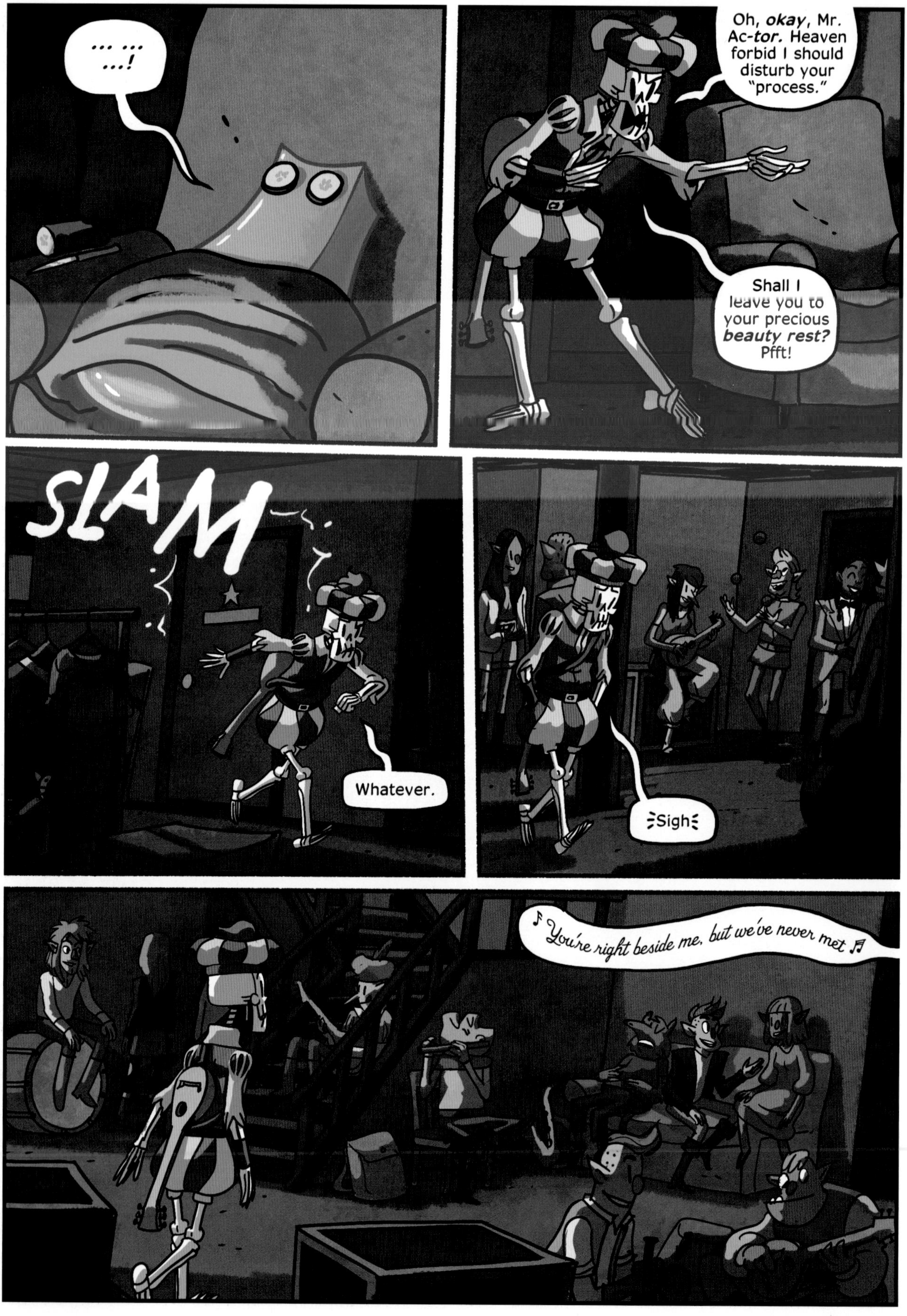
... ...!
Oh, okay, Mr. Ac-tor. Heaven forbid I should disturb your "process."
Shall I leave you to your precious beauty rest? Pfft!
SLAM
Whatever.
Sigh
♪ You're right beside me, but we've never met ♬

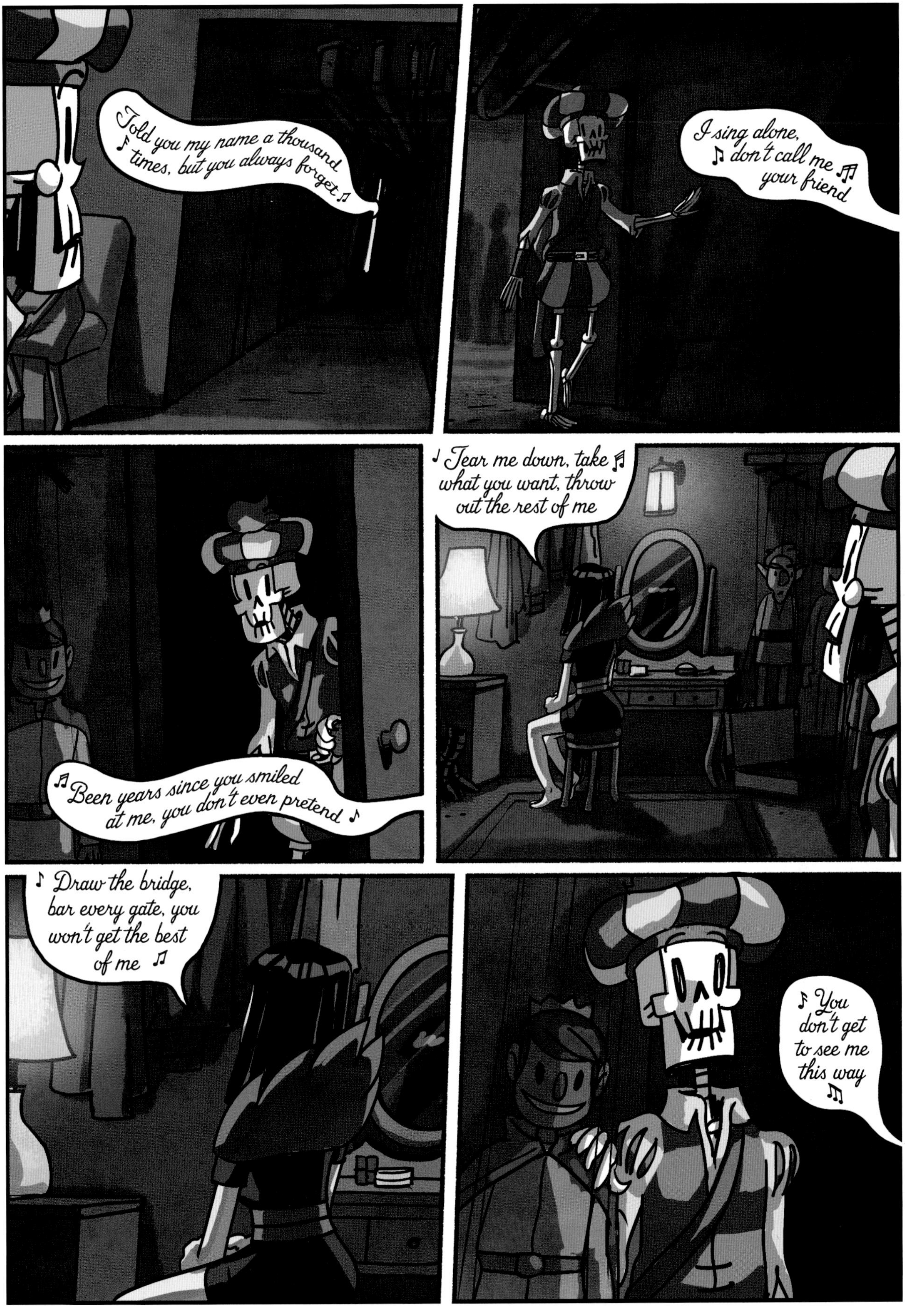
Told you my name a thousand times, but you always forget ♫
I sing alone, ♫ don't call me ♫ your friend
♫ Been years since you smiled at me, you don't even pretend ♪
♩ Tear me down, take ♫ what you want, throw out the rest of me
♪ Draw the bridge, bar every gate, you won't get the best of me ♫
♪ You don't get to see me this way ♫

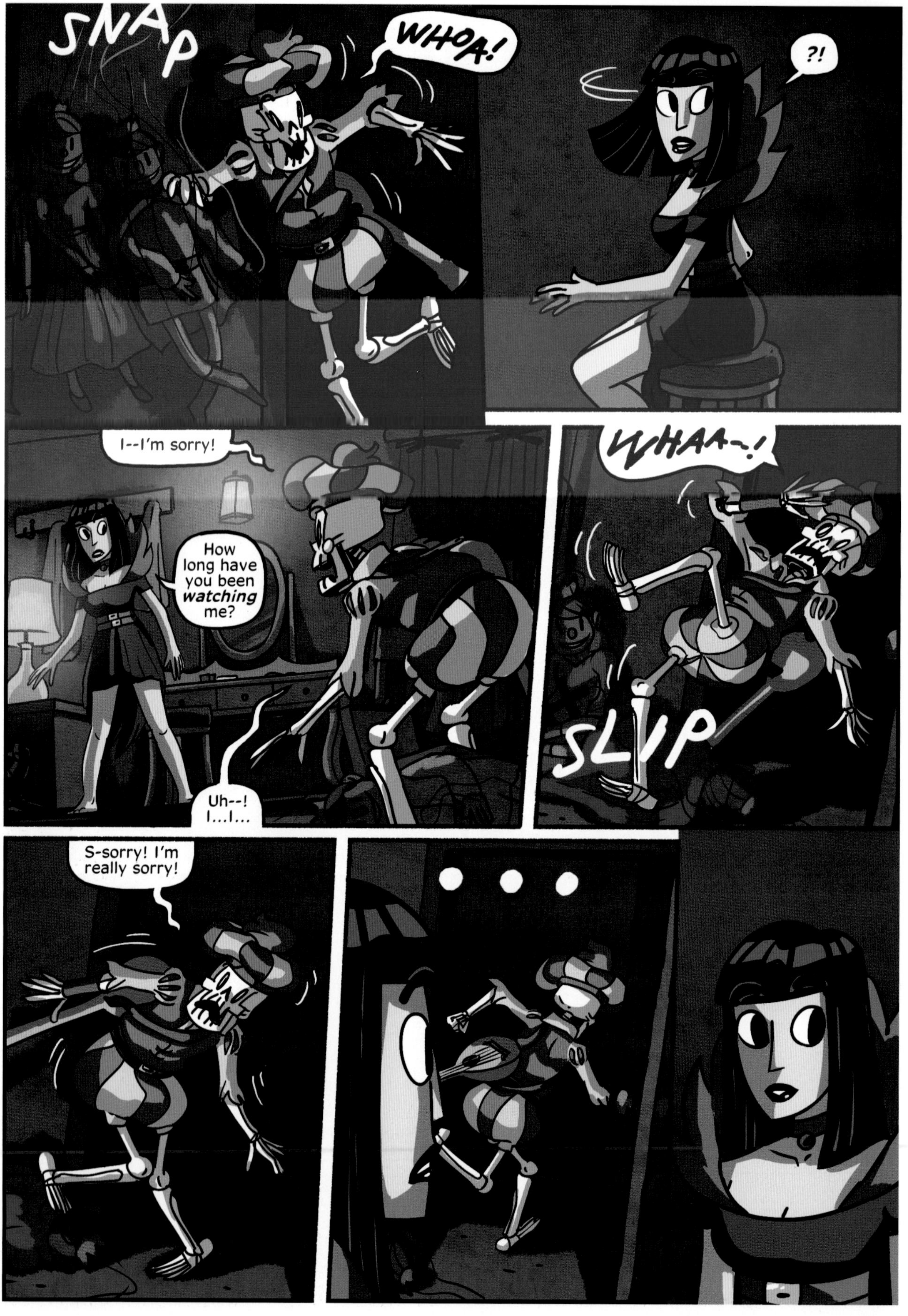
SNAP
WHOA!
?!
I--I'm sorry!
How long have you been ***watching*** me?
Uh--! I...I...
WHAA--!
SLIP
S-sorry! I'm really sorry!
• • •

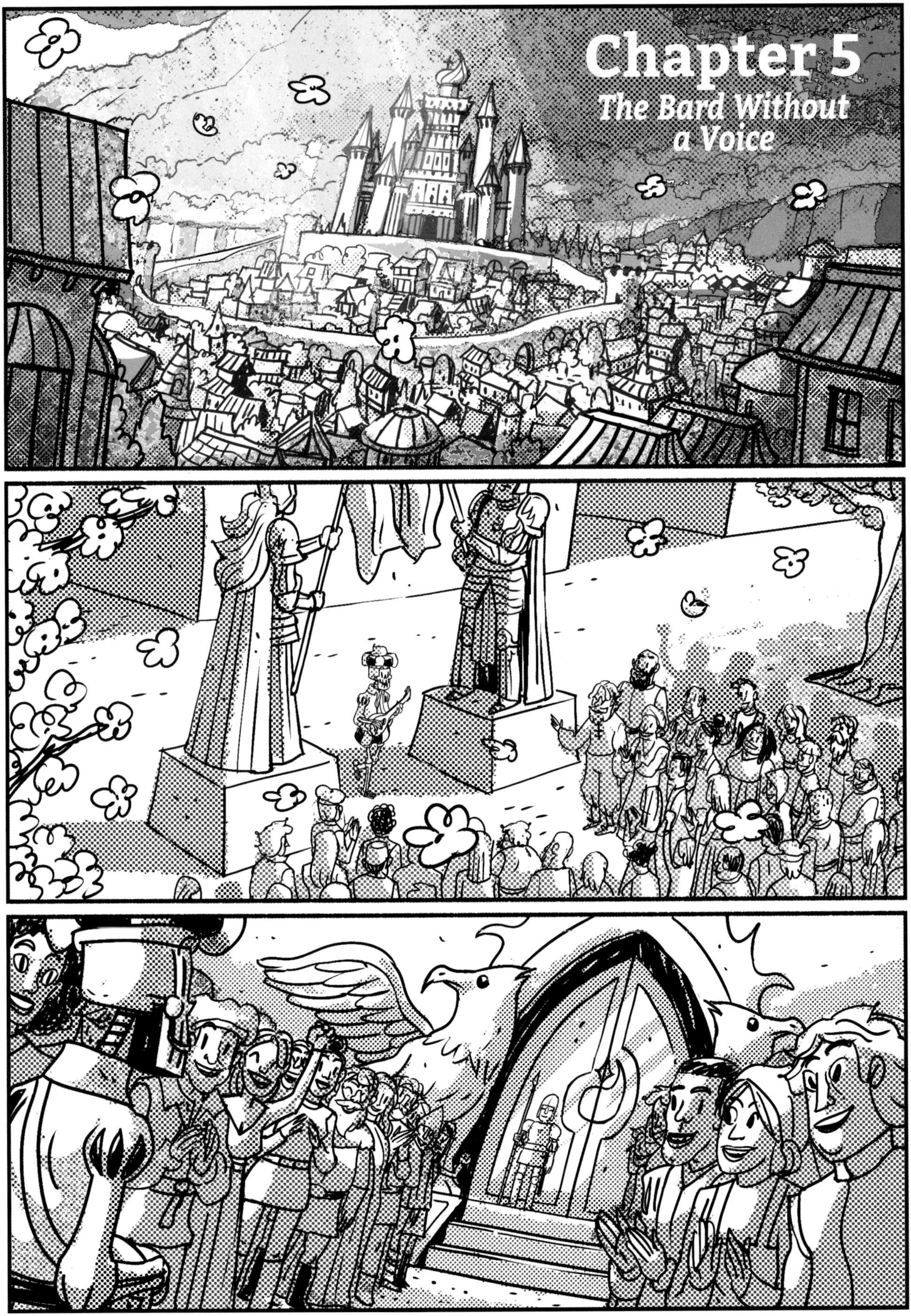
Chapter 5
The Bard Without a Voice

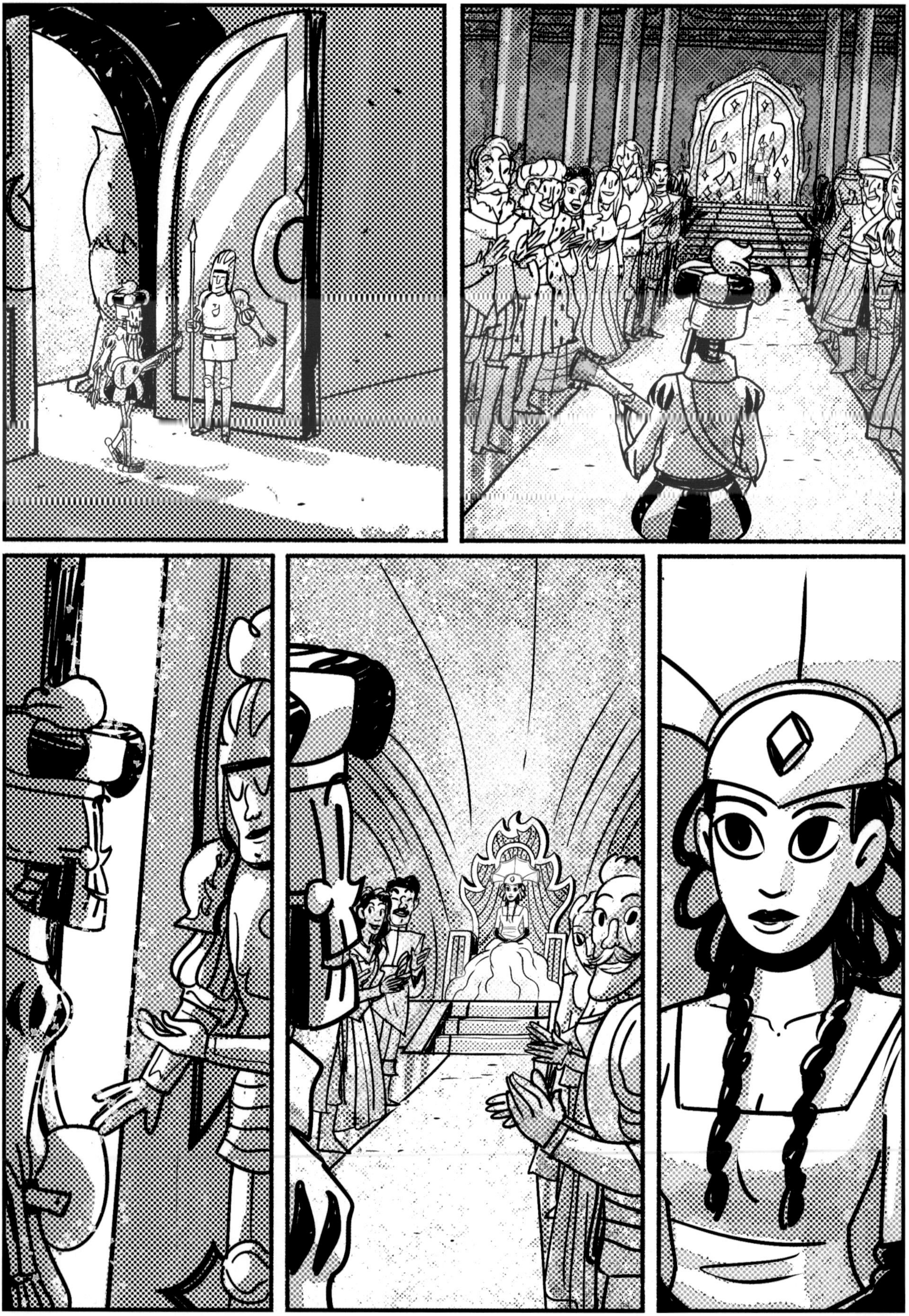

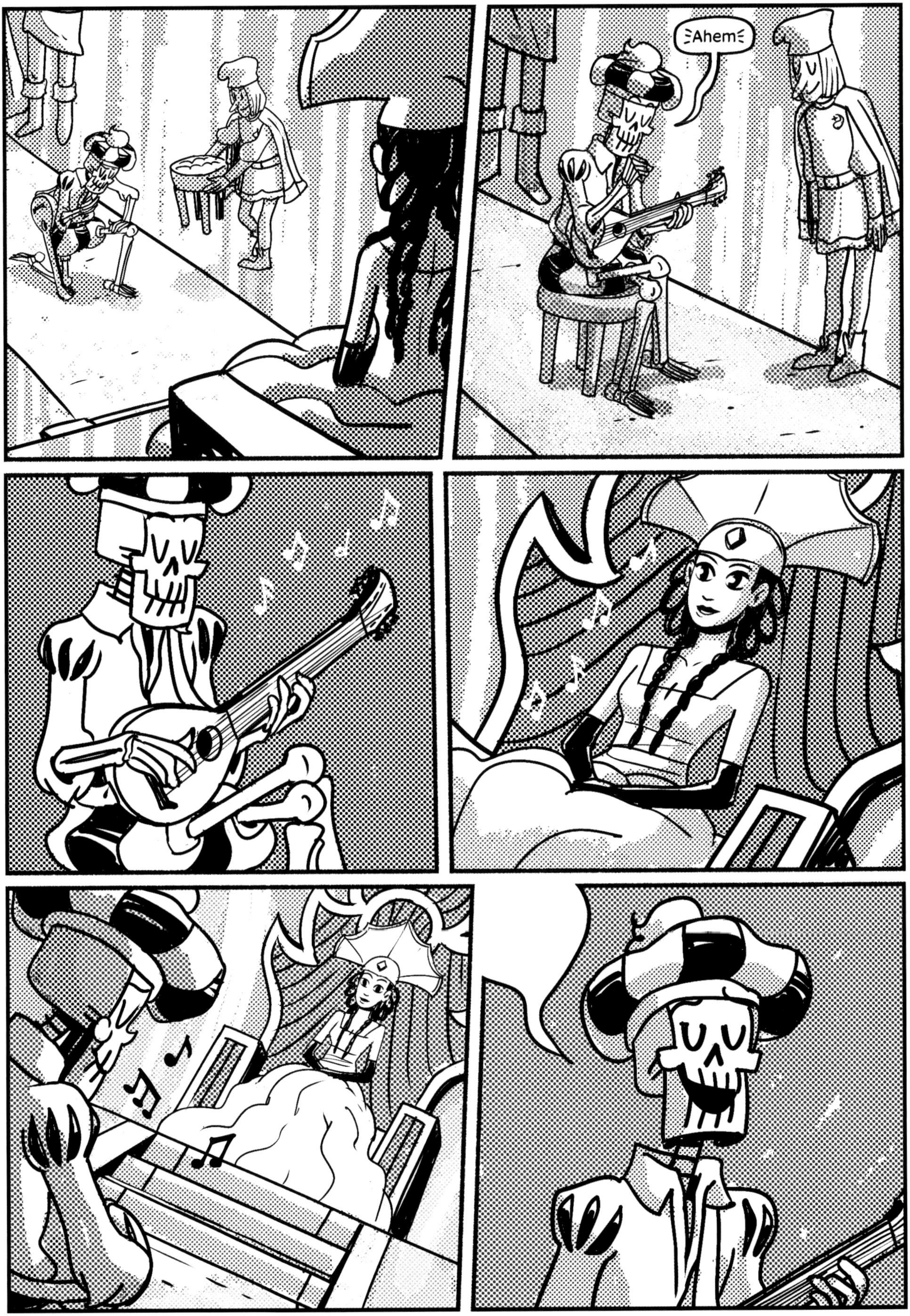
Ahem

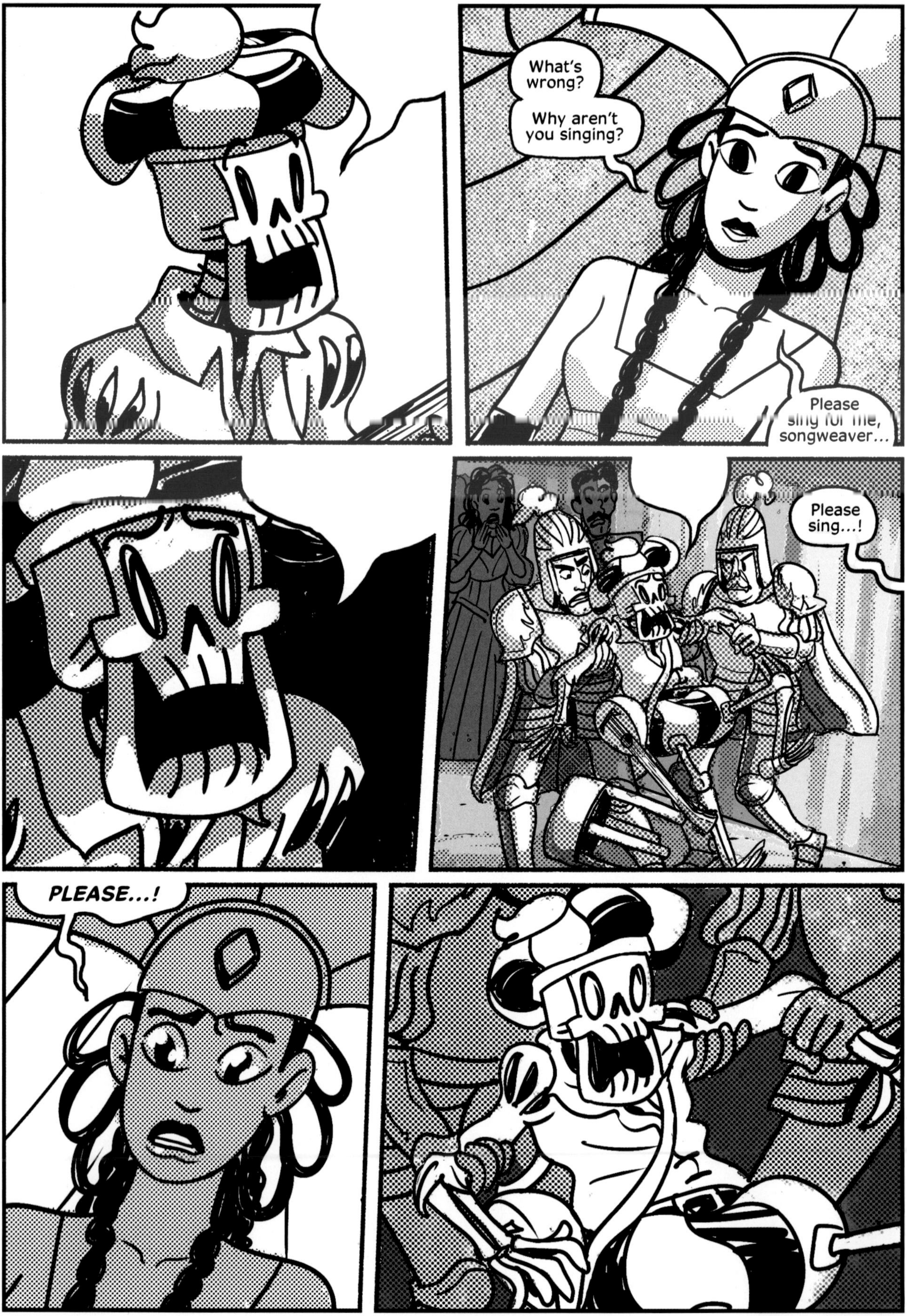
What's wrong?
Why aren't you singing?
Please sing for me, songweaver...
Please sing...!
PLEASE...!

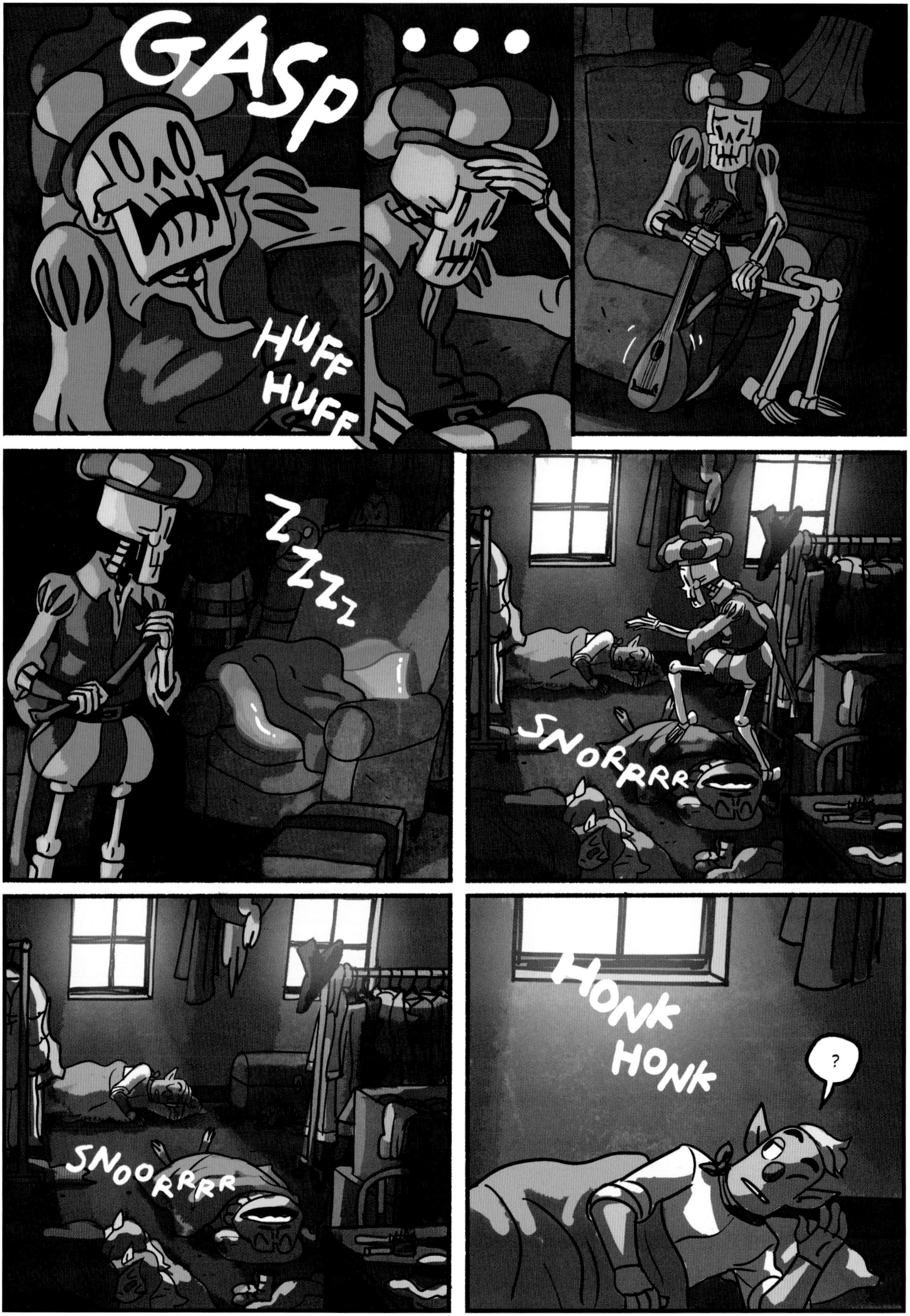
GASP
HUFF HUFF
...
ZZZZ
SNORRRR
SNOORRRR
HONK HONK
?

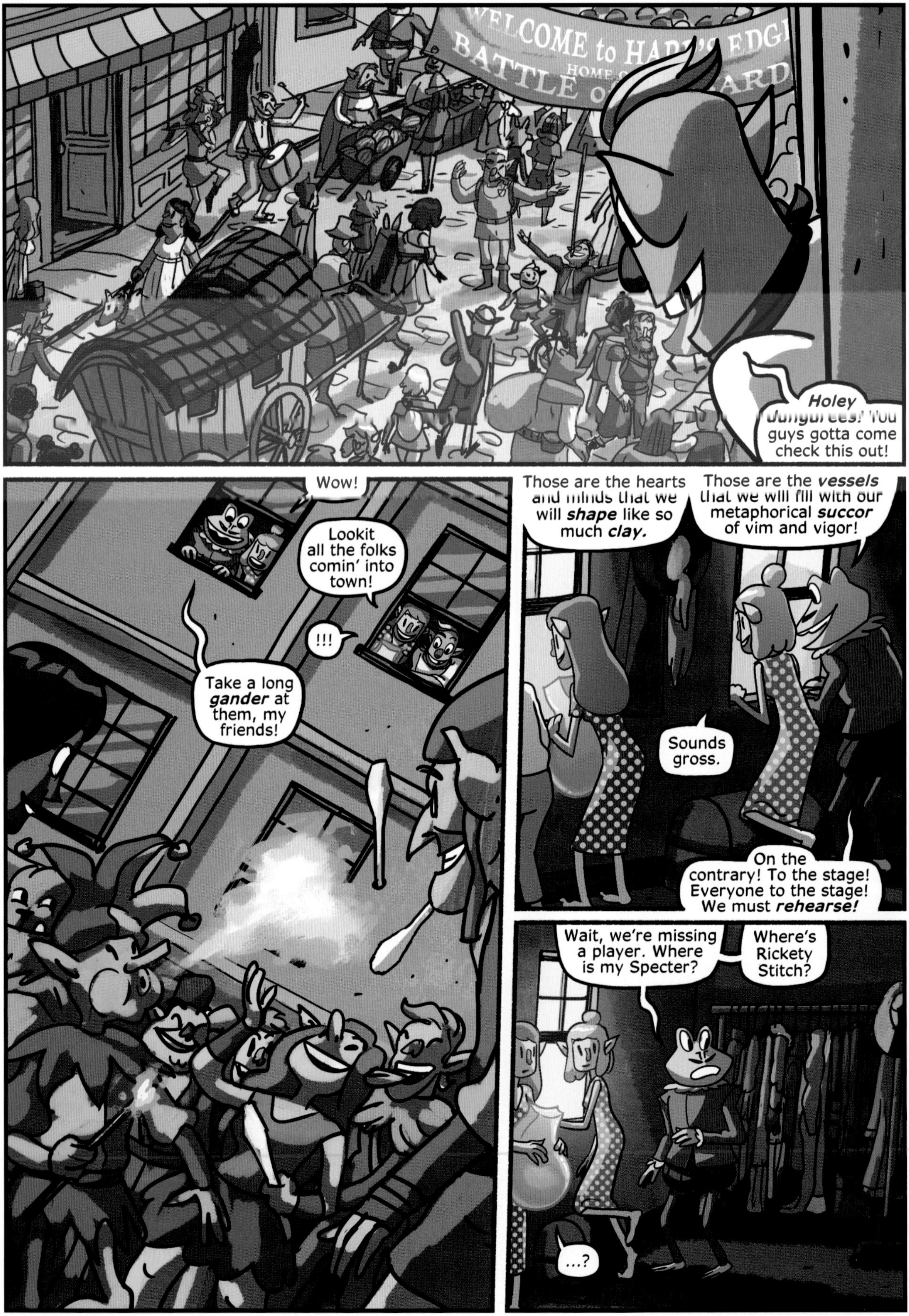
Holey Dungarees! You guys gotta come check this out!
Wow!
Lookit all the folks comin' into town!
!!!
Take a long gander at them, my friends!
Those are the hearts and minds that we will shape like so much clay.
Those are the vessels that we will fill with our metaphorical succor of vim and vigor!
Sounds gross.
On the contrary! To the stage! Everyone to the stage! We must rehearse!
Wait, we're missing a player. Where is my Specter?
Where's Rickety Stitch?
...?

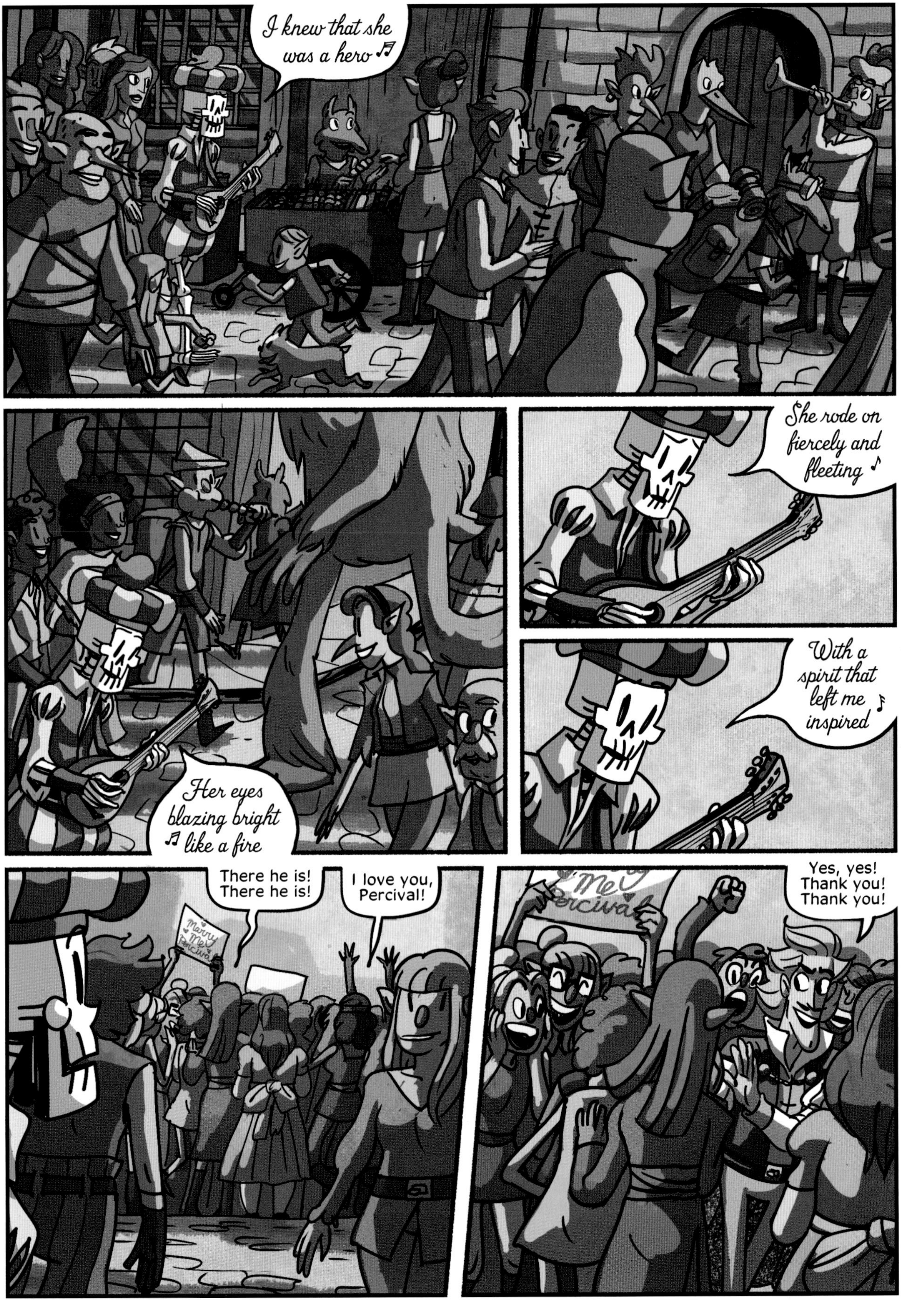

I knew that she was a hero
Her eyes blazing bright like a fire
She rode on fiercely and fleeting
With a spirit that left me inspired
There he is! There he is!
Marry Me Percival
I love you, Percival!
Yes, yes! Thank you! Thank you!

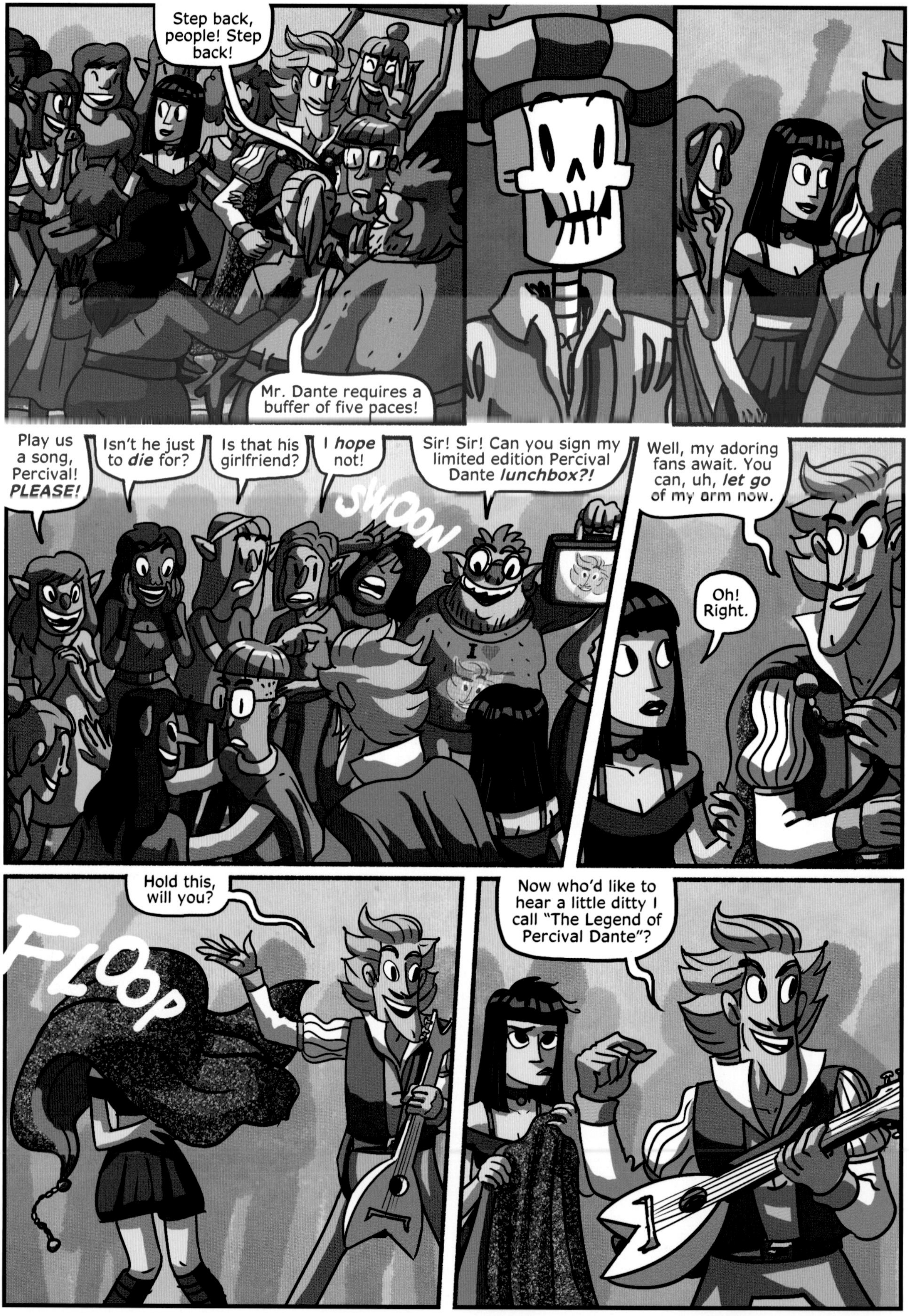
Step back, people! Step back!
Mr. Dante requires a buffer of five paces!
Play us a song, Percival! PLEASE!
Isn't he just to die for?
Is that his girlfriend?
I hope not!
Sir! Sir! Can you sign my limited edition Percival Dante lunchbox?!
SWOON
Well, my adoring fans await. You can, uh, let go of my arm now.
Oh! Right.
Hold this, will you?
FLOOP
Now who'd like to hear a little ditty I call "The Legend of Percival Dante"?

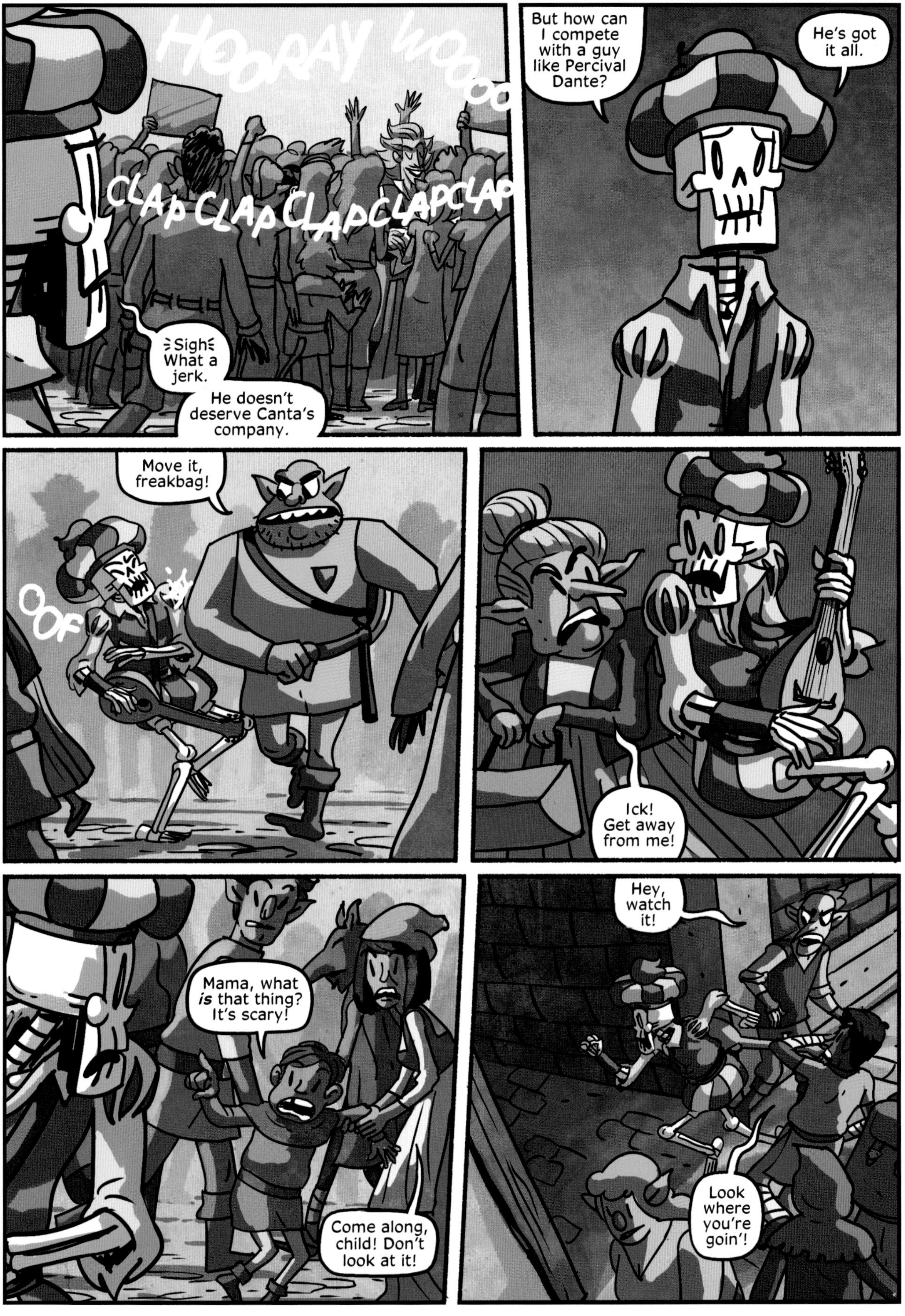
HOORAY
WOOOOO
CLAP CLAP CLAP CLAP CLAP
Sigh
What a jerk.
He doesn't deserve Canta's company.
But how can I compete with a guy like Percival Dante?
He's got it all.
Move it, freakbag!
OOF
Ick! Get away from me!
Mama, what *is* that thing? It's scary!
Come along, child! Don't look at it!
Hey, watch it!
Look where you're goin'!

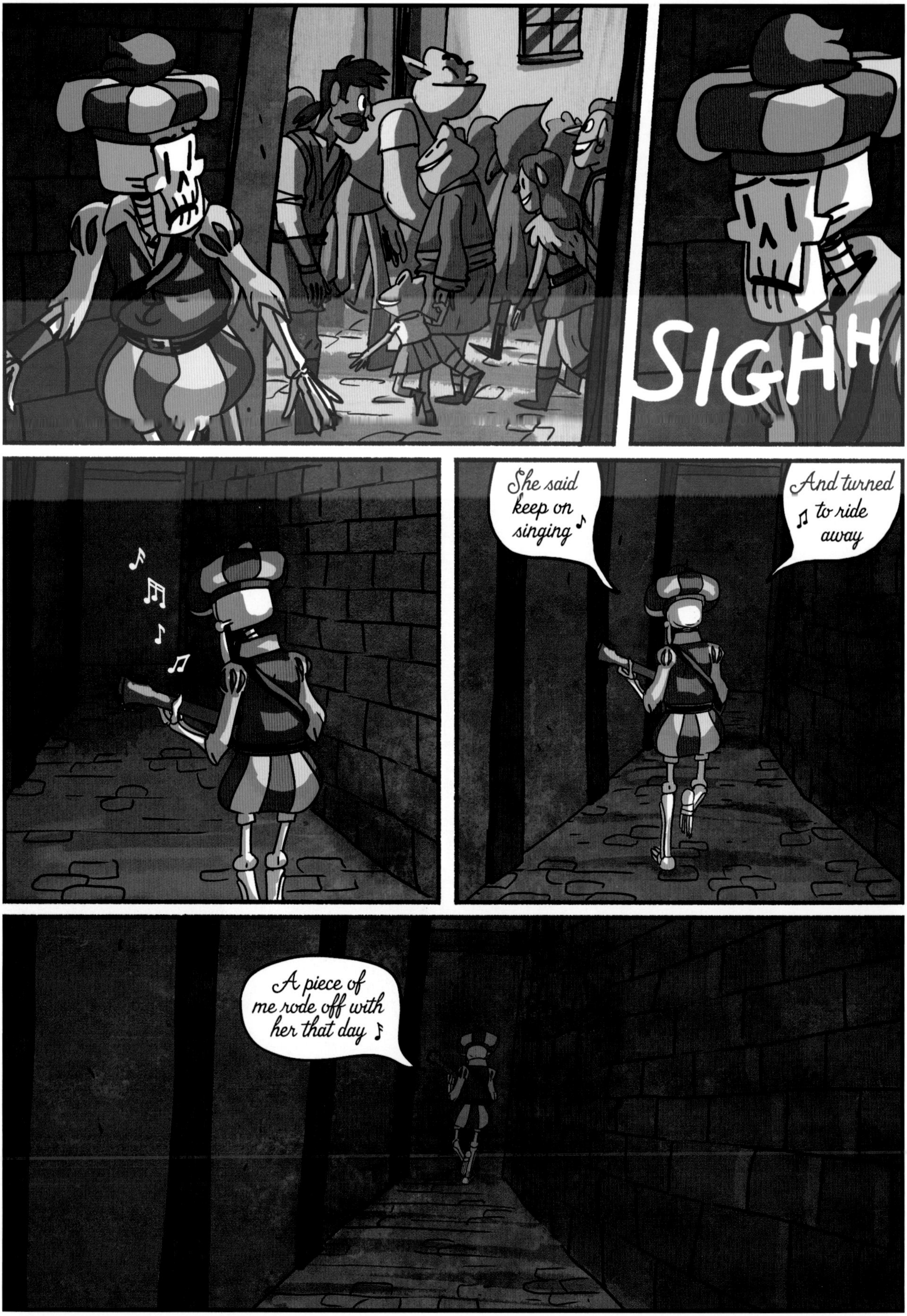

SIGHH
She said keep on singing ♪
And turned ♫ to ride away
A piece of me rode off with her that day ♪

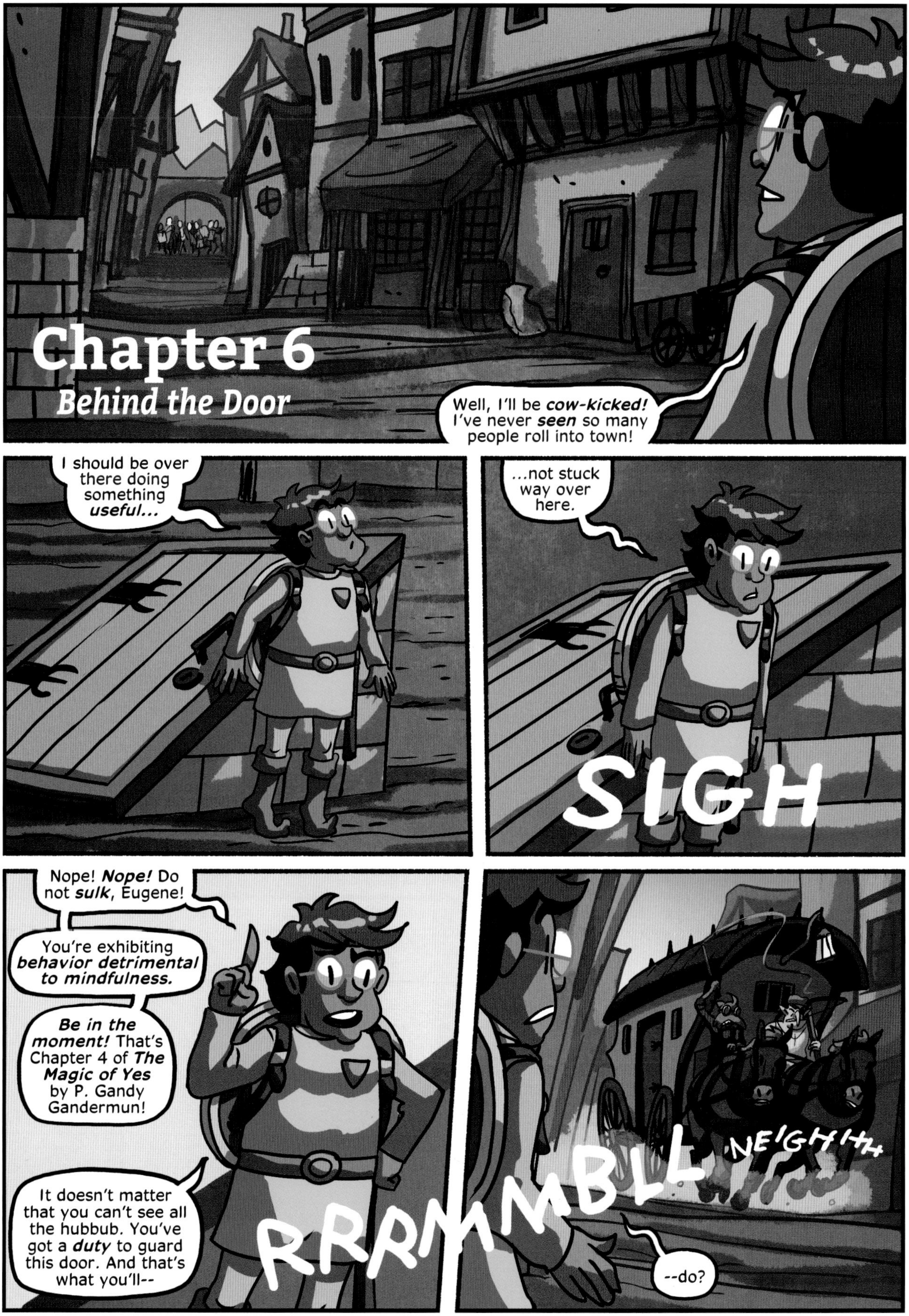
Chapter 6
Behind the Door
Well, I'll be cow-kicked! I've never seen so many people roll into town!
I should be over there doing something useful...
...not stuck way over here.
SIGH
Nope! Nope! Do not sulk, Eugene!
You're exhibiting behavior detrimental to mindfulness.
Be in the moment! That's Chapter 4 of The Magic of Yes by P. Gandy Gandermun!
It doesn't matter that you can't see all the hubbub. You've got a duty to guard this door. And that's what you'll--
RRRMMBLL
NEIGHHH
--do?

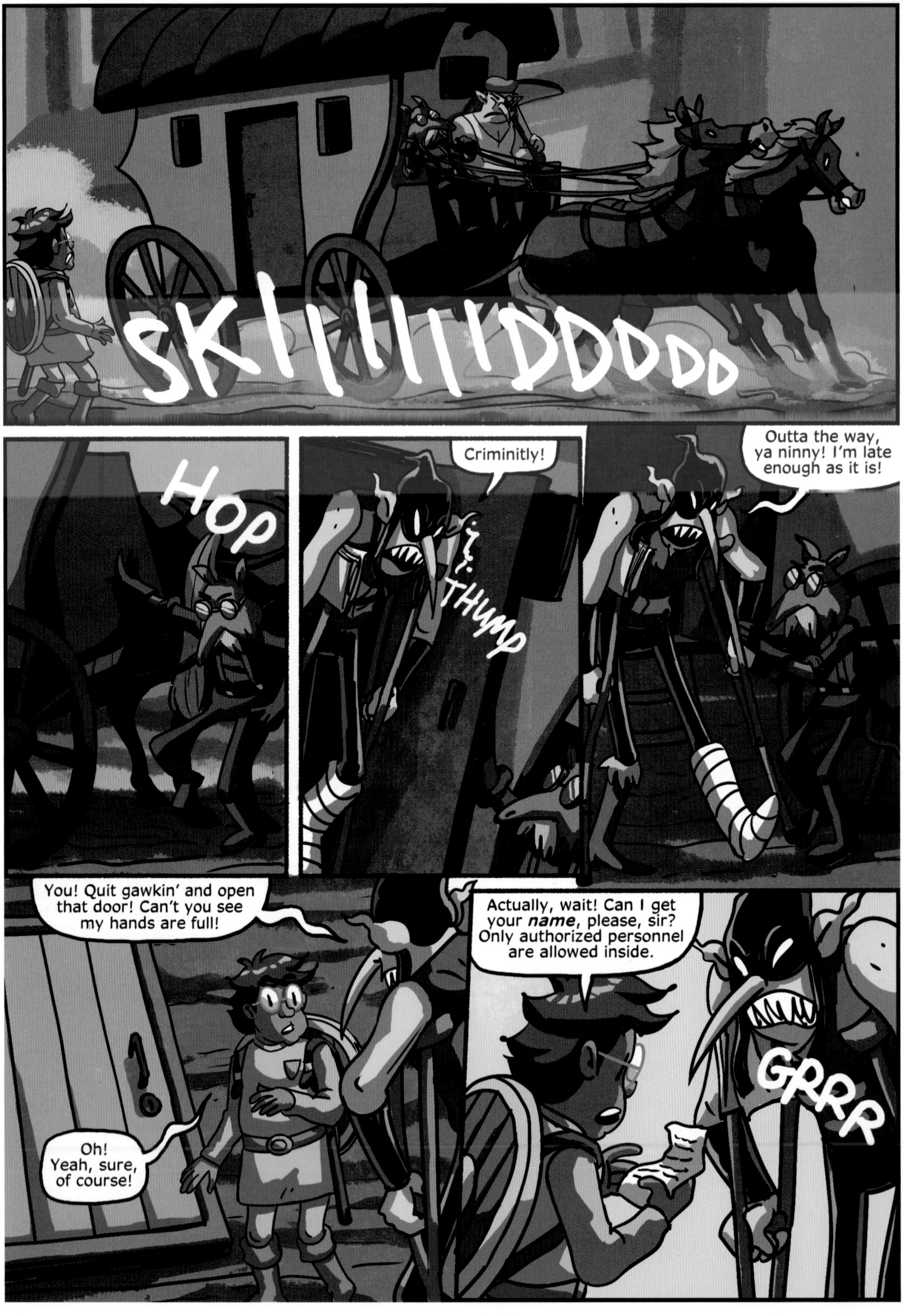
SKIIIIIIDDDDD
HOP
Criminitly!
THUMP
Outta the way, ya ninny! I'm late enough as it is!
You! Quit gawkin' and open that door! Can't you see my hands are full!
Oh! Yeah, sure, of course!
Actually, wait! Can I get your ***name***, please, sir? Only authorized personnel are allowed inside.
GRRR

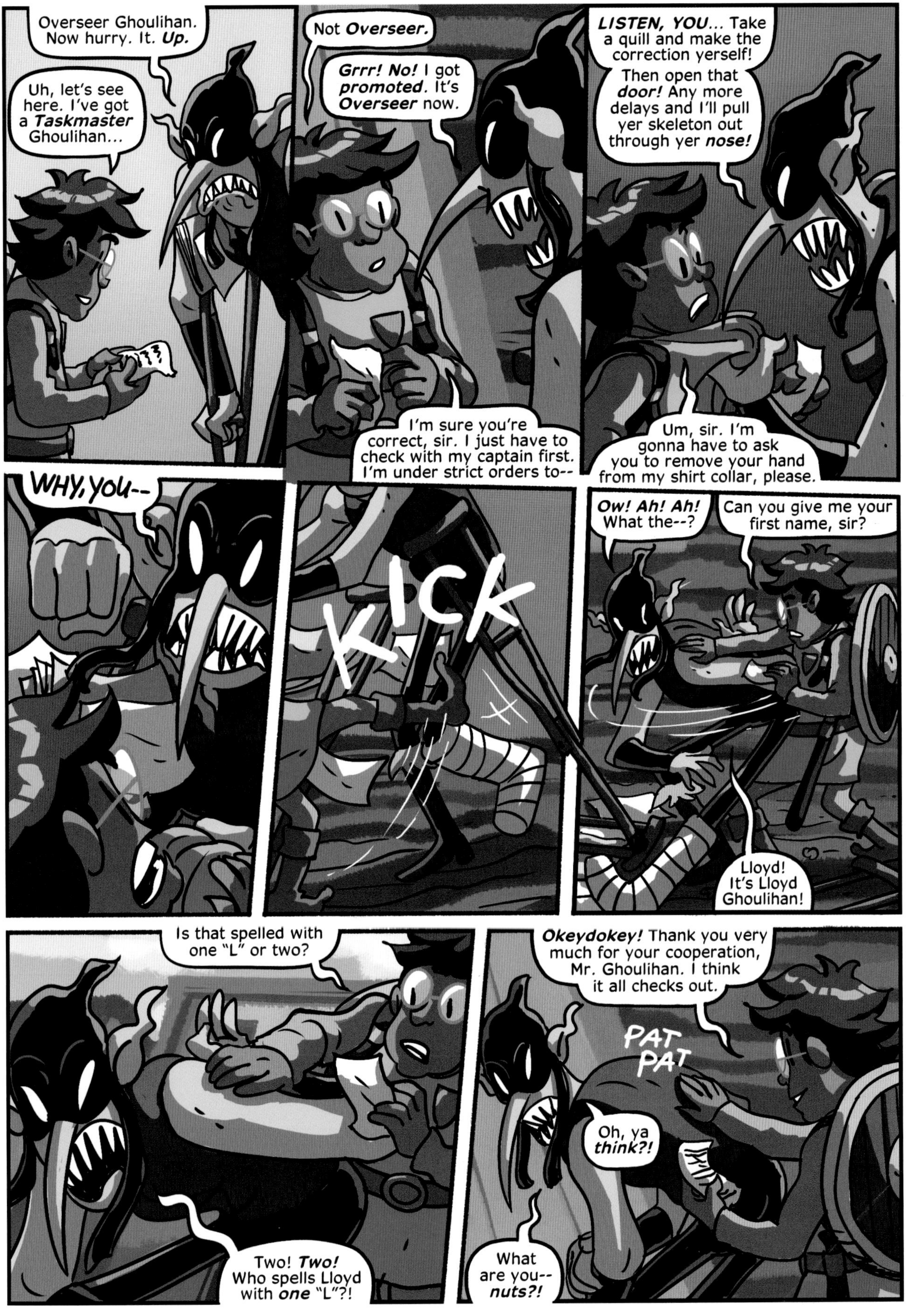
Overseer Ghoulihan. Now hurry. It. *Up.*
Uh, let's see here. I've got a *Taskmaster* Ghoulihan...
Not *Overseer.*
Grrr! No! I got *promoted*. It's *Overseer* now.
I'm sure you're correct, sir. I just have to check with my captain first. I'm under strict orders to--
LISTEN, YOU... Take a quill and make the correction yerself!
Then open that *door!* Any more delays and I'll pull yer skeleton out through yer *nose!*
Um, sir. I'm gonna have to ask you to remove your hand from my shirt collar, please.
WHY, YOU--
KICK
Ow! Ah! Ah! What the--?
Can you give me your first name, sir?
Lloyd! It's Lloyd Ghoulihan!
Is that spelled with one "L" or two?
Two! *Two!* Who spells Lloyd with *one* "L"?!
Okeydokey! Thank you very much for your cooperation, Mr. Ghoulihan. I think it all checks out.
PAT PAT
Oh, ya *think?!*
What are you-- *nuts?!*

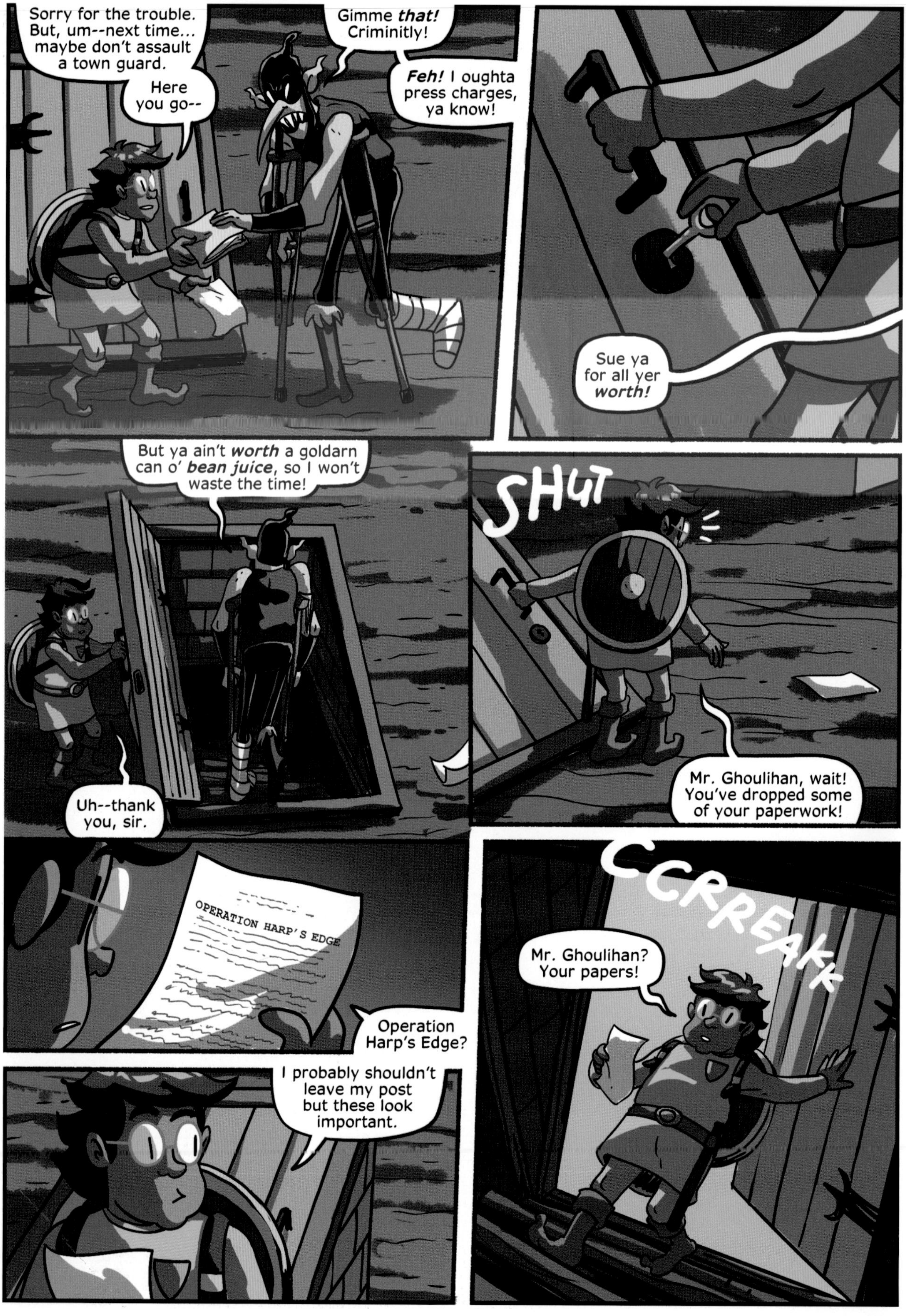
Sorry for the trouble. But, um--next time... maybe don't assault a town guard.
Here you go--
Gimme **that!** Criminitly!
Feh! I oughta press charges, ya know!
Sue ya for all yer ***worth!***
But ya ain't ***worth*** a goldarn can o' ***bean juice***, so I won't waste the time!
Uh--thank you, sir.
SHUT
Mr. Ghoulihan, wait! You've dropped some of your paperwork!
OPERATION HARP'S EDGE
Operation Harp's Edge?
I probably shouldn't leave my post but these look important.
CCRREAKK
Mr. Ghoulihan? Your papers!

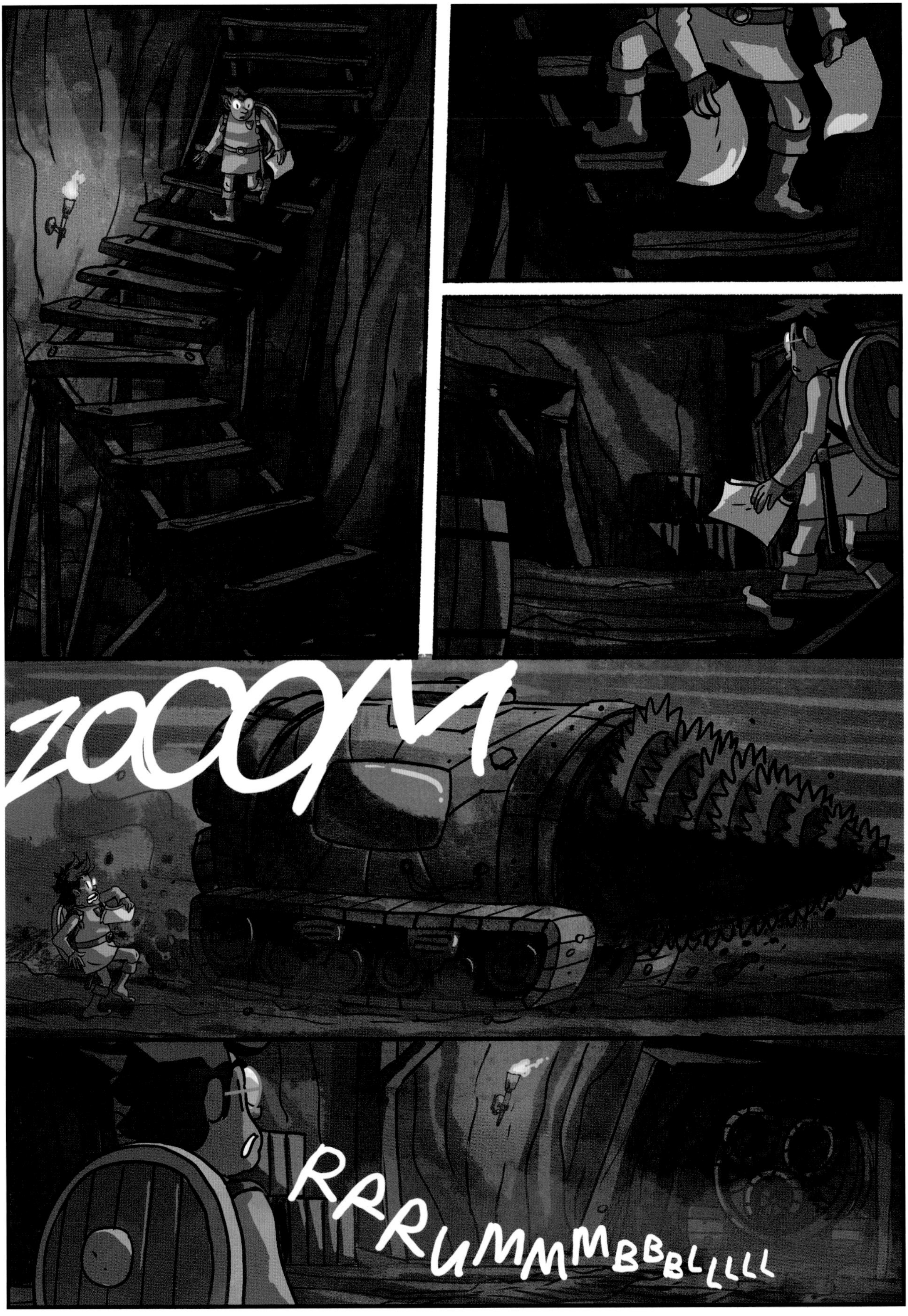
ZOOOM
RRRUMMMMBBBLLLLL

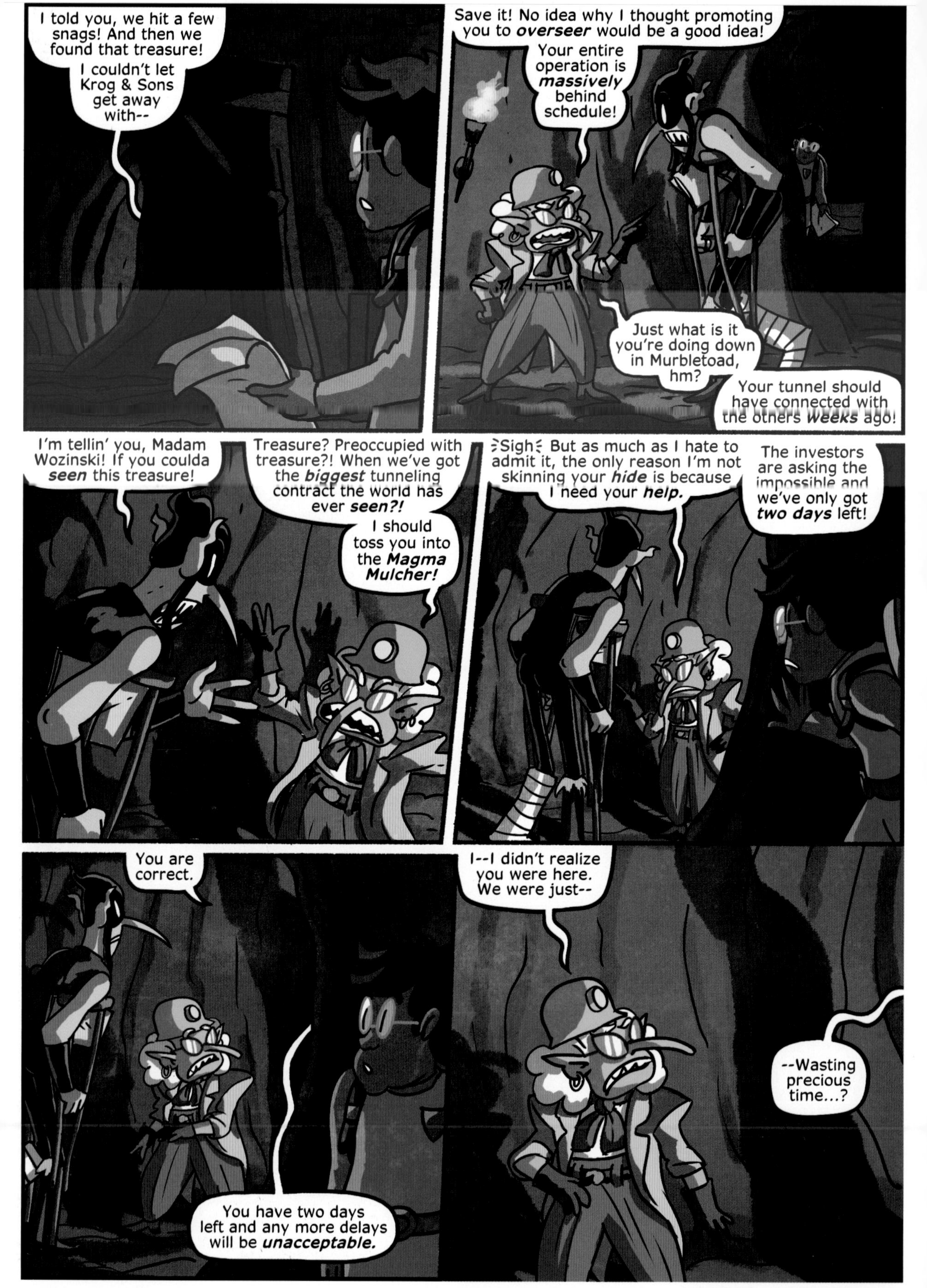
I told you, we hit a few snags! And then we found that treasure!
I couldn't let Krog & Sons get away with--
Save it! No idea why I thought promoting you to *overseer* would be a good idea!
Your entire operation is *massively* behind schedule!
Just what is it you're doing down in Murbletoad, hm?
Your tunnel should have connected with the others *weeks* ago!
I'm tellin' you, Madam Wozinski! If you coulda *seen* this treasure!
Treasure? Preoccupied with treasure?! When we've got the *biggest* tunneling contract the world has ever *seen?!*
I should toss you into the *Magma Mulcher!*
Sigh But as much as I hate to admit it, the only reason I'm not skinning your *hide* is because I need your *help.*
The investors are asking the impossible and we've only got *two days* left!
You are correct.
You have two days left and any more delays will be *unacceptable.*
I--I didn't realize you were here. We were just--
--Wasting precious time...?

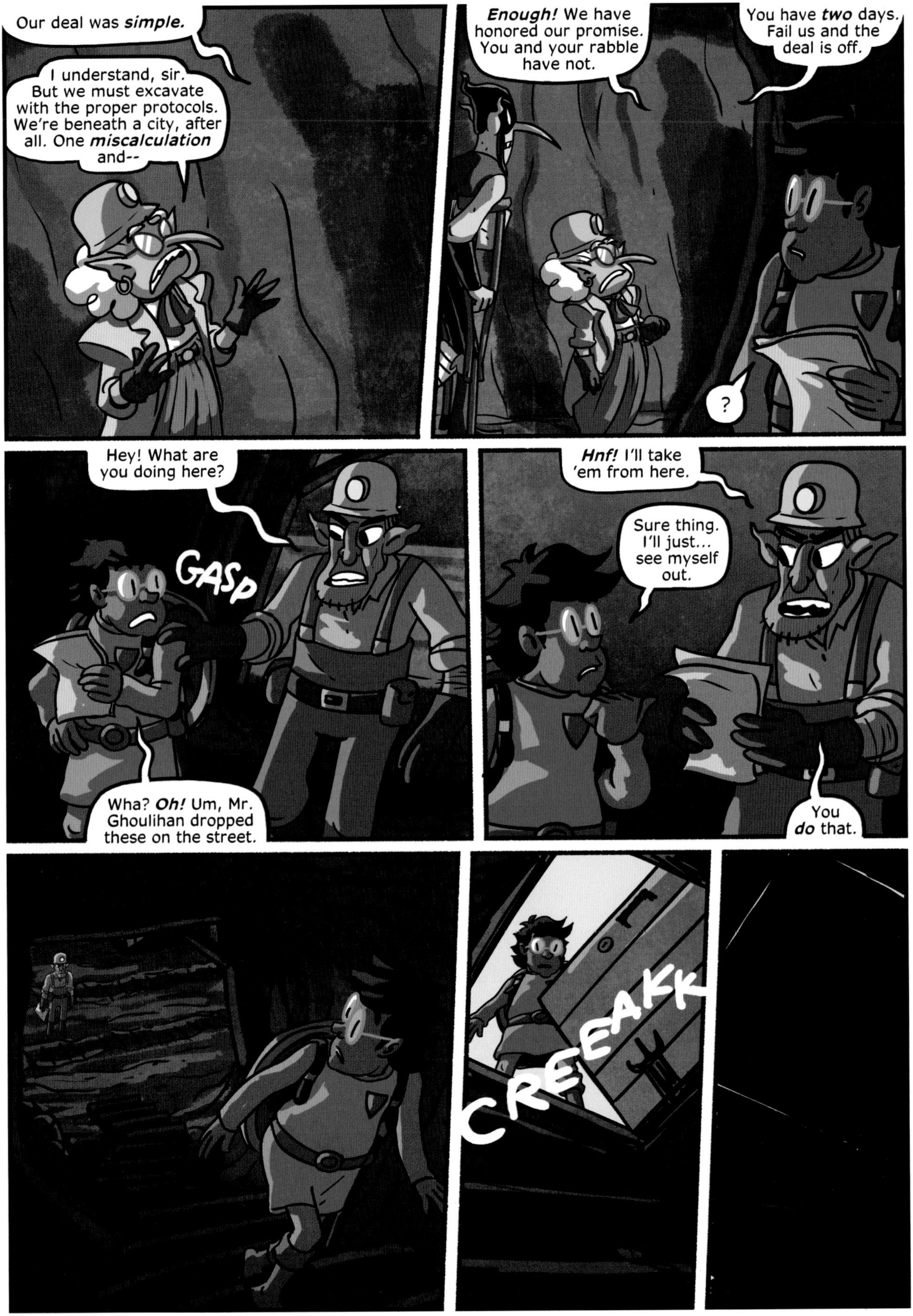

Our deal was *simple.*
I understand, sir. But we must excavate with the proper protocols. We're beneath a city, after all. One *miscalculation* and--
Enough! We have honored our promise. You and your rabble have not.
You have *two* days. Fail us and the deal is off.
?
Hey! What are you doing here?
GASP
Wha? *Oh!* Um, Mr. Ghoulihan dropped these on the street.
Hnf! I'll take 'em from here.
Sure thing. I'll just... see myself out.
You *do* that.
CREEAKK

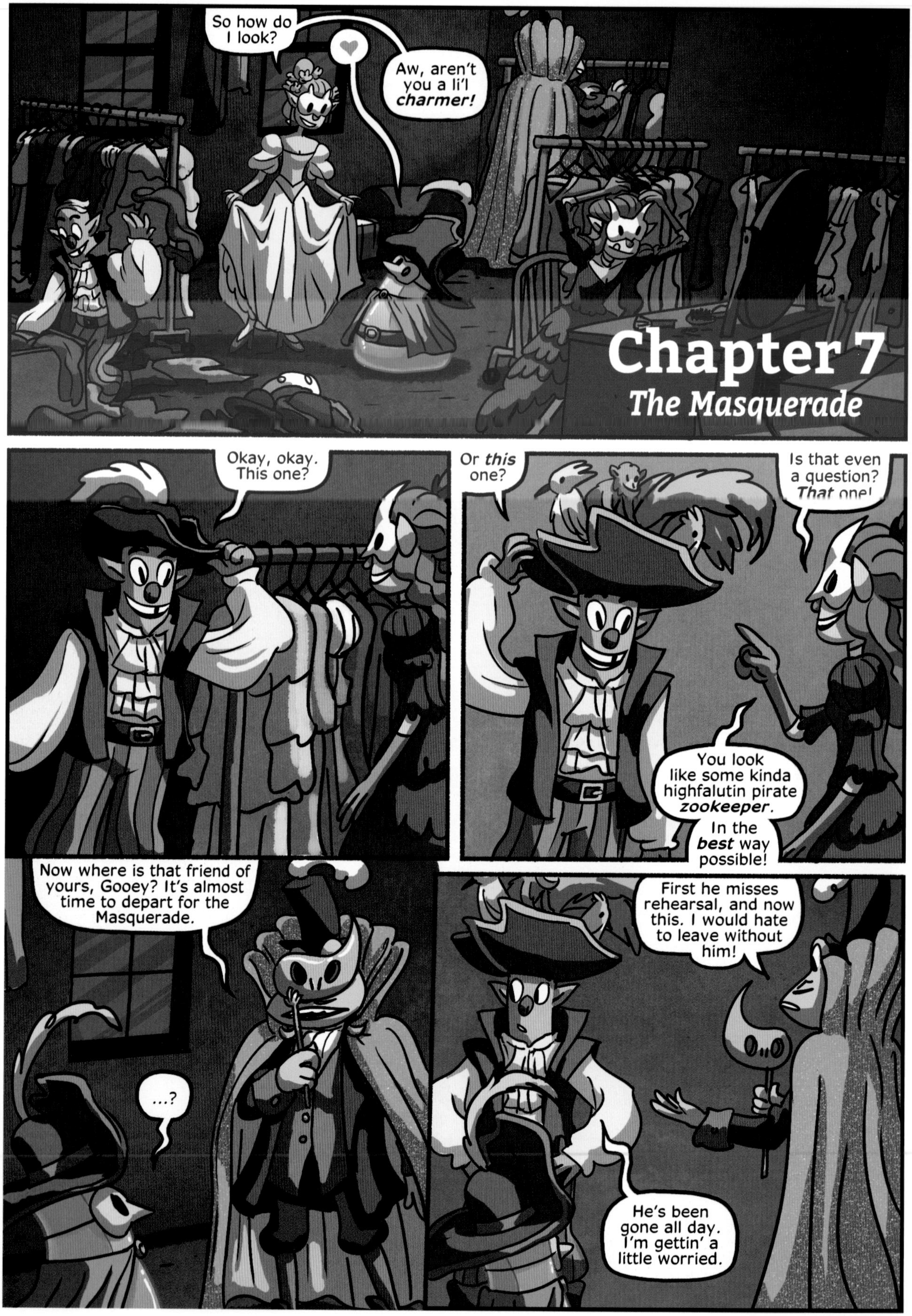

So how do I look?
Aw, aren't you a li'l *charmer!*
Chapter 7
The Masquerade
Okay, okay. This one?
Or *this* one?
Is that even a question? *That* one!
You look like some kinda highfalutin pirate *zookeeper*.
In the *best* way possible!
Now where is that friend of yours, Gooey? It's almost time to depart for the Masquerade.
...?
First he misses rehearsal, and now this. I would hate to leave without him!
He's been gone all day. I'm gettin' a little worried.

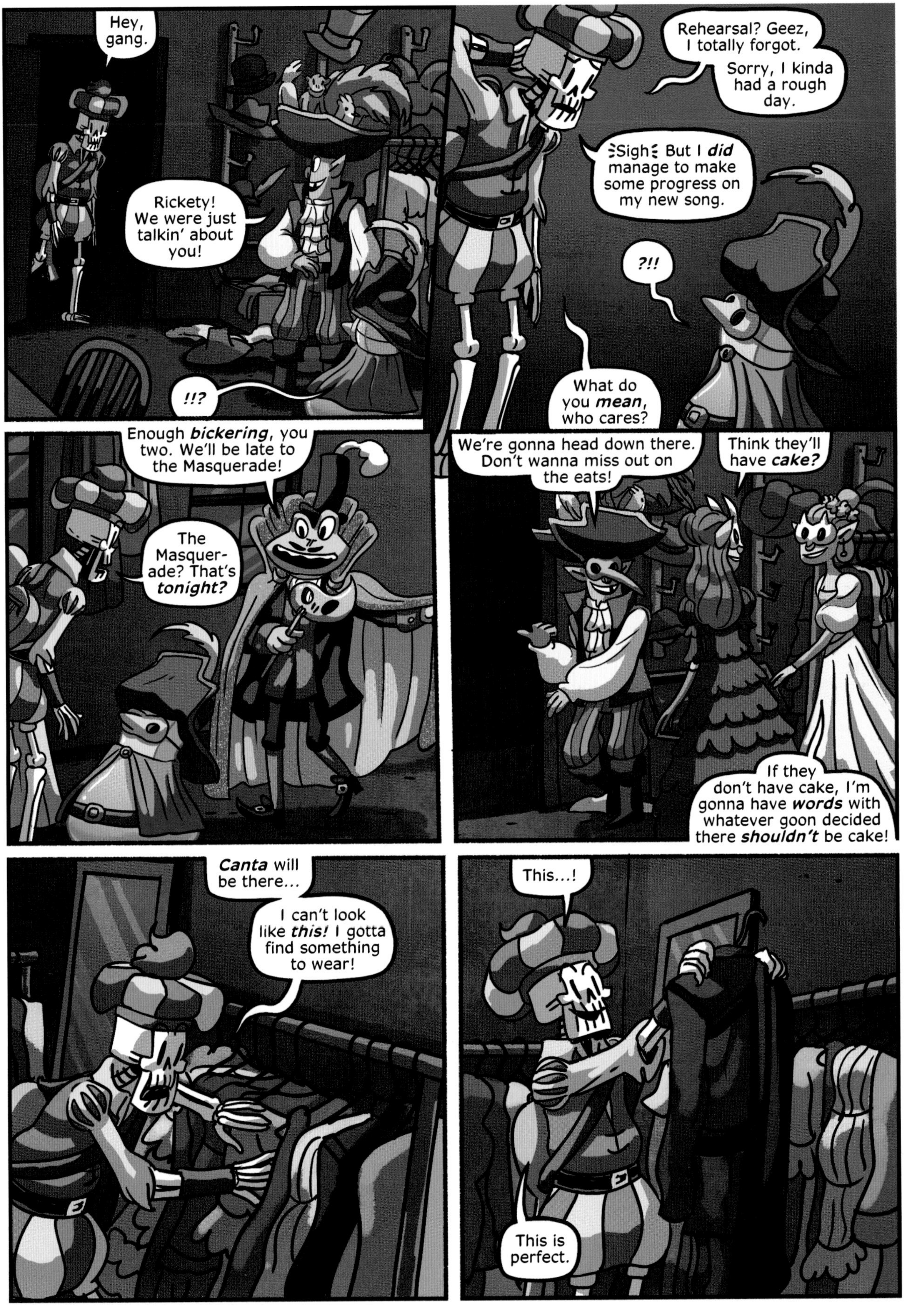

Hey, gang.
Rickety! We were just talkin' about you!
!!?
Rehearsal? Geez, I totally forgot.
Sorry, I kinda had a rough day.
Sigh But I *did* manage to make some progress on my new song.
?!!
What do you *mean*, who cares?
Enough *bickering*, you two. We'll be late to the Masquerade!
The Masquer-ade? That's *tonight?*
We're gonna head down there. Don't wanna miss out on the eats!
Think they'll have *cake?*
If they don't have cake, I'm gonna have *words* with whatever goon decided there *shouldn't* be cake!
Canta will be there...
I can't look like *this!* I gotta find something to wear!
This...!
This is perfect.

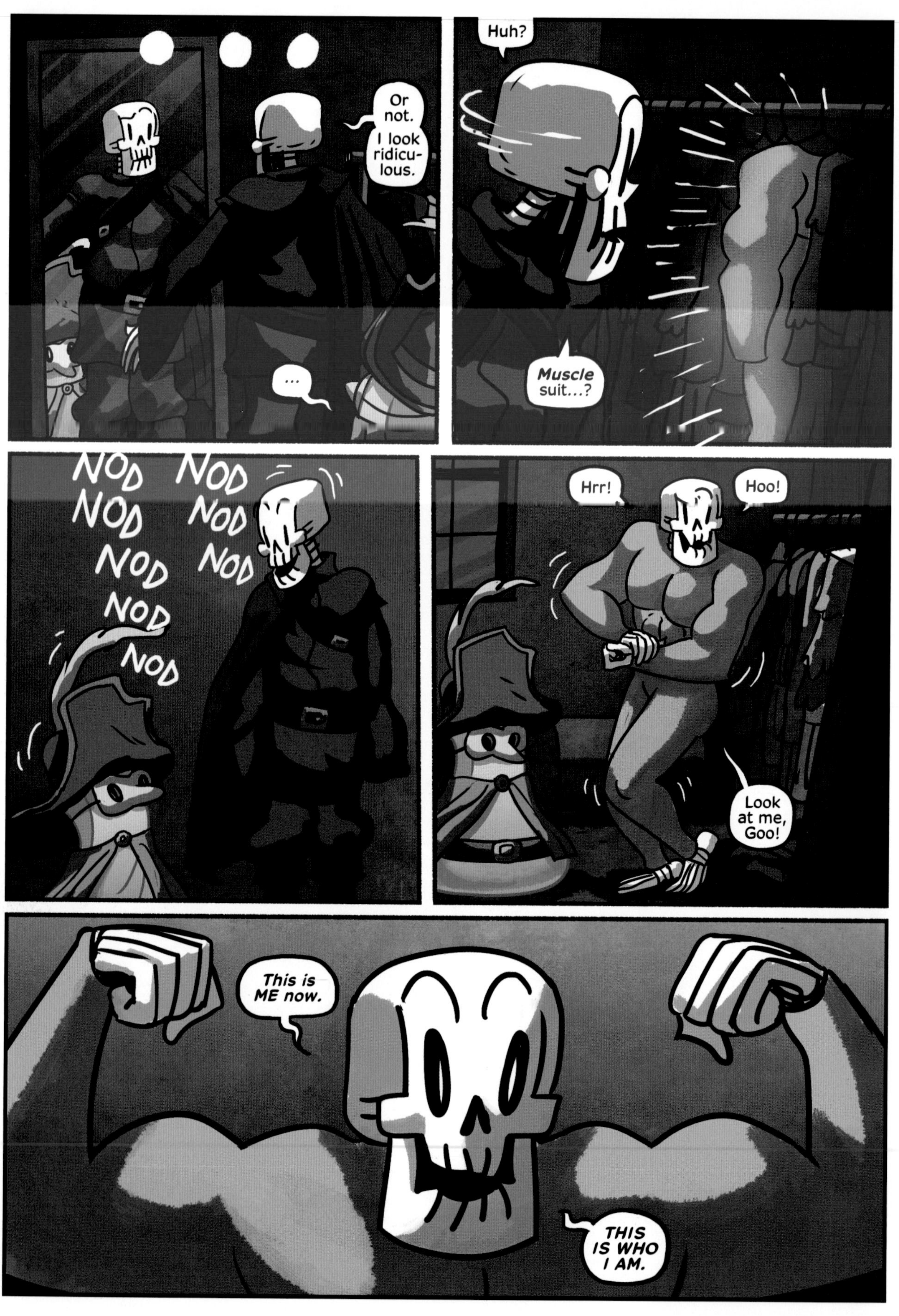
Or not.
I look ridicu-lous.
...
Huh?
Muscle suit...?
NOD NOD NOD NOD NOD NOD NOD NOD
Hrr!
Hoo!
Look at me, Goo!
This is ME now.
THIS IS WHO I AM.

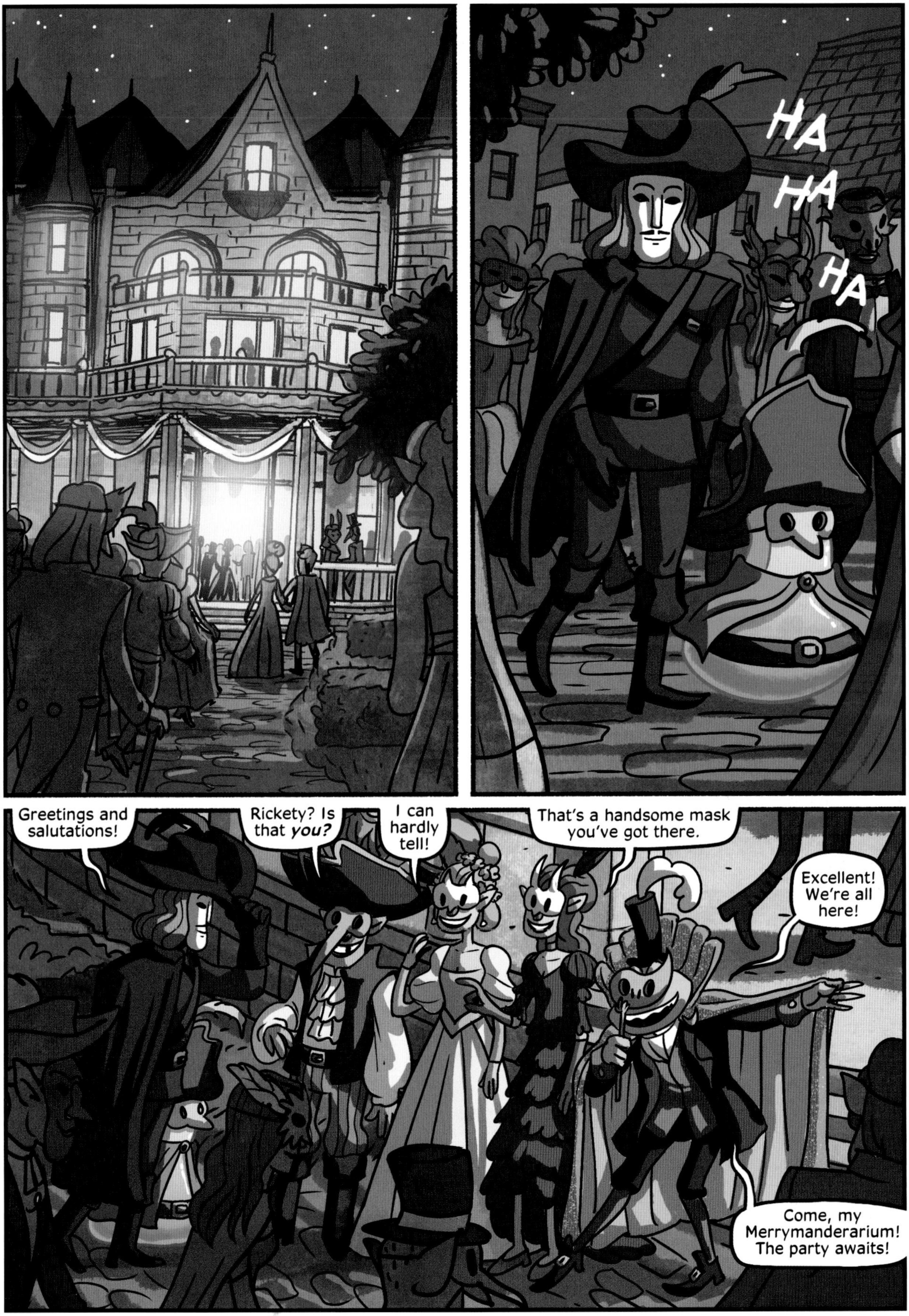
HA HA HA
Greetings and salutations!
Rickety? Is that *you?*
I can hardly tell!
That's a handsome mask you've got there.
Excellent! We're all here!
Come, my Merrymanderarium! The party awaits!

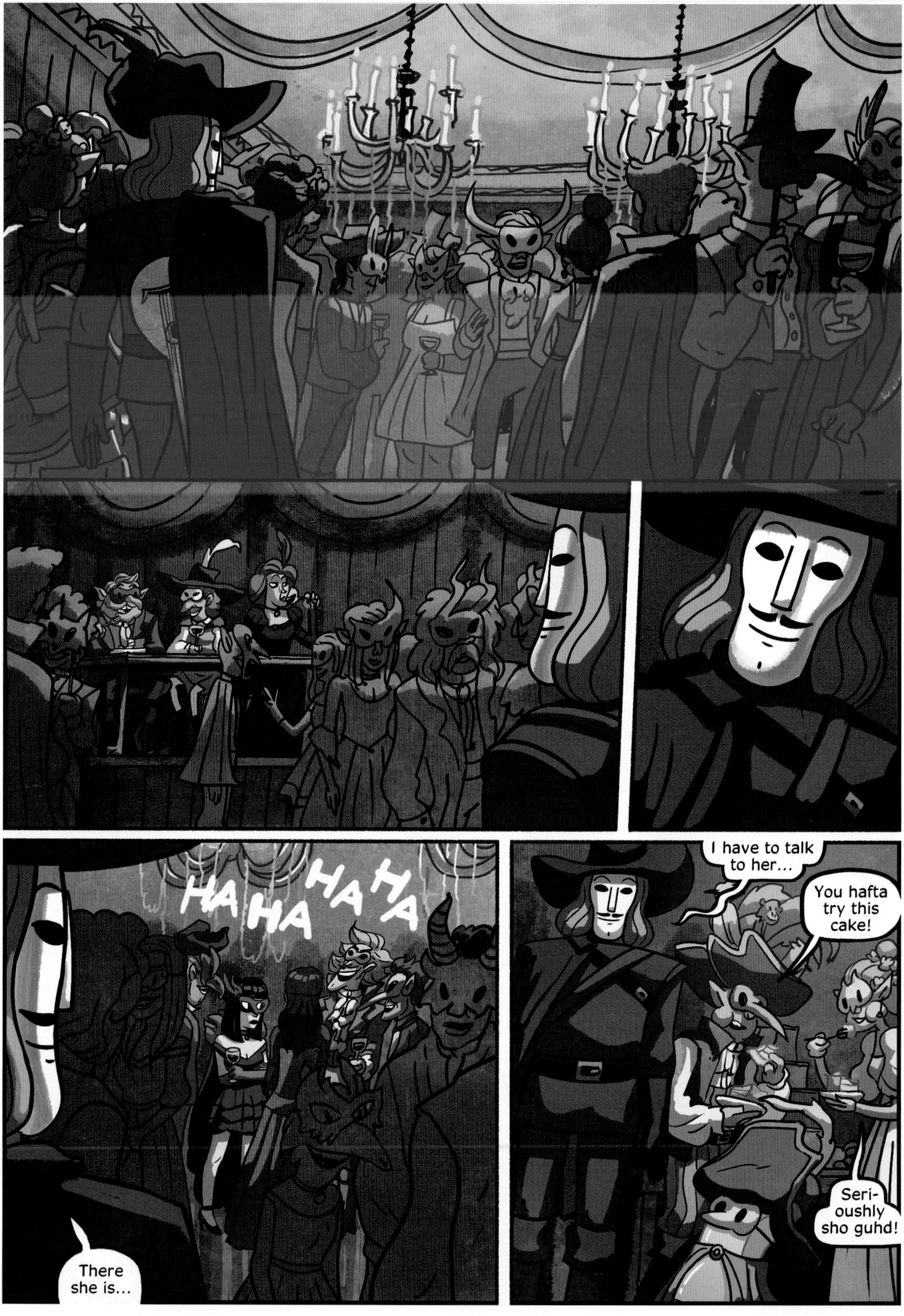
HAHA HAHA
There she is...
I have to talk to her...
You hafta try this cake!
Seri-oushly sho guhd!

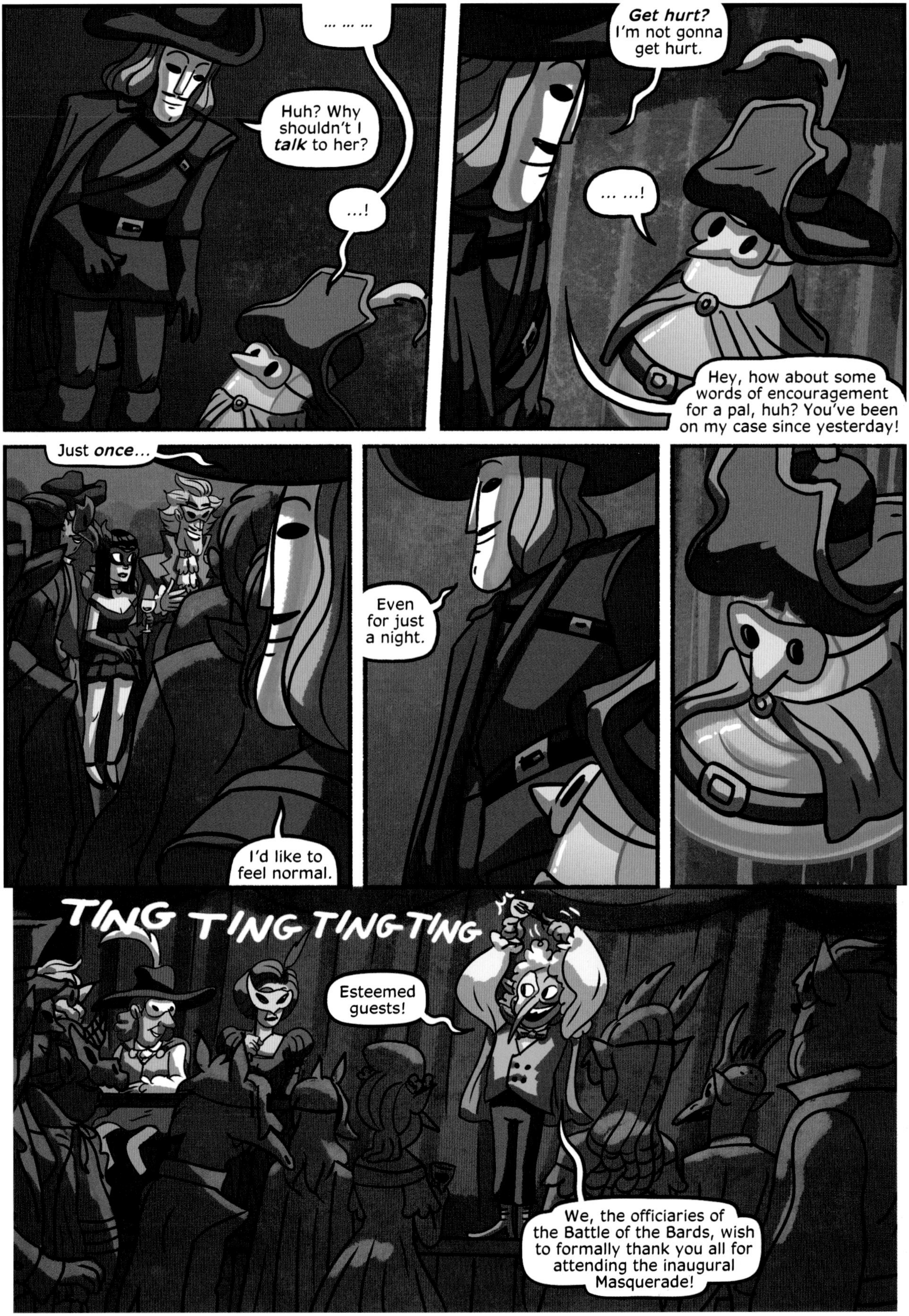
... ...
Huh? Why shouldn't I *talk* to her?
...!
Get hurt? I'm not gonna get hurt.
... ...!
Hey, how about some words of encouragement for a pal, huh? You've been on my case since yesterday!
Just *once*...
I'd like to feel normal.
Even for just a night.
TING TING TING-TING
Esteemed guests!
We, the officiaries of the Battle of the Bards, wish to formally thank you all for attending the inaugural Masquerade!

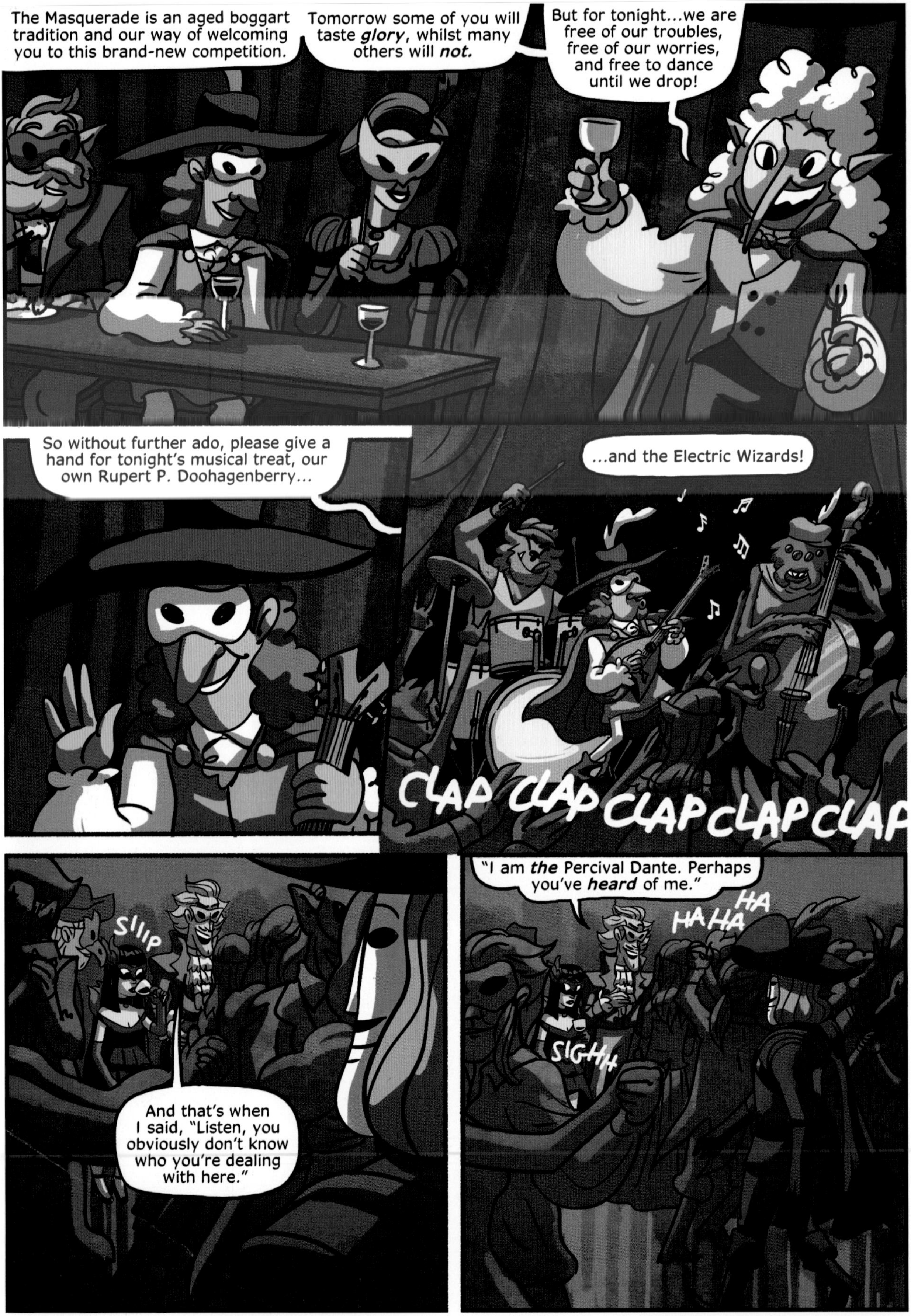
The Masquerade is an aged boggart tradition and our way of welcoming you to this brand-new competition.
Tomorrow some of you will taste *glory*, whilst many others will ***not.***
But for tonight...we are free of our troubles, free of our worries, and free to dance until we drop!
So without further ado, please give a hand for tonight's musical treat, our own Rupert P. Doohagenberry...
...and the Electric Wizards!
CLAP CLAP CLAP CLAP CLAP
SLIIP
And that's when I said, "Listen, you obviously don't know who you're dealing with here."
"I am ***the*** Percival Dante. Perhaps you've ***heard*** of me."
HA HA HA
SIGHH

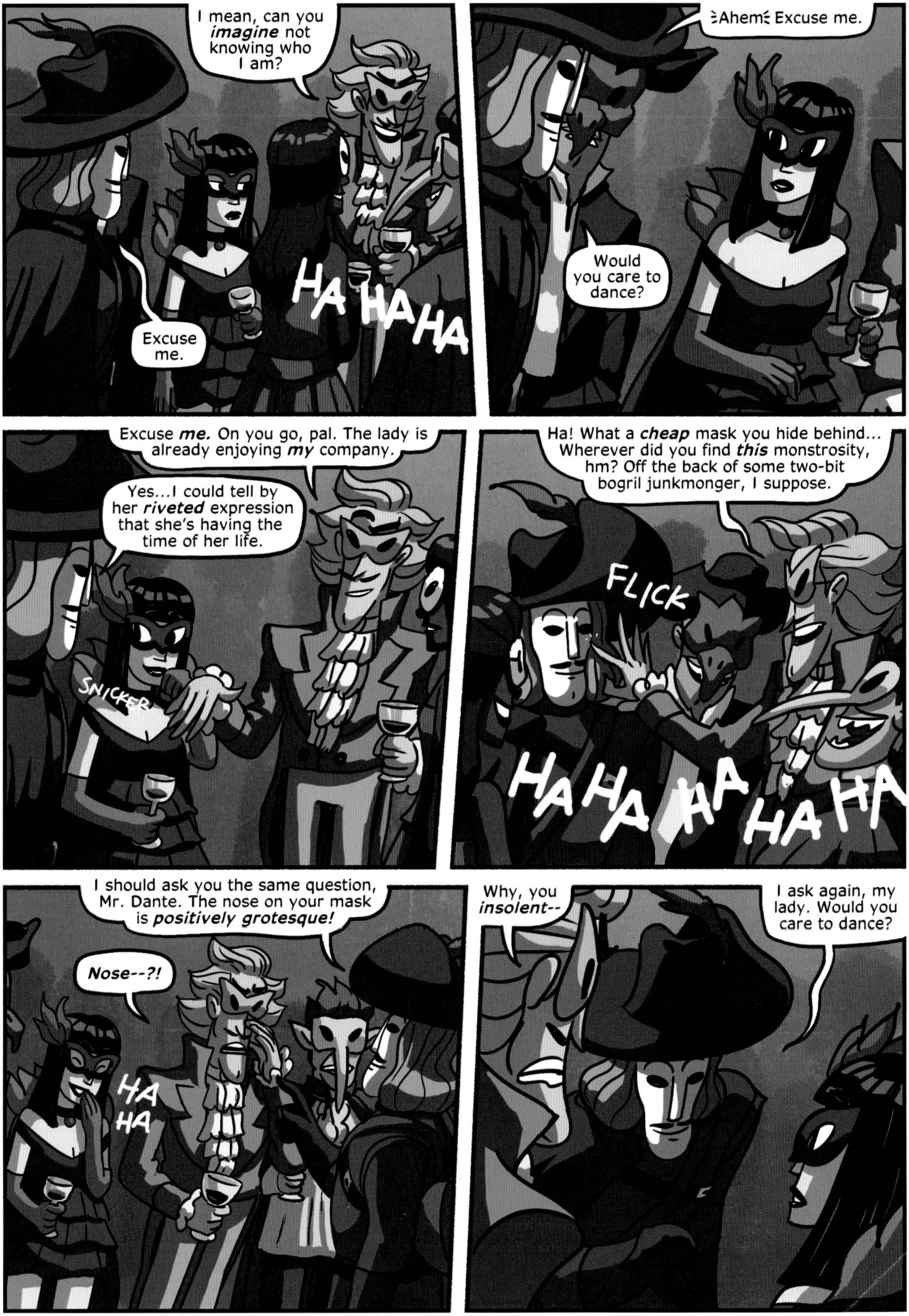
I mean, can you *imagine* not knowing who I am?
Excuse me.
HA HA HA
Ahem Excuse me.
Would you care to dance?
Excuse *me.* On you go, pal. The lady is already enjoying *my* company.
Yes...I could tell by her *riveted* expression that she's having the time of her life.
SNICKER
Ha! What a *cheap* mask you hide behind... Wherever did you find *this* monstrosity, hm? Off the back of some two-bit bogril junkmonger, I suppose.
FLICK
HA HA HA HA HA
I should ask you the same question, Mr. Dante. The nose on your mask is *positively grotesque!*
Nose--?!
HA HA
Why, you *insolent*--
I ask again, my lady. Would you care to dance?

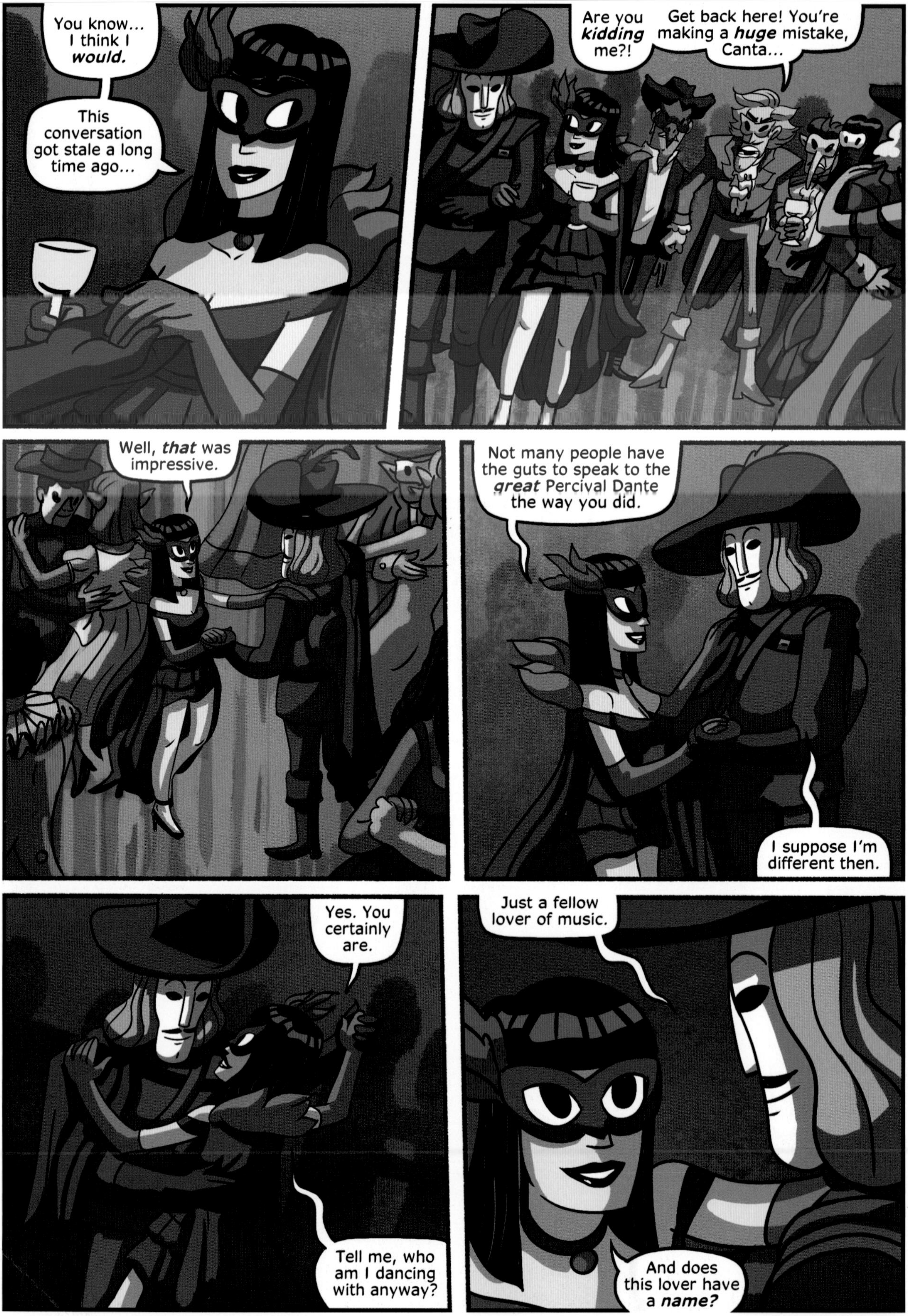
You know... I think I *would.*
This conversation got stale a long time ago...
Are you *kidding* me?!
Get back here! You're making a *huge* mistake, Canta...
Well, *that* was impressive.
Not many people have the guts to speak to the *great* Percival Dante the way you did.
I suppose I'm different then.
Yes. You certainly are.
Tell me, who am I dancing with anyway?
Just a fellow lover of music.
And does this lover have a *name?*

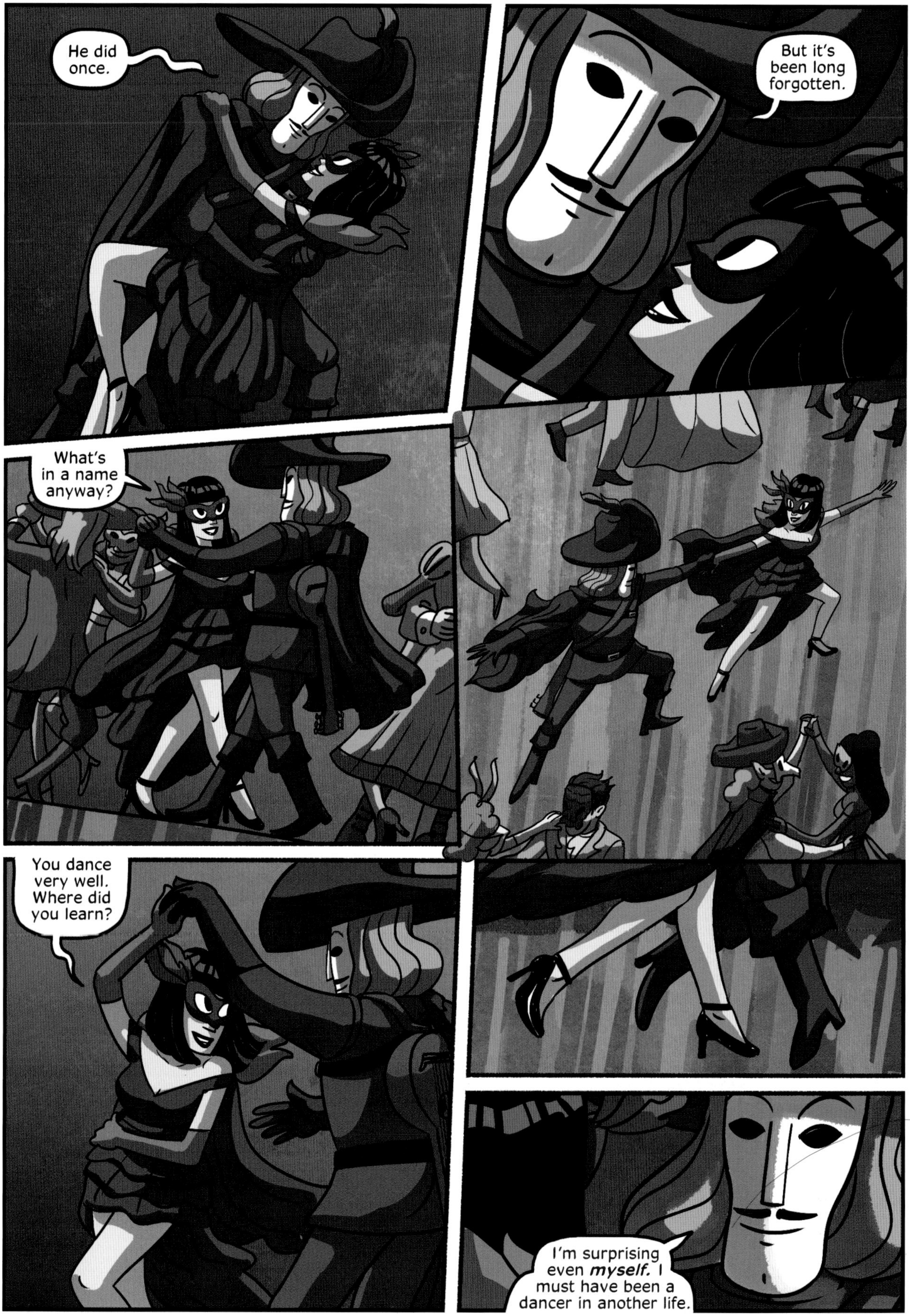
He did once.
But it's been long forgotten.
What's in a name anyway?
You dance very well. Where did you learn?
I'm surprising even ***myself.*** I must have been a dancer in another life.

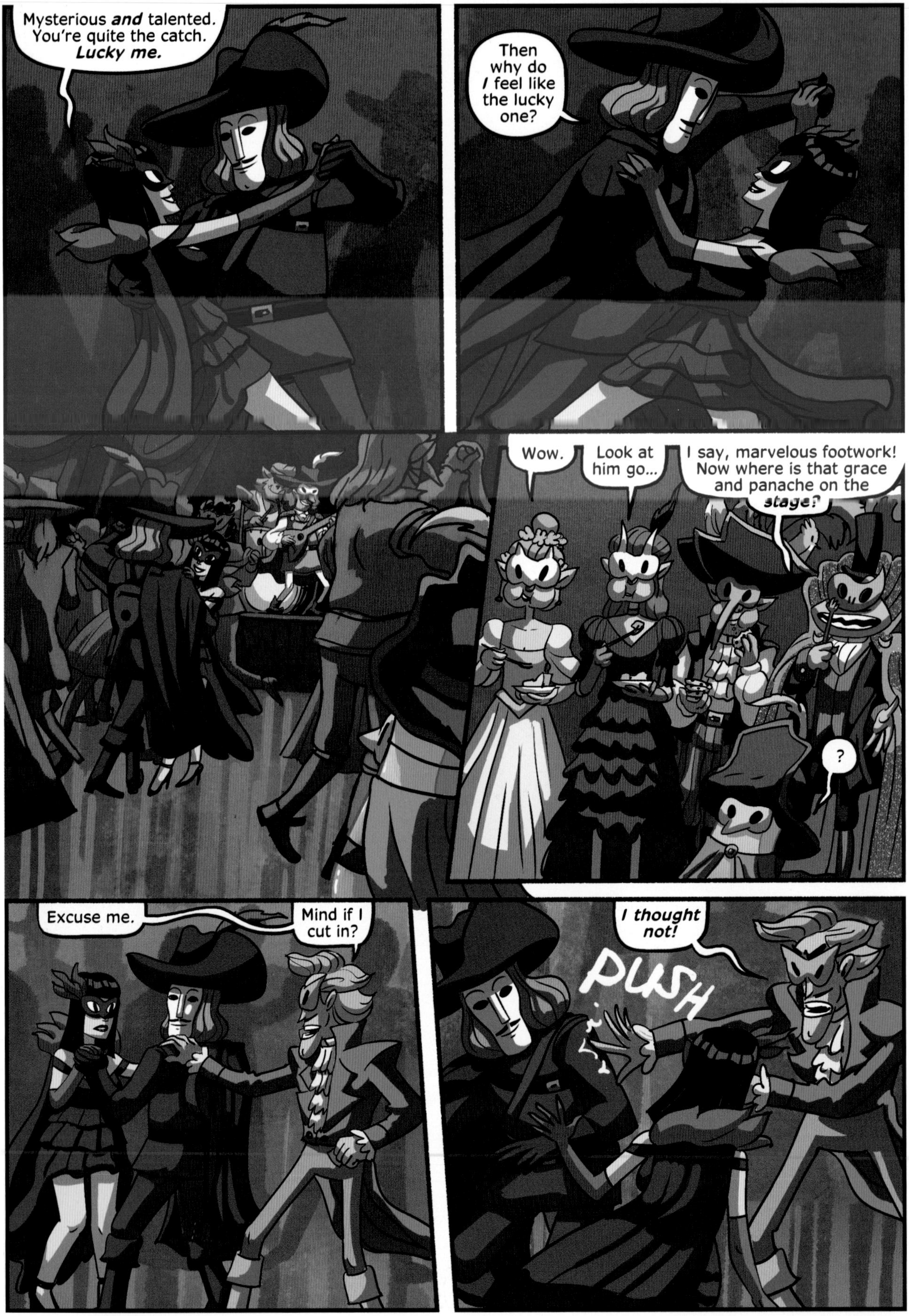
Mysterious *and* talented. You're quite the catch. ***Lucky me.***
Then why do *I* feel like the lucky one?
Wow.
Look at him go...
I say, marvelous footwork! Now where is that grace and panache on the ***stage?***
?
Excuse me.
Mind if I cut in?
I thought not!
PUSH

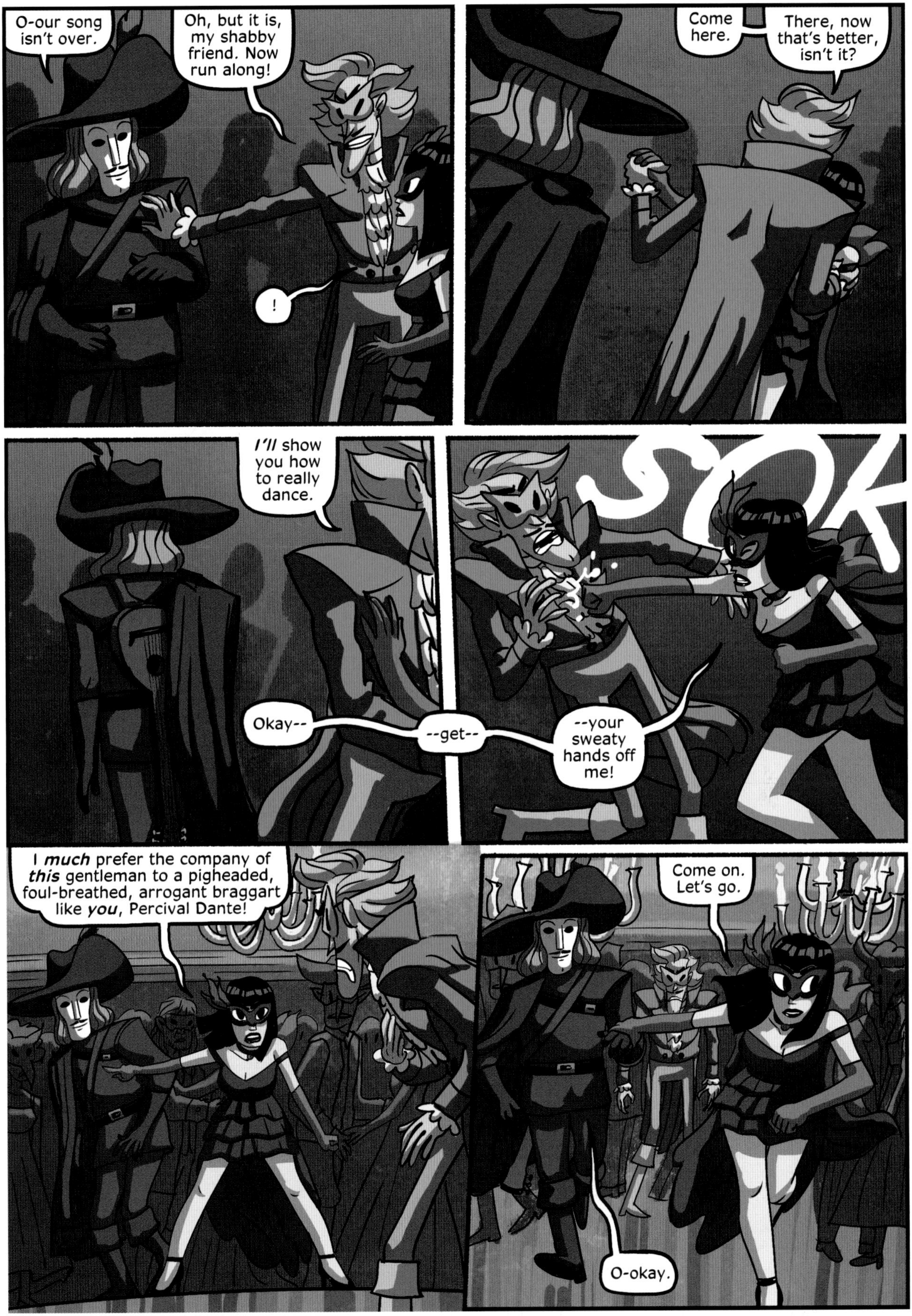

O-our song isn't over.
Oh, but it is, my shabby friend. Now run along!
!
Come here.
There, now that's better, isn't it?
I'll show you how to really dance.
SOK
Okay--
--get--
--your sweaty hands off me!
I ***much*** prefer the company of ***this*** gentleman to a pigheaded, foul-breathed, arrogant braggart like ***you***, Percival Dante!
Come on. Let's go.
O-okay.

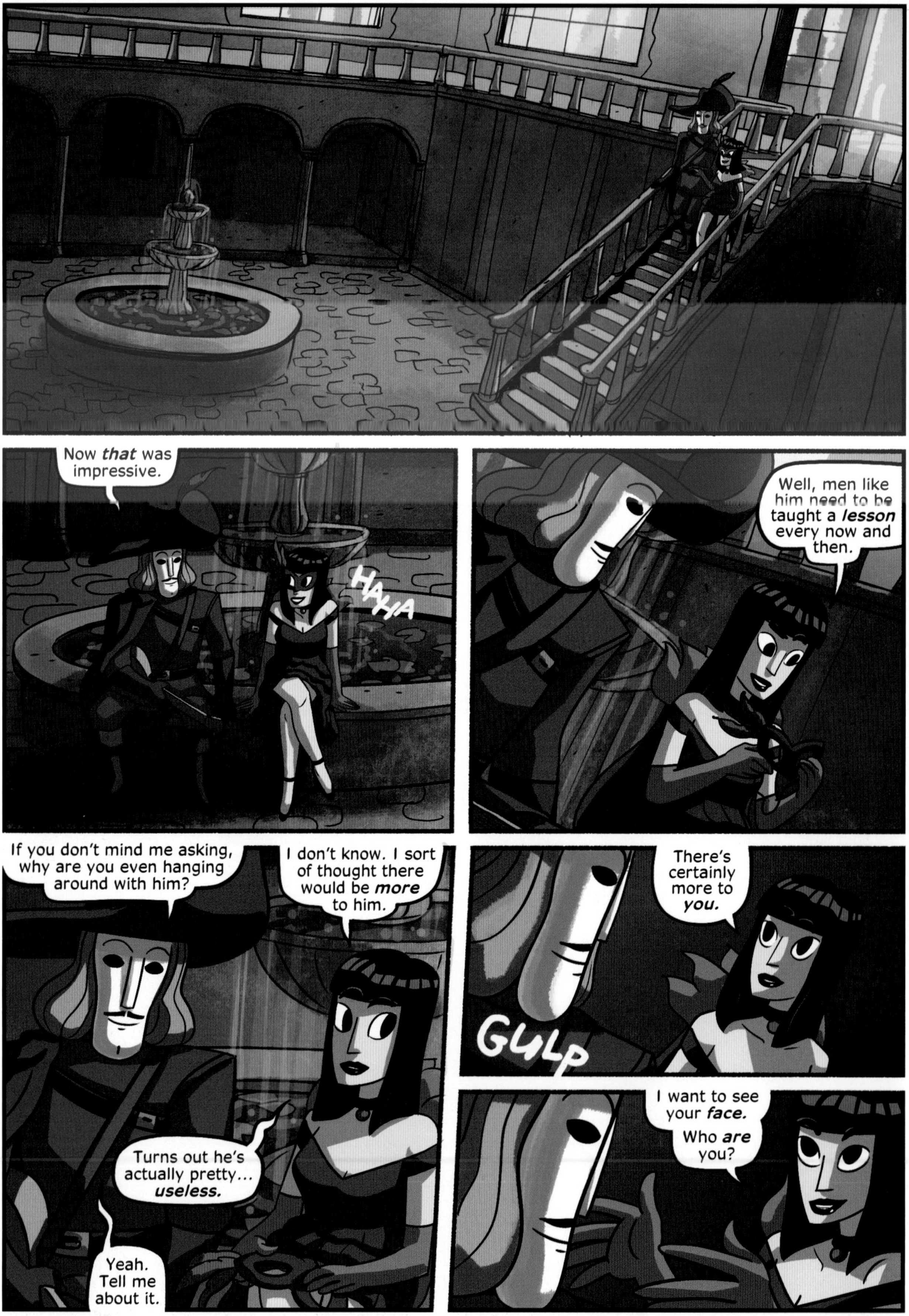
Now *that* was impressive.
HAHA
Well, men like him need to be taught a ***lesson*** every now and then.
If you don't mind me asking, why are you even hanging around with him?
I don't know. I sort of thought there would be ***more*** to him.
Turns out he's actually pretty... ***useless.***
Yeah. Tell me about it.
There's certainly more to ***you.***
GULP
I want to see your ***face.***
Who ***are*** you?

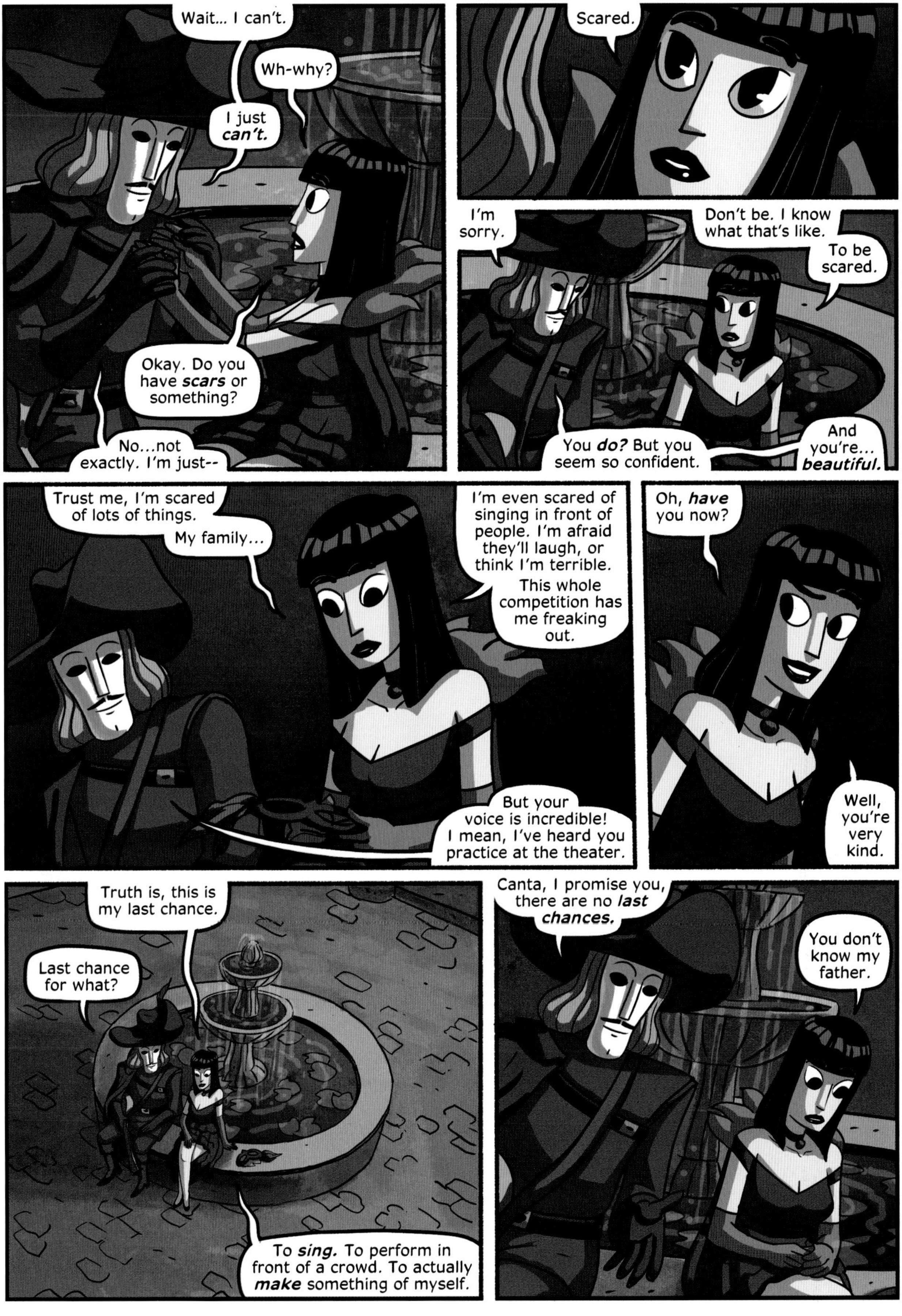
Wait... I can't.
Wh-why?
I just ***can't.***
Okay. Do you have ***scars*** or something?
No...not exactly. I'm just--
Scared.
I'm sorry.
Don't be. I know what that's like.
To be scared.
You ***do?*** But you seem so confident.
And you're... ***beautiful.***
Trust me, I'm scared of lots of things.
My family...
I'm even scared of singing in front of people. I'm afraid they'll laugh, or think I'm terrible.
This whole competition has me freaking out.
But your voice is incredible! I mean, I've heard you practice at the theater.
Oh, ***have*** you now?
Well, you're very kind.
Truth is, this is my last chance.
Last chance for what?
To ***sing.*** To perform in front of a crowd. To actually ***make*** something of myself.
Canta, I promise you, there are no ***last chances.***
You don't know my father.

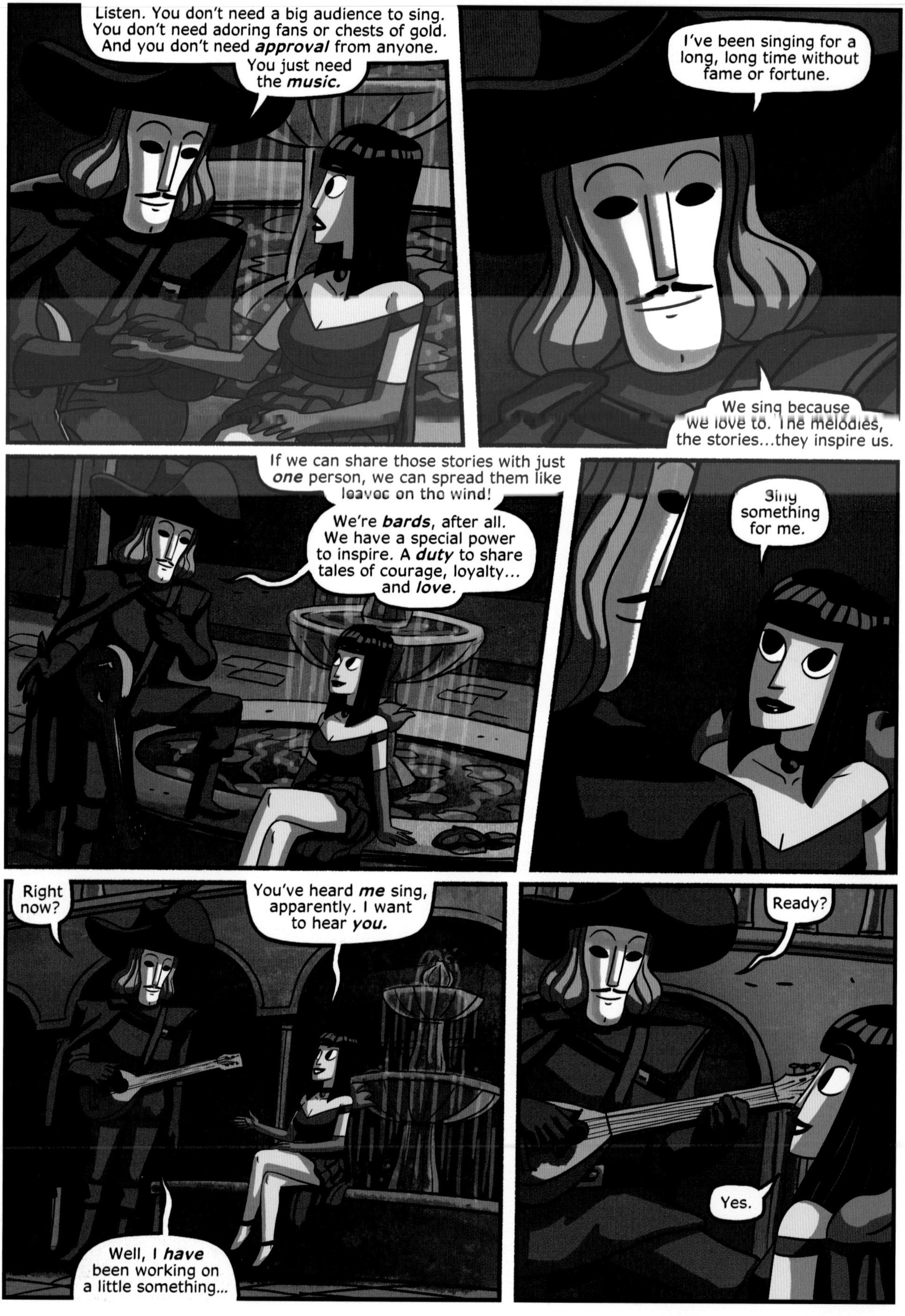
Listen. You don't need a big audience to sing. You don't need adoring fans or chests of gold. And you don't need *approval* from anyone.
You just need the *music.*
I've been singing for a long, long time without fame or fortune.
We sing because we love to. The melodies, the stories...they inspire us.
If we can share those stories with just *one* person, we can spread them like leaves on the wind!
We're *bards*, after all. We have a special power to inspire. A *duty* to share tales of courage, loyalty... and *love.*
Sing something for me.
Right now?
You've heard *me* sing, apparently. I want to hear *you.*
Well, I *have* been working on a little something...
Ready?
Yes.

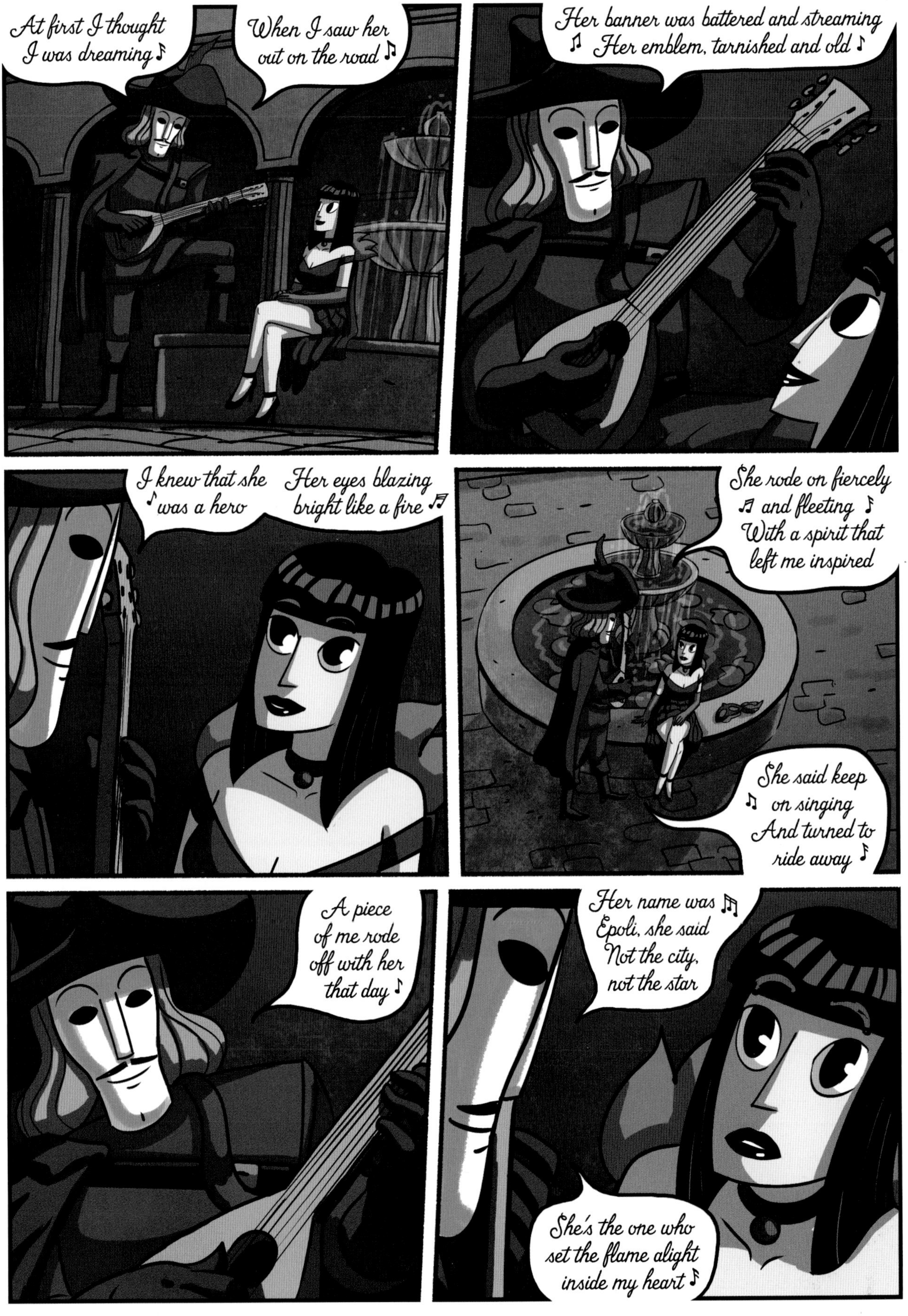
At first I thought I was dreaming ♪
When I saw her out on the road ♫
Her banner was battered and streaming ♫ Her emblem, tarnished and old ♪
I knew that she ♪ was a hero
Her eyes blazing bright like a fire ♬
She rode on fiercely ♫ and fleeting ♪ With a spirit that left me inspired
She said keep ♫ on singing And turned to ride away ♪
A piece of me rode off with her that day ♪
Her name was ♬ Epoli, she said Not the city, not the star
She's the one who set the flame alight inside my heart ♪

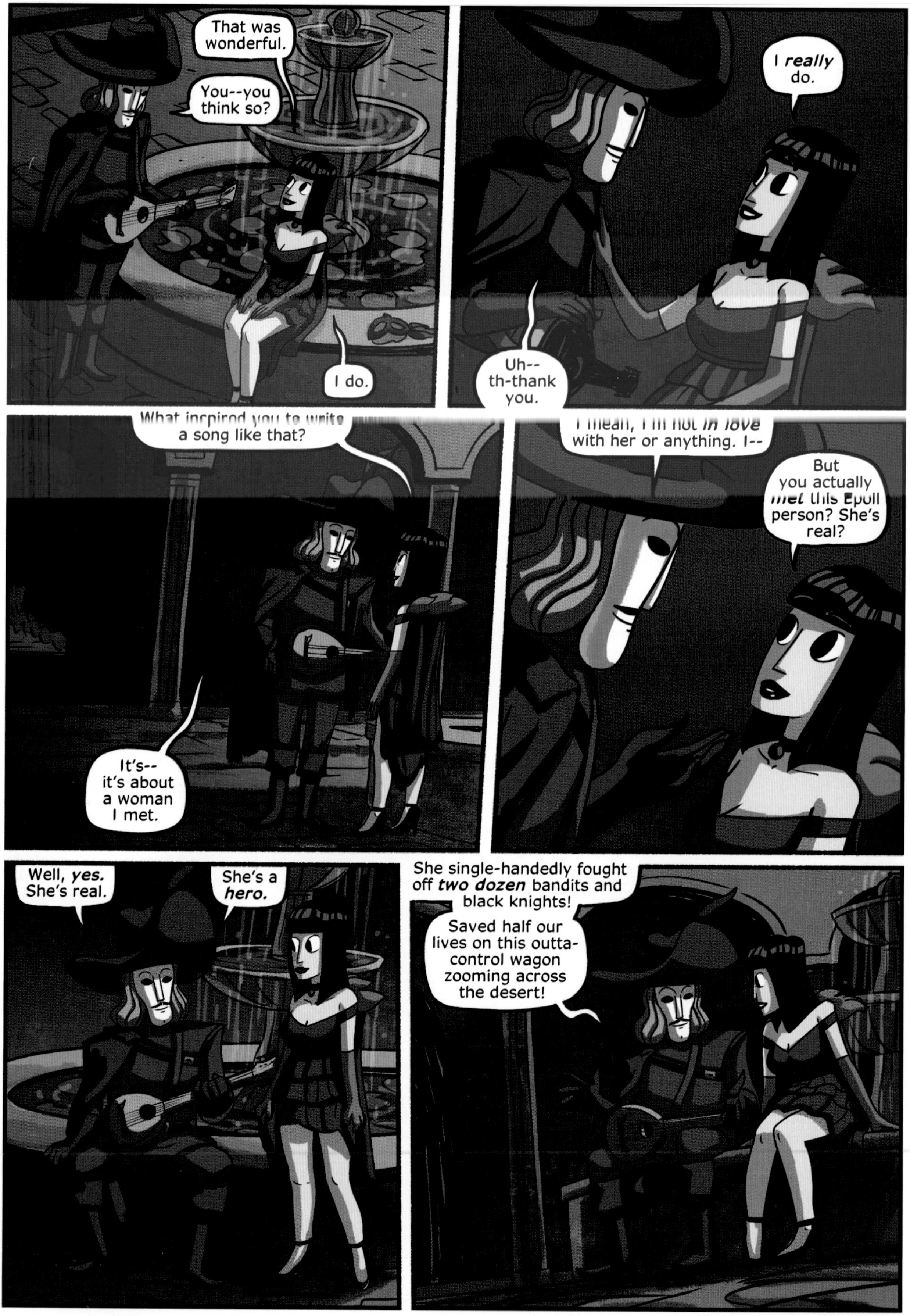
That was wonderful.
You--you think so?
I do.
I *really* do.
Uh-- th-thank you.
What inspired you to write a song like that?
It's-- it's about a woman I met.
I mean, I'm not *in love* with her or anything. I--
But you actually
person? She's real?
Well, *yes.* She's real.
She's a *hero.*
She single-handedly fought off *two dozen* bandits and black knights!
Saved half our lives on this outta-control wagon zooming across the desert!

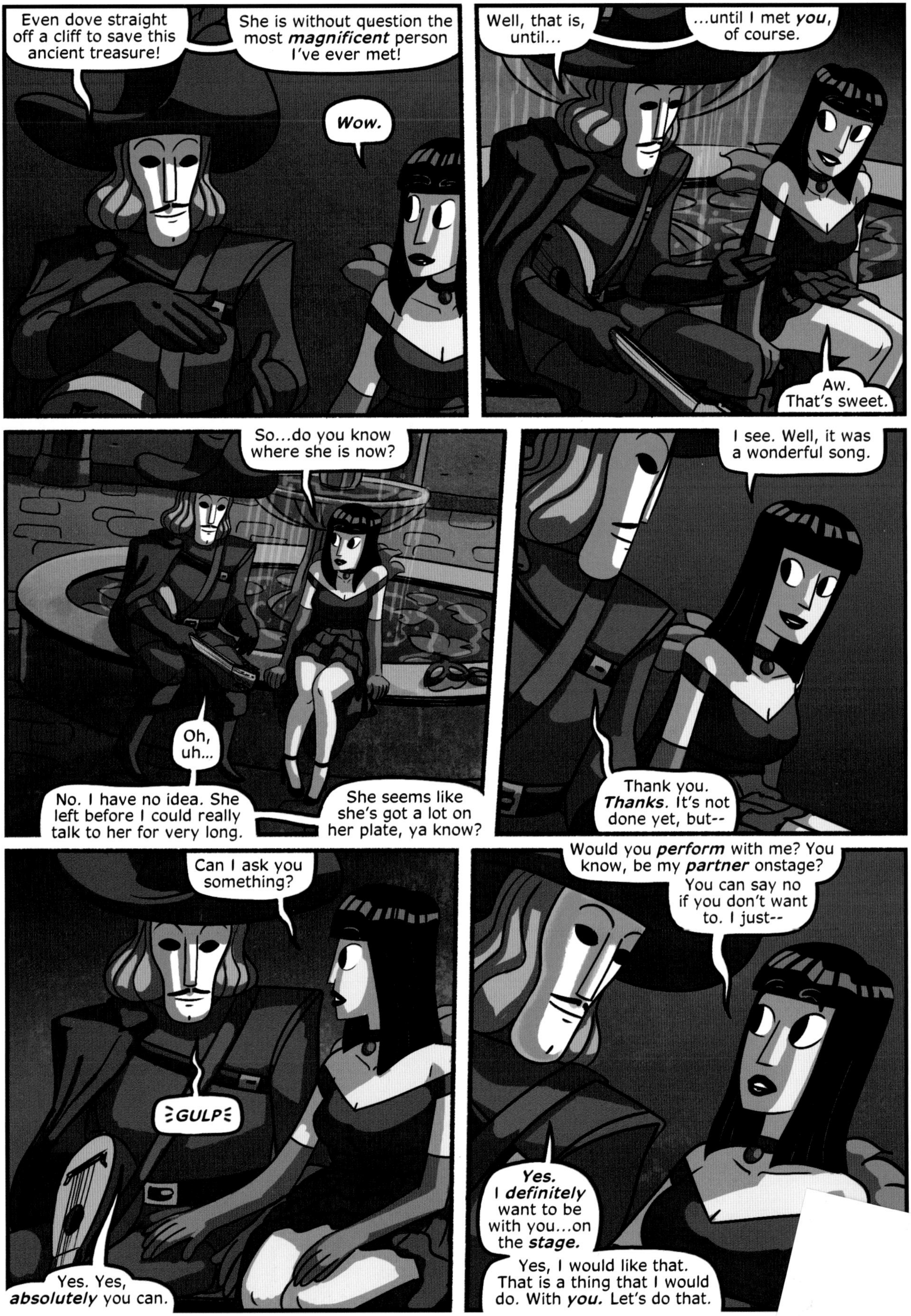
Even dove straight off a cliff to save this ancient treasure!
She is without question the most ***magnificent*** person I've ever met!
Wow.
Well, that is, until...
...until I met ***you***, of course.
Aw. That's sweet.
So...do you know where she is now?
Oh, uh...
No. I have no idea. She left before I could really talk to her for very long.
She seems like she's got a lot on her plate, ya know?
I see. Well, it was a wonderful song.
Thank you. ***Thanks***. It's not done yet, but--
Can I ask you something?
GULP
Yes. Yes, ***absolutely*** you can.
Would you ***perform*** with me? You know, be my ***partner*** onstage?
You can say no if you don't want to. I just--
Yes. I ***definitely*** want to be with you...on the ***stage.***
Yes, I would like that. That is a thing that I would do. With ***you.*** Let's do that.

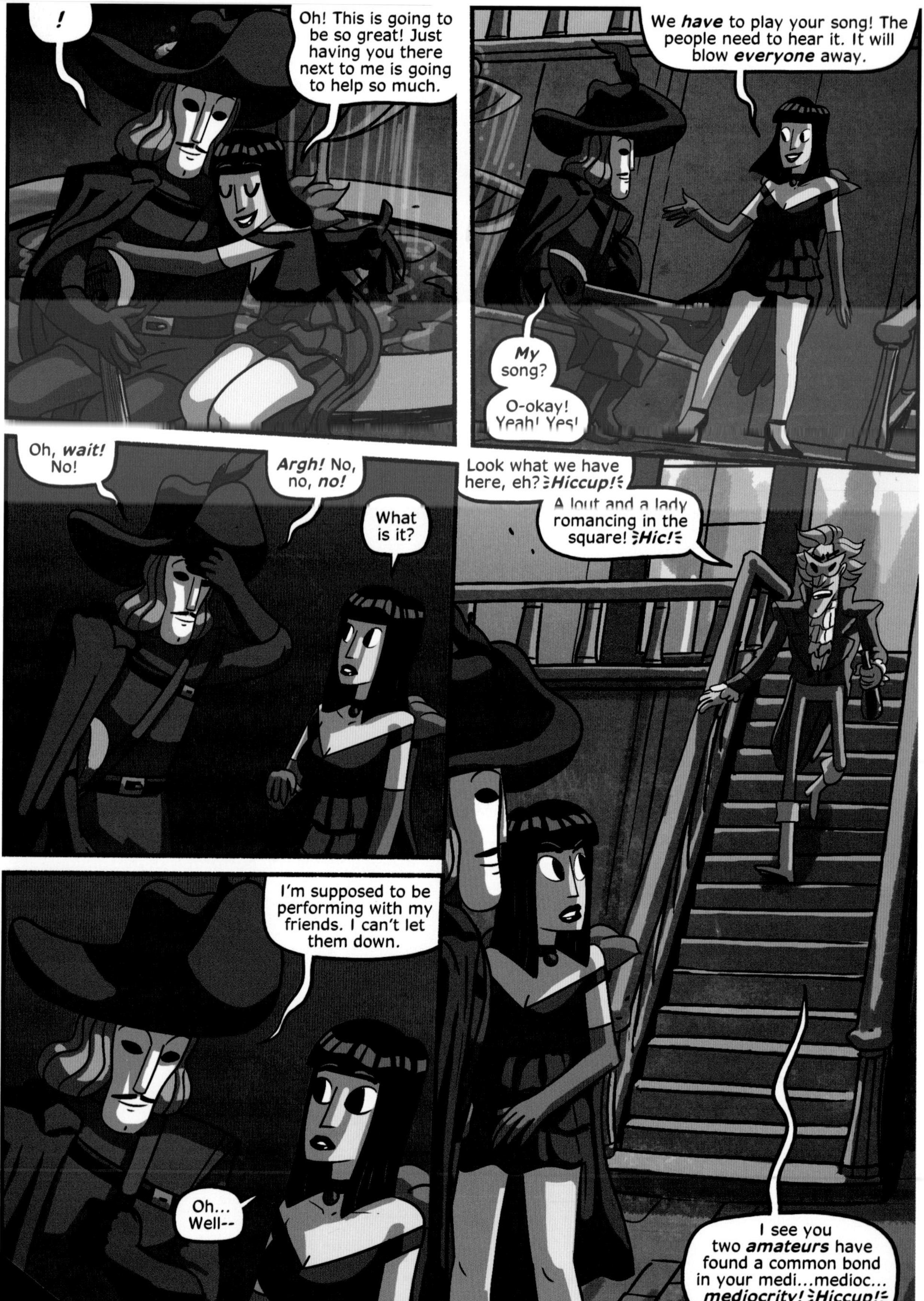
!
Oh! This is going to be so great! Just having you there next to me is going to help so much.
We *have* to play your song! The people need to hear it. It will blow *everyone* away.
My song?
O-okay! Yeah! Yes!
Oh, *wait!* No!
Argh! No, no, *no!*
What is it?
I'm supposed to be performing with my friends. I can't let them down.
Oh... Well--
Look what we have here, eh? *Hiccup!*
A lout and a lady romancing in the square! *Hic!*
I see you two *amateurs* have found a common bond in your medi...medioc... *mediocrity!* *Hiccup!*

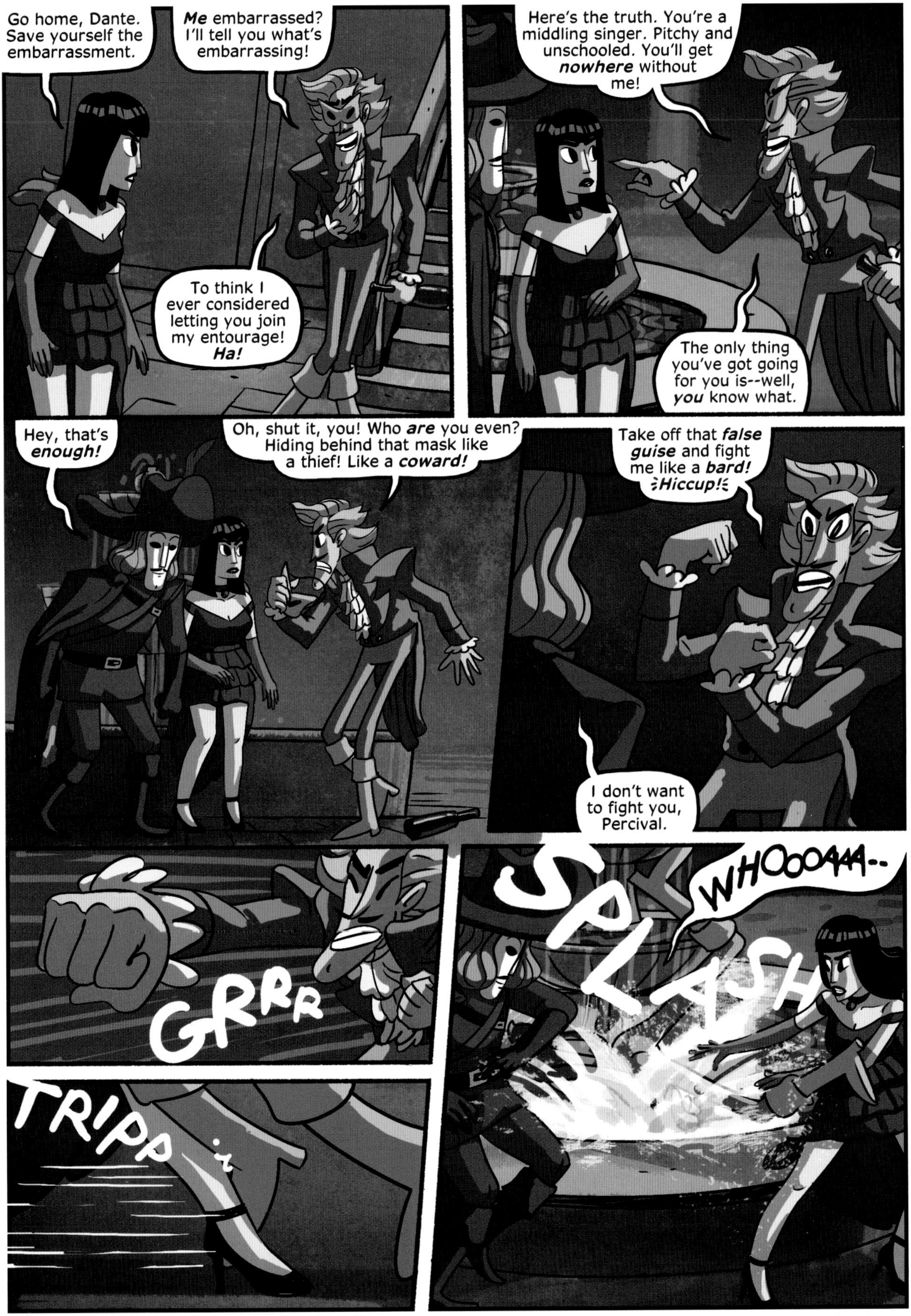
Go home, Dante. Save yourself the embarrassment.
Me embarrassed? I'll tell you what's embarrassing!
To think I ever considered letting you join my entourage! ***Ha!***
Here's the truth. You're a middling singer. Pitchy and unschooled. You'll get ***nowhere*** without me!
The only thing you've got going for you is--well, ***you*** know what.
Hey, that's ***enough!***
Oh, shut it, you! Who ***are*** you even? Hiding behind that mask like a thief! Like a ***coward!***
Take off that ***false guise*** and fight me like a ***bard!*** ***Hiccup!***
I don't want to fight you, Percival.
GRRR
TRIPP
SPLASH
WHOOOAAA--

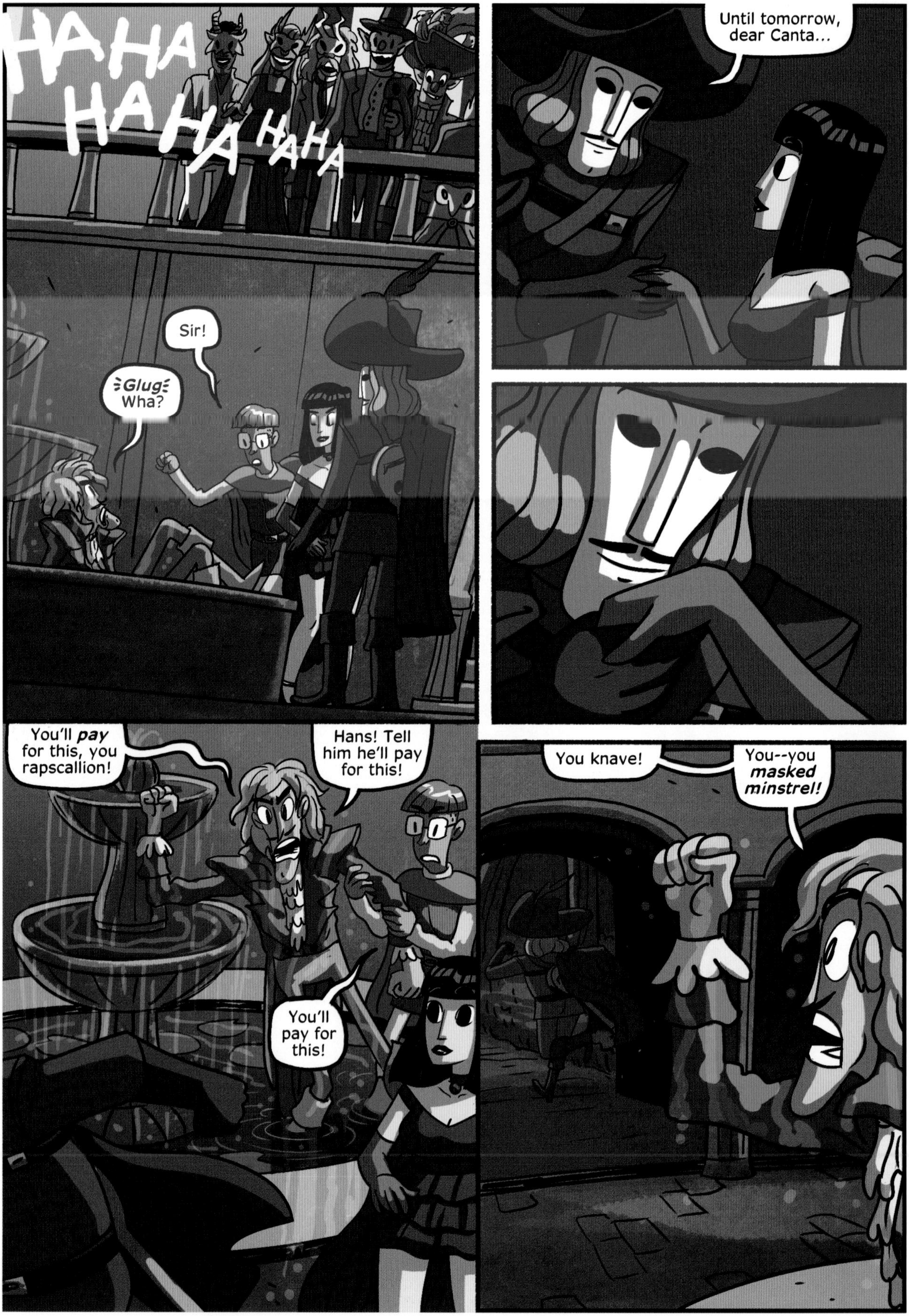

HAHA HAHA HAHA HAHA
Until tomorrow, dear Canta...
Sir!
Glug Wha?
You'll *pay* for this, you rapscallion!
Hans! Tell him he'll pay for this!
You'll pay for this!
You knave!
You--you *masked minstrel!*

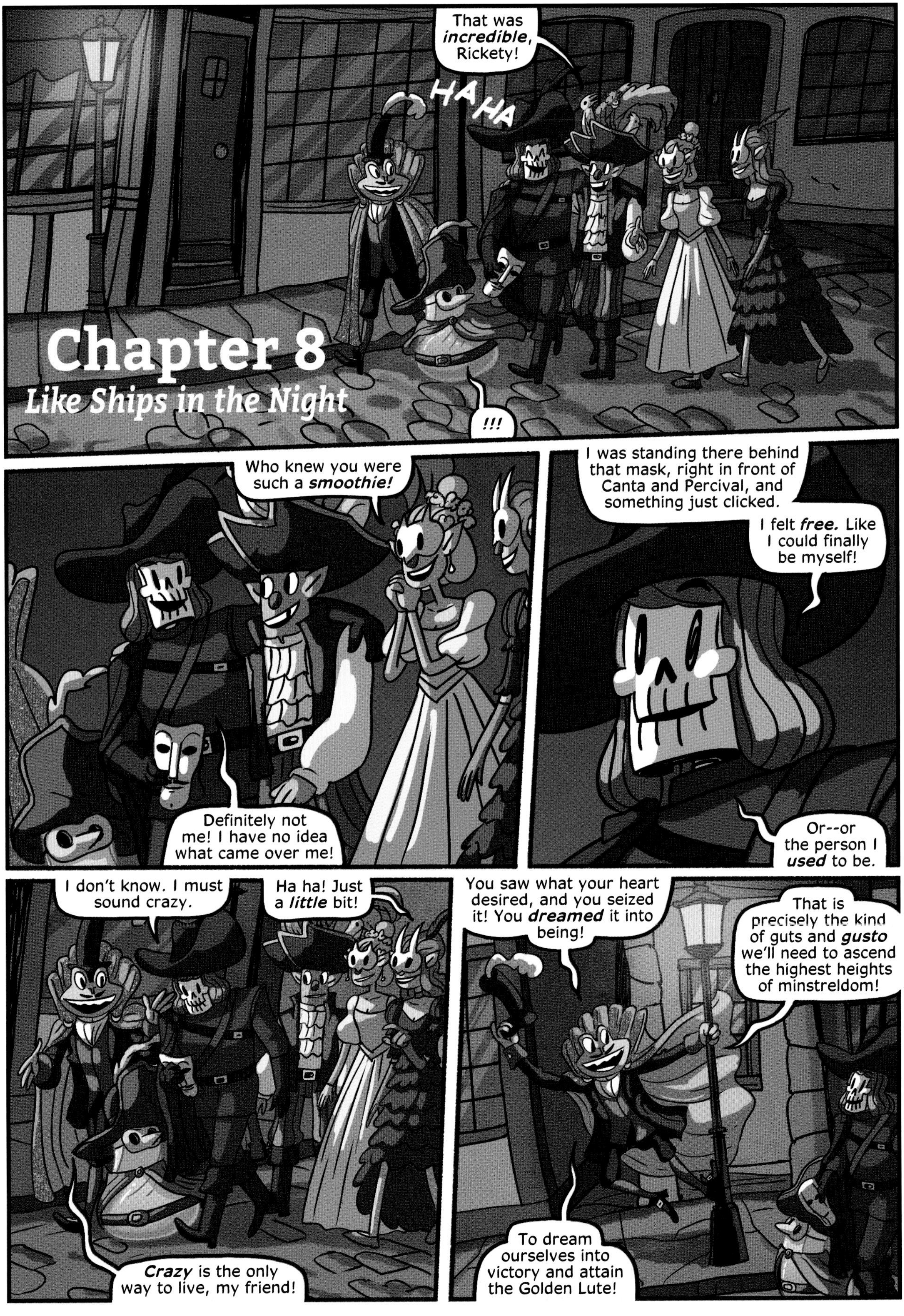

Chapter 8
Like Ships in the Night
That was *incredible*, Rickety!
HA HA
!!!
Who knew you were such a *smoothie!*
Definitely not me! I have no idea what came over me!
I was standing there behind that mask, right in front of Canta and Percival, and something just clicked.
I felt *free.* Like I could finally be myself!
Or--or the person I *used* to be.
I don't know. I must sound crazy.
Ha ha! Just a *little* bit!
Crazy is the only way to live, my friend!
You saw what your heart desired, and you seized it! You *dreamed* it into being!
That is precisely the kind of guts and *gusto* we'll need to ascend the highest heights of minstreldom!
To dream ourselves into victory and attain the Golden Lute!

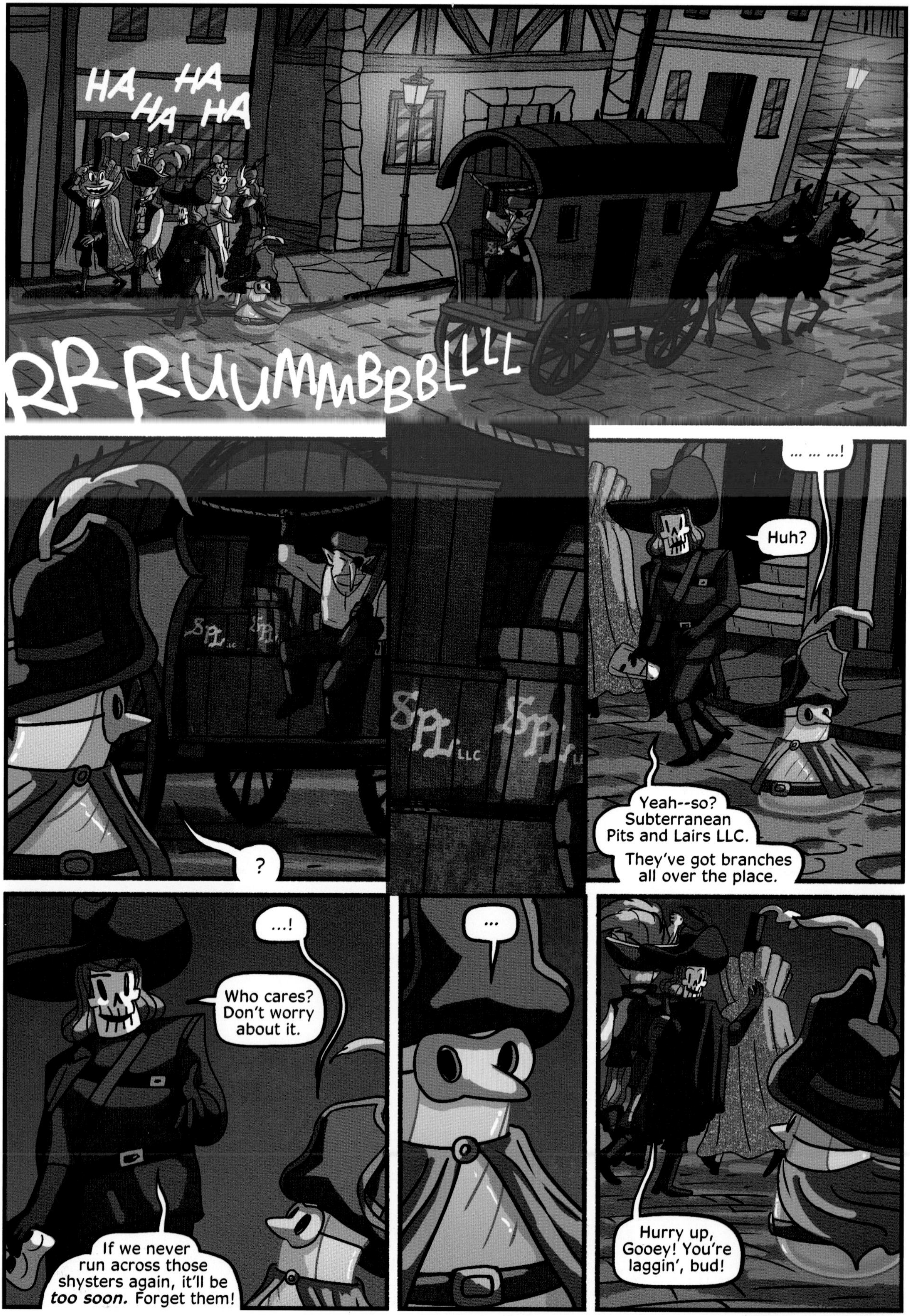
HA HA HA HA
RRRUUMMBBBLLLL
?
... ...!
Huh?
Yeah--so? Subterranean Pits and Lairs LLC.
They've got branches all over the place.
...!
Who cares? Don't worry about it.
If we never run across those shysters again, it'll be *too soon.* Forget them!
...
Hurry up, Gooey! You're laggin', bud!

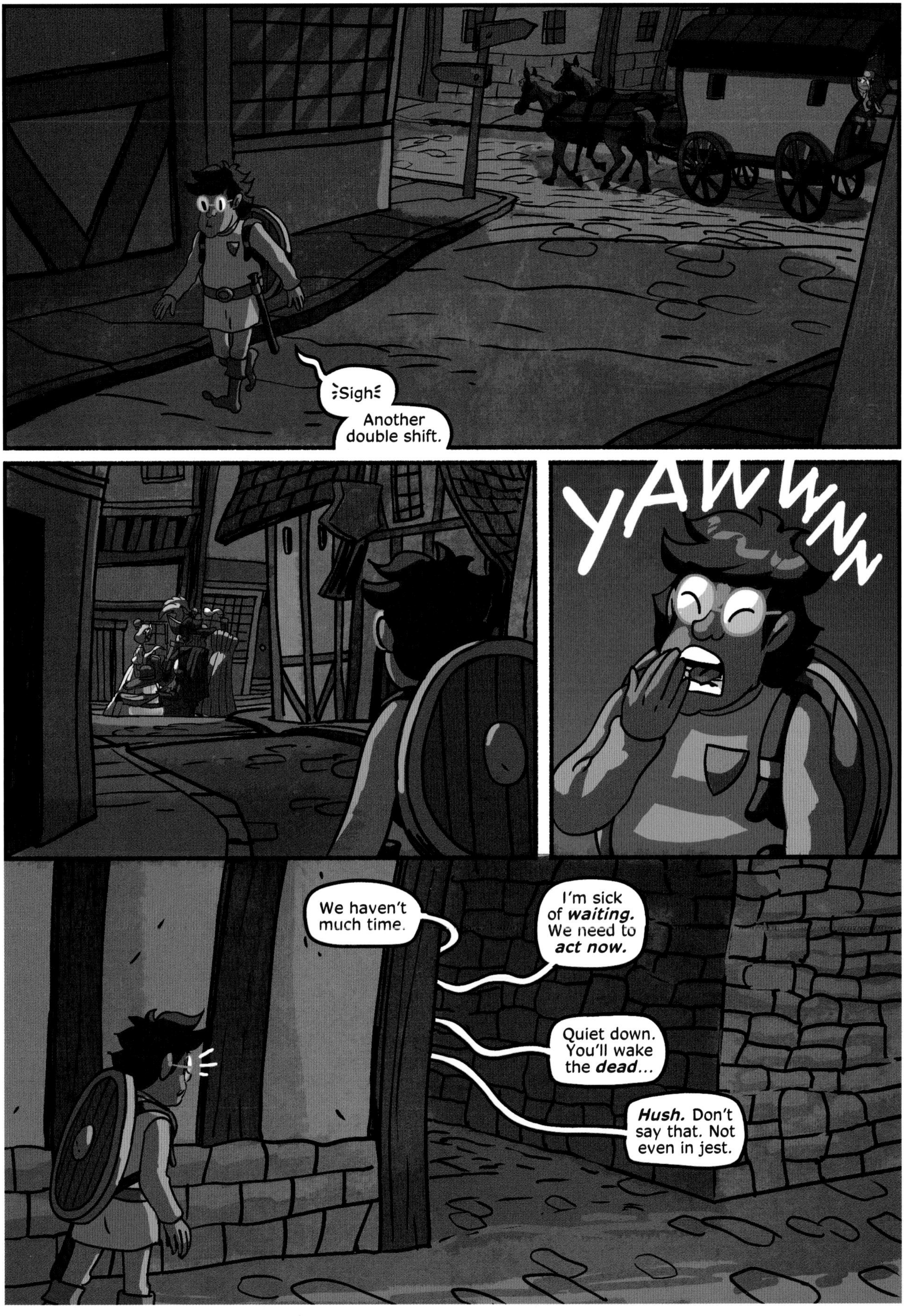

Sigh
Another double shift.
YAWWNN
We haven't much time.
I'm sick of *waiting.* We need to *act now.*
Quiet down. You'll wake the *dead*...
Hush. Don't say that. Not even in jest.

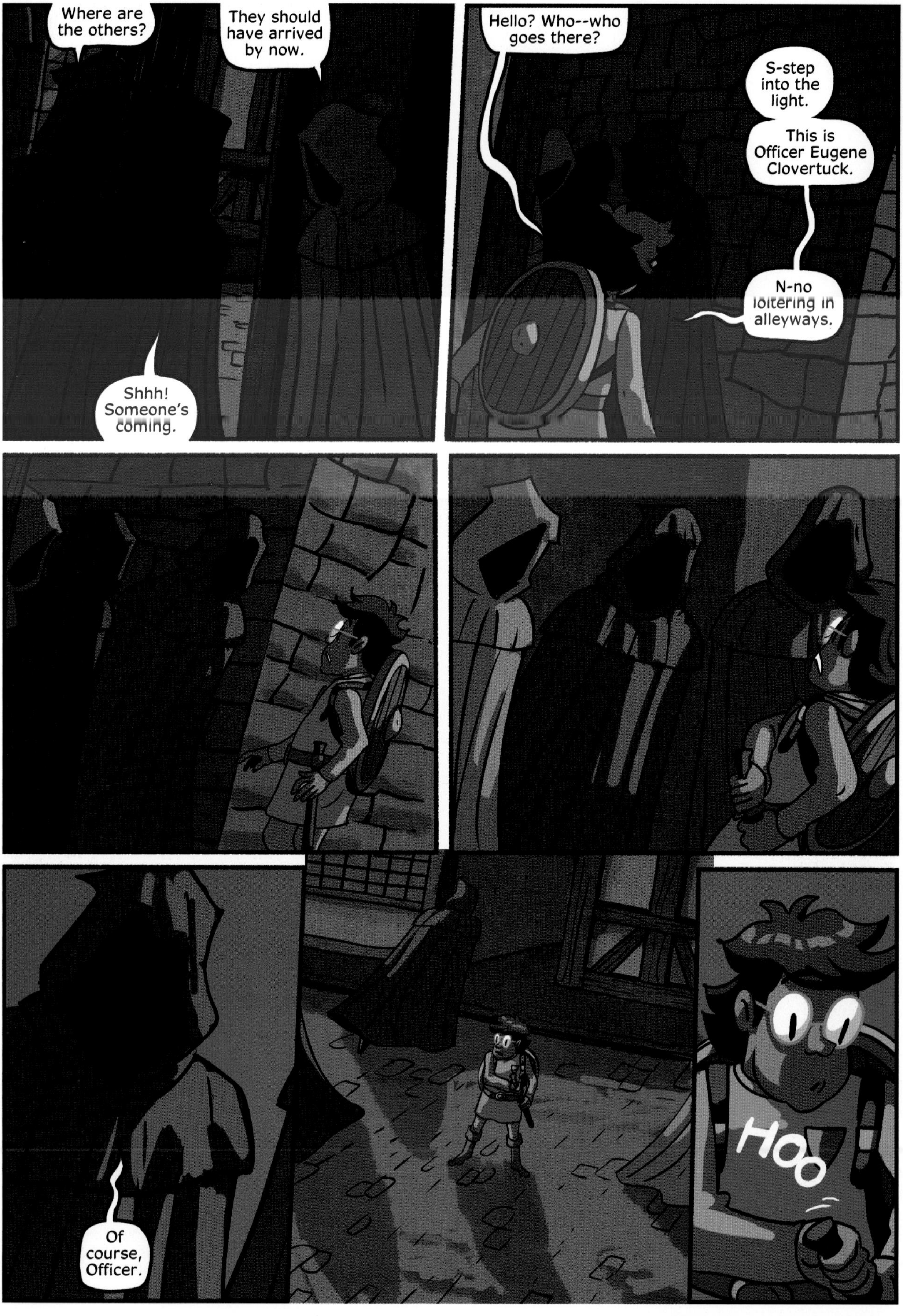
Where are the others?
They should have arrived by now.
Shhh! Someone's coming.
Hello? Who--who goes there?
S-step into the light.
This is Officer Eugene Clovertuck.
N-no loitering in alleyways.
Of course, Officer.
HOO

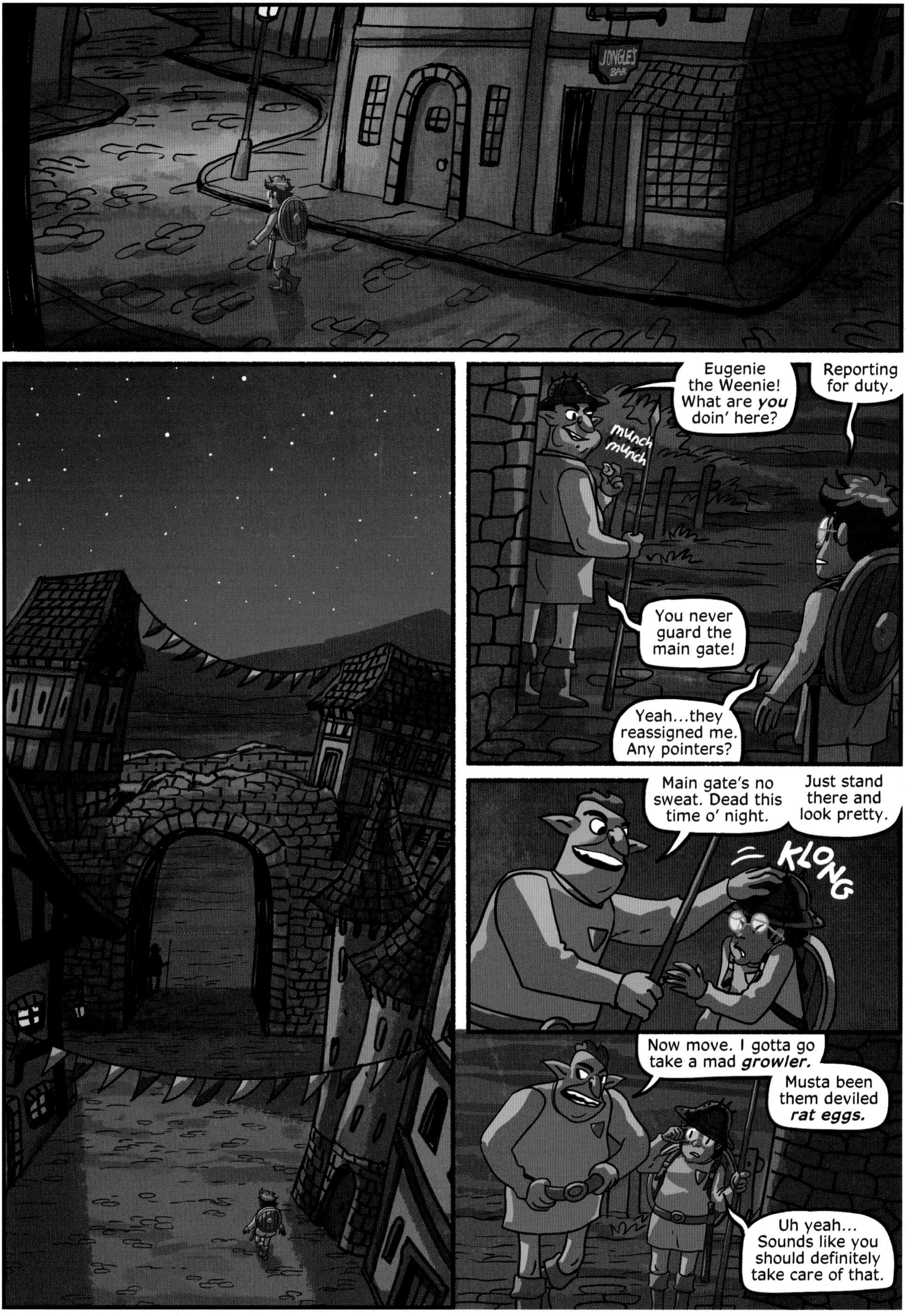
JONGLE'S BAR
Eugenie the Weenie! What are *you* doin' here?
munch munch
Reporting for duty.
You never guard the main gate!
Yeah...they reassigned me. Any pointers?
Main gate's no sweat. Dead this time o' night.
Just stand there and look pretty.
KLONG
Now move. I gotta go take a mad *growler.*
Musta been them deviled *rat eggs.*
Uh yeah... Sounds like you should definitely take care of that.

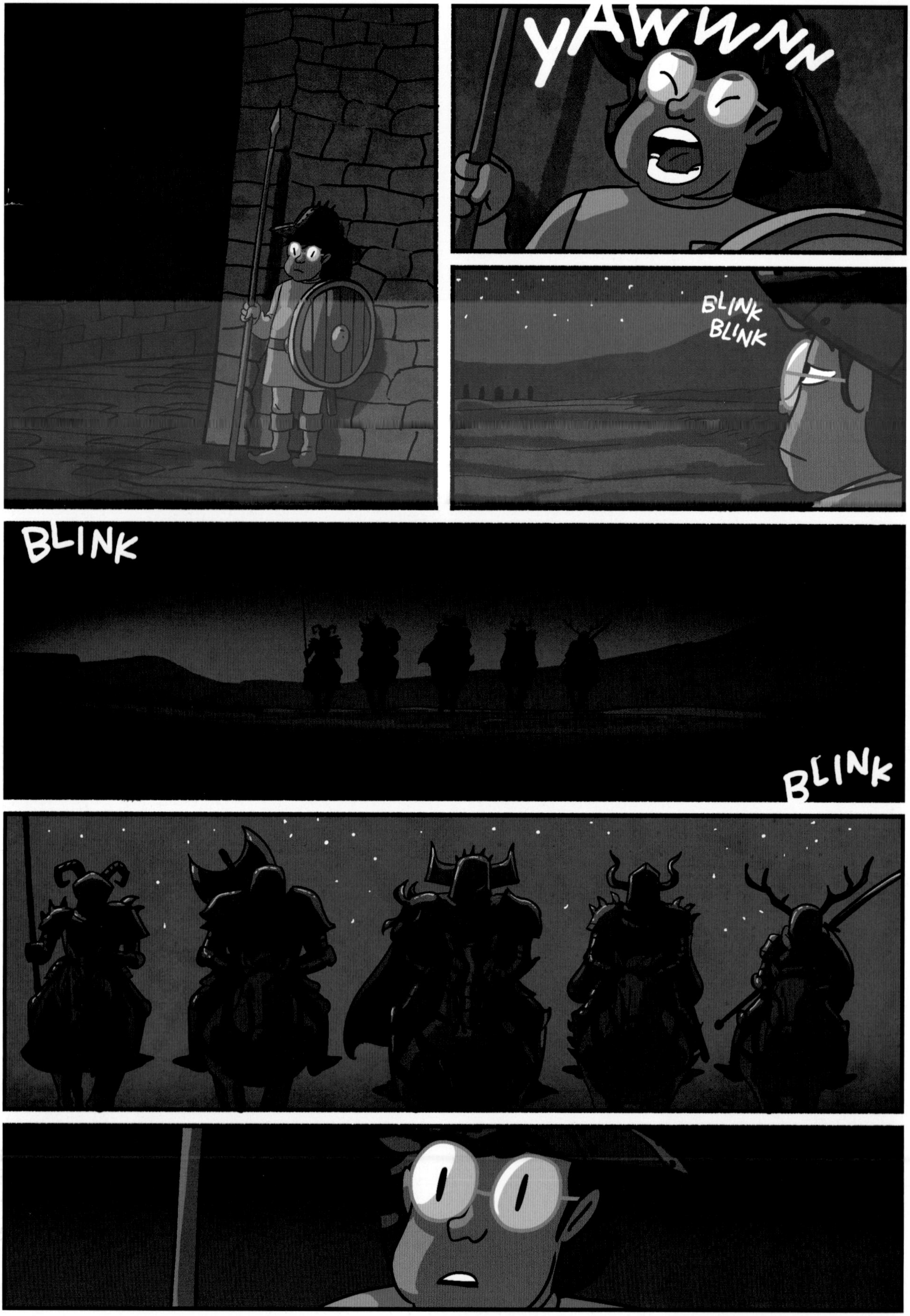
YAWWNN
BLINK
BLINK
BLINK
BLINK

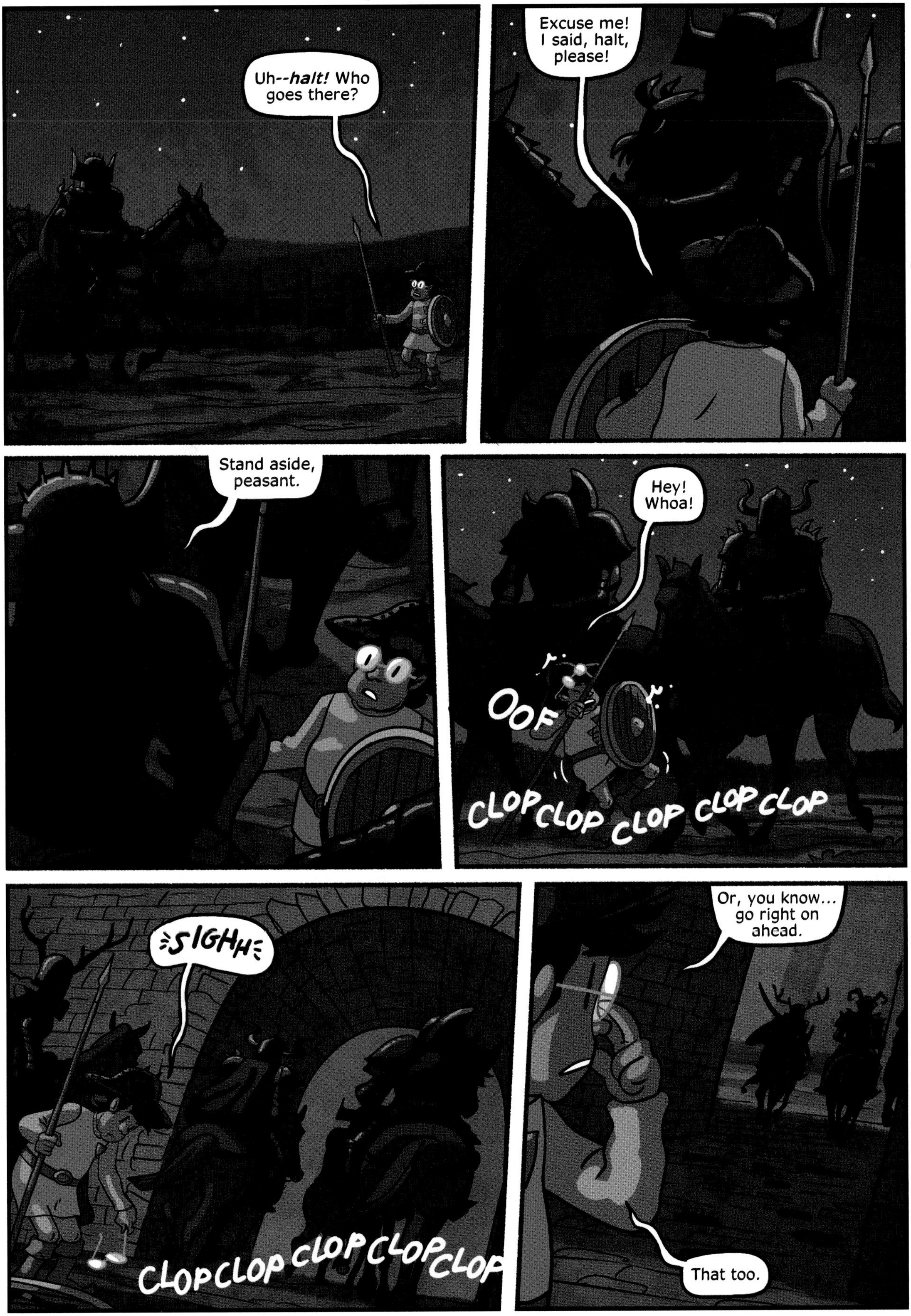
Uh--*halt!* Who goes there?
Excuse me! I said, halt, please!
Stand aside, peasant.
Hey! Whoa!
OOF
CLOP CLOP CLOP CLOP CLOP
SIGHH
CLOP CLOP CLOP CLOP CLOP
Or, you know... go right on ahead.
That too.

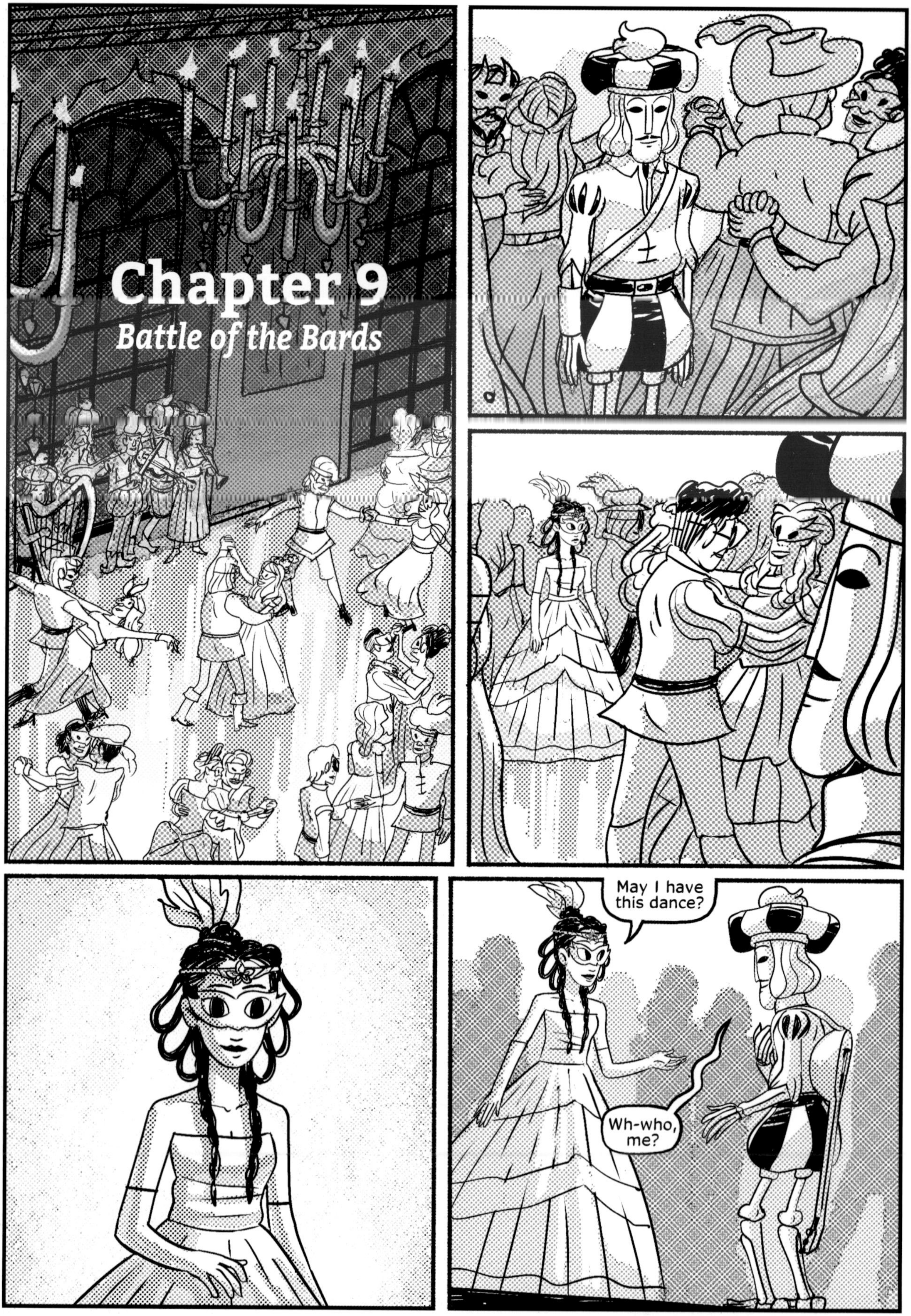
Chapter 9
Battle of the Bards
May I have this dance?
Wh-who, me?

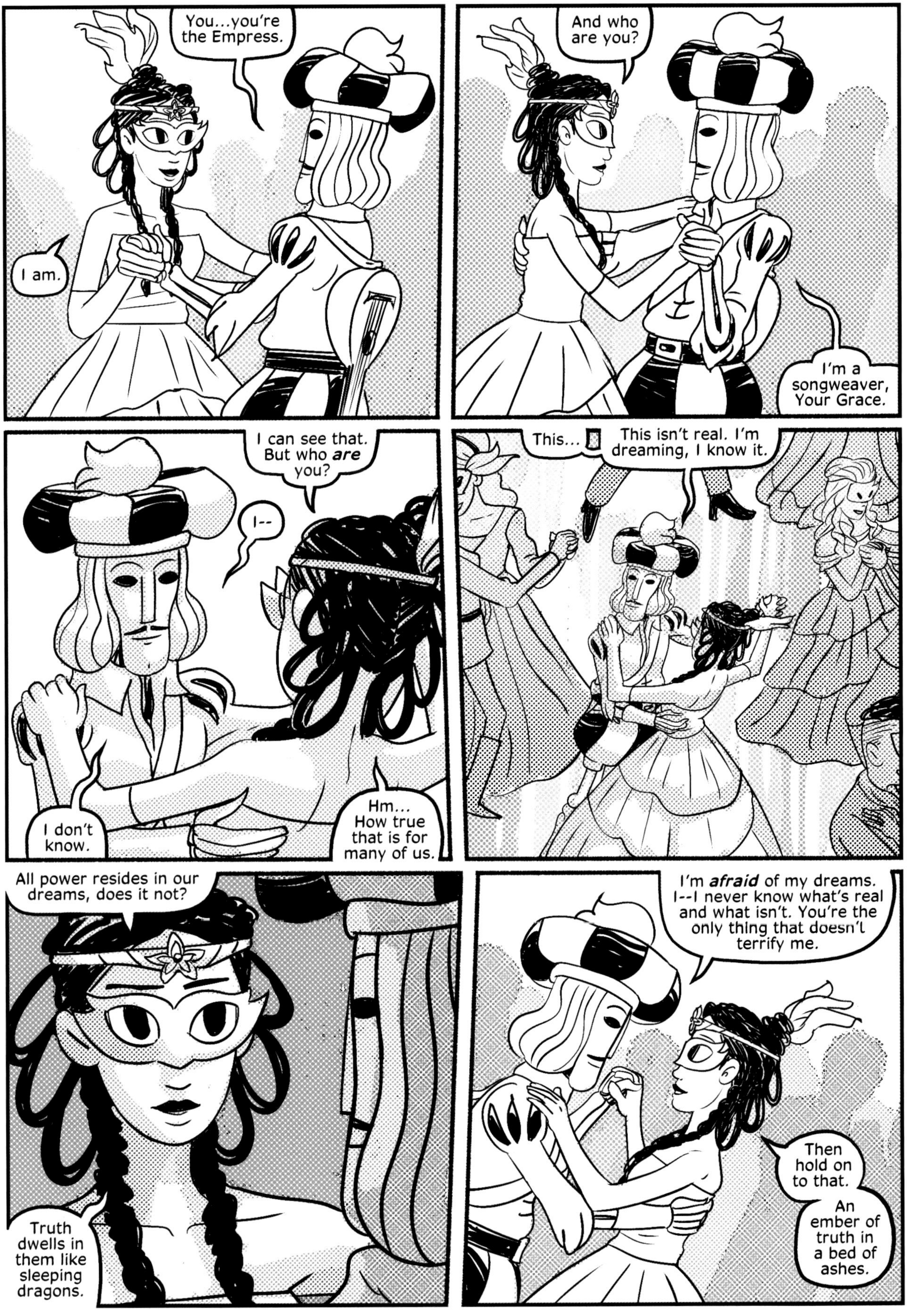
You...you're the Empress.
I am.
And who are you?
I'm a songweaver, Your Grace.
I can see that. But who *are* you?
I--
I don't know.
Hm... How true that is for many of us.
This...
This isn't real. I'm dreaming, I know it.
All power resides in our dreams, does it not?
Truth dwells in them like sleeping dragons.
I'm *afraid* of my dreams. I--I never know what's real and what isn't. You're the only thing that doesn't terrify me.
Then hold on to that.
An ember of truth in a bed of ashes.

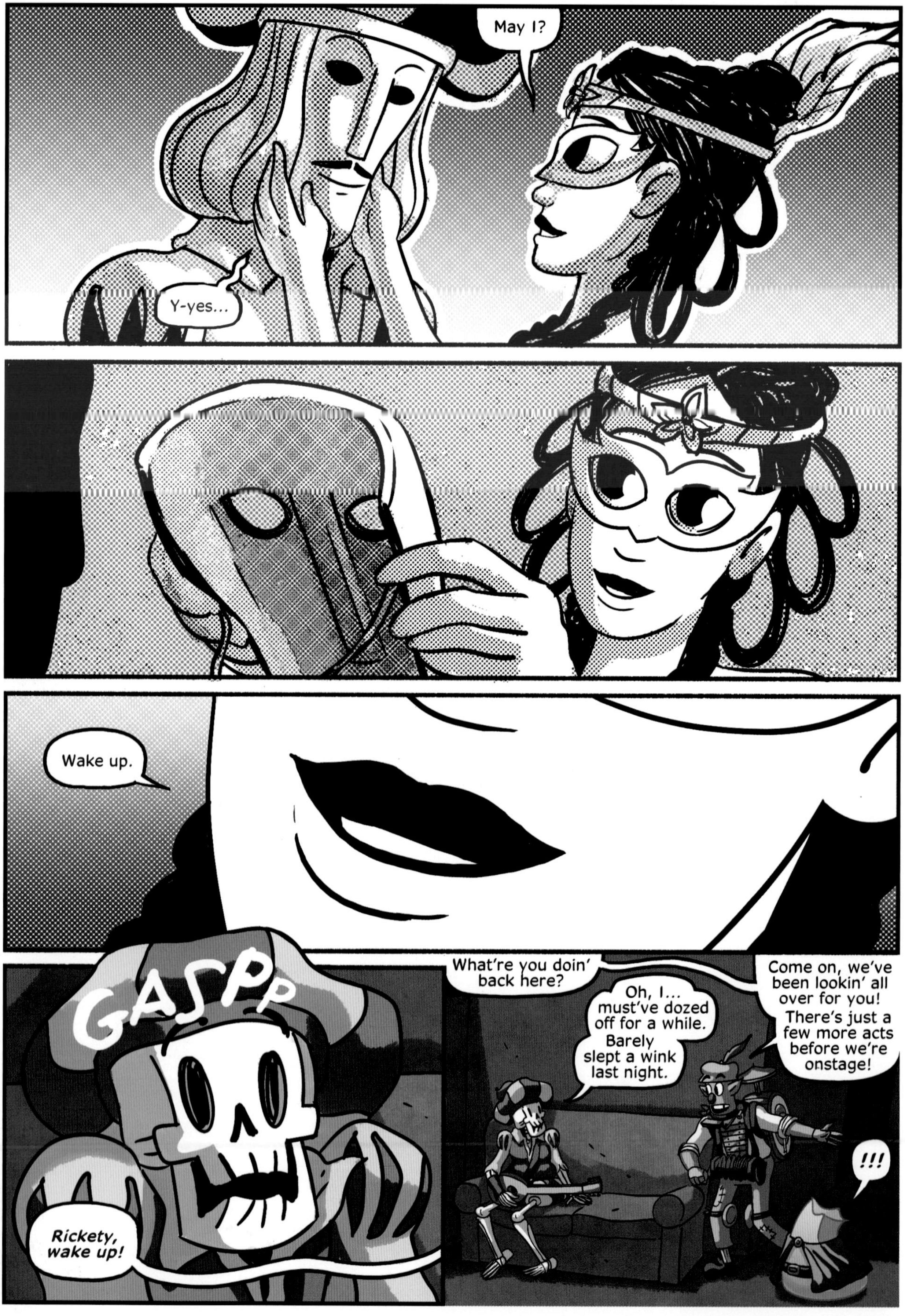
May I?
Y-yes...
Wake up.
GASPp
Rickety, wake up!
What're you doin' back here?
Oh, I... must've dozed off for a while. Barely slept a wink last night.
Come on, we've been lookin' all over for you! There's just a few more acts before we're onstage!
!!!

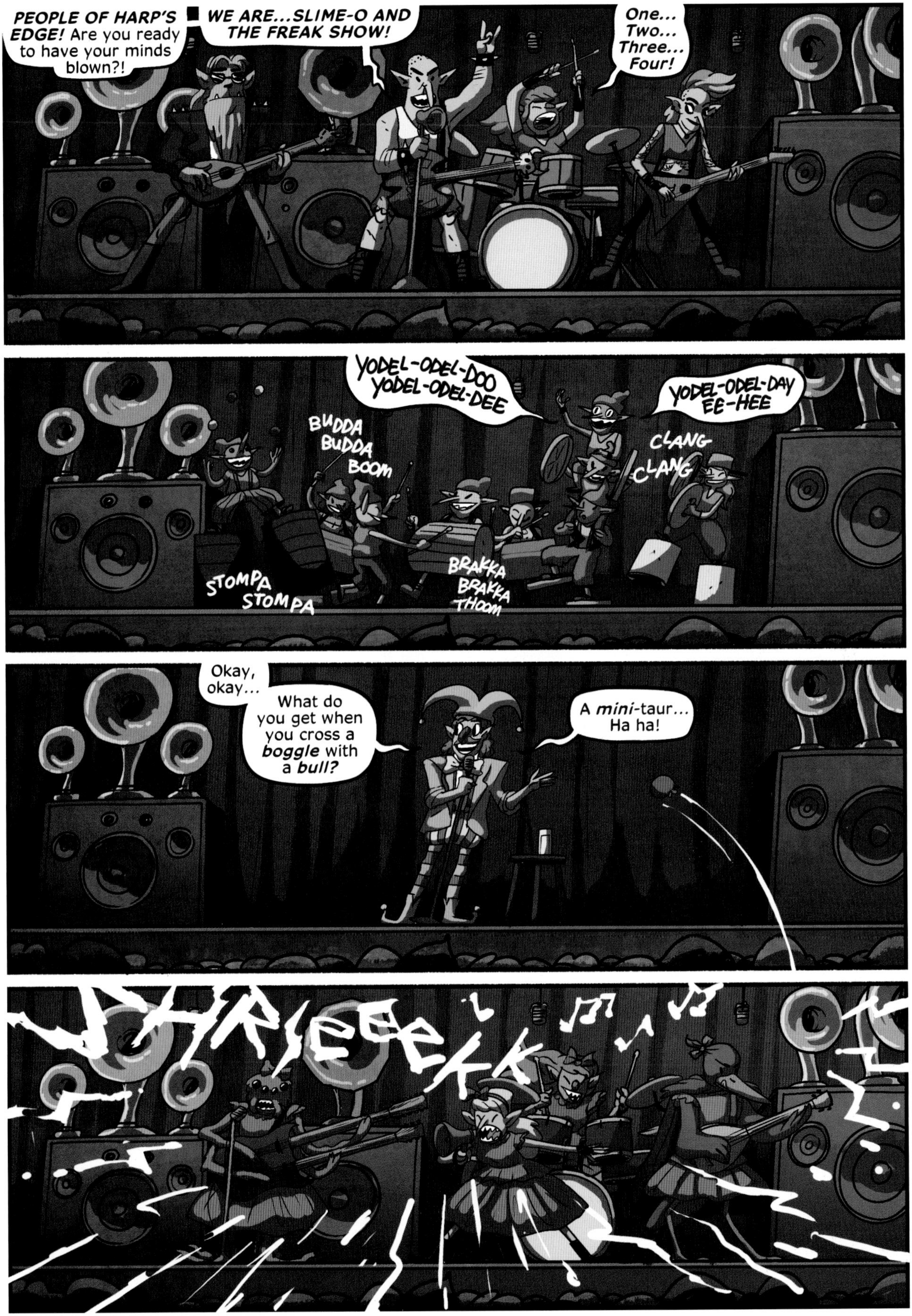
PEOPLE OF HARP'S EDGE! Are you ready to have your minds blown?!
WE ARE...SLIME-O AND THE FREAK SHOW!
One... Two... Three... Four!
YODEL-ODEL-DOO YODEL-ODEL-DEE
YODEL-ODEL-DAY EE-HEE
BUDDA BUDDA BOOM
CLANG CLANG
STOMPA STOMPA
BRAKKA BRAKKA THOOM
Okay, okay...
What do you get when you cross a *boggle* with a *bull?*
A *mini*-taur... Ha ha!
SHRIEEKK

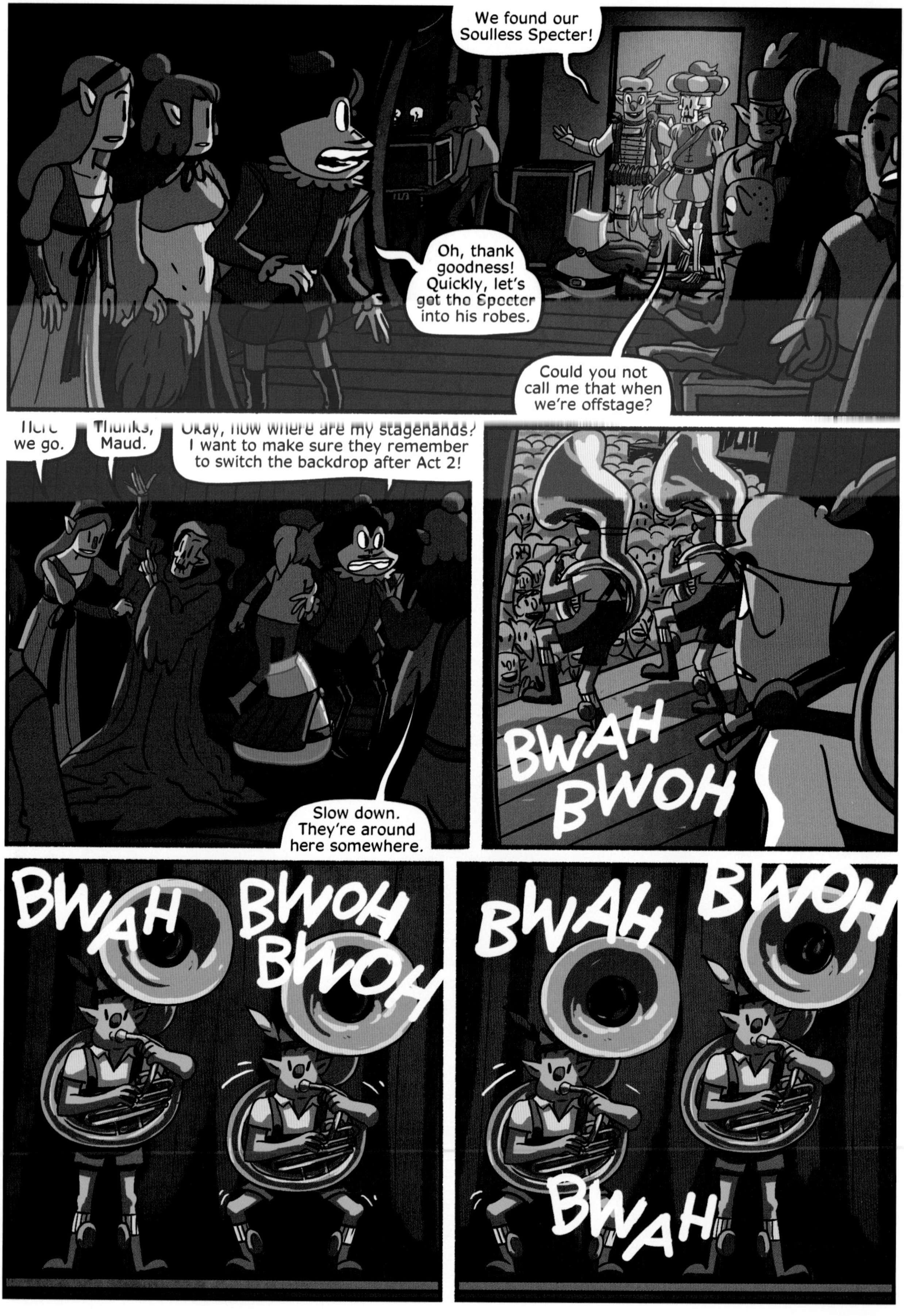

We found our Soulless Specter!
Oh, thank goodness! Quickly, let's get the Specter into his robes.
Could you not call me that when we're offstage?
Here we go.
Thanks, Maud.
Okay, now where are my stagehands? I want to make sure they remember to switch the backdrop after Act 2!
Slow down. They're around here somewhere.
BWAH BWOH
BWAH
BWOH BWOH
BWAH
BWOH
BWAH

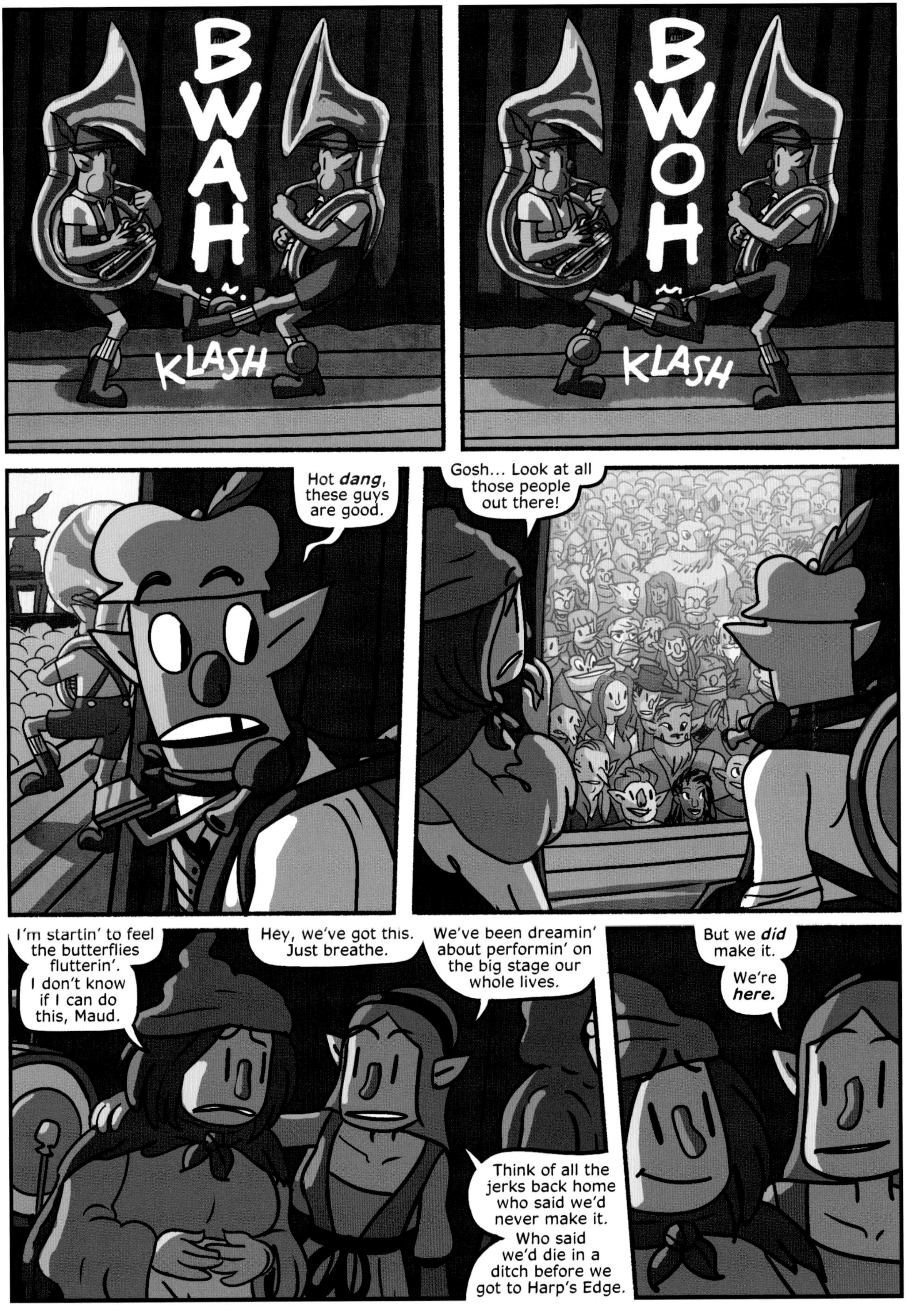
BWAH
KLASH
BWOH
KLASH
Hot *dang*, these guys are good.
Gosh... Look at all those people out there!
I'm startin' to feel the butterflies flutterin'.
I don't know if I can do this, Maud.
Hey, we've got this. Just breathe.
We've been dreamin' about performin' on the big stage our whole lives.
Think of all the jerks back home who said we'd never make it.
Who said we'd die in a ditch before we got to Harp's Edge.
But we *did* make it.
We're ***here.***

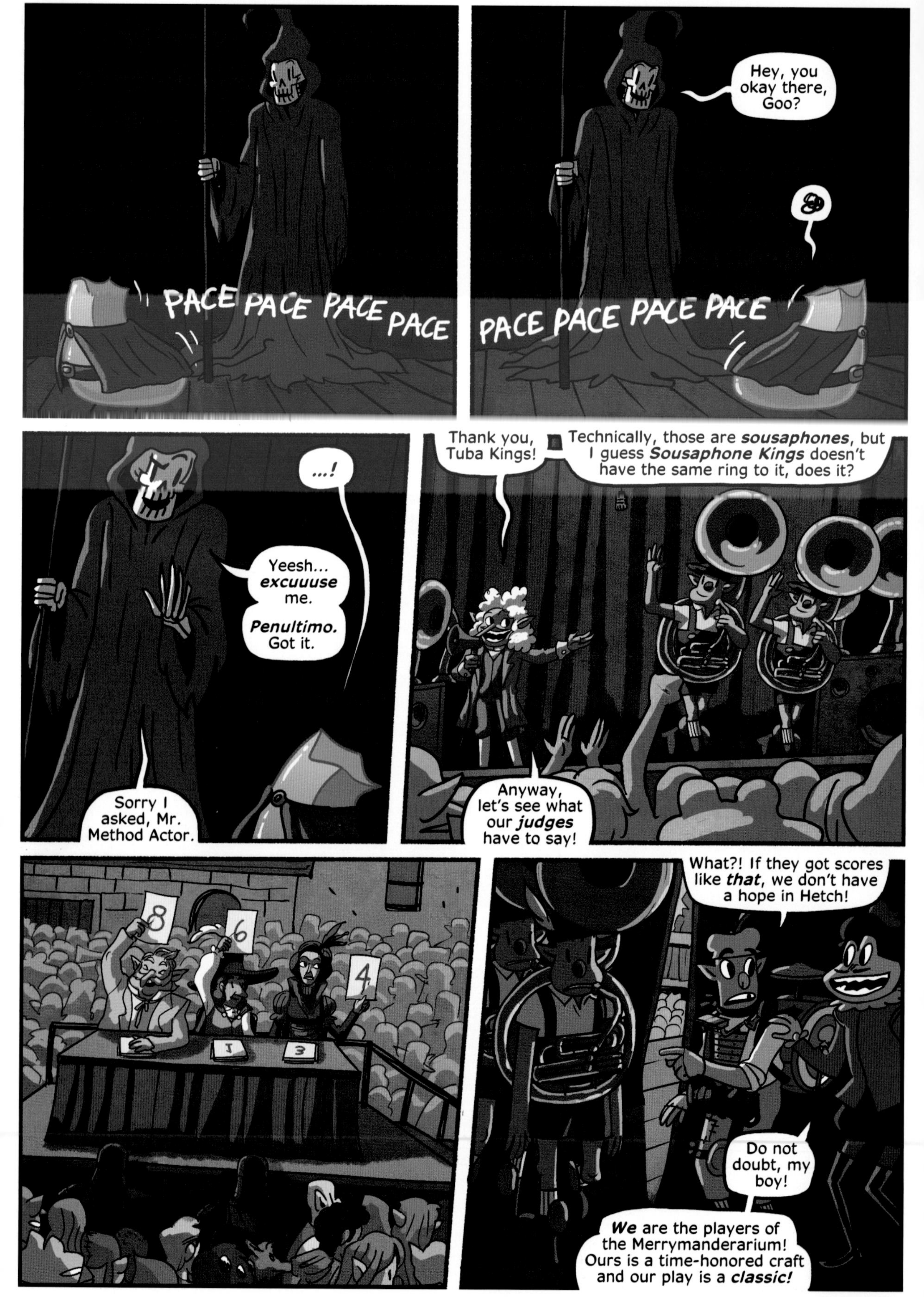
PACE PACE PACE PACE
Hey, you okay there, Goo?
PACE PACE PACE PACE
...!
Yeesh... *excuuuse* me.
Penultimo. Got it.
Sorry I asked, Mr. Method Actor.
Thank you, Tuba Kings!
Technically, those are *sousaphones*, but I guess *Sousaphone Kings* doesn't have the same ring to it, does it?
Anyway, let's see what our *judges* have to say!
8
6
4
J
3
What?! If they got scores like *that*, we don't have a hope in Hetch!
Do not doubt, my boy!
We are the players of the Merrymanderarium! Ours is a time-honored craft and our play is a *classic!*

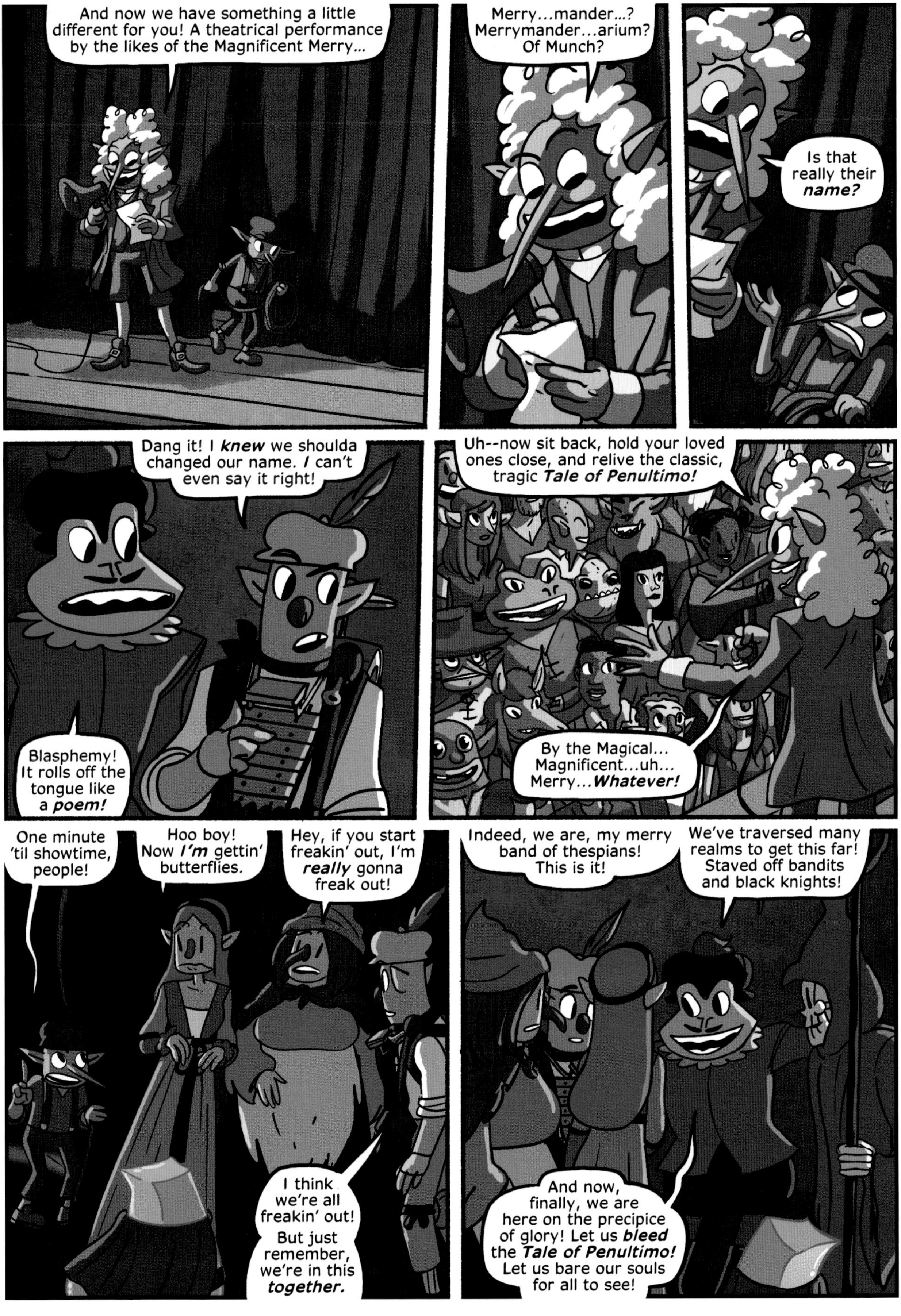

And now we have something a little different for you! A theatrical performance by the likes of the Magnificent Merry...
Merry...mander...? Merrymander...arium? Of Munch?
Is that really their ***name?***
Dang it! I ***knew*** we shoulda changed our name. ***I*** can't even say it right!
Blasphemy! It rolls off the tongue like a ***poem!***
Uh--now sit back, hold your loved ones close, and relive the classic, tragic ***Tale of Penultimo!***
By the Magical... Magnificent...uh... Merry...***Whatever!***
One minute 'til showtime, people!
Hoo boy! Now ***I'm*** gettin' butterflies.
Hey, if you start freakin' out, I'm ***really*** gonna freak out!
I think we're all freakin' out!
But just remember, we're in this ***together.***
Indeed, we are, my merry band of thespians! This is it!
We've traversed many realms to get this far! Staved off bandits and black knights!
And now, finally, we are here on the precipice of glory! Let us ***bleed*** the ***Tale of Penultimo!*** Let us bare our souls for all to see!

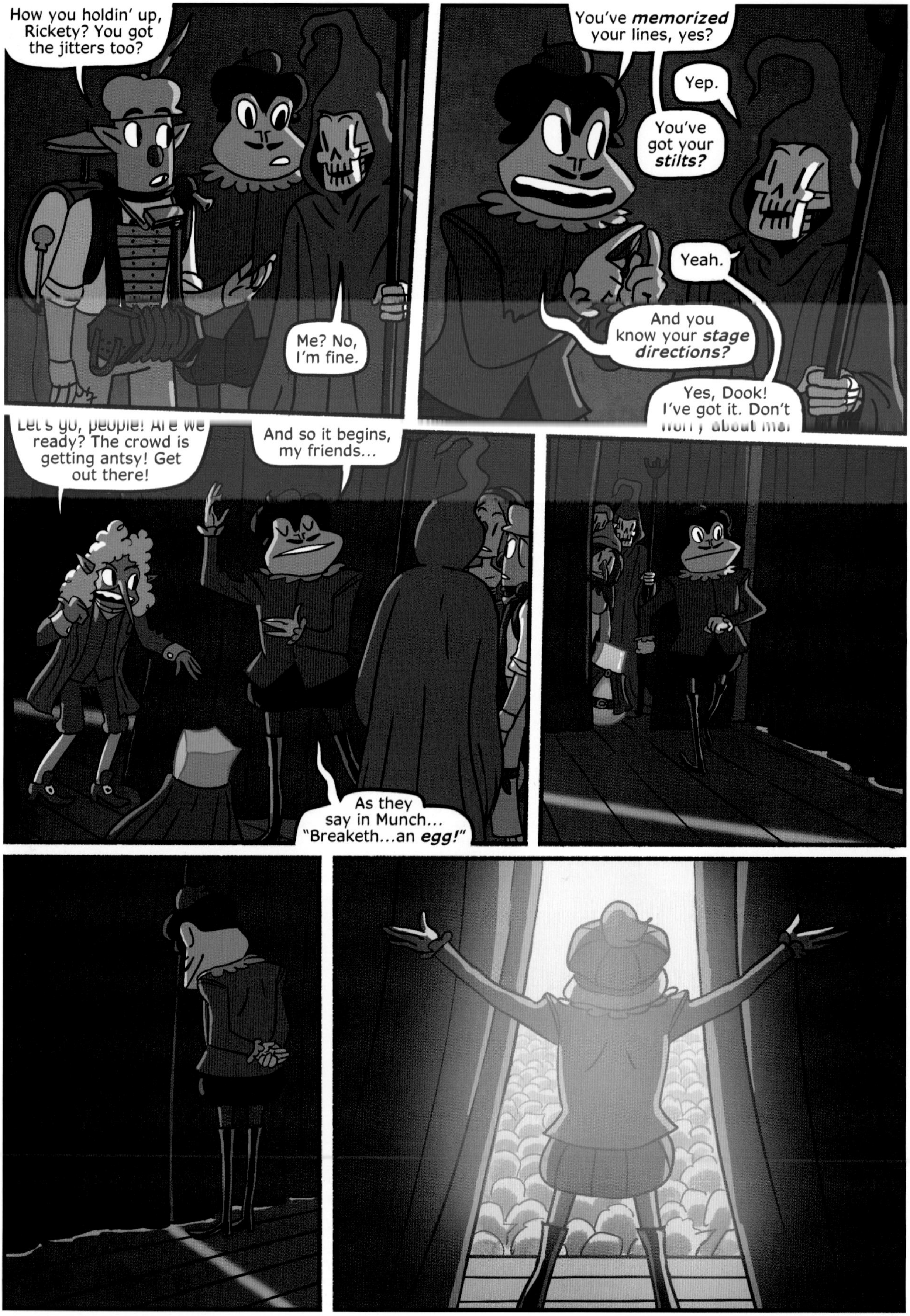
How you holdin' up, Rickety? You got the jitters too?
Me? No, I'm fine.
You've ***memorized*** your lines, yes?
Yep.
You've got your ***stilts?***
Yeah.
And you know your ***stage directions?***
Yes, Dook! I've got it. Don't worry about me!
Let's go, people! Are we ready? The crowd is getting antsy! Get out there!
And so it begins, my friends...
As they say in Munch... "Breaketh...an ***egg!***"

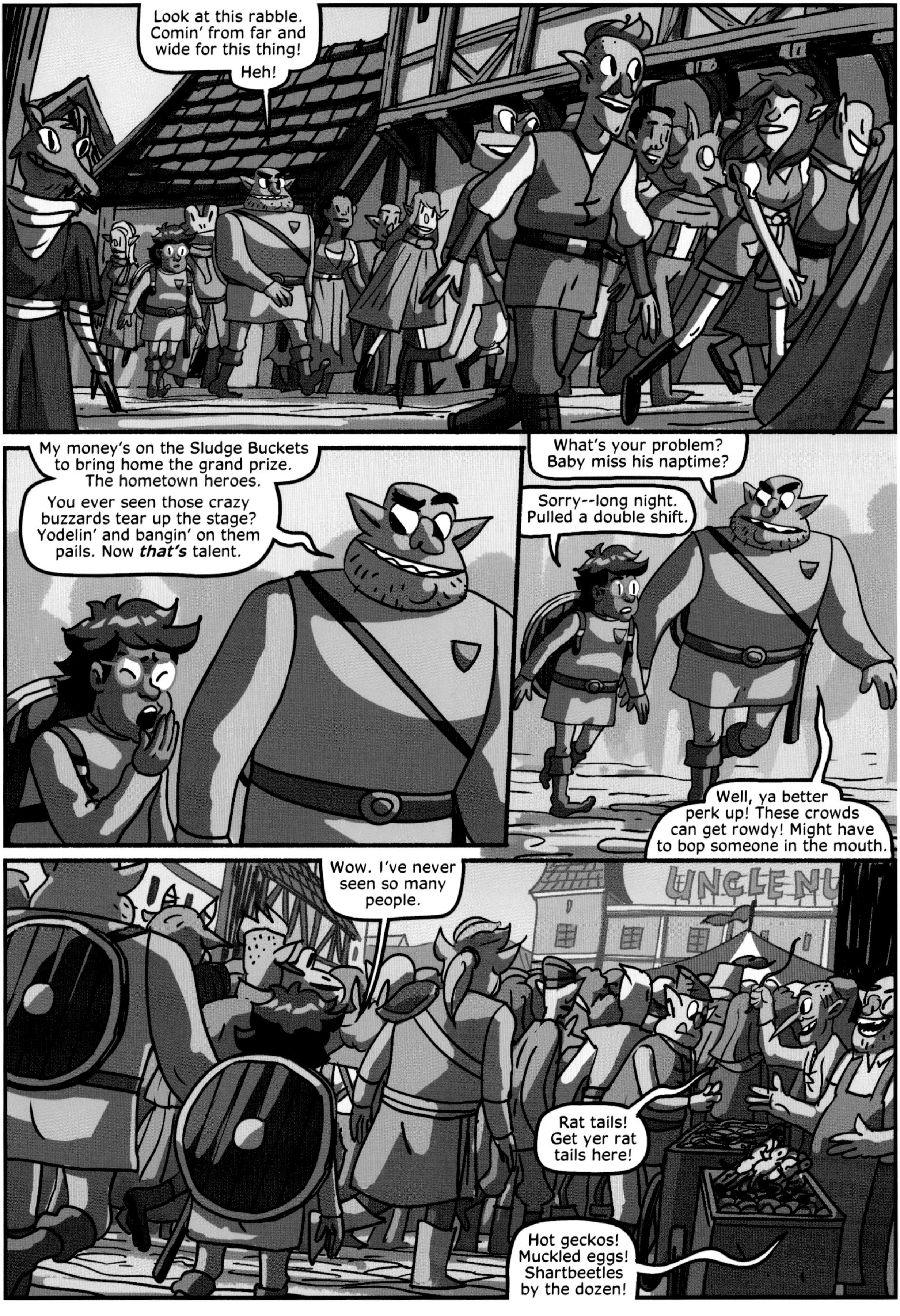
Look at this rabble. Comin' from far and wide for this thing!
Heh!
My money's on the Sludge Buckets to bring home the grand prize. The hometown heroes.
You ever seen those crazy buzzards tear up the stage? Yodelin' and bangin' on them pails. Now *that's* talent.
What's your problem? Baby miss his naptime?
Sorry--long night. Pulled a double shift.
Well, ya better perk up! These crowds can get rowdy! Might have to bop someone in the mouth.
Wow. I've never seen so many people.
UNCLE NU
Rat tails! Get yer rat tails here!
Hot geckos! Muckled eggs! Shartbeetles by the dozen!

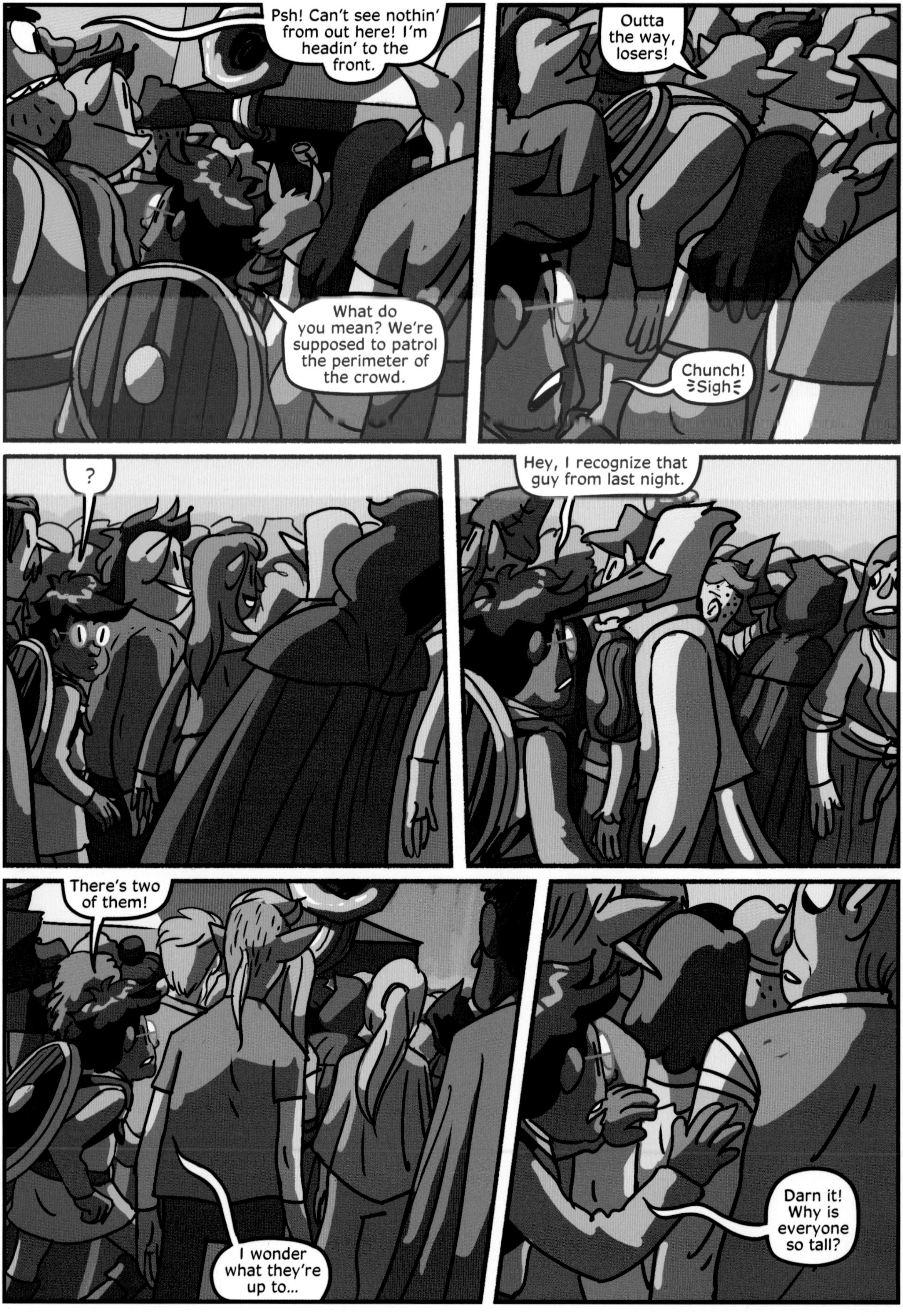
Psh! Can't see nothin' from out here! I'm headin' to the front.
What do you mean? We're supposed to patrol the perimeter of the crowd.
Outta the way, losers!
Chunch! Sigh
?
Hey, I recognize that guy from last night.
There's two of them!
I wonder what they're up to...
Darn it! Why is everyone so tall?

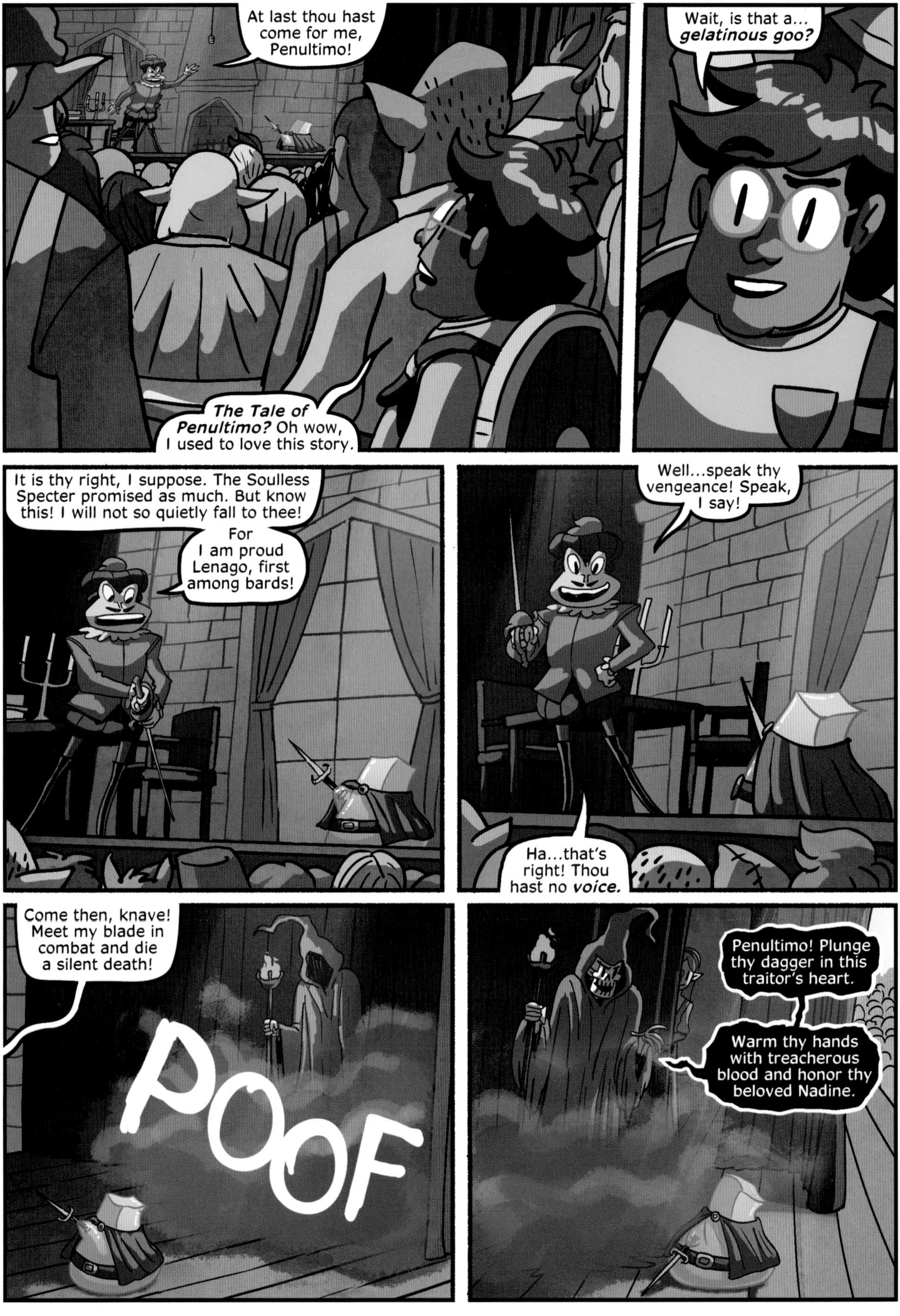

At last thou hast come for me, Penultimo!
The Tale of Penultimo? Oh wow, I used to love this story.
Wait, is that a... *gelatinous goo?*
It is thy right, I suppose. The Soulless Specter promised as much. But know this! I will not so quietly fall to thee!
For I am proud Lenago, first among bards!
Well...speak thy vengeance! Speak, I say!
Ha...that's right! Thou hast no *voice.*
Come then, knave! Meet my blade in combat and die a silent death!
POOF
Penultimo! Plunge thy dagger in this traitor's heart.
Warm thy hands with treacherous blood and honor thy beloved Nadine.

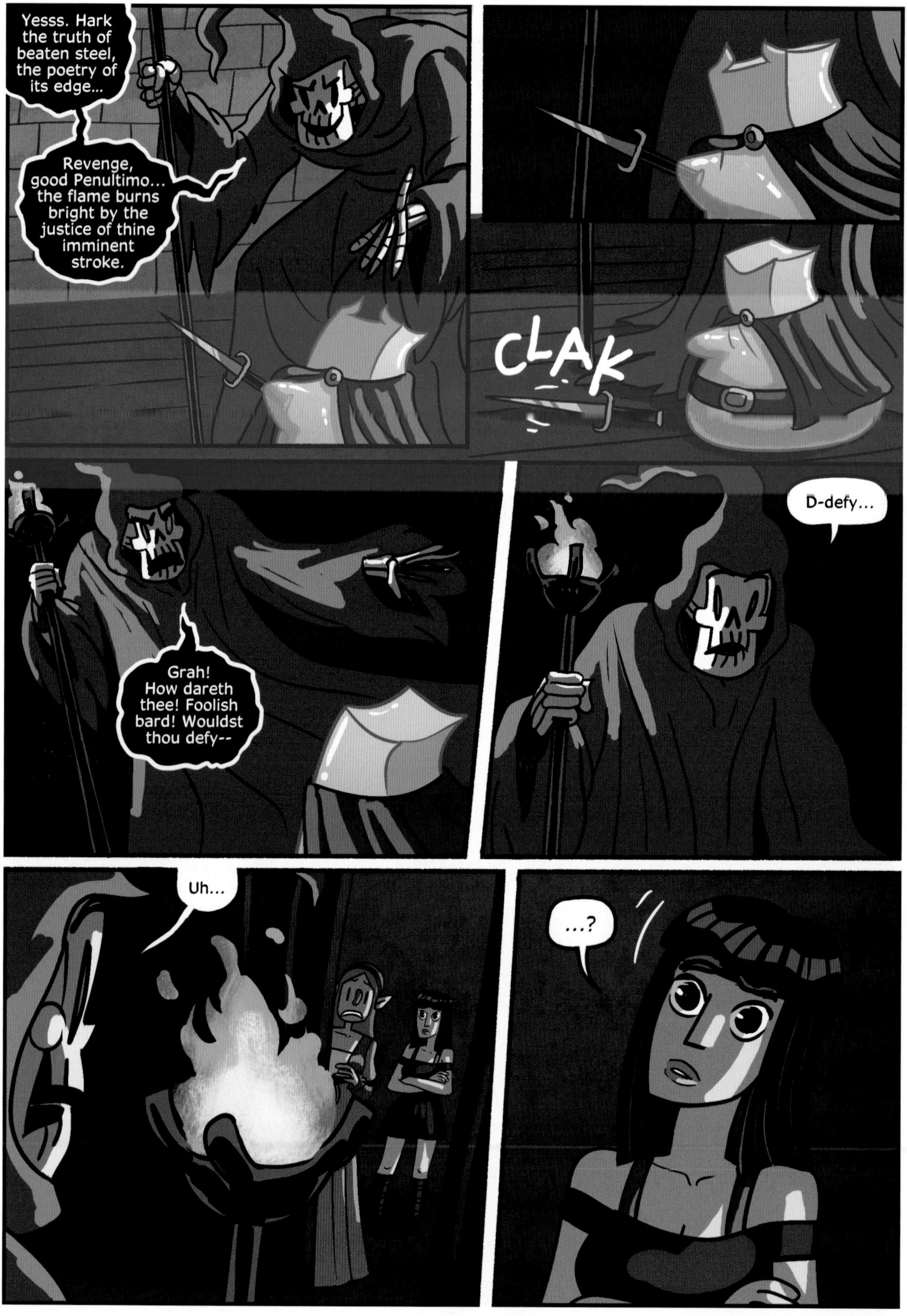
Yesss. Hark the truth of beaten steel, the poetry of its edge...
Revenge, good Penultimo... the flame burns bright by the justice of thine imminent stroke.
CLAK
Grah! How dareth thee! Foolish bard! Wouldst thou defy--
D-defy...
Uh...
...?

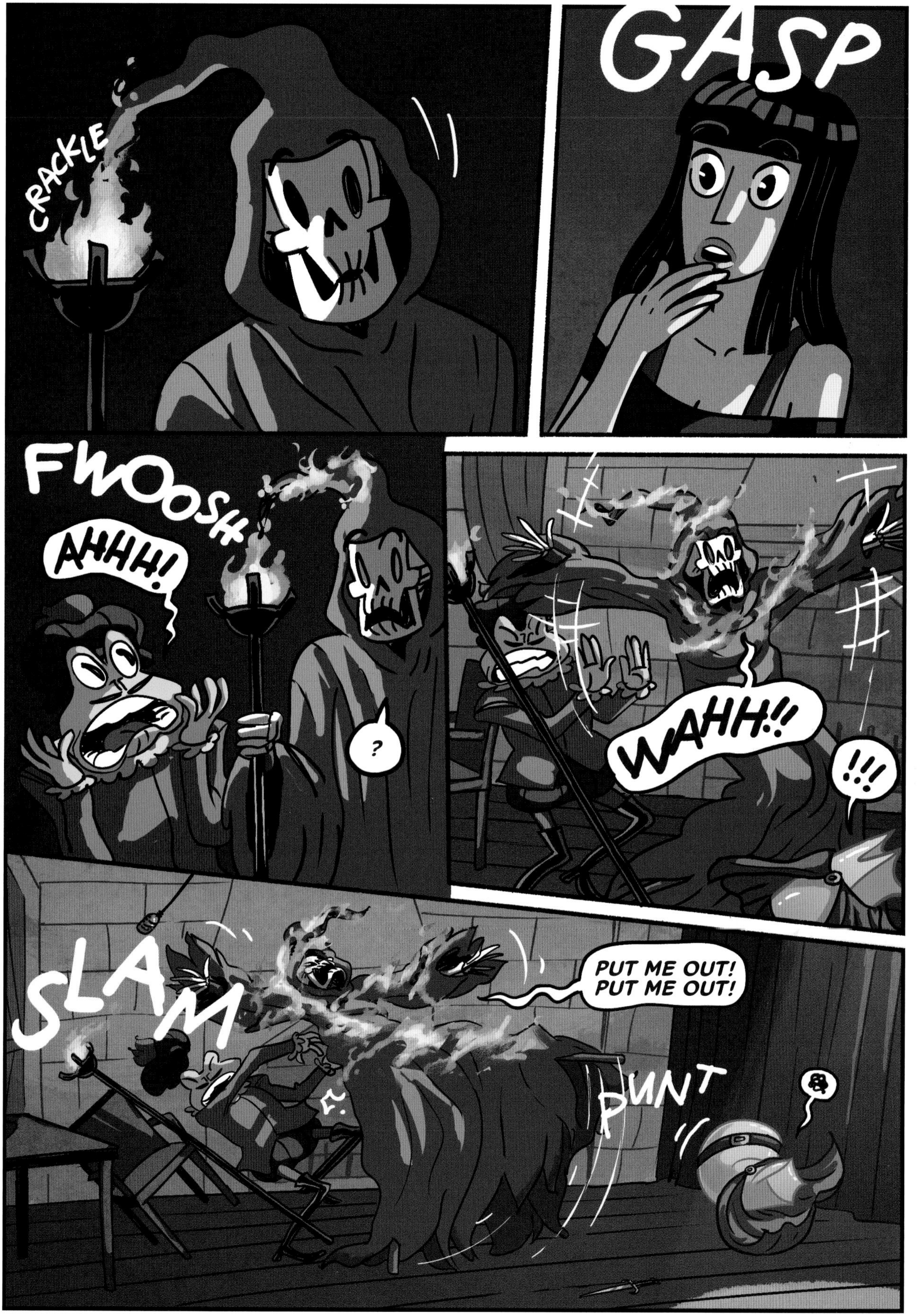
CRACKLE
GASP
FWOOSH
AHHH!
?
WAHH!!
!!!
SLAM
PUT ME OUT! PUT ME OUT!
PUNT

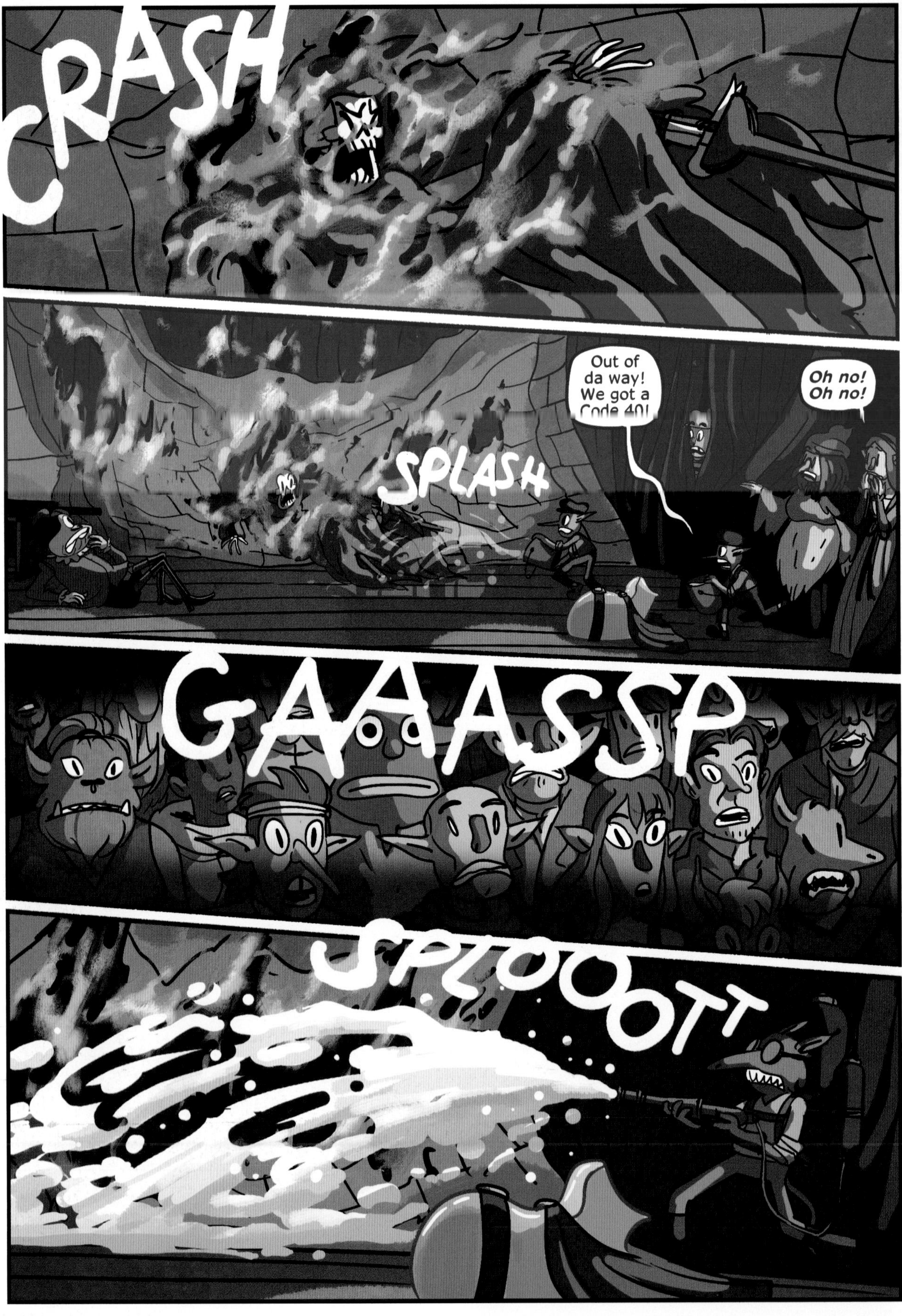
CRASH
SPLASH
Out of da way! We got a Code 40!
Oh no! Oh no!
GAAASSP
SPLOOOTT

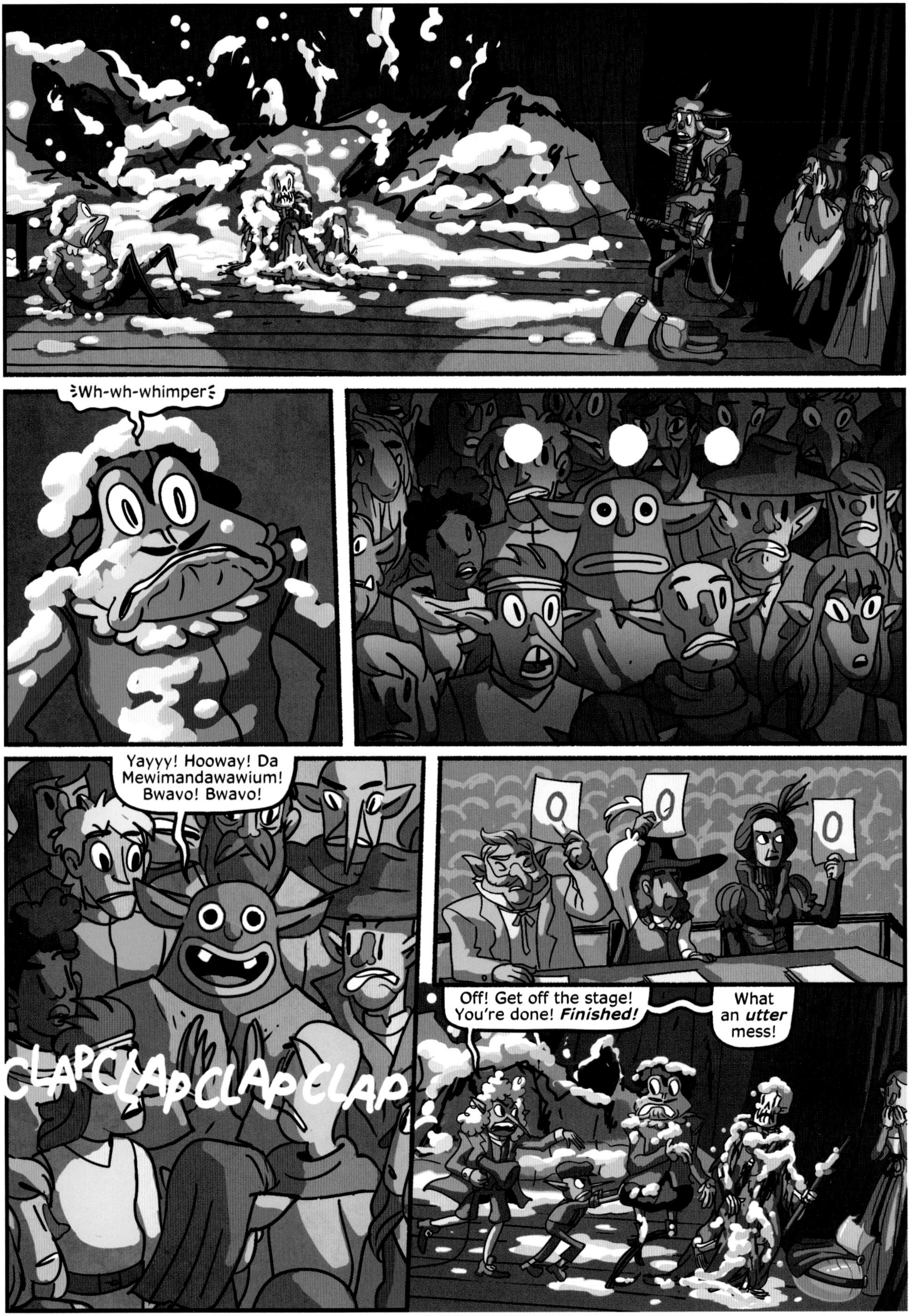
Wh-wh-whimper
Yayyy! Hooway! Da Mewimandawawium! Bwavo! Bwavo!
CLAP CLAP CLAP CLAP
0
0
0
Off! Get off the stage! You're done! *Finished!*
What an *utter* mess!

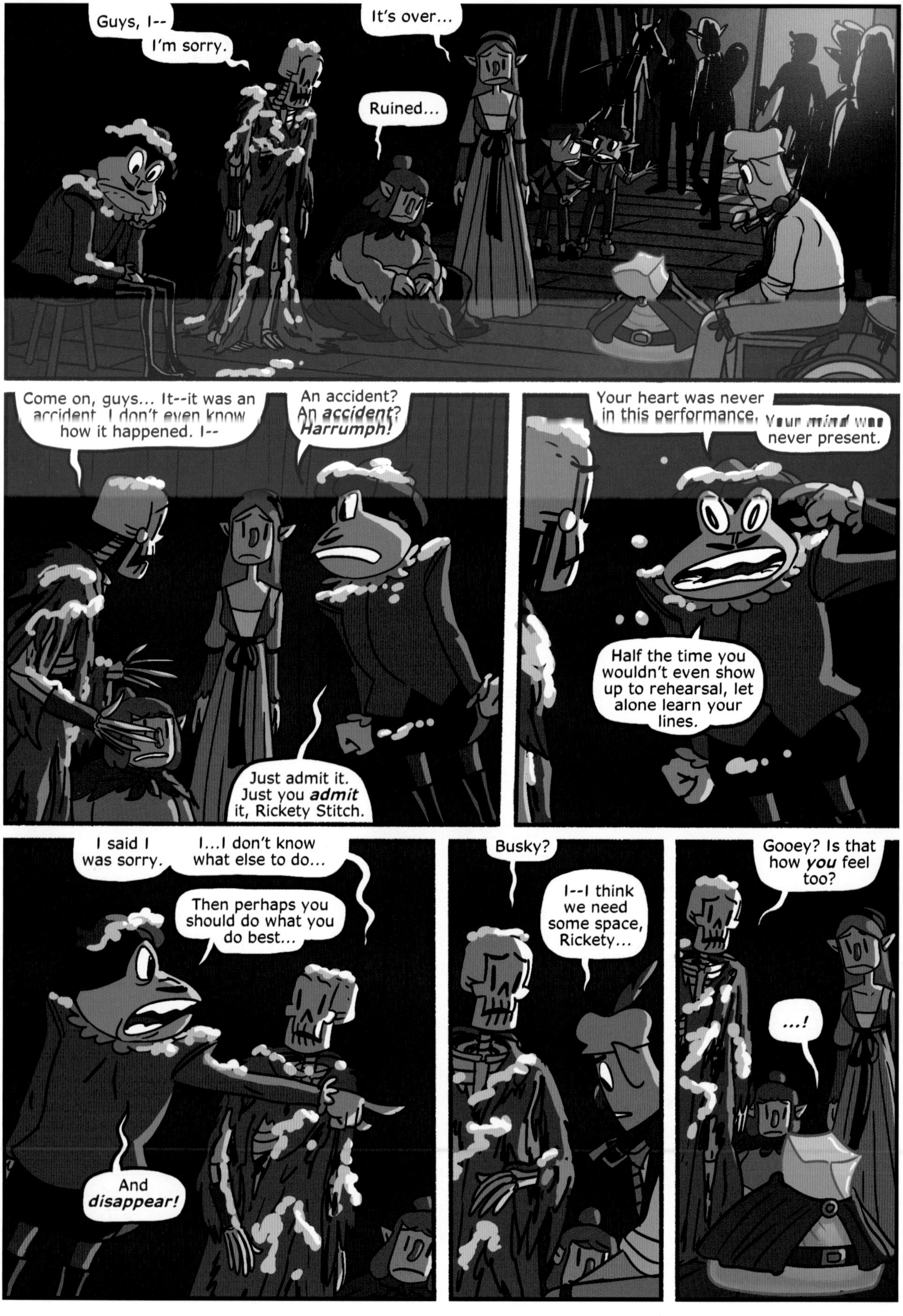

Guys, I--
I'm sorry.
It's over...
Ruined...
Come on, guys... It--it was an accident. I don't even know how it happened. I--
An accident? An *accident*? ***Harrumph!***
Just admit it. Just you ***admit*** it, Rickety Stitch.
Your heart was never in this performance.
Your *mind* was never present.
Half the time you wouldn't even show up to rehearsal, let alone learn your lines.
I said I was sorry.
I...I don't know what else to do...
Then perhaps you should do what you do best...
And ***disappear!***
Busky?
I--I think we need some space, Rickety...
Gooey? Is that how ***you*** feel too?
...!

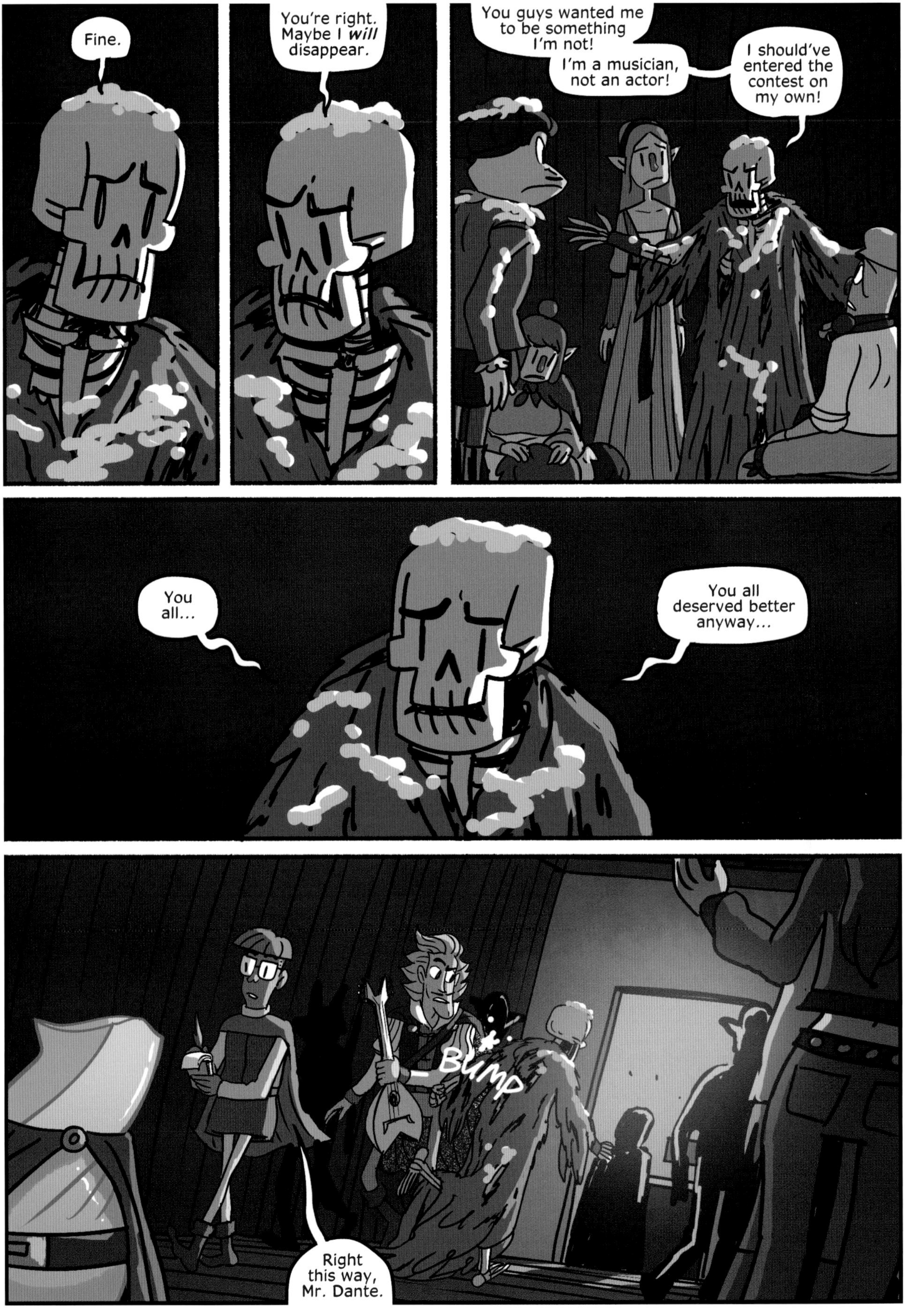
Fine.
You're right. Maybe I *will* disappear.
You guys wanted me to be something I'm not!
I'm a musician, not an actor!
I should've entered the contest on my own!
You all...
You all deserved better anyway...
BUMP
Right this way, Mr. Dante.

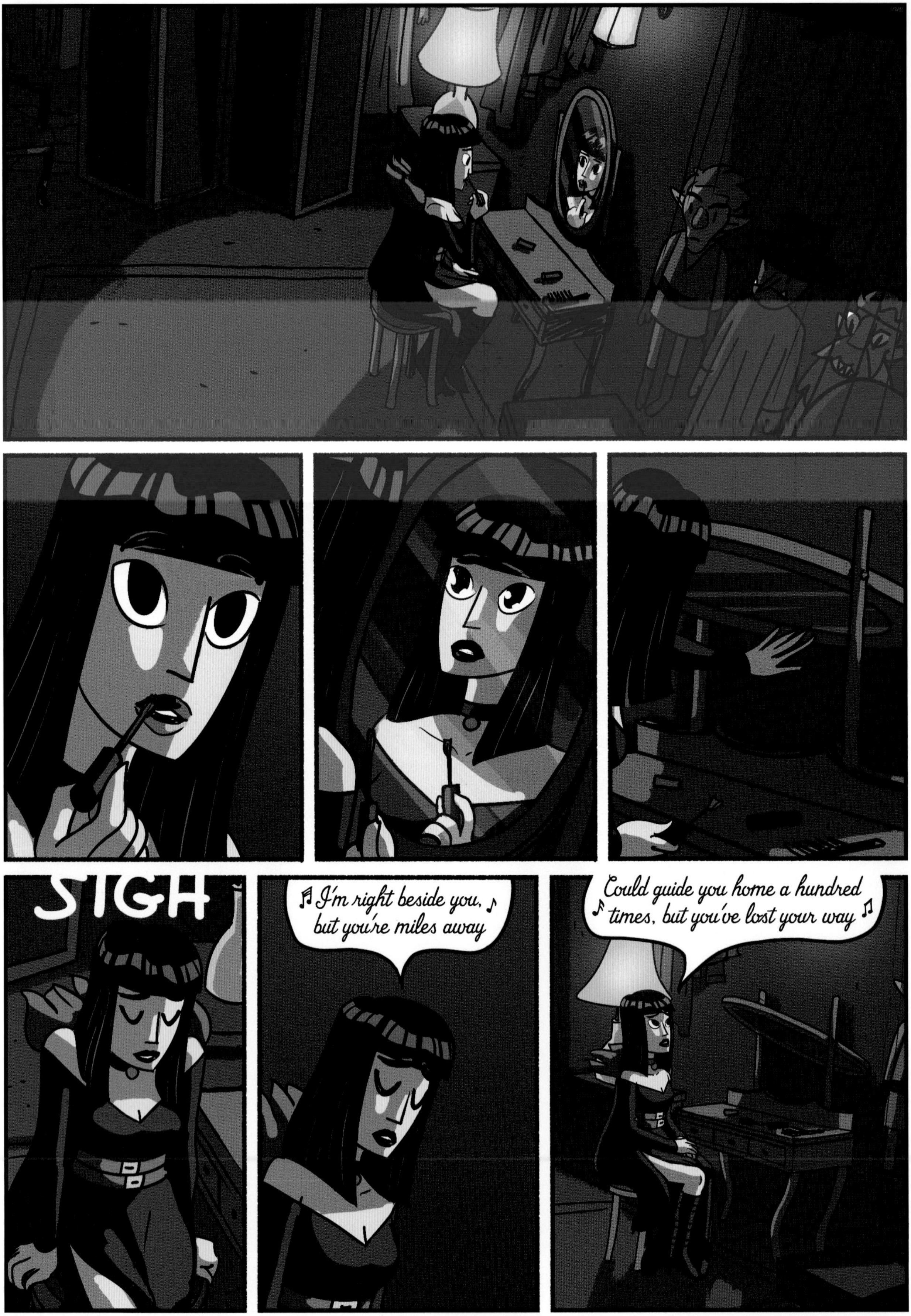
SIGH
♬ I'm right beside you, ♪ but you're miles away
Could guide you home a hundred ♪ times, but you've lost your way ♫

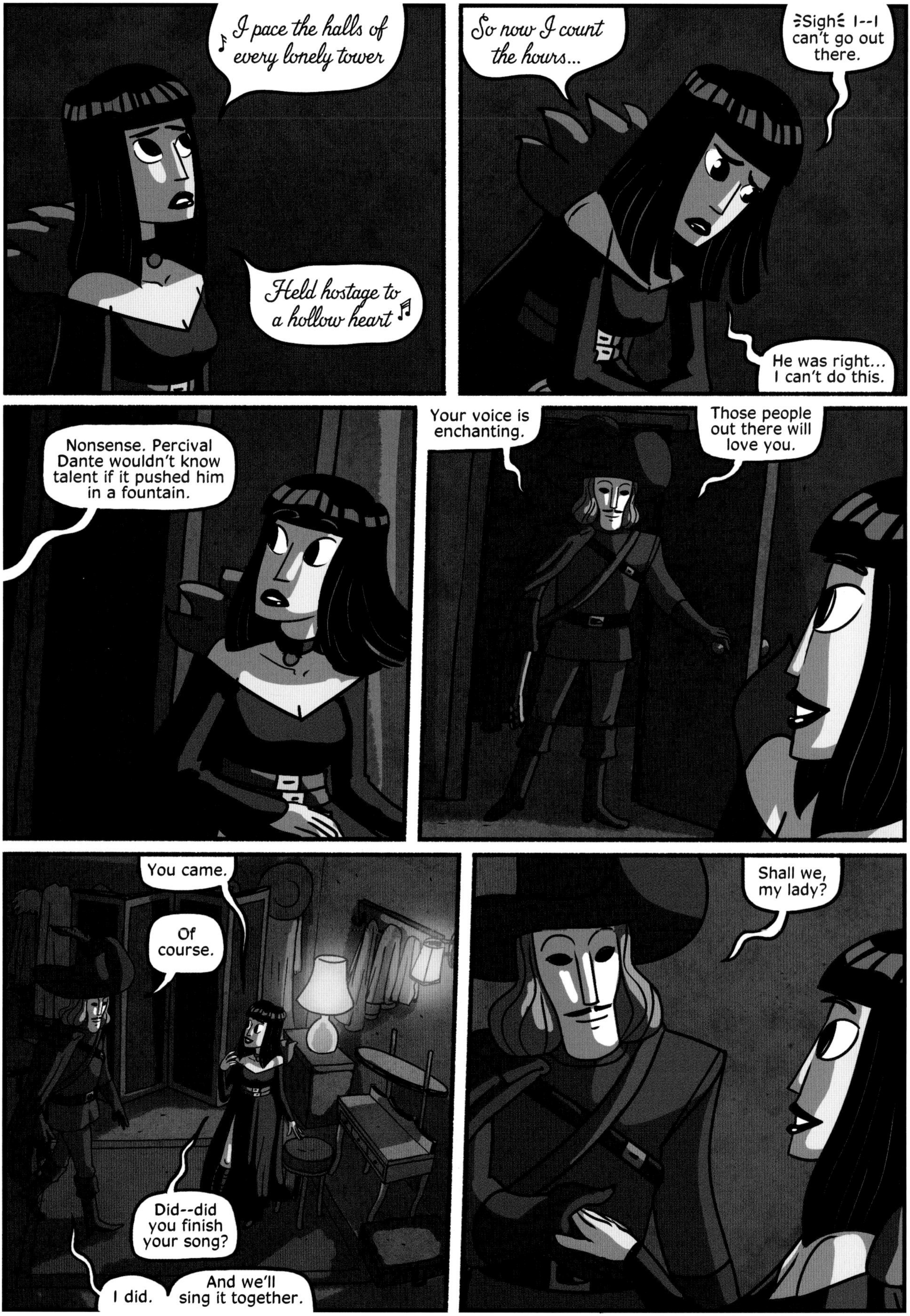
I pace the halls of every lonely tower
Held hostage to a hollow heart
So now I count the hours...
Sigh I--I can't go out there.
He was right... I can't do this.
Nonsense. Percival Dante wouldn't know talent if it pushed him in a fountain.
Your voice is enchanting.
Those people out there will love you.
You came.
Of course.
Did--did you finish your song?
I did.
And we'll sing it together.
Shall we, my lady?

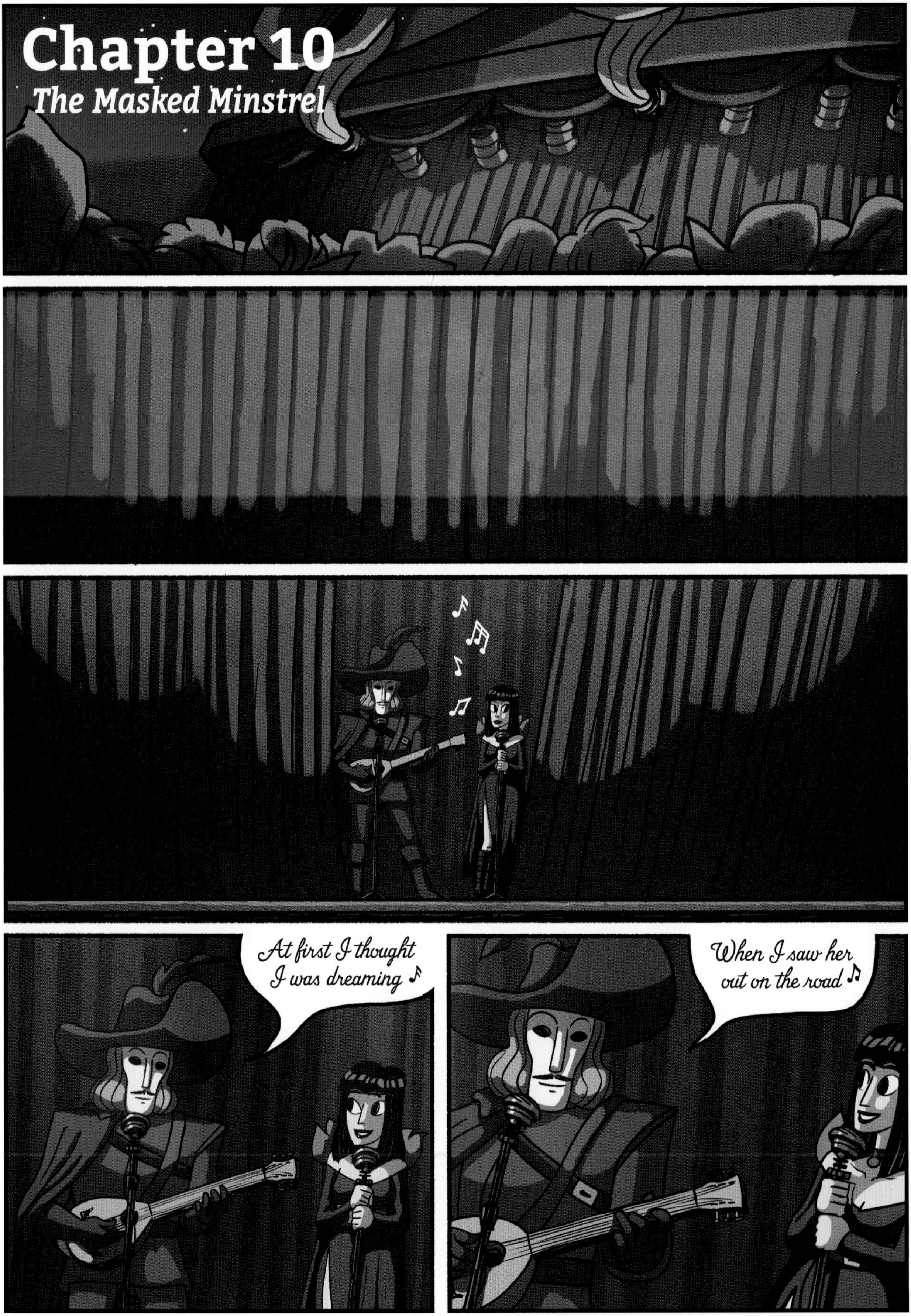
Chapter 10
The Masked Minstrel
At first I thought I was dreaming ♪
When I saw her out on the road ♫

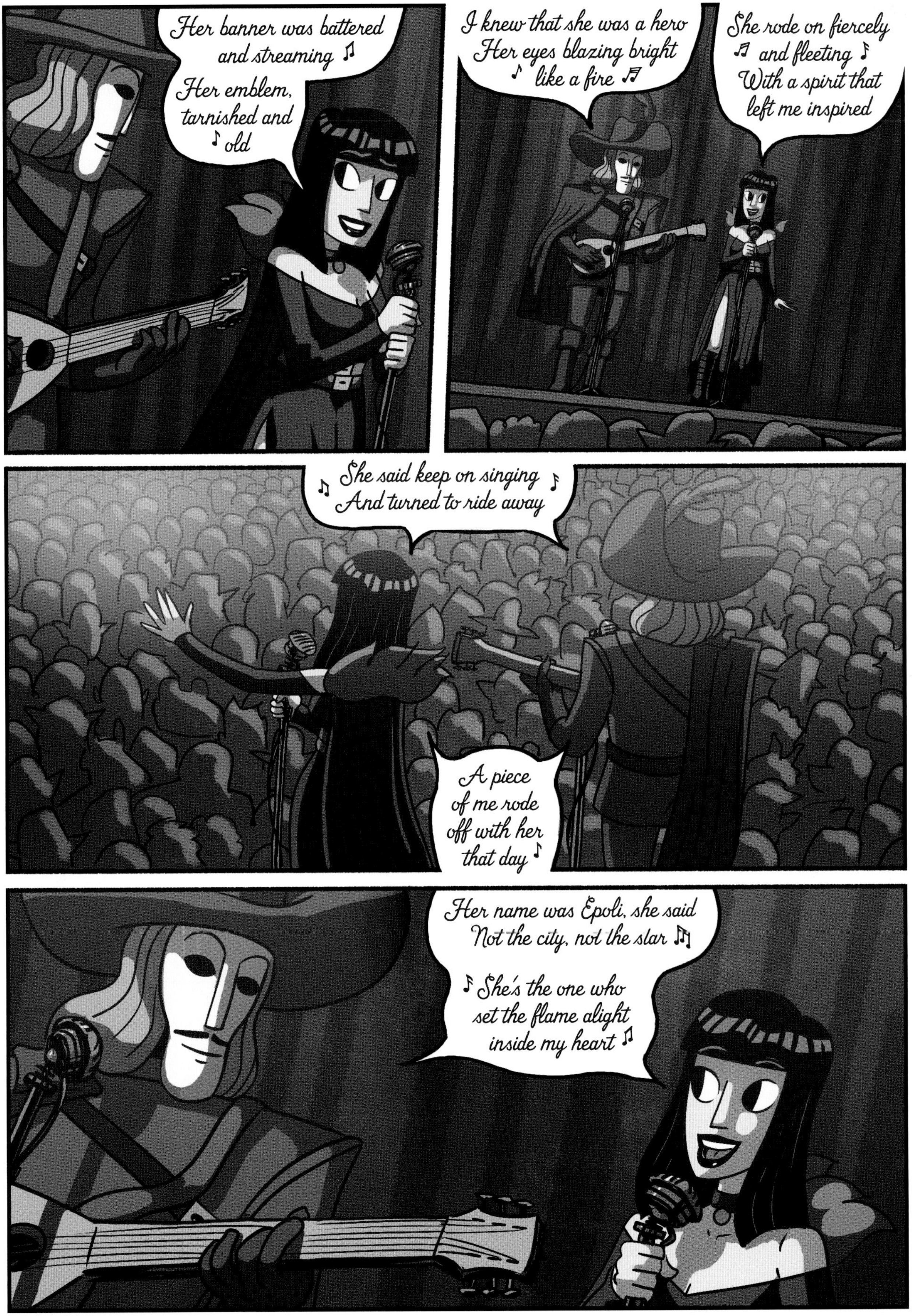
Her banner was battered and streaming ♫ Her emblem, tarnished and ♪ old
I knew that she was a hero Her eyes blazing bright ♪ like a fire ♬
She rode on fiercely ♫ and fleeting ♪ With a spirit that left me inspired
♫ She said keep on singing ♪ And turned to ride away
A piece of me rode off with her that day ♪
Her name was Epoli, she said Not the city, not the star ♬
♪ She's the one who set the flame alight inside my heart ♫

She wasn't my dream ♪ of a hero ♫ Her armor, dusty and worn
A long road ahead without resting ♬ No time to reflect or ♪ to mourn
But her sword and her spirit were fearless ♪ Her heart, courageous and brave ♪
Oh, y'all have to see this.
?!
♪ We said our goodbyes at the seashore ♬ To the crash of the rumbling waves
She said keep ♫ on singing And turned to ride away ♪
A piece of me rode off with her that day ♪
Her name was Epoli, she said ♬ Not the city, not the star
♪ She's the one who set the flame alight inside my heart ♫

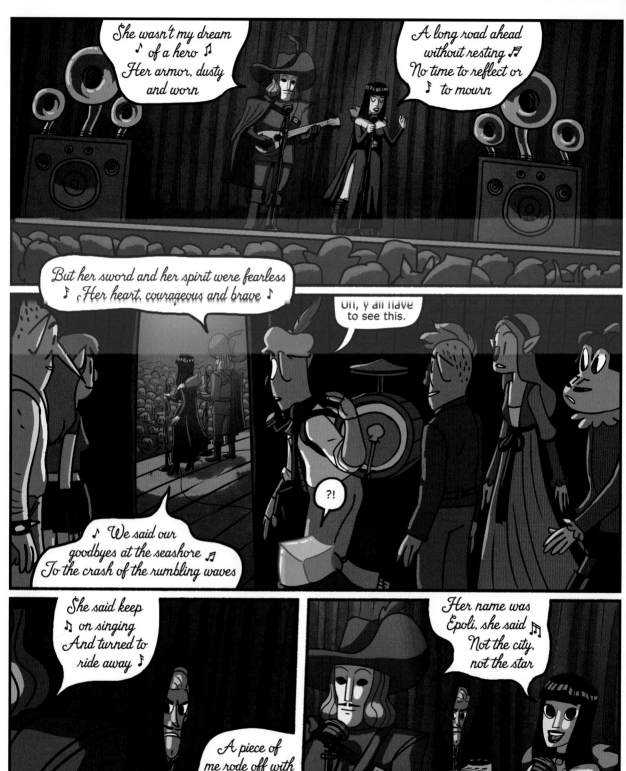

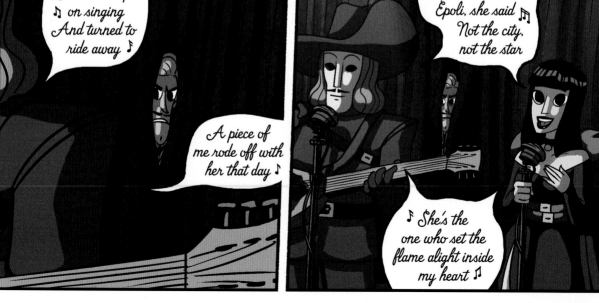

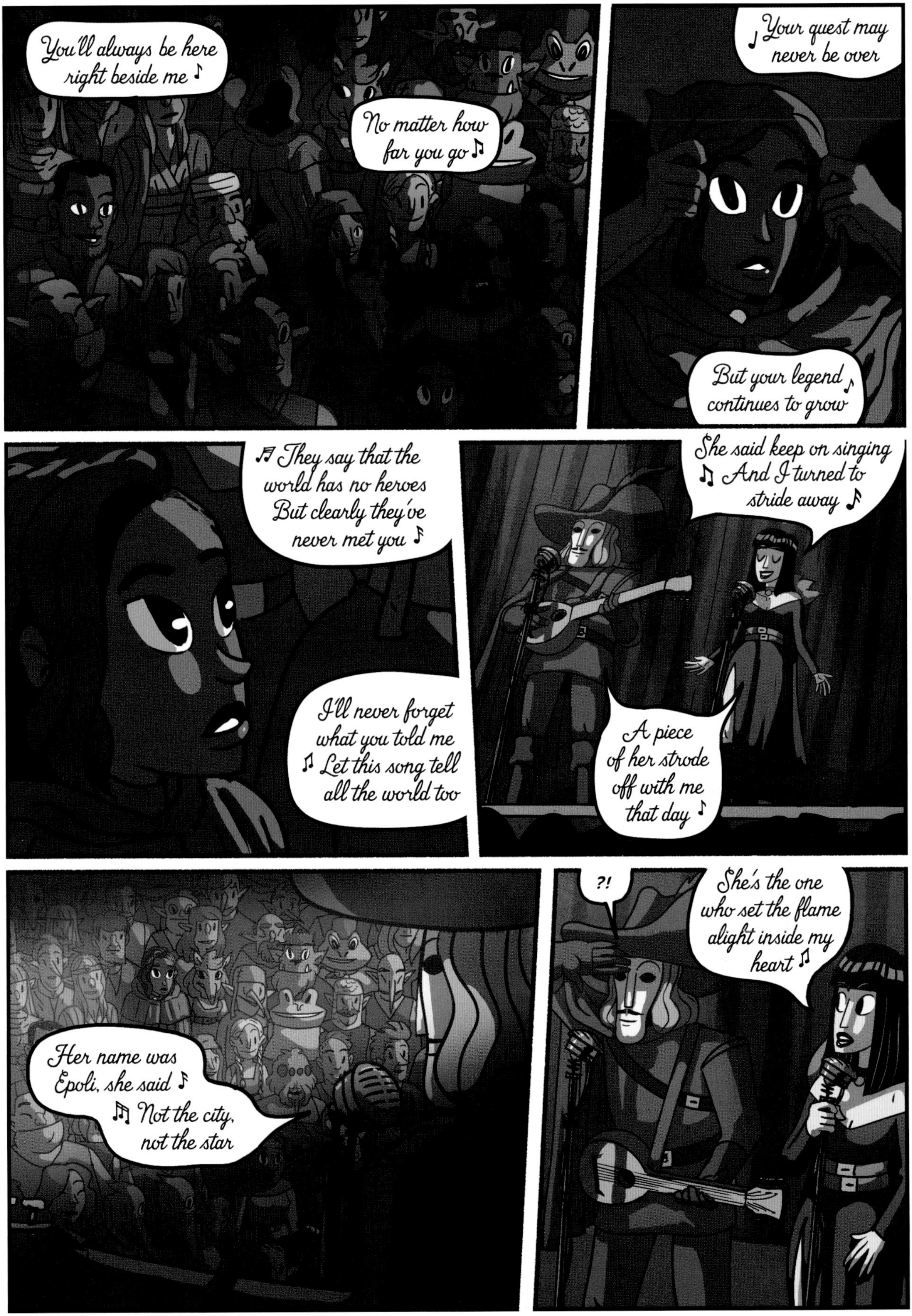

You'll always be here right beside me ♪
No matter how far you go ♫
♩ Your quest may never be over
But your legend ♪ continues to grow
♬ They say that the world has no heroes But clearly they've never met you ♪
I'll never forget what you told me ♫ Let this song tell all the world too
She said keep on singing ♫ And I turned to stride away ♪
A piece of her strode off with me that day ♪
Her name was Epoli, she said ♪
♬ Not the city, not the star
?!
She's the one who set the flame alight inside my heart ♫

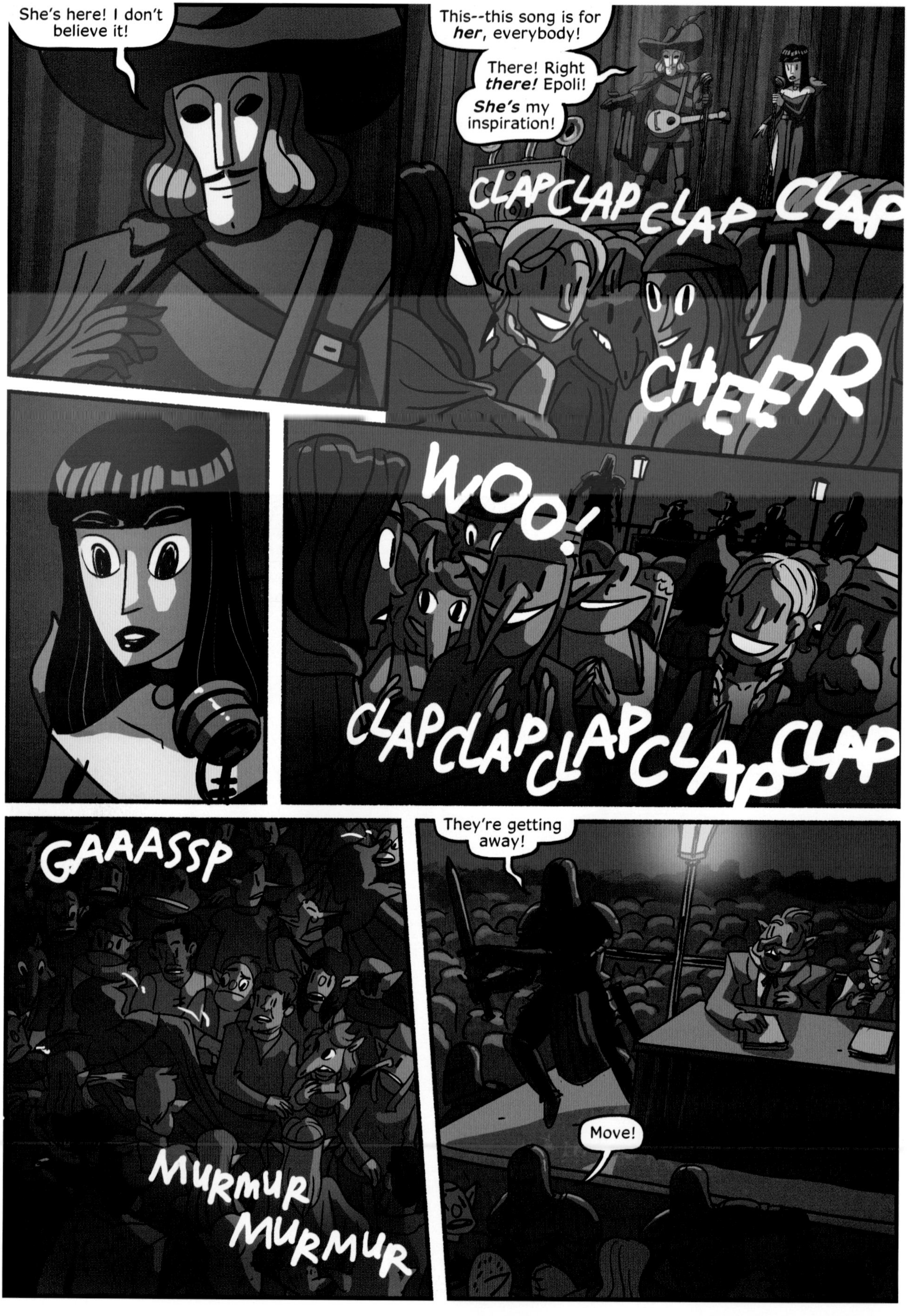

She's here! I don't believe it!
This--this song is for *her*, everybody!
There! Right *there!* Epoli!
She's my inspiration!
CLAPCLAPCLAP CLAP
CHEER
WOO!
CLAPCLAPCLAPCLAPCLAP
GAAASSP
MURMUR MURMUR
They're getting away!
Move!

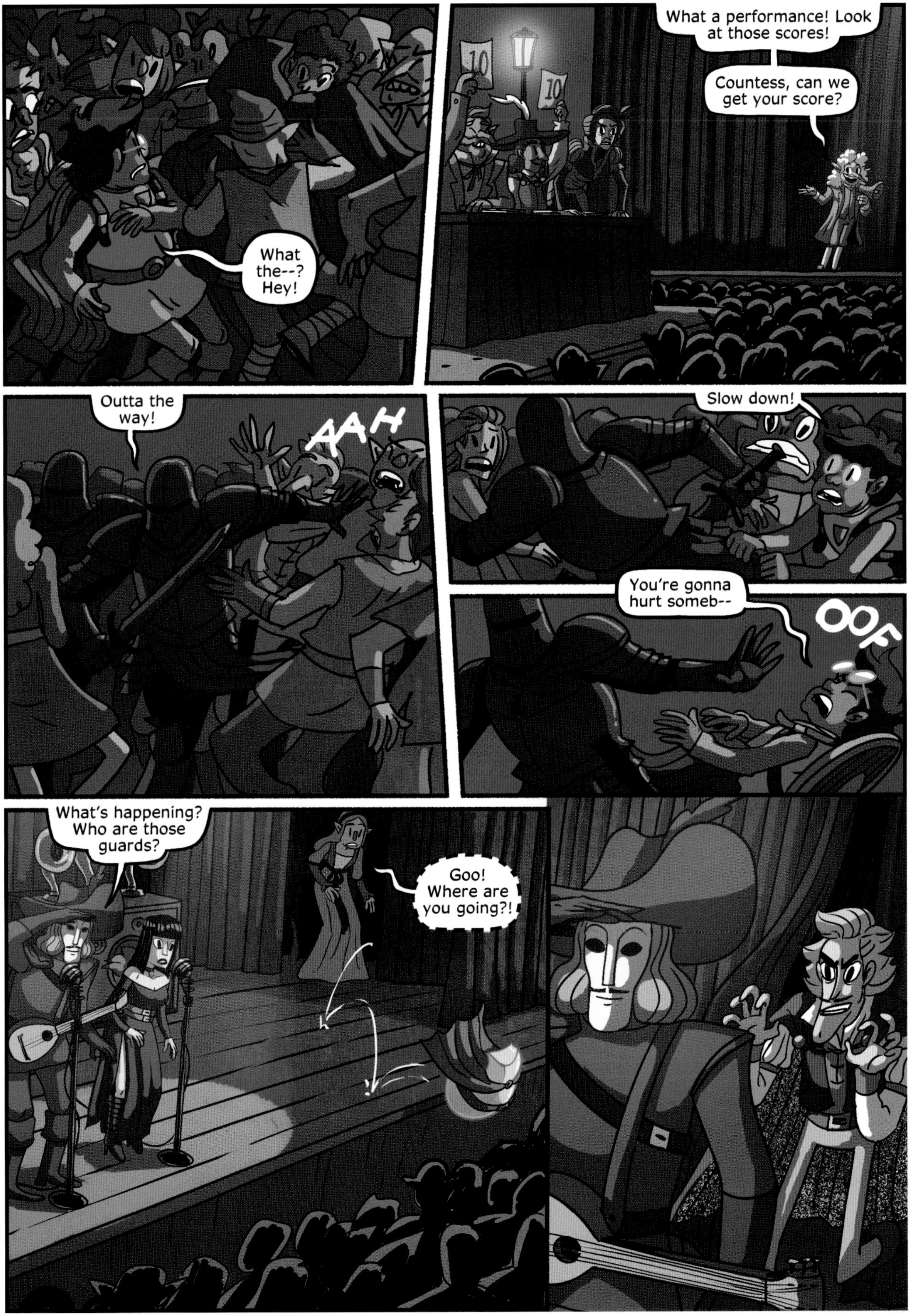
What the--? Hey!
What a performance! Look at those scores!
Countess, can we get your score?
10
10
Outta the way!
AAH
Slow down!
You're gonna hurt someb--
OOF
What's happening? Who are those guards?
Goo! Where are you going?!

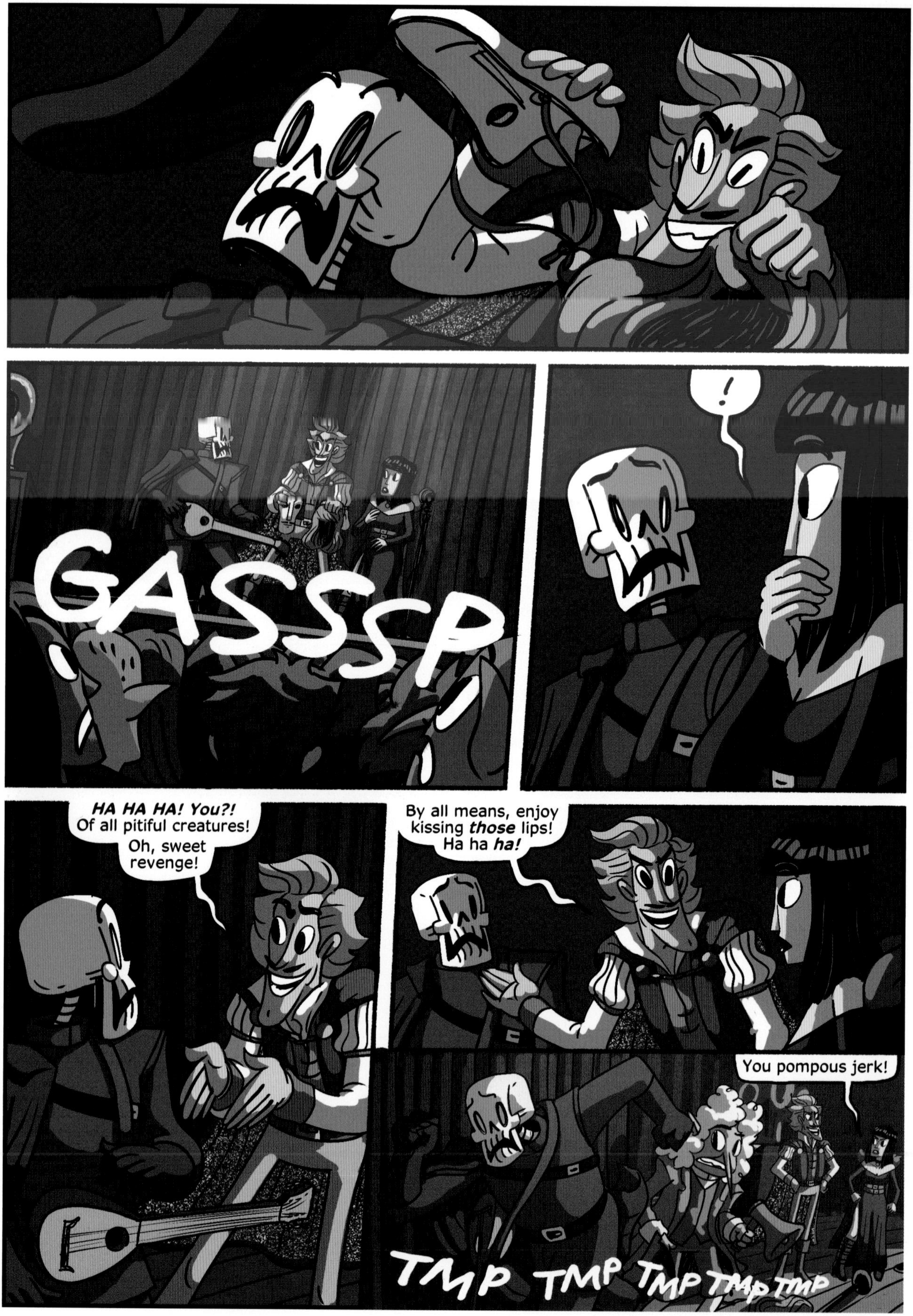
GASSSP
!
HA HA HA! You?!
Of all pitiful creatures!
Oh, sweet revenge!
By all means, enjoy kissing those lips! Ha ha ha!
You pompous jerk!
TMP TMP TMP TMP TMP

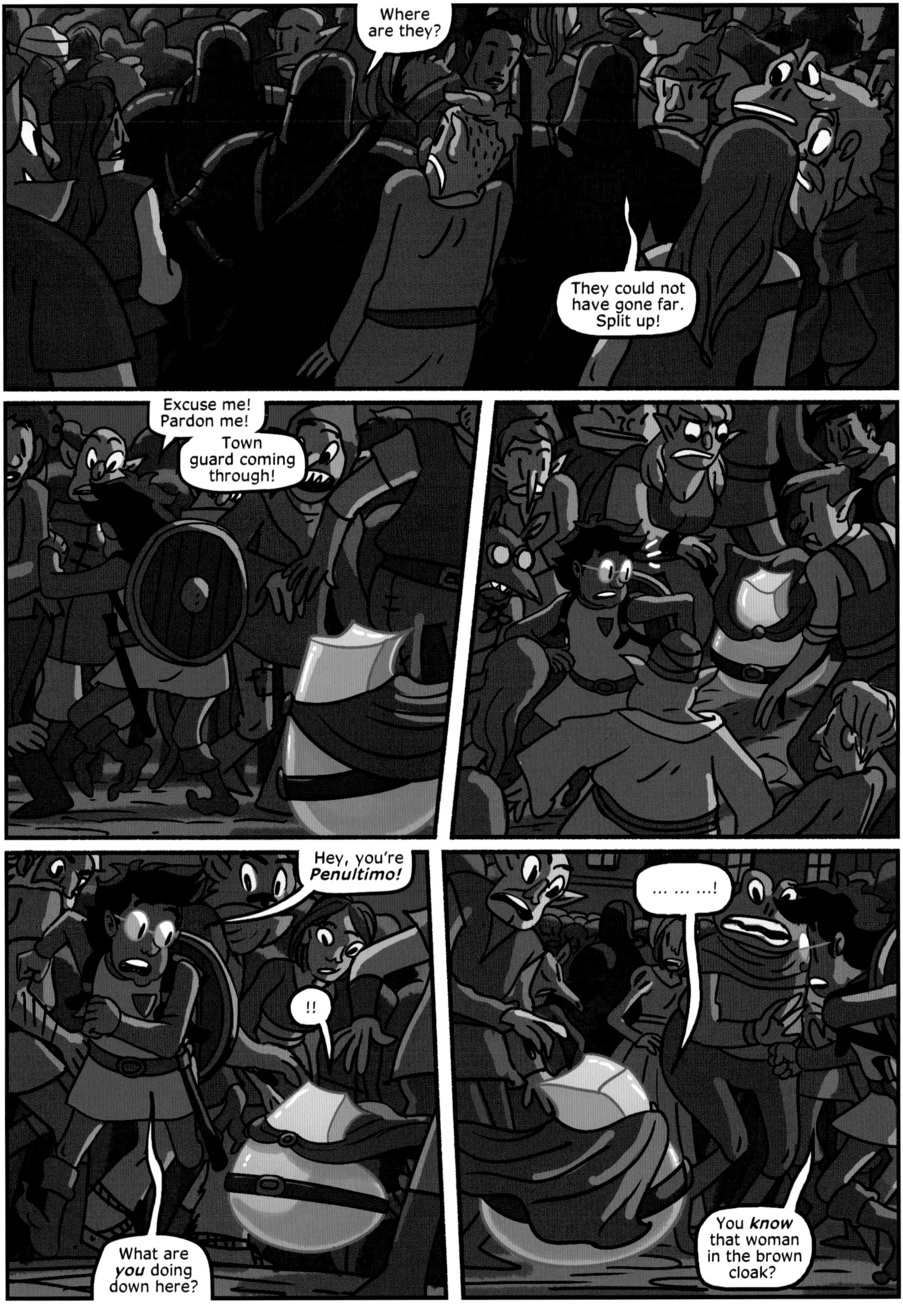
Where are they?
They could not have gone far. Split up!
Excuse me! Pardon me!
Town guard coming through!
Hey, you're *Penultimo!*
!!
What are *you* doing down here?
... ...!
You ***know*** that woman in the brown cloak?

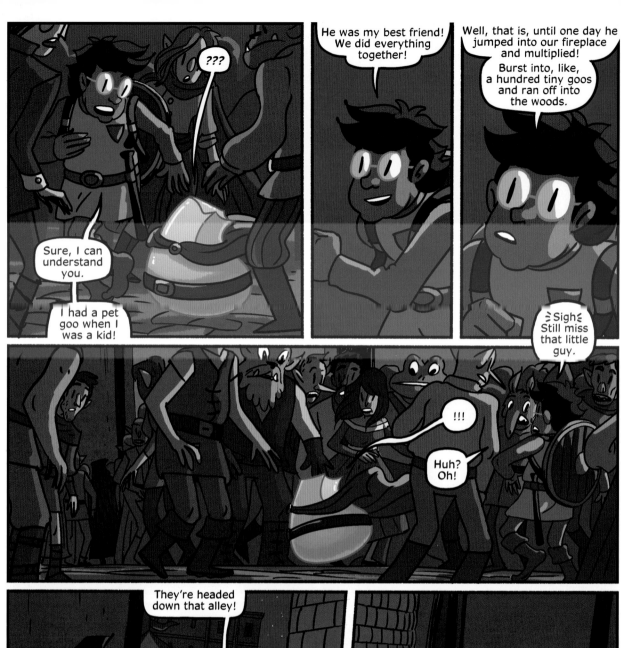

???

Sure, I can understand you.

I had a pet goo when I was a kid!

He was my best friend! We did everything together!

Well, that is, until one day he jumped into our fireplace and multiplied!

Burst into, like, a hundred tiny goos and ran off into the woods.

≷Sigh≷ Still miss that little guy.

!!!

Huh? Oh!

They're headed down that alley!

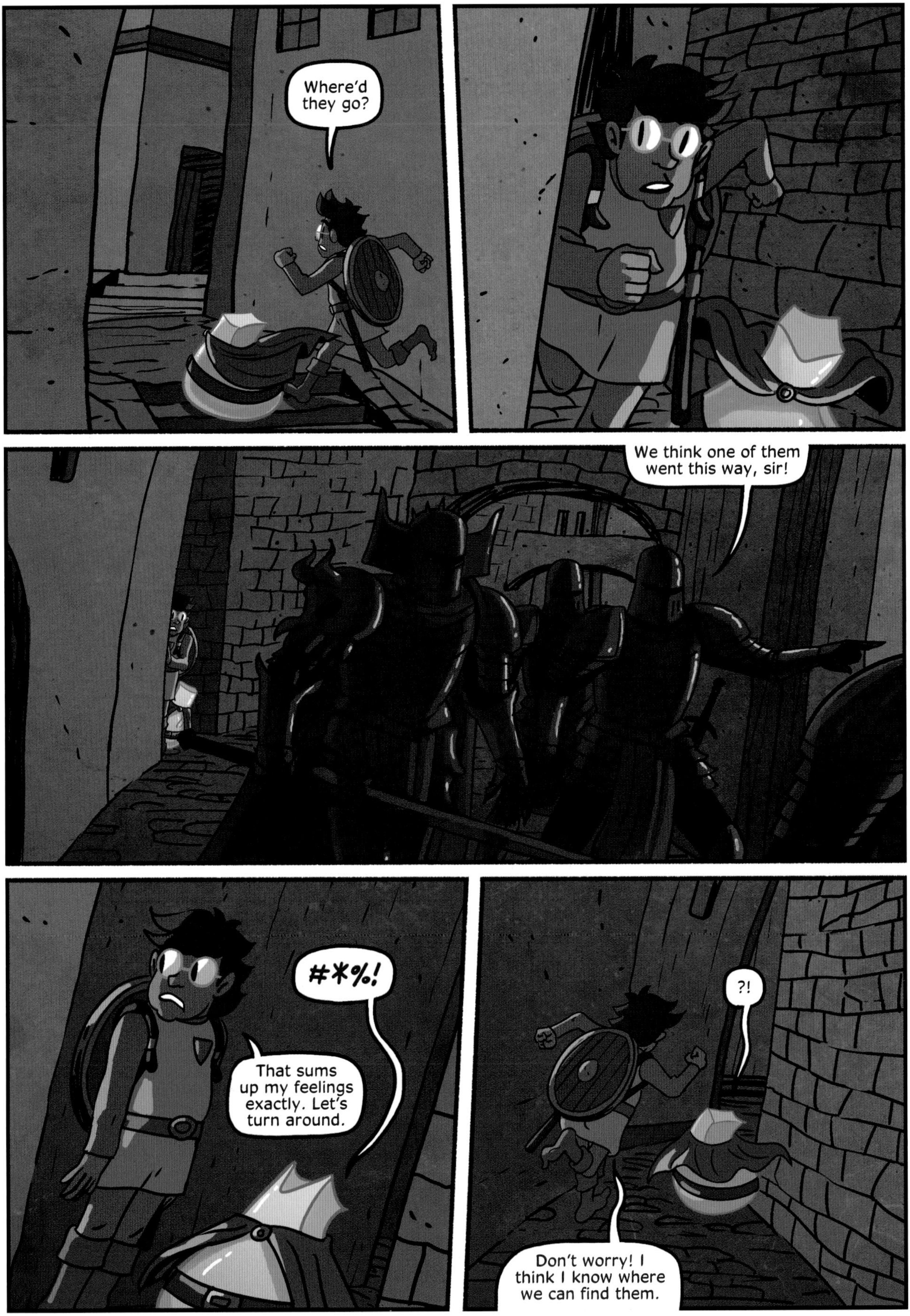

Where'd they go?
We think one of them went this way, sir!
#*%!
That sums up my feelings exactly. Let's turn around.
?!
Don't worry! I think I know where we can find them.

Chapter 11
Monster

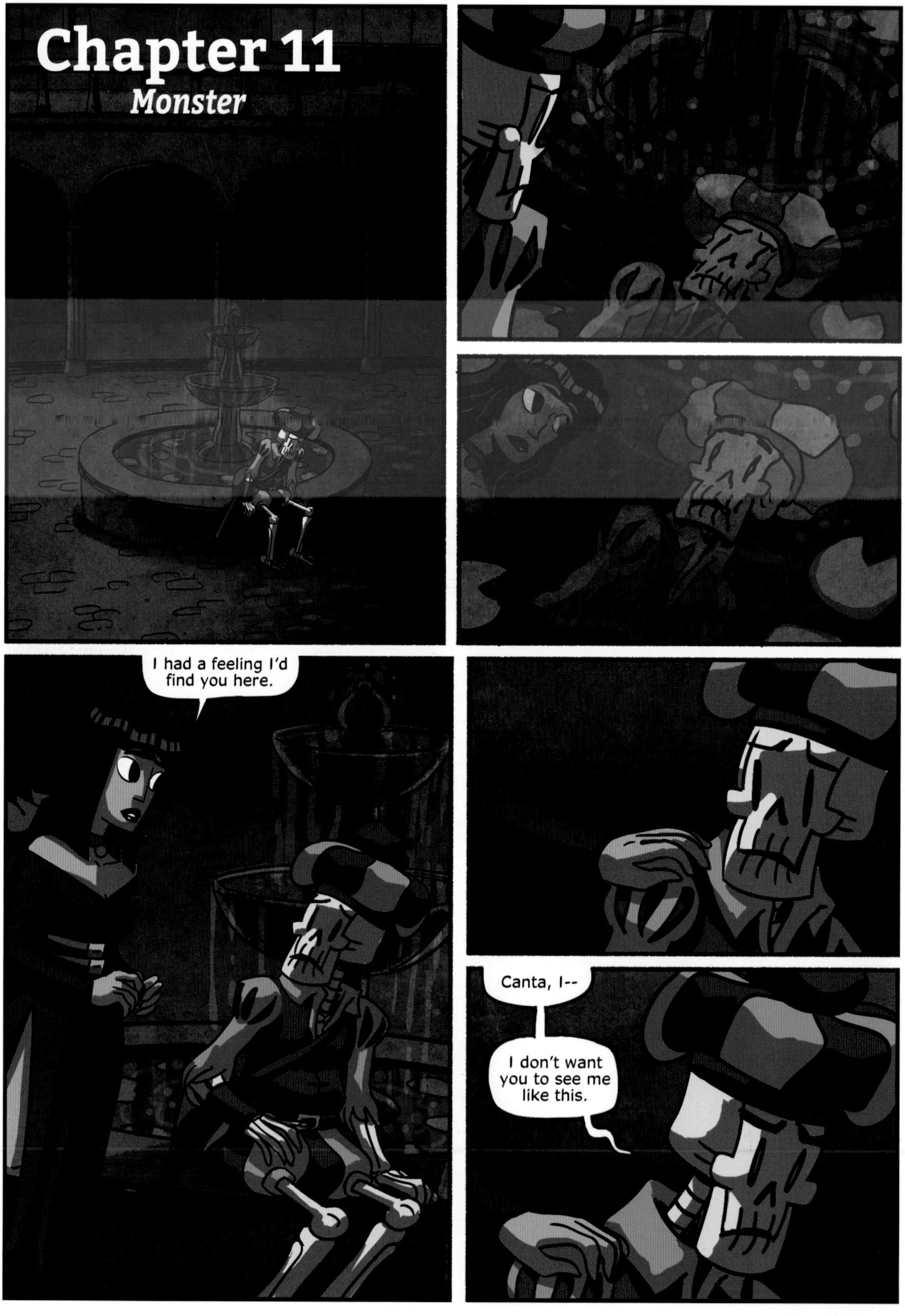
I had a feeling I'd find you here.
Canta, I--
I don't want you to see me like this.

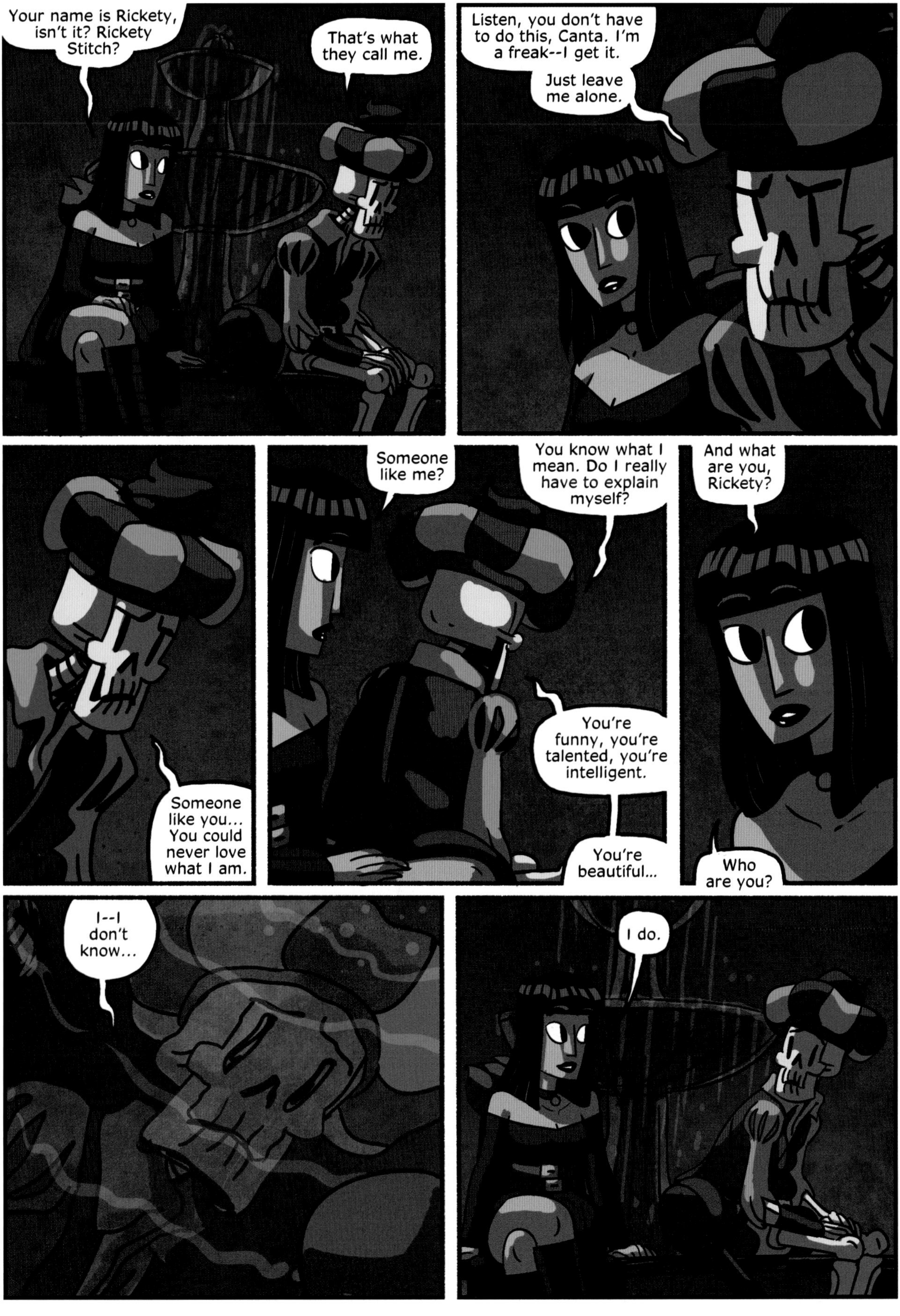

Your name is Rickety, isn't it? Rickety Stitch?
That's what they call me.
Listen, you don't have to do this, Canta. I'm a freak--I get it.
Just leave me alone.
Someone like you... You could never love what I am.
Someone like me?
You know what I mean. Do I really have to explain myself?
You're funny, you're talented, you're intelligent.
You're beautiful...
And what are you, Rickety?
Who are you?
I--I don't know...
I do.

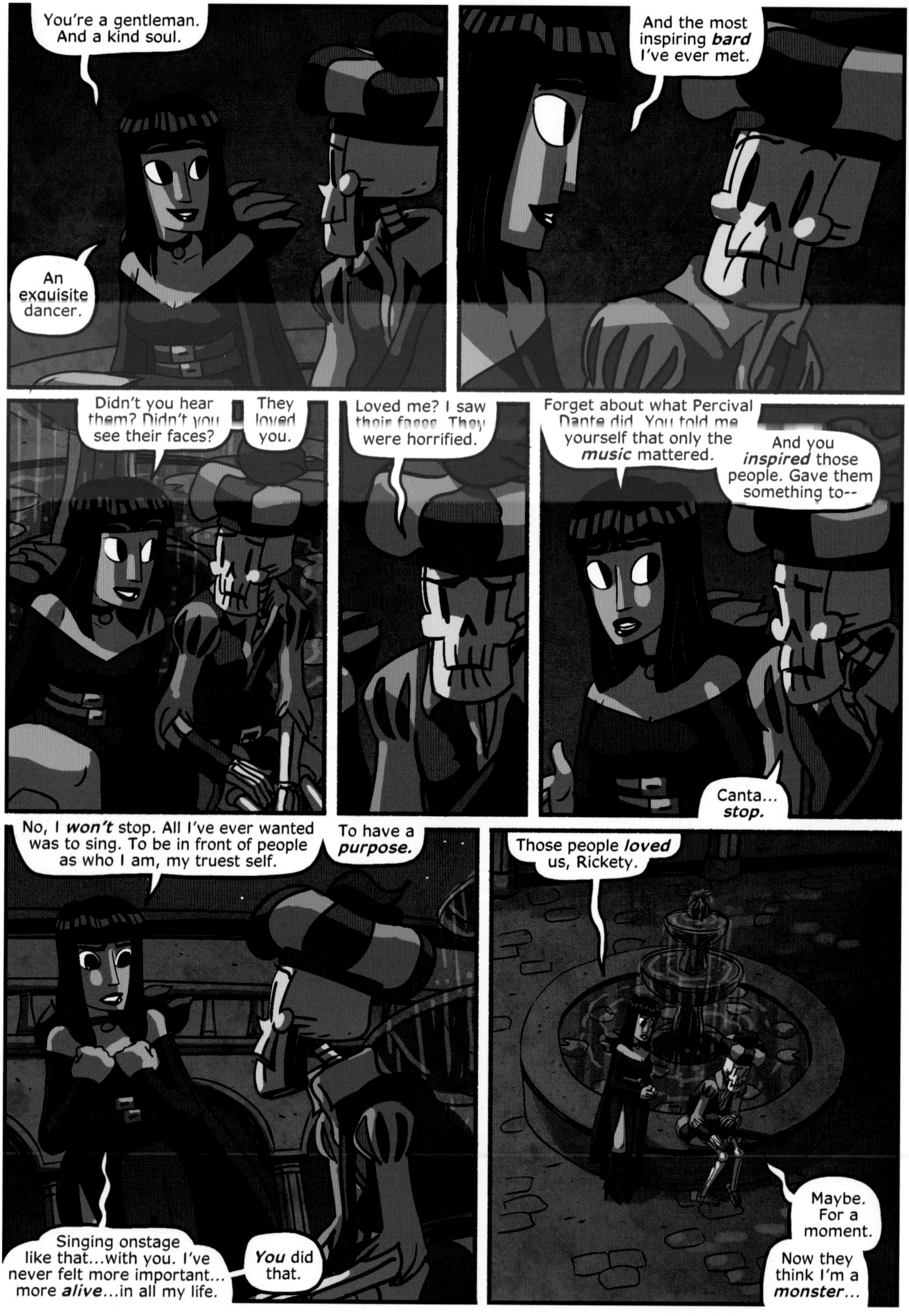

You're a gentleman. And a kind soul.
An exquisite dancer.
And the most inspiring *bard* I've ever met.
Didn't you hear them? Didn't you see their faces?
They loved you.
Loved me? I saw their faces. They were horrified.
Forget about what Percival Dante did. You told me yourself that only the *music* mattered.
And you *inspired* those people. Gave them something to--
Canta... *stop.*
No, I *won't* stop. All I've ever wanted was to sing. To be in front of people as who I am, my truest self.
To have a *purpose.*
Singing onstage like that...with you. I've never felt more important... more *alive*...in all my life.
You did that.
Those people *loved* us, Rickety.
Maybe. For a moment.
Now they think I'm a *monster*...

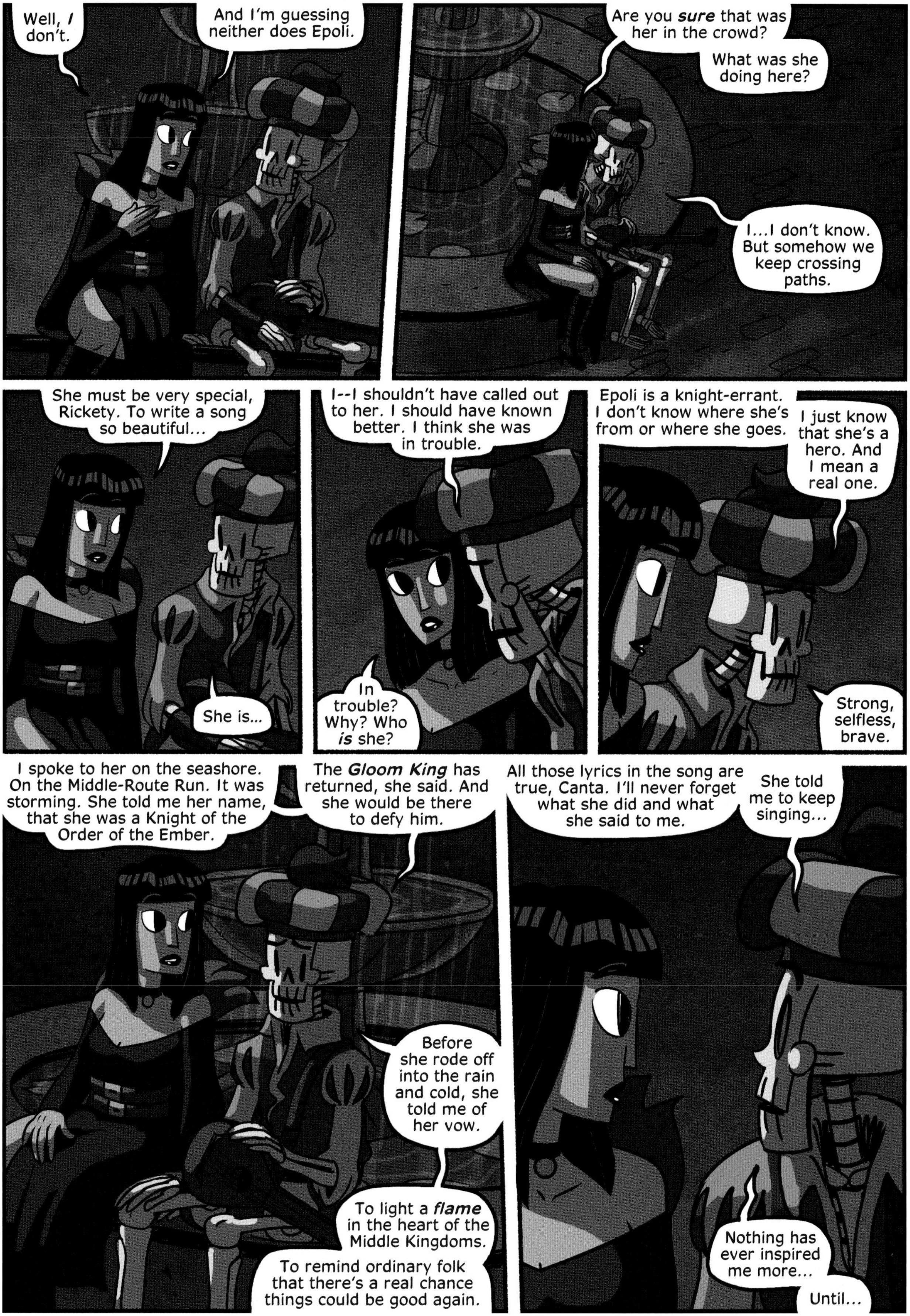
Well, *I* don't.
And I'm guessing neither does Epoli.
Are you *sure* that was her in the crowd?
What was she doing here?
I...I don't know. But somehow we keep crossing paths.
She must be very special, Rickety. To write a song so beautiful...
She is...
I--I shouldn't have called out to her. I should have known better. I think she was in trouble.
In trouble? Why? Who *is* she?
Epoli is a knight-errant. I don't know where she's from or where she goes.
I just know that she's a hero. And I mean a real one.
Strong, selfless, brave.
I spoke to her on the seashore. On the Middle-Route Run. It was storming. She told me her name, that she was a Knight of the Order of the Ember.
The *Gloom King* has returned, she said. And she would be there to defy him.
Before she rode off into the rain and cold, she told me of her vow.
To light a *flame* in the heart of the Middle Kingdoms.
To remind ordinary folk that there's a real chance things could be good again.
All those lyrics in the song are true, Canta. I'll never forget what she did and what she said to me.
She told me to keep singing...
Nothing has ever inspired me more...
Until...

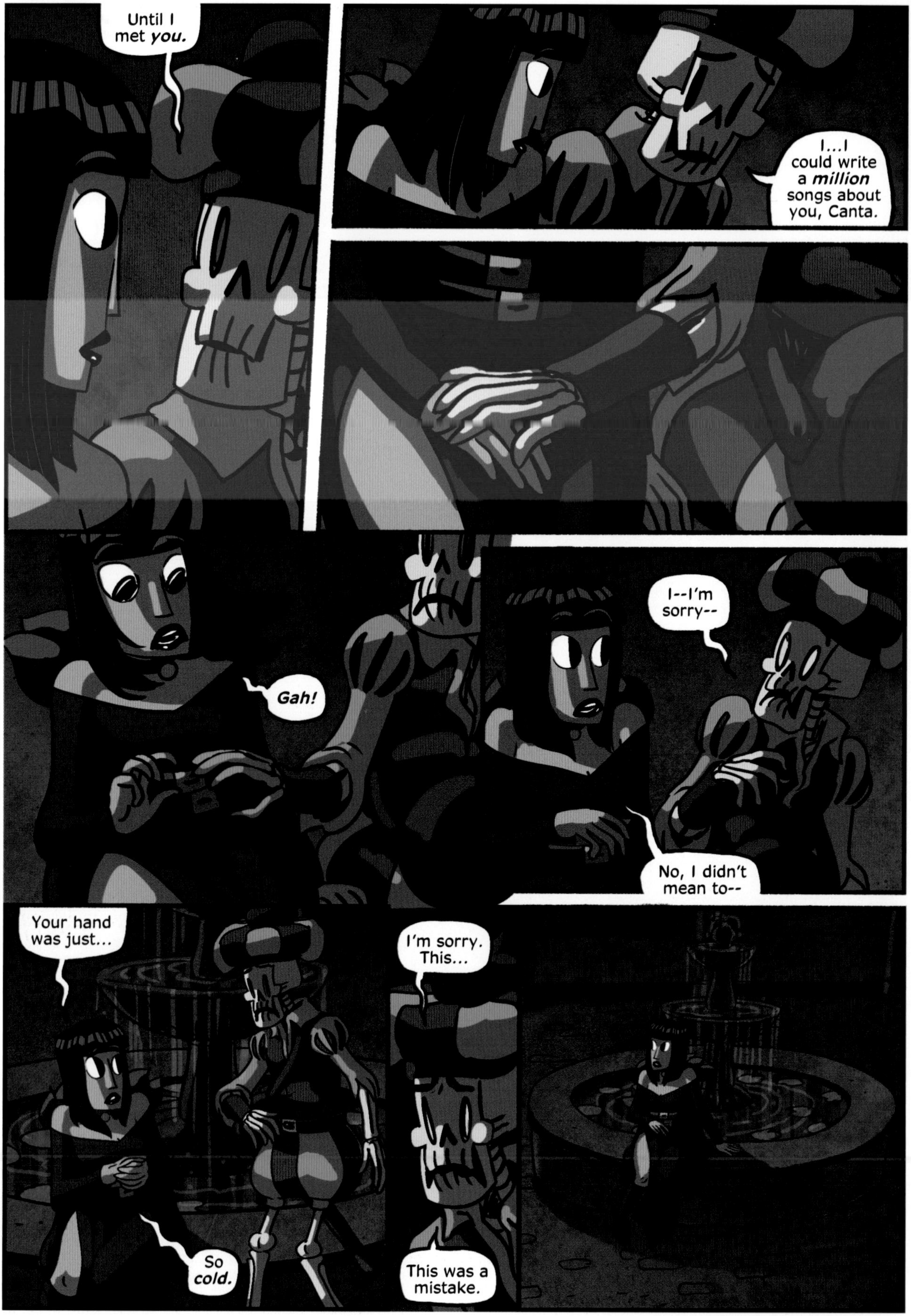

Until I met *you.*
I...I could write a ***million*** songs about you, Canta.
Gah!
I--I'm sorry--
No, I didn't mean to--
Your hand was just...
So ***cold.***
I'm sorry. This...
This was a mistake.

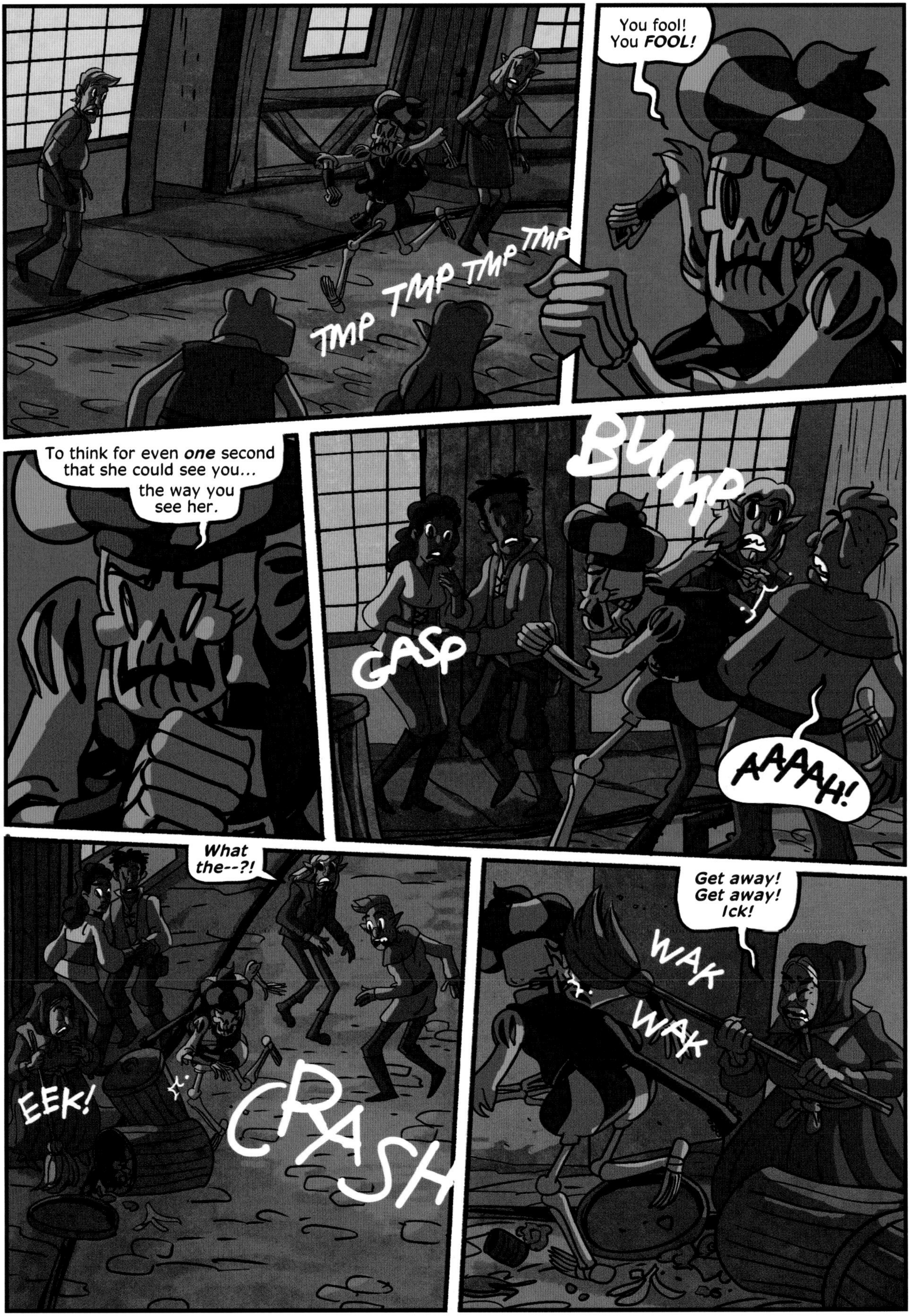

TMP TMP TMP TMP
You fool! You *FOOL!*
To think for even *one* second that she could see you...
the way you see her.
BUMP
GASP
AAAAH!
What the--?!
EEK!
CRASH
Get away! Get away! Ick!
WAK
WAK

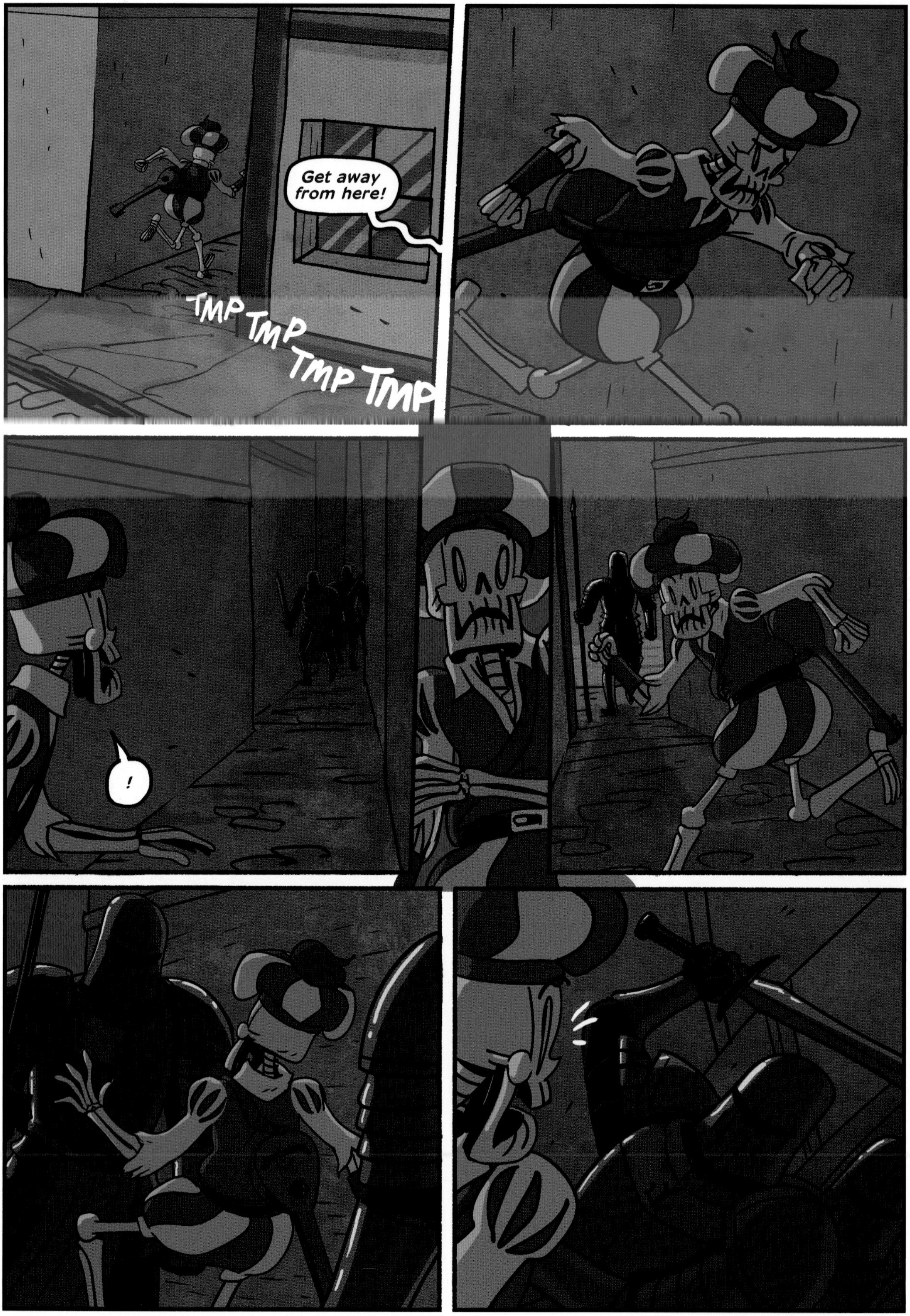
Get away from here!
TMP TMP TMP TMP
!

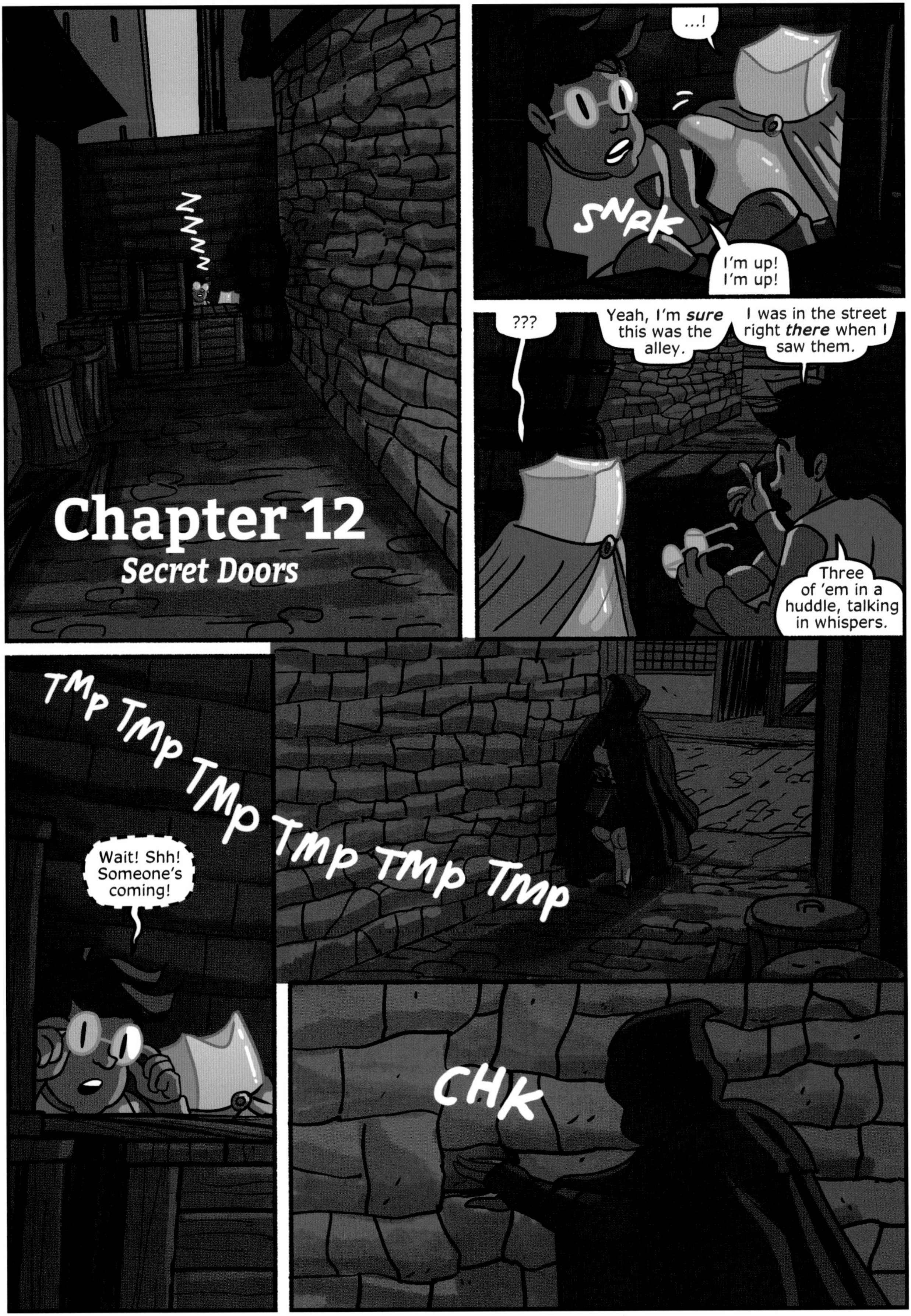

ZZZZ
Chapter 12
Secret Doors
...!
SNRK
I'm up! I'm up!
???
Yeah, I'm ***sure*** this was the alley.
I was in the street right ***there*** when I saw them.
Three of 'em in a huddle, talking in whispers.
TMP TMP TMP TMP TMP TMP TMP
Wait! Shh! Someone's coming!
CHK

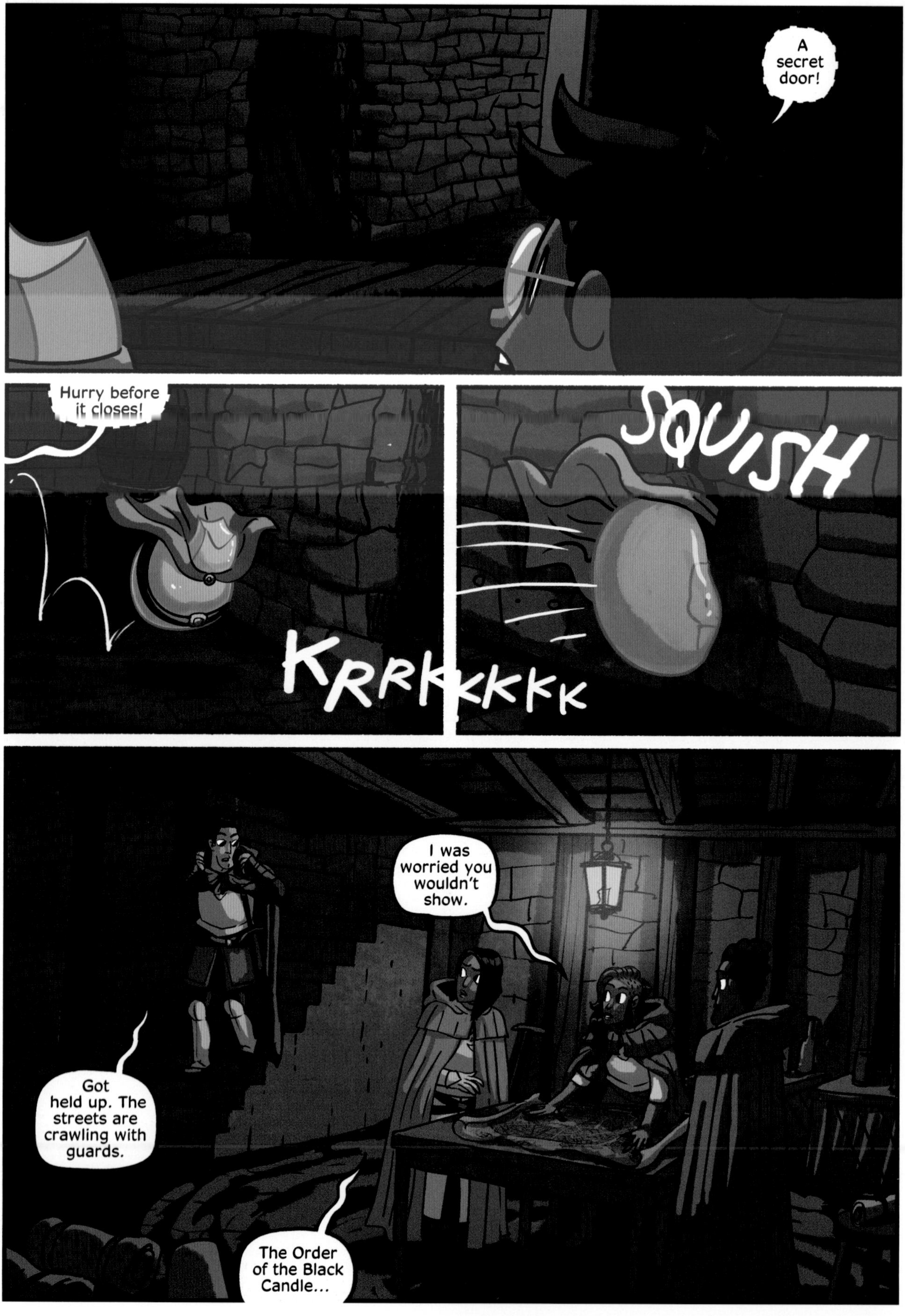
A secret door!
Hurry before it closes!
SQUISH
KRRKKKKK
I was worried you wouldn't show.
Got held up. The streets are crawling with guards.
The Order of the Black Candle...

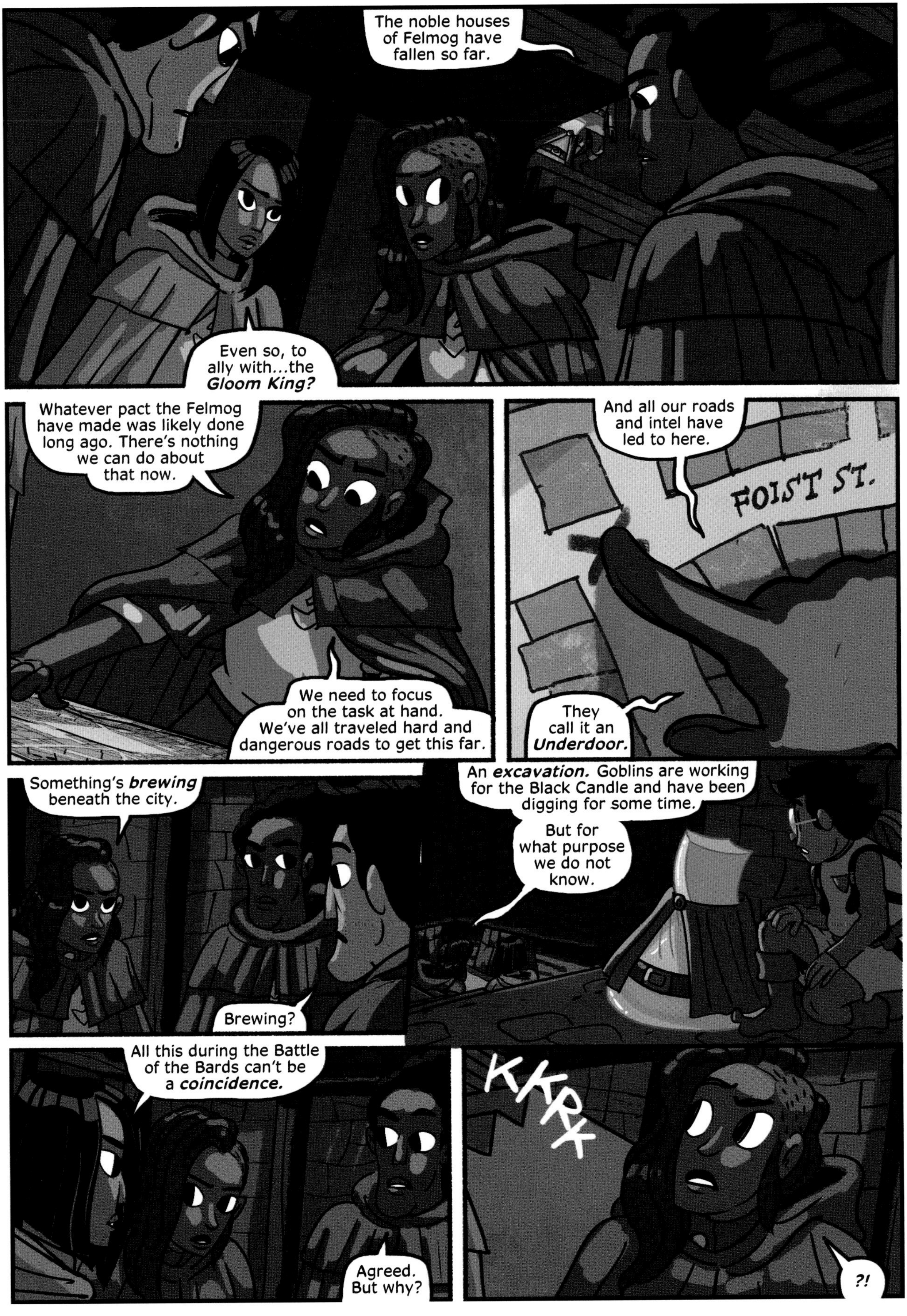
The noble houses of Felmog have fallen so far.
Even so, to ally with...the *Gloom King?*
Whatever pact the Felmog have made was likely done long ago. There's nothing we can do about that now.
We need to focus on the task at hand. We've all traveled hard and dangerous roads to get this far.
And all our roads and intel have led to here.
FOIST ST.
They call it an *Underdoor.*
Something's *brewing* beneath the city.
Brewing?
An *excavation.* Goblins are working for the Black Candle and have been digging for some time.
But for what purpose we do not know.
All this during the Battle of the Bards can't be a *coincidence.*
Agreed. But why?
KKRK
?!

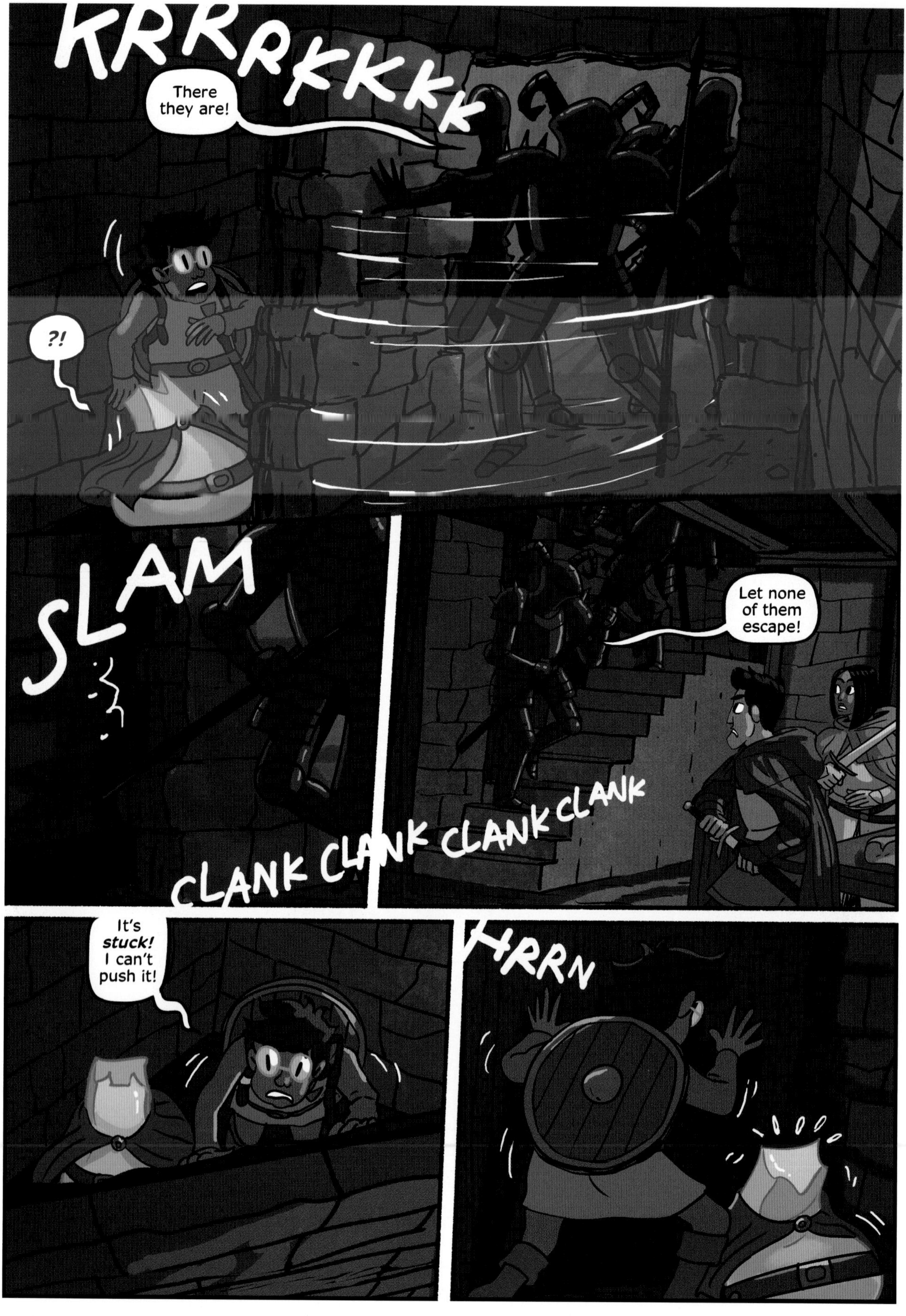
KRRRKKKKK
There they are!
?!
SLAM
Let none of them escape!
CLANK CLANK CLANK CLANK
It's *stuck!* I can't push it!
HRRN

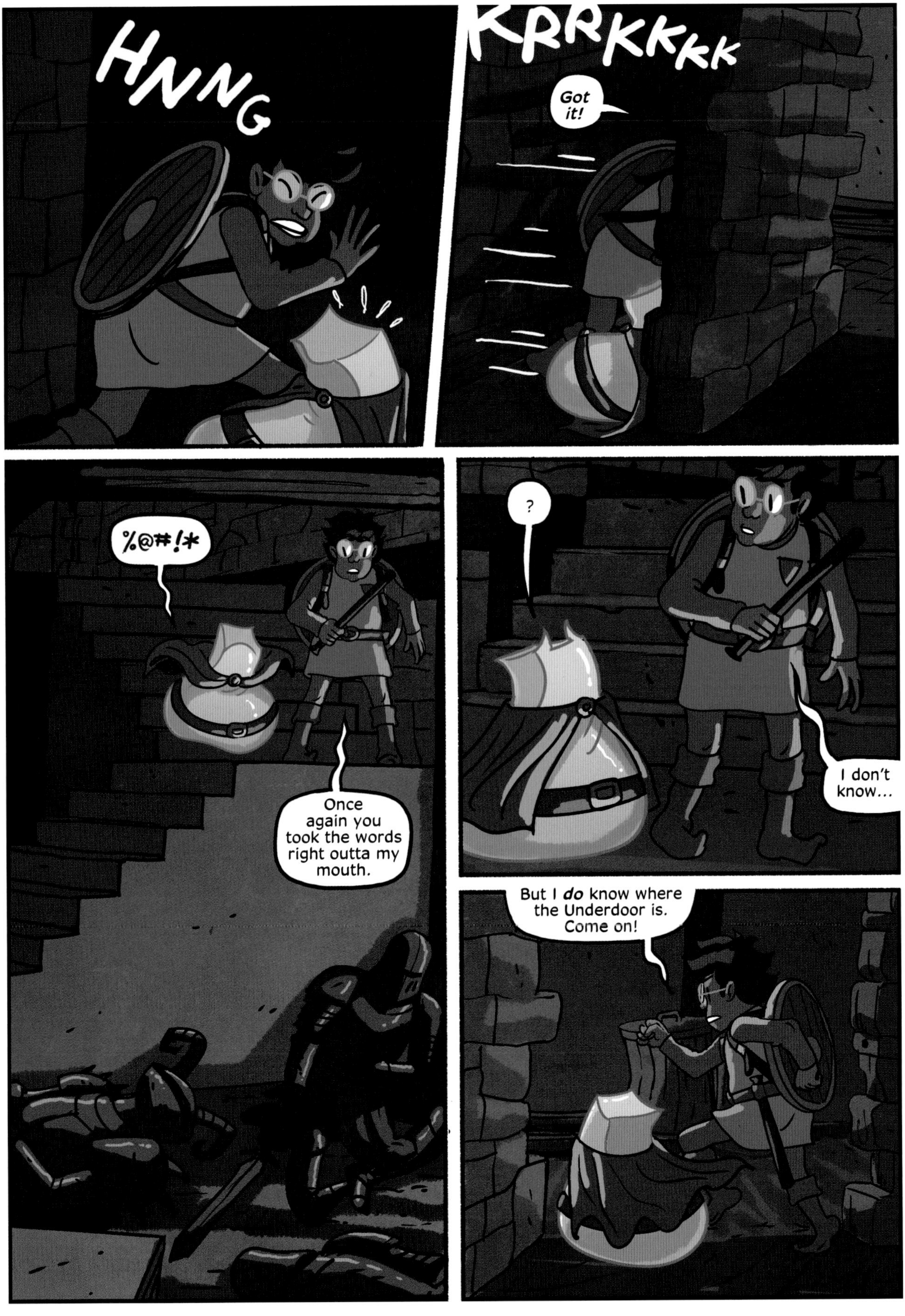
HNNG
KRRKKKK
Got it!
%@#!*
Once again you took the words right outta my mouth.
?
I don't know...
But I *do* know where the Underdoor is. Come on!

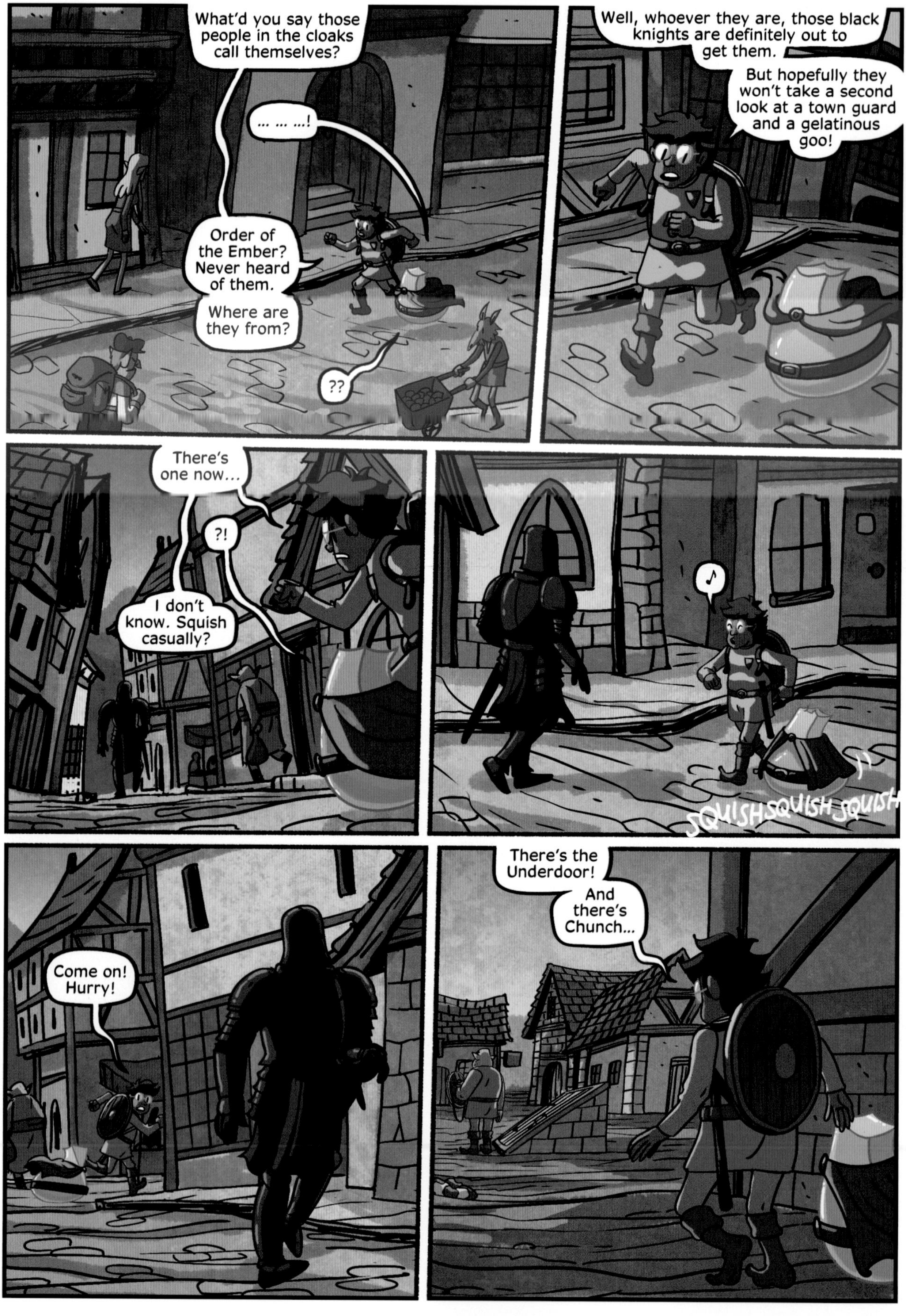
What'd you say those people in the cloaks call themselves?
... ...!
Order of the Ember? Never heard of them.
Where are they from?
??
Well, whoever they are, those black knights are definitely out to get them.
But hopefully they won't take a second look at a town guard and a gelatinous goo!
There's one now...
?!
I don't know. Squish casually?
♪
SQUISH SQUISH SQUISH
Come on! Hurry!
There's the Underdoor!
And there's Chunch...

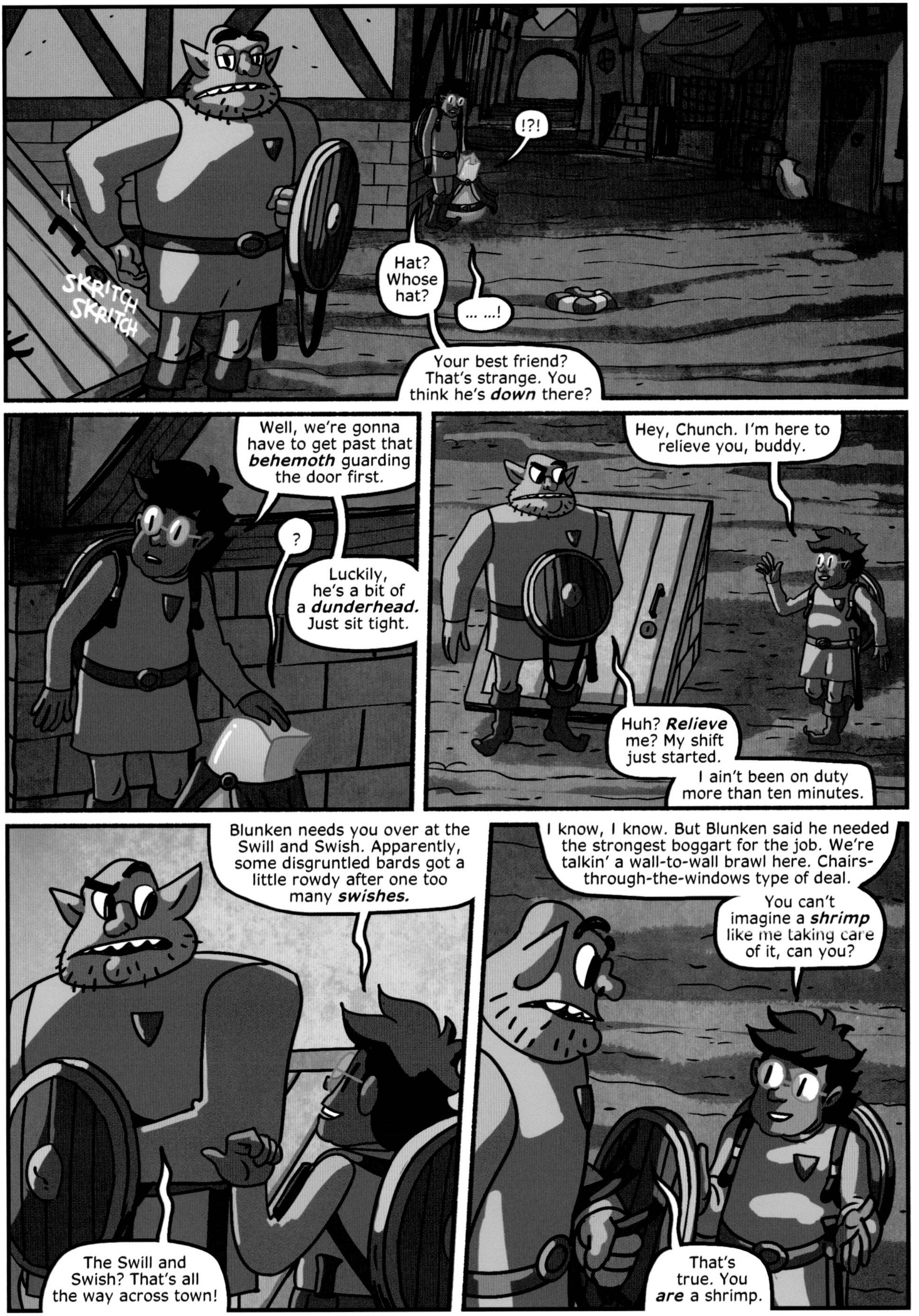

!?!
SKRITCH SKRITCH
Hat? Whose hat?
... ...!
Your best friend? That's strange. You think he's *down* there?
Well, we're gonna have to get past that *behemoth* guarding the door first.
?
Luckily, he's a bit of a *dunderhead.* Just sit tight.
Hey, Chunch. I'm here to relieve you, buddy.
Huh? *Relieve* me? My shift just started.
I ain't been on duty more than ten minutes.
Blunken needs you over at the Swill and Swish. Apparently, some disgruntled bards got a little rowdy after one too many *swishes.*
The Swill and Swish? That's all the way across town!
I know, I know. But Blunken said he needed the strongest boggart for the job. We're talkin' a wall-to-wall brawl here. Chairs-through-the-windows type of deal.
You can't imagine a *shrimp* like me taking care of it, can you?
That's true. You *are* a shrimp.

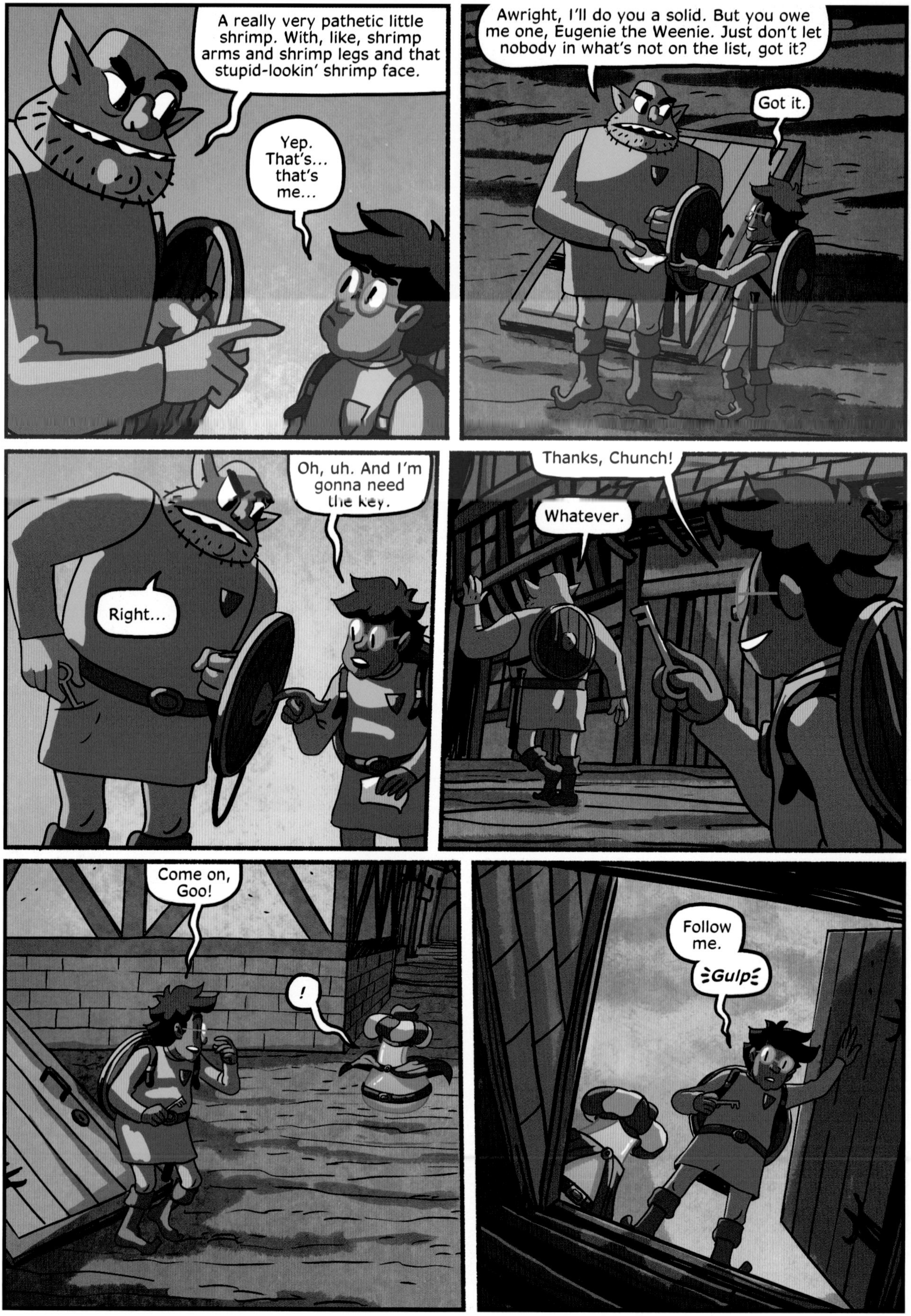
A really very pathetic little shrimp. With, like, shrimp arms and shrimp legs and that stupid-lookin' shrimp face.
Yep. That's... that's me...
Awright, I'll do you a solid. But you owe me one, Eugenie the Weenie. Just don't let nobody in what's not on the list, got it?
Got it.
Oh, uh. And I'm gonna need the key.
Right...
Thanks, Chunch!
Whatever.
Come on, Goo!
!
Follow me.
Gulp

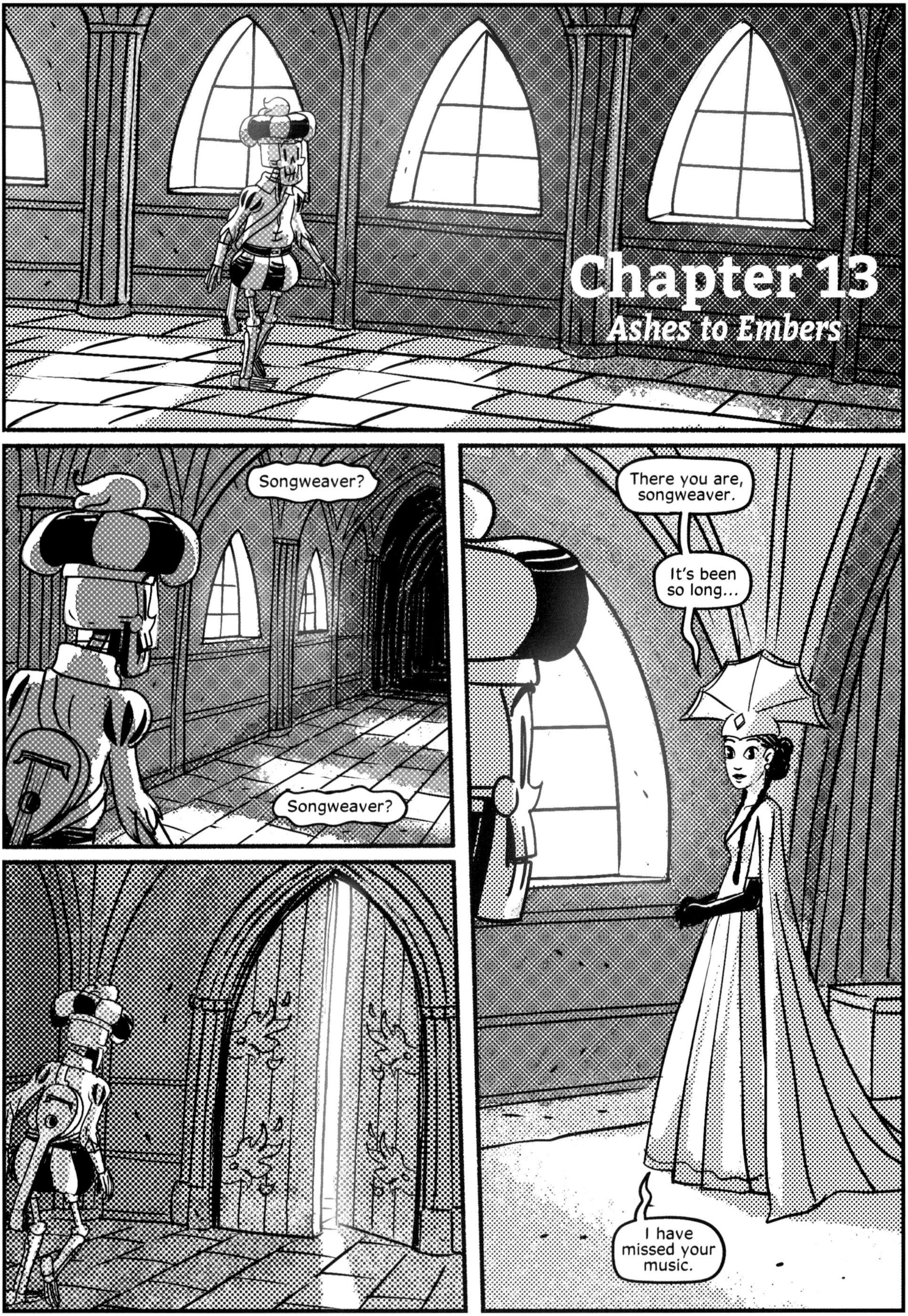
Chapter 13
Ashes to Embers
Songweaver?
Songweaver?
There you are, songweaver.
It's been so long...
I have missed your music.

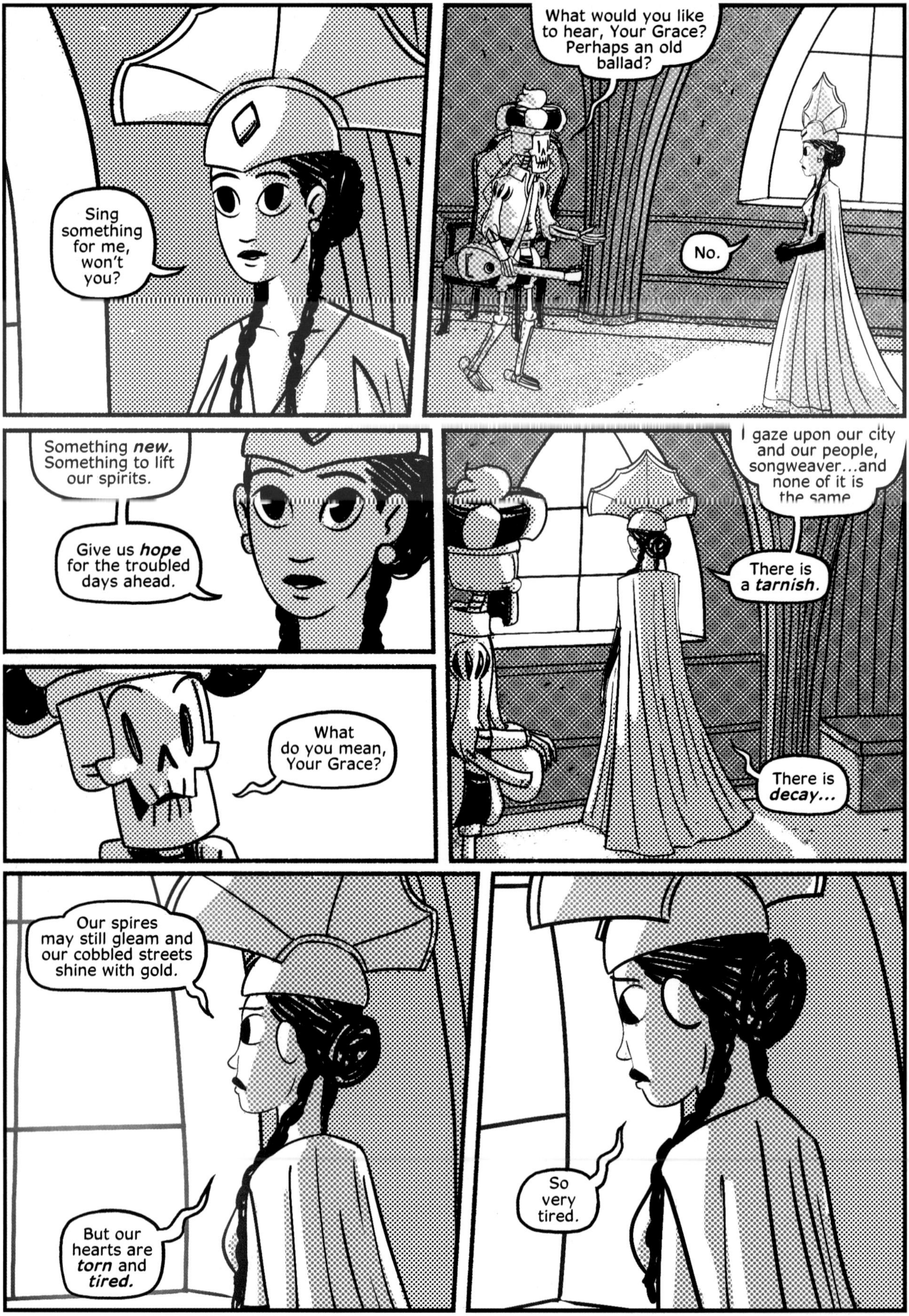
Sing something for me, won't you?
What would you like to hear, Your Grace? Perhaps an old ballad?
No.
Something *new.* Something to lift our spirits.
Give us *hope* for the troubled days ahead.
What do you mean, Your Grace?
I gaze upon our city and our people, songweaver...and none of it is the same.
There is a *tarnish*.
There is *decay...*
Our spires may still gleam and our cobbled streets shine with gold.
But our hearts are *torn* and *tired.*
So very tired.

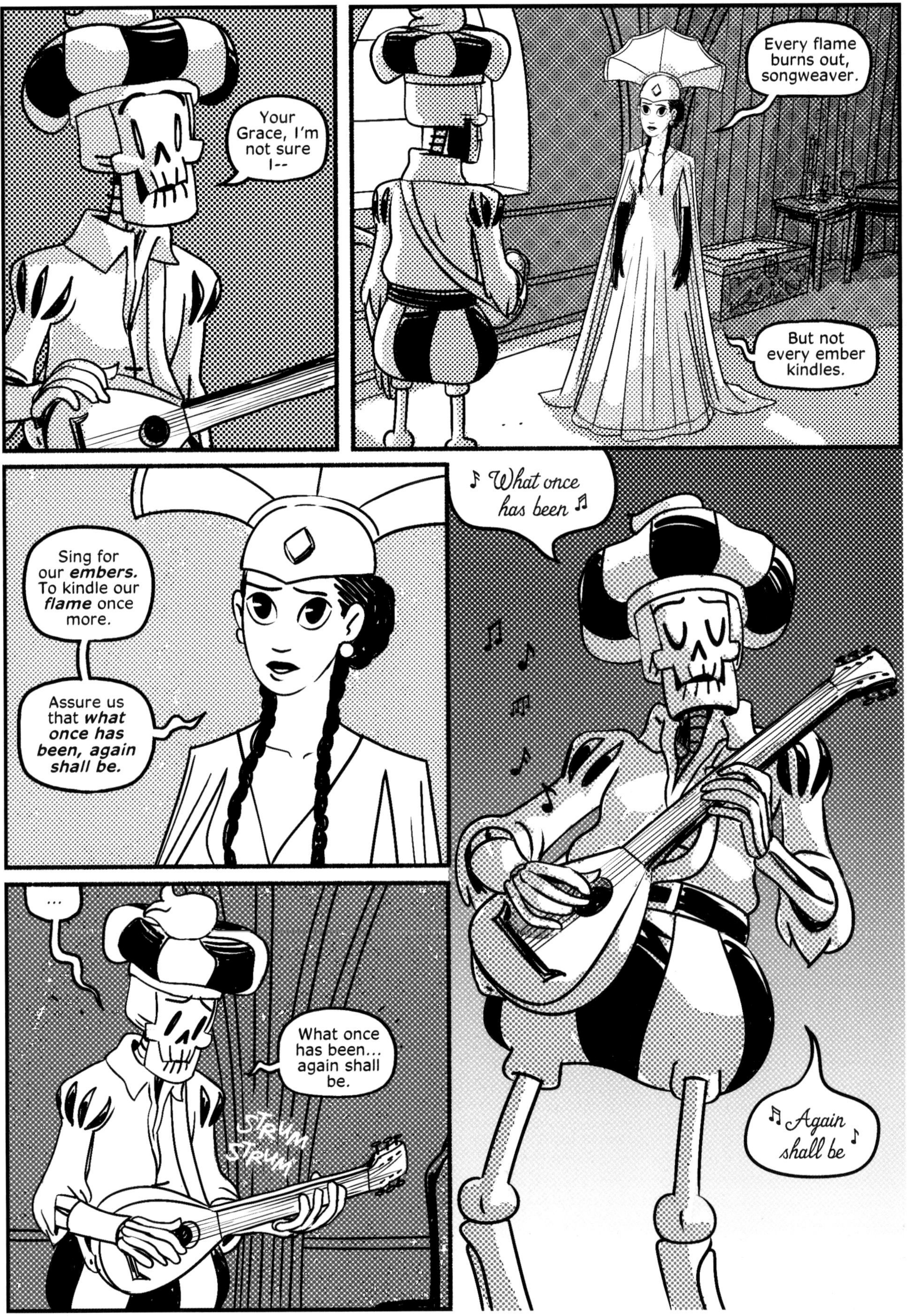
Your Grace, I'm not sure I--
Every flame burns out, songweaver.
But not every ember kindles.
Sing for our *embers.* To kindle our *flame* once more.
Assure us that *what once has been, again shall be.*
♪ What once has been ♫
...
What once has been... again shall be.
STRUM STRUM
♫ Again shall be ♪

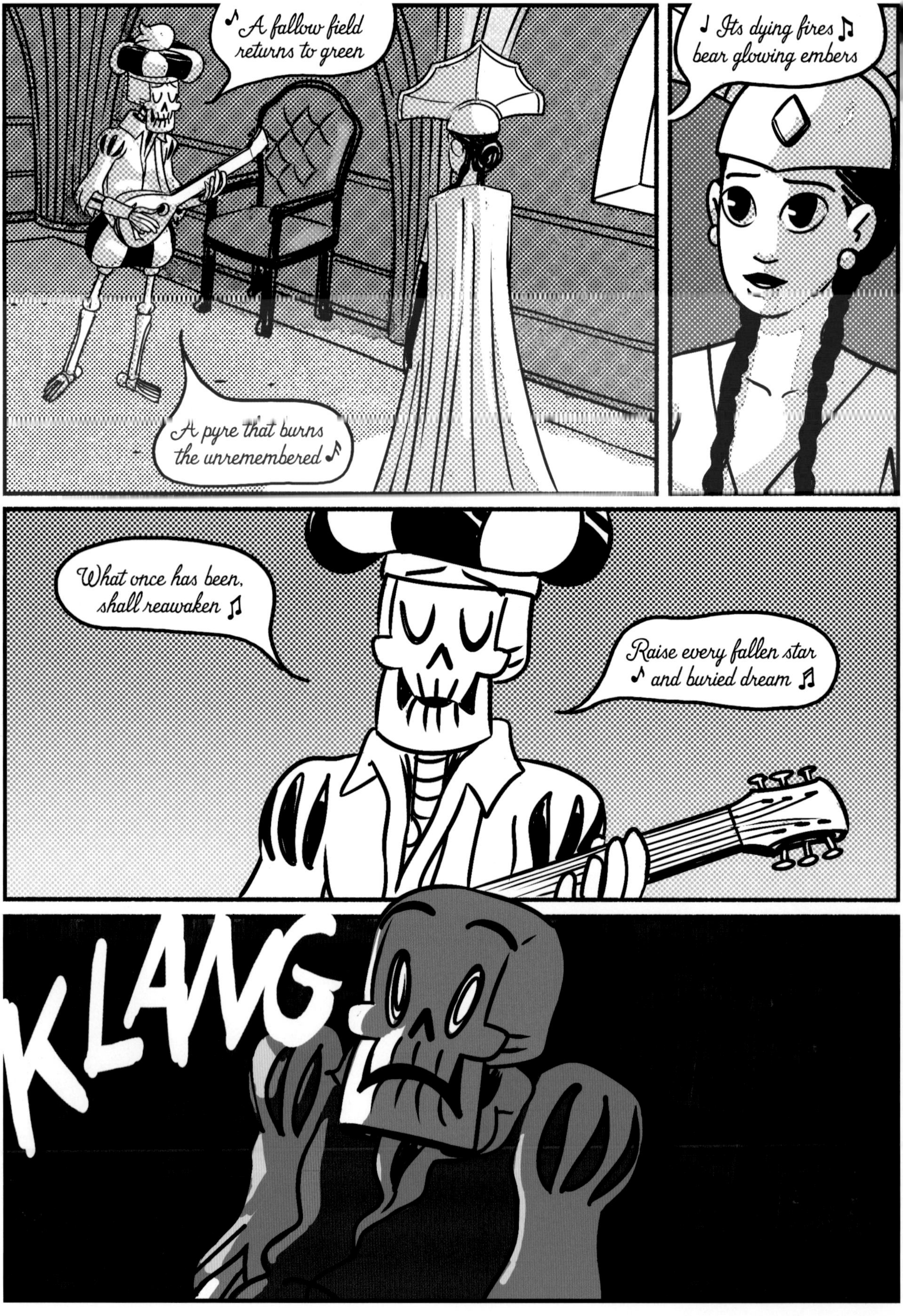
♪ A fallow field returns to green
A pyre that burns the unremembered ♪
♩ Its dying fires bear glowing embers ♫
What once has been, shall reawaken ♫
Raise every fallen star ♪ and buried dream ♫
KLANG

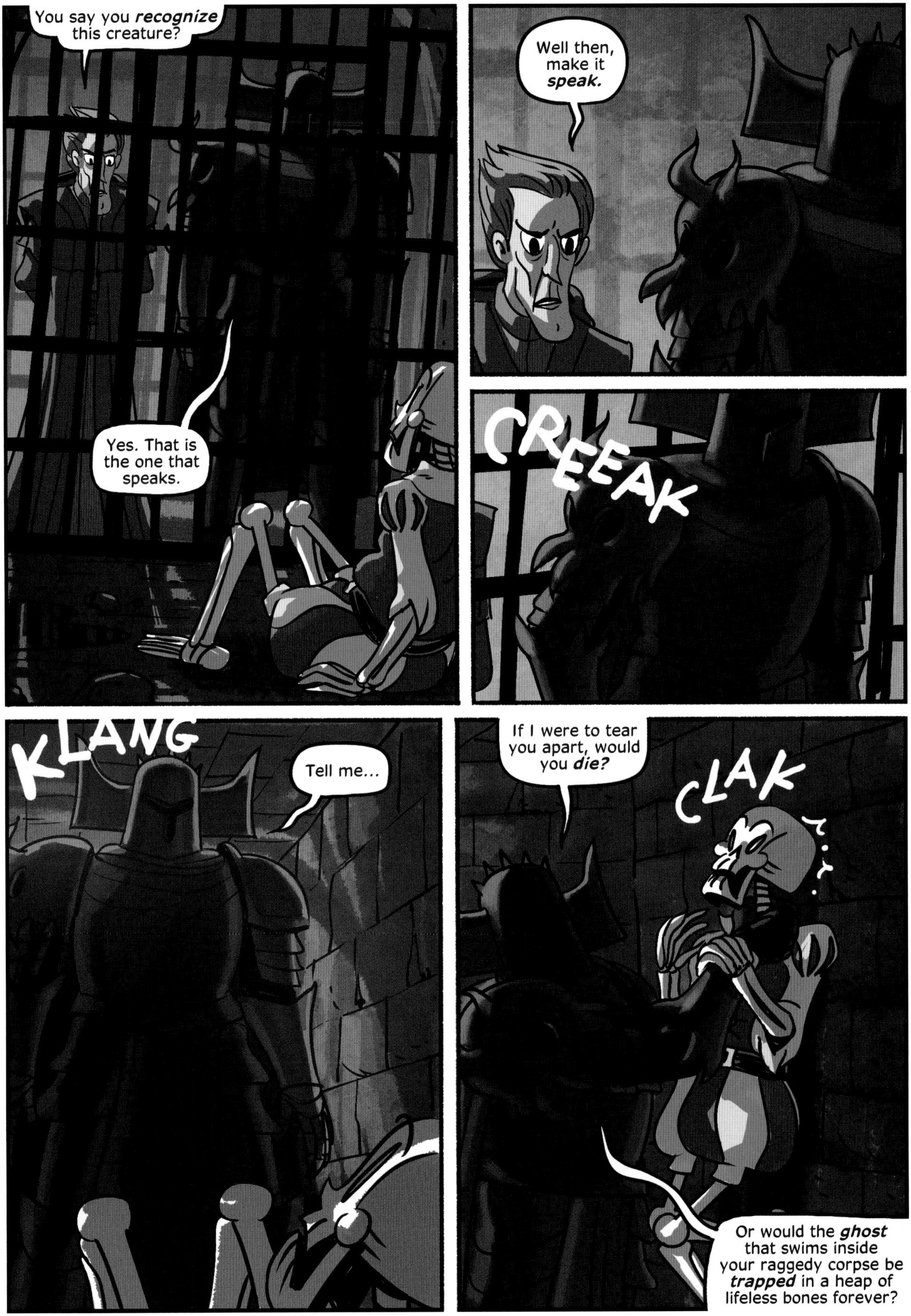
You say you ***recognize*** this creature?
Yes. That is the one that speaks.
Well then, make it ***speak.***
CREEAK
KLANG
Tell me...
If I were to tear you apart, would you ***die?***
CLAK
Or would the ***ghost*** that swims inside your raggedy corpse be ***trapped*** in a heap of lifeless bones forever?

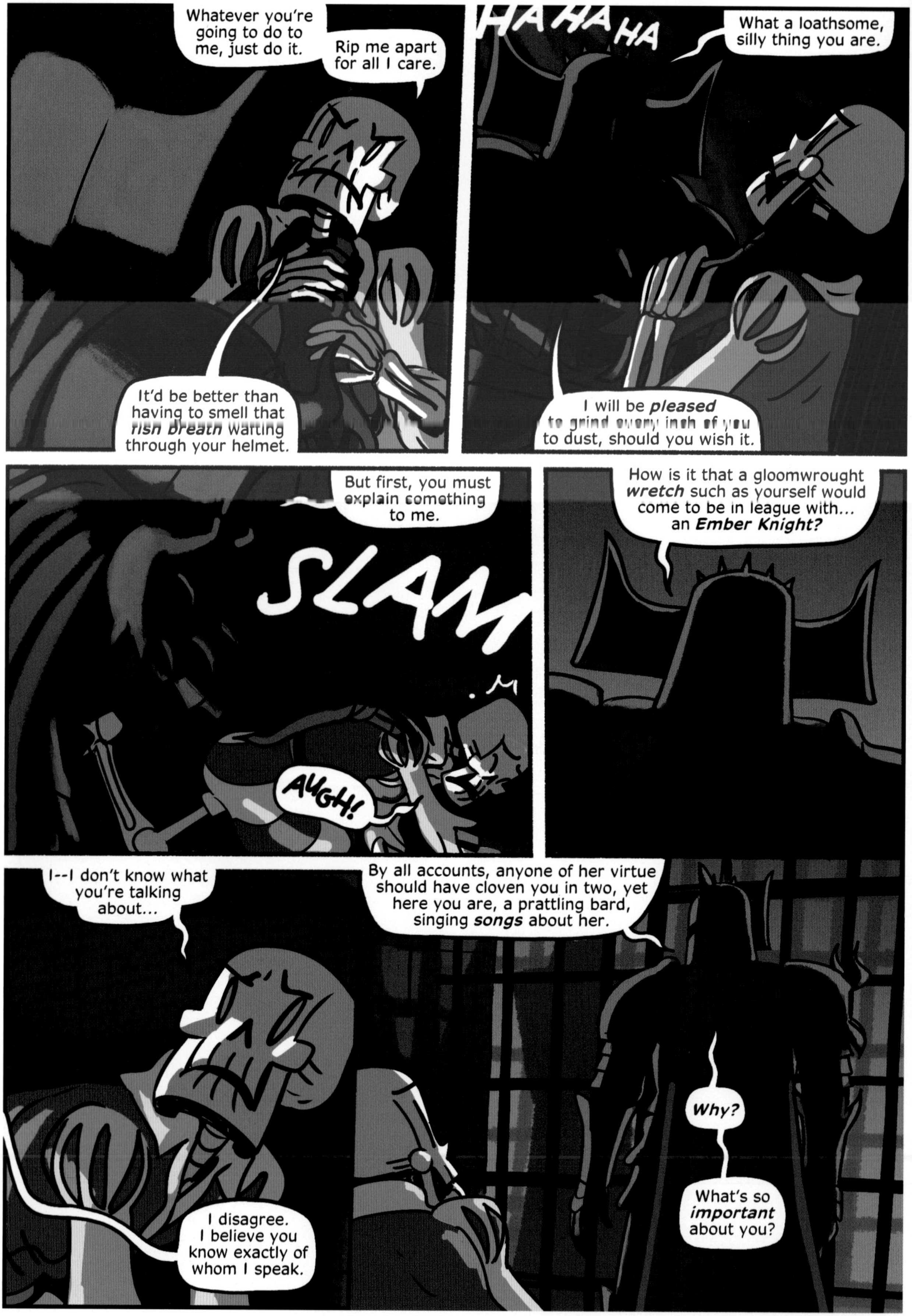
Whatever you're going to do to me, just do it.
Rip me apart for all I care.
It'd be better than having to smell that fish breath wafting through your helmet.
HA HA HA HA
What a loathsome, silly thing you are.
I will be *pleased* to grind every inch of you to dust, should you wish it.
But first, you must explain something to me.
SLAM
AUGH!
How is it that a gloomwrought *wretch* such as yourself would come to be in league with... an *Ember Knight?*
I--I don't know what you're talking about...
By all accounts, anyone of her virtue should have cloven you in two, yet here you are, a prattling bard, singing *songs* about her.
I disagree. I believe you know exactly of whom I speak.
Why?
What's so *important* about you?

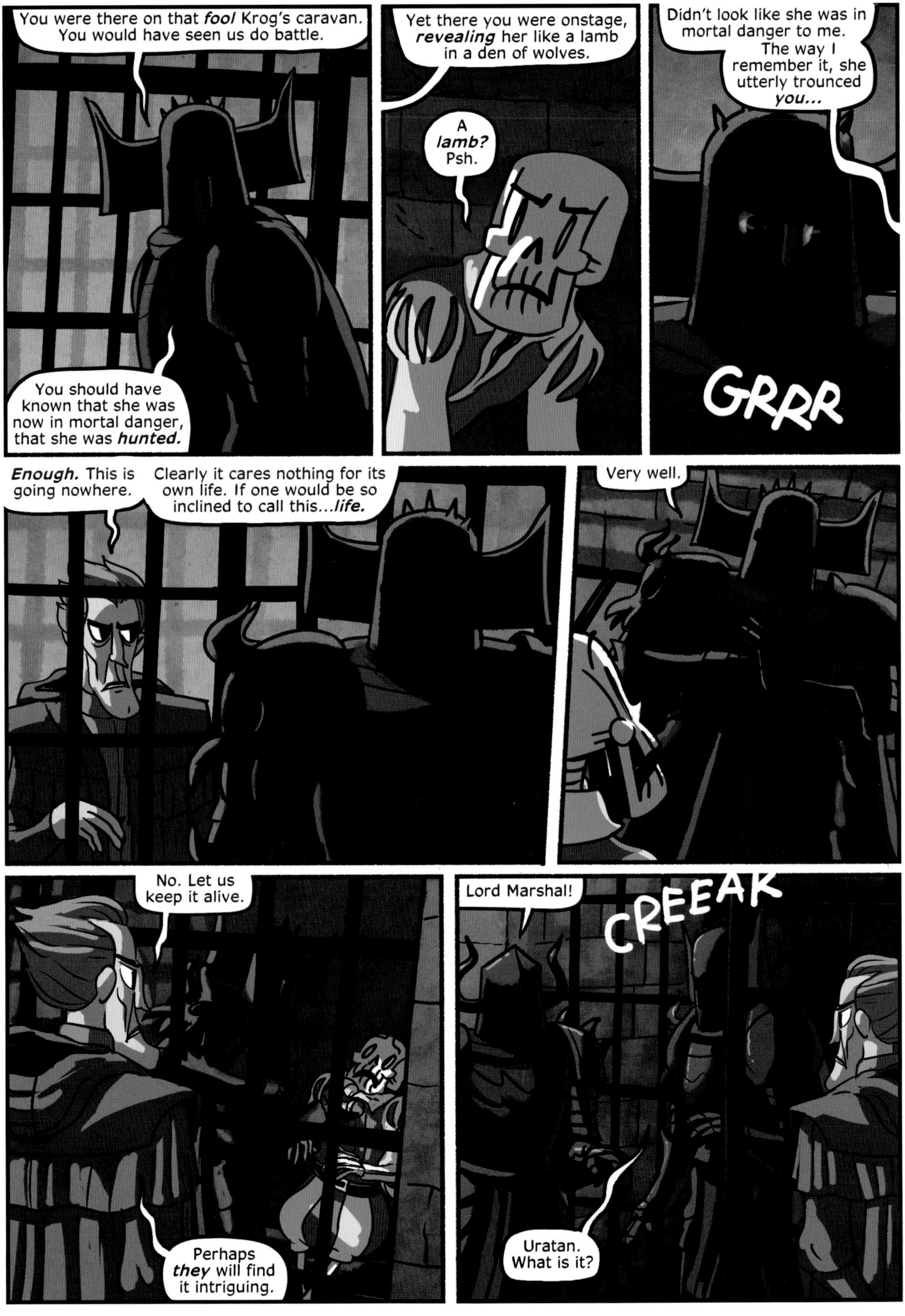
You were there on that *fool* Krog's caravan. You would have seen us do battle.
You should have known that she was now in mortal danger, that she was ***hunted.***
Yet there you were onstage, ***revealing*** her like a lamb in a den of wolves.
A ***lamb?*** Psh.
Didn't look like she was in mortal danger to me.
The way I remember it, she utterly trounced ***you...***
GRRR
Enough. This is going nowhere.
Clearly it cares nothing for its own life. If one would be so inclined to call this...***life.***
Very well.
No. Let us keep it alive.
Perhaps ***they*** will find it intriguing.
Lord Marshal!
CREEAK
Uratan. What is it?

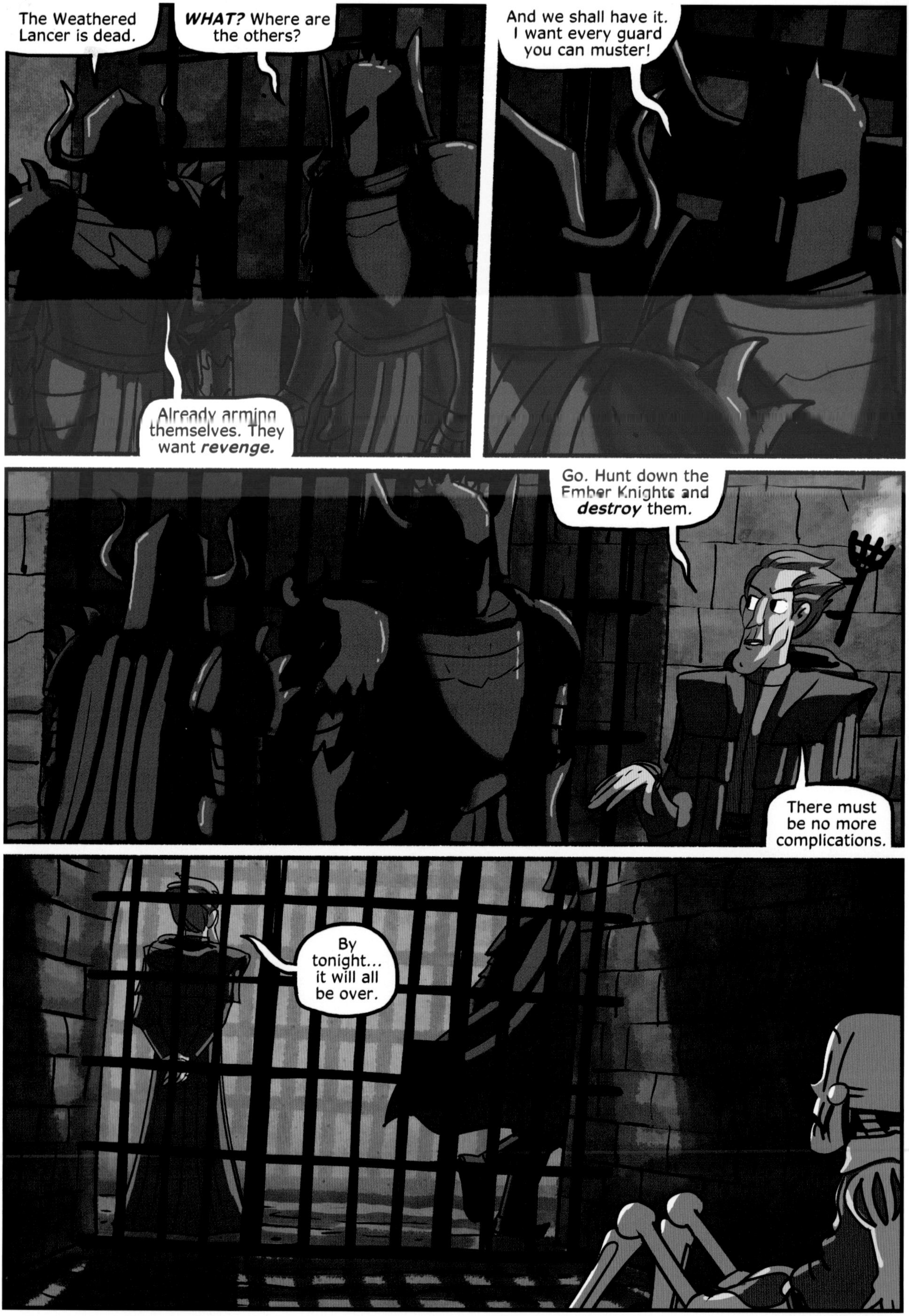
The Weathered Lancer is dead.
WHAT? Where are the others?
Already arming themselves. They want *revenge.*
And we shall have it. I want every guard you can muster!
Go. Hunt down the Ember Knights and *destroy* them.
There must be no more complications.
By tonight... it will all be over.

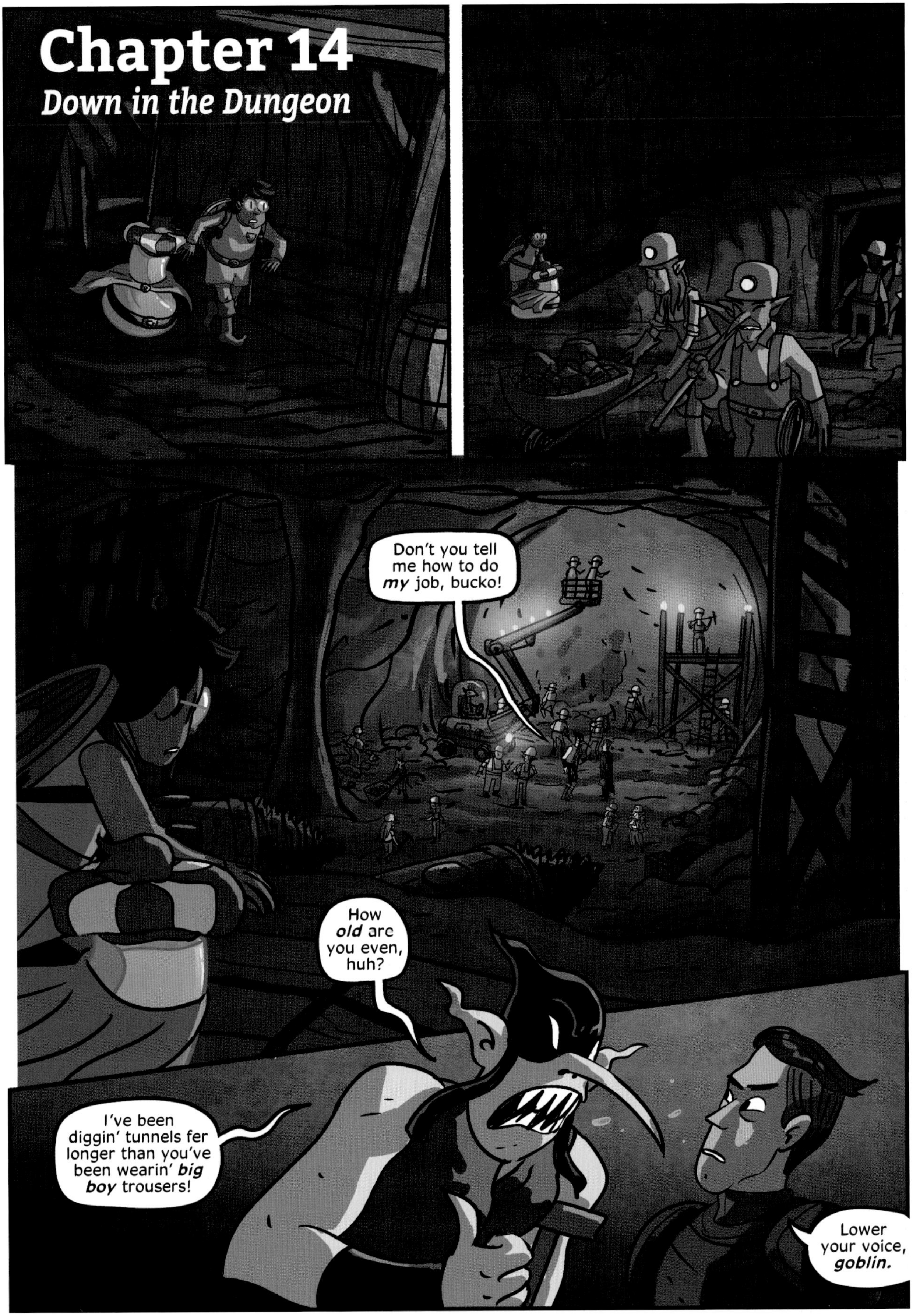

Chapter 14
Down in the Dungeon
Don't you tell me how to do *my* job, bucko!
How *old* are you even, huh?
I've been diggin' tunnels fer longer than you've been wearin' *big boy* trousers!
Lower your voice, *goblin.*

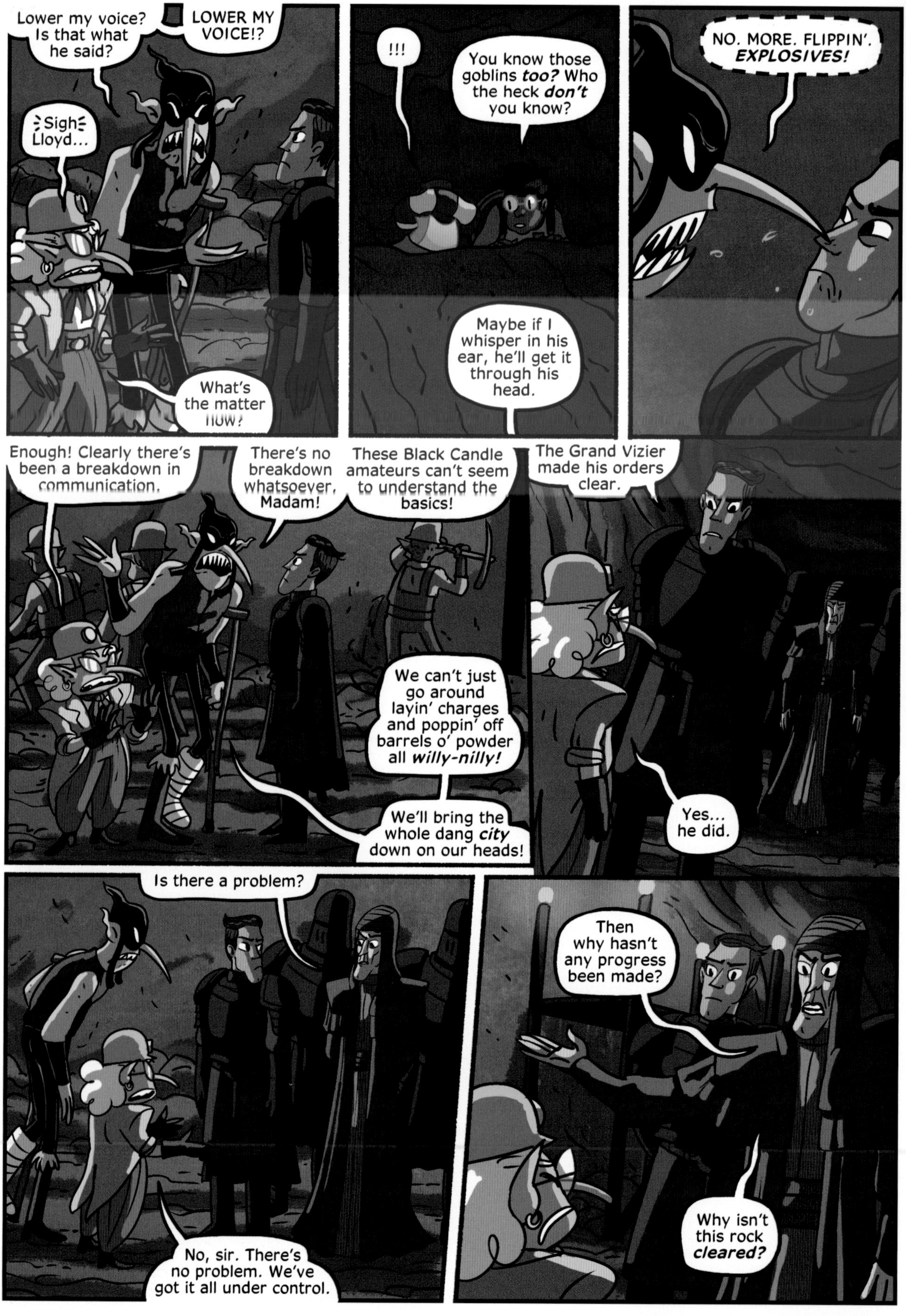
Lower my voice? Is that what he said?
LOWER MY VOICE!?
Sigh Lloyd...
What's the matter now?
!!!
You know those goblins *too?* Who the heck *don't* you know?
Maybe if I whisper in his ear, he'll get it through his head.
NO. MORE. FLIPPIN'. *EXPLOSIVES!*
Enough! Clearly there's been a breakdown in communication.
There's no breakdown whatsoever, Madam!
These Black Candle amateurs can't seem to understand the basics!
We can't just go around layin' charges and poppin' off barrels o' powder all *willy-nilly!*
We'll bring the whole dang *city* down on our heads!
The Grand Vizier made his orders clear.
Yes... he did.
Is there a problem?
No, sir. There's no problem. We've got it all under control.
Then why hasn't any progress been made?
Why isn't this rock *cleared?*

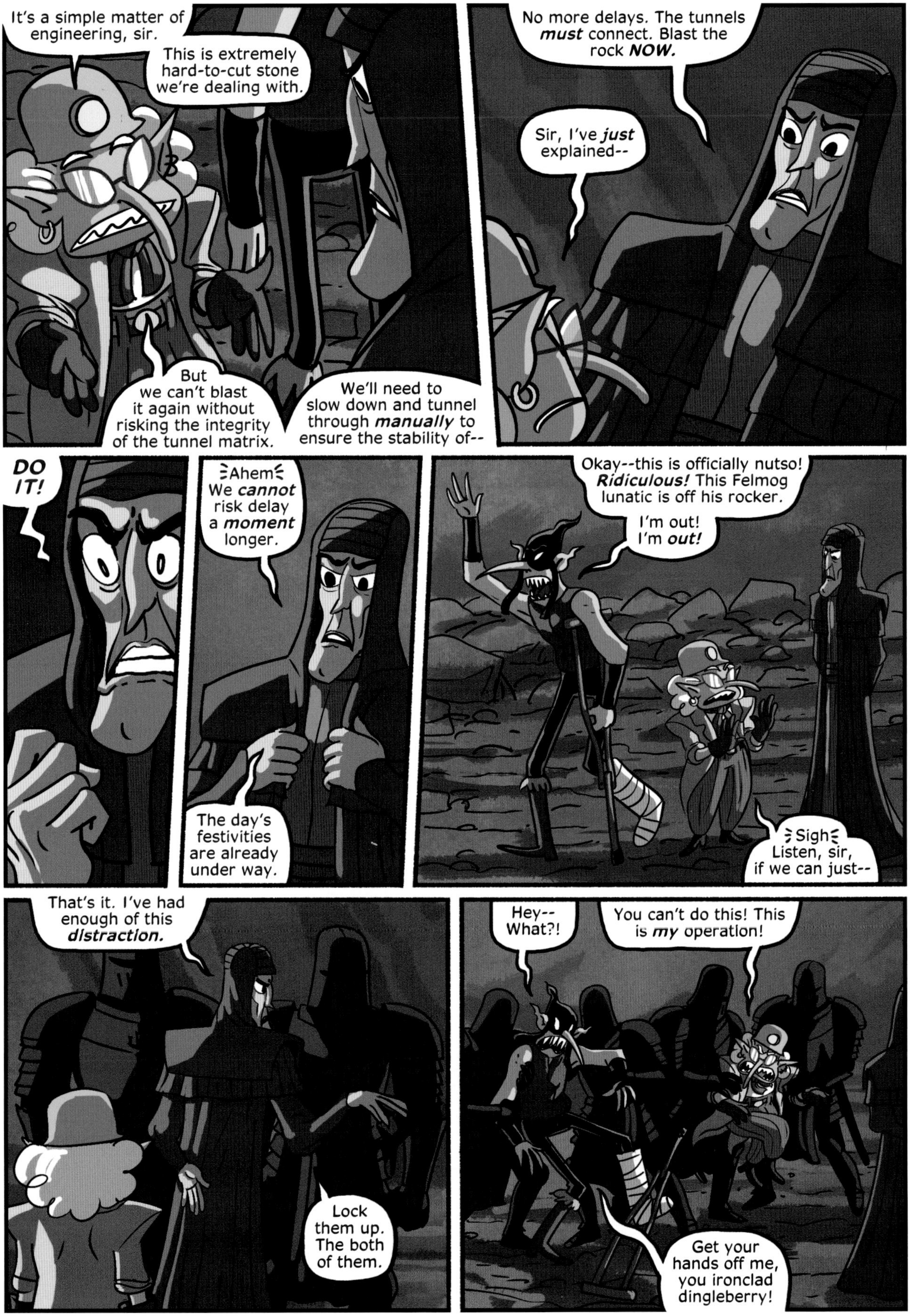

It's a simple matter of engineering, sir.
This is extremely hard-to-cut stone we're dealing with.
But we can't blast it again without risking the integrity of the tunnel matrix.
We'll need to slow down and tunnel through *manually* to ensure the stability of--
No more delays. The tunnels *must* connect. Blast the rock ***NOW.***
Sir, I've *just* explained--
DO IT!
Ahem
We *cannot* risk delay a *moment* longer.
The day's festivities are already under way.
Okay--this is officially nutso! ***Ridiculous!*** This Felmog lunatic is off his rocker.
I'm out! I'm ***out!***
Sigh
Listen, sir, if we can just--
That's it. I've had enough of this ***distraction.***
Lock them up. The both of them.
Hey-- What?!
You can't do this! This is *my* operation!
Get your hands off me, you ironclad dingleberry!

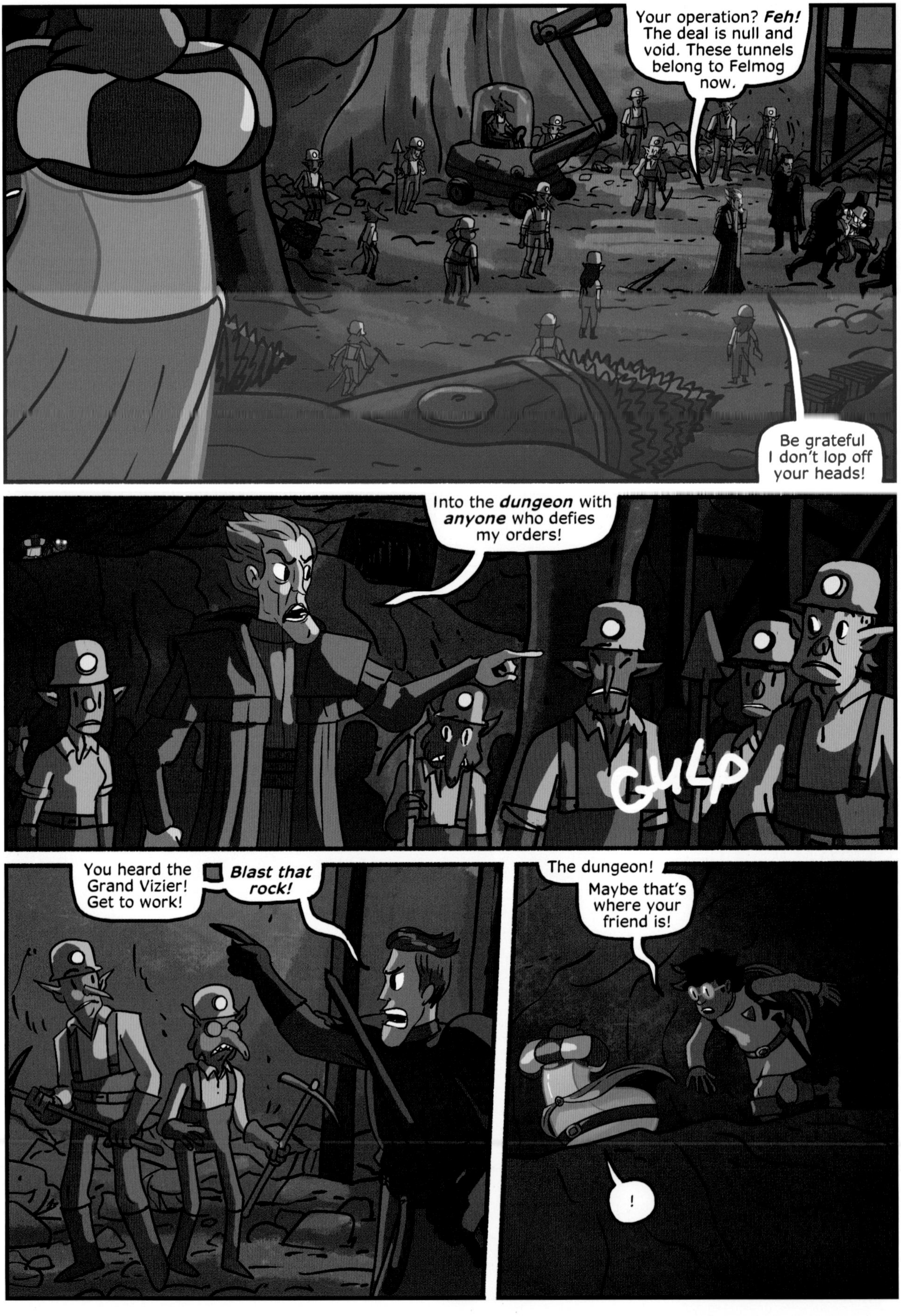
Your operation? ***Feh!*** The deal is null and void. These tunnels belong to Felmog now.
Be grateful I don't lop off your heads!
Into the ***dungeon*** with ***anyone*** who defies my orders!
GULP
You heard the Grand Vizier! Get to work!
Blast that rock!
The dungeon!
Maybe that's where your friend is!
!

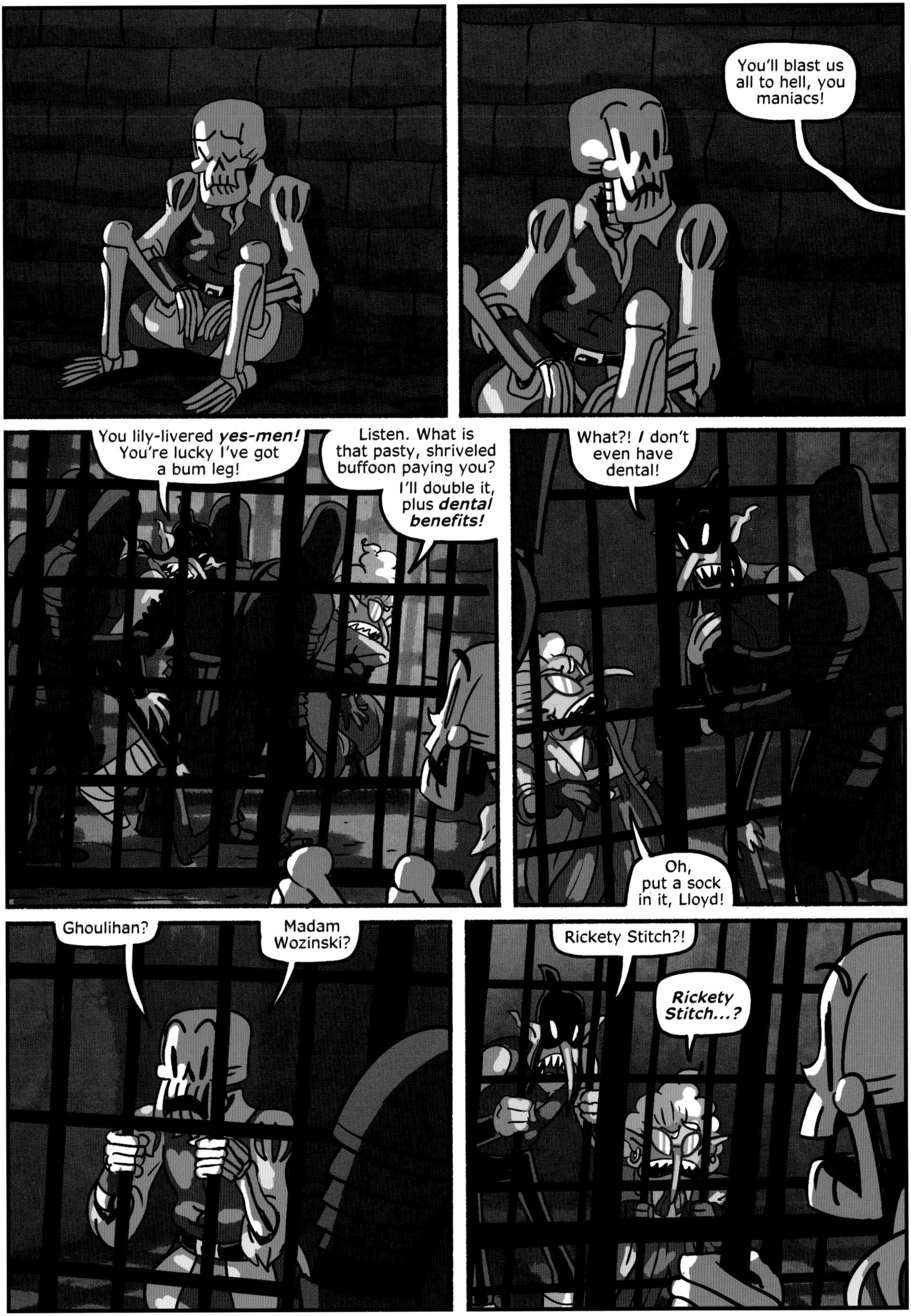

You'll blast us all to hell, you maniacs!
You lily-livered *yes-men!* You're lucky I've got a bum leg!
Listen. What is that pasty, shriveled buffoon paying you?
I'll double it, plus ***dental benefits!***
What?! *I* don't even have dental!
Oh, put a sock in it, Lloyd!
Ghoulihan?
Madam Wozinski?
Rickety Stitch?!
Rickety Stitch...?

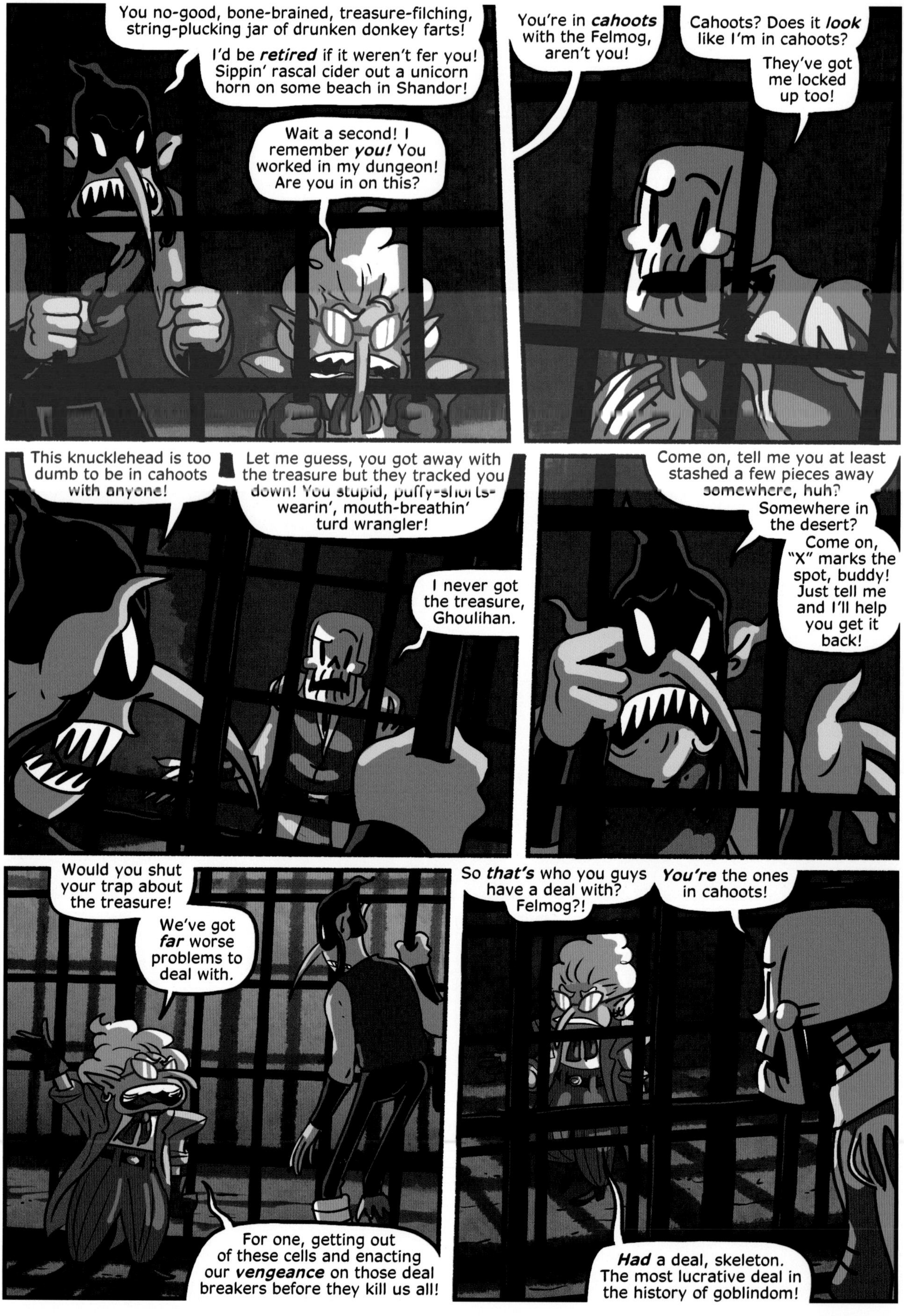

You no-good, bone-brained, treasure-filching, string-plucking jar of drunken donkey farts!
I'd be *retired* if it weren't fer you! Sippin' rascal cider out a unicorn horn on some beach in Shandor!
Wait a second! I remember *you!* You worked in my dungeon! Are you in on this?
You're in *cahoots* with the Felmog, aren't you!
Cahoots? Does it *look* like I'm in cahoots?
They've got me locked up too!
This knucklehead is too dumb to be in cahoots with anyone!
Let me guess, you got away with the treasure but they tracked you down! You stupid, puffy-shorts-wearin', mouth-breathin' turd wrangler!
I never got the treasure, Ghoulihan.
Come on, tell me you at least stashed a few pieces away somewhere, huh?
Somewhere in the desert?
Come on, "X" marks the spot, buddy! Just tell me and I'll help you get it back!
Would you shut your trap about the treasure!
We've got *far* worse problems to deal with.
For one, getting out of these cells and enacting our *vengeance* on those deal breakers before they kill us all!
So *that's* who you guys have a deal with? Felmog?!
You're the ones in cahoots!
Had a deal, skeleton. The most lucrative deal in the history of goblindom!

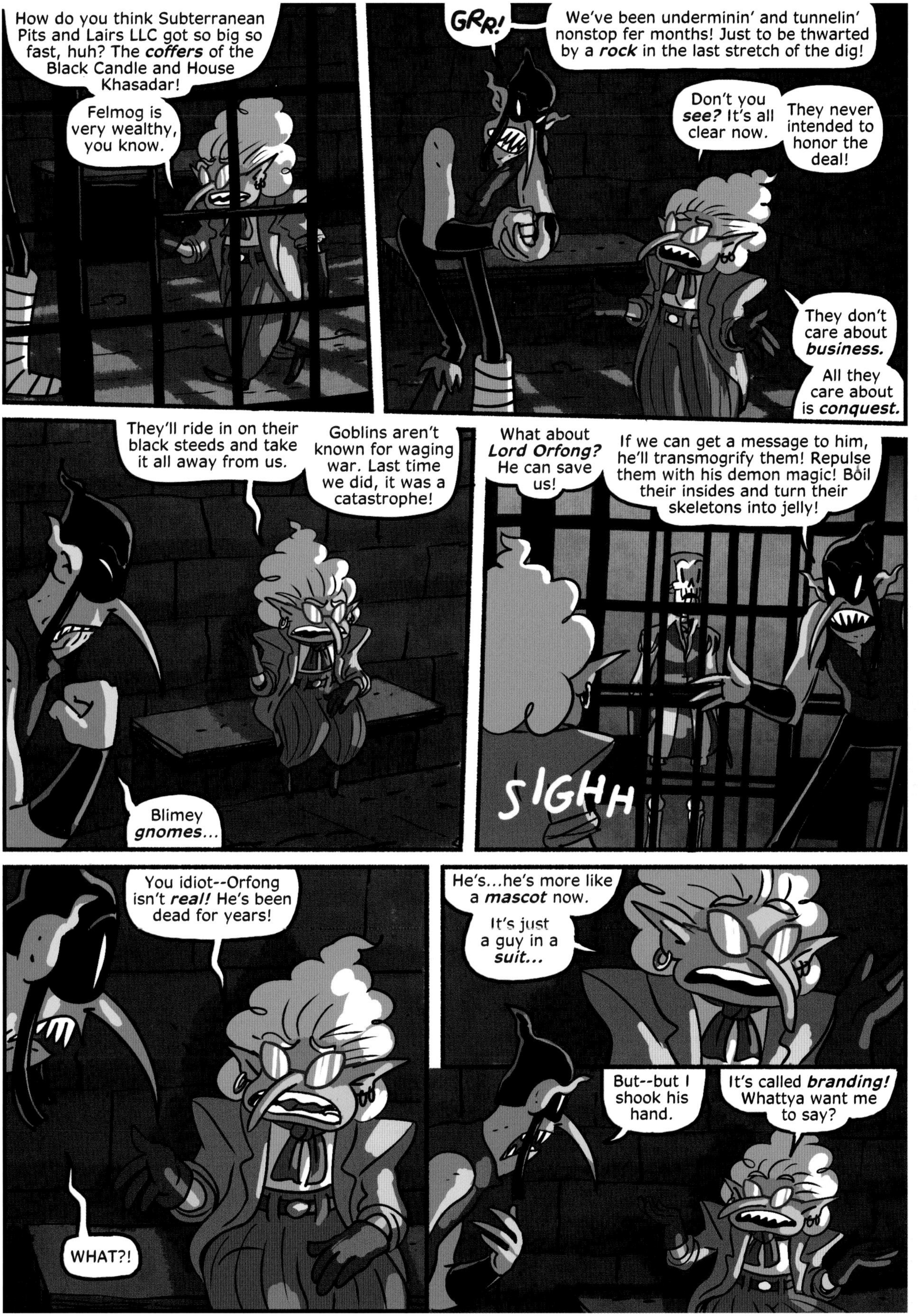
How do you think Subterranean Pits and Lairs LLC got so big so fast, huh? The *coffers* of the Black Candle and House Khasadar!
Felmog is very wealthy, you know.
GRR!
We've been underminin' and tunnelin' nonstop fer months! Just to be thwarted by a *rock* in the last stretch of the dig!
Don't you *see?* It's all clear now.
They never intended to honor the deal!
They don't care about *business.*
All they care about is *conquest.*
They'll ride in on their black steeds and take it all away from us.
Goblins aren't known for waging war. Last time we did, it was a catastrophe!
Blimey *gnomes*...
What about *Lord Orfong?* He can save us!
If we can get a message to him, he'll transmogrify them! Repulse them with his demon magic! Boil their insides and turn their skeletons into jelly!
SIGHH
You idiot--Orfong isn't *real!* He's been dead for years!
WHAT?!
He's...he's more like a *mascot* now.
It's just a guy in a *suit...*
But--but I shook his hand.
It's called *branding!* Whattya want me to say?

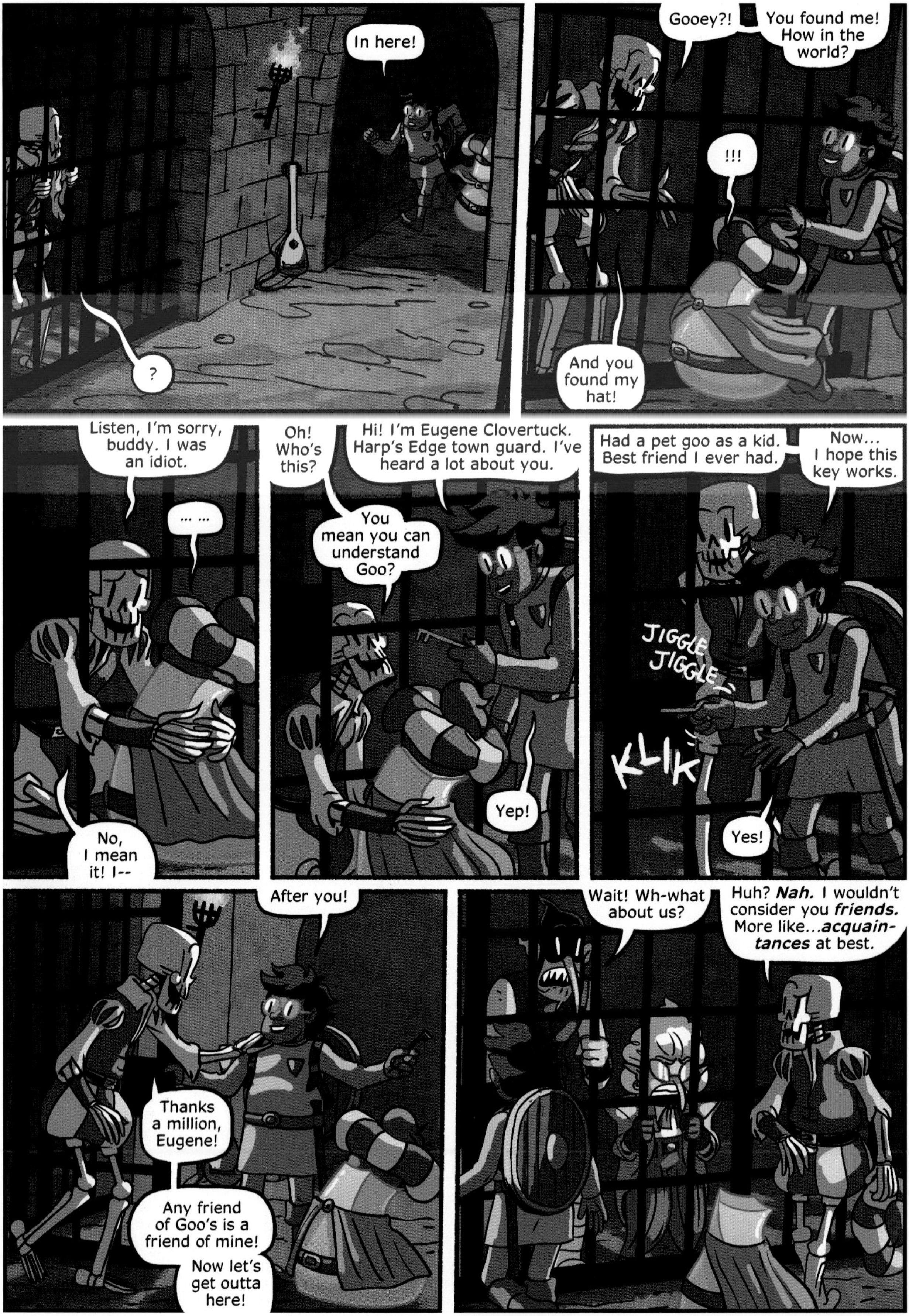
In here!
?
Gooey?!
You found me! How in the world?
!!!
And you found my hat!
Listen, I'm sorry, buddy. I was an idiot.
... ...
No, I mean it! I--
Oh! Who's this?
Hi! I'm Eugene Clovertuck. Harp's Edge town guard. I've heard a lot about you.
You mean you can understand Goo?
Yep!
Had a pet goo as a kid. Best friend I ever had.
Now... I hope this key works.
JIGGLE JIGGLE
KLIK
Yes!
After you!
Thanks a million, Eugene!
Any friend of Goo's is a friend of mine!
Now let's get outta here!
Wait! Wh-what about us?
Huh? ***Nah.*** I wouldn't consider you ***friends.*** More like...***acquaintances*** at best.

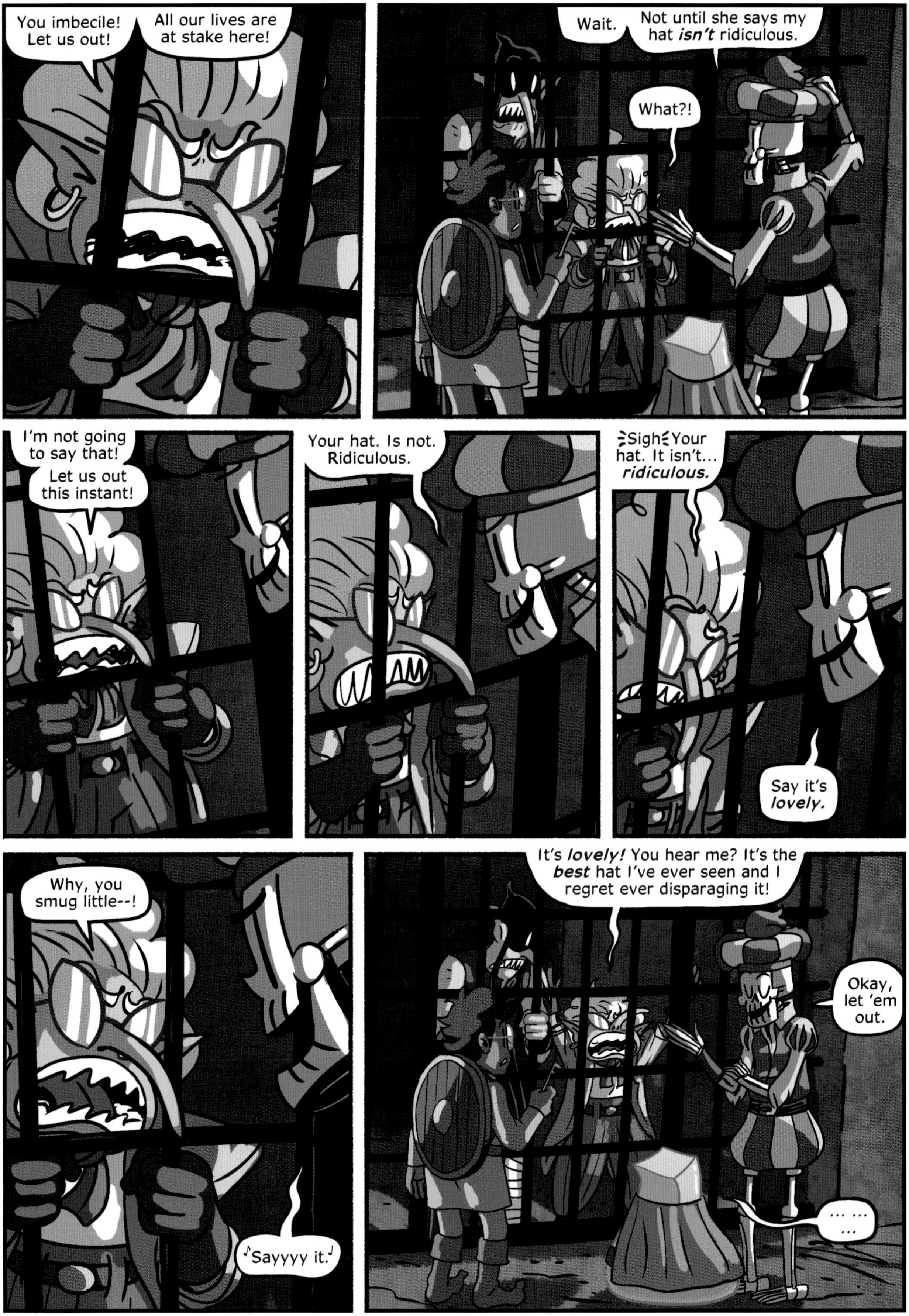

You imbecile! Let us out!
All our lives are at stake here!
Wait.
Not until she says my hat *isn't* ridiculous.
What?!
I'm not going to say that!
Let us out this instant!
Your hat. Is not. Ridiculous.
Sigh Your hat. It isn't... *ridiculous.*
Say it's *lovely.*
Why, you smug little--!
♪Sayyyy it.♪
It's *lovely!* You hear me? It's the *best* hat I've ever seen and I regret ever disparaging it!
Okay, let 'em out.
... ...

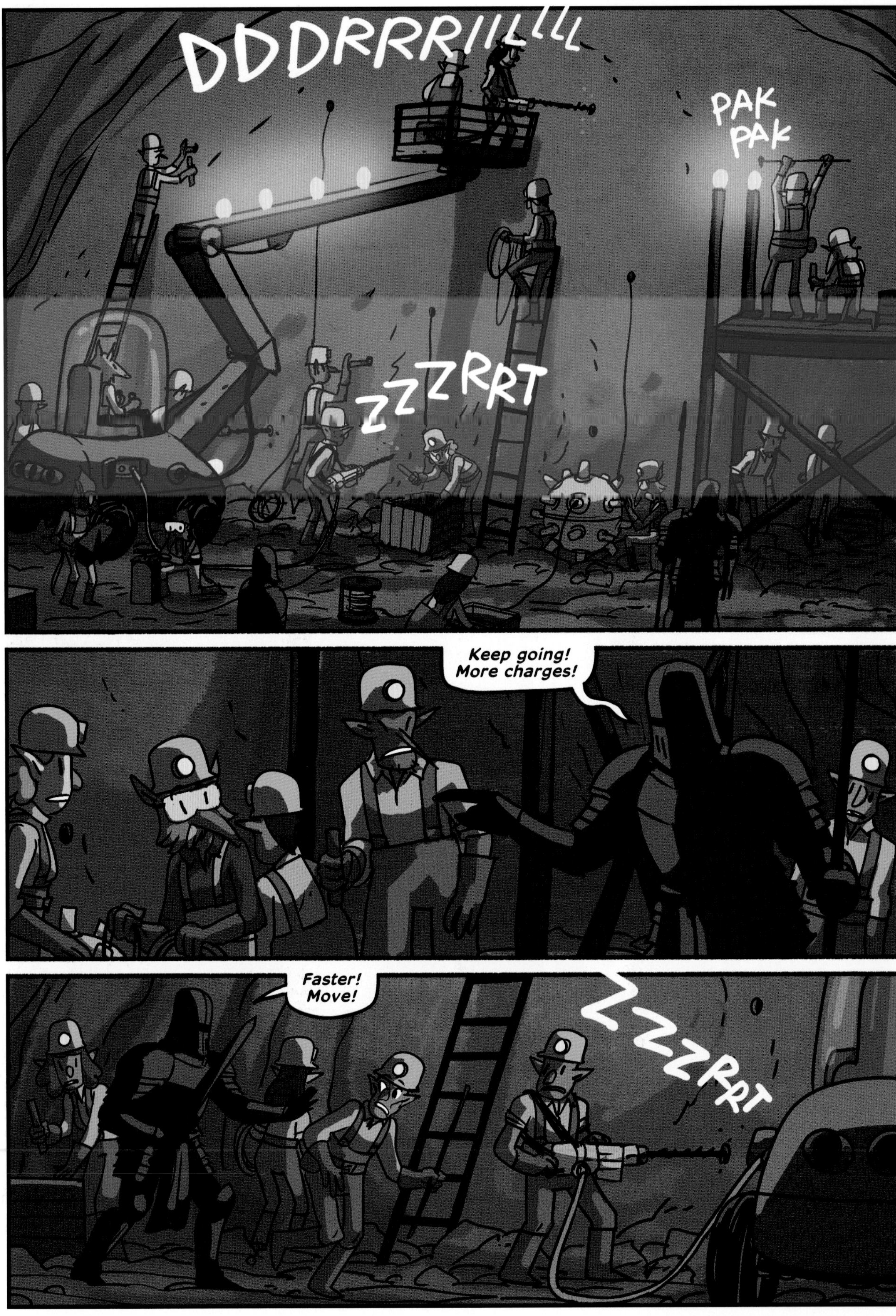
DDDRRRRIIILLLL
PAK PAK
ZZZRRT
Keep going! More charges!
Faster! Move!
ZZZRRT

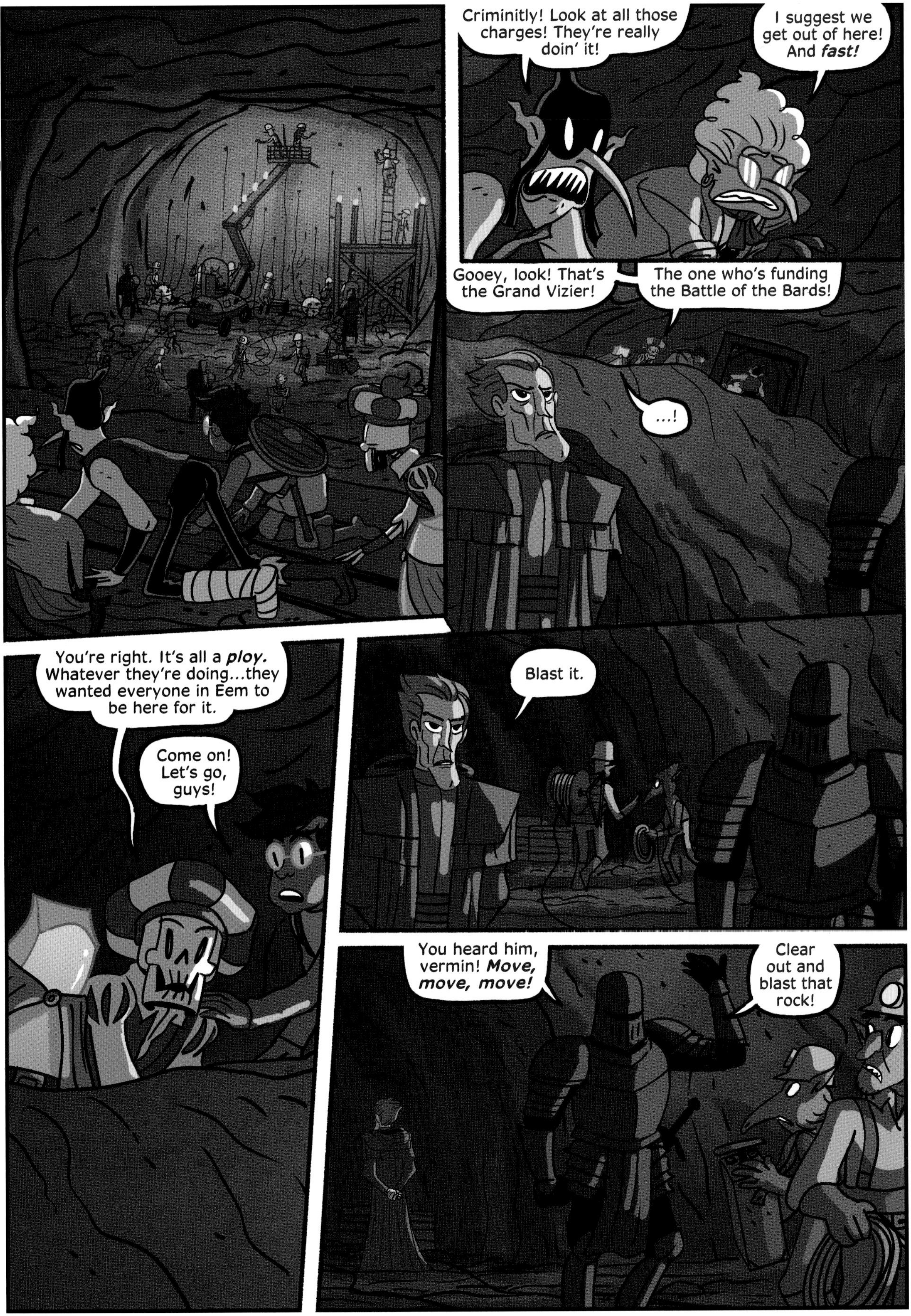
Criminitly! Look at all those charges! They're really doin' it!
I suggest we get out of here! And *fast!*
Gooey, look! That's the Grand Vizier!
The one who's funding the Battle of the Bards!
...!
You're right. It's all a *ploy.* Whatever they're doing...they wanted everyone in Eem to be here for it.
Come on! Let's go, guys!
Blast it.
You heard him, vermin! ***Move, move, move!***
Clear out and blast that rock!

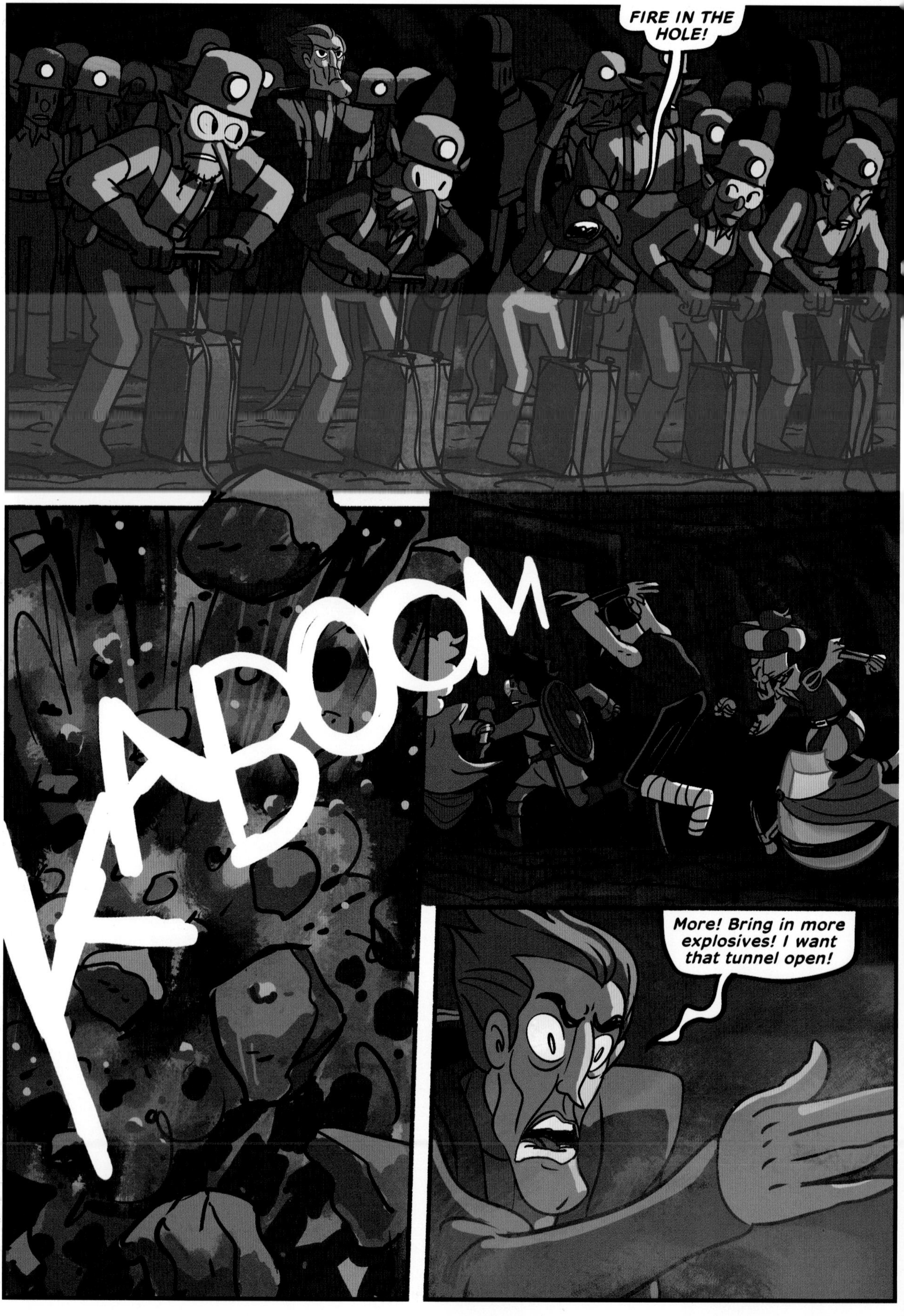
FIRE IN THE HOLE!
KABOOM
More! Bring in more explosives! I want that tunnel open!

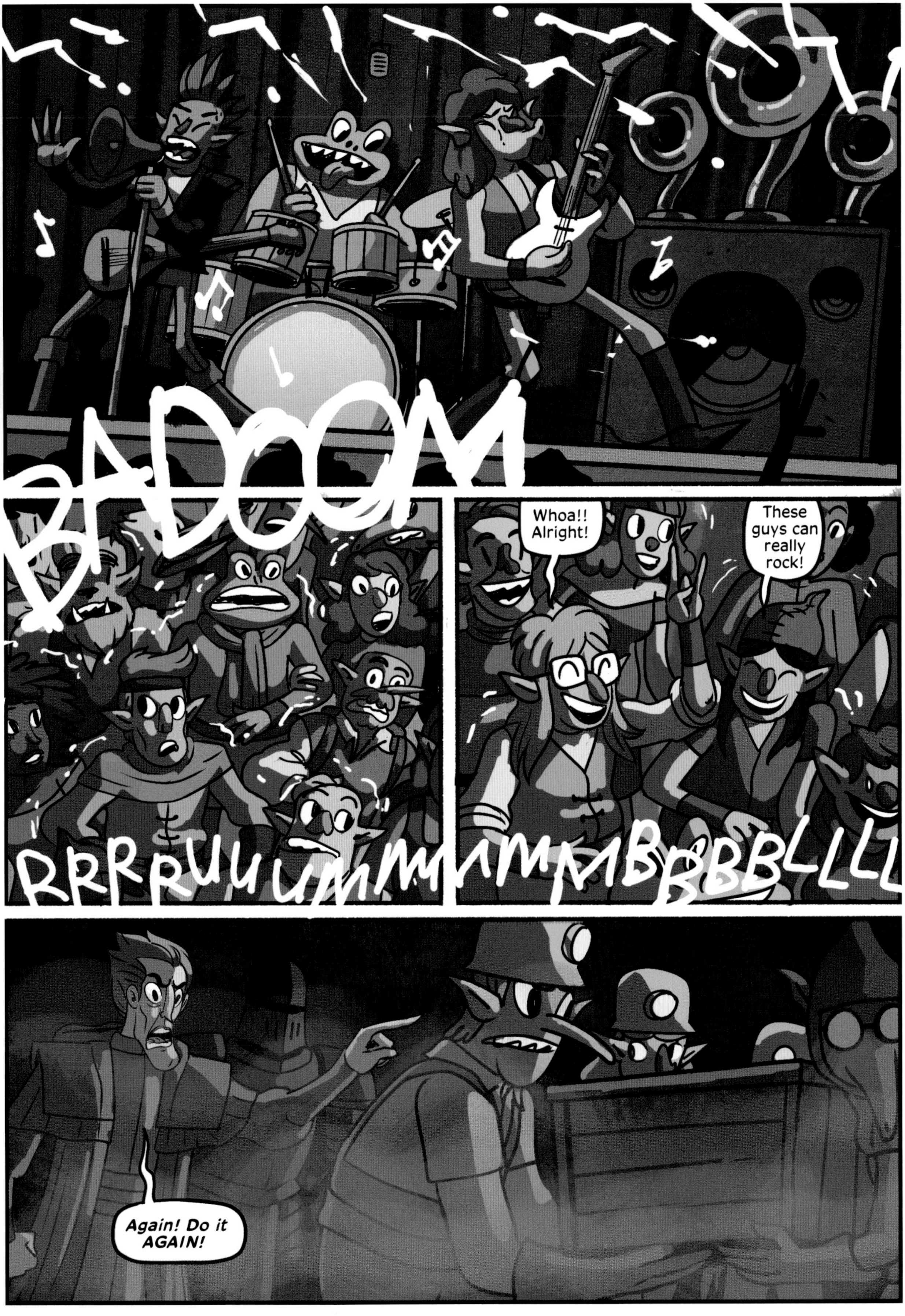
BADOOM
Whoa!! Alright!
These guys can really rock!
RRRRUUUUMMMMMMBBBBLLLL
Again! Do it AGAIN!

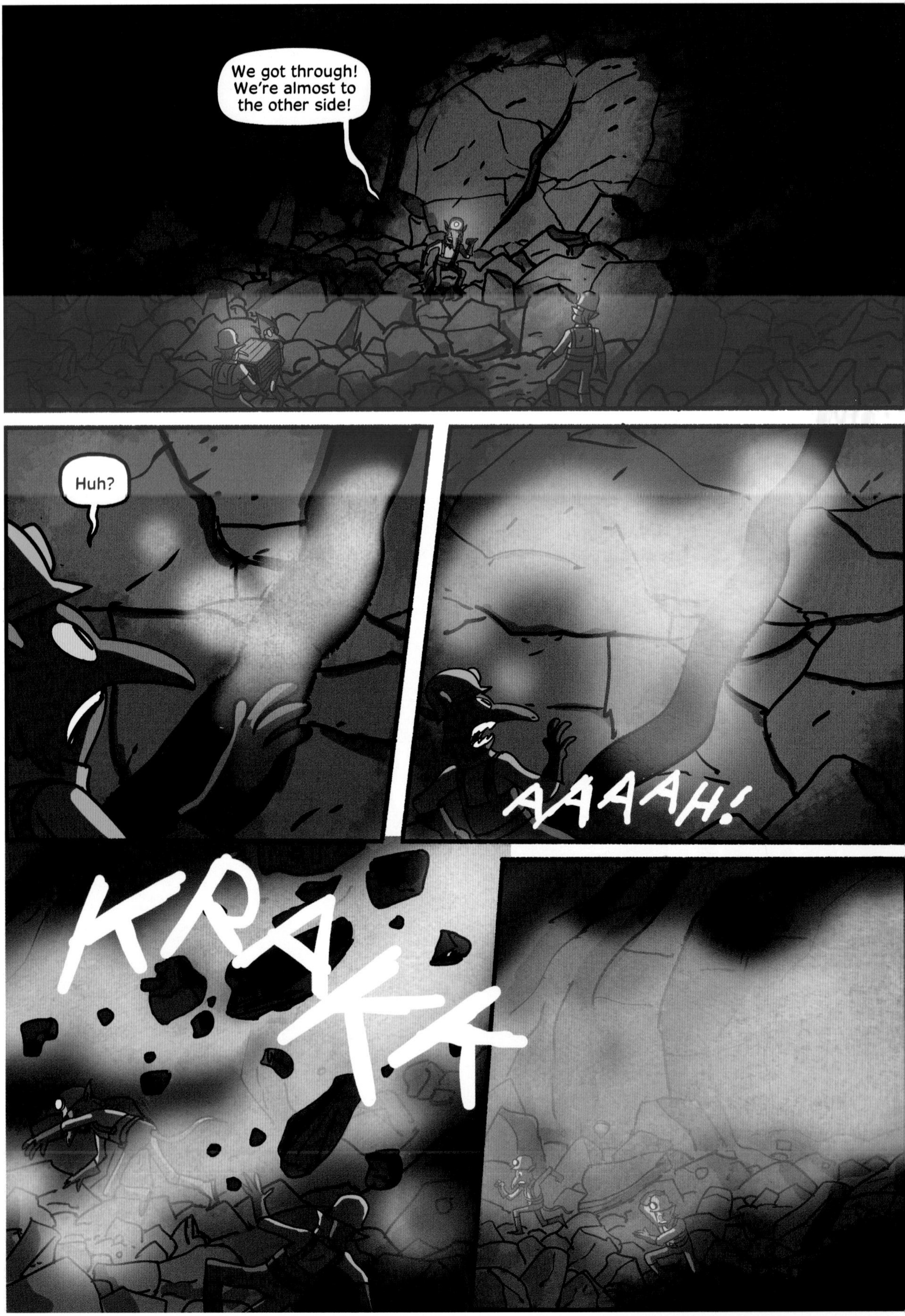
We got through! We're almost to the other side!
Huh?
AAAAH!
KRAKK

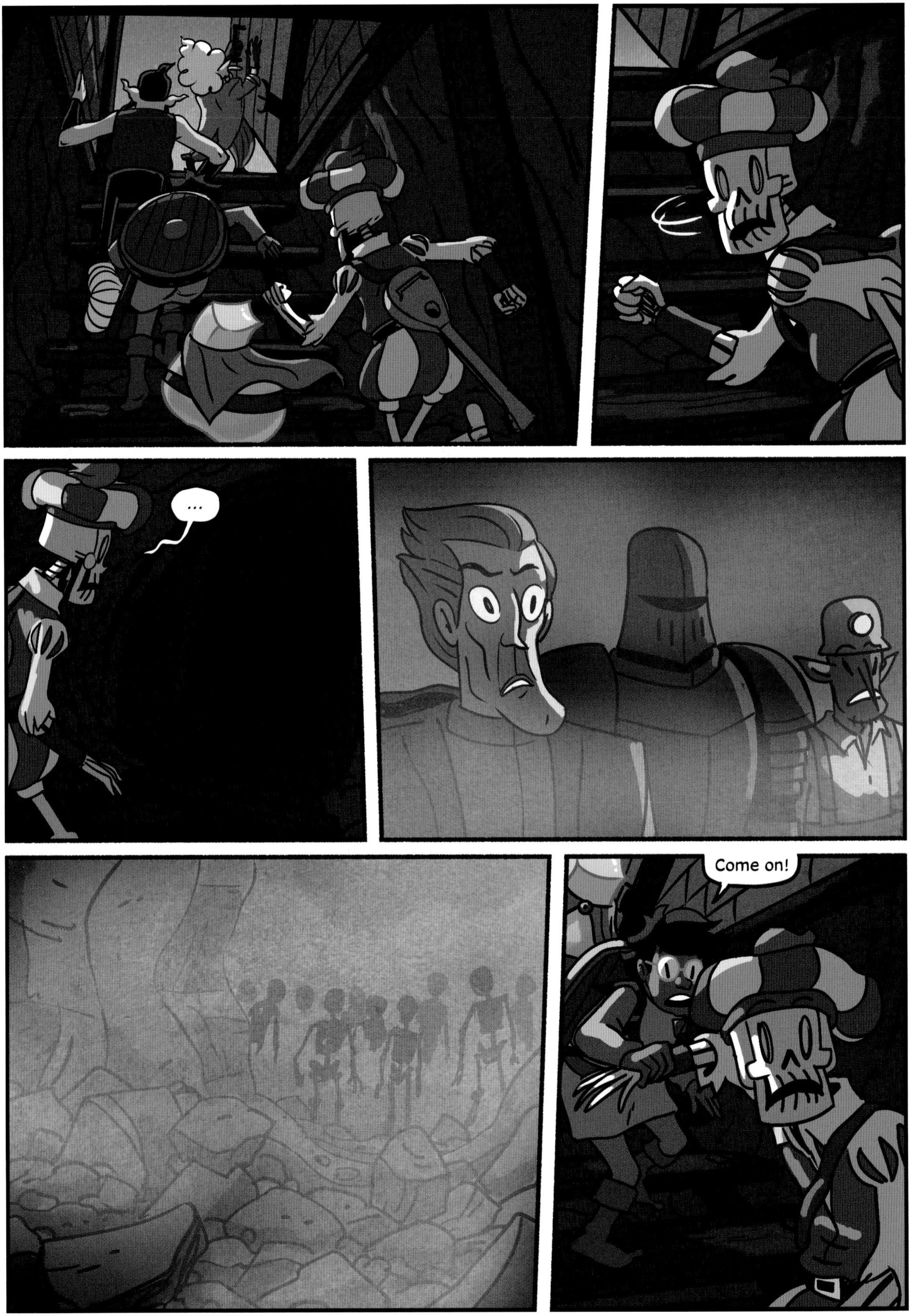
...
Come on!

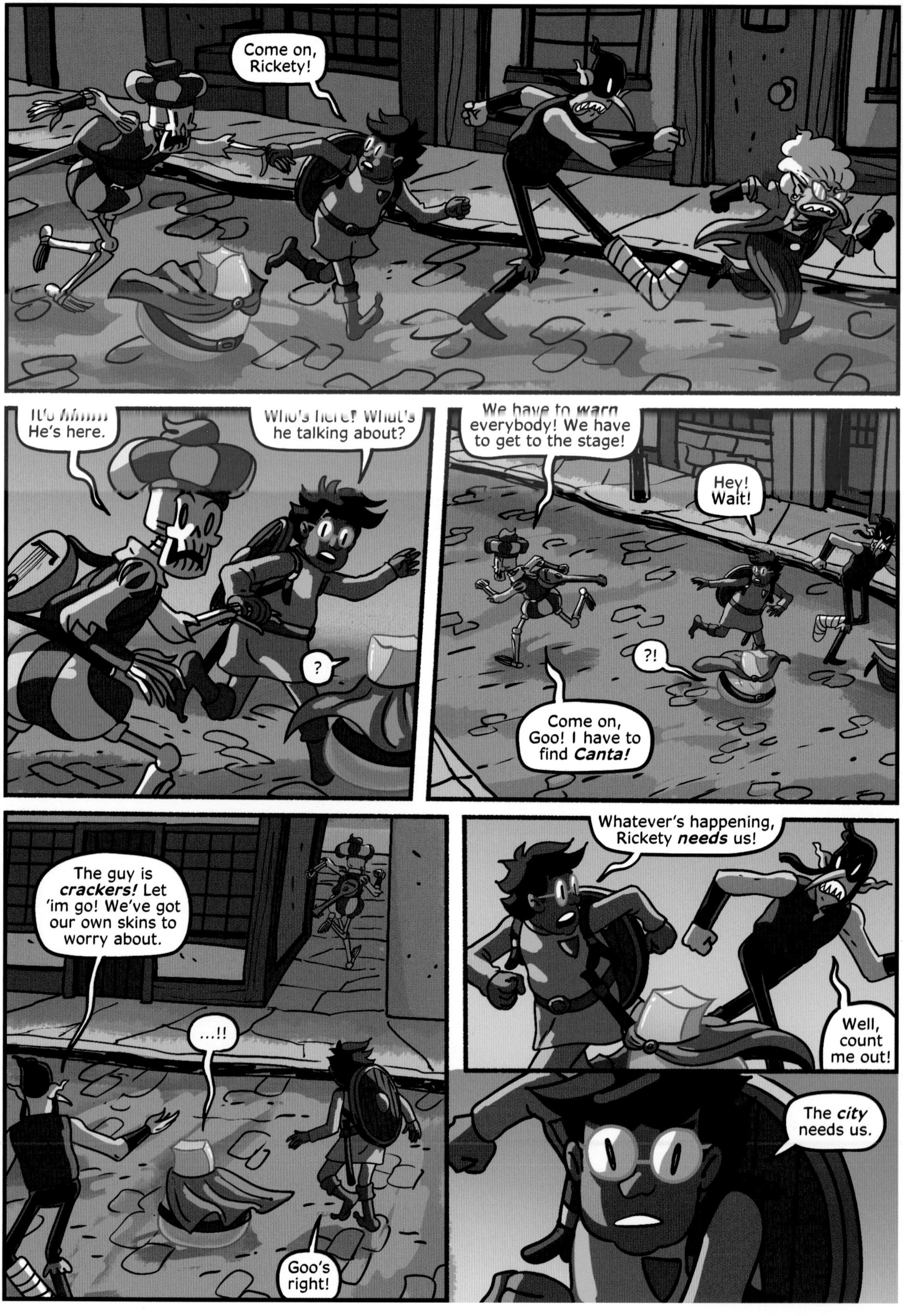
Come on, Rickety!
He's here.
Who's here? What's he talking about?
?
We have to warn everybody! We have to get to the stage!
Hey! Wait!
?!
Come on, Goo! I have to find *Canta!*
The guy is *crackers!* Let 'im go! We've got our own skins to worry about.
...!!
Goo's right!
Whatever's happening, Rickety *needs* us!
Well, count me out!
The *city* needs us.

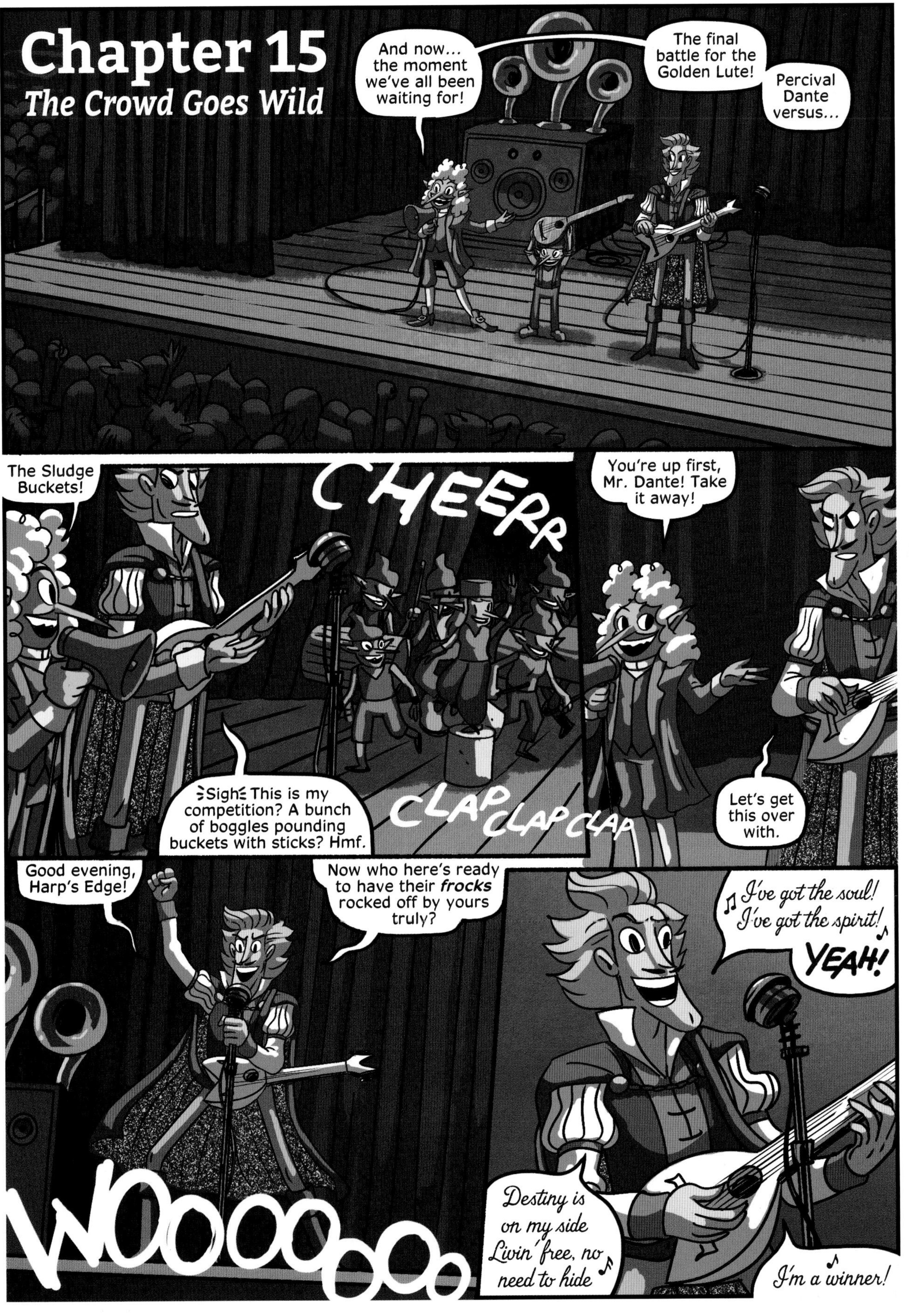
Chapter 15
The Crowd Goes Wild
And now... the moment we've all been waiting for!
The final battle for the Golden Lute!
Percival Dante versus...
The Sludge Buckets!
CHEERR
ⵈSighⵈ This is my competition? A bunch of boggles pounding buckets with sticks? Hmf.
CLAP CLAP CLAP
You're up first, Mr. Dante! Take it away!
Let's get this over with.
Good evening, Harp's Edge!
Now who here's ready to have their *frocks* rocked off by yours truly?
WOOOOOOO
♫ I've got the soul! I've got the spirit! ♪
YEAH!
Destiny is on my side
Livin' free, no need to hide ♪
I'm a winner! ♪

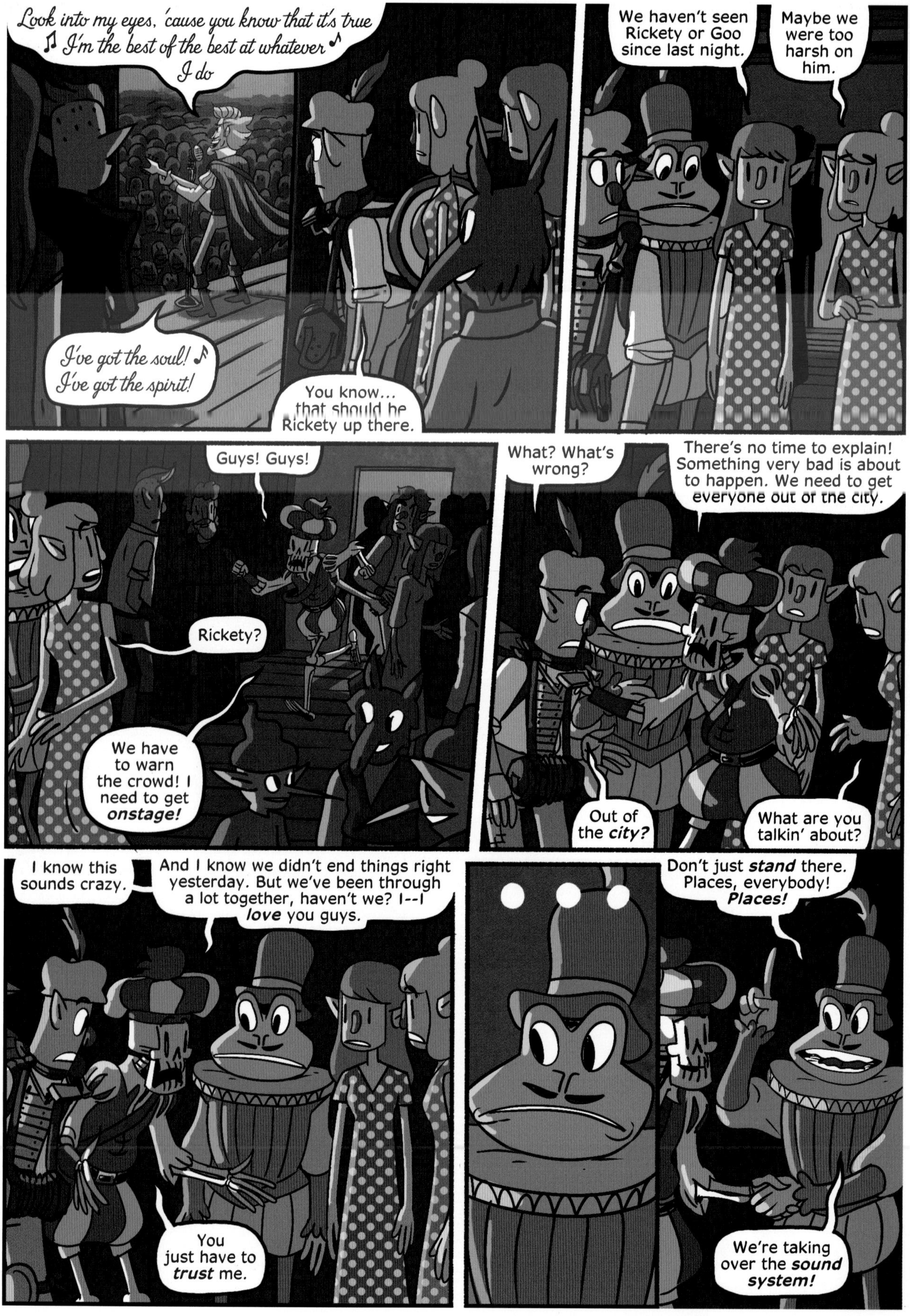

Look into my eyes, 'cause you know that it's true ♫ I'm the best of the best at whatever ♪ I do
I've got the soul! ♪ I've got the spirit!
You know... that should be Rickety up there.
We haven't seen Rickety or Goo since last night.
Maybe we were too harsh on him.
Guys! Guys!
Rickety?
We have to warn the crowd! I need to get *onstage!*
What? What's wrong?
There's no time to explain! Something very bad is about to happen. We need to get everyone out of the city.
Out of the *city?*
What are you talkin' about?
I know this sounds crazy.
And I know we didn't end things right yesterday. But we've been through a lot together, haven't we? I--I *love* you guys.
You just have to *trust* me.
Don't just *stand* there. Places, everybody! *Places!*
We're taking over the *sound system!*

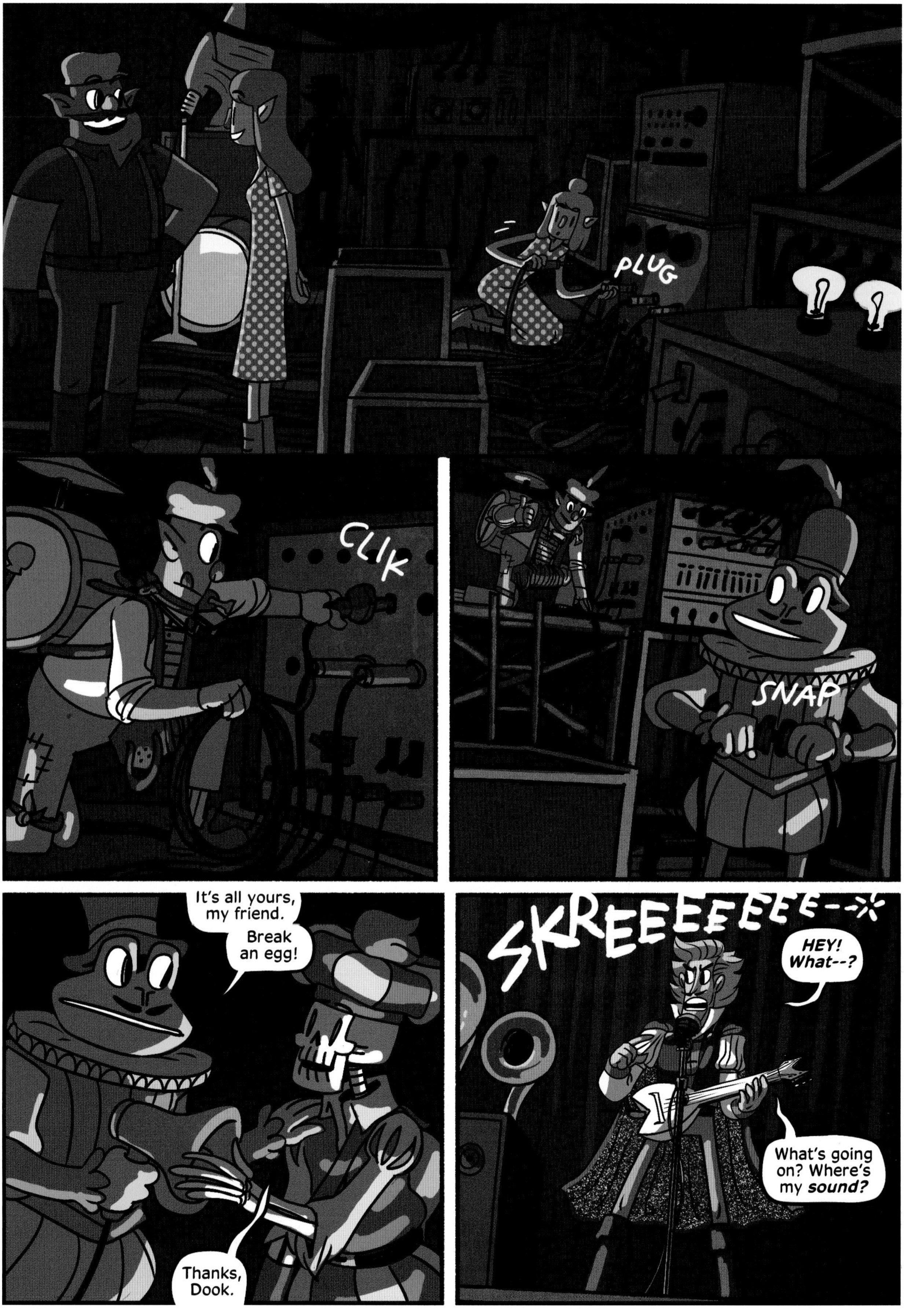
PLUG
CLIK
SNAP
It's all yours, my friend.
Break an egg!
Thanks, Dook.
SKREEEEEEE--
HEY! What--?
What's going on? Where's my *sound?*

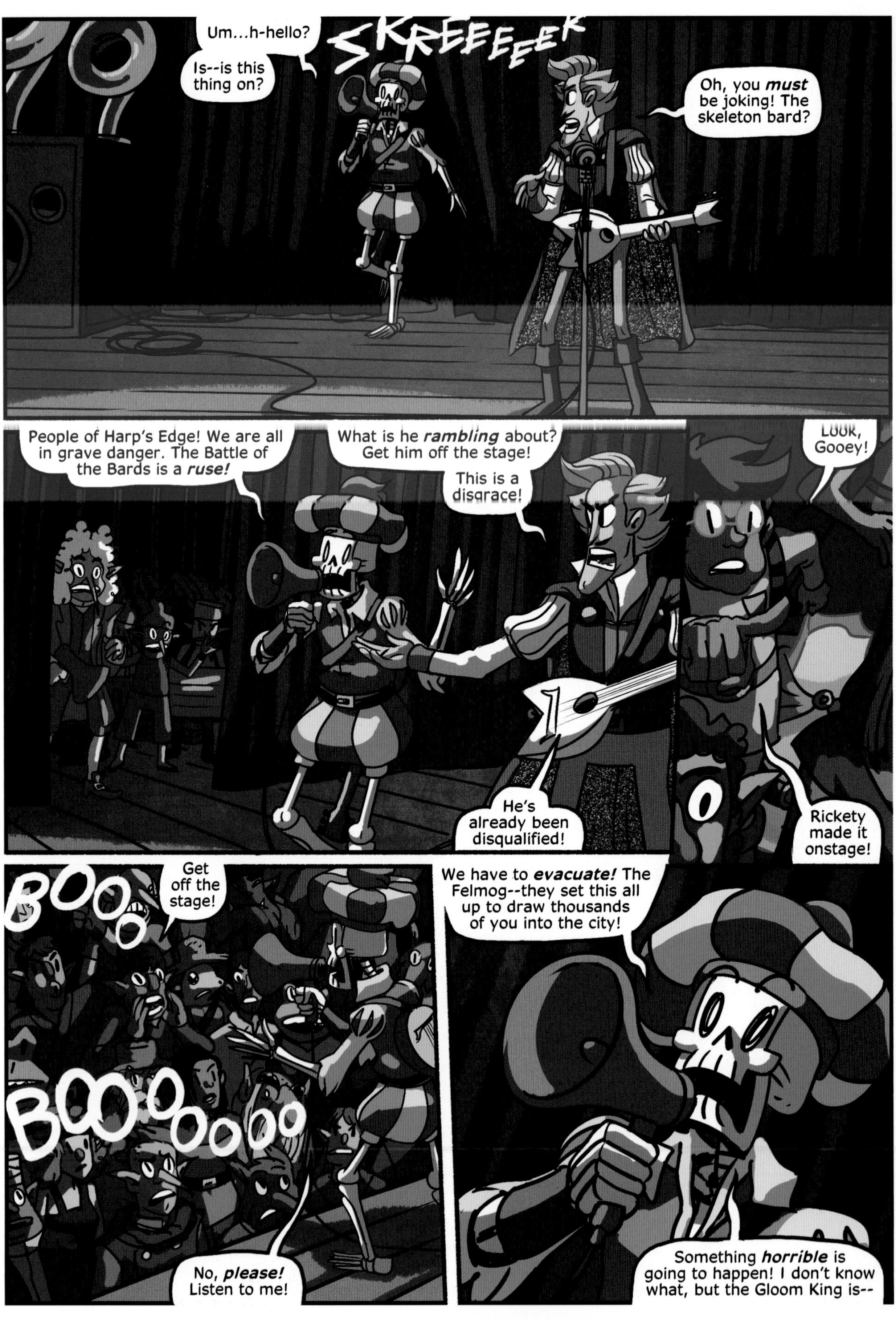
Um...h-hello?
Is--is this thing on?
SKREEEEEEK
Oh, you *must* be joking! The skeleton bard?
People of Harp's Edge! We are all in grave danger. The Battle of the Bards is a *ruse!*
What is he *rambling* about? Get him off the stage!
This is a disgrace!
He's already been disqualified!
Look, Gooey!
Rickety made it onstage!
BOOO
Get off the stage!
BOOOOOOOO
No, *please!* Listen to me!
We have to *evacuate!* The Felmog--they set this all up to draw thousands of you into the city!
Something *horrible* is going to happen! I don't know what, but the Gloom King is--

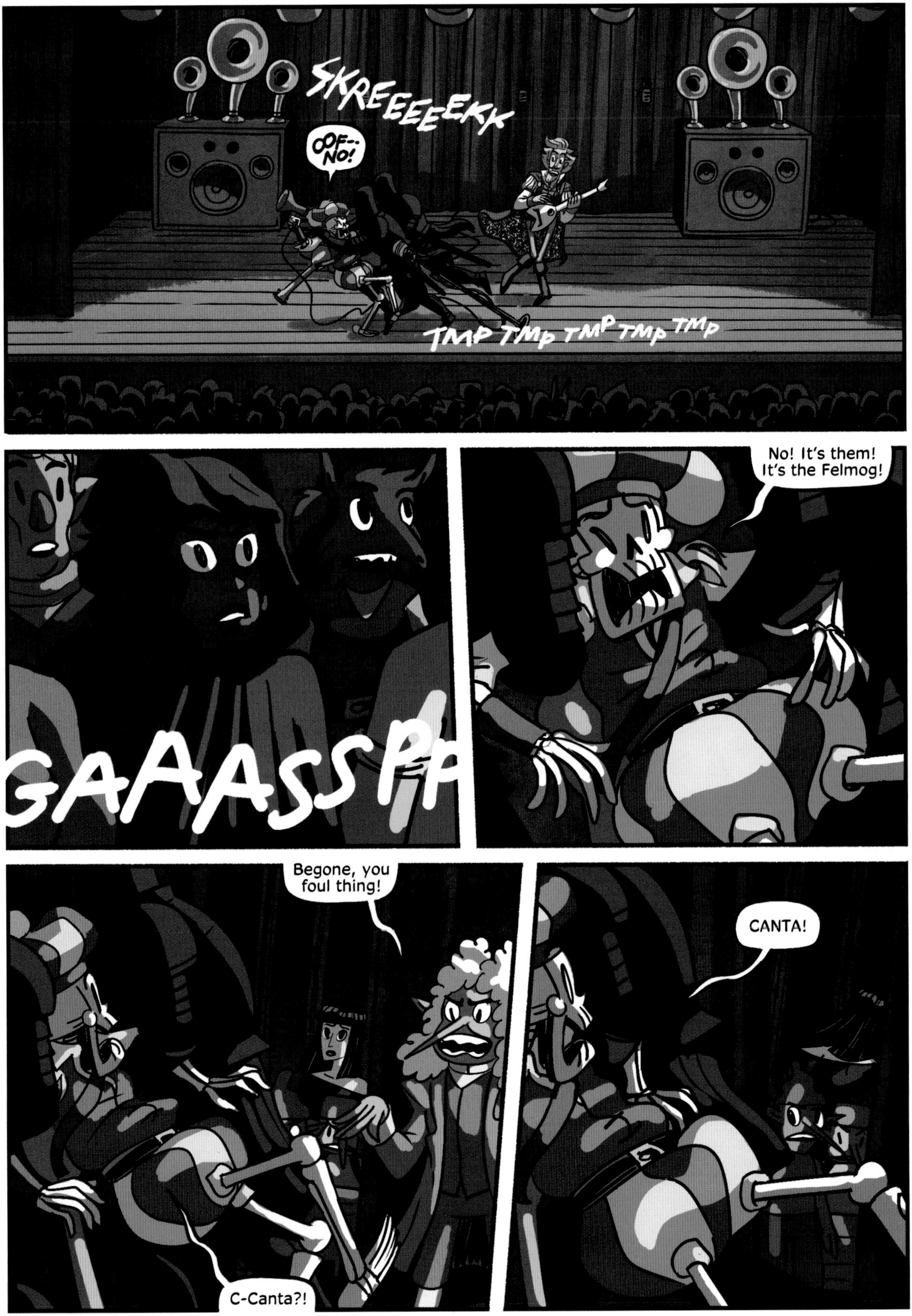

SKREEEEEEKK
OOF-- NO!
TMP TMP TMP TMP TMP
GAAASSPP
No! It's them! It's the Felmog!
Begone, you foul thing!
C-Canta?!
CANTA!

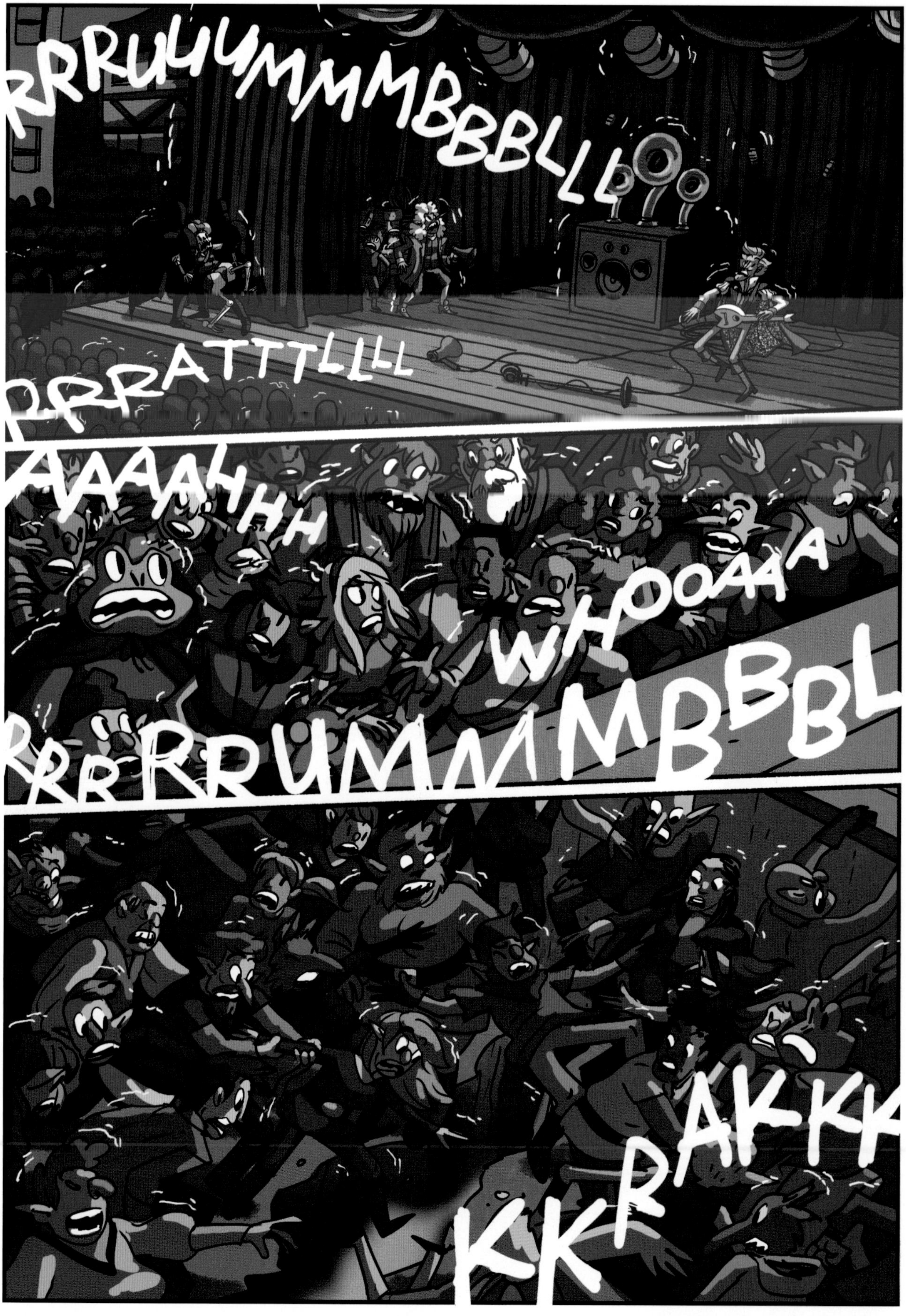
RRRUUUMMMBBBLLL
RRRATTTLLL
AAAAHHH
WHOOAAA
RRRRRUMMMBBBL
KKRAKKK

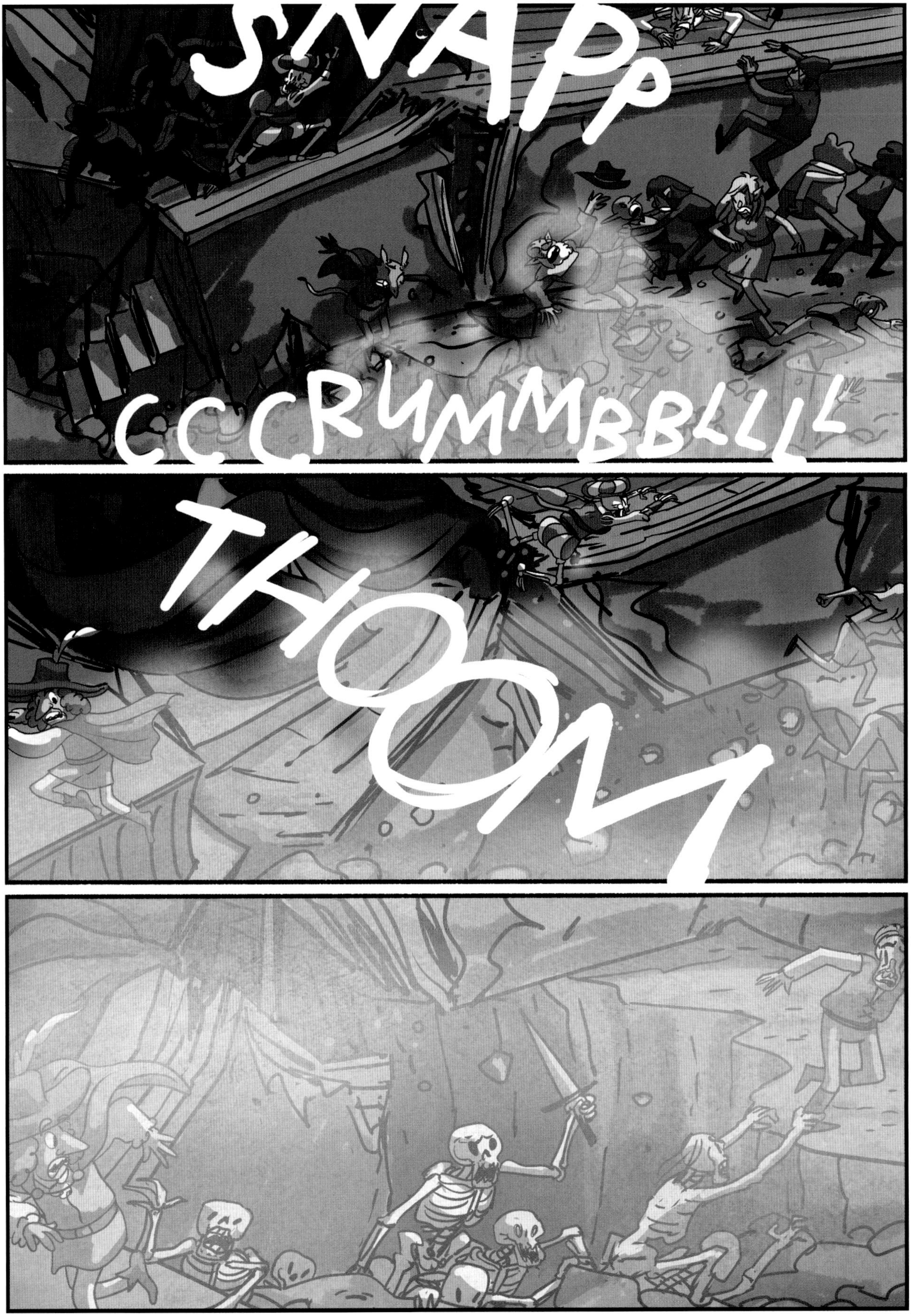
SNAPP
CCCRUMMBBLLLL
THOOM

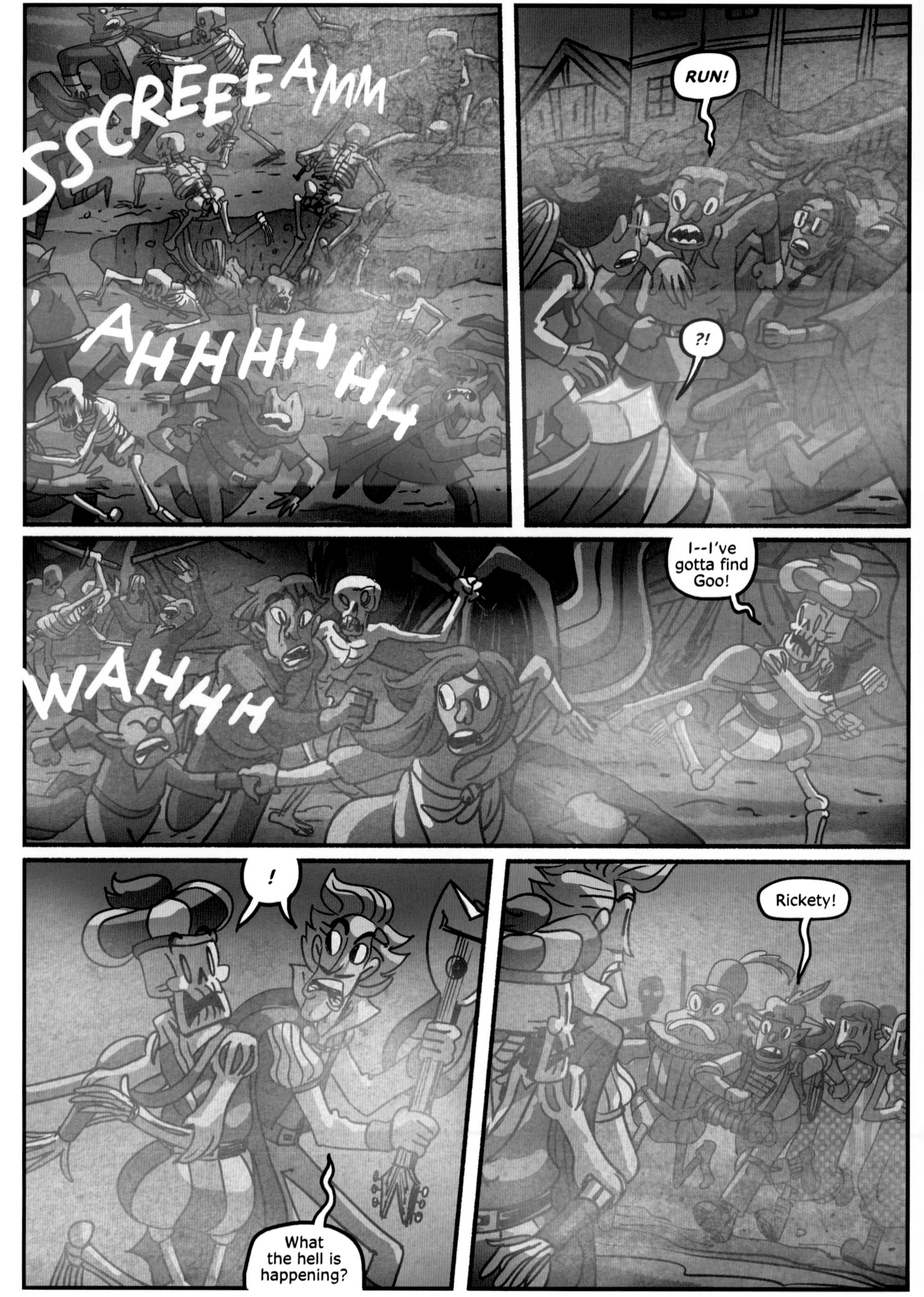
SSCREEEAMM
AHHHHHH
RUN!
?!
WAHHH
I--I've gotta find Goo!
!
What the hell is happening?
Rickety!

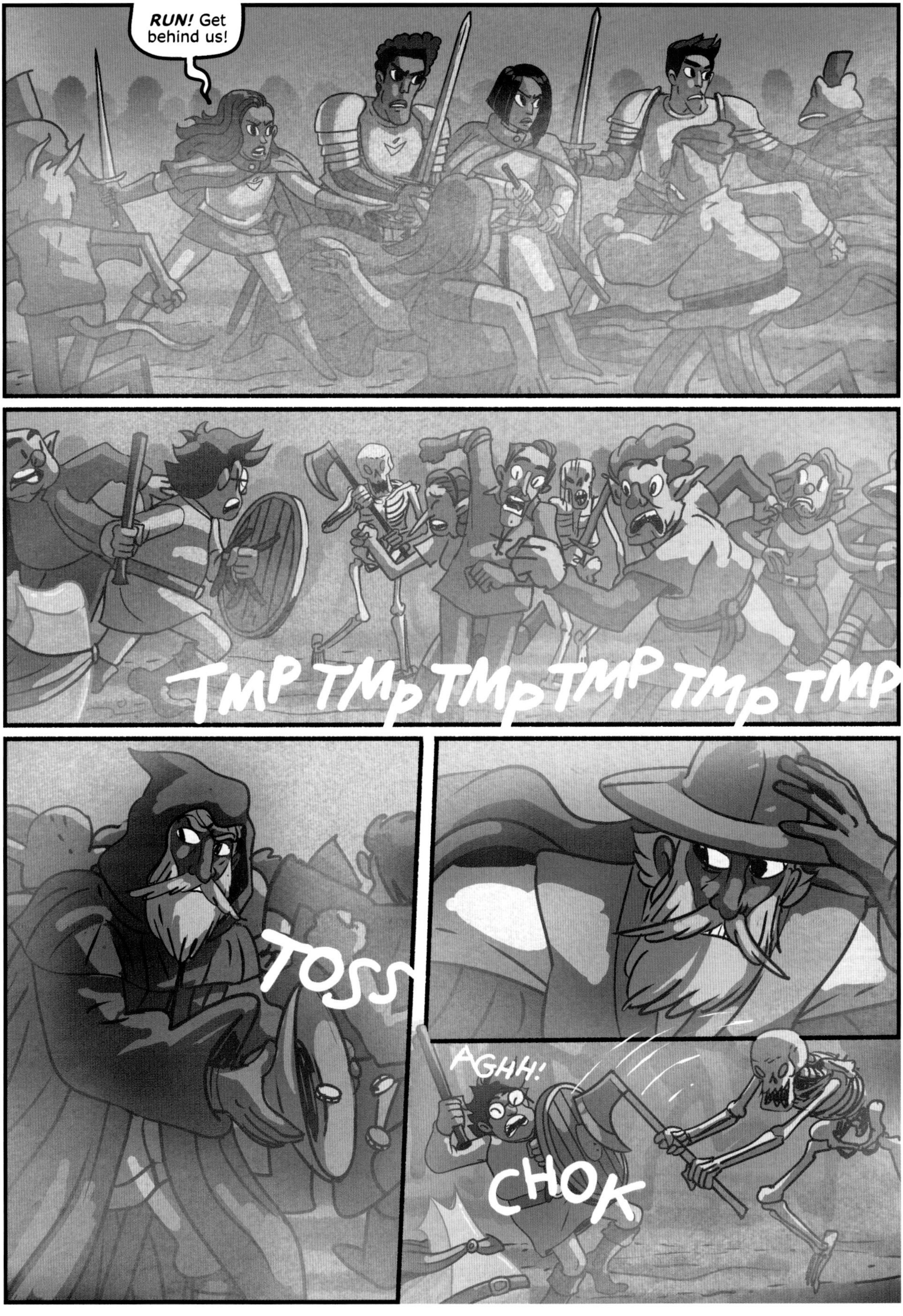
RUN! Get behind us!
TMP TMP TMP TMP TMP TMP
TOSS
AGHH!
CHOK

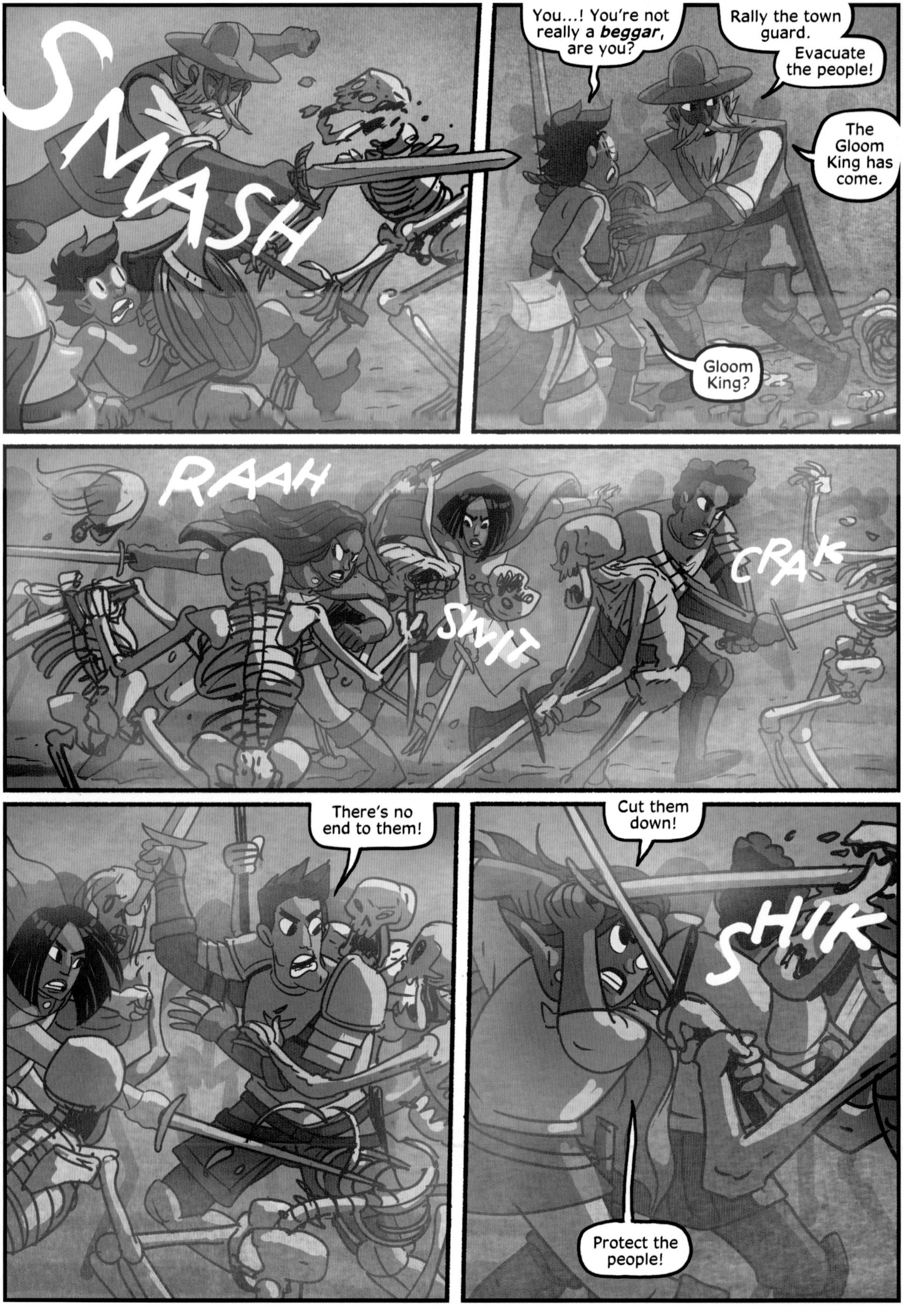

SMASH
You...! You're not really a *beggar*, are you?
Rally the town guard.
Evacuate the people!
The Gloom King has come.
Gloom King?
RAAH
SWIT
CRAK
There's no end to them!
Cut them down!
SHIK
Protect the people!

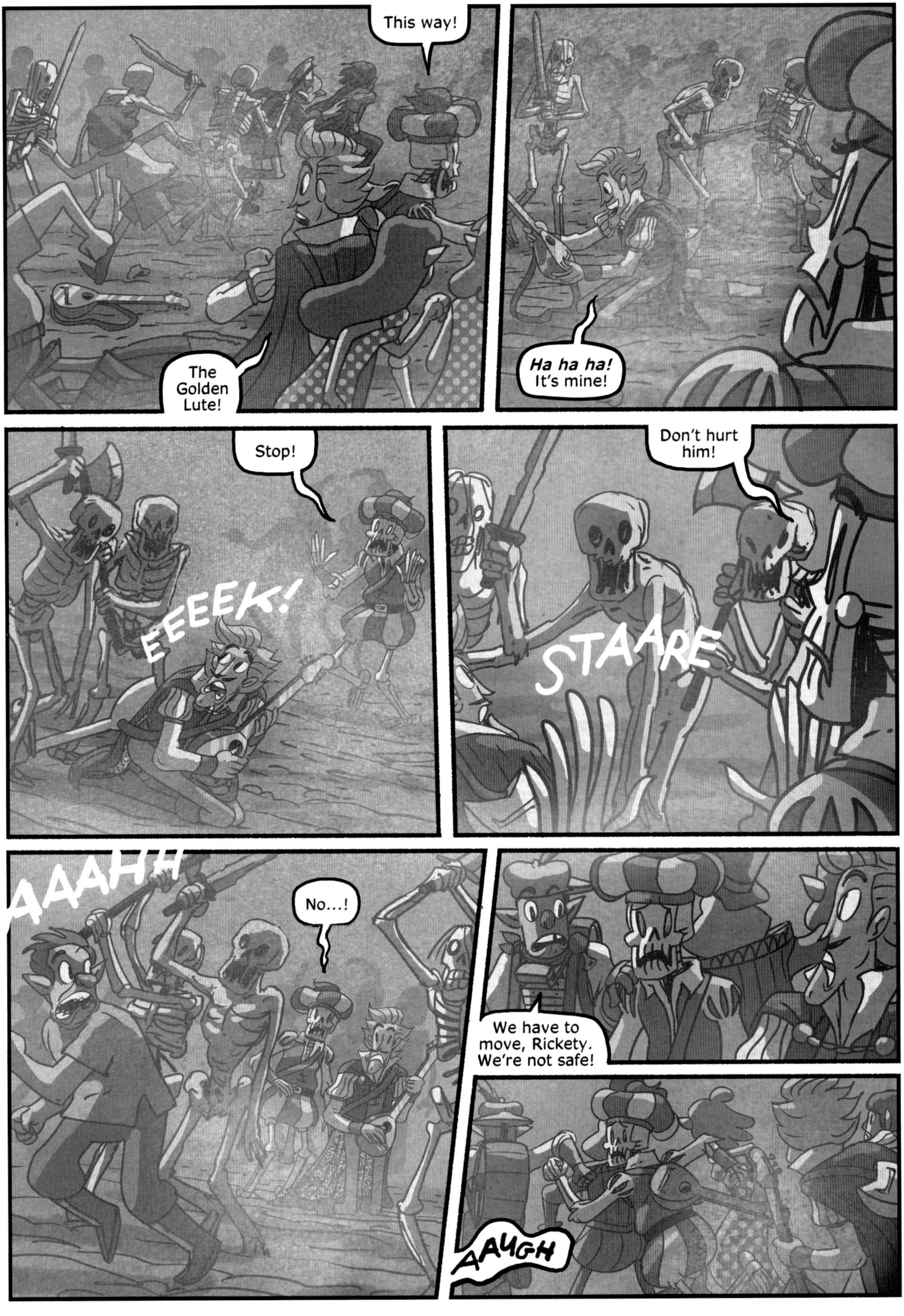
This way!
The Golden Lute!
Ha ha ha! It's mine!
Stop!
EEEEK!
Don't hurt him!
STAARE
AAAAHH
No...!
We have to move, Rickety. We're not safe!
AAUGH

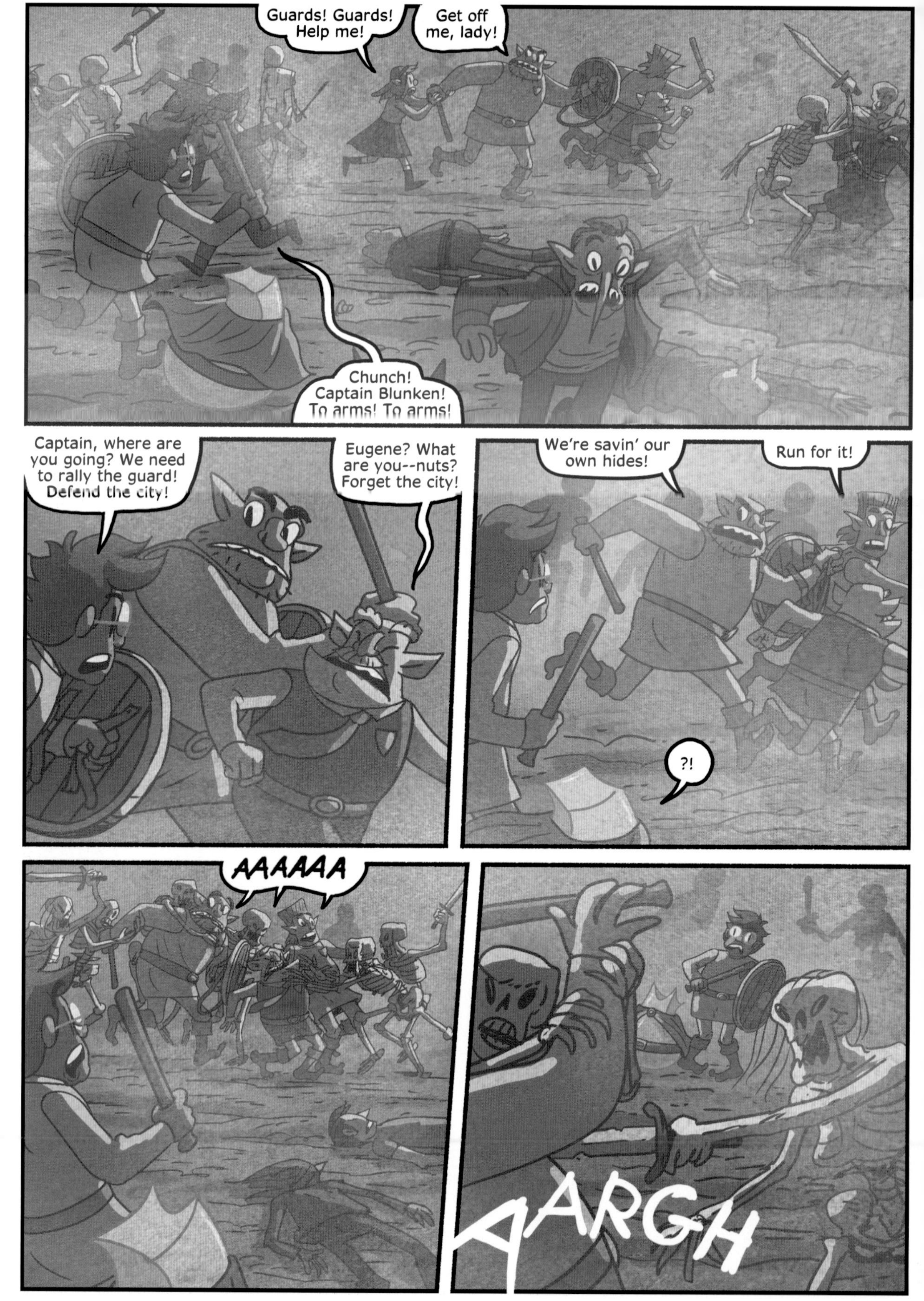
Guards! Guards! Help me!
Get off me, lady!
Chunch! Captain Blunken! To arms! To arms!
Captain, where are you going? We need to rally the guard! Defend the city!
Eugene? What are you--nuts? Forget the city!
We're savin' our own hides!
Run for it!
?!
AAAAAA
AARGH

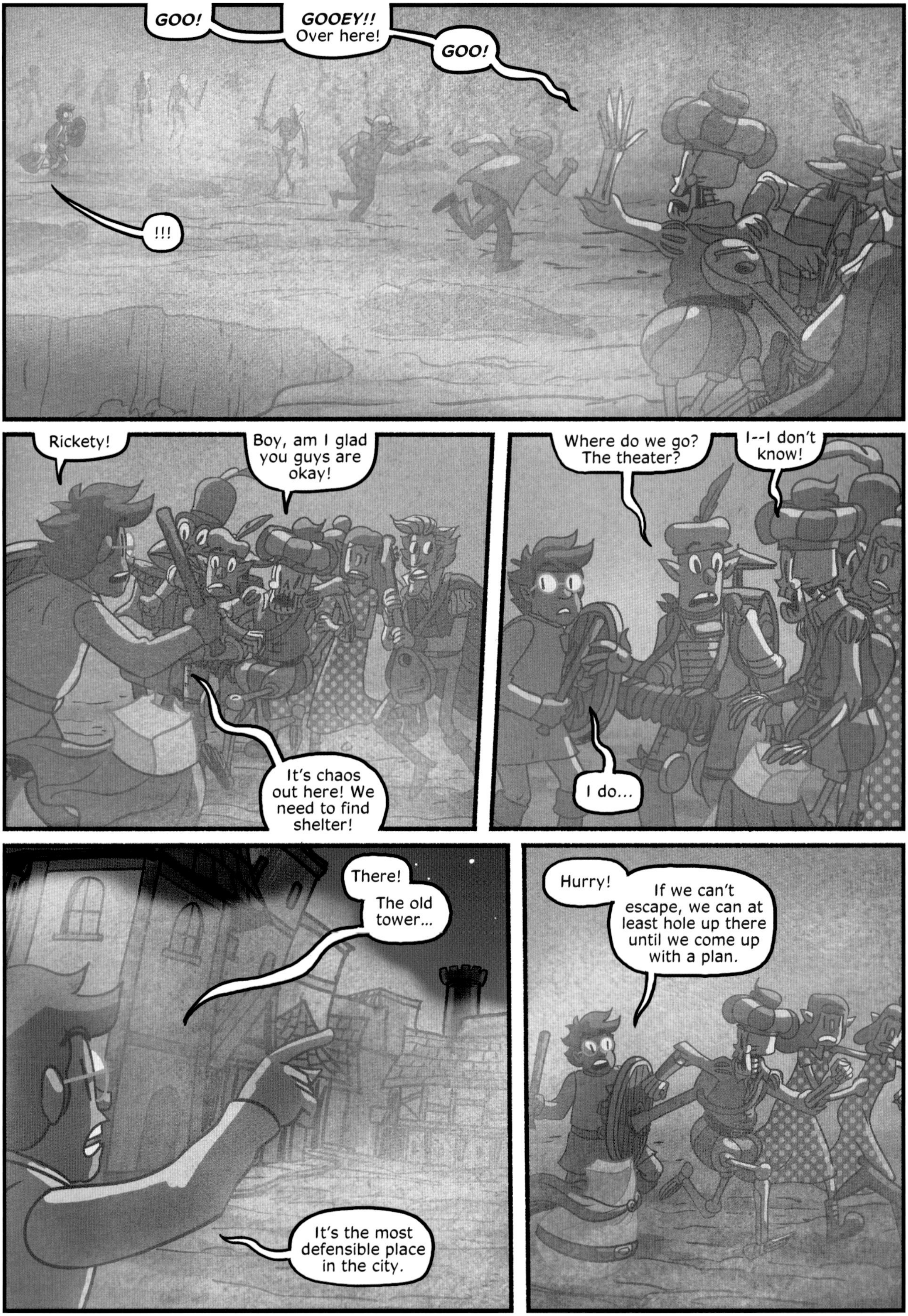
GOO!
GOOEY!! Over here!
GOO!
!!!
Rickety!
Boy, am I glad you guys are okay!
It's chaos out here! We need to find shelter!
Where do we go? The theater?
I--I don't know!
I do...
There!
The old tower...
It's the most defensible place in the city.
Hurry!
If we can't escape, we can at least hole up there until we come up with a plan.

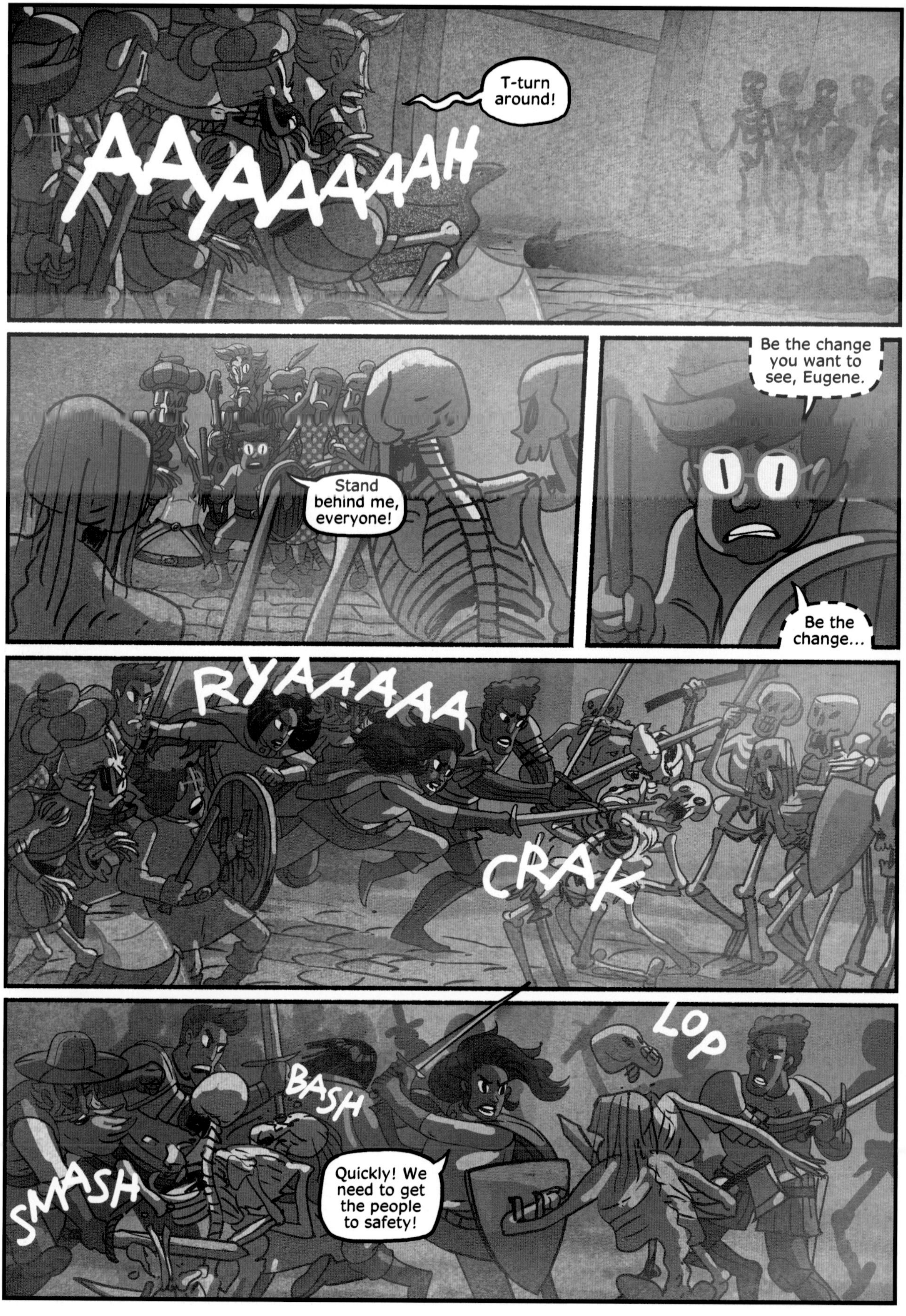
T-turn around!
AAAAAAAAH
Stand behind me, everyone!
Be the change you want to see, Eugene.
Be the change...
RYAAAAA
CRAK
LOP
BASH
SMASH
Quickly! We need to get the people to safety!

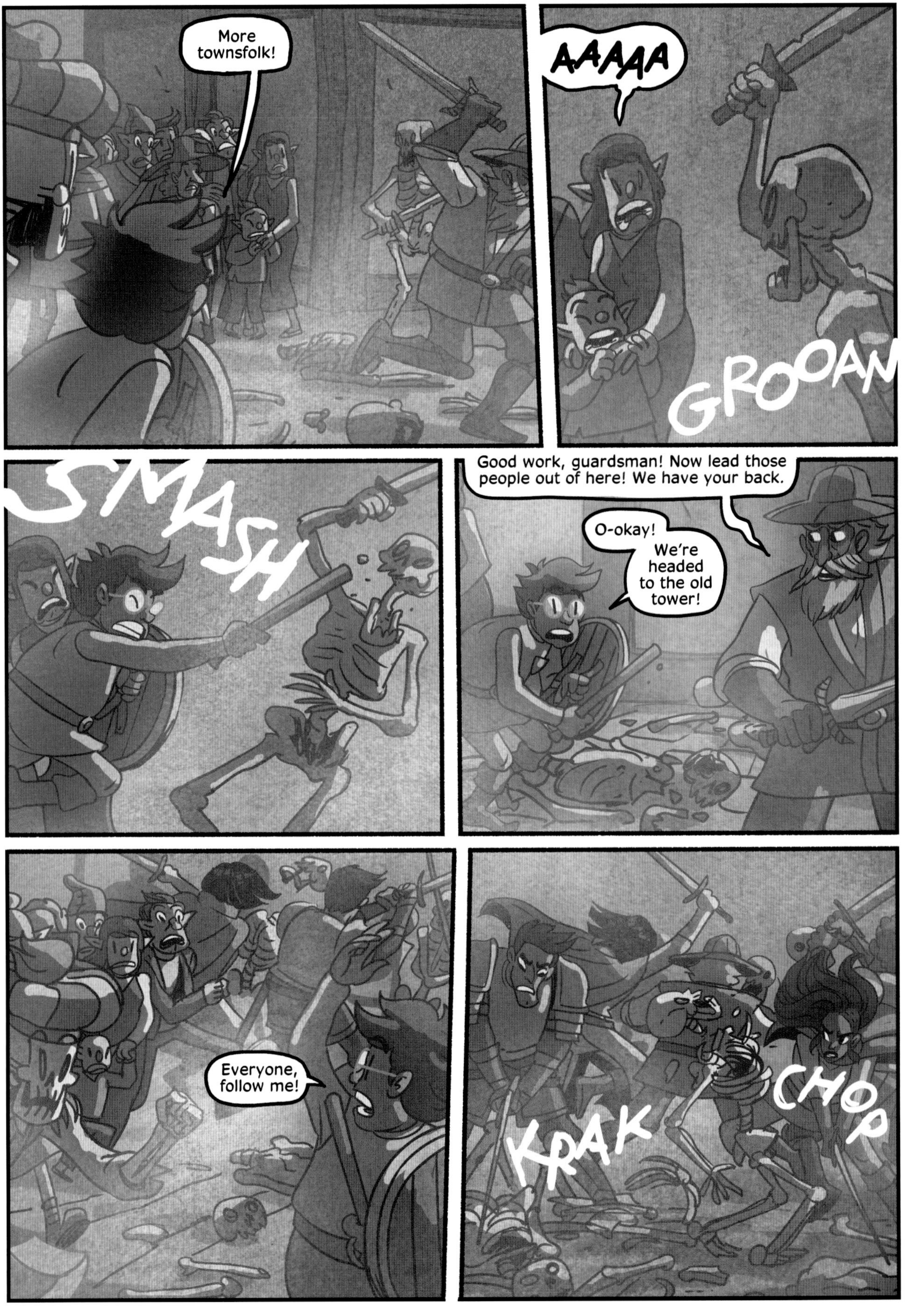
More townsfolk!
AAAAA
GROOAN
SMASH
Good work, guardsman! Now lead those people out of here! We have your back.
O-okay!
We're headed to the old tower!
Everyone, follow me!
KRAK
CHOP

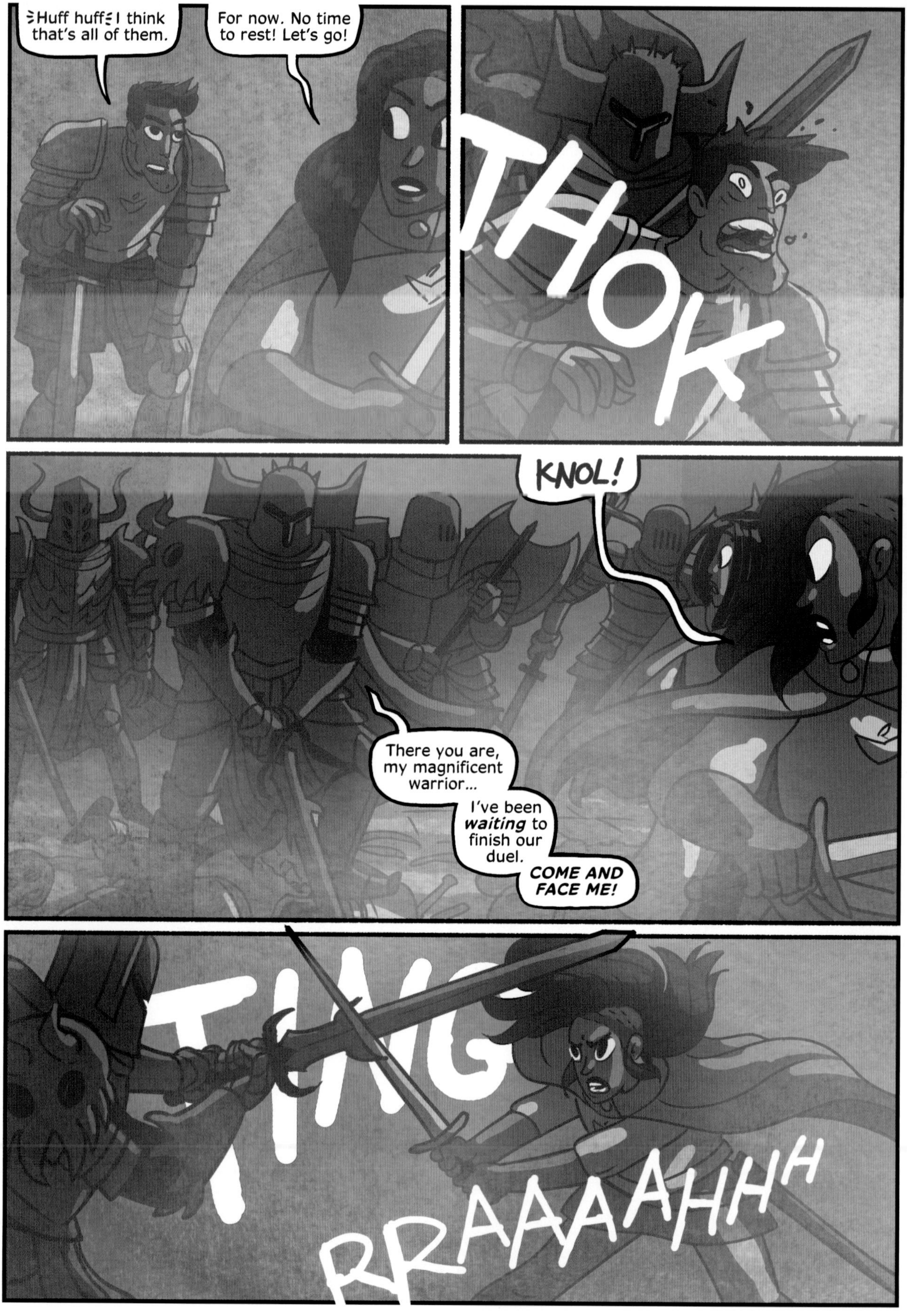

Huff huff I think that's all of them.
For now. No time to rest! Let's go!
THOK
KNOL!
There you are, my magnificent warrior...
I've been *waiting* to finish our duel.
COME AND FACE ME!
TING
RRAAAAHHH

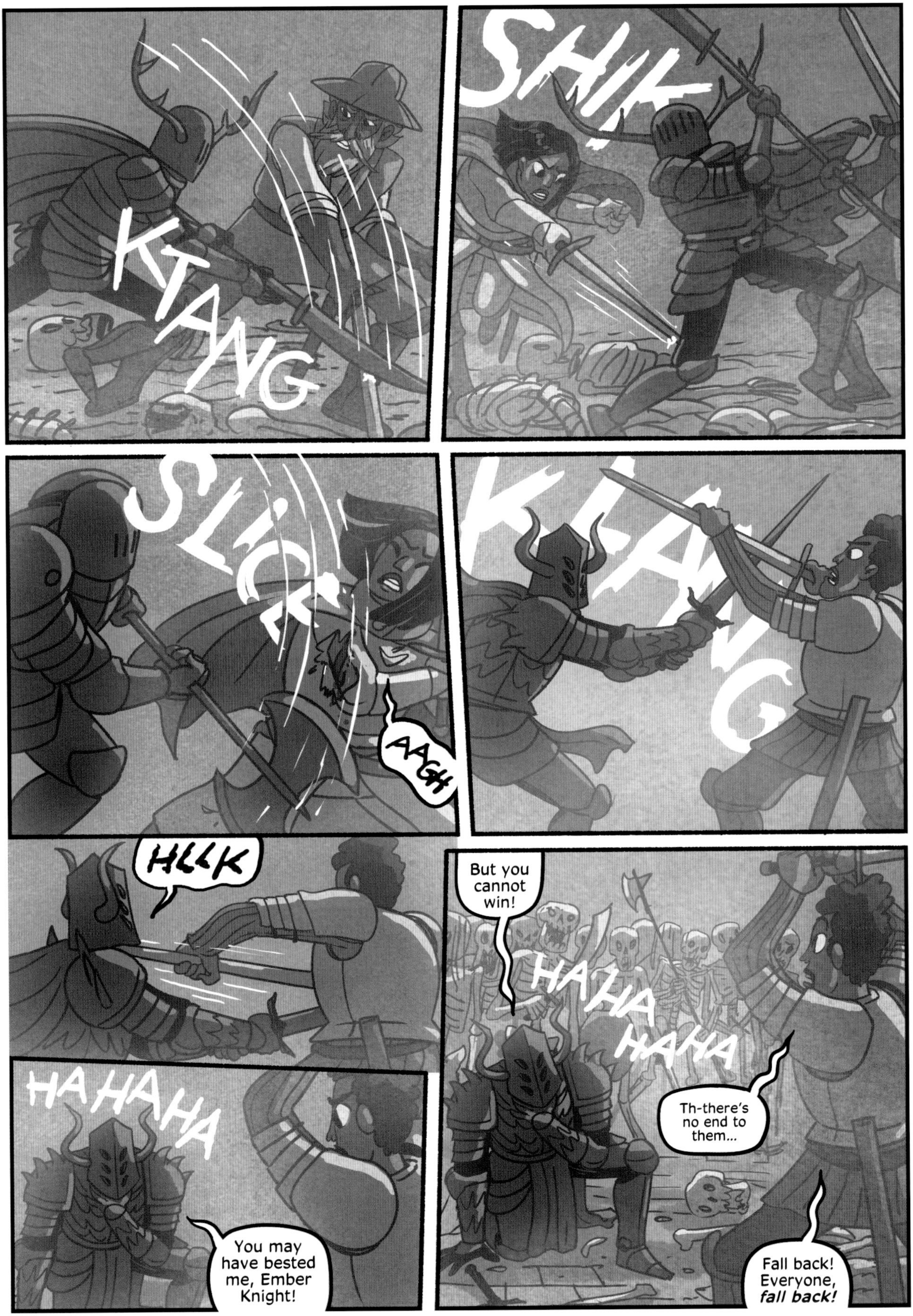
KTANG
SHIK
SLICE
AAGH
KTANG
HLLK
But you cannot win!
HAHA HAHA
Th-there's no end to them...
Fall back! Everyone, *fall back!*
HAHAHAHA
You may have bested me, Ember Knight!

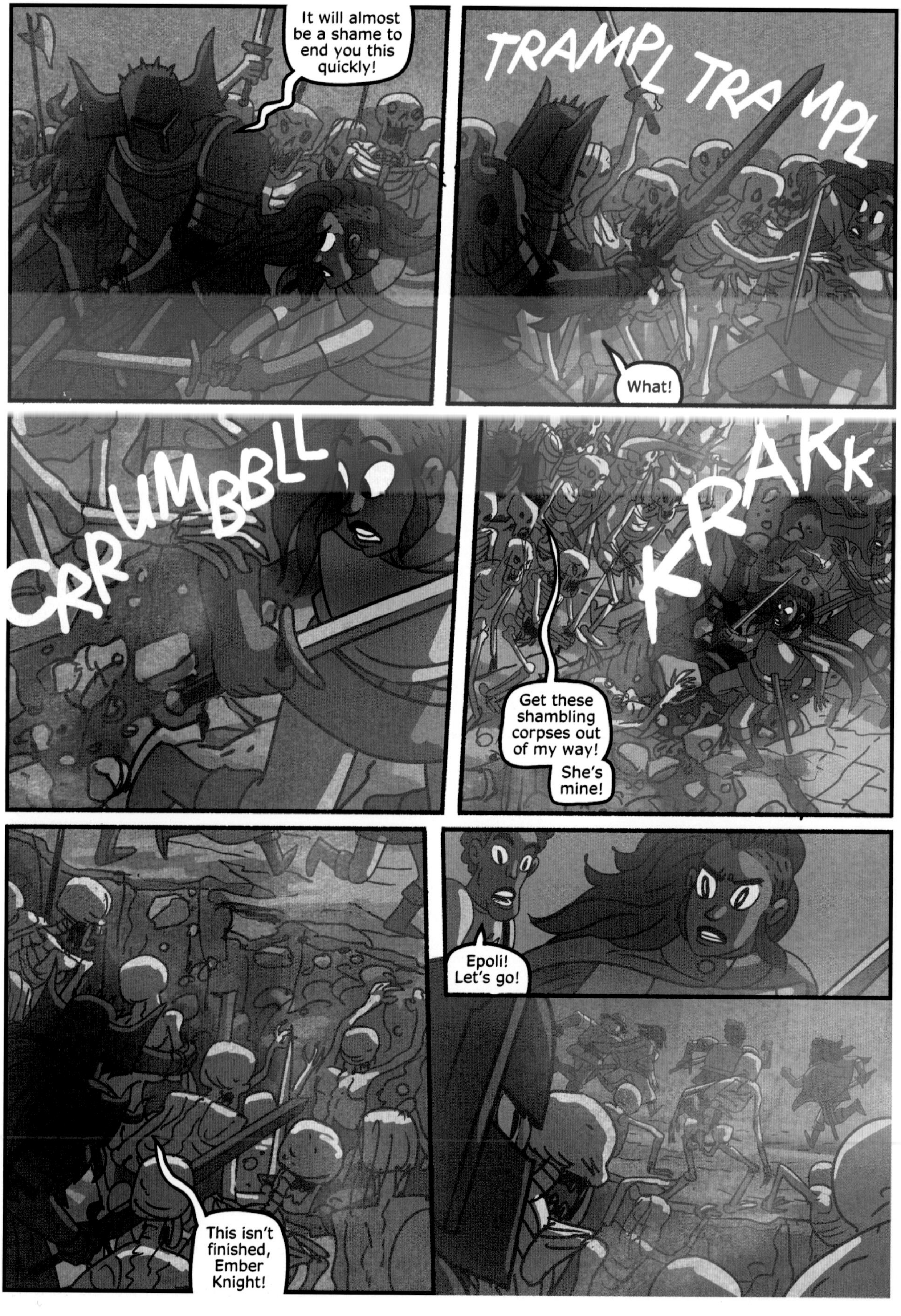
It will almost be a shame to end you this quickly!
TRAMPL TRAMPL
What!
CRRUMBBLL
KRAKK
Get these shambling corpses out of my way!
She's mine!
Epoli! Let's go!
This isn't finished, Ember Knight!

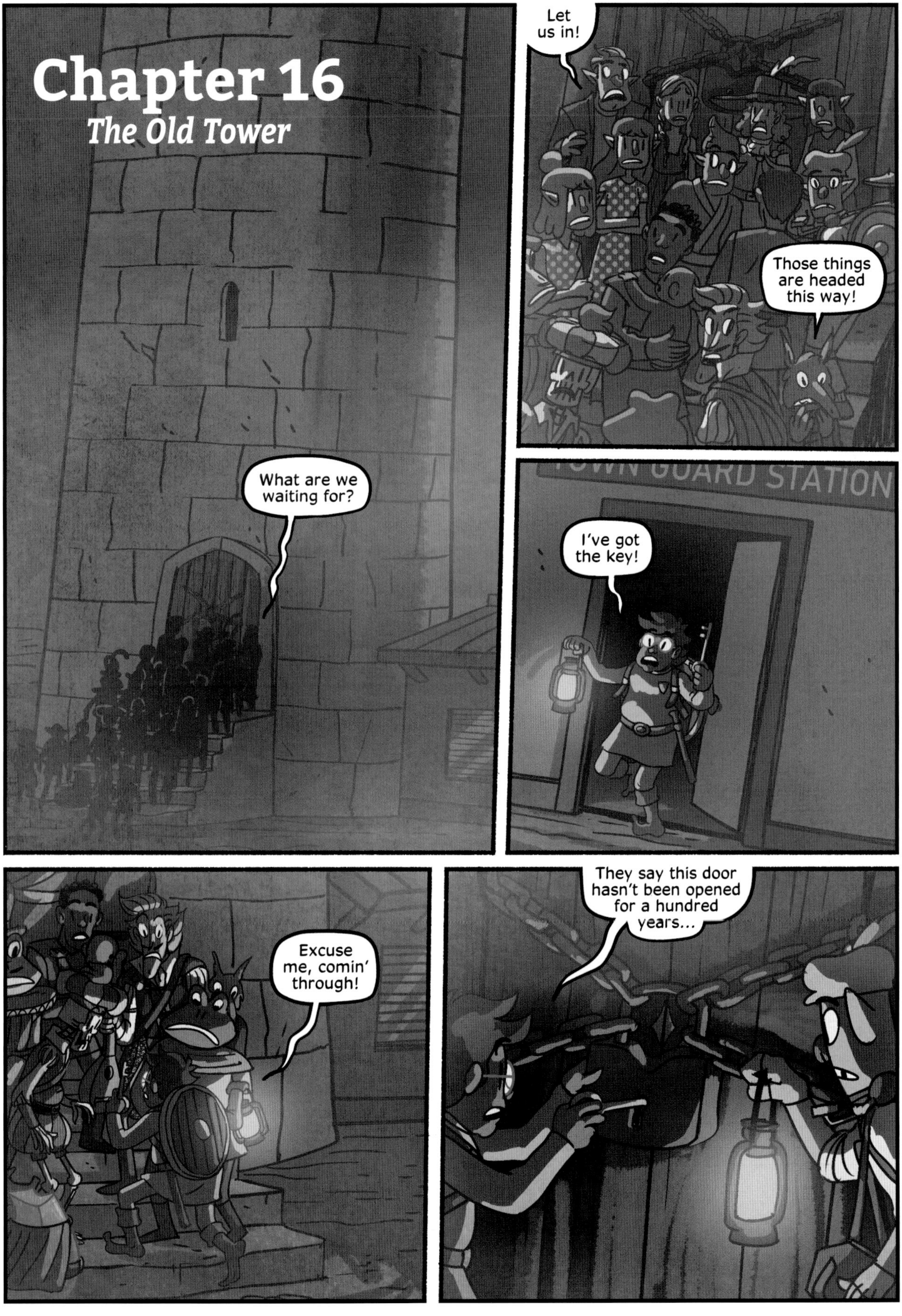

Chapter 16
The Old Tower
What are we waiting for?
Let us in!
Those things are headed this way!
TOWN GUARD STATION
I've got the key!
Excuse me, comin' through!
They say this door hasn't been opened for a hundred years...

Is that...the *Star and Flame of Epoli?*

!!

Towers like this used to stand in every city in the Middle Kingdoms.

E-Epoli!

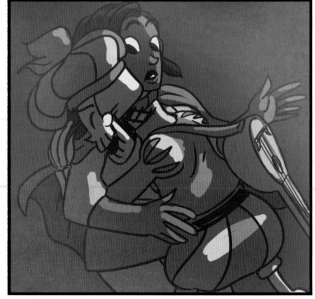

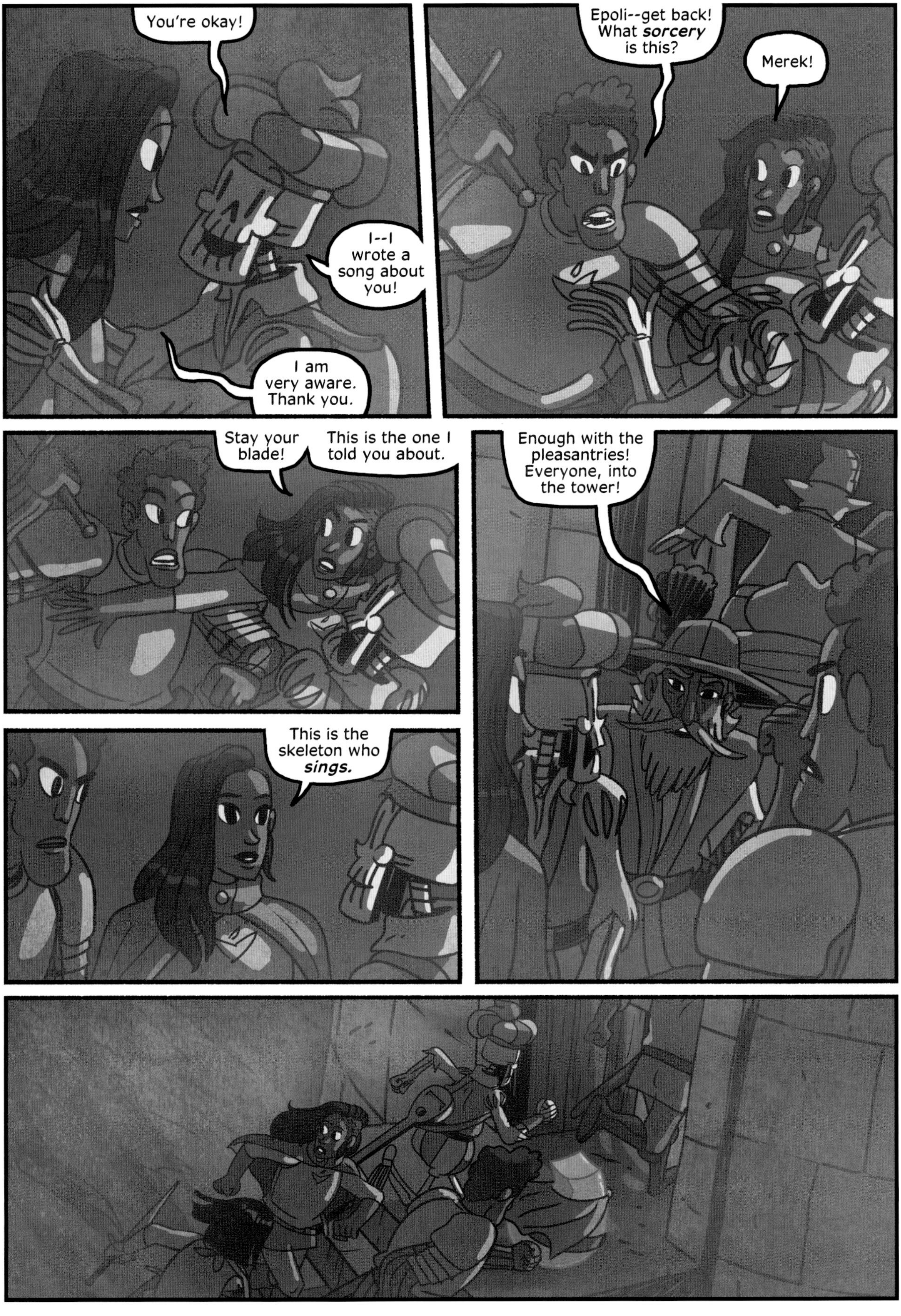
You're okay!
I--I wrote a song about you!
I am very aware. Thank you.
Epoli--get back! What *sorcery* is this?
Merek!
Stay your blade!
This is the one I told you about.
This is the skeleton who *sings.*
Enough with the pleasantries! Everyone, into the tower!

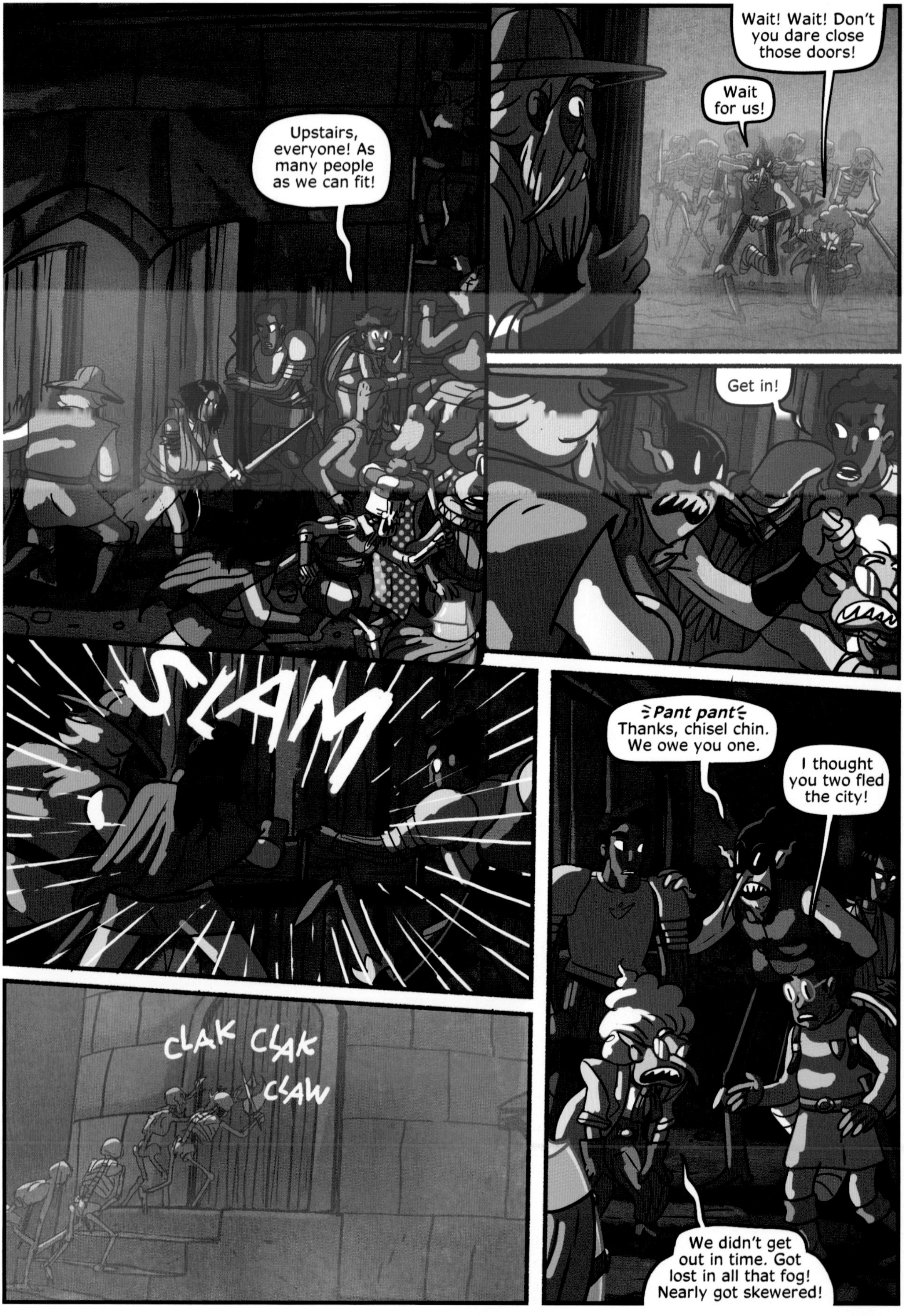

Upstairs, everyone! As many people as we can fit!
Wait! Wait! Don't you dare close those doors!
Wait for us!
Get in!
SLAM
CLAK CLAK CLAW
Pant pant
Thanks, chisel chin. We owe you one.
I thought you two fled the city!
We didn't get out in time. Got lost in all that fog! Nearly got skewered!

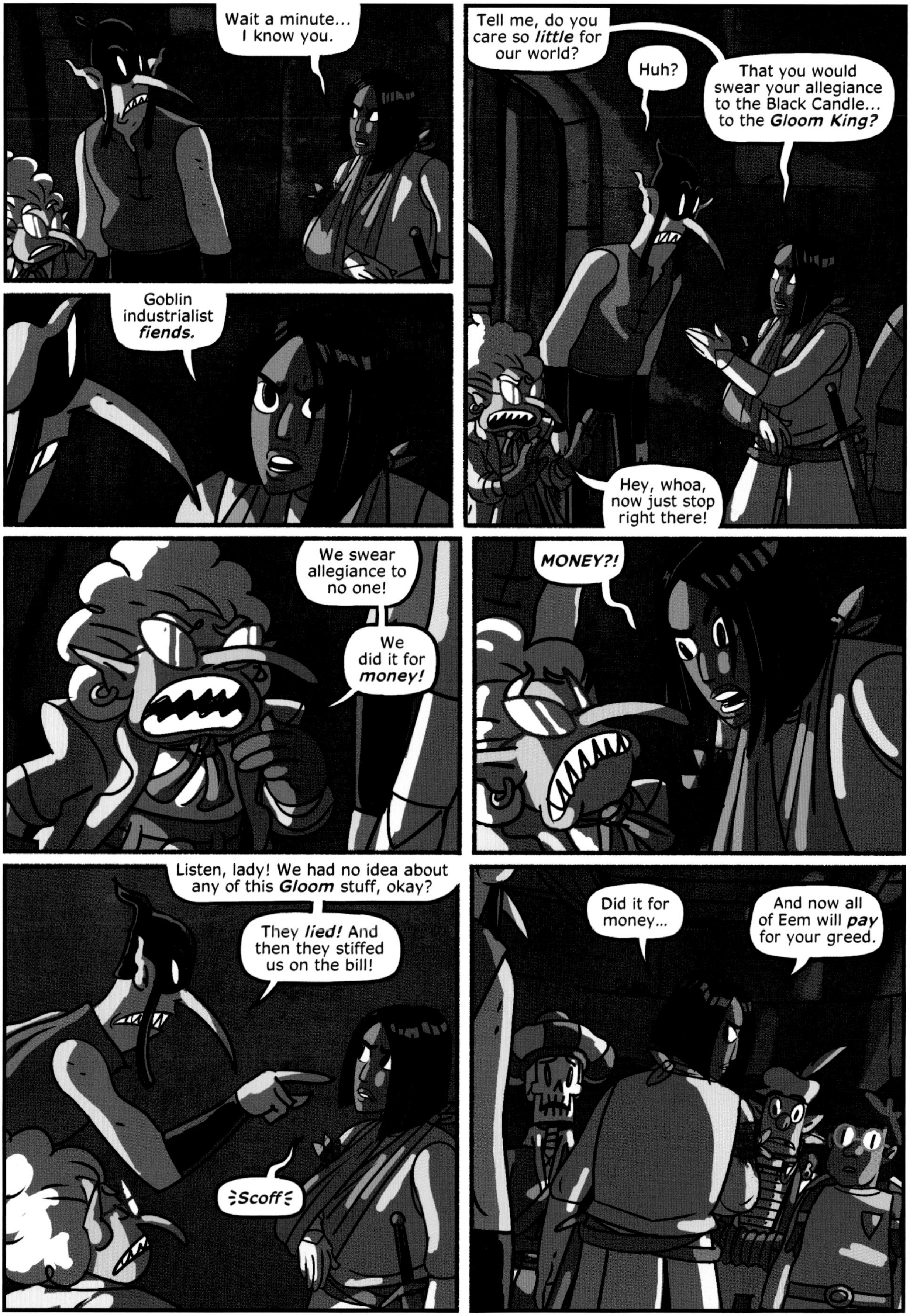

Wait a minute... I know you.
Goblin industrialist *fiends.*
Tell me, do you care so *little* for our world?
Huh?
That you would swear your allegiance to the Black Candle... to the ***Gloom King?***
Hey, whoa, now just stop right there!
We swear allegiance to no one!
We did it for ***money!***
MONEY?!
Listen, lady! We had no idea about any of this ***Gloom*** stuff, okay?
They ***lied!*** And then they stiffed us on the bill!
Scoff
Did it for money...
And now all of Eem will ***pay*** for your greed.

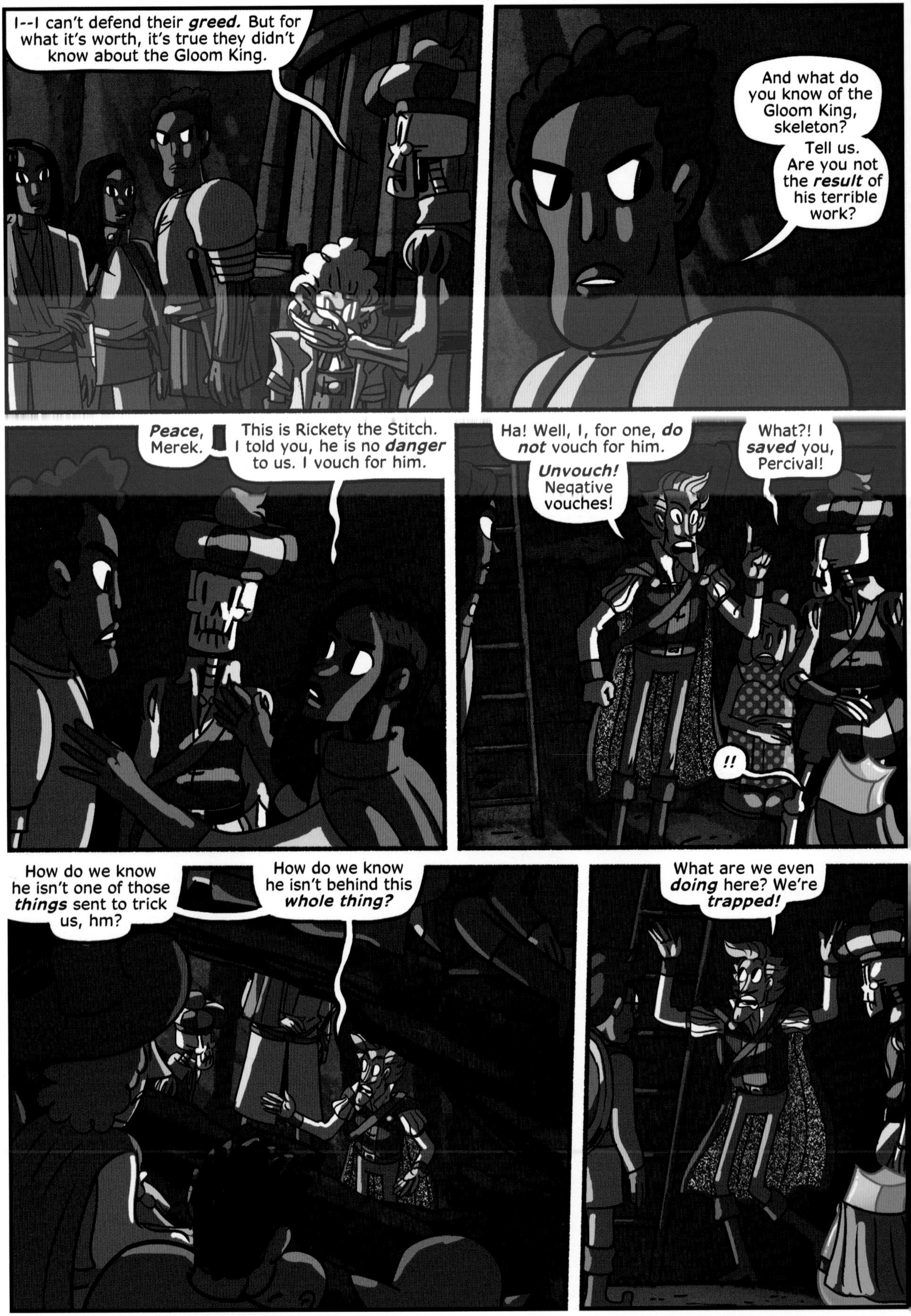
I--I can't defend their *greed.* But for what it's worth, it's true they didn't know about the Gloom King.
And what do you know of the Gloom King, skeleton?
Tell us. Are you not the *result* of his terrible work?
Peace, Merek.
This is Rickety the Stitch. I told you, he is no *danger* to us. I vouch for him.
Ha! Well, I, for one, *do not* vouch for him.
Unvouch! Negative vouches!
What?! I *saved* you, Percival!
!!
How do we know he isn't one of those *things* sent to trick us, hm?
How do we know he isn't behind this *whole thing?*
What are we even *doing* here? We're *trapped!*

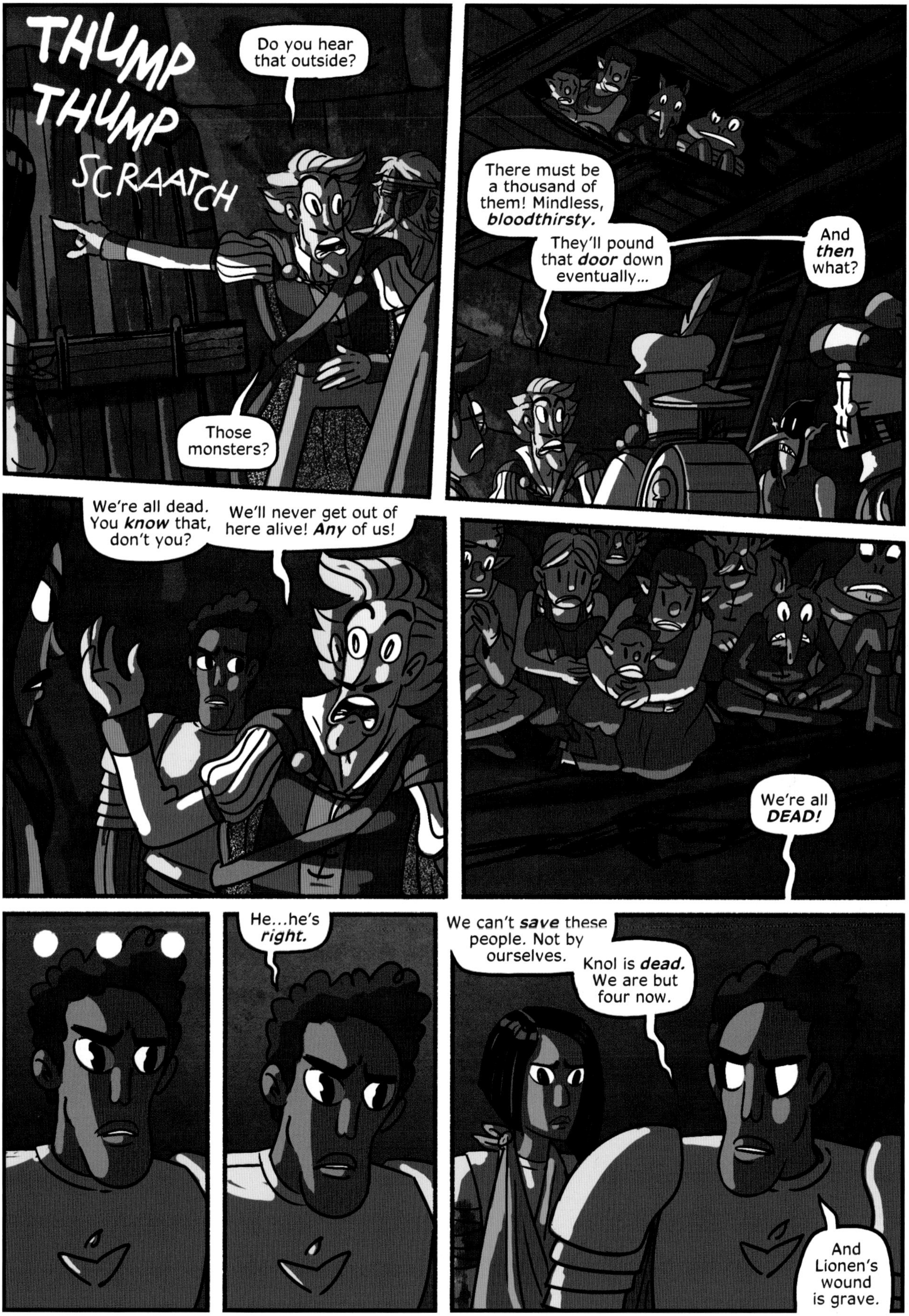
THUMP
THUMP
SCRAATCH
Do you hear that outside?
Those monsters?
There must be a thousand of them! Mindless, ***bloodthirsty.***
They'll pound that ***door*** down eventually...
And ***then*** what?
We're all dead. You ***know*** that, don't you?
We'll never get out of here alive! ***Any*** of us!
We're all ***DEAD!***
He...he's ***right.***
We can't ***save*** these people. Not by ourselves.
Knol is ***dead.*** We are but four now.
And Lionen's wound is grave.

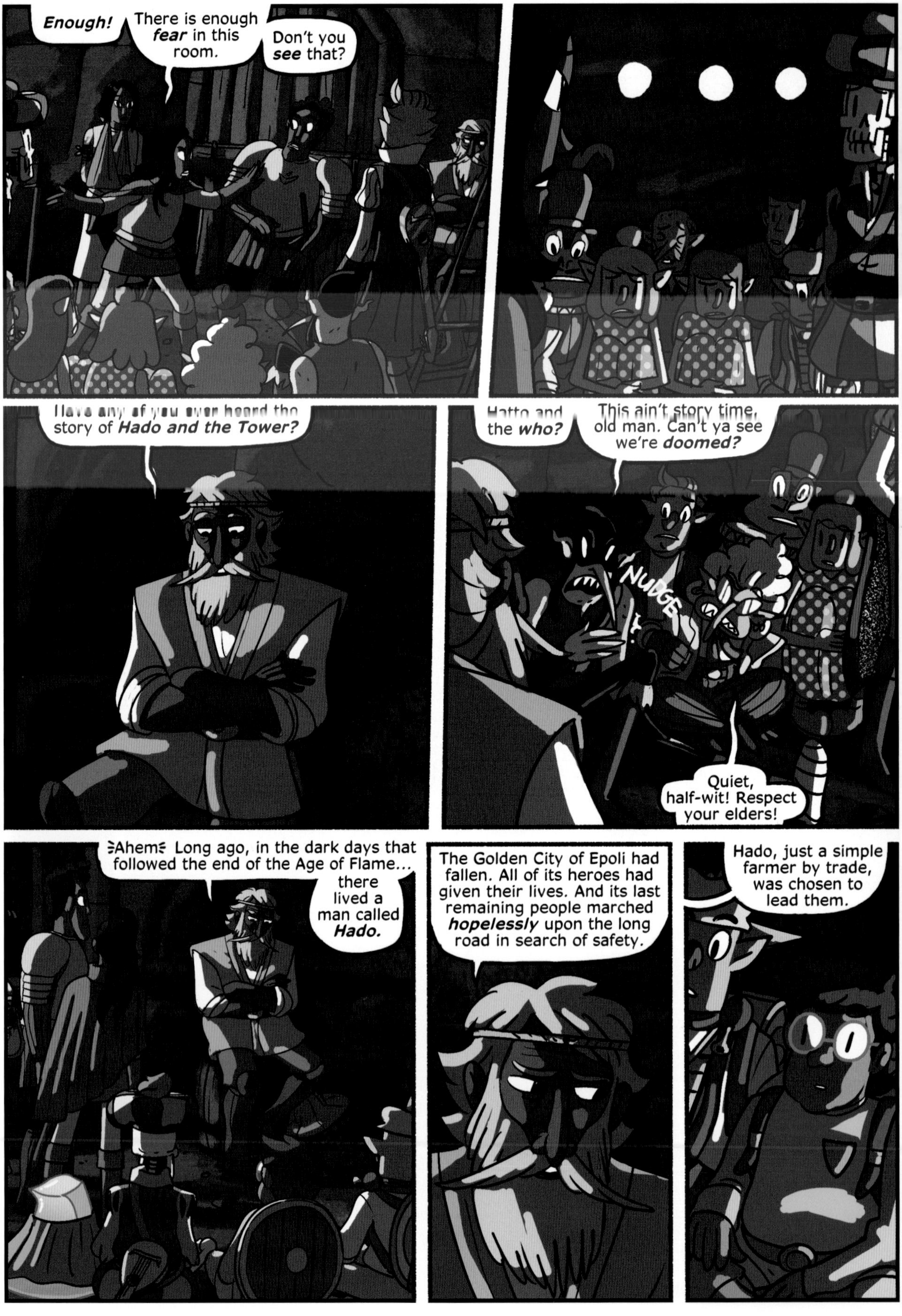

Enough!
There is enough *fear* in this room.
Don't you *see* that?
Have any of you ever heard the story of *Hado and the Tower?*
Hatto and the *who?*
This ain't story time, old man. Can't ya see we're *doomed?*
NUDGE
Quiet, half-wit! Respect your elders!
≥Ahem≤ Long ago, in the dark days that followed the end of the Age of Flame...
there lived a man called *Hado.*
The Golden City of Epoli had fallen. All of its heroes had given their lives. And its last remaining people marched *hopelessly* upon the long road in search of safety.
Hado, just a simple farmer by trade, was chosen to lead them.

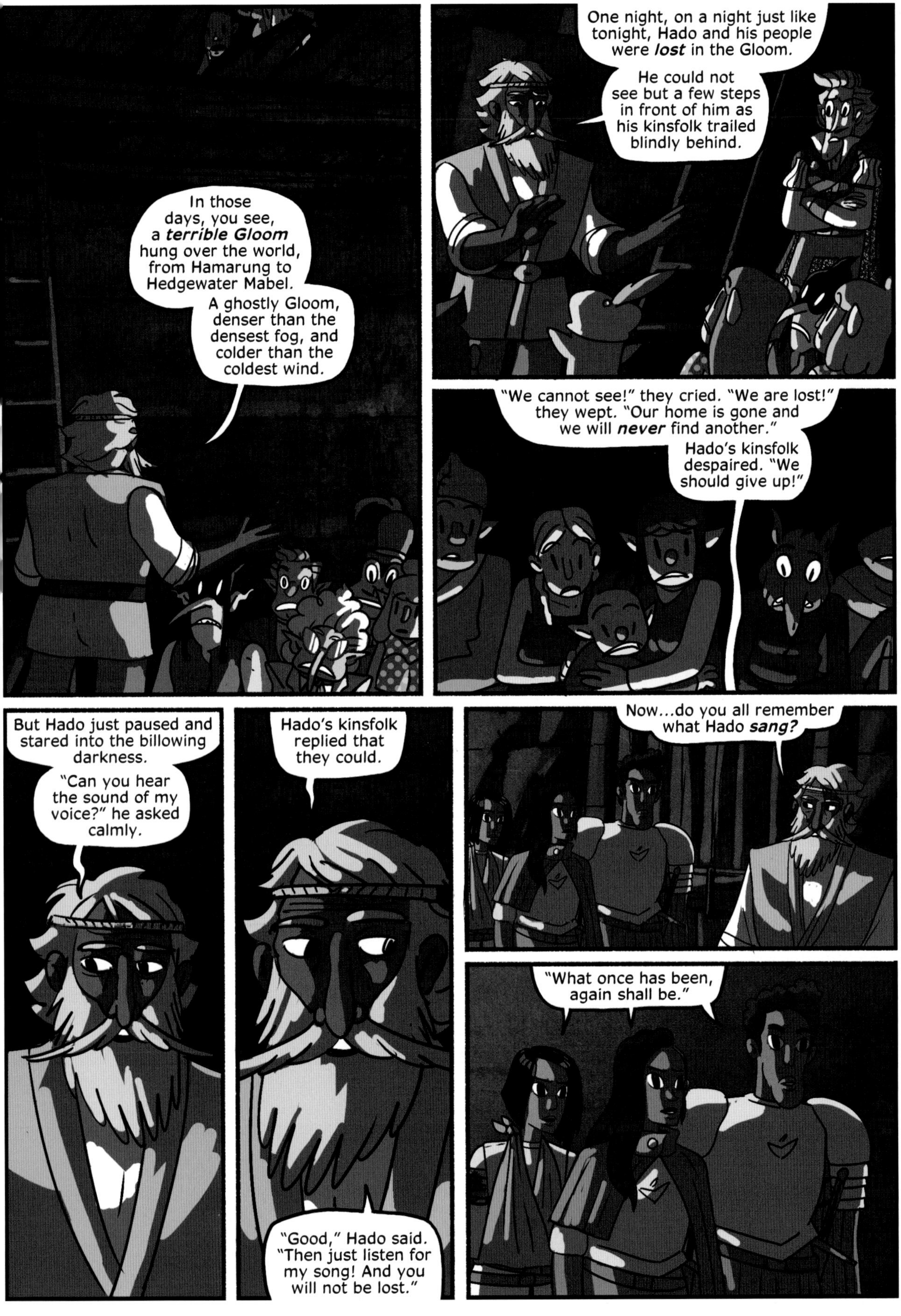
In those days, you see, a *terrible Gloom* hung over the world, from Hamarung to Hedgewater Mabel.
A ghostly Gloom, denser than the densest fog, and colder than the coldest wind.
One night, on a night just like tonight, Hado and his people were *lost* in the Gloom.
He could not see but a few steps in front of him as his kinsfolk trailed blindly behind.
"We cannot see!" they cried. "We are lost!" they wept. "Our home is gone and we will *never* find another."
Hado's kinsfolk despaired. "We should give up!"
But Hado just paused and stared into the billowing darkness.
"Can you hear the sound of my voice?" he asked calmly.
Hado's kinsfolk replied that they could.
"Good," Hado said. "Then just listen for my song! And you will not be lost."
Now...do you all remember what Hado *sang?*
"What once has been, again shall be."

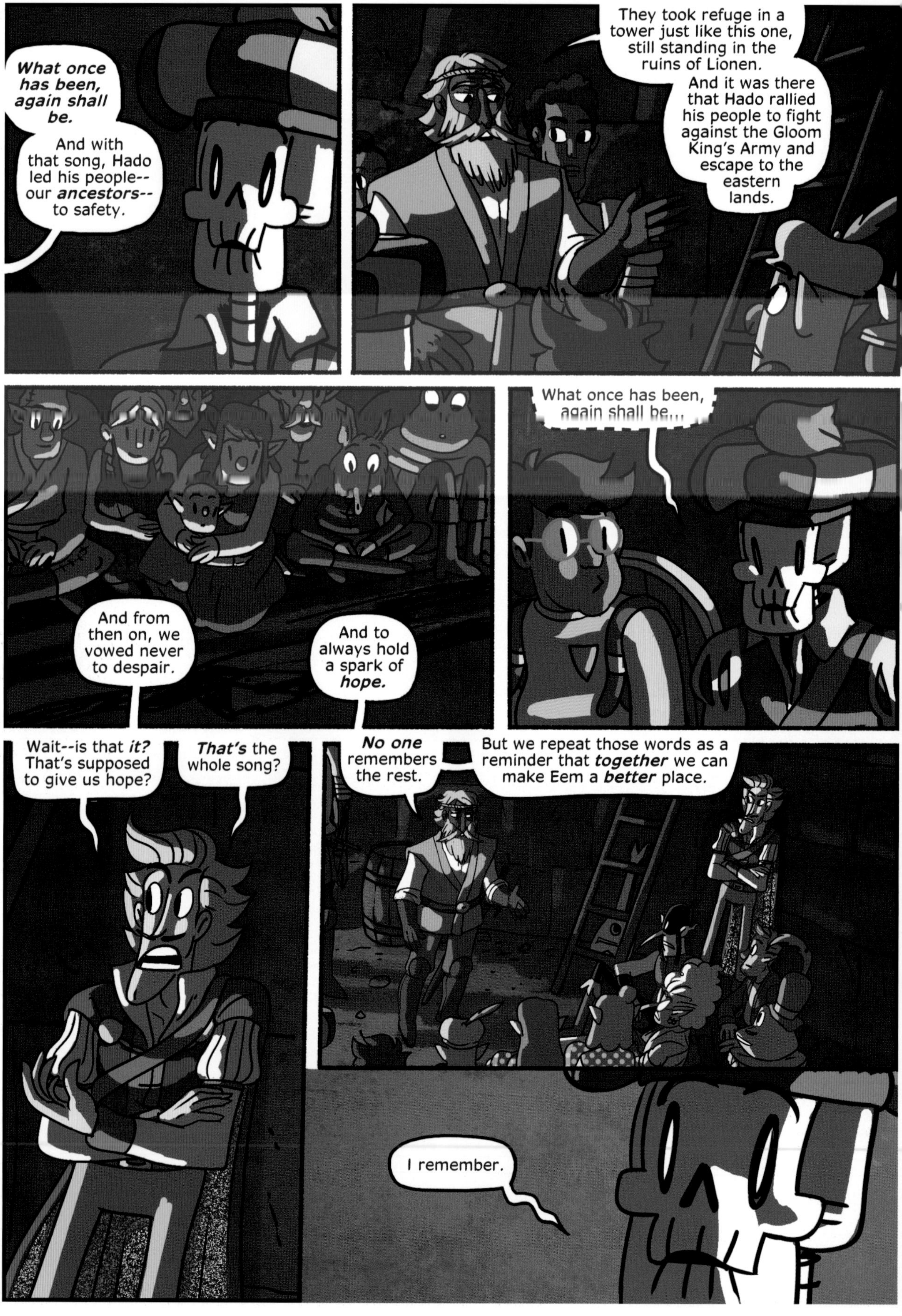
What once has been, again shall be.
And with that song, Hado led his people-- our ancestors-- to safety.
They took refuge in a tower just like this one, still standing in the ruins of Lionen.
And it was there that Hado rallied his people to fight against the Gloom King's Army and escape to the eastern lands.
And from then on, we vowed never to despair.
And to always hold a spark of hope.
What once has been, again shall be...
Wait--is that it? That's supposed to give us hope?
That's the whole song?
No one remembers the rest.
But we repeat those words as a reminder that together we can make Eem a better place.
I remember.

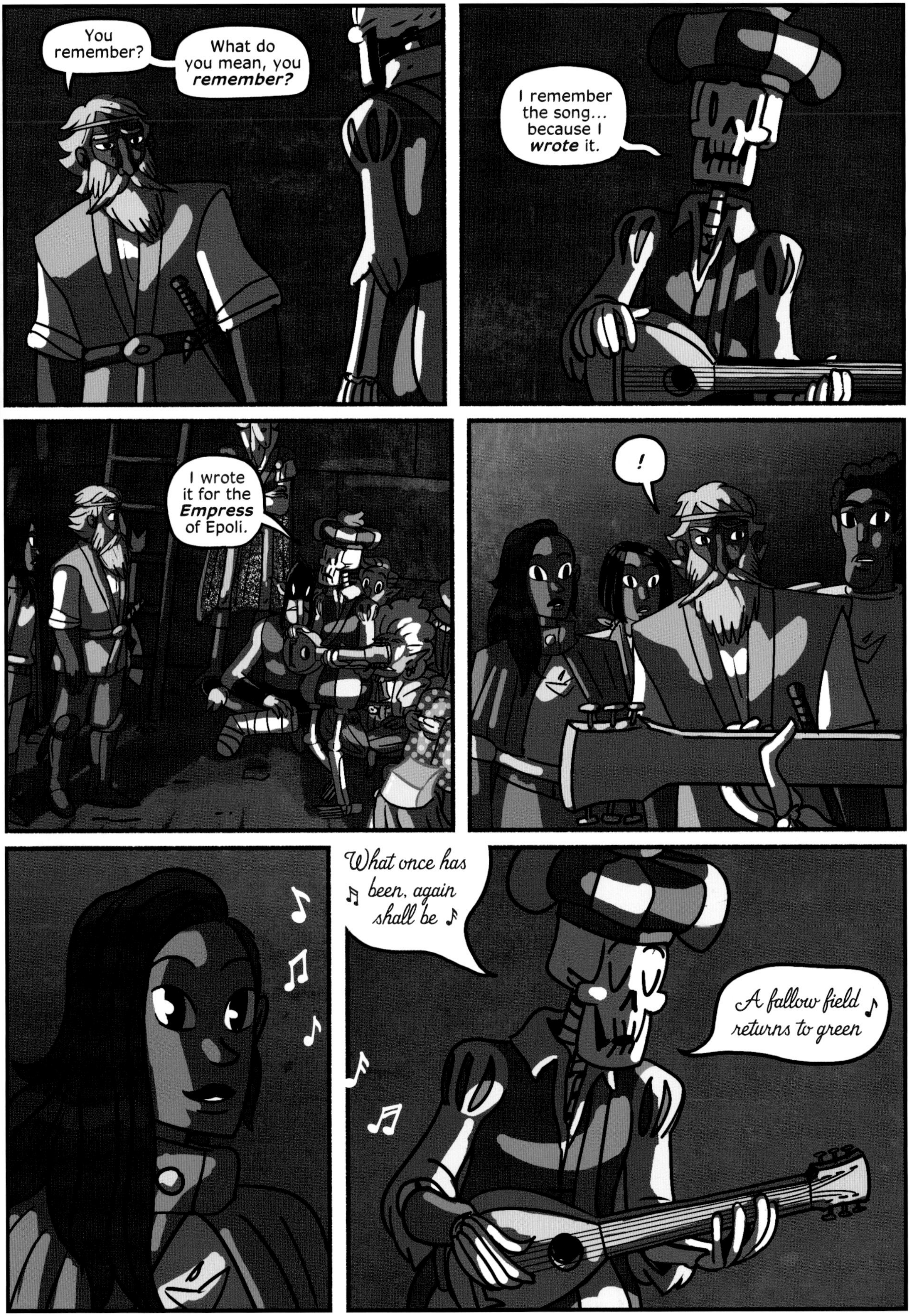
You remember?
What do you mean, you *remember?*
I remember the song... because I *wrote* it.
I wrote it for the *Empress* of Epoli.
!
What once has been, again shall be ♪
A fallow field returns to green ♪

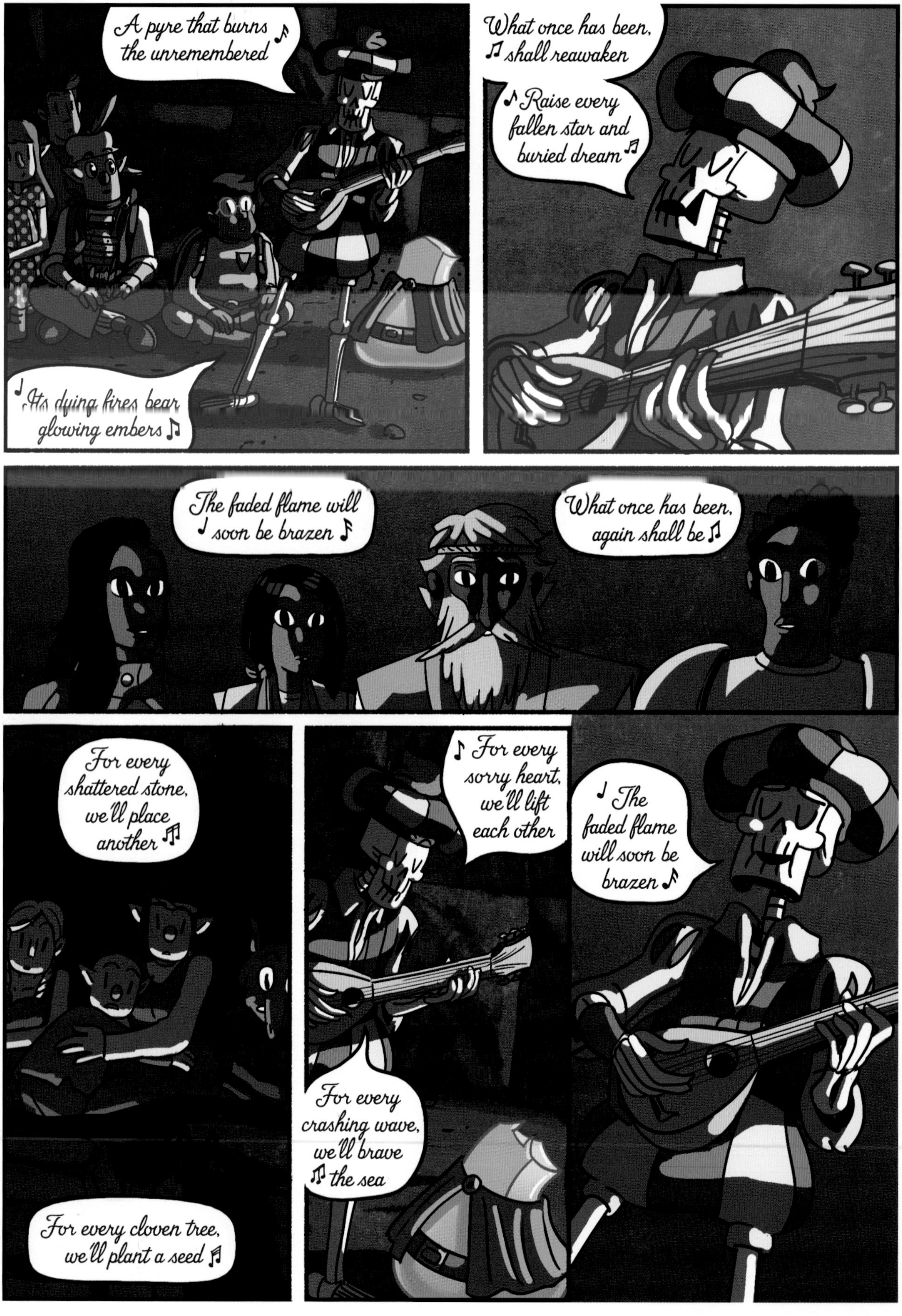
A pyre that burns the unremembered
It's dying fires bear glowing embers
What once has been, shall reawaken
Raise every fallen star and buried dream
The faded flame will soon be brazen
What once has been, again shall be
For every shattered stone, we'll place another
For every cloven tree, we'll plant a seed
For every sorry heart, we'll lift each other
For every crashing wave, we'll brave the sea
The faded flame will soon be brazen

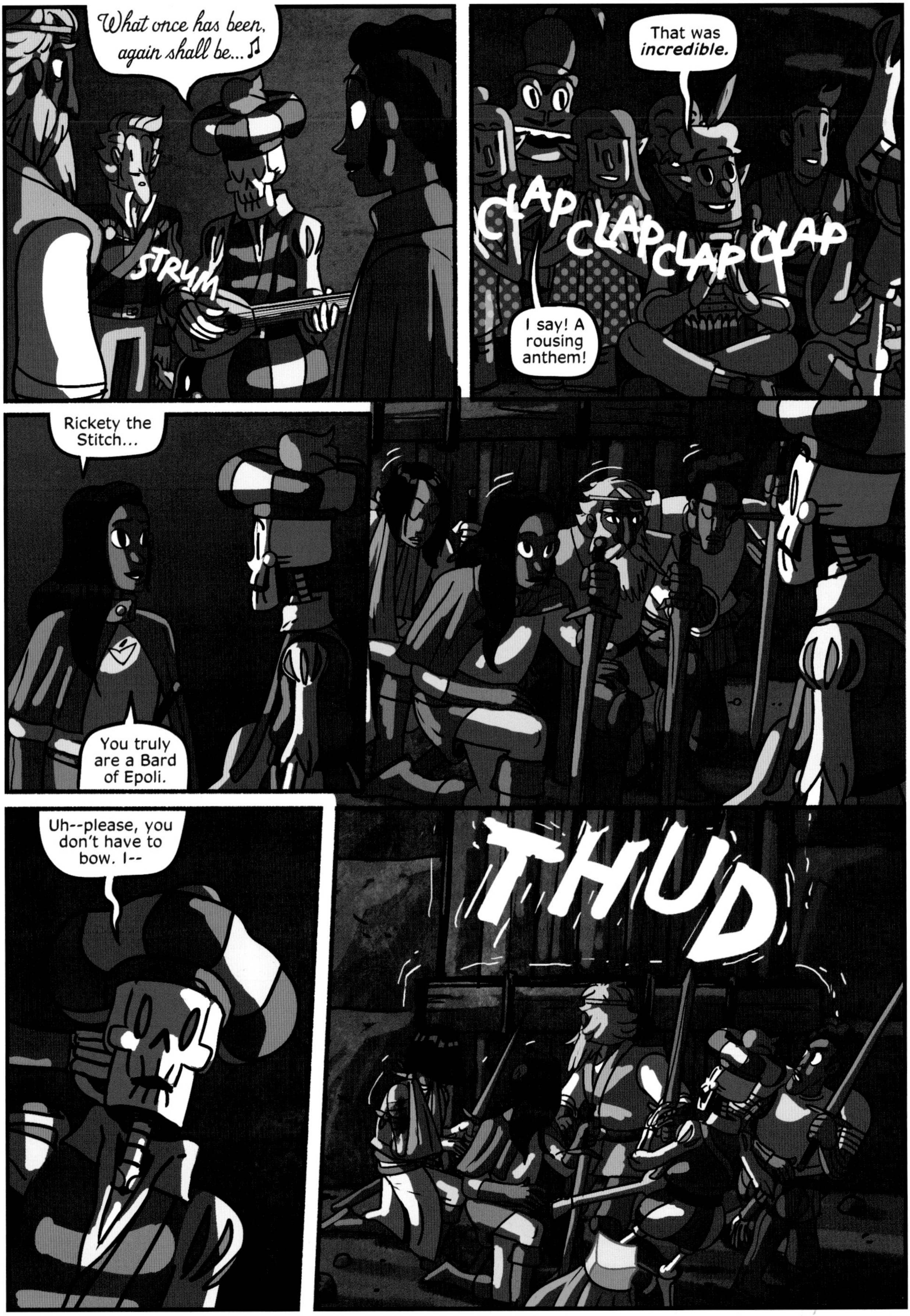
What once has been, again shall be...♫
STRUM
That was incredible.
CLAP CLAP CLAP CLAP
I say! A rousing anthem!
Rickety the Stitch...
You truly are a Bard of Epoli.
Uh--please, you don't have to bow. I--
THUD

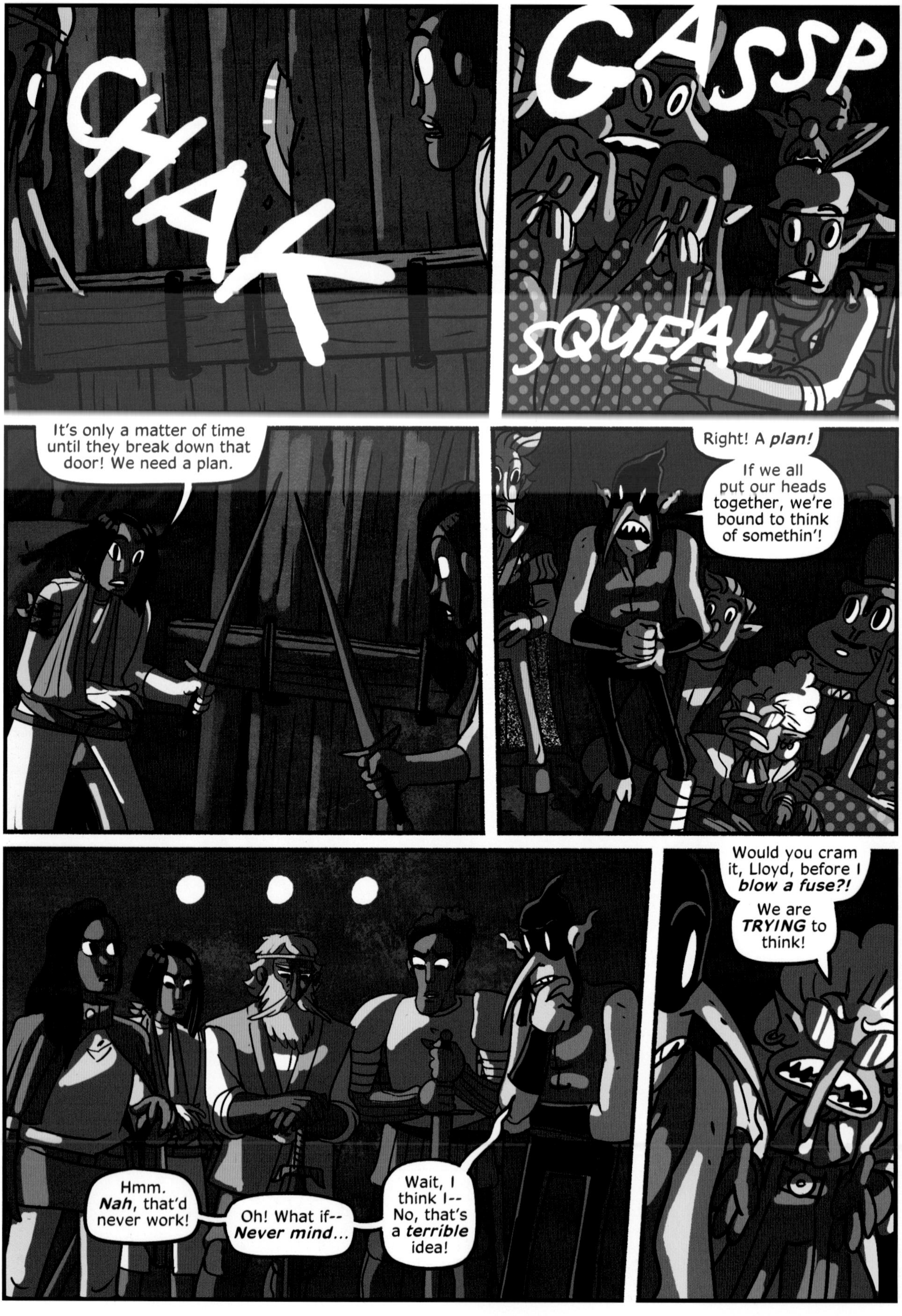
CHAK
GASSP
SQUEAL
It's only a matter of time until they break down that door! We need a plan.
Right! A *plan!*
If we all put our heads together, we're bound to think of somethin'!
Hmm. ***Nah***, that'd never work!
Oh! What if-- ***Never mind...***
Wait, I think I-- No, that's a ***terrible*** idea!
Would you cram it, Lloyd, before I ***blow a fuse?!***
We are ***TRYING*** to think!

!!!
...

... ...!

What? Blow a fuse...?

...!
... ...
... ...!!

What's he saying?

HOP   HOP

... ...!

He's saying there's a way we can **stop** those hordes of skeletons.

But it's pretty drastic.

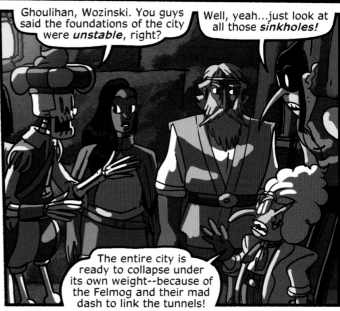

Ghoulihan, Wozinski. You guys said the foundations of the city were **unstable**, right?

Well, yeah...just look at all those **sinkholes!**

The entire city is ready to collapse under its own weight--because of the Felmog and their mad dash to link the tunnels!

Tunnels? Link what tunnels?

From the north!

They're spreading the Gloom...

That's their plan.

Spread the Gloom underground...

And unleash it upon the world before we ever knew what hit us.

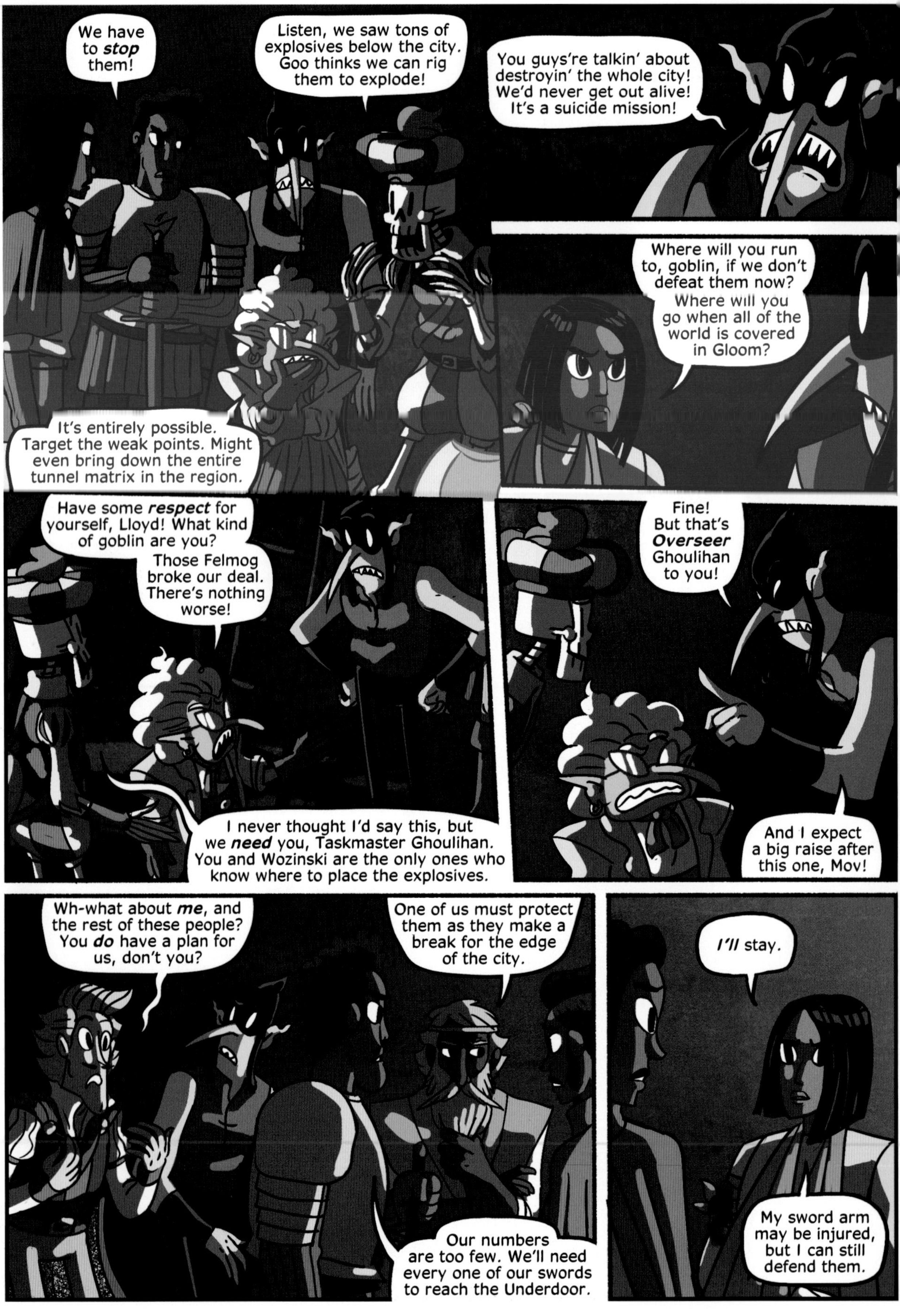
We have to *stop* them!
Listen, we saw tons of explosives below the city. Goo thinks we can rig them to explode!
It's entirely possible. Target the weak points. Might even bring down the entire tunnel matrix in the region.
You guys're talkin' about destroyin' the whole city! We'd never get out alive! It's a suicide mission!
Where will you run to, goblin, if we don't defeat them now?
Where will you go when all of the world is covered in Gloom?
Have some *respect* for yourself, Lloyd! What kind of goblin are you?
Those Felmog broke our deal. There's nothing worse!
I never thought I'd say this, but we *need* you, Taskmaster Ghoulihan. You and Wozinski are the only ones who know where to place the explosives.
Fine! But that's *Overseer* Ghoulihan to you!
And I expect a big raise after this one, Mov!
Wh-what about *me*, and the rest of these people? You *do* have a plan for us, don't you?
One of us must protect them as they make a break for the edge of the city.
Our numbers are too few. We'll need every one of our swords to reach the Underdoor.
I'll stay.
My sword arm may be injured, but I can still defend them.

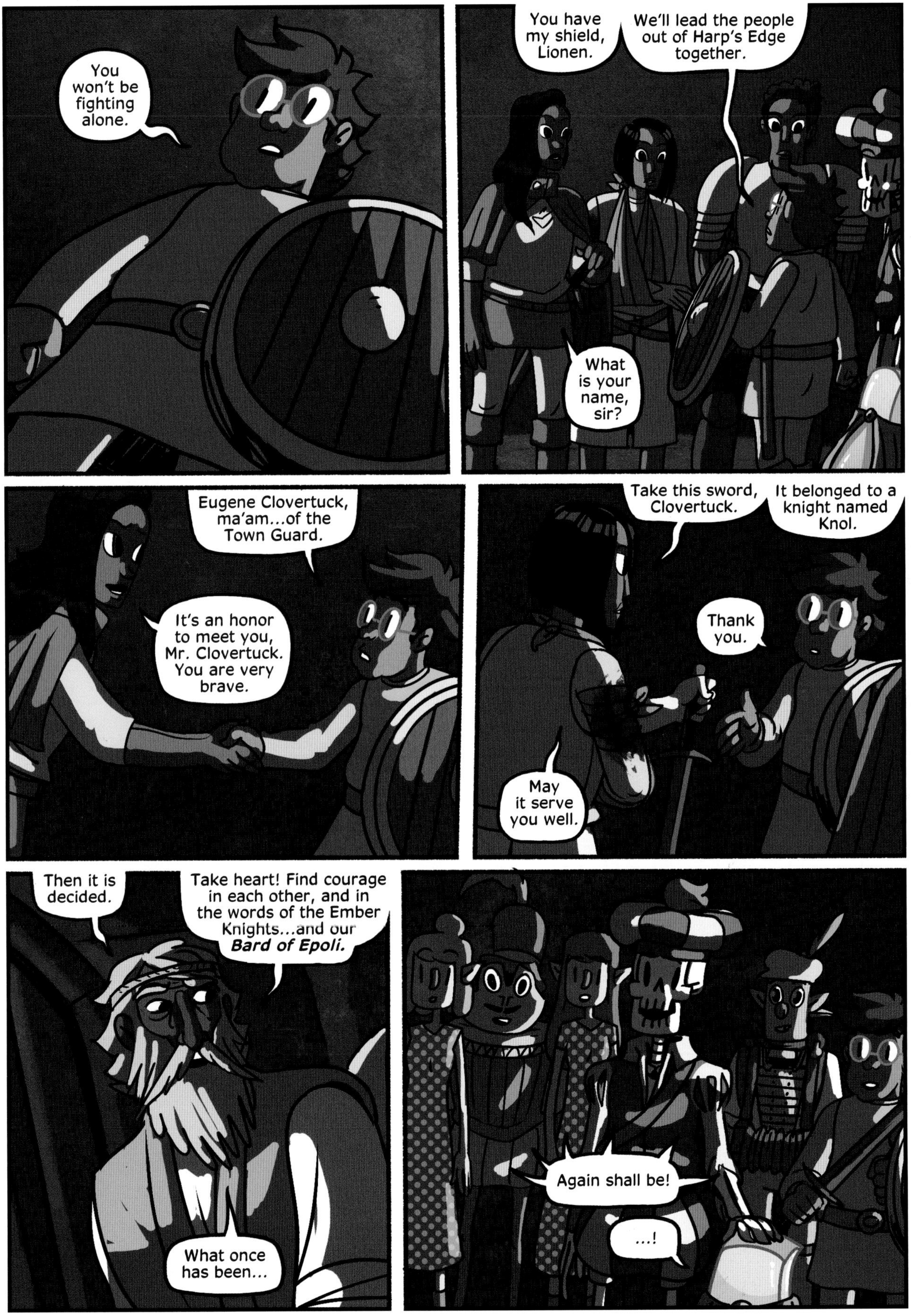
You won't be fighting alone.
You have my shield, Lionen.
We'll lead the people out of Harp's Edge together.
What is your name, sir?
Eugene Clovertuck, ma'am...of the Town Guard.
It's an honor to meet you, Mr. Clovertuck. You are very brave.
Take this sword, Clovertuck.
It belonged to a knight named Knol.
Thank you.
May it serve you well.
Then it is decided.
Take heart! Find courage in each other, and in the words of the Ember Knights...and our *Bard of Epoli.*
What once has been...
Again shall be!
...!

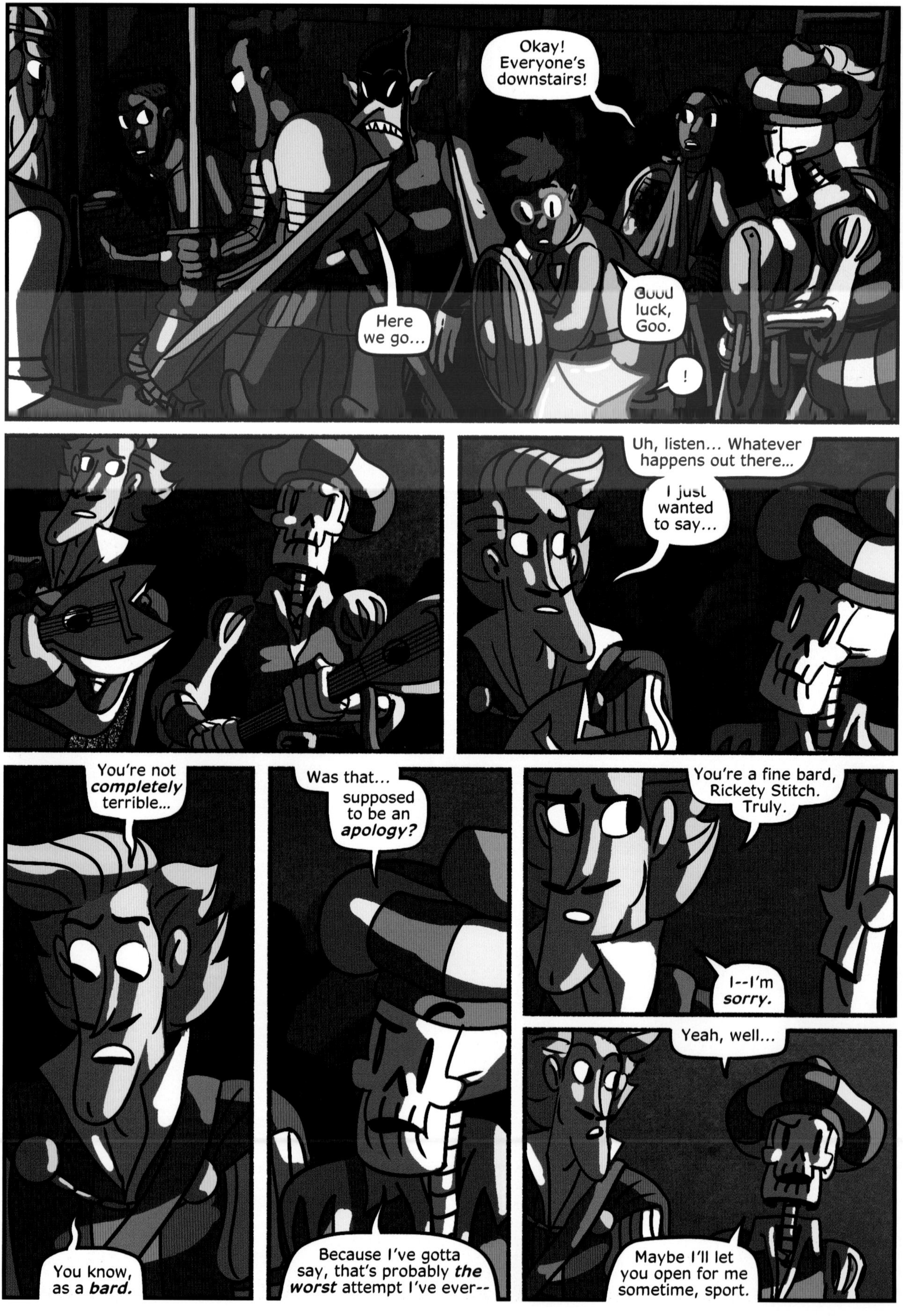

Okay! Everyone's downstairs!
Here we go...
Good luck, Goo.
!
Uh, listen... Whatever happens out there...
I just wanted to say...
You're not *completely* terrible...
You know, as a *bard.*
Was that...
supposed to be an *apology?*
Because I've gotta say, that's probably *the worst* attempt I've ever--
You're a fine bard, Rickety Stitch. Truly.
I--I'm *sorry.*
Yeah, well...
Maybe I'll let you open for me sometime, sport.

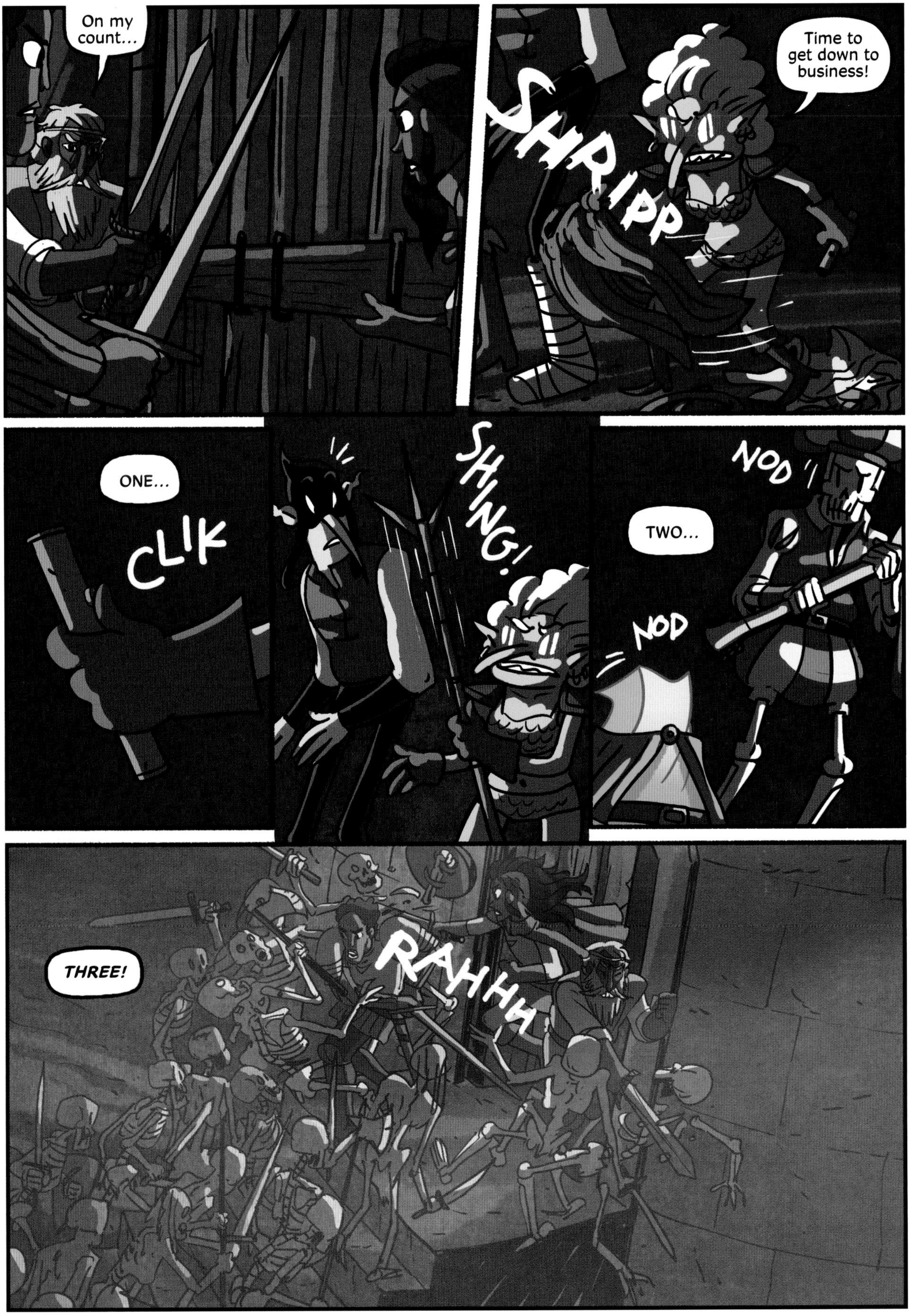

On my count...
SHRIPP
Time to get down to business!
ONE...
CLIK
SHING!
TWO...
NOD
NOD
THREE!
RAHHH

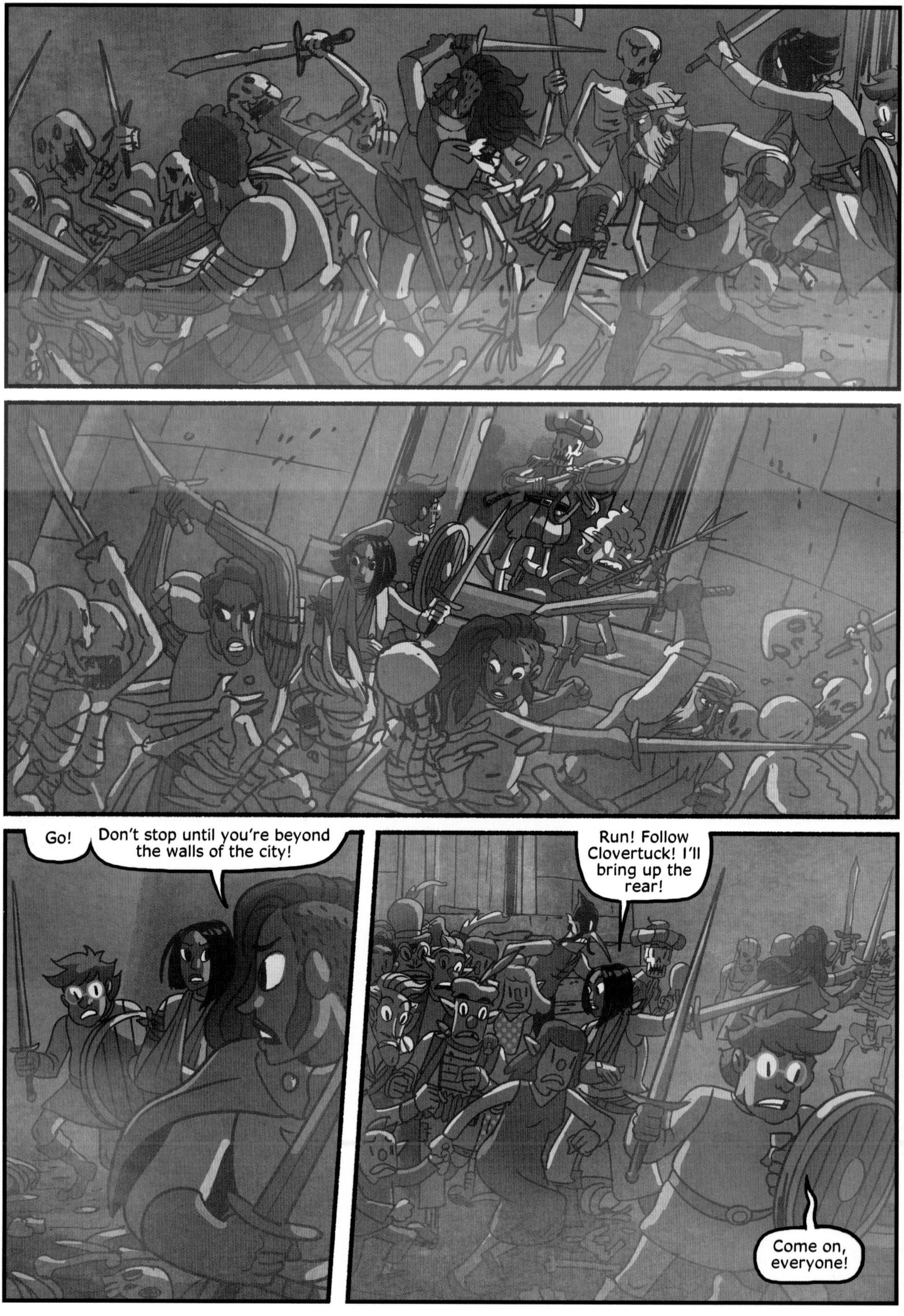
Go!
Don't stop until you're beyond the walls of the city!
Run! Follow Clovertuck! I'll bring up the rear!
Come on, everyone!

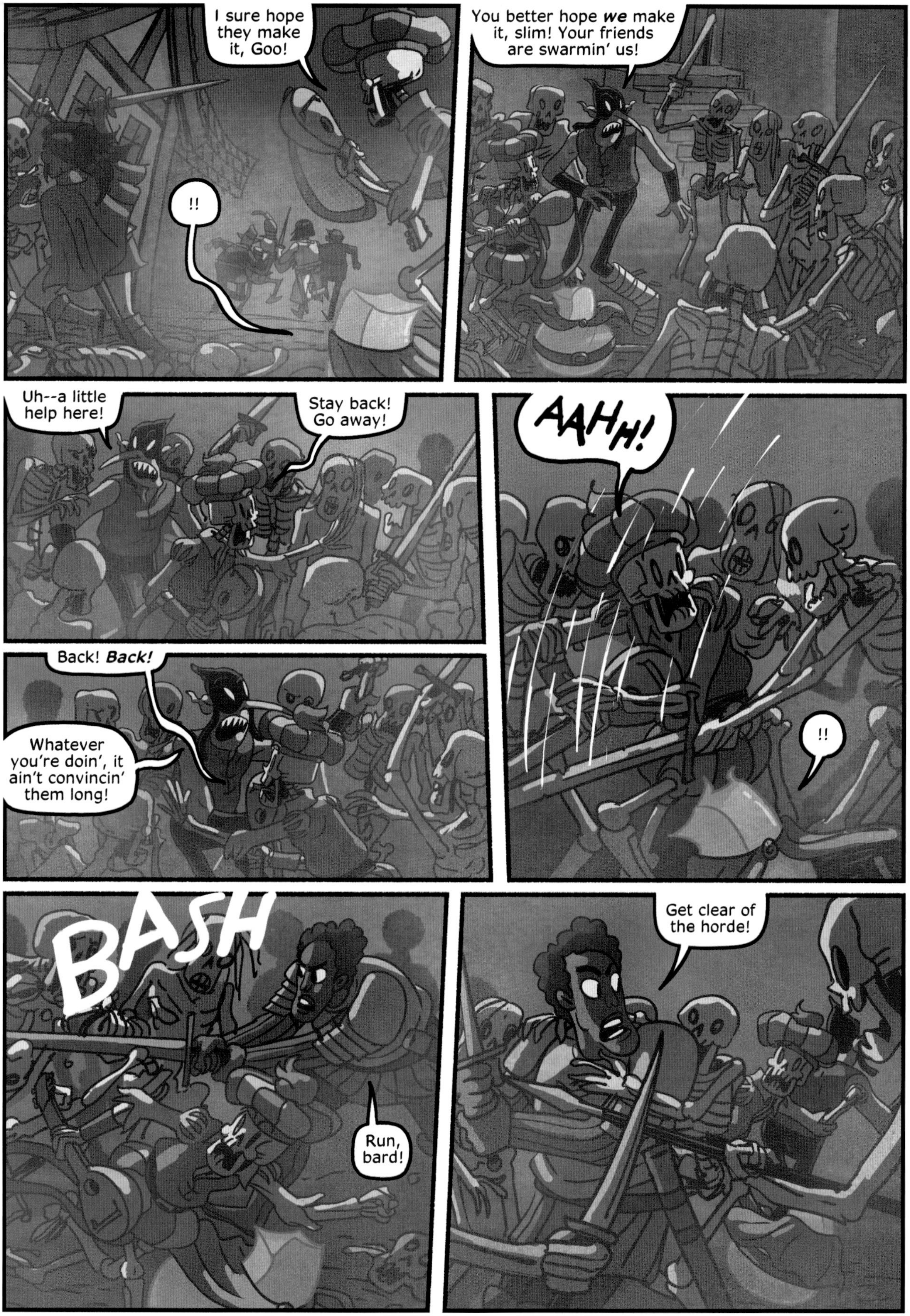
I sure hope they make it, Goo!
!!
You better hope **we** make it, slim! Your friends are swarmin' us!
Uh--a little help here!
Stay back! Go away!
AAHH!
Back! **Back!**
Whatever you're doin', it ain't convincin' them long!
!!
BASH
Run, bard!
Get clear of the horde!

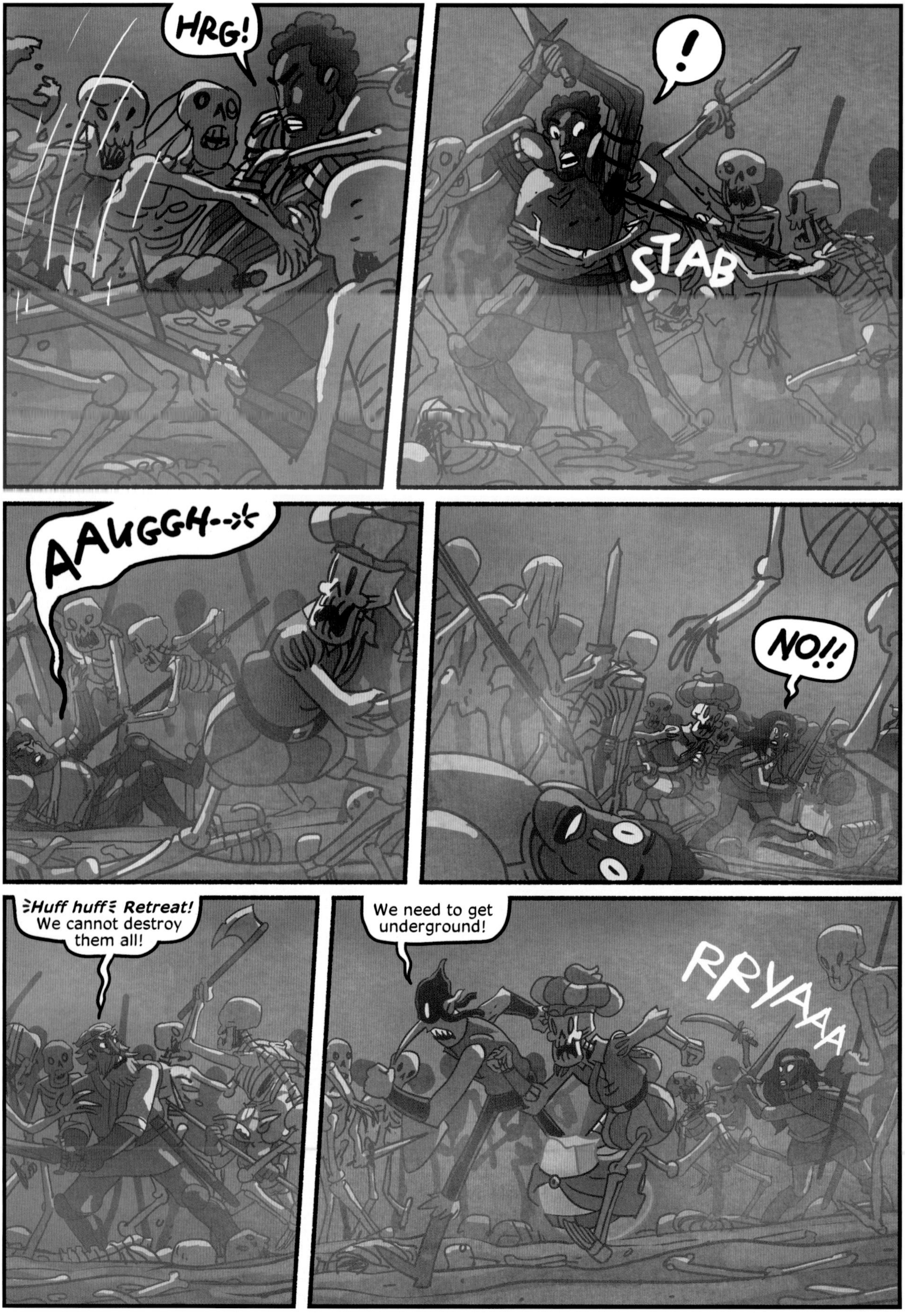
HRG!
!
STAB
AAUGGH--
NO!!
Huff huff Retreat! We cannot destroy them all!
We need to get underground!
RRYAAA

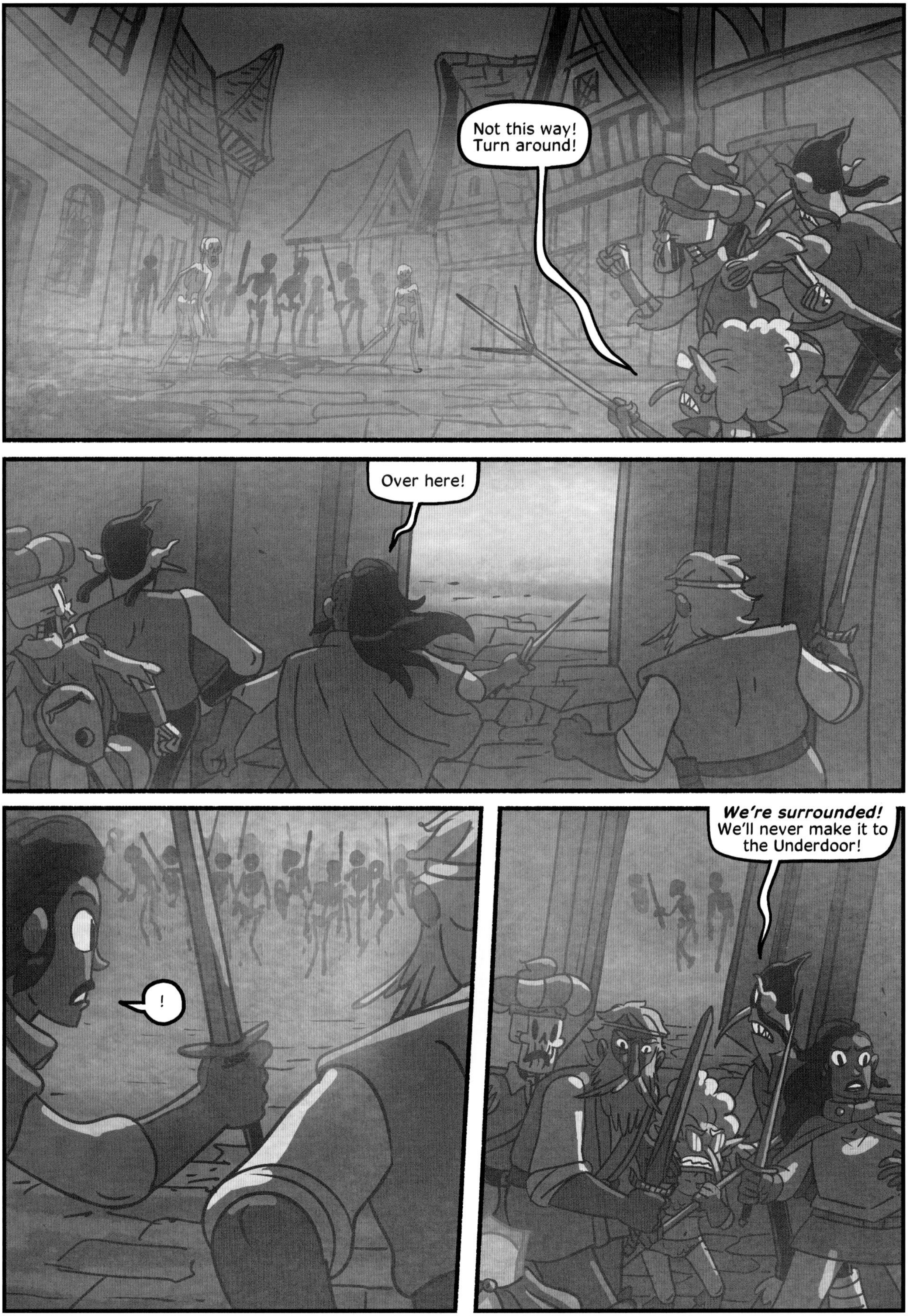
Not this way! Turn around!
Over here!
!
We're surrounded! We'll never make it to the Underdoor!

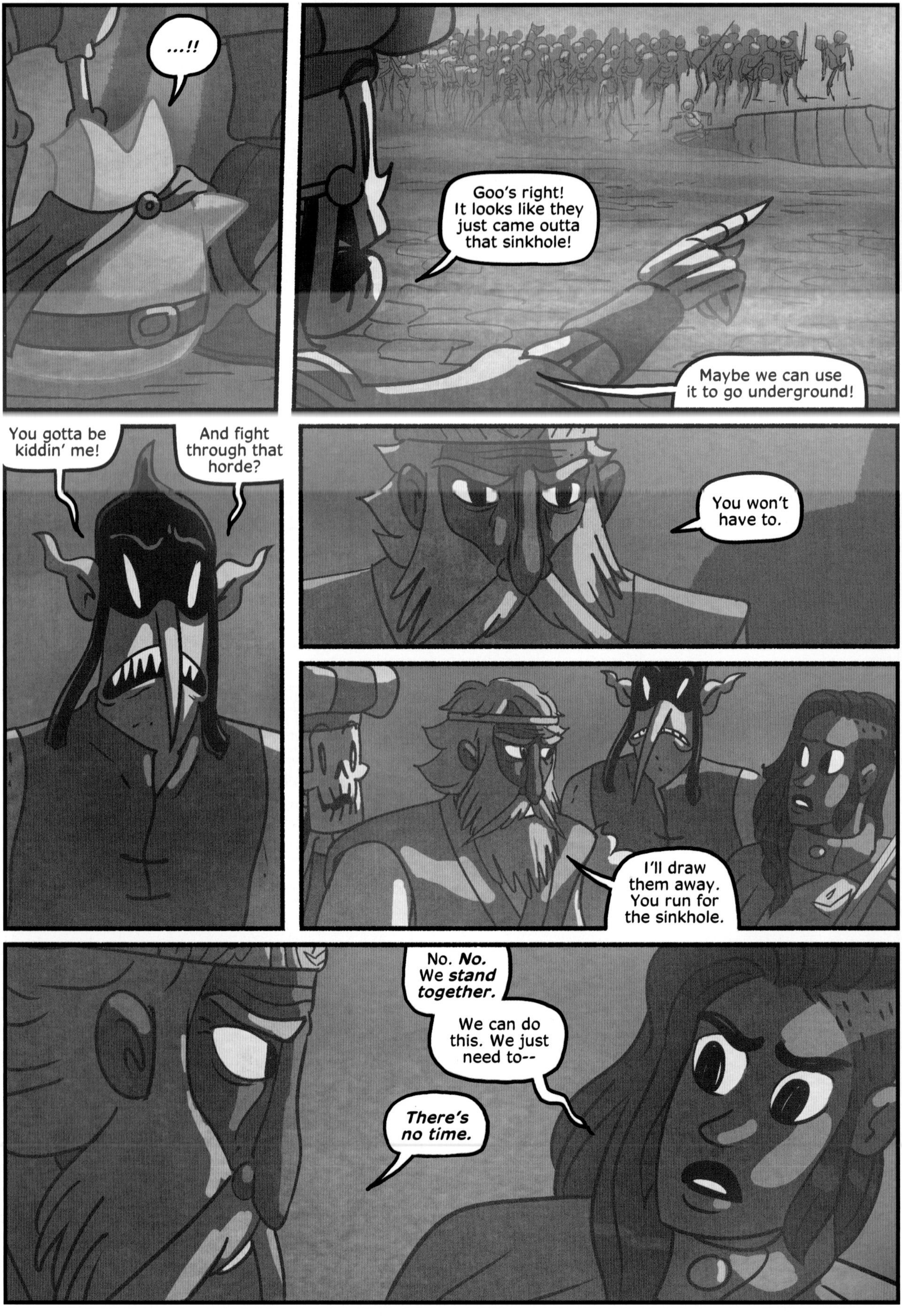
...!!
Goo's right! It looks like they just came outta that sinkhole!
Maybe we can use it to go underground!
You gotta be kiddin' me!
And fight through that horde?
You won't have to.
I'll draw them away. You run for the sinkhole.
No. *No.* We *stand together.*
We can do this. We just need to--
There's no time.

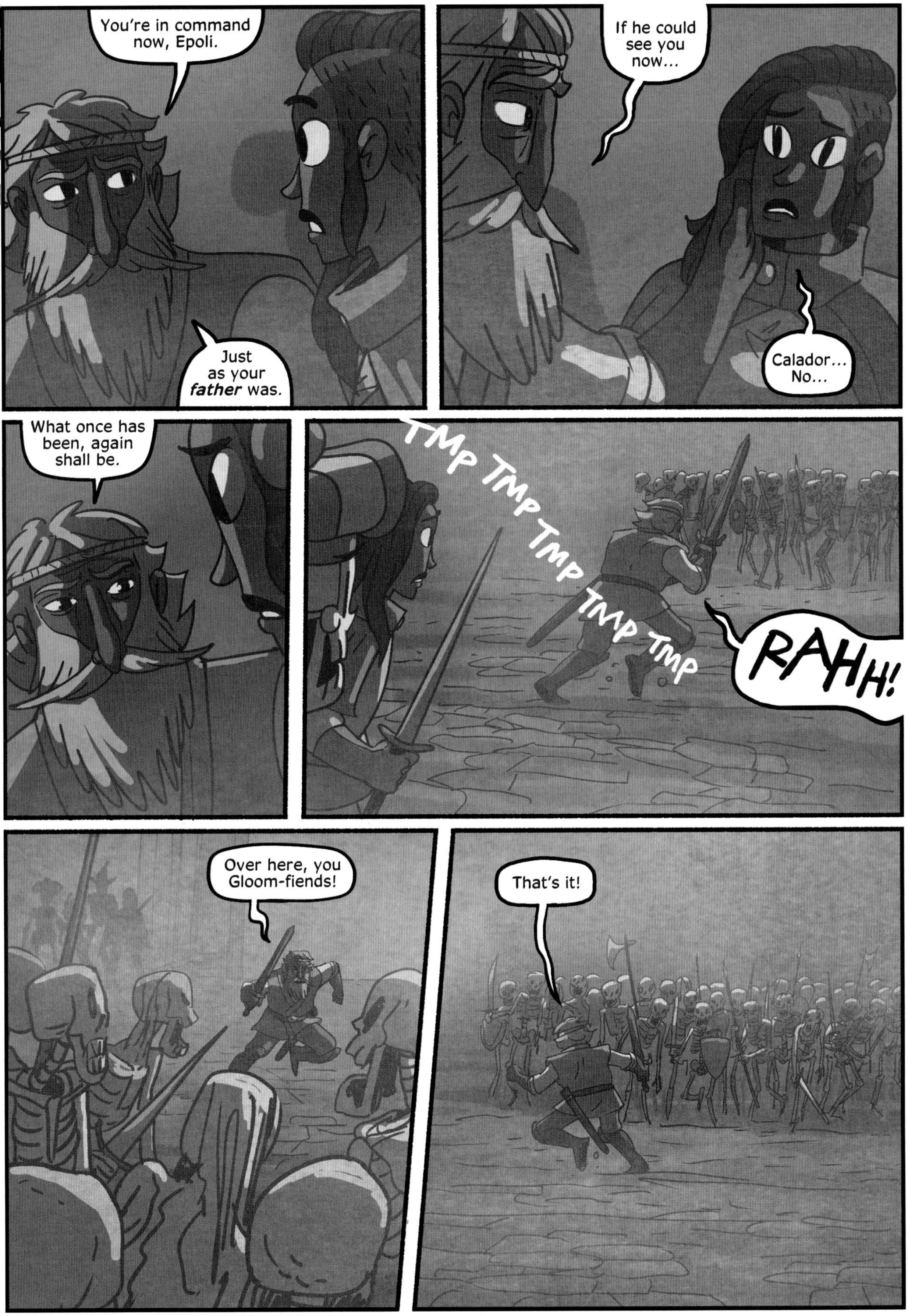
You're in command now, Epoli.
Just as your *father* was.
If he could see you now...
Calador... No...
What once has been, again shall be.
TMP TMP TMP TMP TMP TMP TMP
RAHH!
Over here, you Gloom-fiends!
That's it!

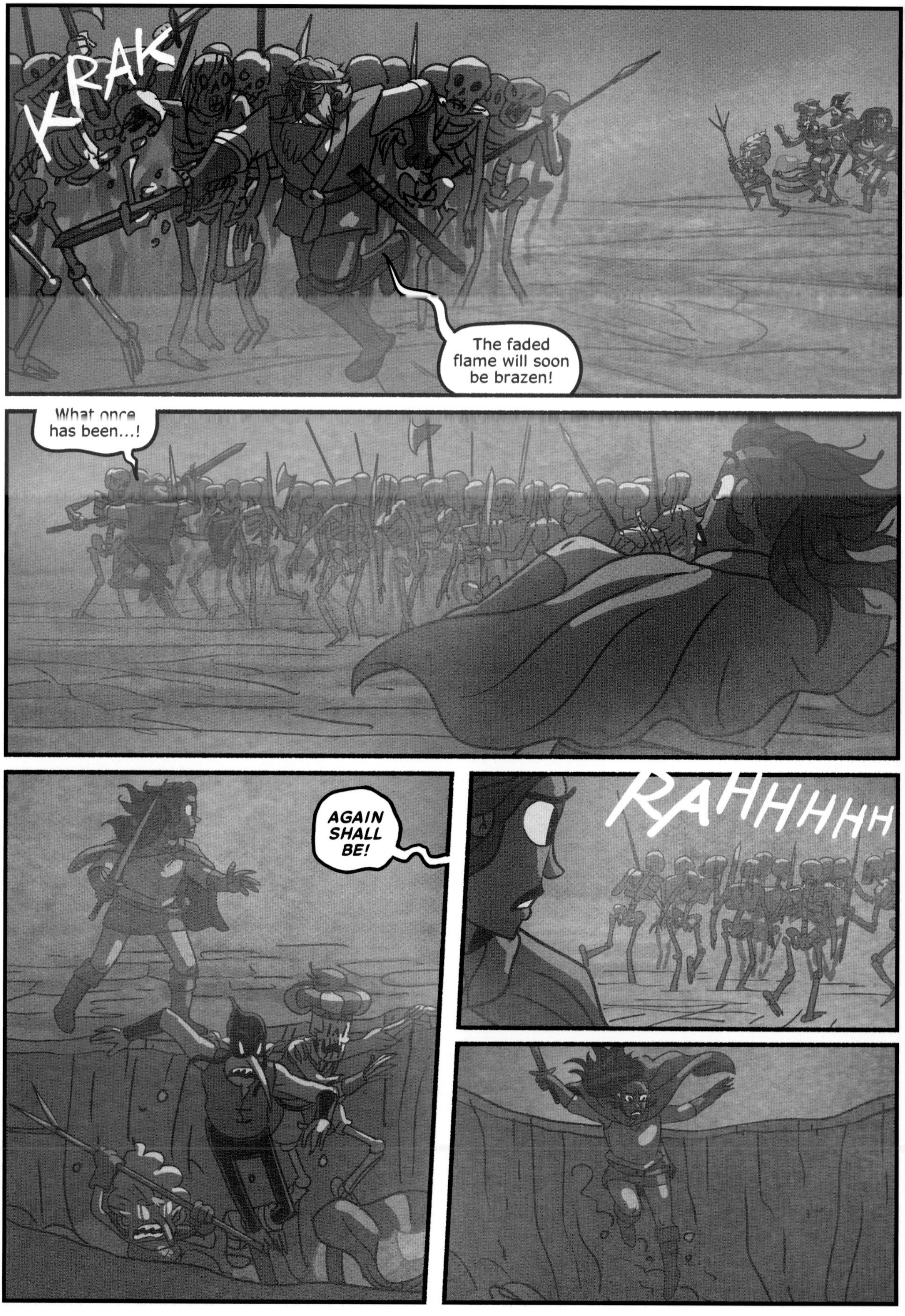
KRAK
The faded flame will soon be brazen!
What once has been...!
AGAIN SHALL BE!
RAHHHHH

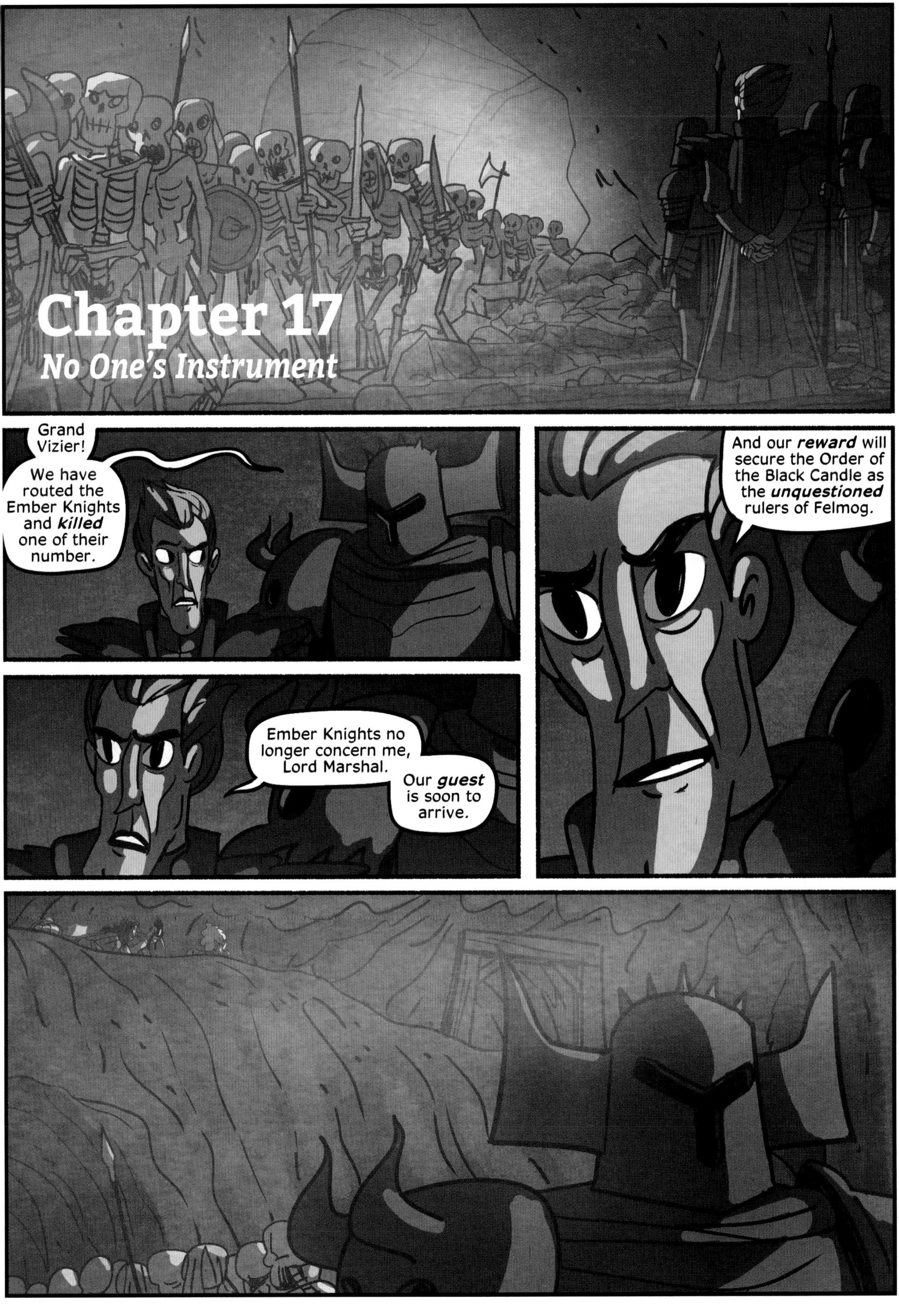
Chapter 17
No One's Instrument
Grand Vizier!
We have routed the Ember Knights and *killed* one of their number.
And our *reward* will secure the Order of the Black Candle as the *unquestioned* rulers of Felmog.
Ember Knights no longer concern me, Lord Marshal.
Our *guest* is soon to arrive.

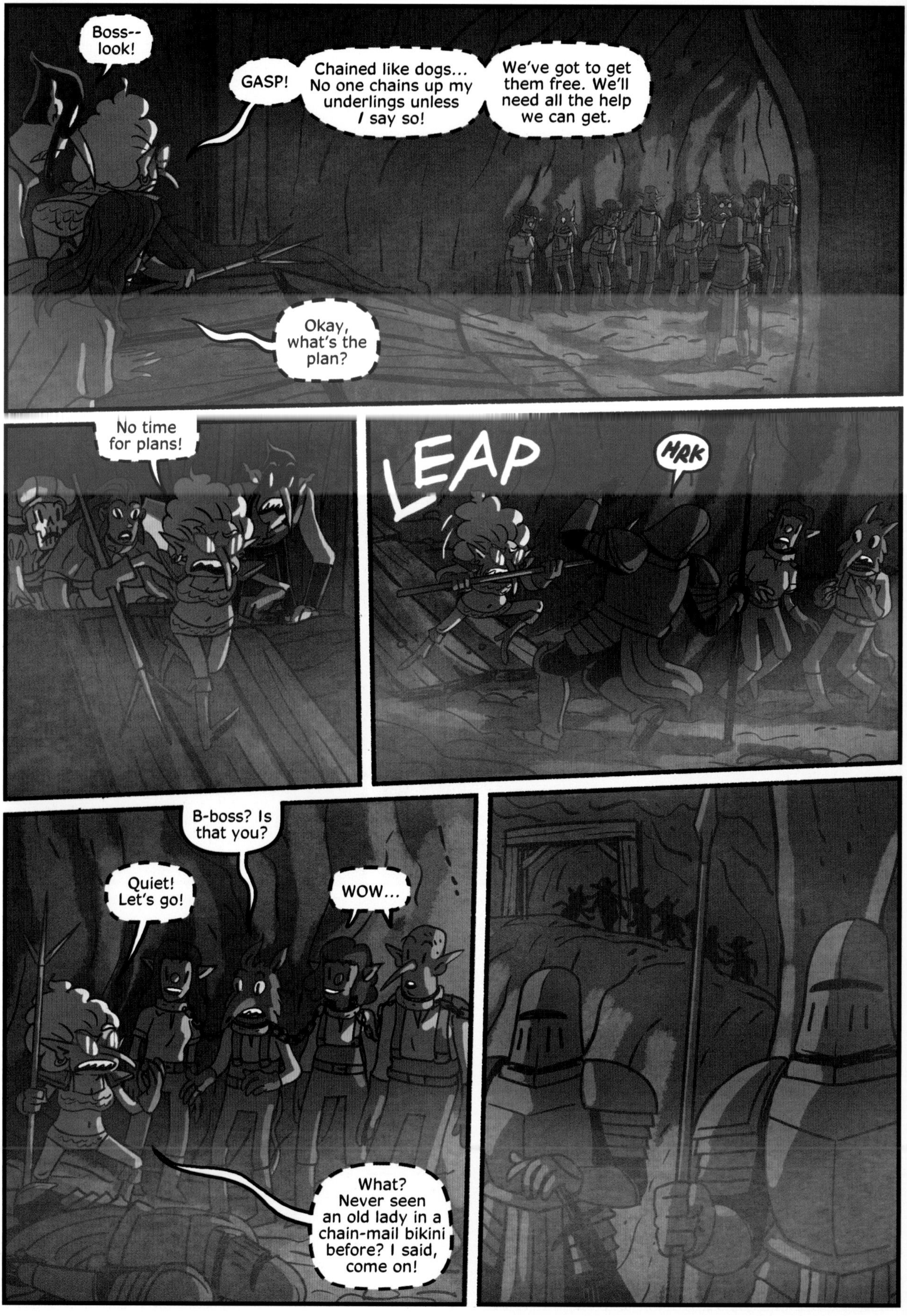
Boss-- look!
GASP!
Chained like dogs... No one chains up my underlings unless *I* say so!
We've got to get them free. We'll need all the help we can get.
Okay, what's the plan?
No time for plans!
LEAP
HRK
B-boss? Is that you?
Quiet! Let's go!
WOW...
!
What? Never seen an old lady in a chain-mail bikini before? I said, come on!

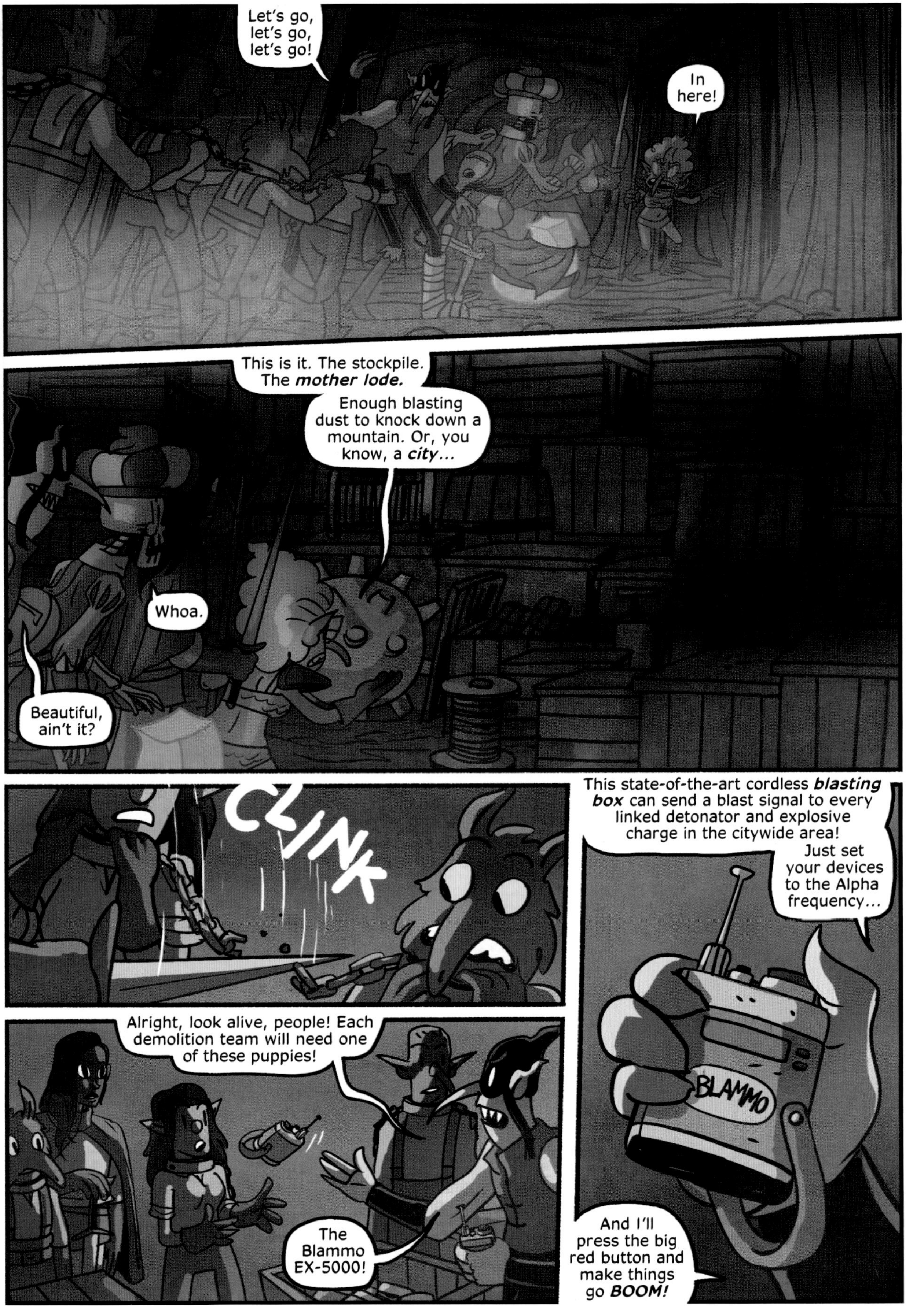
Let's go, let's go, let's go!
In here!
This is it. The stockpile. The *mother lode.*
Enough blasting dust to knock down a mountain. Or, you know, a *city*...
Whoa.
Beautiful, ain't it?
CLINK
This state-of-the-art cordless *blasting box* can send a blast signal to every linked detonator and explosive charge in the citywide area!
Just set your devices to the Alpha frequency...
BLAMMO
Alright, look alive, people! Each demolition team will need one of these puppies!
The Blammo EX-5000!
And I'll press the big red button and make things go *BOOM!*

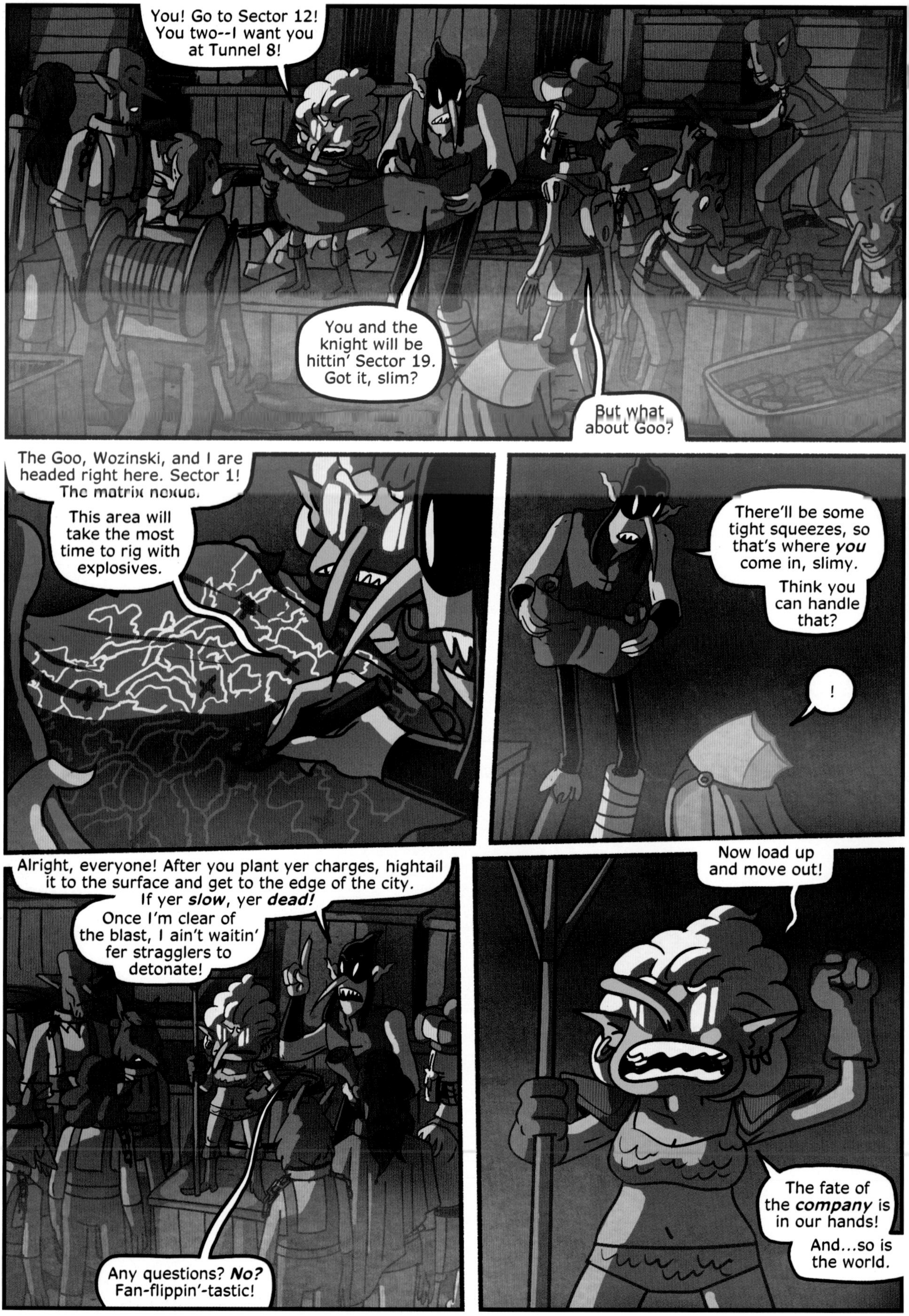
You! Go to Sector 12! You two--I want you at Tunnel 8!
You and the knight will be hittin' Sector 19. Got it, slim?
But what about Goo?
The Goo, Wozinski, and I are headed right here. Sector 1! The matrix nexus.
This area will take the most time to rig with explosives.
There'll be some tight squeezes, so that's where *you* come in, slimy.
Think you can handle that?
!
Alright, everyone! After you plant yer charges, hightail it to the surface and get to the edge of the city.
If yer *slow*, yer ***dead!***
Once I'm clear of the blast, I ain't waitin' fer stragglers to detonate!
Any questions? ***No?*** Fan-flippin'-tastic!
Now load up and move out!
The fate of the ***company*** is in our hands!
And...so is the world.

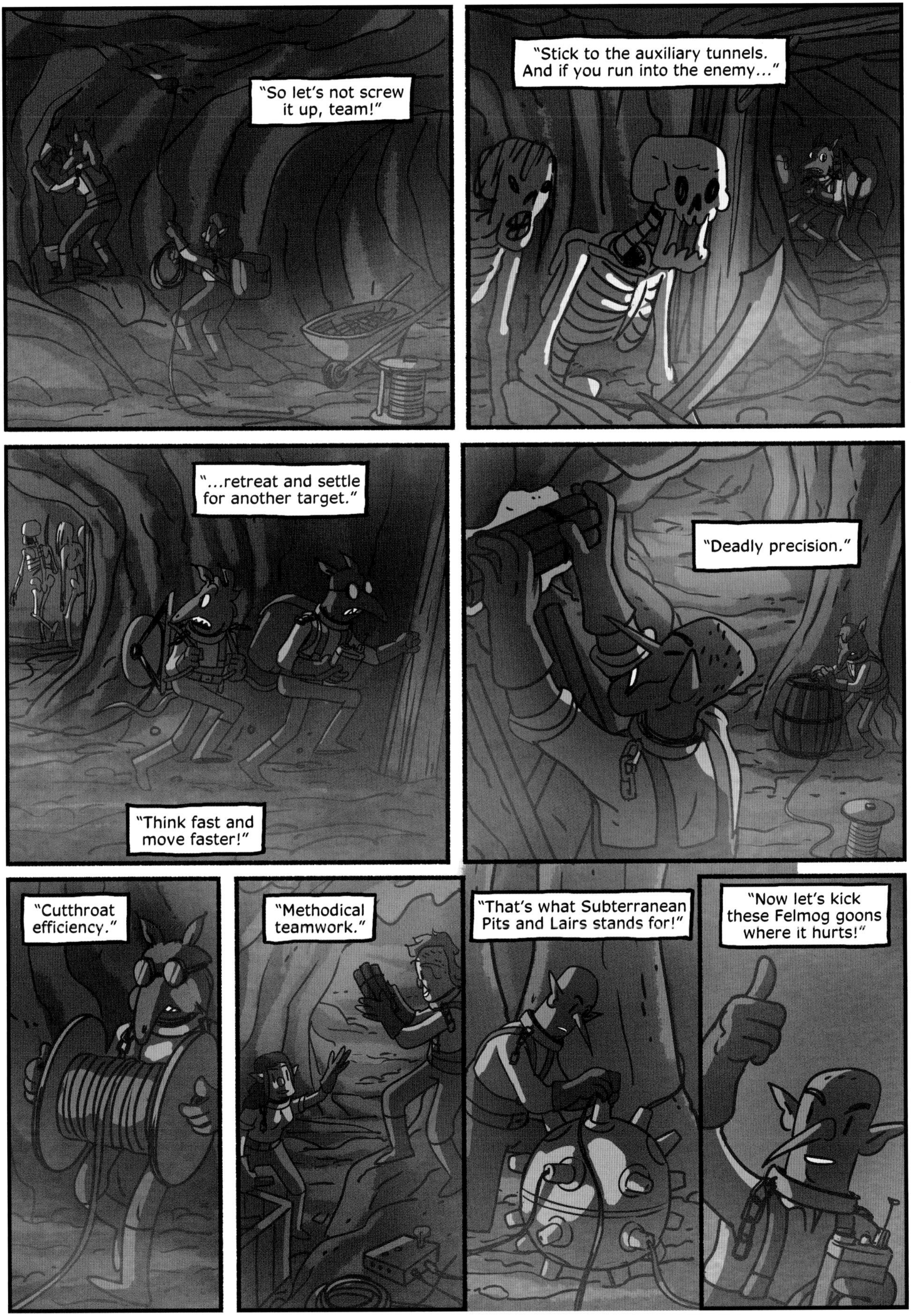
"So let's not screw it up, team!"
"Stick to the auxiliary tunnels. And if you run into the enemy..."
"...retreat and settle for another target."
"Think fast and move faster!"
"Deadly precision."
"Cutthroat efficiency."
"Methodical teamwork."
"That's what Subterranean Pits and Lairs stands for!"
"Now let's kick these Felmog goons where it hurts!"

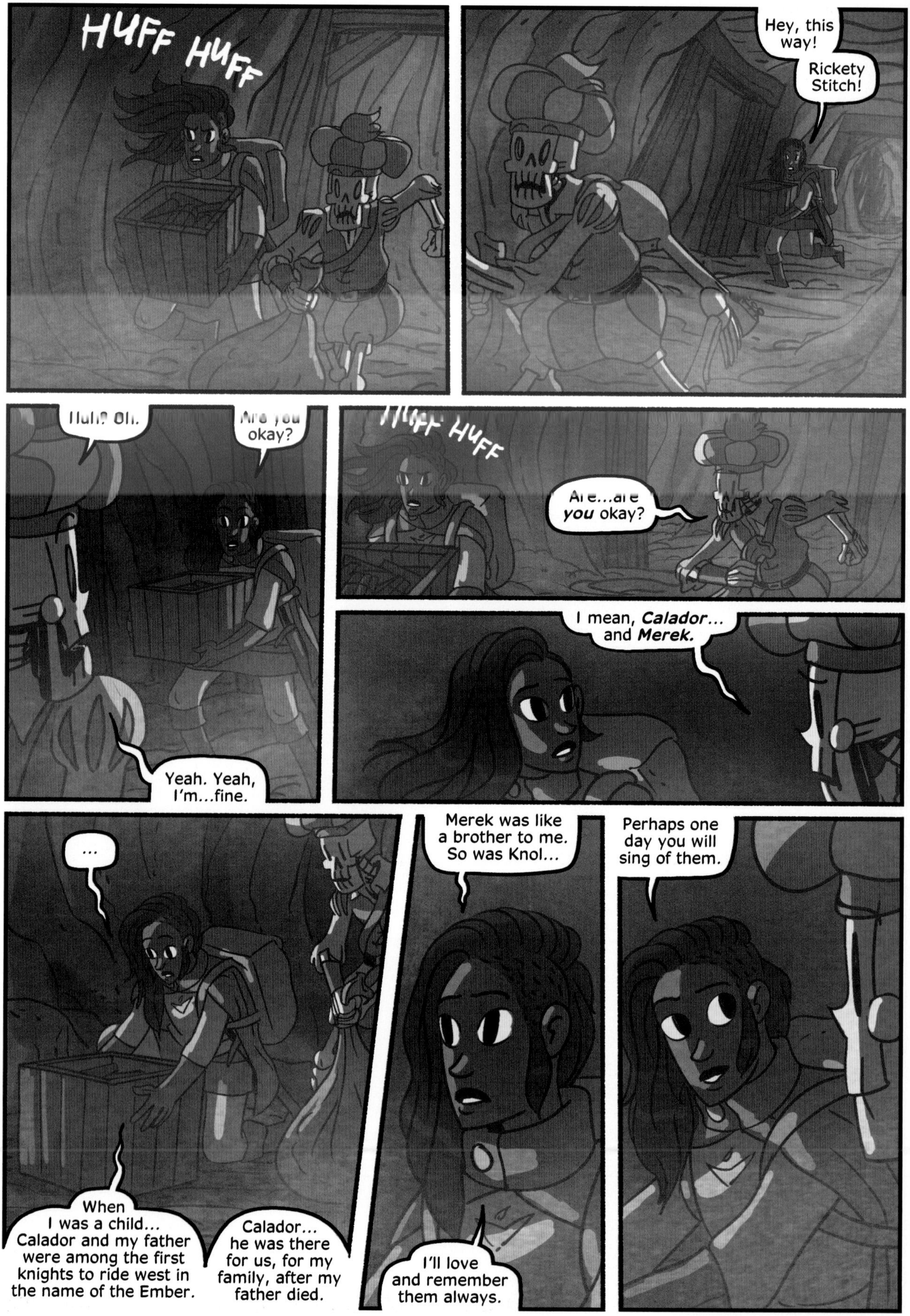
HUFF HUFF
Hey, this way!
Rickety Stitch!
Huh? Oh.
Are you okay?
Yeah. Yeah, I'm...fine.
HUFF HUFF
Are...are *you* okay?
I mean, ***Calador***... and ***Merek.***
...
When I was a child... Calador and my father were among the first knights to ride west in the name of the Ember.
Calador... he was there for us, for my family, after my father died.
Merek was like a brother to me. So was Knol...
I'll love and remember them always.
Perhaps one day you will sing of them.

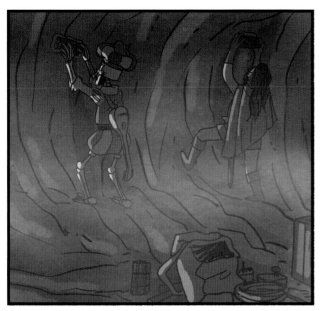

It--it's him. He's calling to me...

Rickety...?

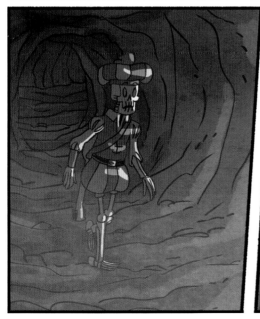

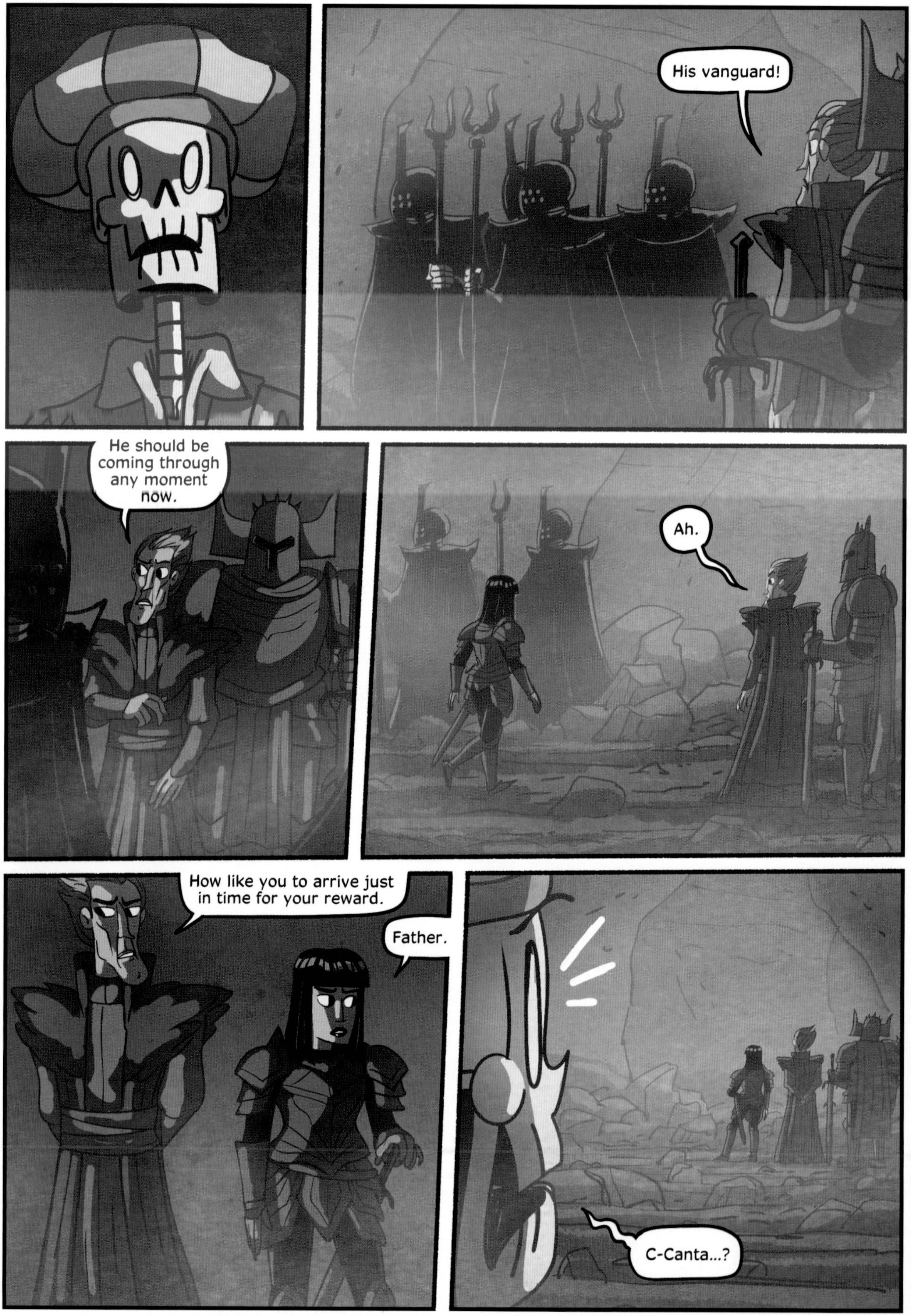
His vanguard!
He should be coming through any moment now.
Ah.
How like you to arrive just in time for your reward.
Father.
C-Canta...?

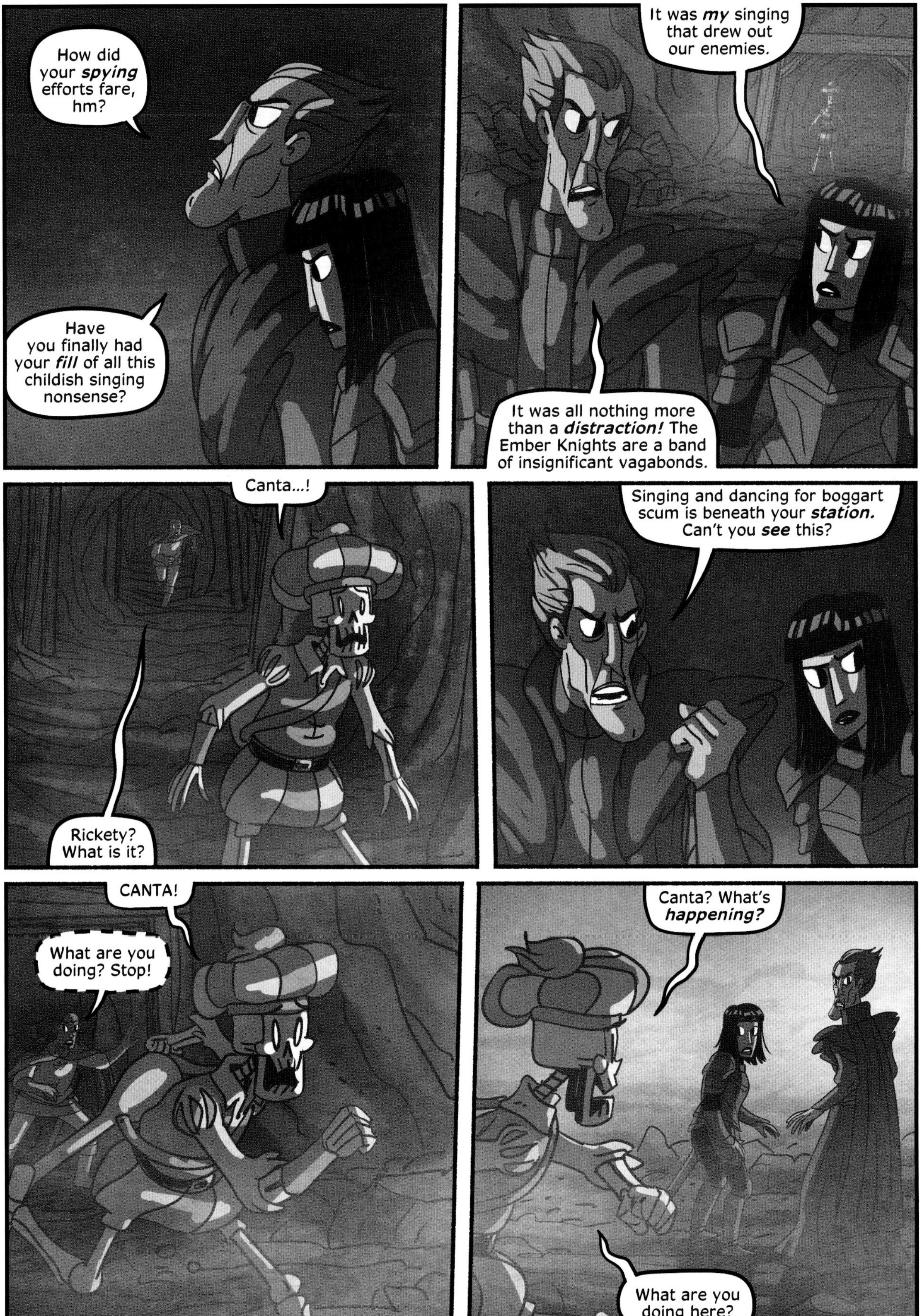
How did your *spying* efforts fare, hm?
Have you finally had your *fill* of all this childish singing nonsense?
It was *my* singing that drew out our enemies.
It was all nothing more than a *distraction!* The Ember Knights are a band of insignificant vagabonds.
Canta...!
Rickety? What is it?
Singing and dancing for boggart scum is beneath your *station.* Can't you *see* this?
CANTA!
What are you doing? Stop!
Canta? What's *happening?*
What are you doing here?

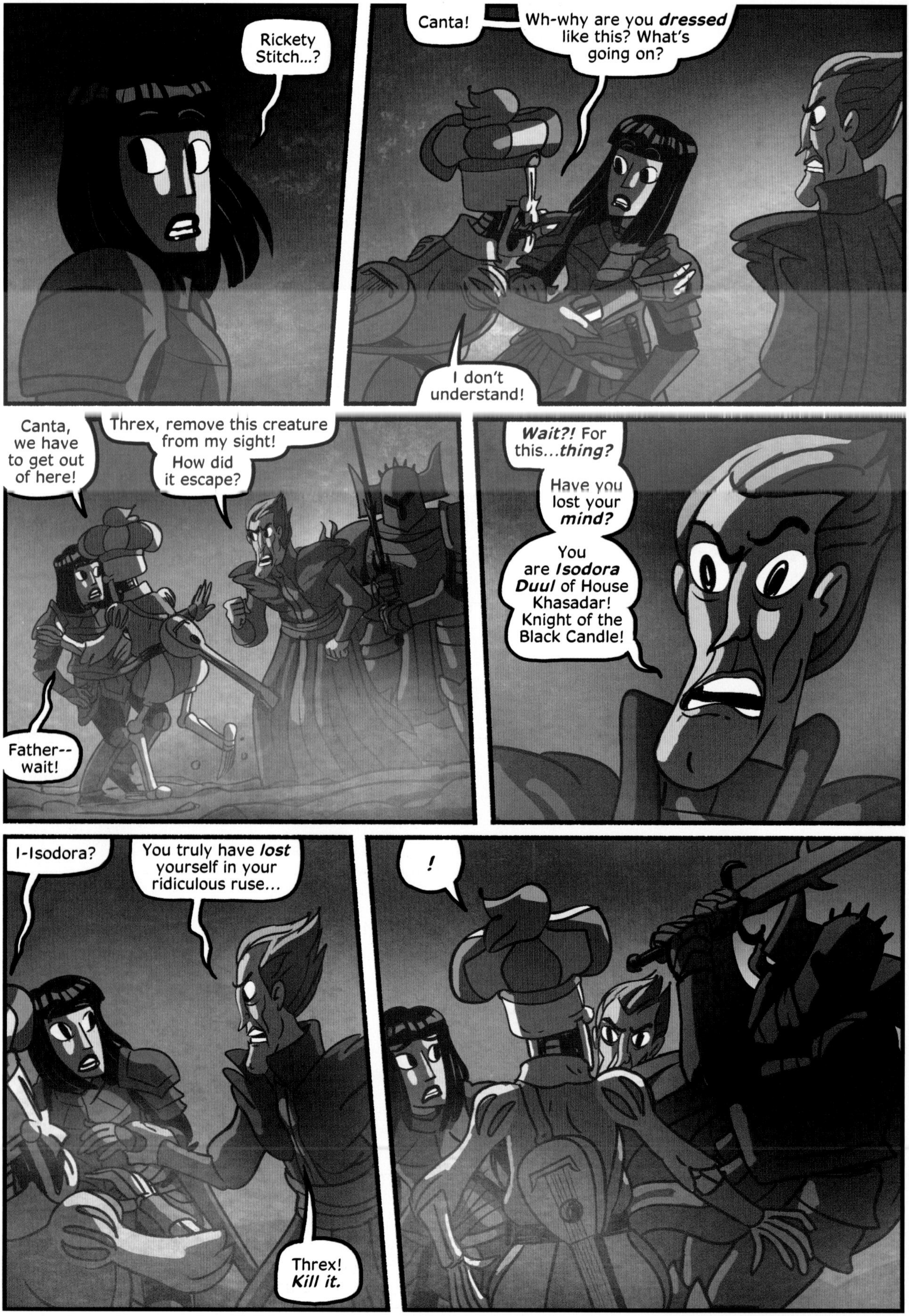

Rickety Stitch...?
Canta!
Wh-why are you *dressed* like this? What's going on?
I don't understand!
Canta, we have to get out of here!
Threx, remove this creature from my sight!
How did it escape?
Father--wait!
Wait?! For this...*thing?*
Have you lost your *mind?*
You are *Isodora Duul* of House Khasadar! Knight of the Black Candle!
I-Isodora?
You truly have *lost* yourself in your ridiculous ruse...
Threx! *Kill it.*
!

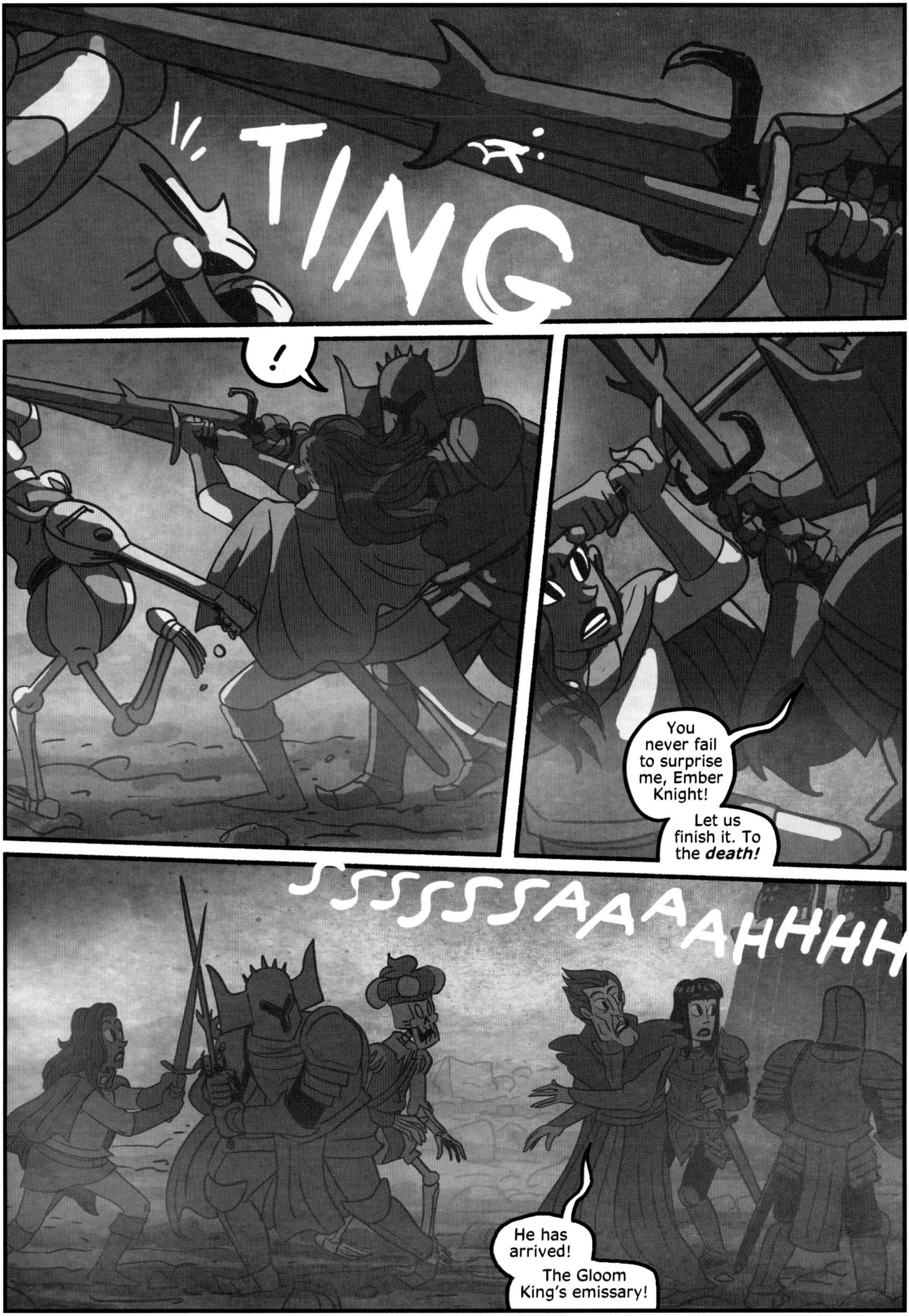
TING
!
You never fail to surprise me, Ember Knight!
Let us finish it. To the ***death!***
SSSSSAAAAHHHH
He has arrived!
The Gloom King's emissary!

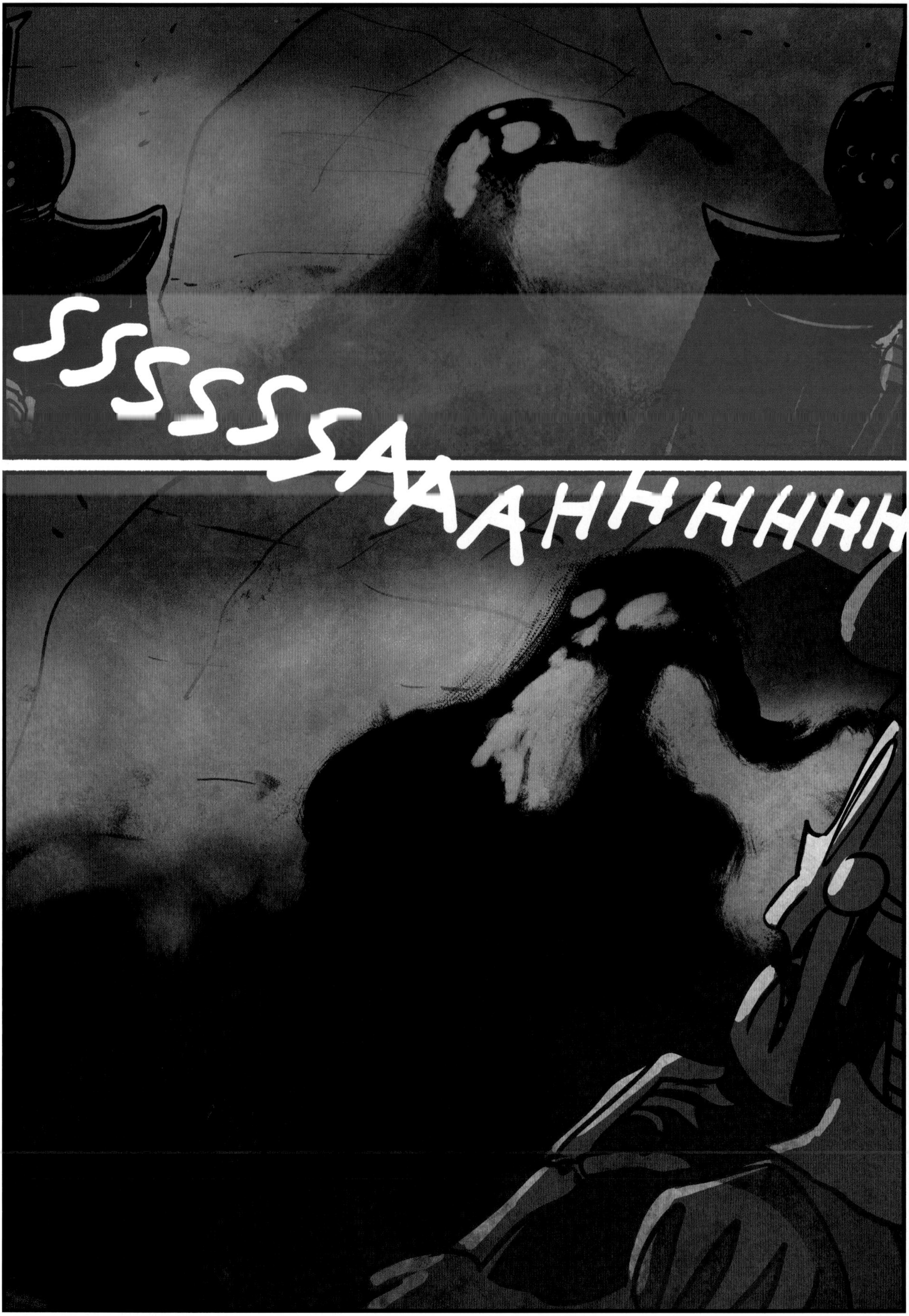
SSSSSSAAAHHHHHH

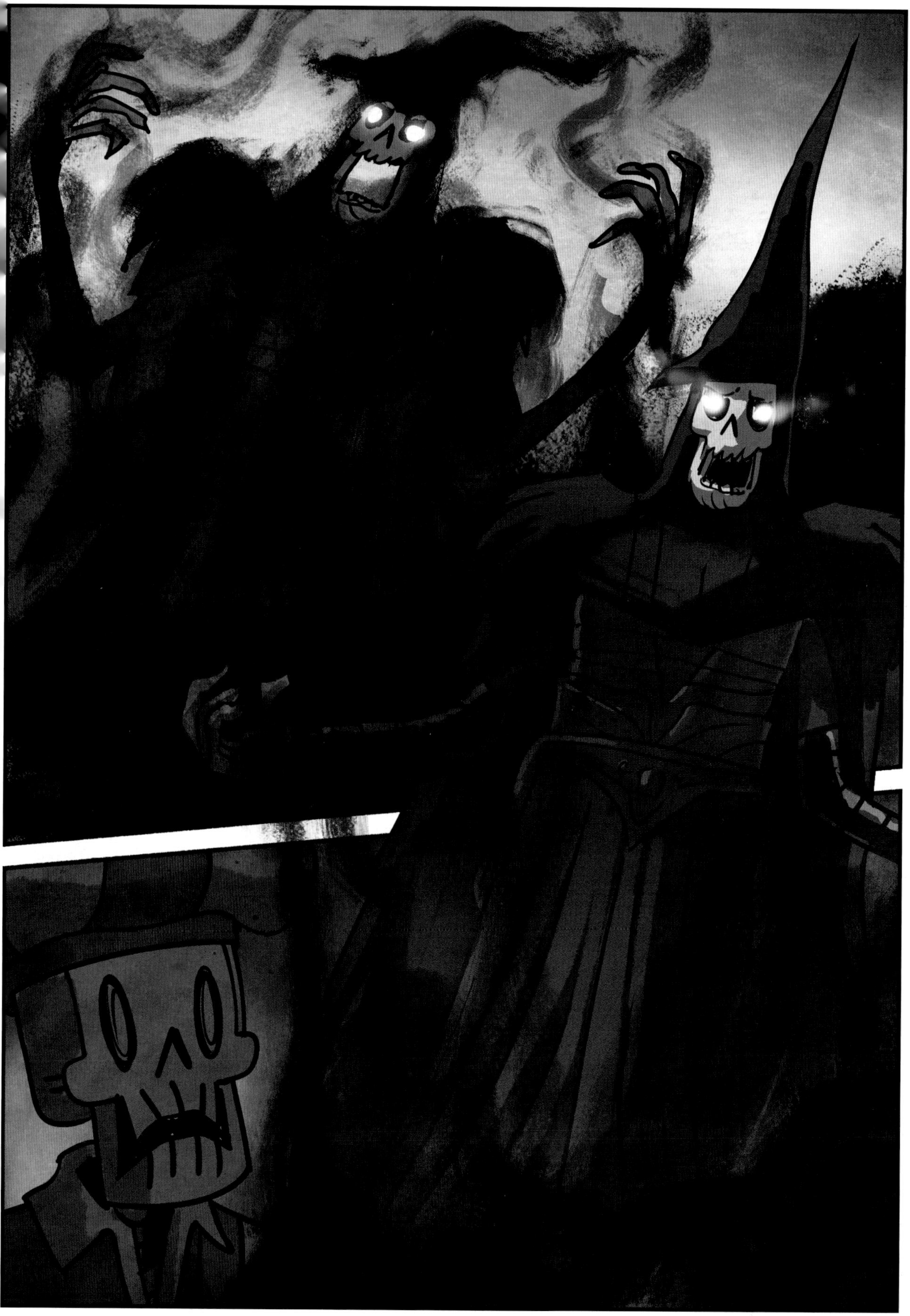

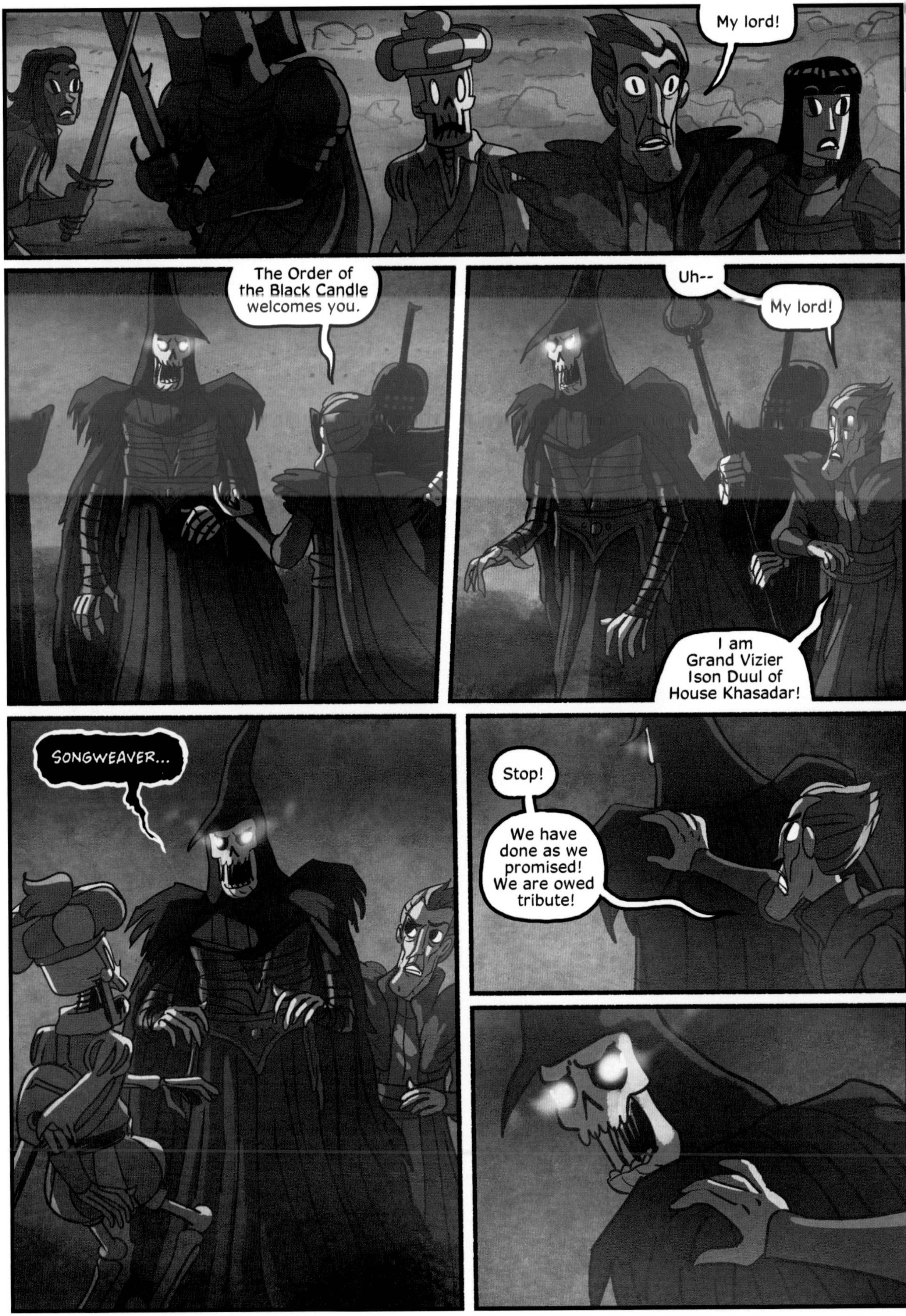
My lord!
The Order of the Black Candle welcomes you.
Uh--
My lord!
I am Grand Vizier Ison Duul of House Khasadar!
SONGWEAVER...
Stop!
We have done as we promised! We are owed tribute!

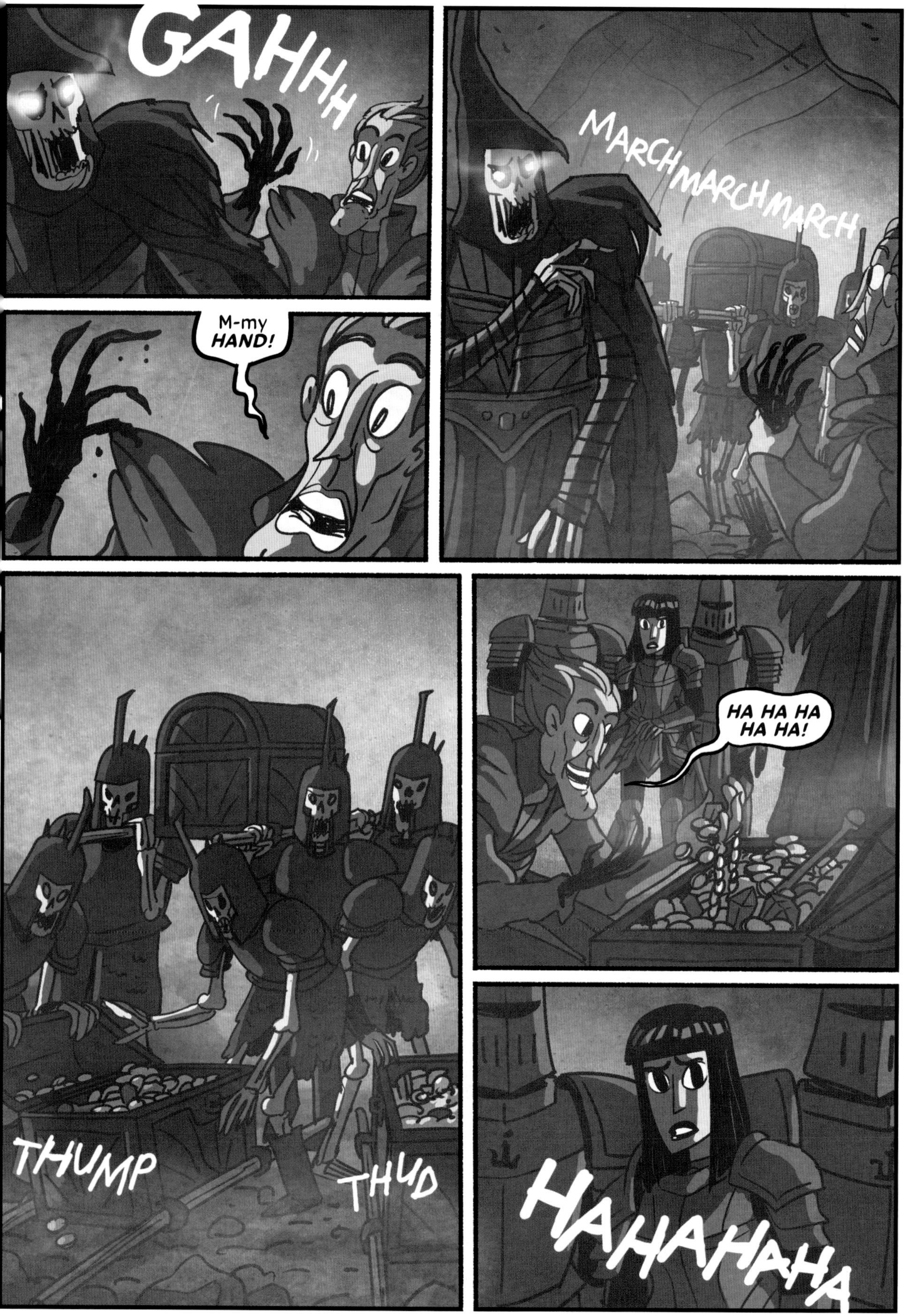
GAHHH
MARCHMARCHMARCH
M-my HAND!
THUMP
THUD
HA HA HA HA HA!
HAHAHAHA

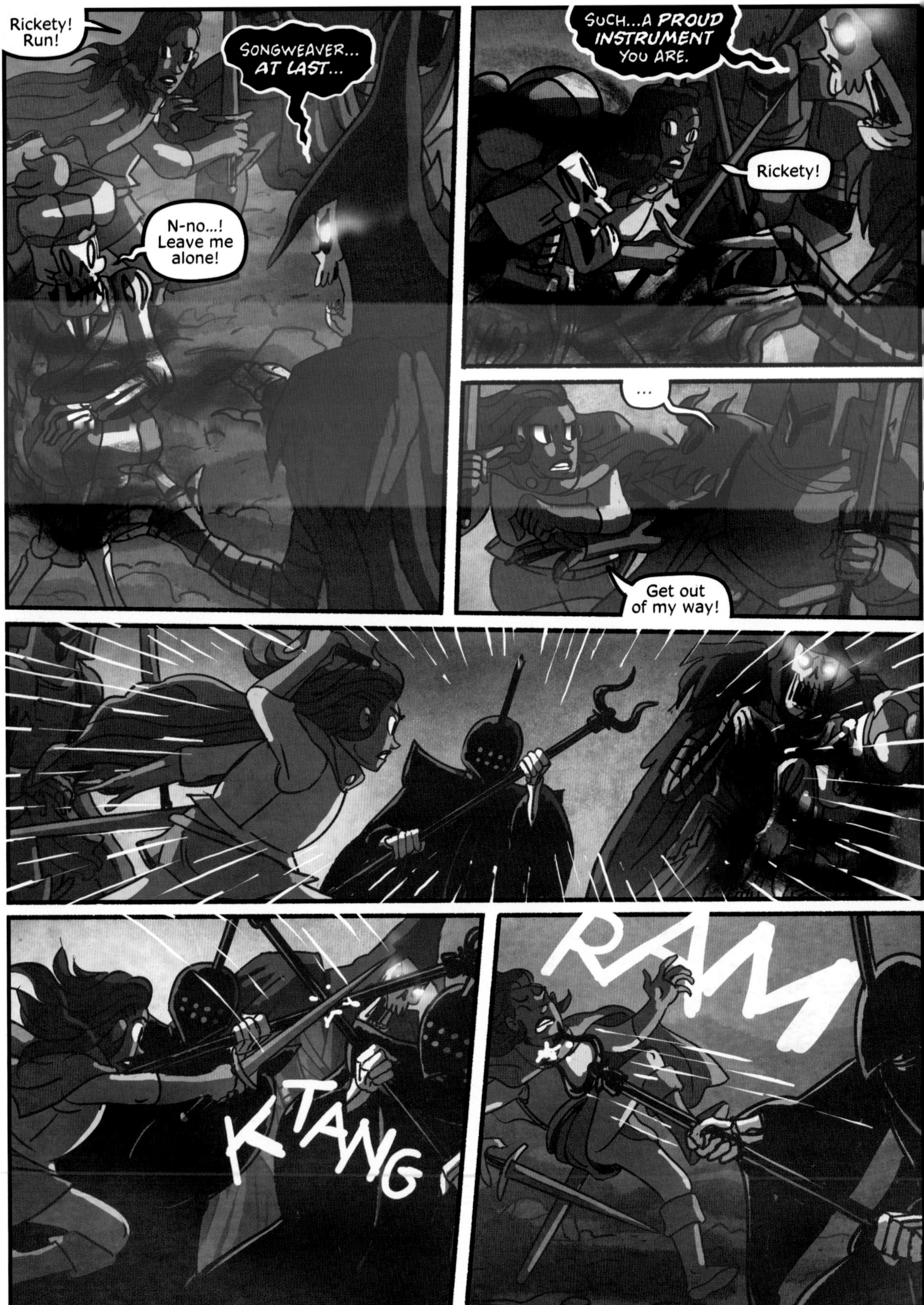
Rickety! Run!
SONGWEAVER... AT LAST...
N-no...! Leave me alone!
SUCH...A PROUD INSTRUMENT YOU ARE.
Rickety!
...
Get out of my way!
KTANG
RAM

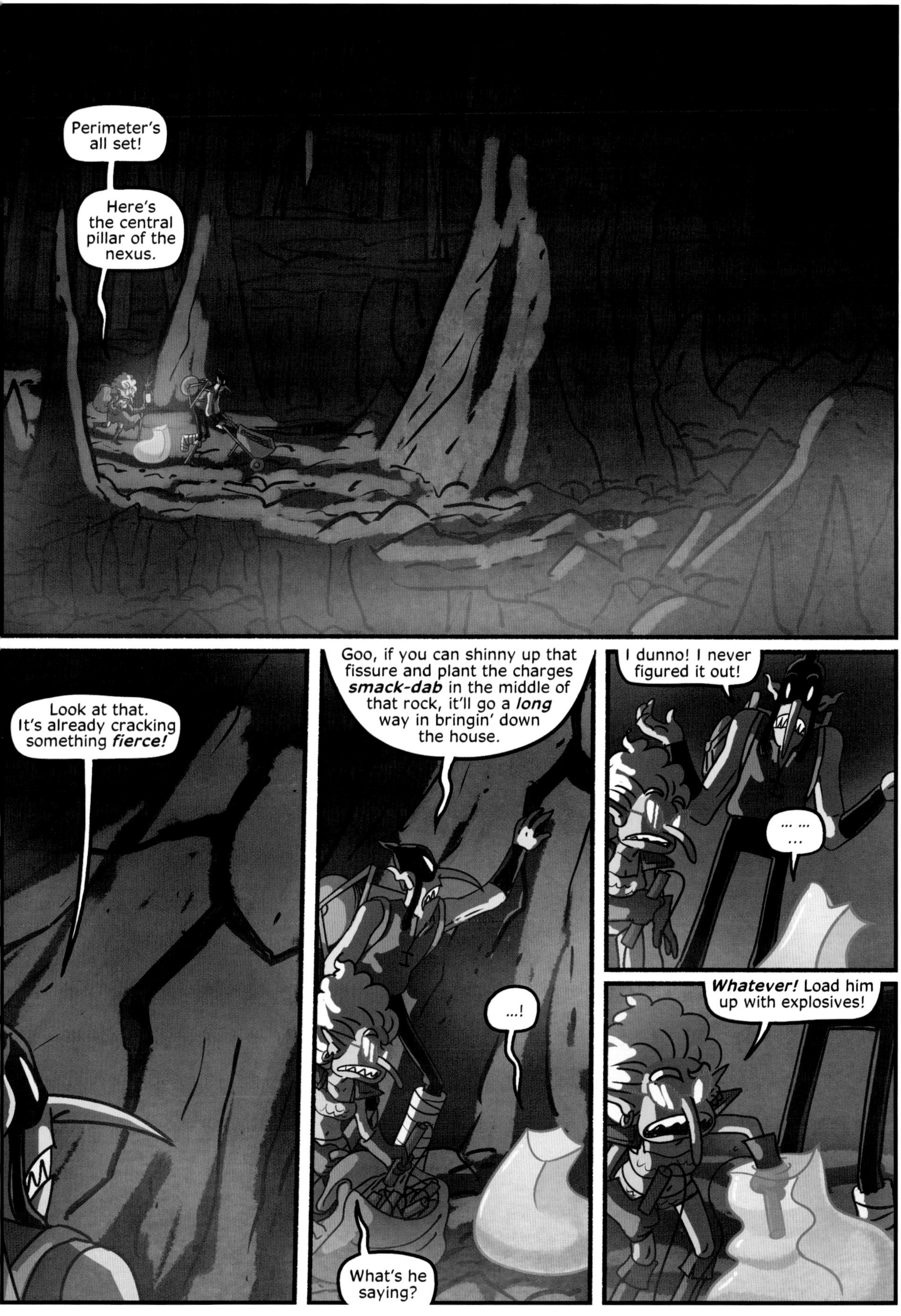
Perimeter's all set!
Here's the central pillar of the nexus.
Look at that. It's already cracking something *fierce!*
Goo, if you can shinny up that fissure and plant the charges ***smack-dab*** in the middle of that rock, it'll go a ***long*** way in bringin' down the house.
...!
What's he saying?
I dunno! I never figured it out!
... ...
Whatever! Load him up with explosives!

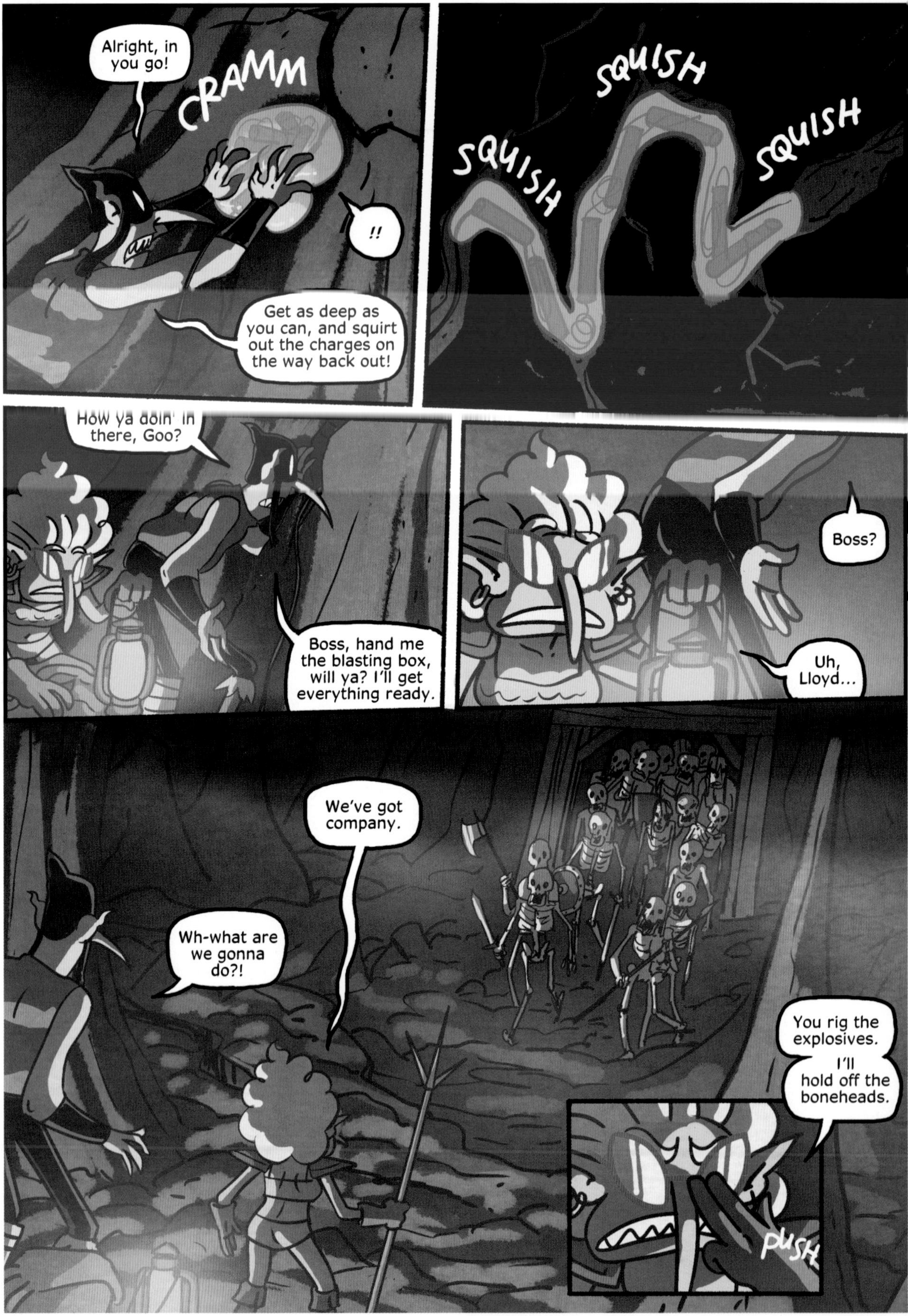
Alright, in you go!
CRAMM
!!
Get as deep as you can, and squirt out the charges on the way back out!
SQUISH
SQUISH
SQUISH
How ya doin' in there, Goo?
Boss, hand me the blasting box, will ya? I'll get everything ready.
Boss?
Uh, Lloyd...
We've got company.
Wh-what are we gonna do?!
You rig the explosives. I'll hold off the boneheads.
PUSH

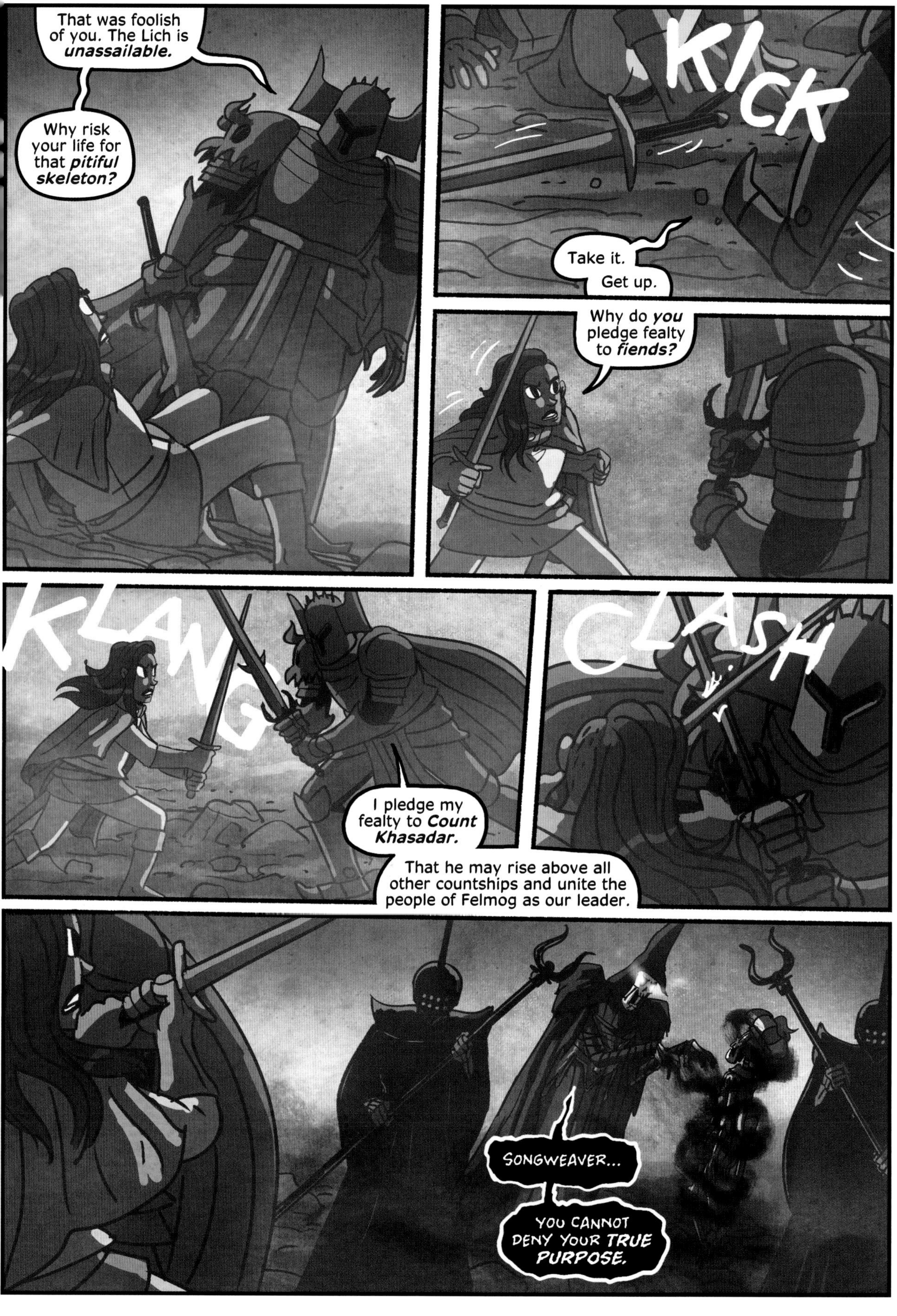

That was foolish of you. The Lich is *unassailable.*
Why risk your life for that *pitiful skeleton?*
KICK
Take it.
Get up.
Why do *you* pledge fealty to *fiends?*
KLANG
I pledge my fealty to ***Count Khasadar.***
CLASH
That he may rise above all other countships and unite the people of Felmog as our leader.
SONGWEAVER...
YOU CANNOT DENY YOUR ***TRUE PURPOSE.***

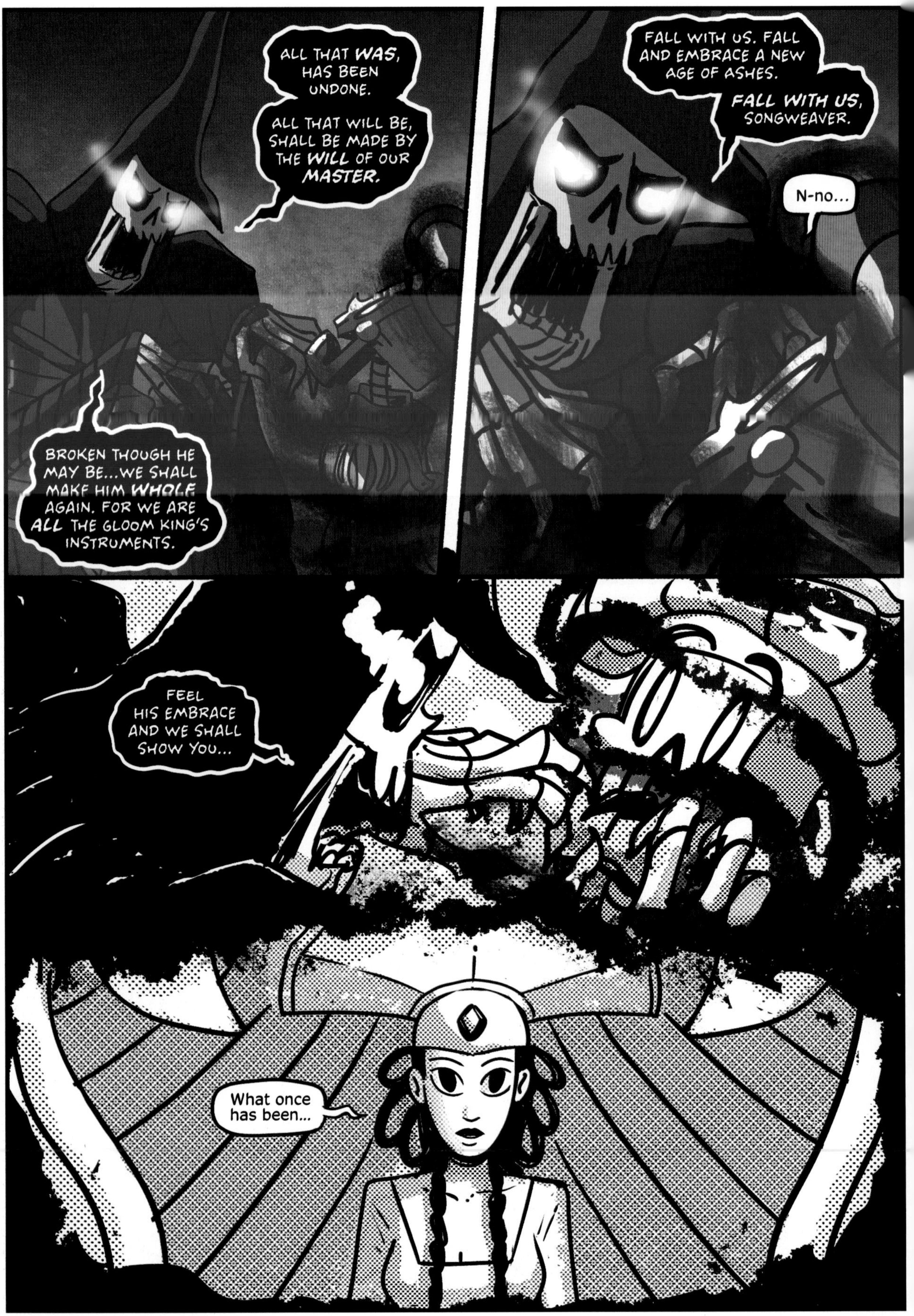
ALL THAT WAS, HAS BEEN UNDONE.
ALL THAT WILL BE, SHALL BE MADE BY THE WILL OF OUR MASTER.
BROKEN THOUGH HE MAY BE...WE SHALL MAKE HIM WHOLE AGAIN. FOR WE ARE ALL THE GLOOM KING'S INSTRUMENTS.
FALL WITH US. FALL AND EMBRACE A NEW AGE OF ASHES.
FALL WITH US, SONGWEAVER.
N-no...
FEEL HIS EMBRACE AND WE SHALL SHOW YOU...
What once has been...

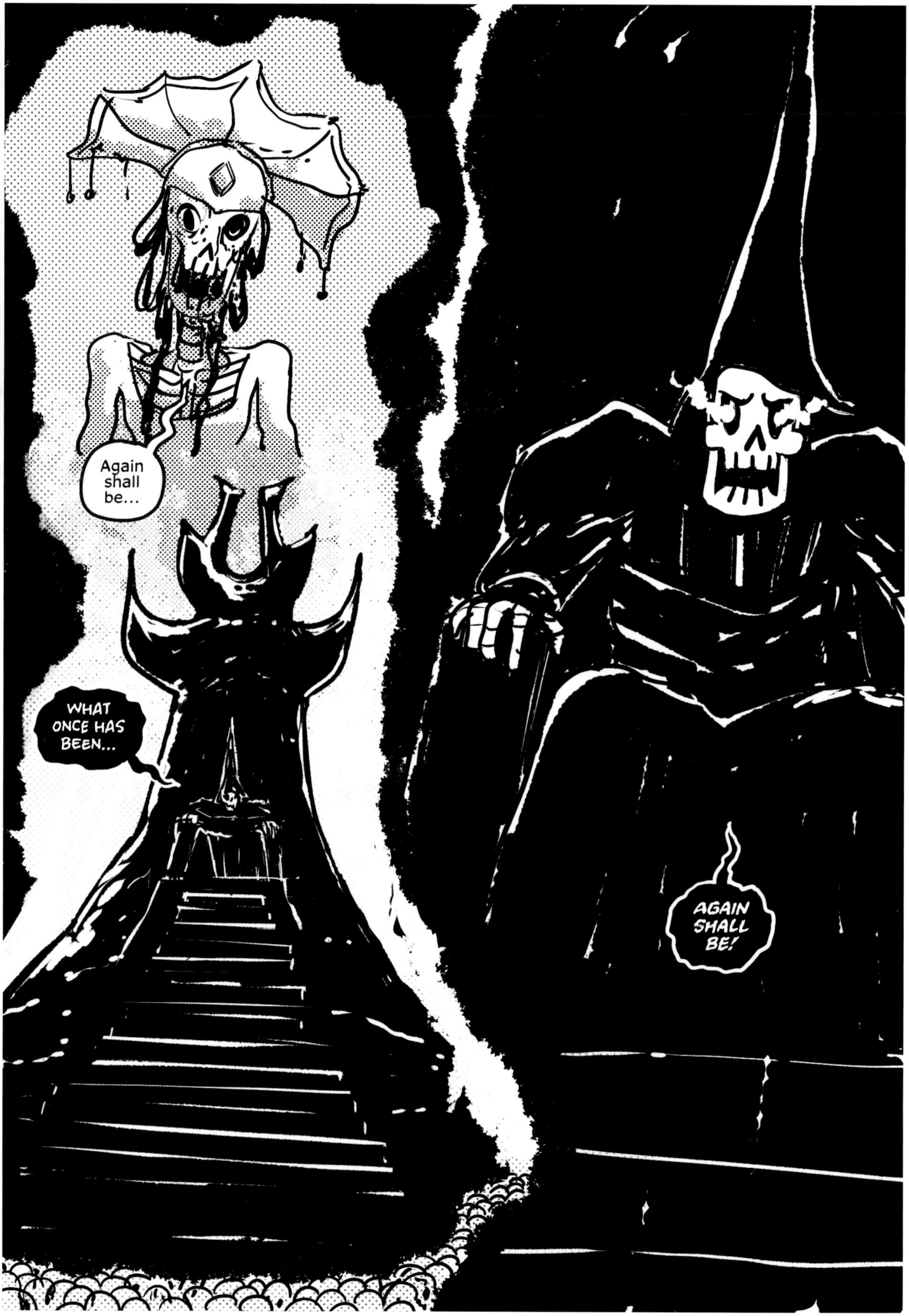
Again shall be...
WHAT ONCE HAS BEEN...
AGAIN SHALL BE!

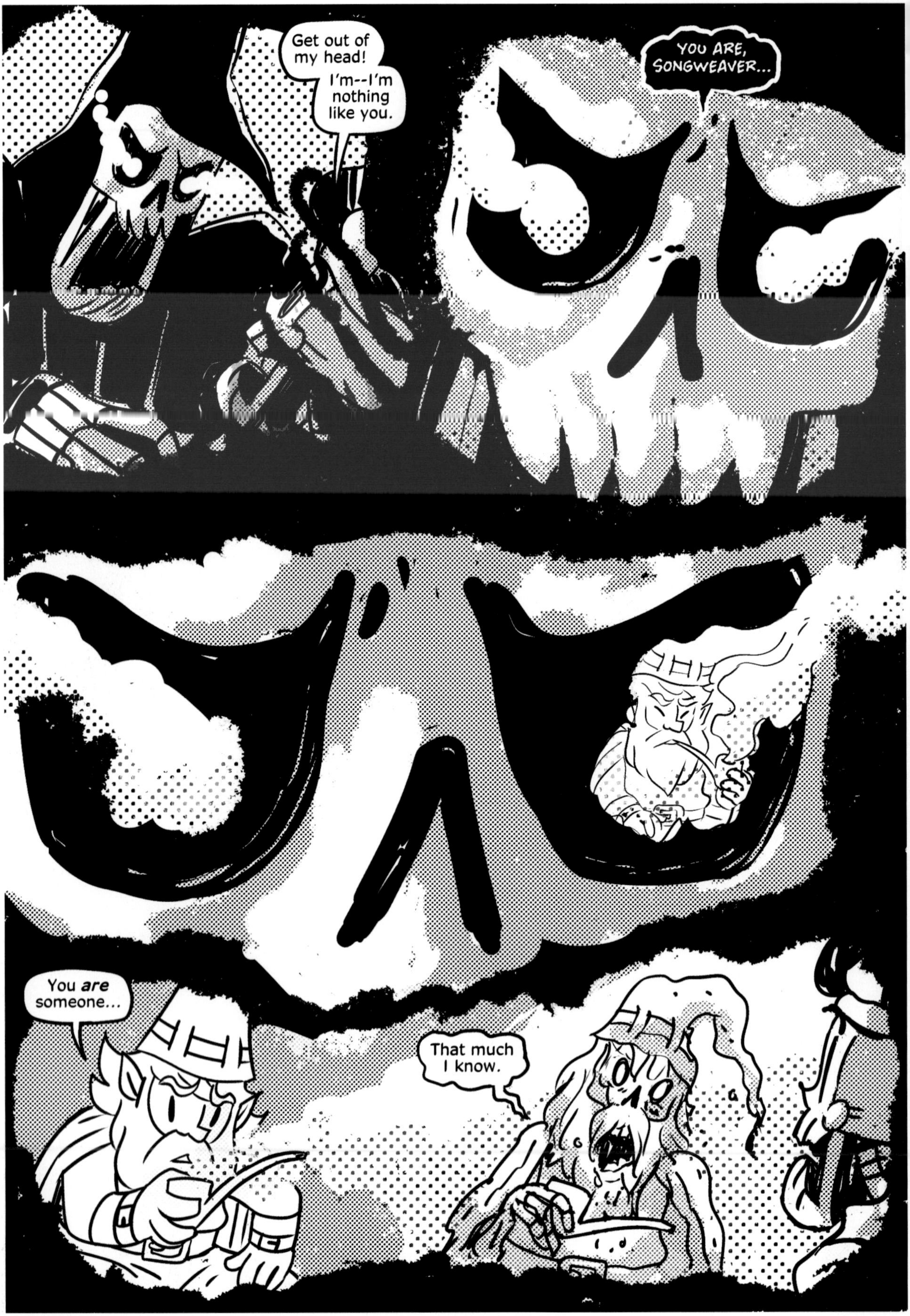
Get out of my head!
I'm--I'm nothing like you.
YOU ARE, SONGWEAVER...
You *are* someone...
That much I know.

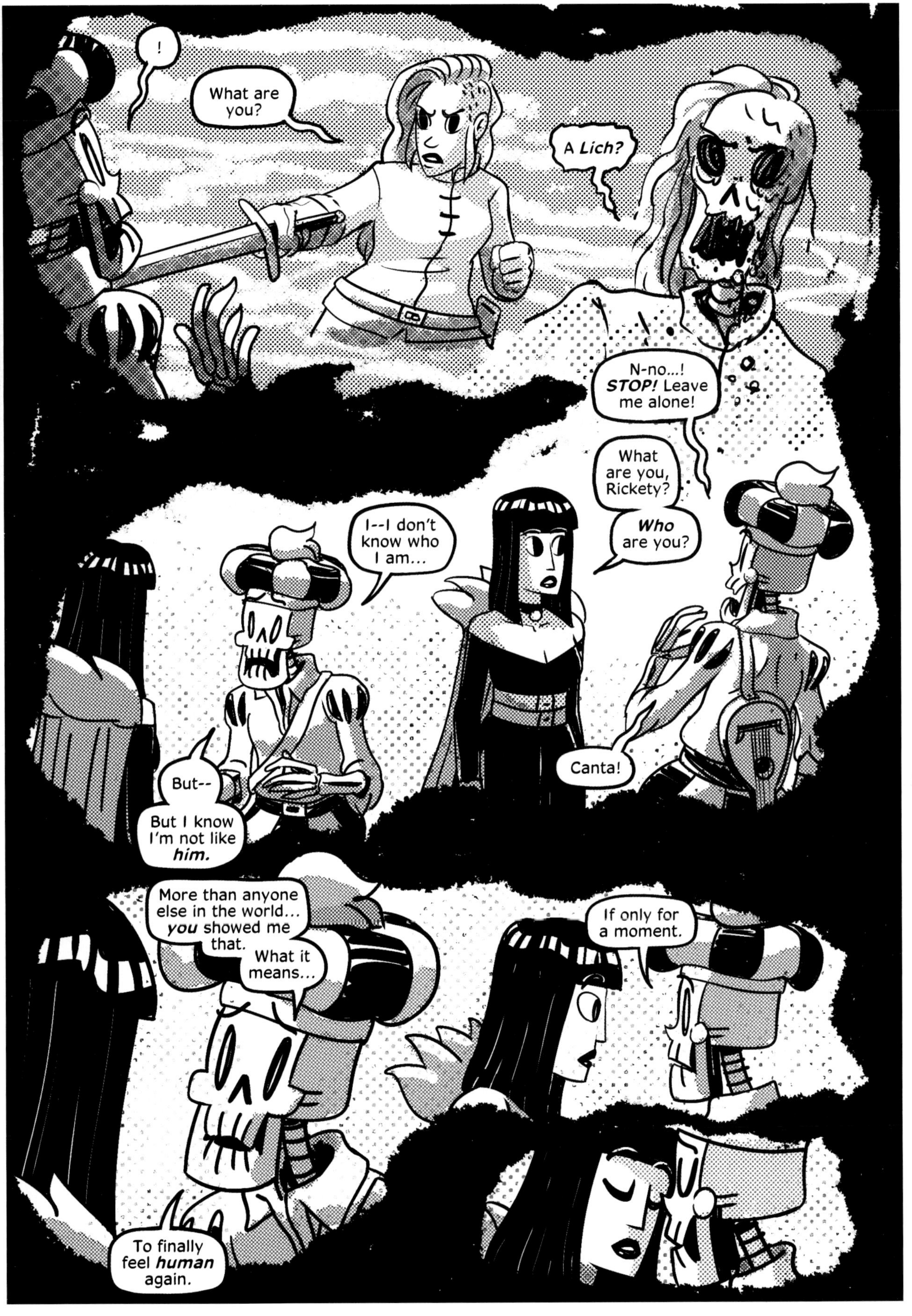
!
What are you?
A *Lich?*
N-no...! ***STOP!*** Leave me alone!
What are you, Rickety?
Who are you?
I--I don't know who I am...
Canta!
But--
But I know I'm not like ***him.***
More than anyone else in the world... ***you*** showed me that.
What it means...
If only for a moment.
To finally feel ***human*** again.

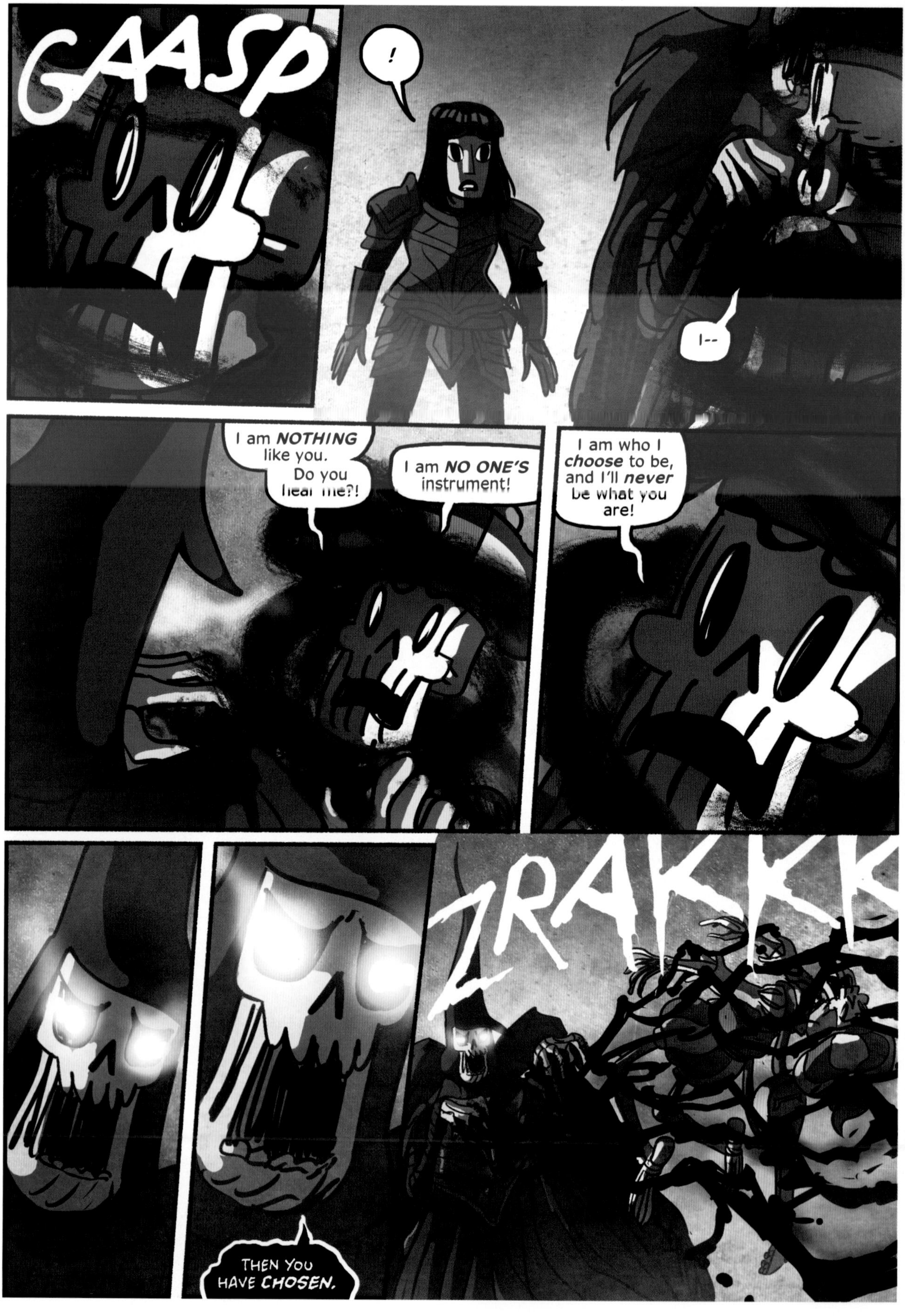
GAASP
!
I--
I am NOTHING like you. Do you hear me?!
I am NO ONE'S instrument!
I am who I choose to be, and I'll never be what you are!
THEN YOU HAVE CHOSEN.
ZRAKKK

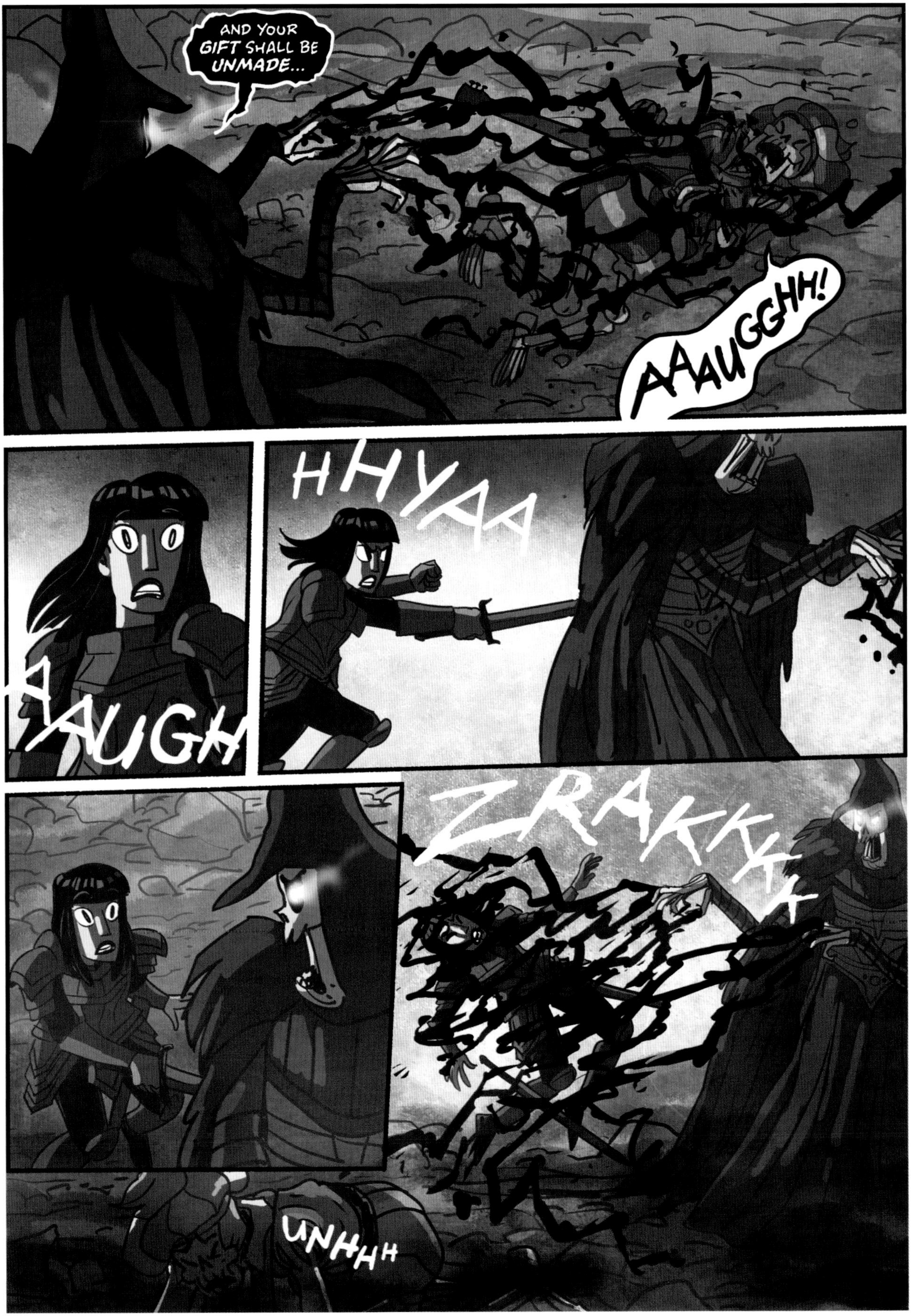
AND YOUR GIFT SHALL BE UNMADE...
AAAUGGHH!
AAUGH
HHYAA
ZRAKKKK
UNHHH

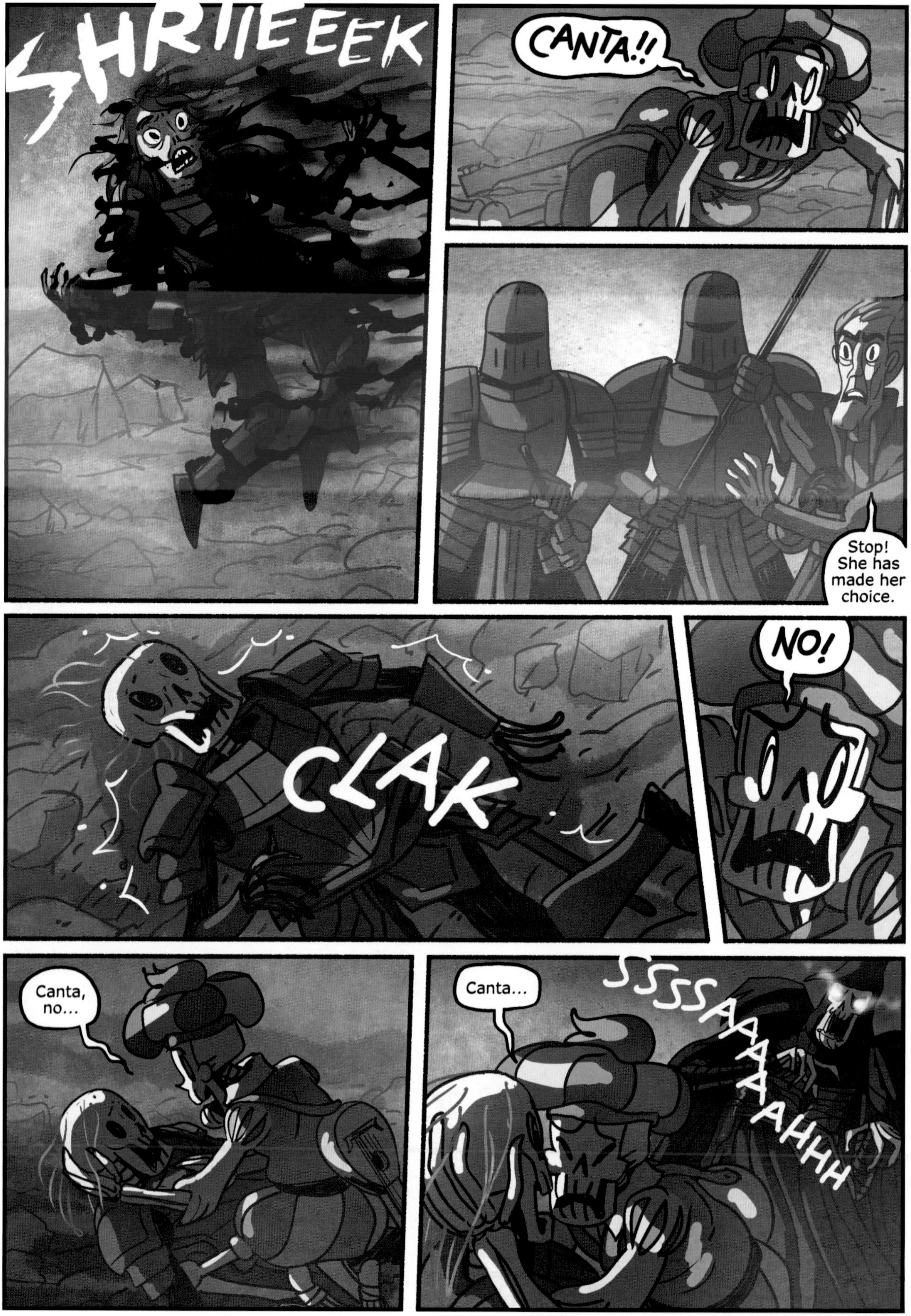
SHRIIEEEK
CANTA!!
Stop! She has made her choice.
CLAK
NO!
Canta, no...
Canta...
SSSSAAAAAAHHH

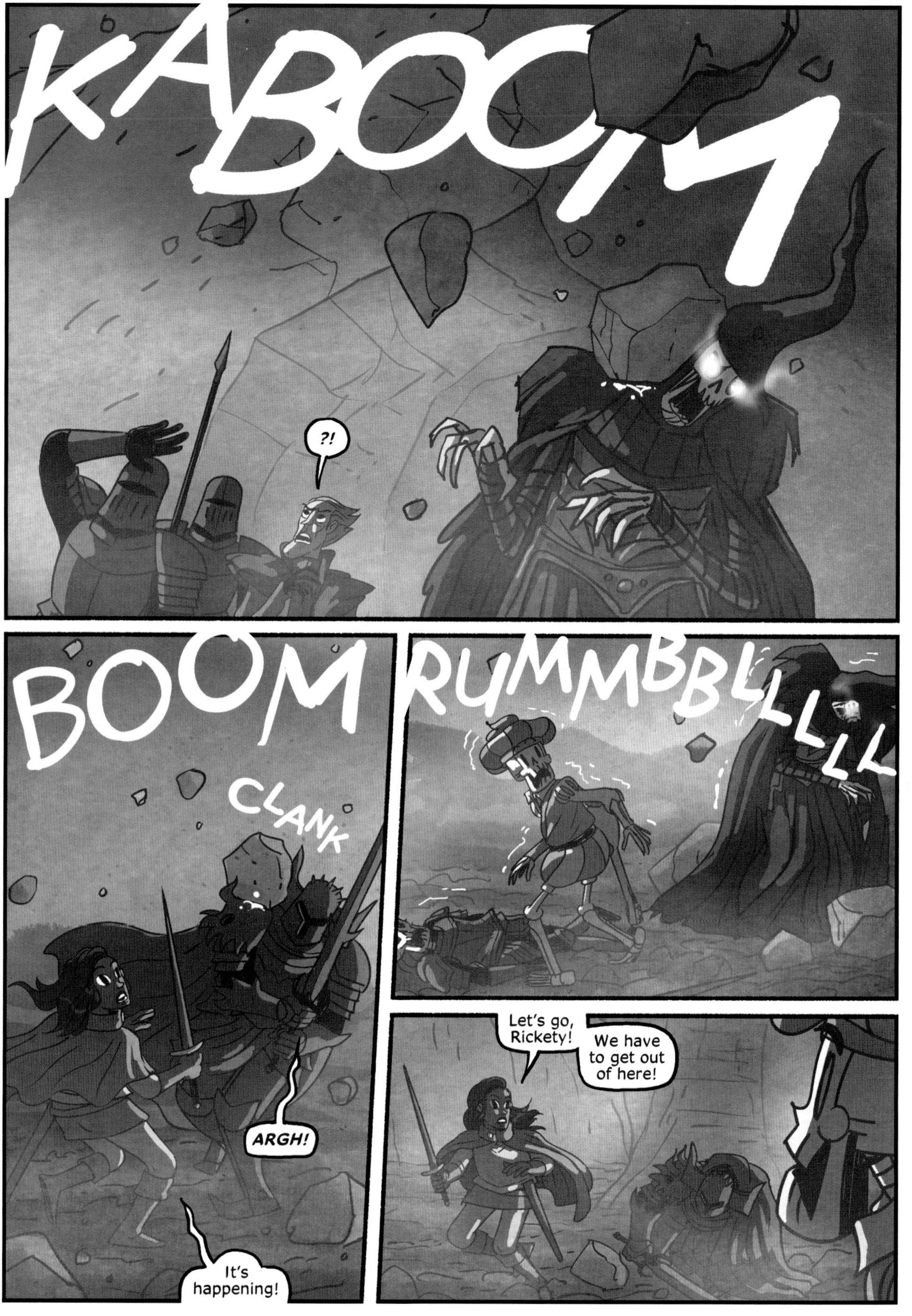
KABOOM
?!
BOOM
CLANK
ARGH!
It's happening!
RUMMBBLLLLL
Let's go, Rickety!
We have to get out of here!

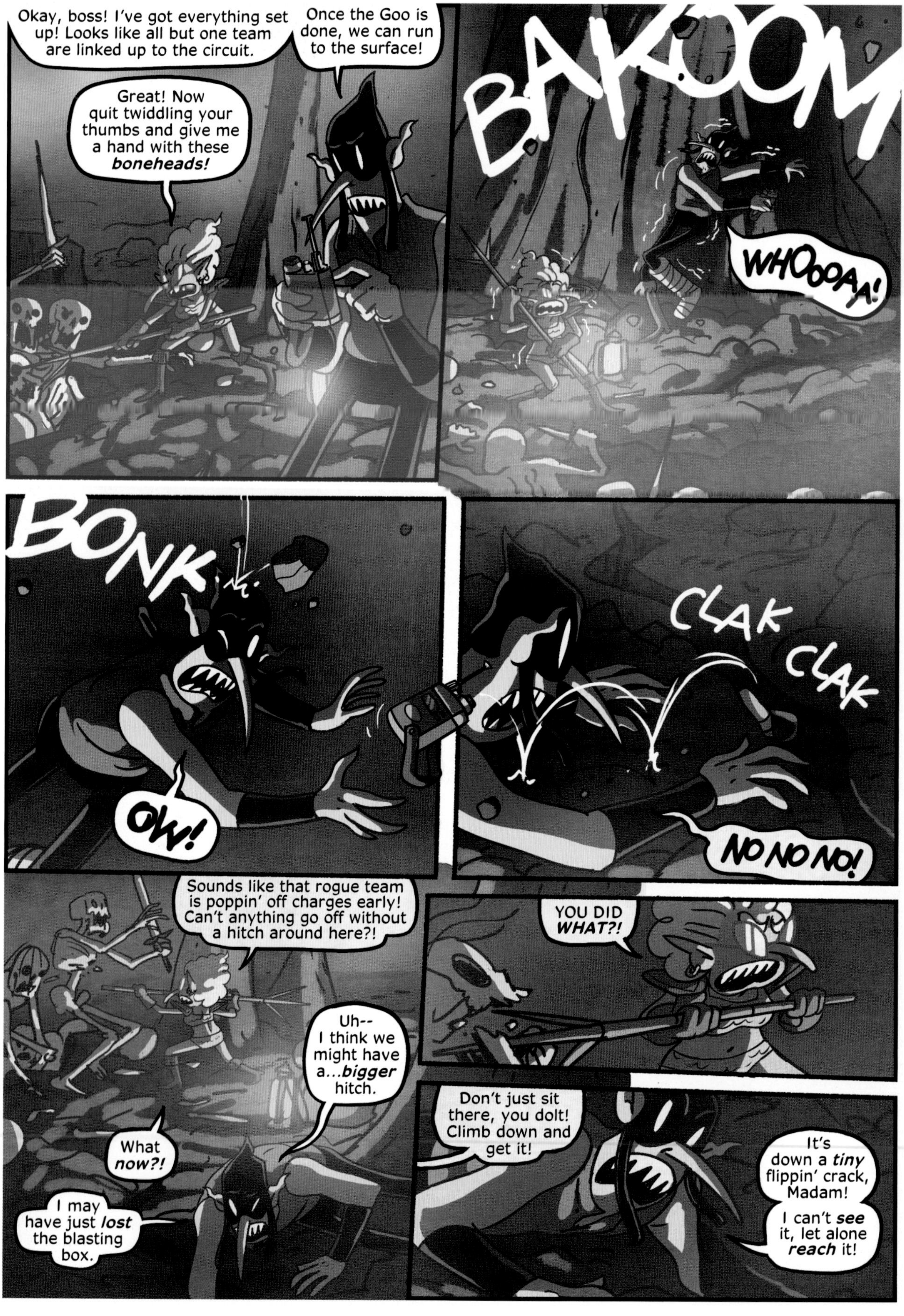
Okay, boss! I've got everything set up! Looks like all but one team are linked up to the circuit.
Once the Goo is done, we can run to the surface!
Great! Now quit twiddling your thumbs and give me a hand with these *boneheads!*
BAKOOM
WHOOOOAA!
BONK
OW!
CLAK CLAK CLAK
NO NO NO!
Sounds like that rogue team is poppin' off charges early! Can't anything go off without a hitch around here?!
Uh-- I think we might have a...*bigger* hitch.
What *now?!*
I may have just *lost* the blasting box.
YOU DID *WHAT?!*
Don't just sit there, you dolt! Climb down and get it!
It's down a *tiny* flippin' crack, Madam!
I can't *see* it, let alone *reach* it!

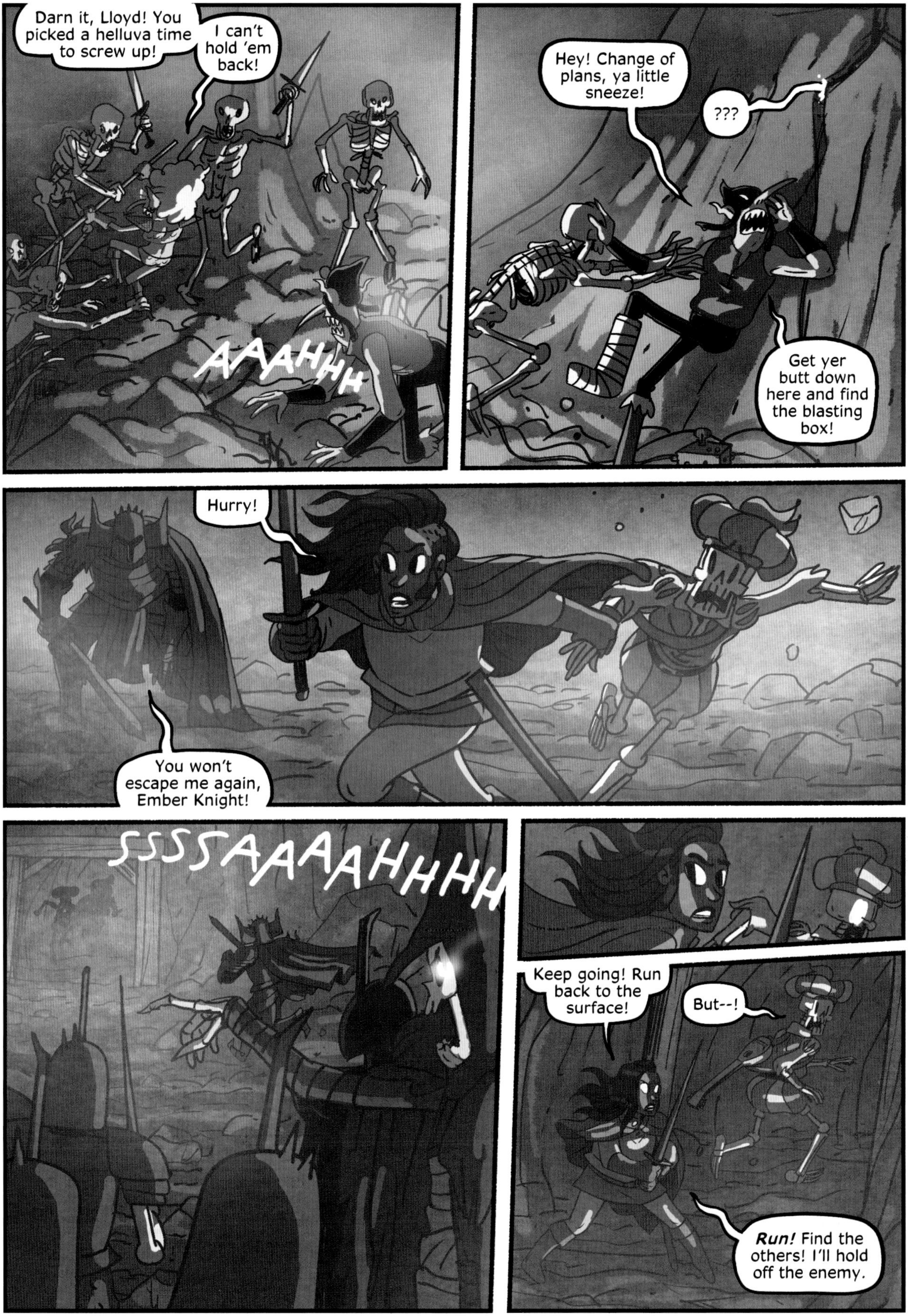
Darn it, Lloyd! You picked a helluva time to screw up!
I can't hold 'em back!
AAAHHH
Hey! Change of plans, ya little sneeze!
???
Get yer butt down here and find the blasting box!
Hurry!
You won't escape me again, Ember Knight!
SSSSAAAAHHHHH
Keep going! Run back to the surface!
But--!
Run! Find the others! I'll hold off the enemy.

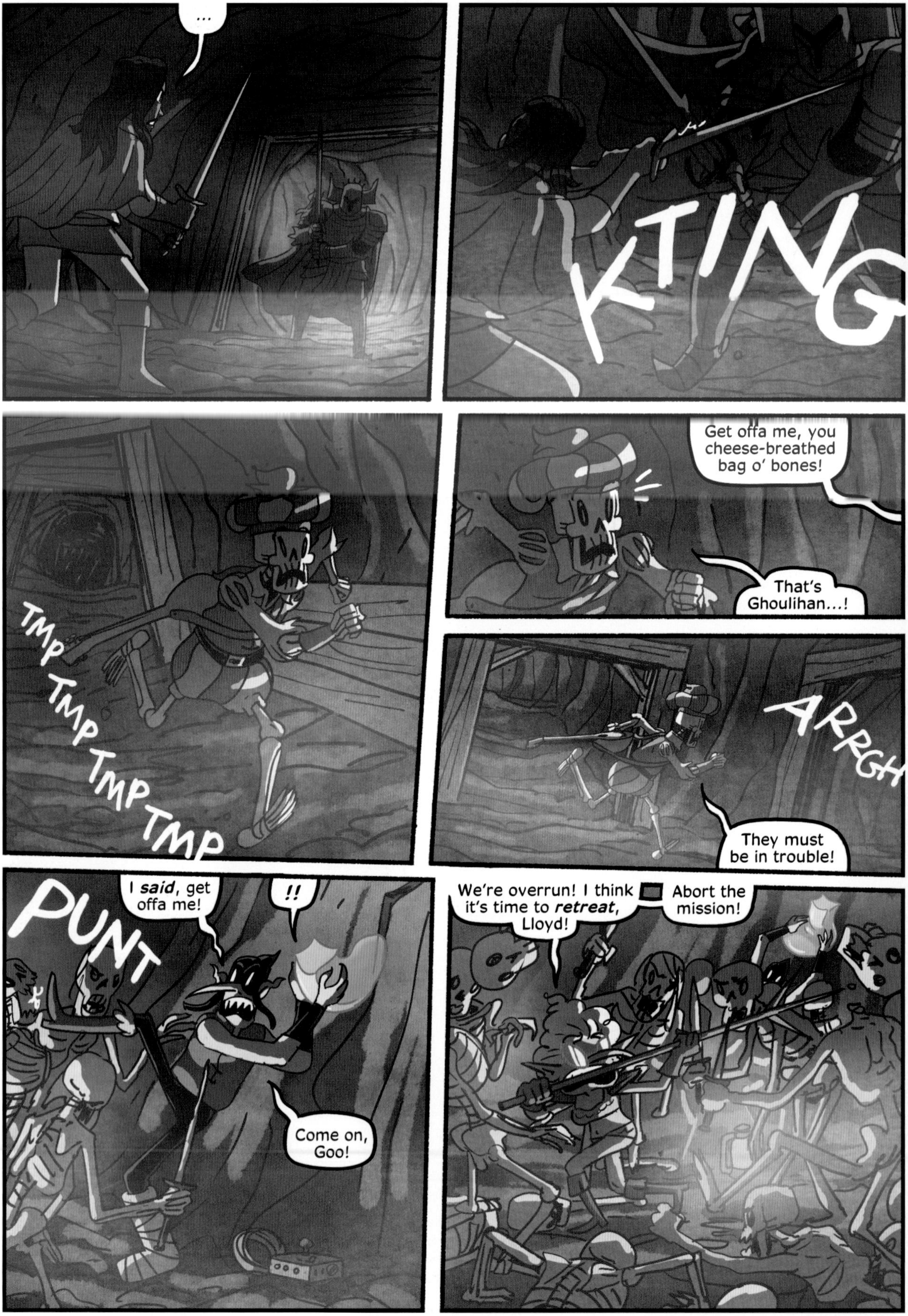
...
KTING
TMP TMP TMP TMP-TMP
Get offa me, you cheese-breathed bag o' bones!
That's Ghoulihan...!
ARRGH
They must be in trouble!
PUNT
I *said*, get offa me!
!!
Come on, Goo!
We're overrun! I think it's time to *retreat*, Lloyd!
Abort the mission!

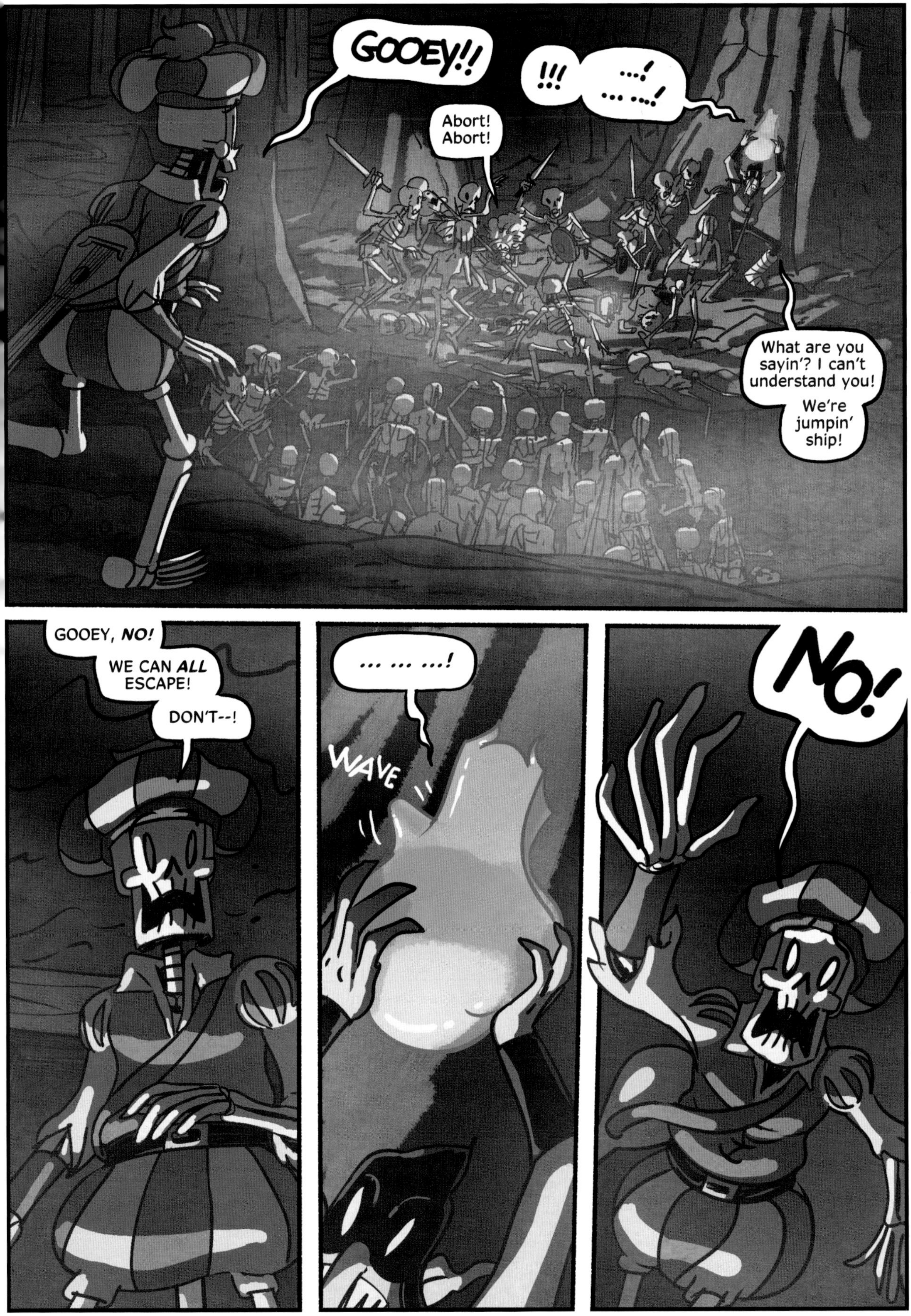
GOOEY!!
Abort! Abort!
!!!
...! ... ...!
What are you sayin'? I can't understand you!
We're jumpin' ship!
GOOEY, **NO!**
WE CAN ***ALL*** ESCAPE!
DON'T--!
... ...!
WAVE
NO!

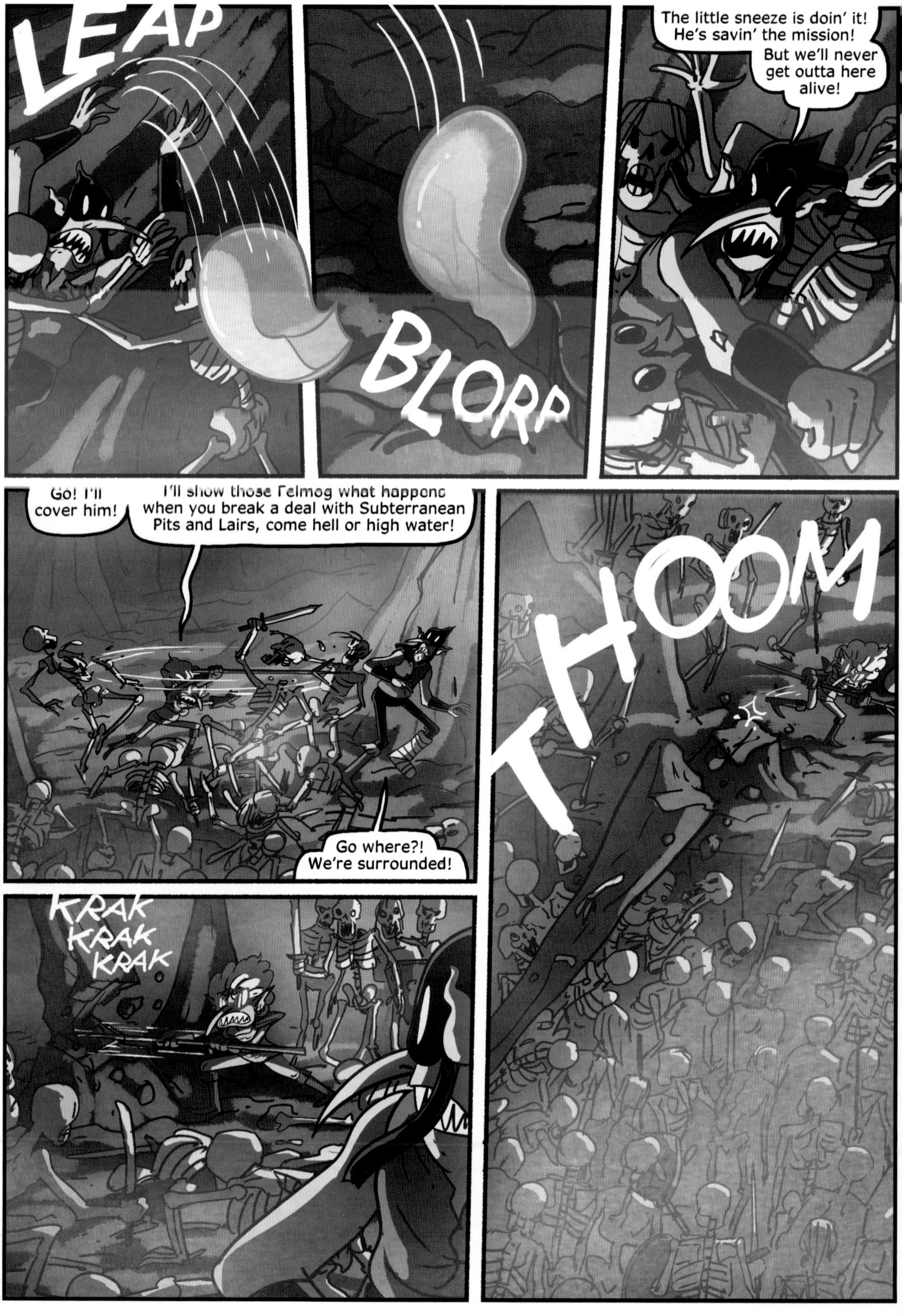

LEAP
BLORP
The little sneeze is doin' it! He's savin' the mission!
But we'll never get outta here alive!
Go! I'll cover him!
I'll show those Felmog what happens when you break a deal with Subterranean Pits and Lairs, come hell or high water!
Go where?! We're surrounded!
THOOM
KRAK
KRAK
KRAK

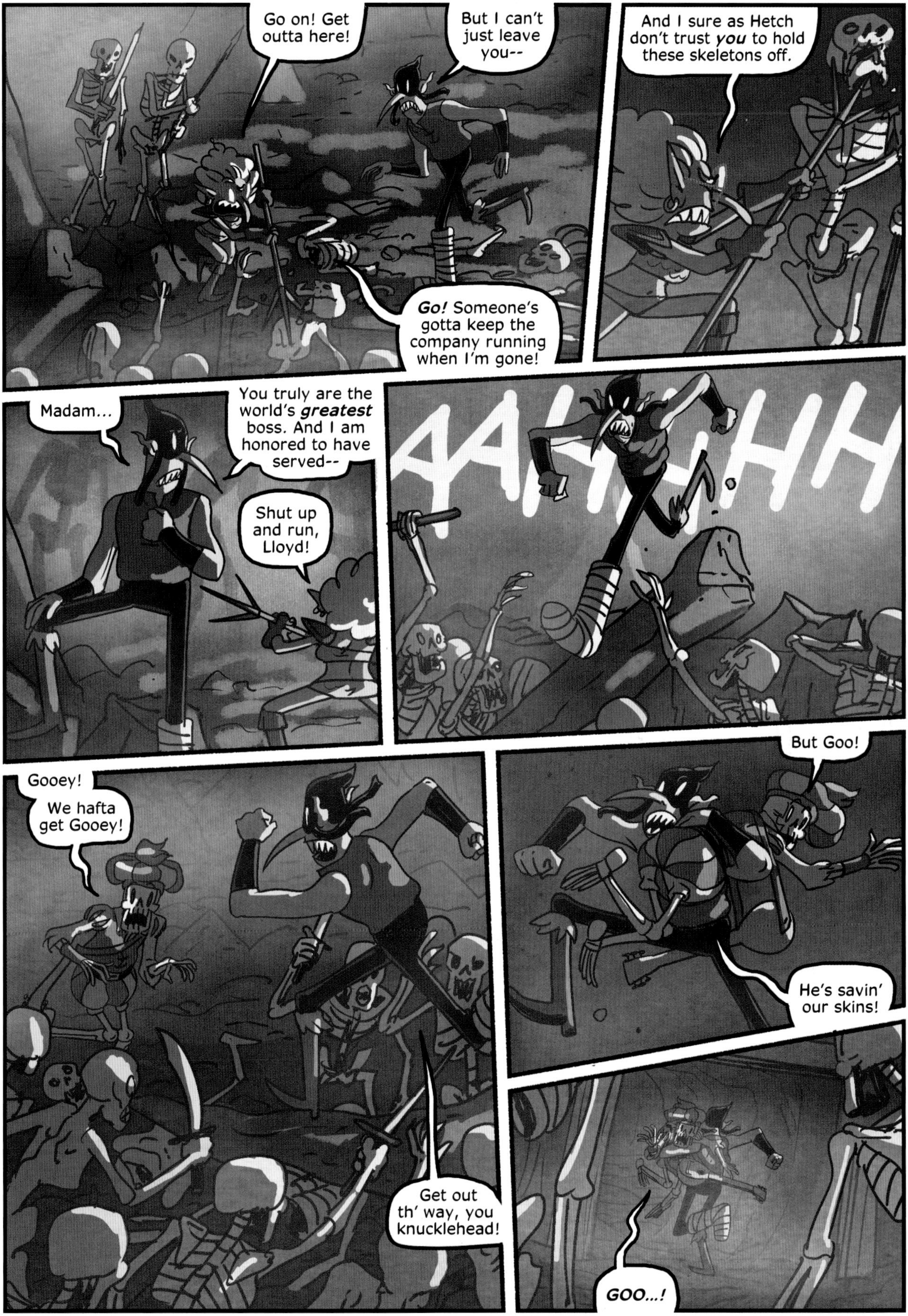
Go on! Get outta here!
But I can't just leave you--
Go! Someone's gotta keep the company running when I'm gone!
And I sure as Hetch don't trust *you* to hold these skeletons off.
Madam...
You truly are the world's ***greatest*** boss. And I am honored to have served--
Shut up and run, Lloyd!
AAHHHH
Gooey!
We hafta get Gooey!
Get out th' way, you knucklehead!
But Goo!
He's savin' our skins!
GOO...!

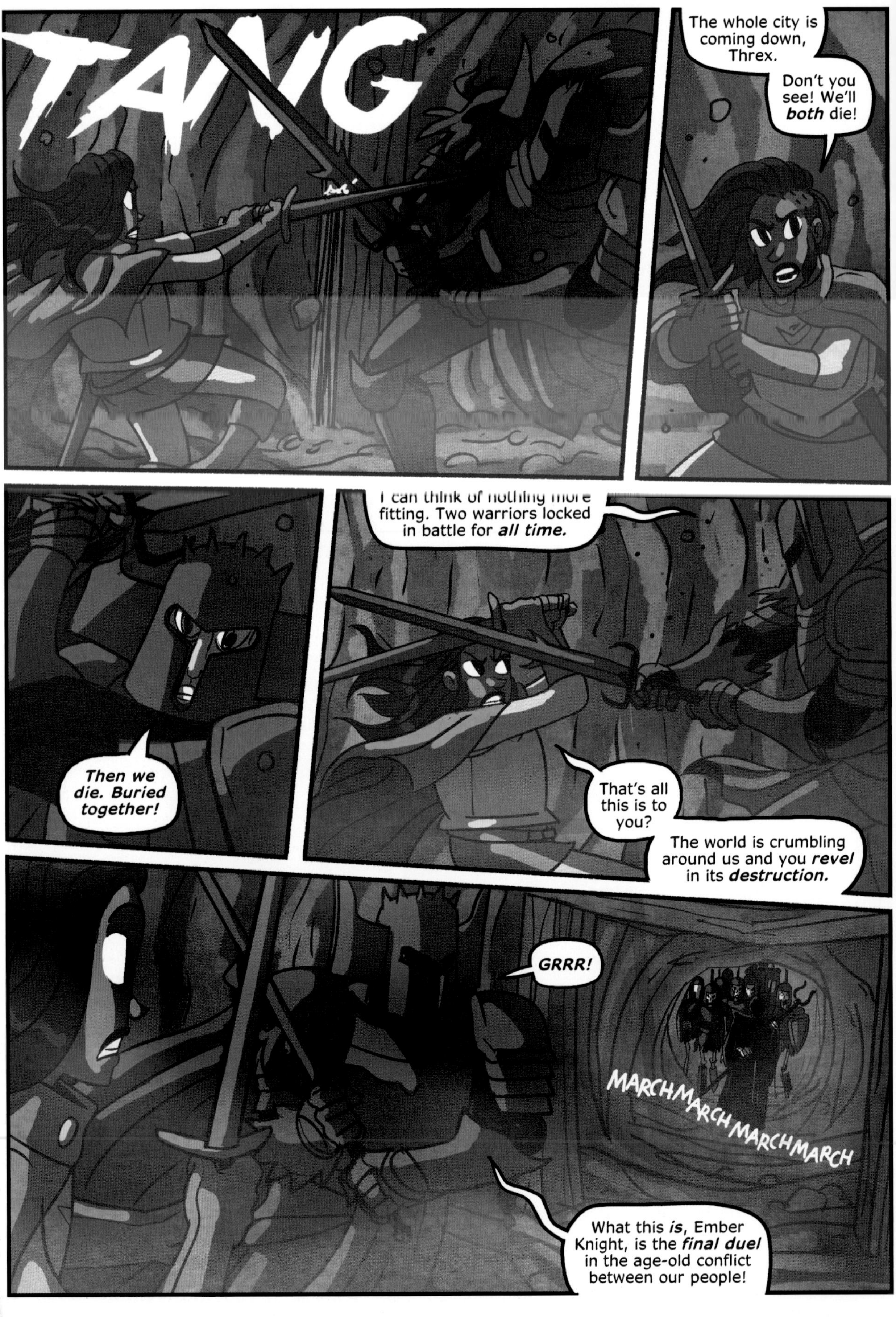
TANG
The whole city is coming down, Threx.
Don't you see! We'll *both* die!
Then we die. Buried together!
I can think of nothing more fitting. Two warriors locked in battle for *all time.*
That's all this is to you?
The world is crumbling around us and you *revel* in its *destruction.*
GRRR!
MARCHMARCHMARCHMARCHMARCH
What this *is*, Ember Knight, is the *final duel* in the age-old conflict between our people!

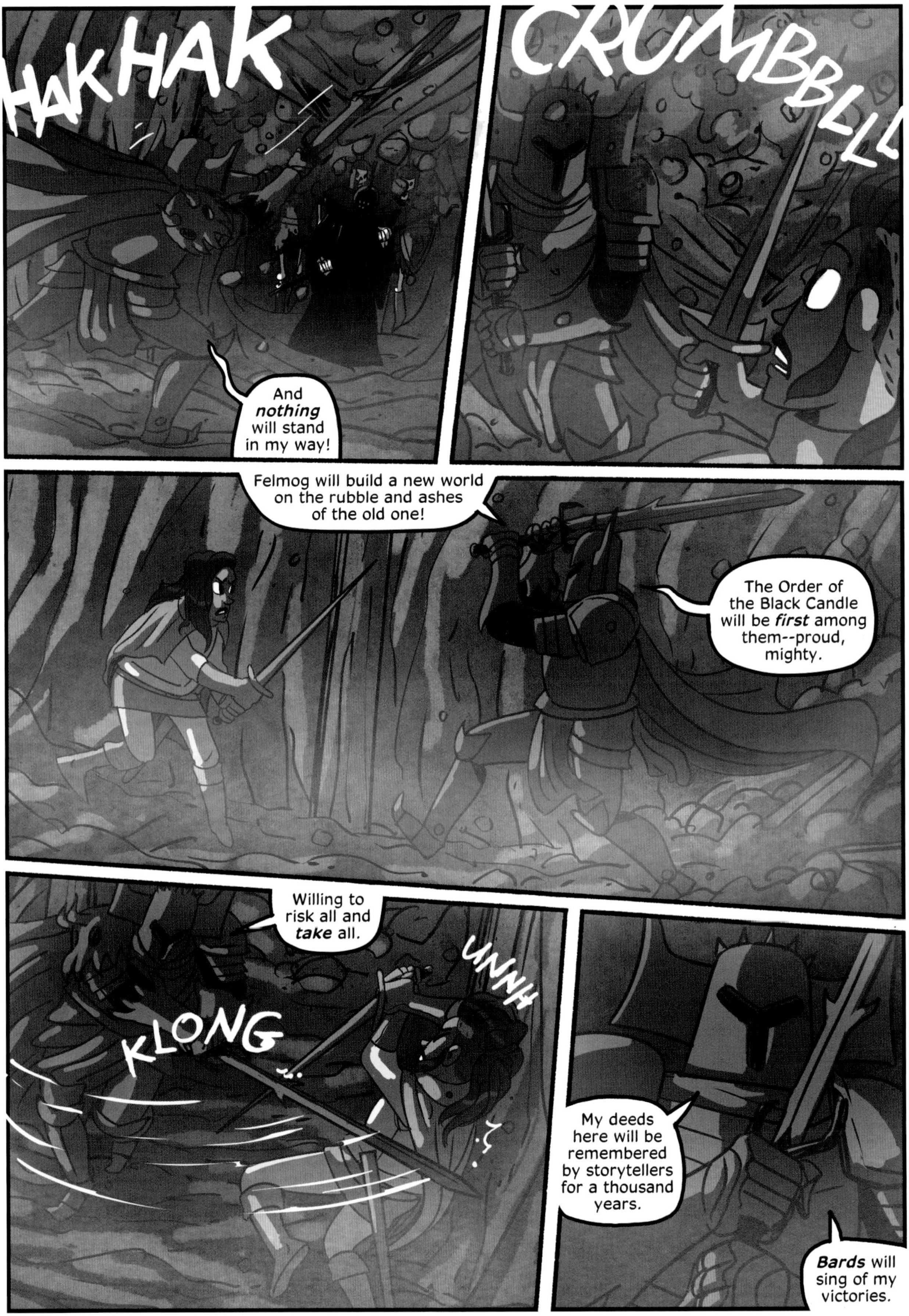
HAK HAK
And *nothing* will stand in my way!
CRUMBBLLL
Felmog will build a new world on the rubble and ashes of the old one!
The Order of the Black Candle will be *first* among them--proud, mighty.
Willing to risk all and *take* all.
UNNH
KLONG
My deeds here will be remembered by storytellers for a thousand years.
Bards will sing of my victories.

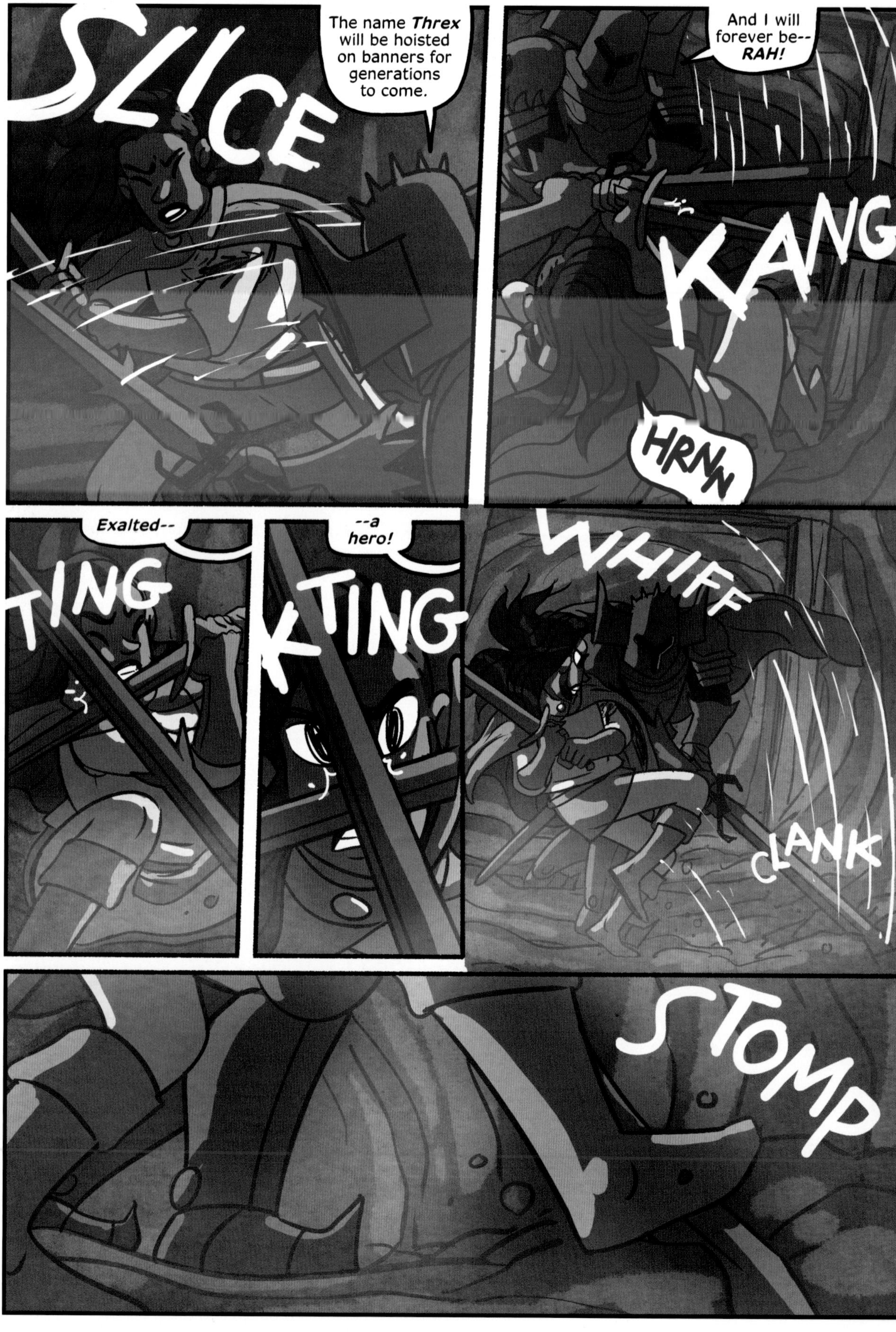
SLICE
The name *Threx* will be hoisted on banners for generations to come.
And I will forever be-- *RAH!*
KANG
HRNNN
Exalted--
TING
--a hero!
KTING
WHIFF
CLANK
STOMP

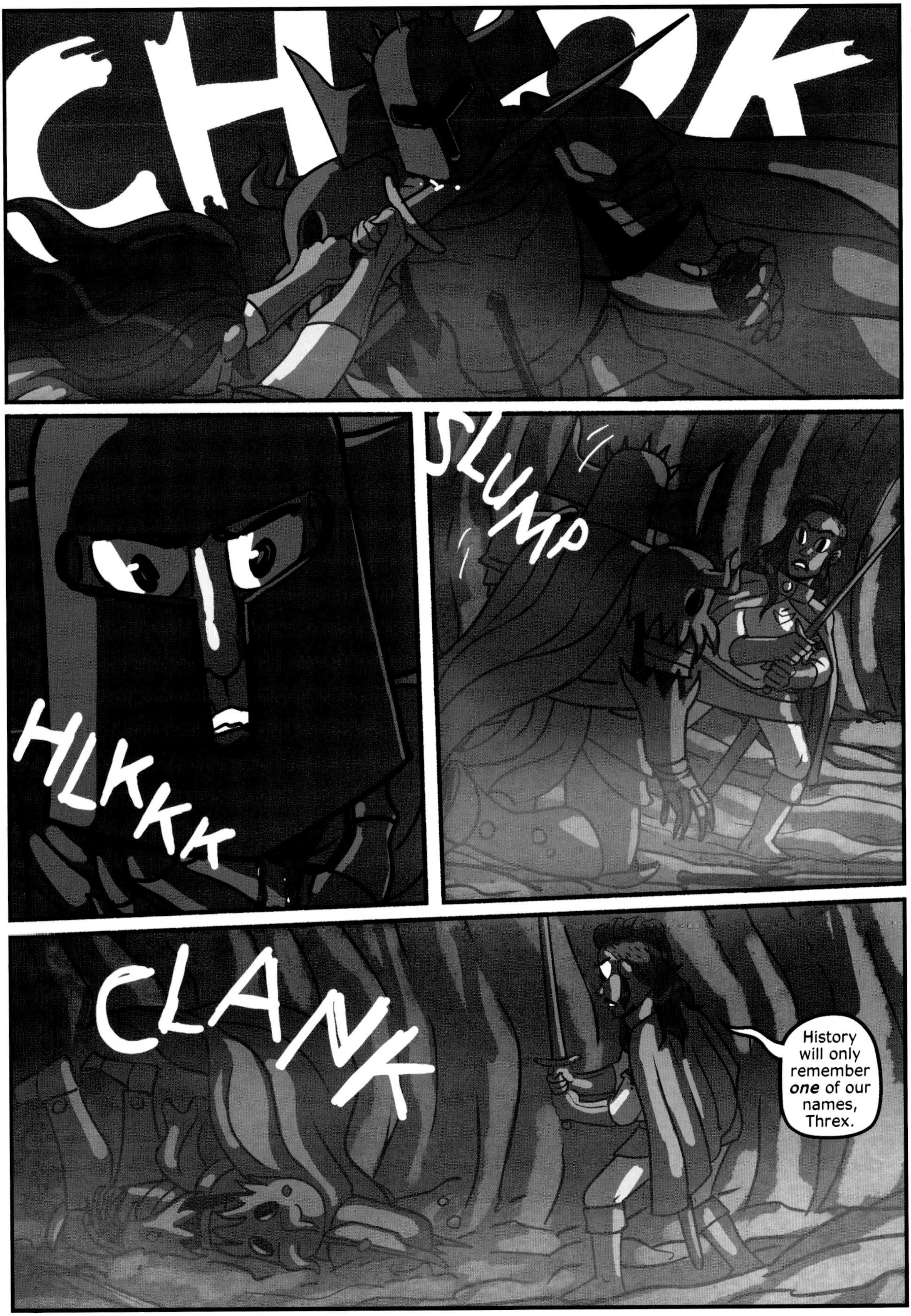
HLKKK
SLUMP
CLANK
History will only remember *one* of our names, Threx.

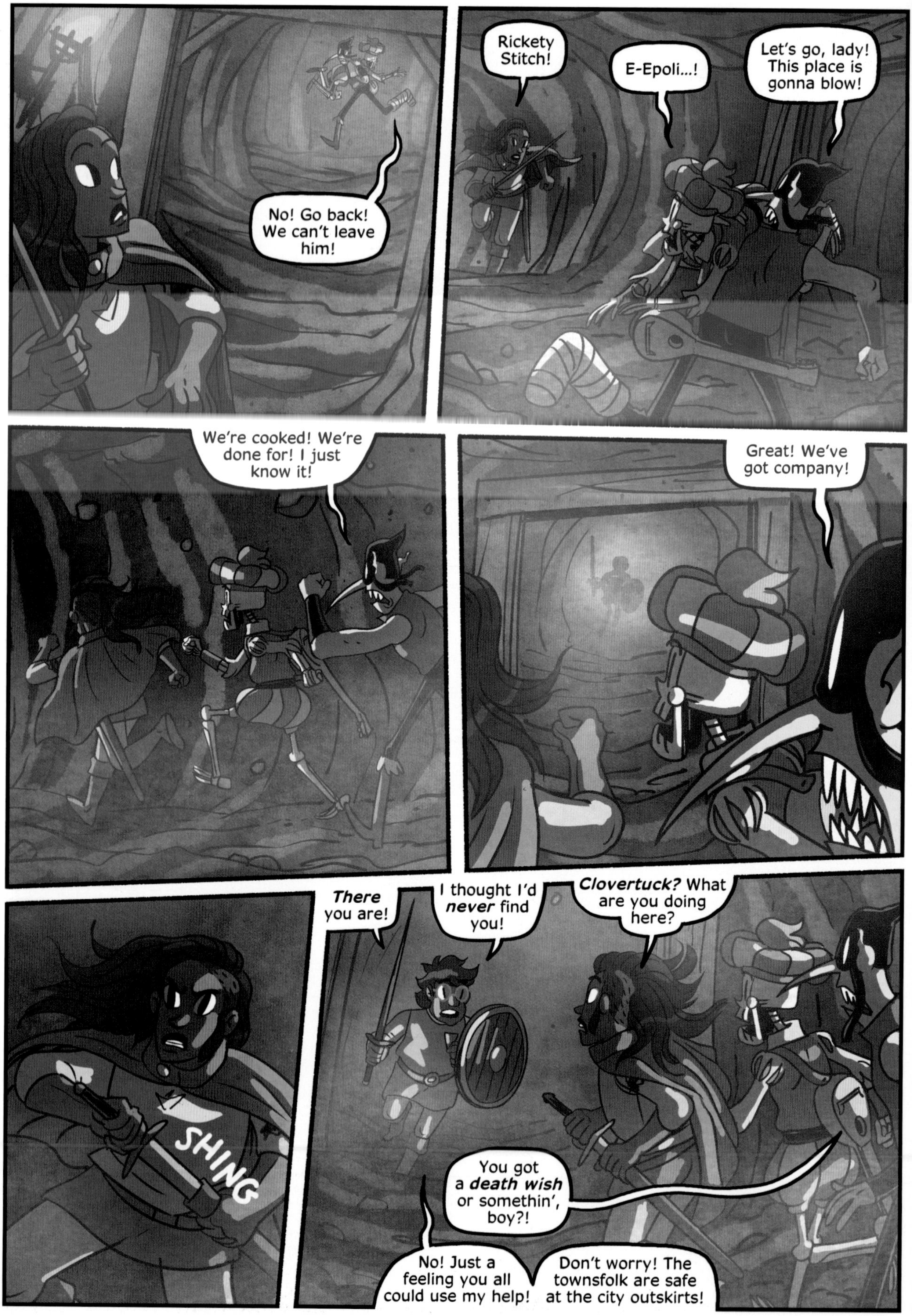
No! Go back! We can't leave him!
Rickety Stitch!
E-Epoli...!
Let's go, lady! This place is gonna blow!
We're cooked! We're done for! I just know it!
Great! We've got company!
SHING
There you are!
I thought I'd *never* find you!
Clovertuck? What are you doing here?
You got a *death wish* or somethin', boy?!
No! Just a feeling you all could use my help!
Don't worry! The townsfolk are safe at the city outskirts!

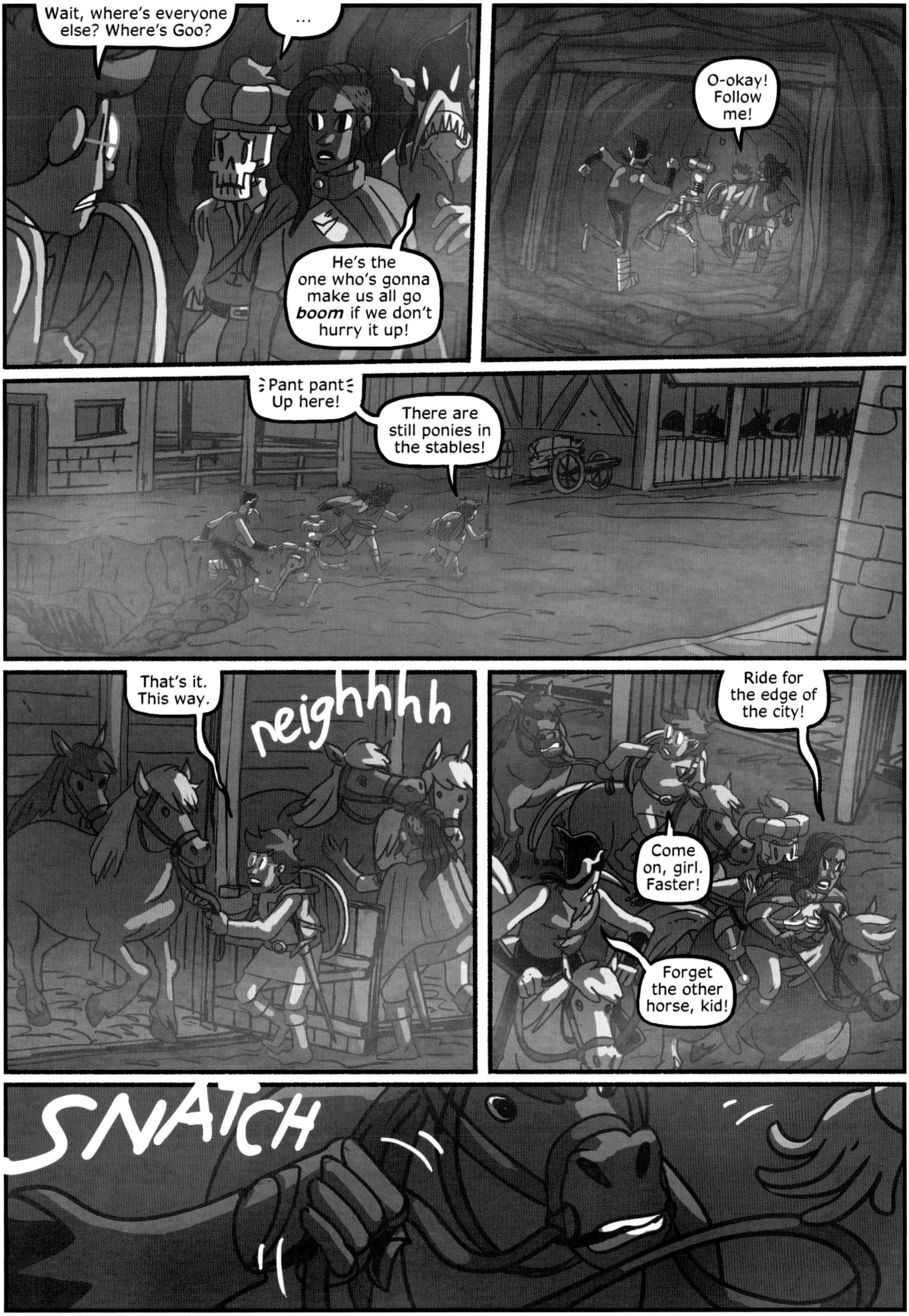
Wait, where's everyone else? Where's Goo?
...
He's the one who's gonna make us all go **boom** if we don't hurry it up!
O-okay! Follow me!
Pant pant Up here!
There are still ponies in the stables!
That's it. This way.
neighhhh
Ride for the edge of the city!
Come on, girl. Faster!
Forget the other horse, kid!
SNATCH

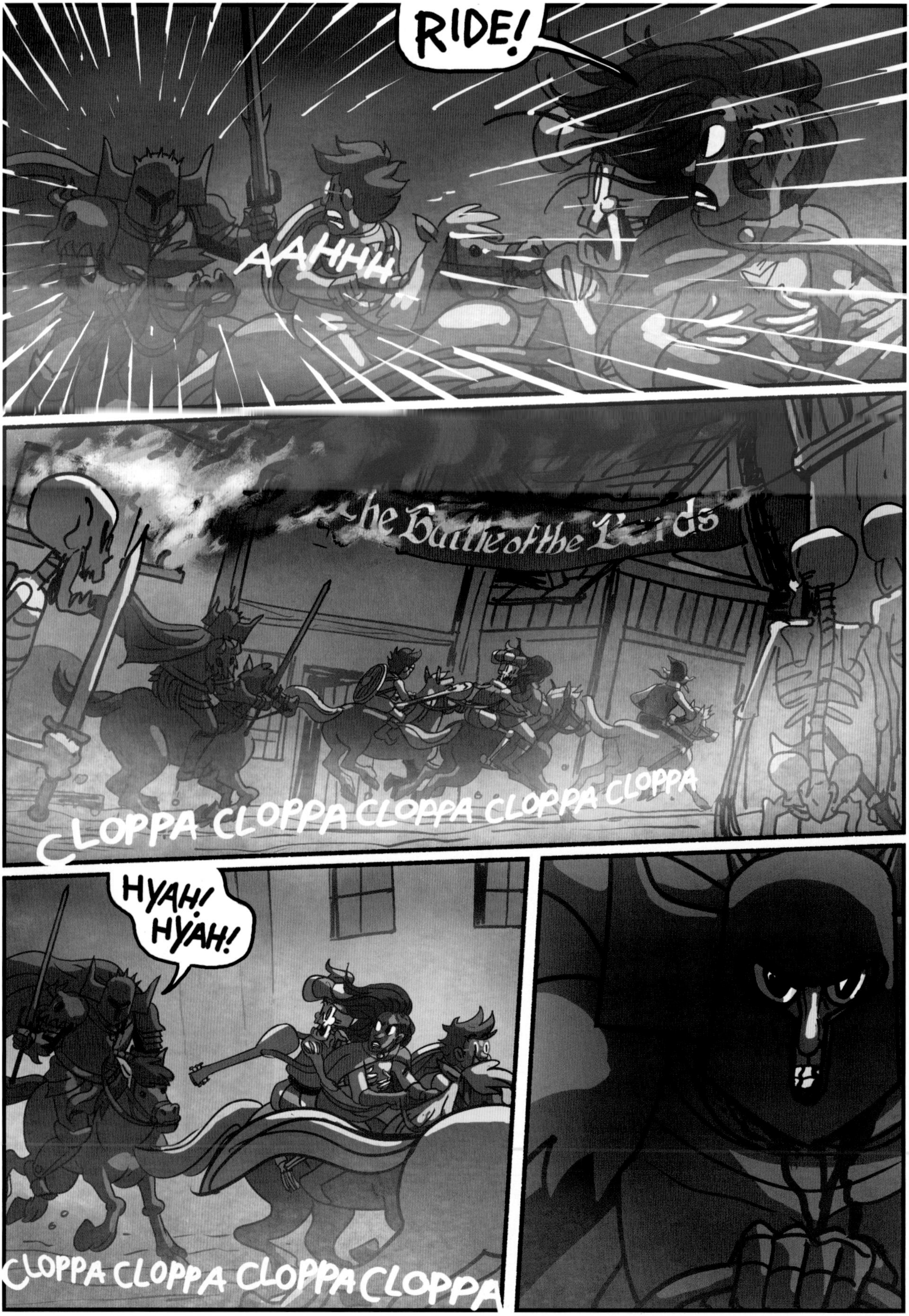
RIDE!
AAHHH
he Battle of the
CLOPPA CLOPPA CLOPPA CLOPPA CLOPPA
HYAH! HYAH!
CLOPPA CLOPPA CLOPPA CLOPPA

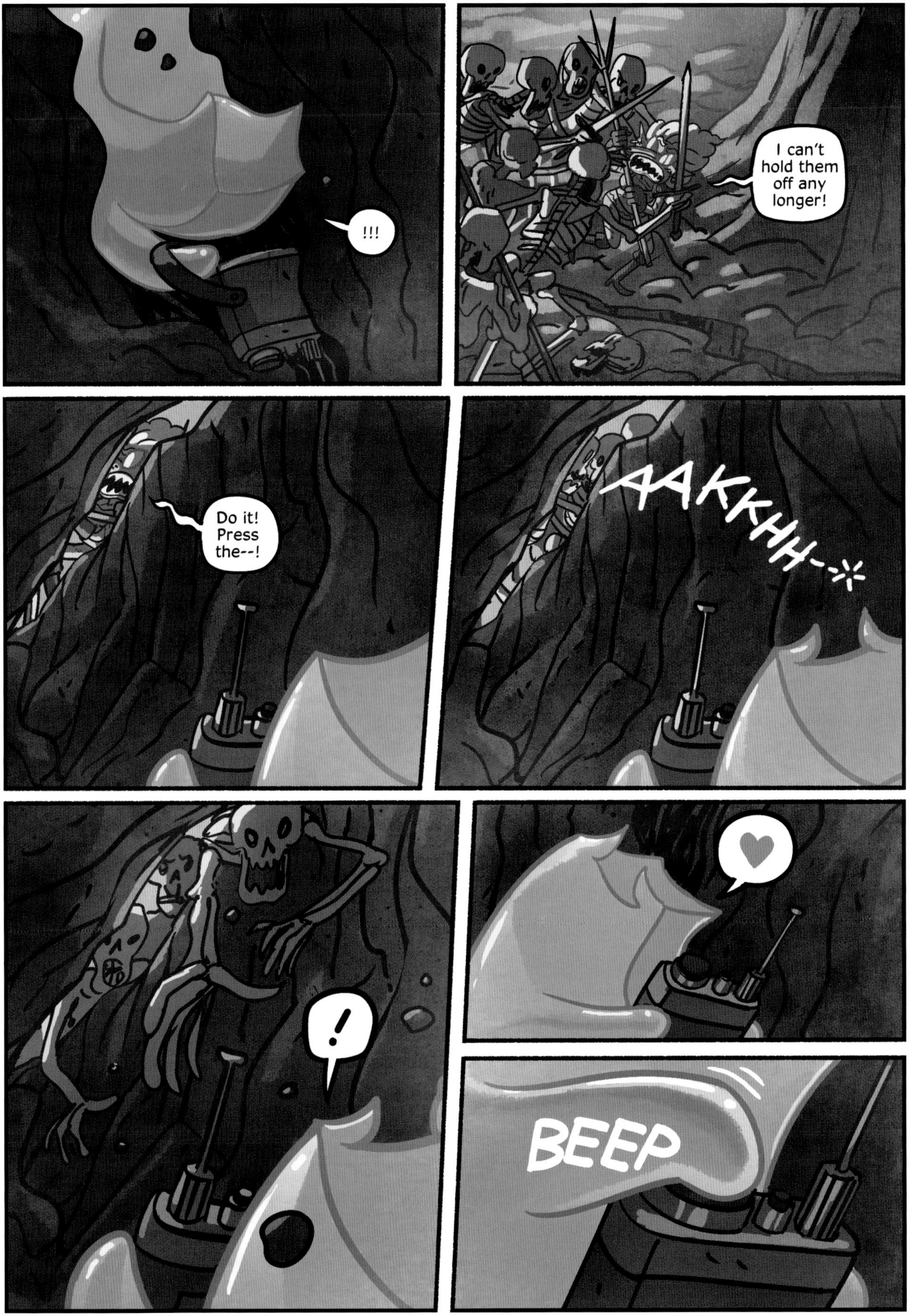
!!!
I can't hold them off any longer!
Do it! Press the--!
AAKKHH--
!
BEEP

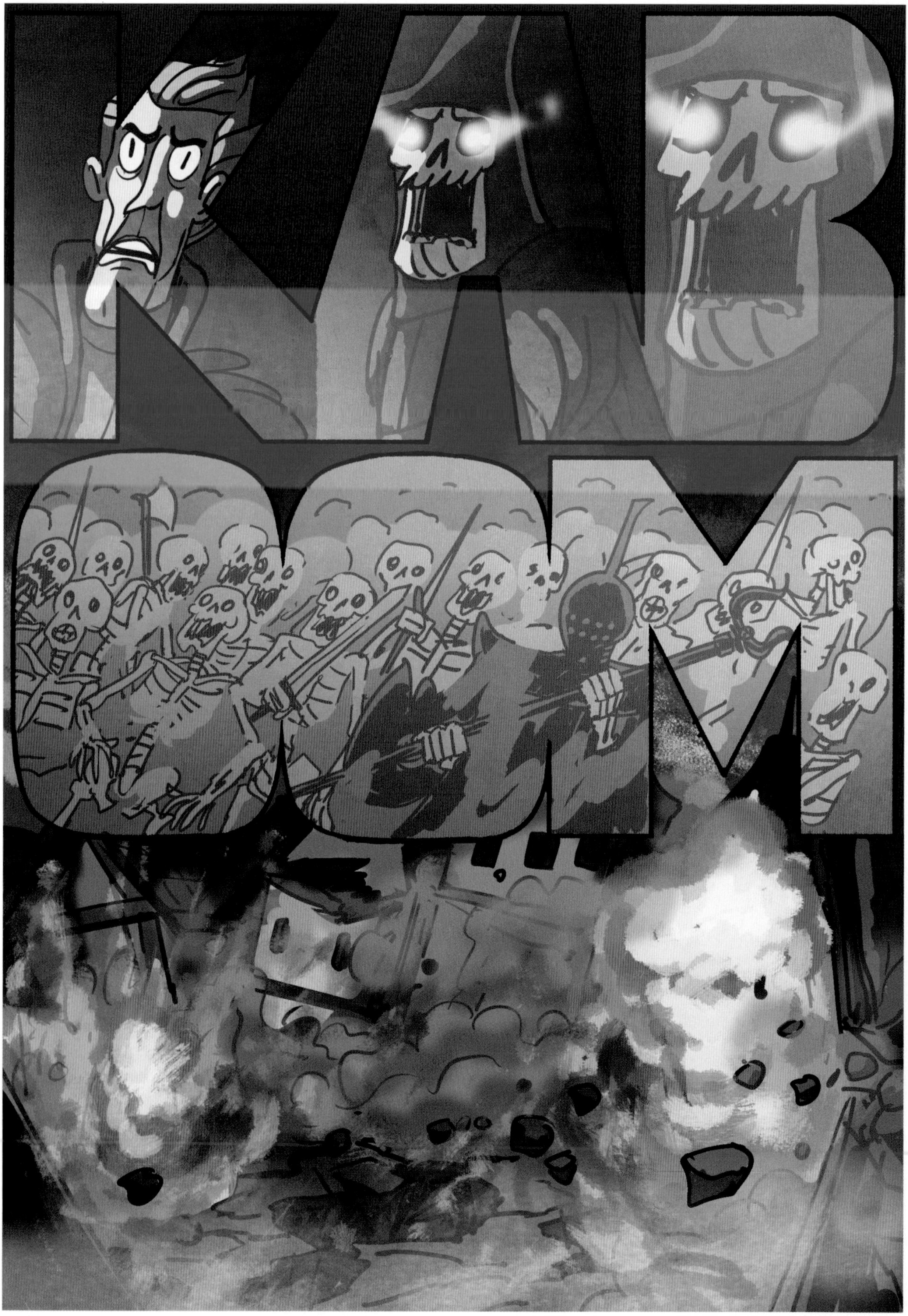
KABOOM

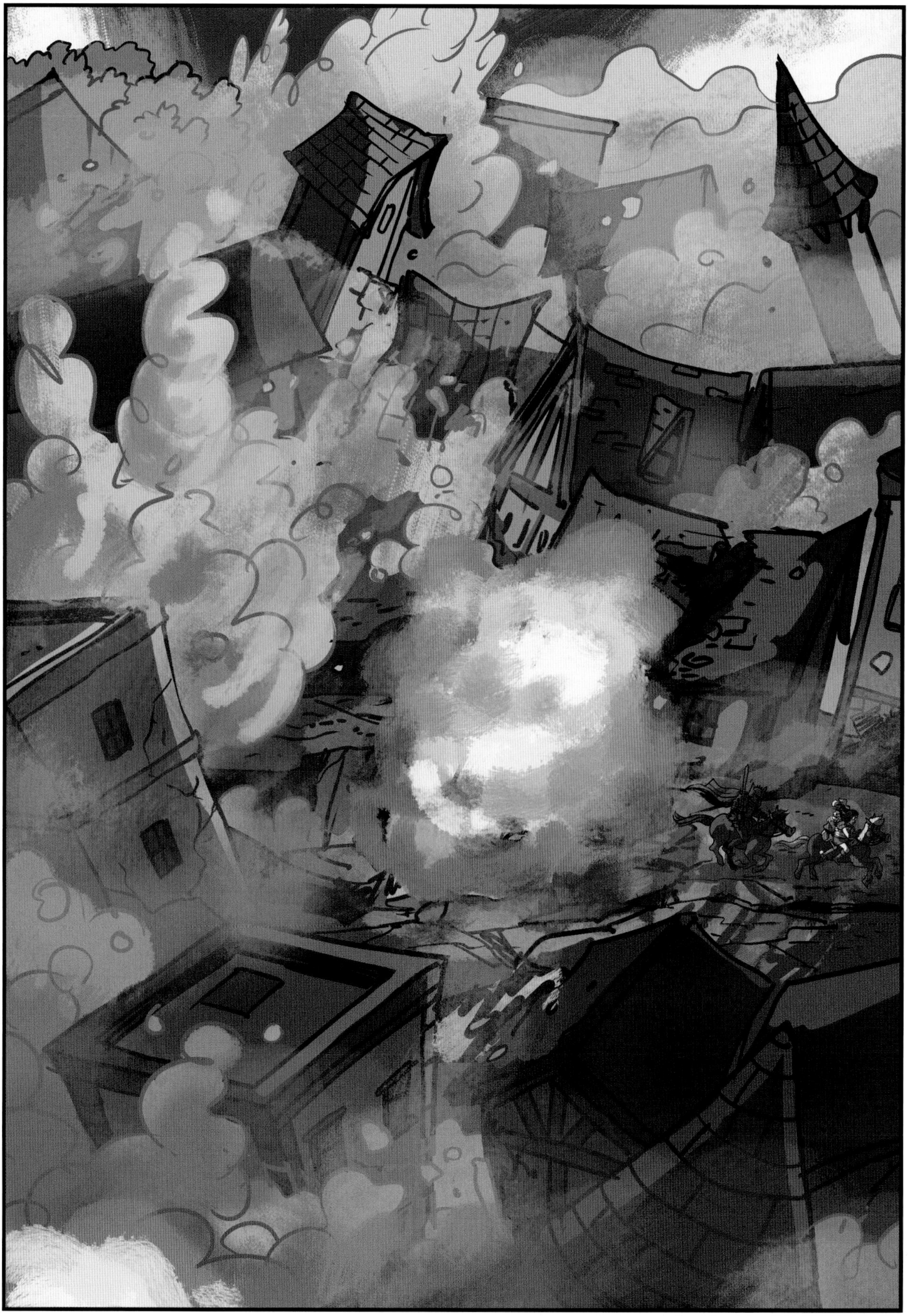

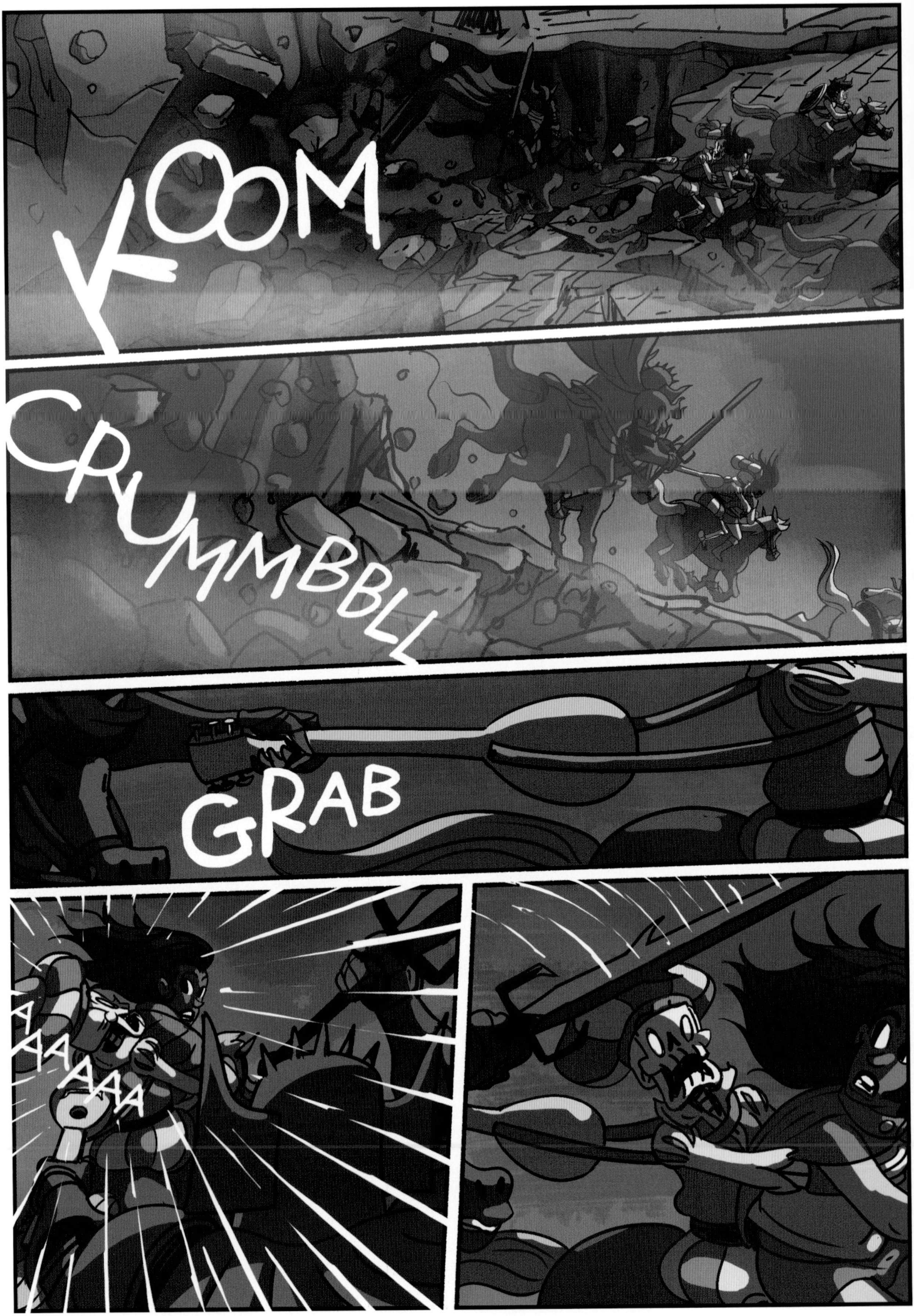
KOOM
CRUMMBBLL
GRAB
AAAAAAA

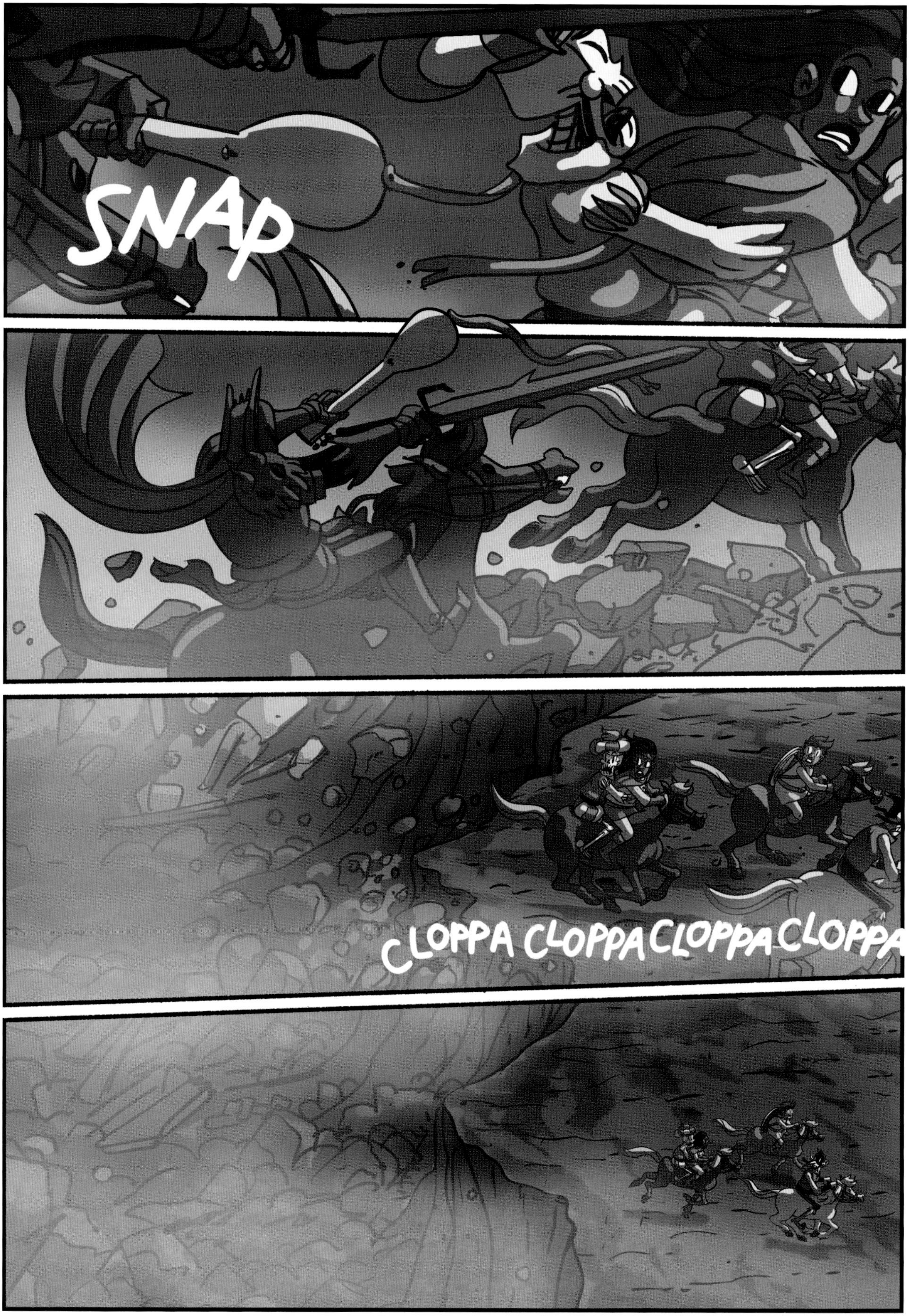
SNAP
CLOPPA CLOPPA CLOPPA CLOPPA

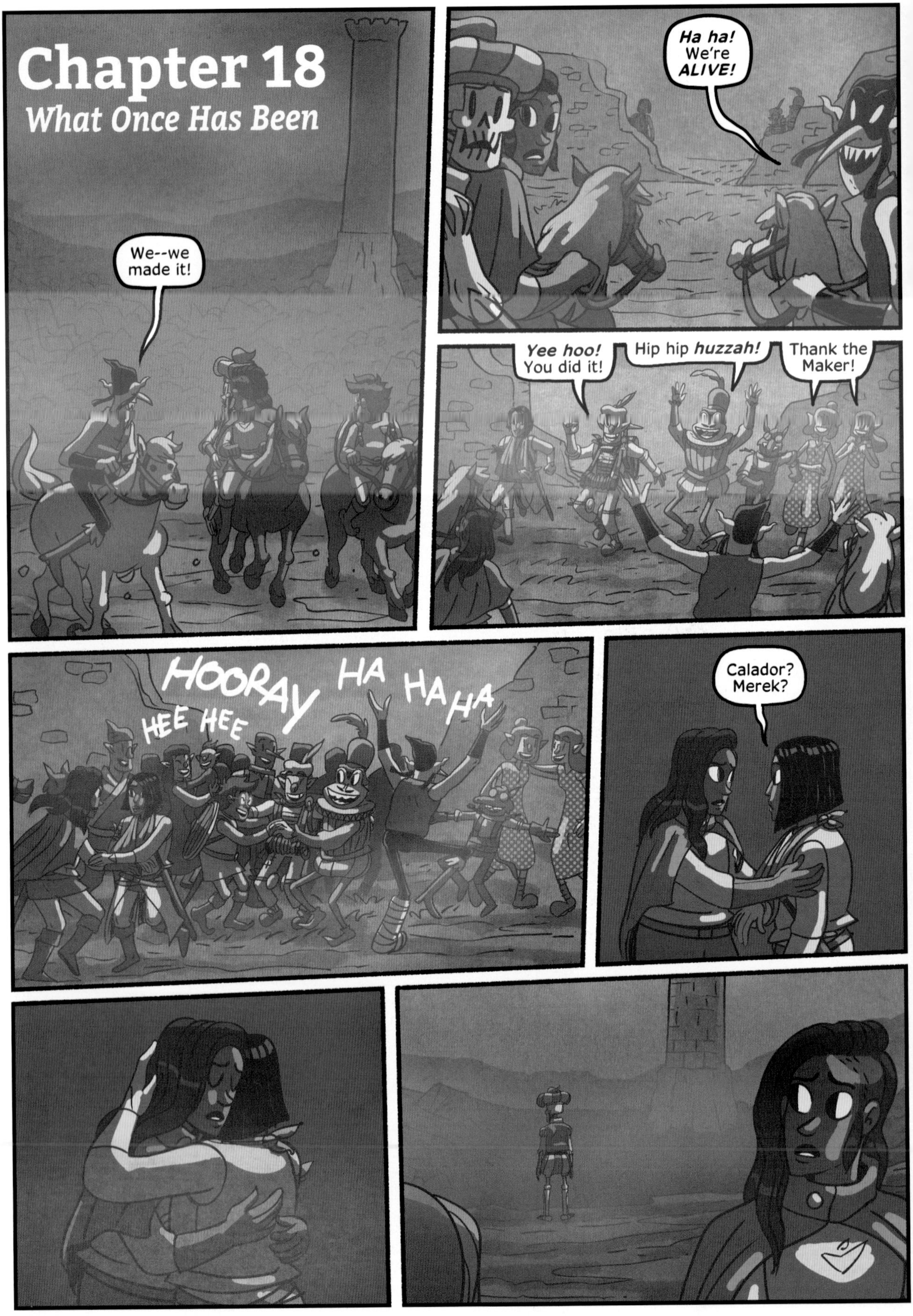
Chapter 18
What Once Has Been
We--we made it!
Ha ha! We're ALIVE!
Yee hoo! You did it!
Hip hip huzzah!
Thank the Maker!
HOORAY
HA HA HA HA
HEE HEE
Calador? Merek?

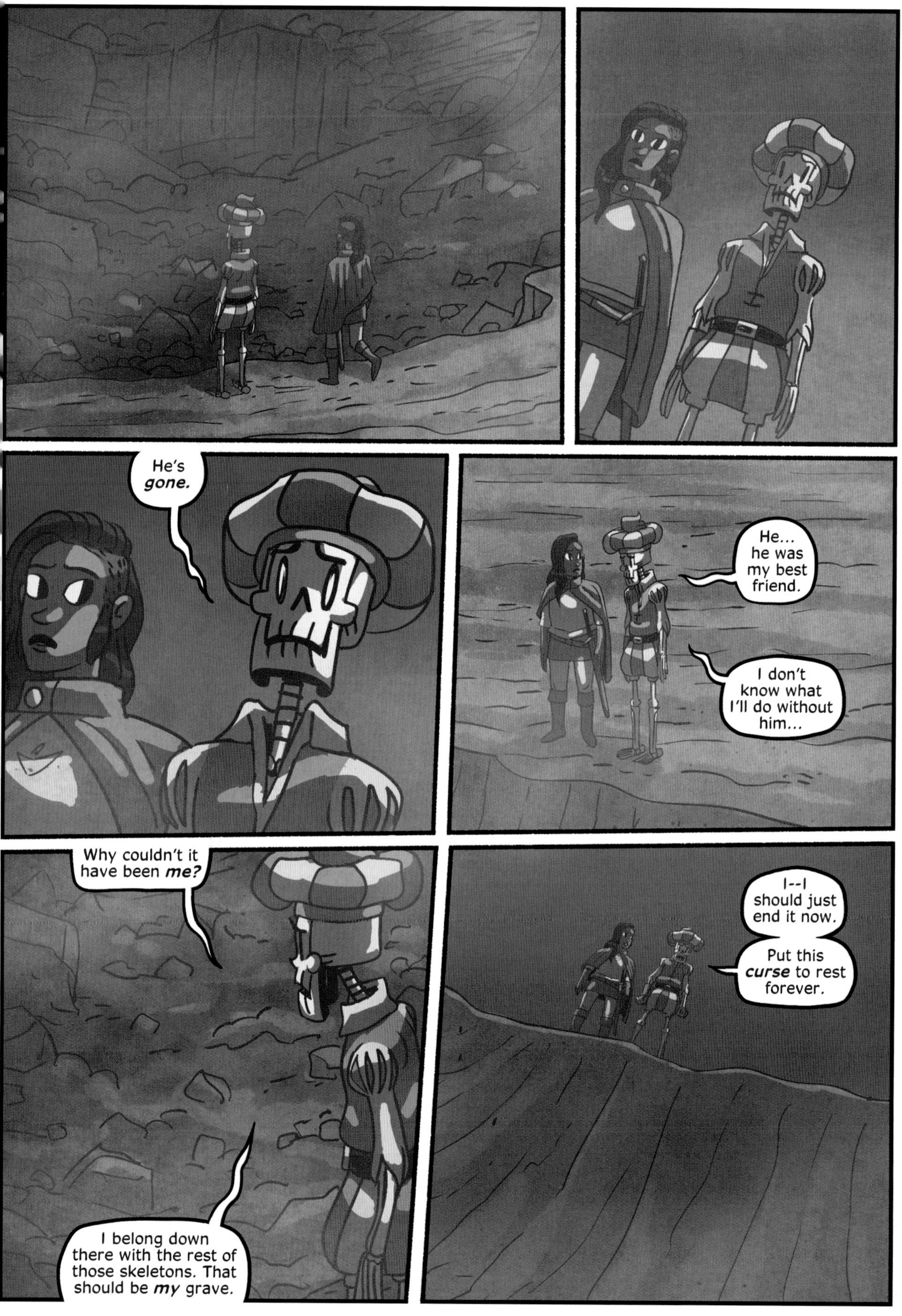
He's *gone.*
He... he was my best friend.
I don't know what I'll do without him...
Why couldn't it have been *me?*
I belong down there with the rest of those skeletons. That should be *my* grave.
I--I should just end it now.
Put this *curse* to rest forever.

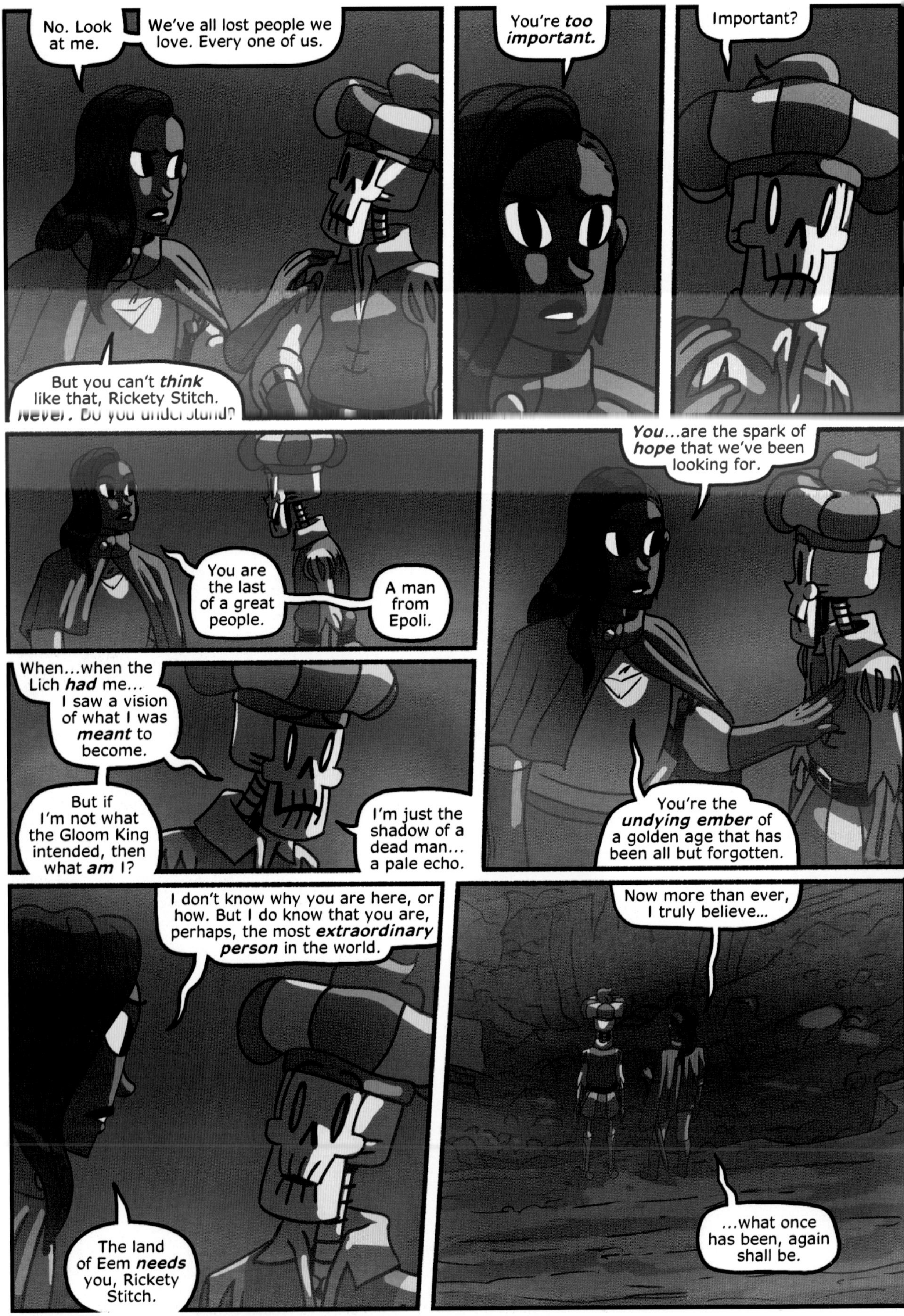
No. Look at me.
We've all lost people we love. Every one of us.
But you can't *think* like that, Rickety Stitch. *Never.* Do you understand?
You're *too important.*
Important?
You are the last of a great people.
A man from Epoli.
You...are the spark of *hope* that we've been looking for.
When...when the Lich *had* me...
I saw a vision of what I was *meant* to become.
But if I'm not what the Gloom King intended, then what *am* I?
I'm just the shadow of a dead man... a pale echo.
You're the *undying ember* of a golden age that has been all but forgotten.
I don't know why you are here, or how. But I do know that you are, perhaps, the most *extraordinary person* in the world.
The land of Eem *needs* you, Rickety Stitch.
Now more than ever, I truly believe...
...what once has been, again shall be.

POP
POP
POP
POP
POP
POP
POP
What? What's all *this?*
SPRONG
BOING
BOING
What's happening?
Goo? Is this ***YOU?!***
HOP
BOING
HOP
!!!
GASP
BOING
HOP
GOOEY! My loyal chum! My man-at-arms!
Ha-HA! I don't believe it! I thought I lost you!
!
HOP
BOUNCE
I thought I lost you...

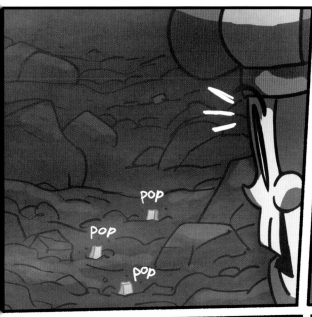

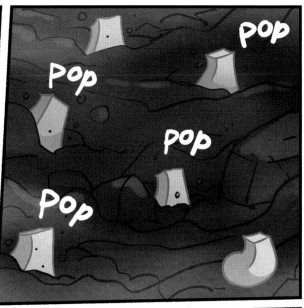

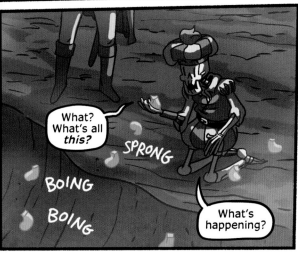

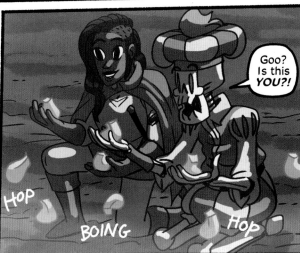

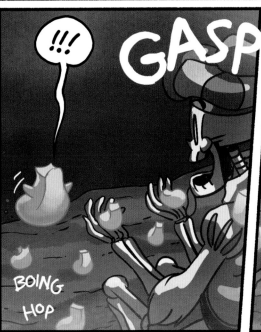

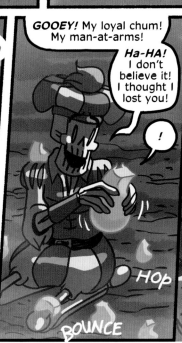

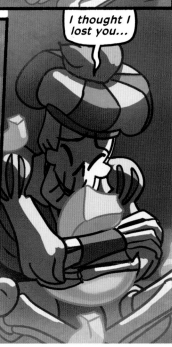

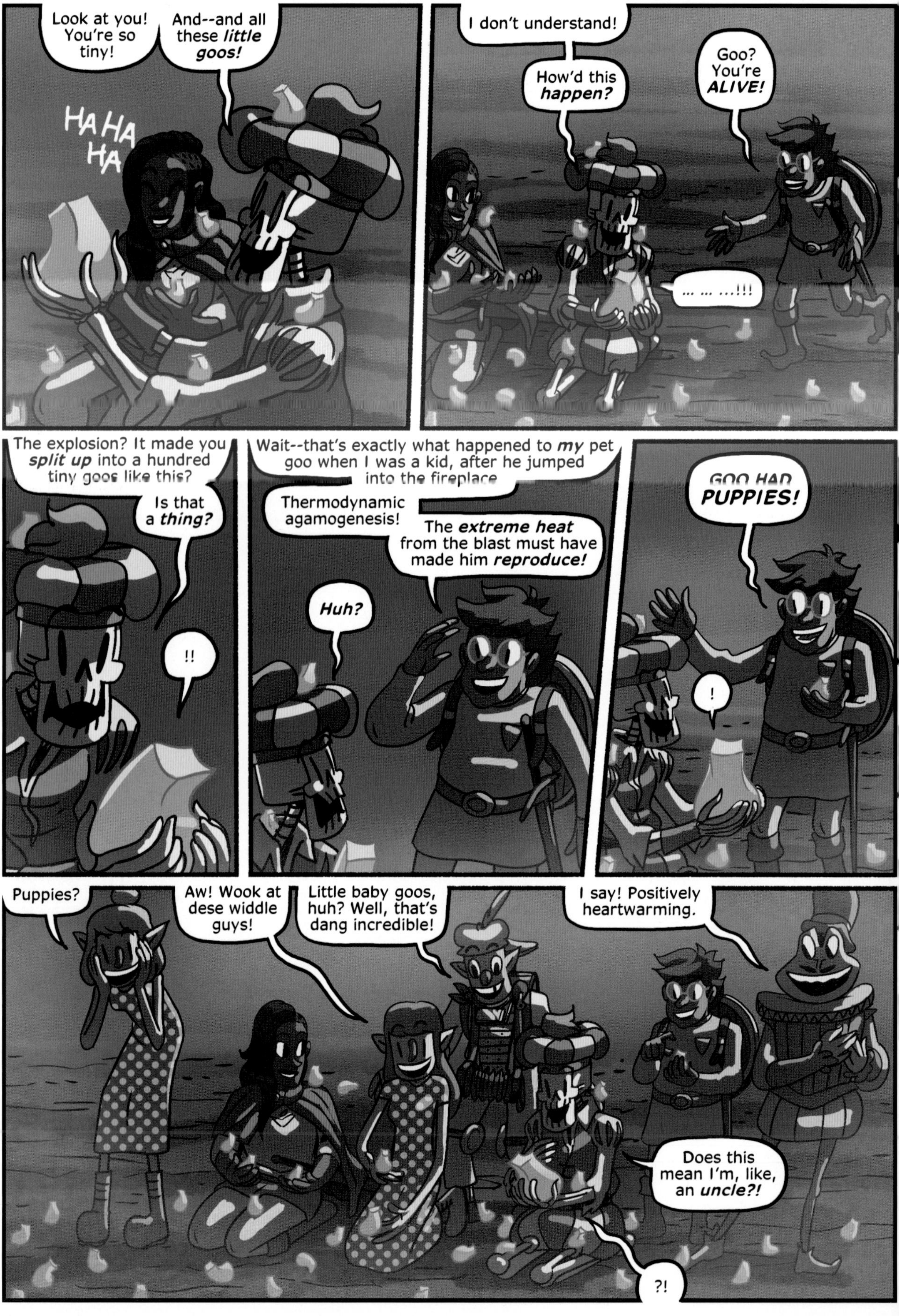

Look at you! You're so tiny!
And--and all these *little goos!*
HA HA HA
I don't understand!
How'd this *happen?*
Goo? You're *ALIVE!*
... ...!!!
The explosion? It made you *split up* into a hundred tiny goos like this?
Is that a *thing?*
!!
Wait--that's exactly what happened to *my* pet goo when I was a kid, after he jumped into the fireplace
Thermodynamic agamogenesis!
The *extreme heat* from the blast must have made him *reproduce!*
Huh?
GOO HAD PUPPIES!
!
Puppies?
Aw! Wook at dese widdle guys!
Little baby goos, huh? Well, that's dang incredible!
I say! Positively heartwarming.
Does this mean I'm, like, an *uncle?!*
?!

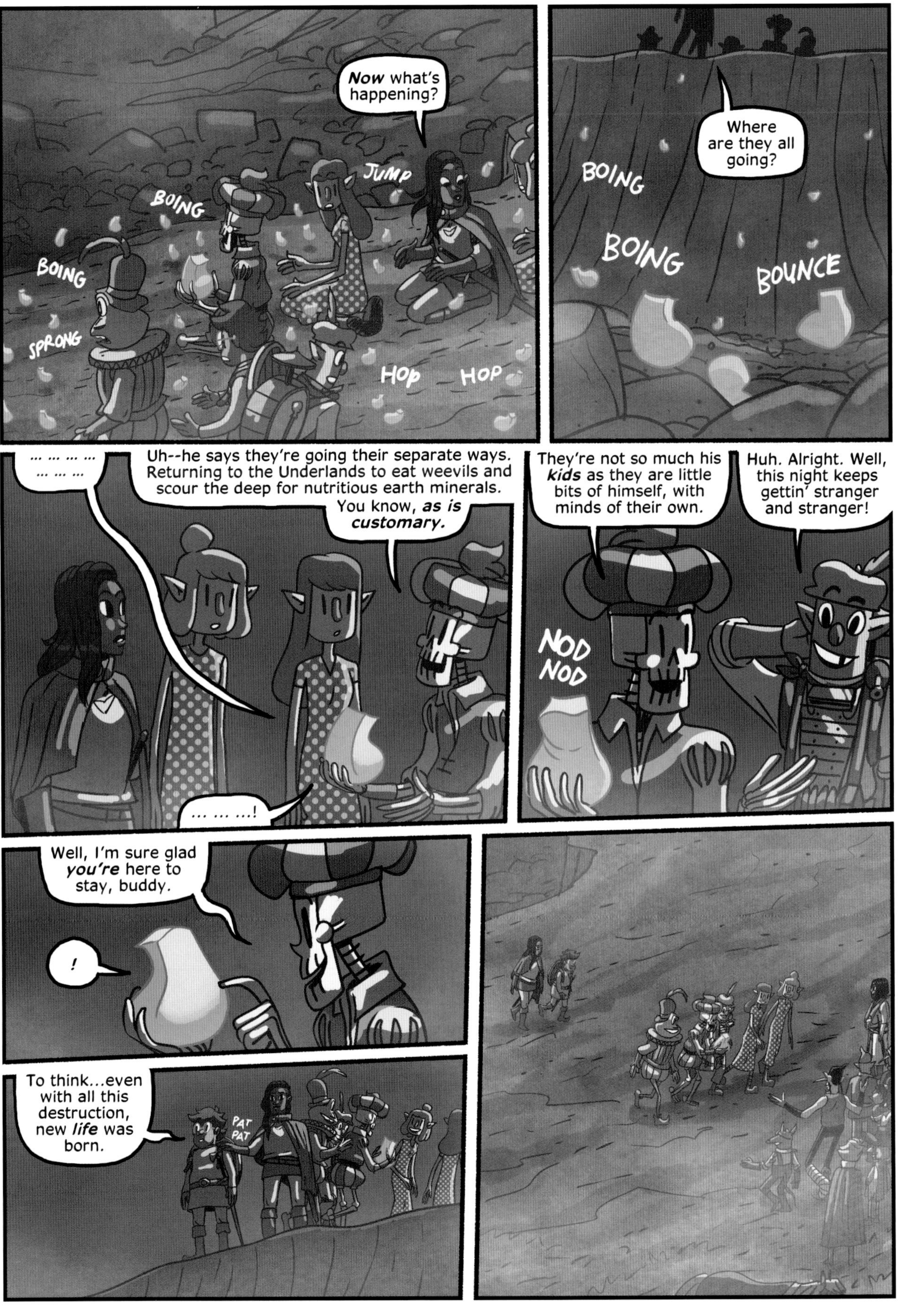
Now what's happening?
JUMP
BOING
BOING
SPRONG
HOP
HOP
Where are they all going?
BOING
BOING
BOUNCE
... ...
Uh--he says they're going their separate ways. Returning to the Underlands to eat weevils and scour the deep for nutritious earth minerals.
You know, ***as is customary.***
... ...!
They're not so much his *kids* as they are little bits of himself, with minds of their own.
NOD NOD
Huh. Alright. Well, this night keeps gettin' stranger and stranger!
Well, I'm sure glad *you're* here to stay, buddy.
!
To think...even with all this destruction, new *life* was born.
PAT PAT

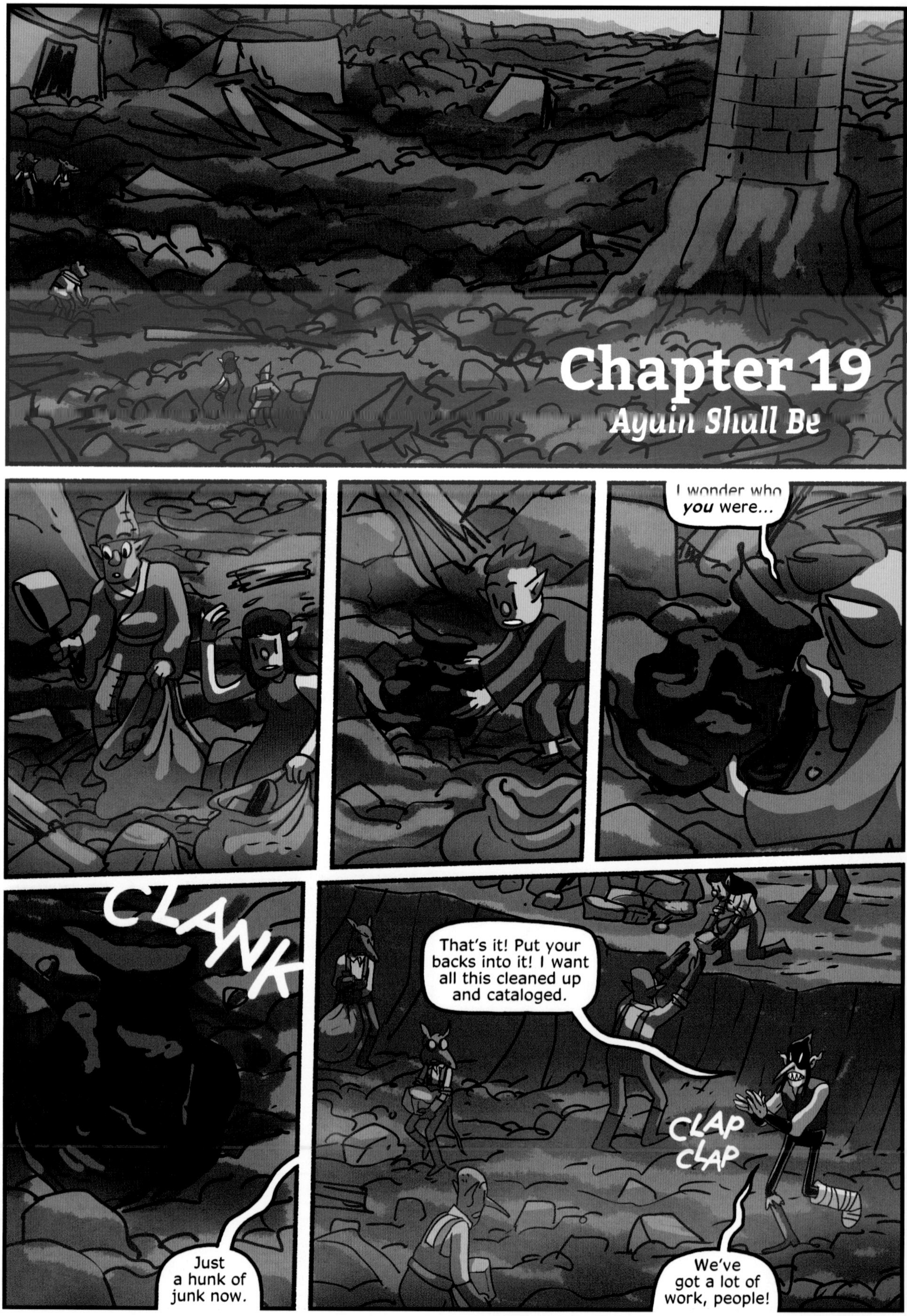
Chapter 19
Again Shall Be
I wonder who *you* were...
CLANK
Just a hunk of junk now.
That's it! Put your backs into it! I want all this cleaned up and cataloged.
CLAP CLAP
We've got a lot of work, people!

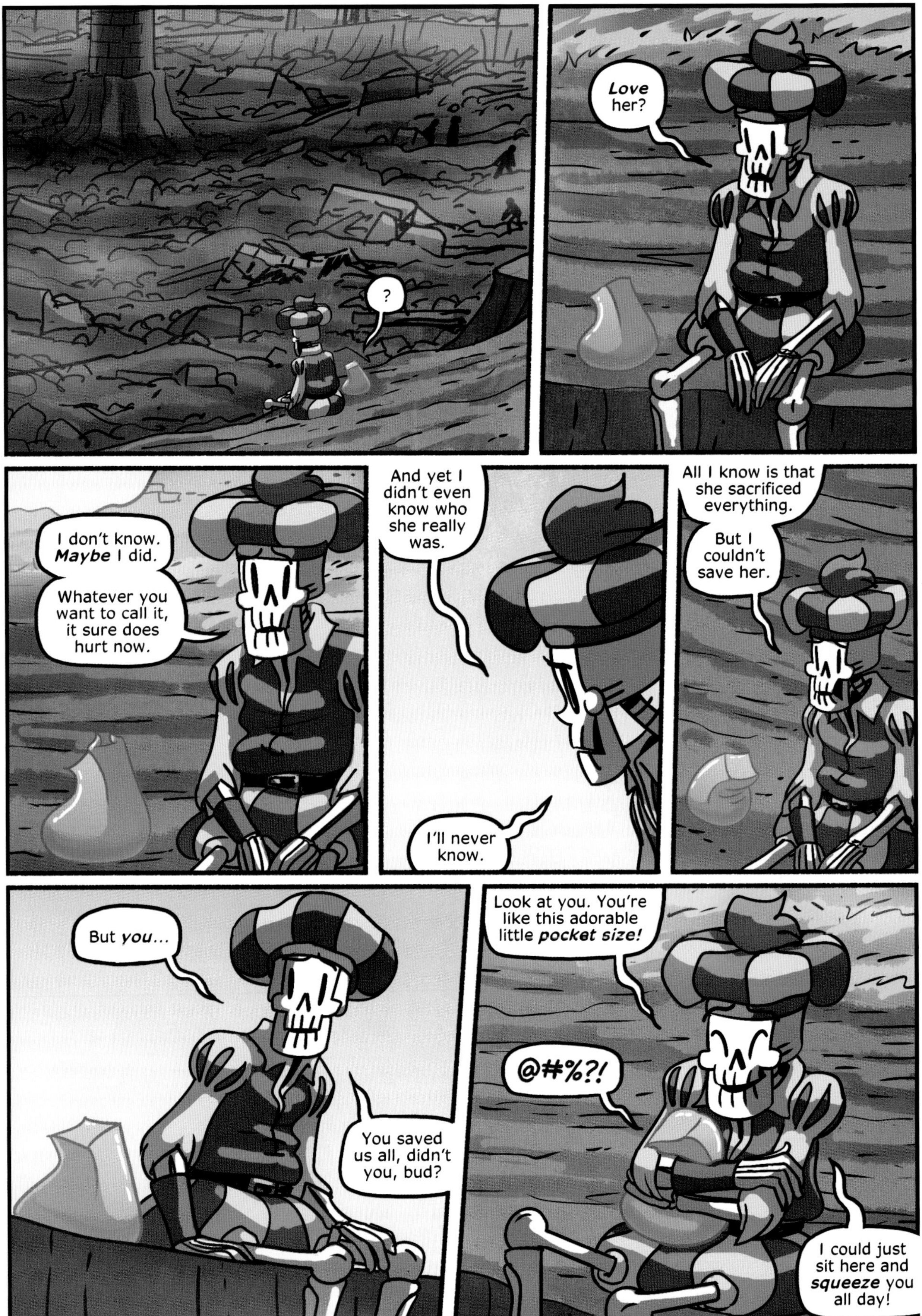
?
Love her?
I don't know. *Maybe* I did.
Whatever you want to call it, it sure does hurt now.
And yet I didn't even know who she really was.
I'll never know.
All I know is that she sacrificed everything.
But I couldn't save her.
But *you*...
You saved us all, didn't you, bud?
Look at you. You're like this adorable little *pocket size!*
@#%?!
I could just sit here and *squeeze* you all day!

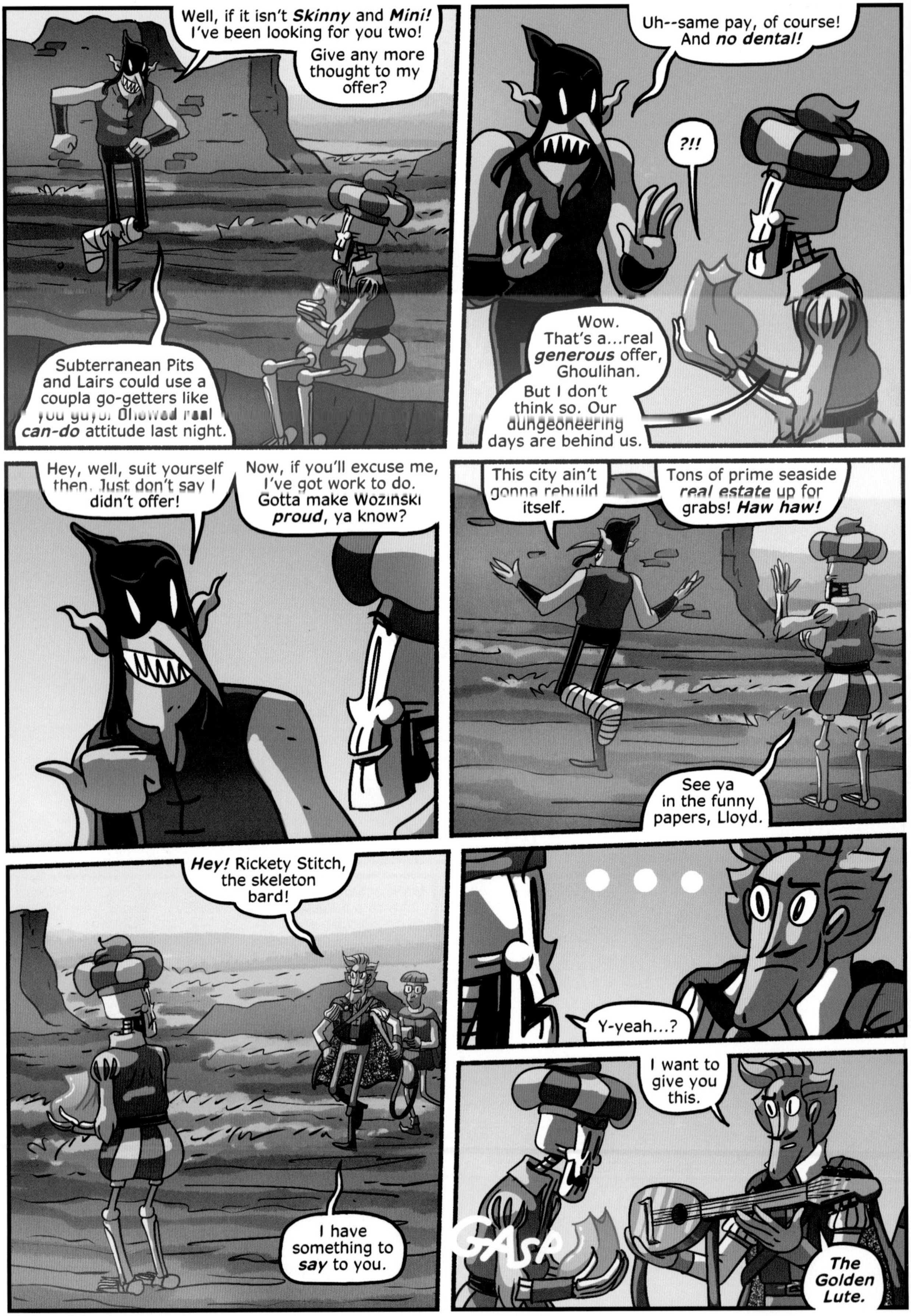
Well, if it isn't *Skinny* and *Mini!* I've been looking for you two!
Give any more thought to my offer?
Subterranean Pits and Lairs could use a coupla go-getters like you guys! Showed real *can-do* attitude last night.
Uh--same pay, of course! And *no dental!*
?!!
Wow. That's a...real *generous* offer, Ghoulihan.
But I don't think so. Our dungeoneering days are behind us.
Hey, well, suit yourself then. Just don't say I didn't offer!
Now, if you'll excuse me, I've got work to do. Gotta make Wozinski *proud*, ya know?
This city ain't gonna rebuild itself.
Tons of prime seaside *real estate* up for grabs! *Haw haw!*
See ya in the funny papers, Lloyd.
Hey! Rickety Stitch, the skeleton bard!
I have something to *say* to you.
Y-yeah...?
I want to give you this.
GASP
The Golden Lute.

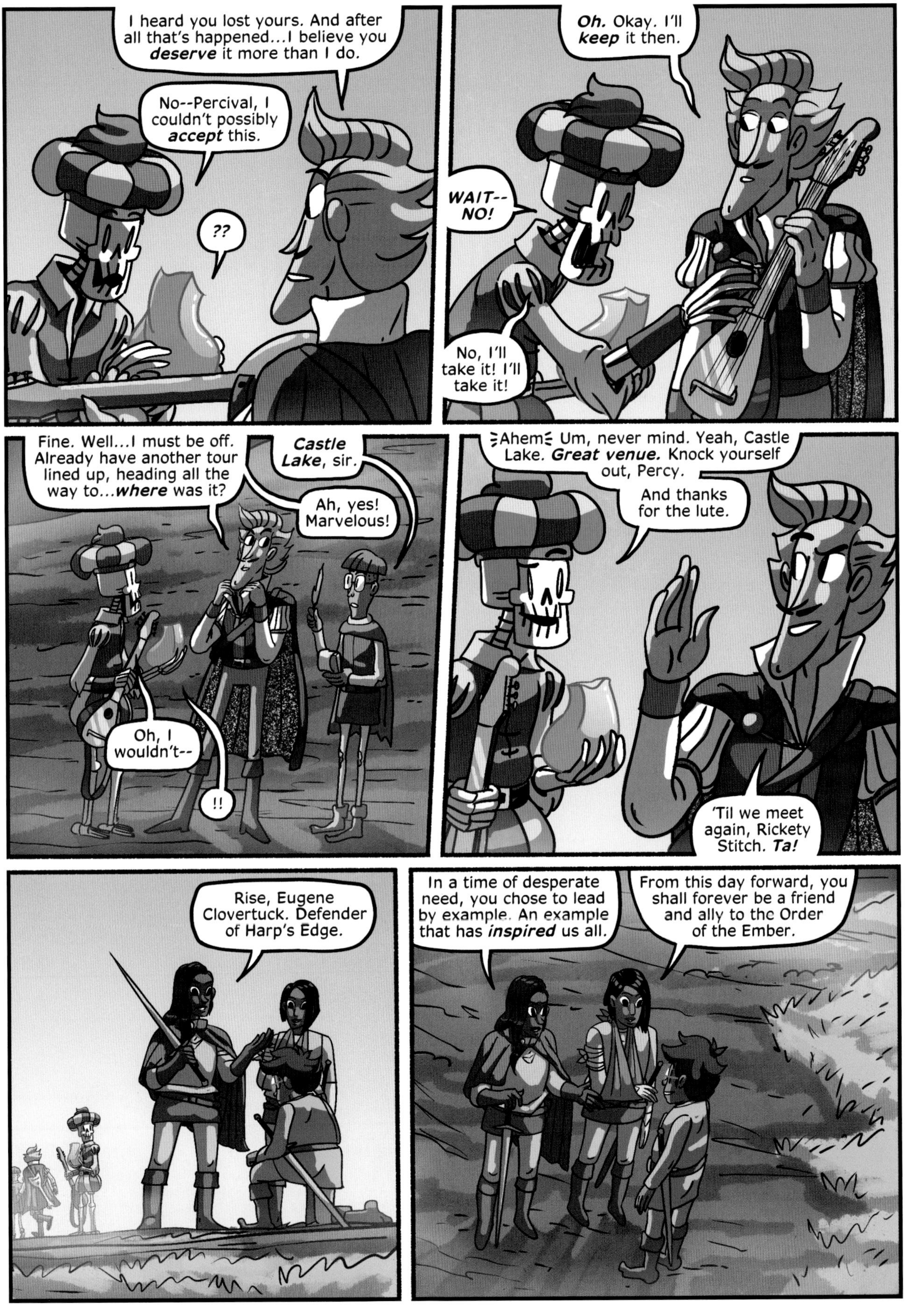
I heard you lost yours. And after all that's happened...I believe you *deserve* it more than I do.
No--Percival, I couldn't possibly *accept* this.
??
Oh. Okay. I'll *keep* it then.
WAIT-- NO!
No, I'll take it! I'll take it!
Fine. Well...I must be off. Already have another tour lined up, heading all the way to...*where* was it?
Castle Lake, sir.
Ah, yes! Marvelous!
Oh, I wouldn't--
!!
Ahem Um, never mind. Yeah, Castle Lake. *Great venue.* Knock yourself out, Percy.
And thanks for the lute.
'Til we meet again, Rickety Stitch. *Ta!*
Rise, Eugene Clovertuck. Defender of Harp's Edge.
In a time of desperate need, you chose to lead by example. An example that has *inspired* us all.
From this day forward, you shall forever be a friend and ally to the Order of the Ember.

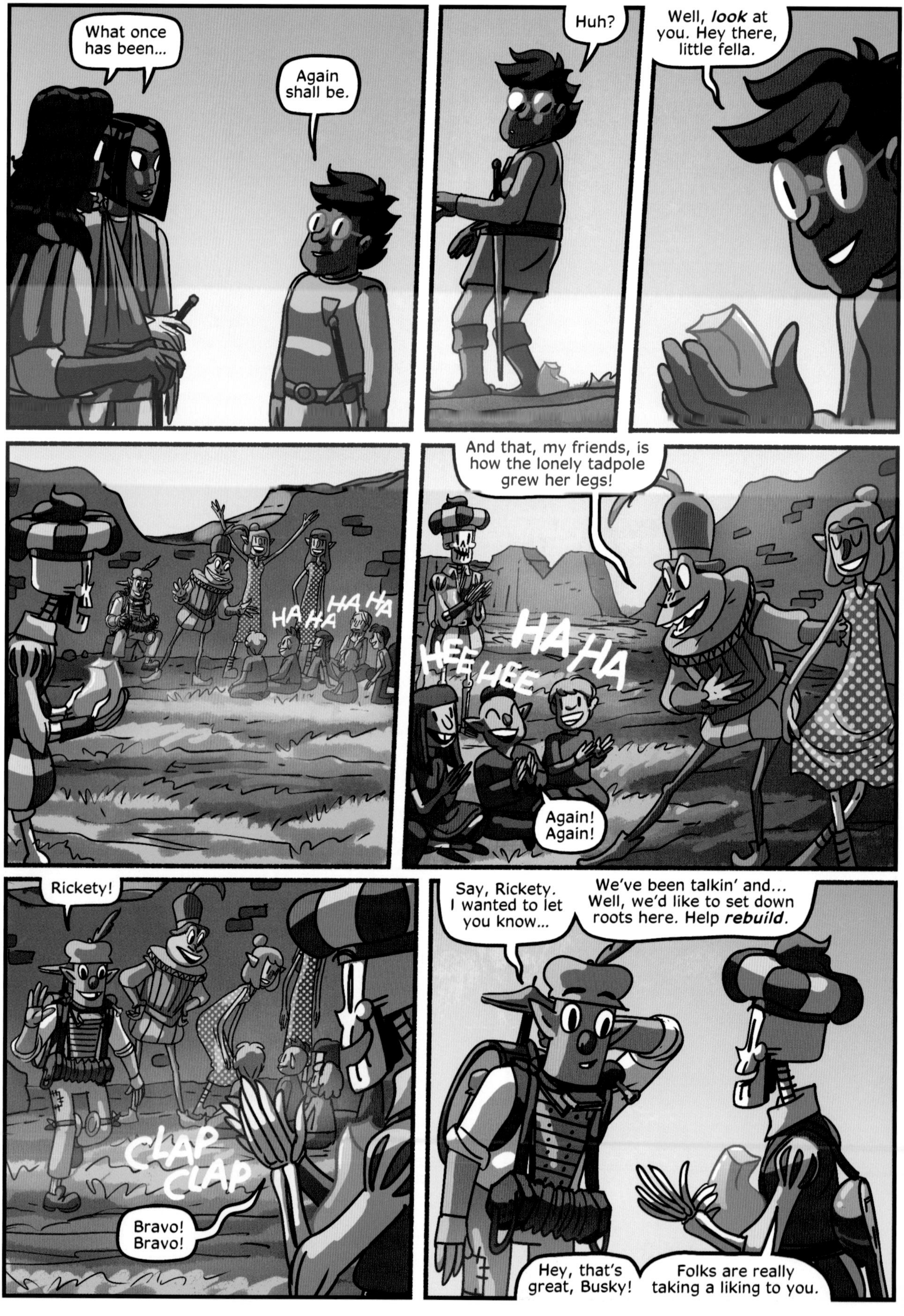

What once has been...
Again shall be.
Huh?
Well, *look* at you. Hey there, little fella.
And that, my friends, is how the lonely tadpole grew her legs!
HA HA HA HA
HA HA
HEE HEE
Again! Again!
Rickety!
CLAP CLAP
Bravo! Bravo!
Say, Rickety. I wanted to let you know...
We've been talkin' and... Well, we'd like to set down roots here. Help *rebuild*.
Hey, that's great, Busky!
Folks are really taking a liking to you.

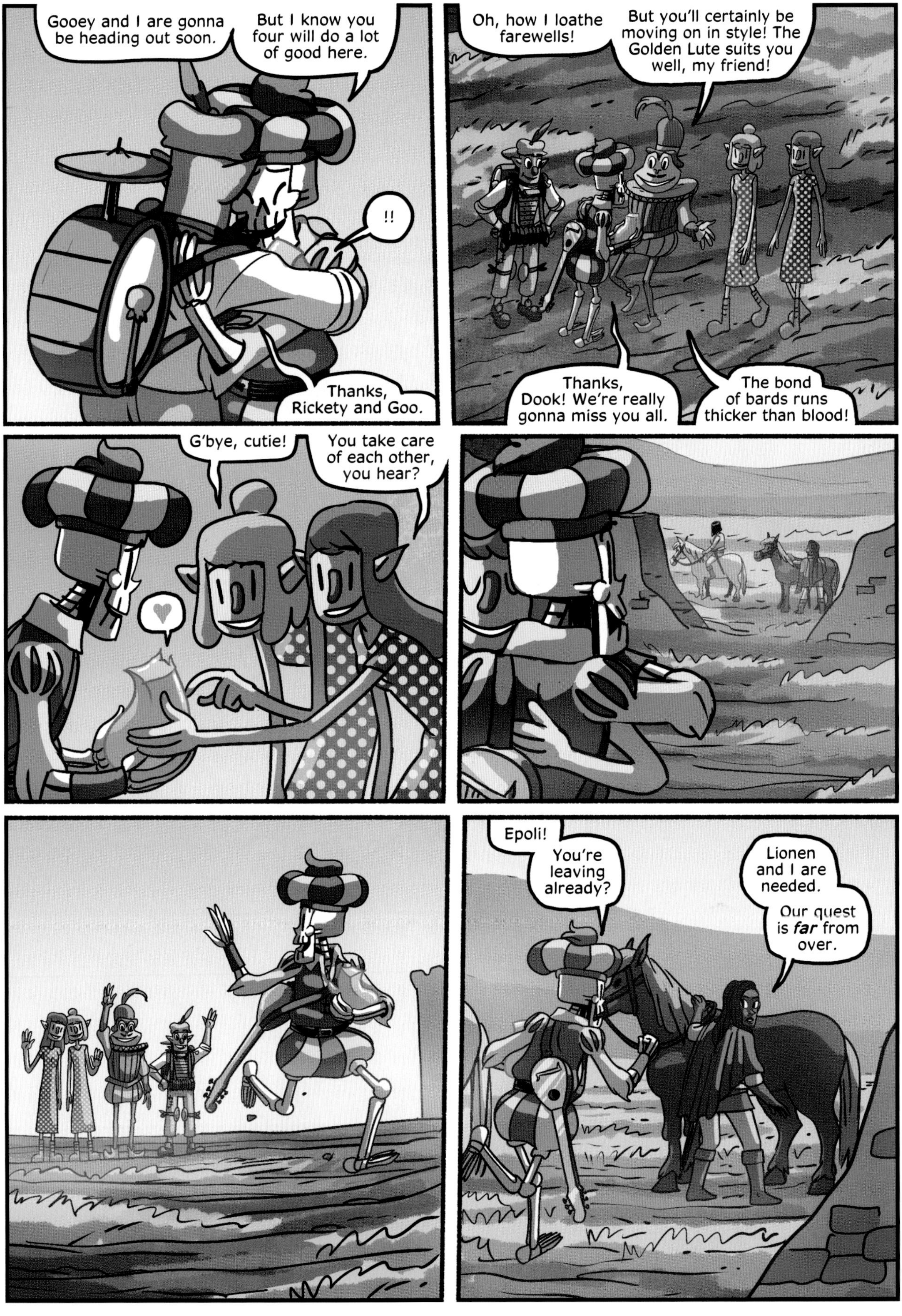
Gooey and I are gonna be heading out soon.
But I know you four will do a lot of good here.
!!
Thanks, Rickety and Goo.
Oh, how I loathe farewells!
But you'll certainly be moving on in style! The Golden Lute suits you well, my friend!
Thanks, Dook! We're really gonna miss you all.
The bond of bards runs thicker than blood!
G'bye, cutie!
You take care of each other, you hear?
Epoli!
You're leaving already?
Lionen and I are needed.
Our quest is *far* from over.

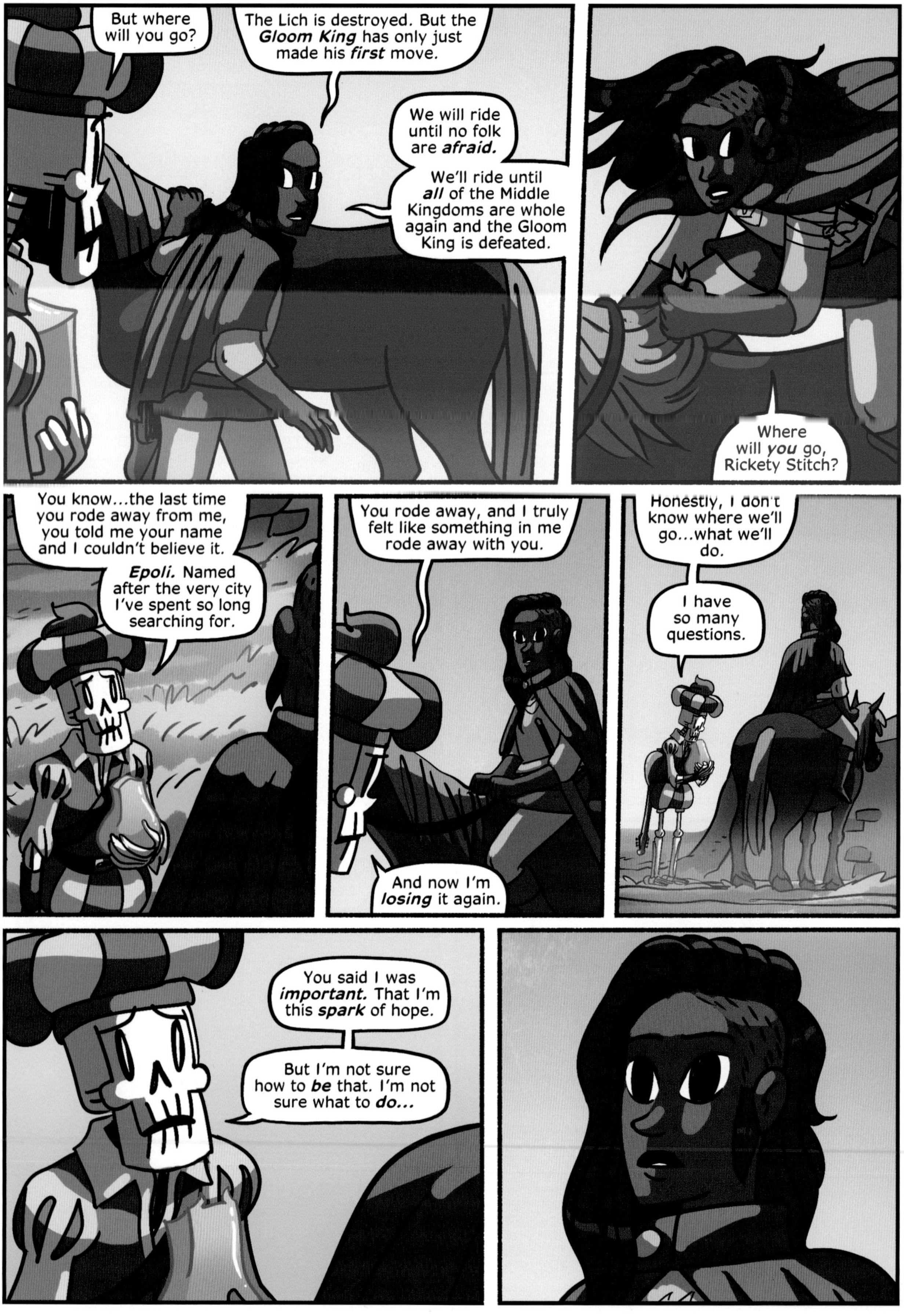
But where will you go?
The Lich is destroyed. But the *Gloom King* has only just made his *first* move.
We will ride until no folk are *afraid.*
We'll ride until *all* of the Middle Kingdoms are whole again and the Gloom King is defeated.
Where will *you* go, Rickety Stitch?
You know...the last time you rode away from me, you told me your name and I couldn't believe it.
Epoli. Named after the very city I've spent so long searching for.
You rode away, and I truly felt like something in me rode away with you.
And now I'm *losing* it again.
Honestly, I don't know where we'll go...what we'll do.
I have so many questions.
You said I was *important.* That I'm this *spark* of hope.
But I'm not sure how to *be* that. I'm not sure what to *do...*

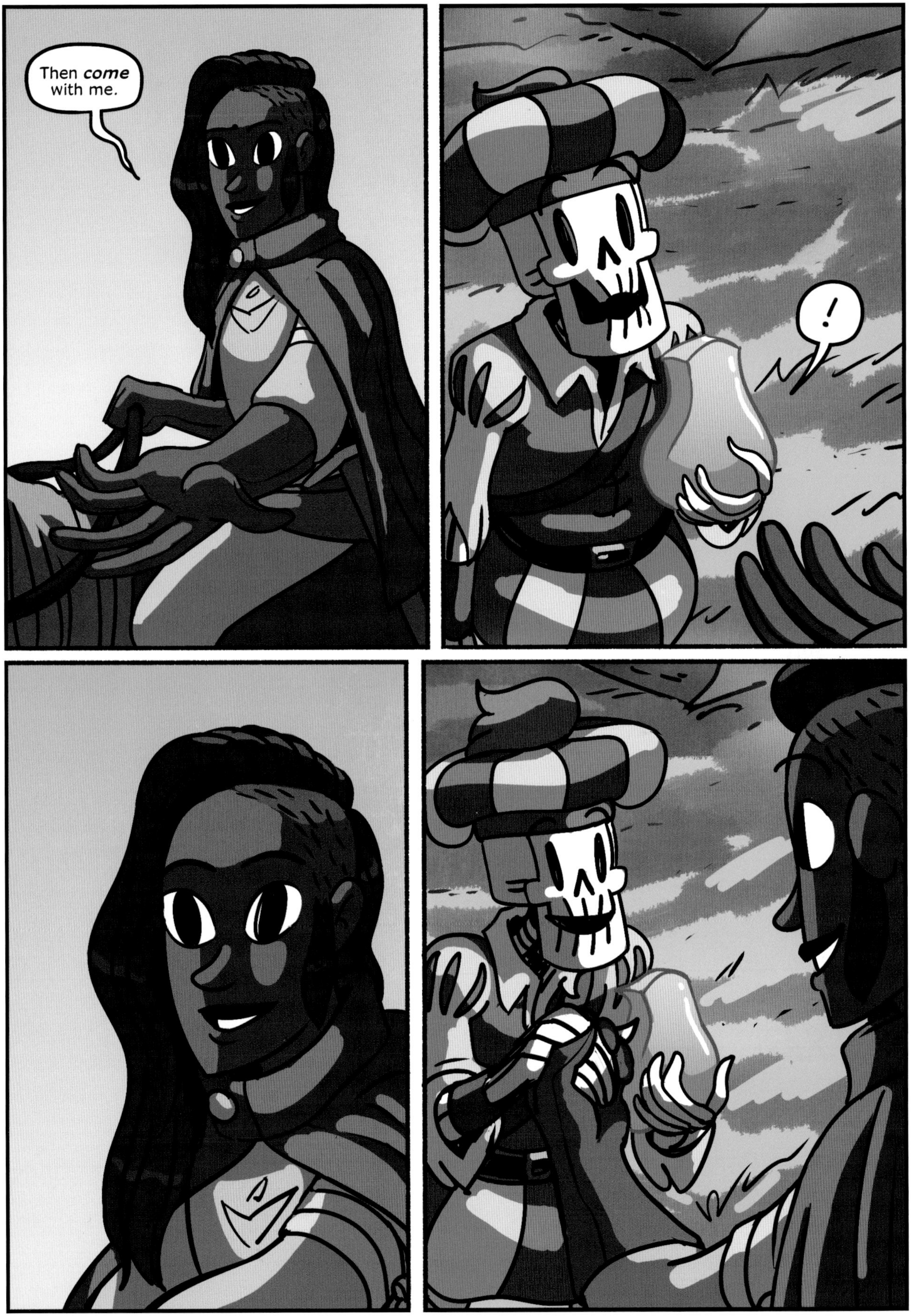
Then *come* with me.
!

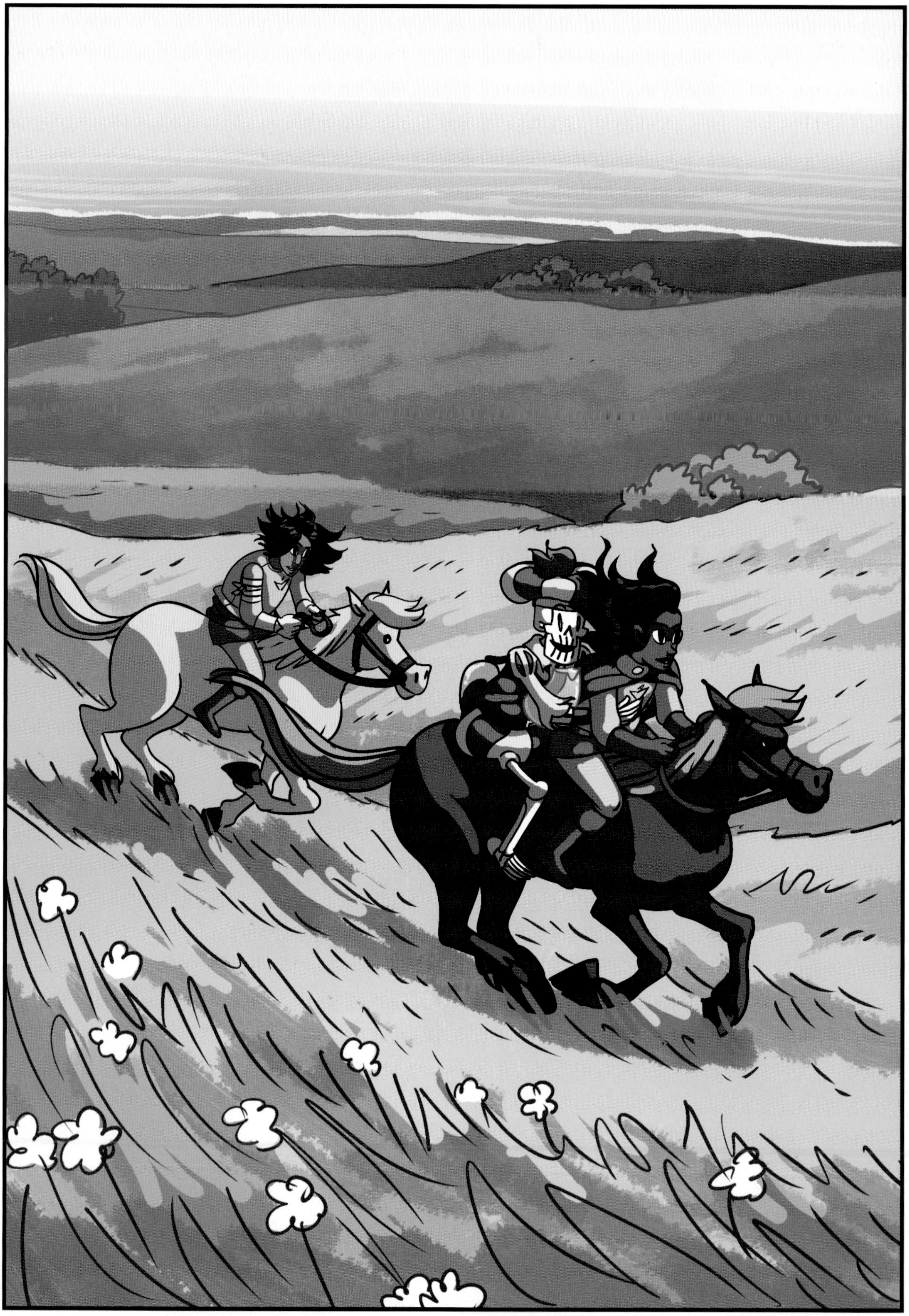

A Hero Named Epoli

Music written and performed by Darren Korb
Lyrics by Ben Costa & James Parks & Darren Korb

At first I thought I was dreaming
When I saw her out on the road
Her banner was battered and streaming
Her emblem, tarnished and old

I knew that she was a hero
Her eyes blazing bright like a fire
She rode on fiercely and fleeting
With a spirit that left me inspired

She said keep on singing
And turned to ride away
A piece of me rode off with her that day
Her name was Epoli, she said
Not the city, not the star
She's the one who set the flame alight inside my heart

She wasn't my dream of a hero
Her armor, dusty and worn
A long road ahead without resting
No time to reflect or to mourn

But her sword and her spirit were fearless
Her heart, courageous and brave
We said our goodbyes at the seashore
To the crash of the rumbling waves

She said keep on singing
And turned to ride away
A piece of me rode off with her that day
Her name was Epoli, she said
Not the city, not the star
She's the one who set the flame alight inside my heart

You'll always be here right beside me
No matter how far you go
Your quest may never be over
But your legend continues to grow

They say that the world has no heroes
But clearly they've never met you
I'll never forget what you told me
Let this song tell all the world too

She said keep on singing
And I turned to stride away
A piece of her strode off with me that day
Her name was Epoli, she said
Not the city, not the star
She's the one who set the flame alight inside my heart

What Once Has Been, Again Shall Be

Music written and performed by Evin Wolverton
Lyrics by Ben Costa & James Parks & Evin Wolverton

What once has been, again shall be
A fallow field returns to green
A pyre that burns the unremembered
Its dying fires bear glowing embers

What once has been, shall reawaken
Raise every fallen star and buried dream
The faded flame will soon be brazen
What once has been, again shall be

A castle falls, its soldiers doomed
Where heroes rest, gold flowers bloom
All dreams must end when we are woken
But time will heal and mend the broken

What once has been, shall reawaken
Raise every fallen star and buried dream
The faded flame will soon be brazen
What once has been, again shall be

For every shattered stone, we'll place another
For every cloven tree, we'll plant a seed
For every sorry heart, we'll lift each other
For every crashing wave, we'll brave the sea

What once has been, shall reawaken
Raise every fallen star and buried dream
The faded flame will soon be brazen
What once has been, again shall be

LISTEN
for FREE at
RicketyStitch.com/songs

Acknowledgments

We could not have finished this book without the hard work of our color-flatting assistant, Svetik Petushkova, who diligently colored one billion crowd scenes.

Special thanks also go to Evin Wolverton, Darren Korb, Estelle Kim, Denya Ciuffo Rose, Dan Lazar, Angela Cheng Caplan, Jeffrey Brown, Kieu Nguyen, Heidi Chen, and our loving families.

And more special thanks to all of our Wizards of Eem on Patreon, especially Jona Kay Dul, Amir Rao, Elliot Block, George Higgins, Darren Korb (again), and the Seventh Tavern.

This book is dedicated to the promise of a better tomorrow and to the people who work tirelessly for our communities, even when challenges seem insurmountable.